FALLING

BACK

TO

ONE

FALLING BACK TO ONE

RANDY MASON

A GENUINE ARCHER BOOK

ARCHER/RARE BIRD

453 South Spring Street · Suite 302 · Los Angeles · CA 90013
archerlit.com

Copyright © 2017 by Randy Mason

FIRST HARDCOVER EDITION

Cover Photograph by Sasin Paraksa

Set in Minion
Printed in the United States

"The River Runs" by Randy Mason
© 1995 Randy Mason (Scattered Light Publishing)
Lyrics used by permission. All rights reserved.

"Night" by Randy Mason
© 1998 Scattered Light Publishing
Lyrics used by permission. All rights reserved.

This is a work of fiction. Names, characters, places, and incidents either are the product of the author's imagination or are used fictitiously; and any resemblance to actual persons, living or dead, businesses, companies, events, or locales is entirely coincidental.

10 9 8 7 6 5 4 3 2 1

Publisher's Cataloging-in-Publication data

Names: Mason, Randy, author.
Title: Falling back to one / Randy Mason.
Description: A Genuine Archer Book | First Trade Paperback Original Edition | New York, NY, Los Angeles, CA : Archer, Rare Bird Books, 2017.
Identifiers: ISBN 9781941729182
Subjects: LCSH Police—Fiction. | Juvenile delinquents—Fiction. | New York (N.Y.)—Fiction. | Suspense fiction. | Suspense fiction. | BISAC FICTION / Suspense. | FICTION / Literary.
Classification: LCC PS3613.A81755 F35 2017 | DDC 813.6—dc23

To Dr. Ceci, who first encouraged me, so very many years ago, to write down this story that I, alone, could tell.

Chapter 1

EVEN THE STARS THEMSELVES were dying. Beautiful as they were—brilliant sparkles of pure energy shining through light-years of space—they were each destined to one day disappear, some in a spectacular explosion, ultimately pulling whatever was around them into a lightless, lifeless void. As if they'd never existed. Several of the ones she saw glittering right now were already gone—they just didn't know it yet.

She lowered her gaze and turned her head away. But in that last hour of darkness, there were miles to go with nothing to do except stare out the dirty, wire-meshed window. So as the minibus continued to roll down the highway, she went back to watching the shadows streaking by, black against black—a cool shiver creeping slowly up her spine. Less than four months ago, as if for the very first time, she'd opened her eyes in the gloom of just such early morning hours. Slouched in a boarded-up doorway, she'd been sleeping in an alley. Black against black had been the shadows there, too, one sliding into the other—a huge two-dimensional mass. Until her eyes had adjusted.

Garbage was strewn everywhere, a collage of anything and everything people used and threw away. A twisted bicycle frame. A broken sink. An old tire. Torn black bags with garbage cascading out. There were planks of rotting wood and pieces of plastic. And glass—lots of glass—that reflected the minimal light seeping down from the street at the other end.

Something rustled nearby, and she flinched, grimacing as stiff muscles objected. But it was only a cat, and she watched as it poked its nose inside the debris. But when it crossed through a patch of moonlight that had casually slipped through an absent roof and glassless window, she jumped to her feet, pulse racing, eyes wide. It wasn't a cat.

Time stammered and dragged. Alone with the rat. Which was blocking her way while the space turned darker. The moon, continuing its descent, was falling out of alignment with the building's gaps and holes. And though she wanted to keep her eyes on the enormous rodent going in and out of the trash, its tiny nose sniffing and nudging every object in sight, she found herself looking around at the deepening shadows: strange, ill-defined forms in a strange and unfamiliar place. For she had no idea where she was or how she'd gotten there. No idea how to get home.

Home.

Not a single image came to mind. Not a single memory. Nothing. She breathed in: not even her own name. Breaking out in a thin film of sweat, she jammed her hands into the pockets of her jeans—all empty. And nothing on the ground looked like it could've belonged to her. She paused, eyes fixed on the assortment of broken glass littering the pavement, bits and pieces in different shapes and sizes, moving away, getting smaller and smaller. She felt light-headed and very tall. Weightless, like she was floating. Like in a dream.

A gunshot ripped through the night, and then another, piercing the muffled haze. There were shouts and more gunshots, like little pops. Finally a police siren wailed—stunningly loud.

It wasn't a dream.

But the rat was gone.

Steps cautious, she moved down the alley, hearing voices as she neared the end. And once she'd reached the street, she stuck her head out just enough to have a clear line of sight. There was no one to the left, but, further down and to the right, three teenage boys in faded jeans and denim jackets were hanging out on the corner and smoking. At first she thought they were arguing, then realized they were teasing each other, following their jokes with playful slaps and punches. She glanced behind her, but the alley only swallowed itself up in the darkness of a dead end.

She settled back to wait for the boys to leave, the night air not warm enough for merely a T-shirt, her hiding place smelly and gross. But just as she was about to take another look outside, something brushed against her leg, and she jumped, tripping over a box full of rusted metal parts. Heart in her throat, she hugged the wall, but heard nothing—absolutely nothing. And then the stillness grew, pulsing and pressing, until she plunged into the light, every muscle in motion, every nerve on fire. The boys were shouting from close behind: "C'mon, let's get 'er." "Yeah, we gonna have us some fun." "Hey, momma, whatchu runnin fo'?"

She flew down the cracked and ravaged sidewalks, randomly turning corners, the background a washed-out, meaningless blur. And though she tore through several areas that were teeming with people—people selling drugs, selling themselves—heads barely turned. Block after block the pavement disappeared beneath her, and she heard, as if from a great distance, the heavy, labored breathing that was her own. She felt the pounding of her feet and the motion of her body running—like it could run that way forever.

But her pace began to falter. And when she reached an especially dark street, where all but one lonely lamp had been shot out, she ducked into a narrow alley. Deserted and forgotten, relinquished to the night, the buildings on either side of her were completely dark—crumbling, burned-out shells of brick and cement. But with their damaged, aging walls as protection, she slowly picked her way through the blackness and the rubble, trying not to make a sound, trying to control the ragged rhythm of her breath.

After what seemed like hours, she emerged in the back and found a fire escape ladder hanging down, her sneakers tap-tapping ever so lightly as she clambered up the rungs. And when she reached the first landing, she went to pull the metal steps up behind her, only to stop: the noise would give her away. But it wasn't until she paused a few flights later that she thought to strain her ears for sounds of her pursuers. Perhaps they'd given up. For all she knew, she'd been running for blocks with no one behind her. She started to smile. And upon thinking she might be safe, she nearly succumbed to a fit of nervous giggles. Safe? She was considering breaking into a condemned building where rats traced mazes in the yard below.

She peered into the gaping window before her, but it was too dark to see anything, the night still blanketing the city, the moon having disappeared from the horizon. And with the world gone black, and the streets now quiet, she sat with her back against the wall, the rough bricks cool and solid behind her sweat-soaked shirt. But her hair felt unpleasantly damp, and her eyelids were drooping. Hugging her knees to her chest to fend off the encroaching chill, she stared across the roofs, fighting to stay awake.

Hardly noticeable at first, the sky began to glow: a soft smudge of dusty pink, a faded ribbon of aqua lazily melting into deeper shades of blue. Minutes passed in tranquil pastels. And then the cloudy sky bloomed, her dull gaze widening as fiery streaks of color blazed above the buildings. But as the sun rose higher, the vivid hues retreated. And when she looked through the window again, pale morning rays were illuminating the interior.

High above walls covered with graffiti, bare bulbs dangled from a ceiling of chipped and peeling paint. The floor was littered with matchbooks, empty cigarette packs, cigarette butts, candy wrappers, crumpled magazines, beer cans… Her eyes settled on the red vinyl sofa in the middle of the room, its yellow foam stuffing— turning orange—pushing through several large rips in the material.

She climbed through the window only to hesitate: the building was falling apart; the very floor she was standing on might give way. But then she looked at all of the stuff lying around: proof that plenty of people had been there. Not letting herself think about the dust, the dirt, or whatever might be crawling all over the floor, she went to the sofa, cleared a space, and lay down to sleep.

But only a few hours later, a shadow fell across her eyes, which fluttered open to a large fist wrapped around the handle of a knife. Slowly, her gaze shifted upward from a pair of worn, torn jeans to a mane of dirty blond hair that fell slightly below tensed shoulders, two penetrating blue eyes staring back from a rugged, stubbled face.

That was how she'd met Tim Reilly.

THE BUS HIT A nasty pothole, jarring her out of her reverie. In the blush of dawn, they'd reached the southern section of the Bronx. One after another, decaying, abandoned buildings passed by, some with fake windows painted onto panels of wood to replace the missing panes of glass—like that really looked any better. An eerie sensation crept over her: these were the very streets she'd come from.

"We'll be there in about thirty minutes or so." It was the only thing the guard had said to her since they'd boarded the bus, though he and the female driver had been flirting since the trip began.

Micki was the only passenger.

And while it first seemed as if they were heading to someplace in Queens, they ultimately drove through a tunnel and went crosstown on the city's relatively quiet and desolate pre-rush-hour streets. Through the window, Micki could feel the dark side of Manhattan, lying in wait, calmly watching through bloodthirsty eyes. The knot in her stomach tightened. If she could've, she would've gotten up and moved around a little, but her left hand was cuffed to the seat. At least they hadn't shackled her feet together, too.

The guard, who was standing at the front of the bus, was laughing at something the driver had said. Micki looked at him in his uniform: the gun, the cuffs, the baton... But she was leaving all that behind, getting out of that hellhole they politely called a reform school. What she didn't know was exactly what she was getting into. At first they'd told her her release would be on a trial basis; then they'd said it would be for a whole year—unless she violated the terms. First they said she'd be living with her legal guardian; then they said she'd be living alone, claiming she was old enough—which made it sound more like parole. She knew something wasn't right, but what the hell. She just nodded in agreement with whatever they said, essentially yes-ing them to death: yes, she'd take a full high-school-senior program; yes, she'd also work a job after school to support herself; yes, she wouldn't use any drugs or alcohol; wouldn't associate with criminals; would honor a ten o'clock curfew (set late to accommodate her job)... And on and on it went, an endless litany of rules.

They'd refused to tell her anything about her guardian except that he was a cop. She was surprised it was going to be a man. What if he—

With a jolt and a screech of brakes, the bus came to its final stop. They were in front of a midtown precinct, a full array of police vehicles around them. The guard walked back. "Get up." He uncuffed her from the seat, then loosely cuffed her hands together in front. "Let's go."

Stomach in a twist, she walked down the aisle ahead of him, then awkwardly descended the steps. She hated the damn handcuffs.

"Good luck," the bus driver called after her, and handed the guard the gym bag containing Micki's few possessions. The staff shrink had provided the cheap duffle to replace the standard paper bag—a going-away present of sorts.

"Be back in a few," the guard said to the driver. "Let's catch some breakfast before we hit the road again." The two smiled at each other.

The guard took Micki's arm and led her into the station house. None of the air conditioners were working, and the air, already heavy and sticky with the promise of another post–Labor Day scorcher, felt worse than it had outside. Micki scanned the room and saw a lot of people moving around, but no one was paying any attention to her; no one looked like they'd been waiting for her to arrive. The pain in her stomach grew stronger.

The guard pulled her along until they reached the desk sergeant, who was talking to a cop with a scruffy-looking suspect in tow. Micki waited with the guard to the side of the massive wooden desk, which seemed too large for the size of the room. But when she ran her finger around one of the ornate black curls that formed the heavy iron railing in front of it, the guard jerked her hand away: "Don't touch anything." And once it was their turn to approach, he made a point of leaning in to talk, the men's voices so low she couldn't hear what they were saying.

"C'mon." He grabbed her upper arm and tugged her back toward the door.

"Wait. Where're we going?"

He yanked her along more roughly. "We're too early, that's all."

She stopped resisting, but kept looking at him from the corner of her eye.

Outside, the bus driver scowled at their joint return and swept her blonde bangs out of her eyes. "What happened?" Sitting on the steps of the old, dinged-up vehicle, she'd been taking advantage of its shady interior. She pushed herself up and dusted off the ample seat of her uniform.

"Nothing," the guard said. "We just got here too soon. Let's find a place to eat. I'm starving."

So the lanky guard and the bus driver, with Micki in between, headed down the street past closed and gated wholesale stores selling mostly furs and leather goods. On the corner they found an open coffee shop, crowded and noisy with a bunch of early-early midtown office workers and some cops from the next shift. Several solitary diners were reading newspapers while gulping down greasy food and strong coffee.

The three took a booth in the corner, and, in less than a minute, the table was cleared, wiped, and reset. Micki sat near the wall, the guard next to her, and the driver across from him. Their waitress—in a pink-and-white uniform, wisps of hair floating free from her bun—came by with a pot of coffee and immediately filled their cups. She set the carafe down with a thud, then pulled out her pad and pen.

"Ready to order?"

The bus driver said she'd have waffles with a side of bacon.

The guard ordered the Spanish omelet.

But Micki had barely read the first part of the oversized, laminated menu. Going on for four pages, the list of platters and variations seemed endless. She'd found the pancakes under "From the Griddle," but even then: plain, banana, blueberry, silver dollar... With all eyes upon her, waiting, she could feel the heat rising in her face. "I'll just have the coffee," she said.

The waitress scooped up the menus and whisked the pot away.

The bus driver reached for the container of sugar.

The guard took a sip from his mug and unfolded his napkin.

And Micki, once she saw no one else making a move for it, reached for the creamer, nearly knocking over her cup. When she caught several civilians at a nearby table stealing glances, she gave them a nasty look, then held her cuffed hands out to the guard. "Can't you take these things off me now?"

"Forget it. It's my ass on the line until I hand you over."

"But where am I gonna go? I can't get out unless you get up."

"Just forget it. I don't want any trouble."

The set of his jaw and the hard look he gave her made her turn to the bus driver. But the woman quickly looked down and opened two packets of Sweet'N Low. So Micki sat back, the couple's conversation blending into the restaurant's hum and clatter, the thick, white china comfortably hot between her palms. Blasting on high, the air conditioning was like a sweet blessing, and sometimes, when she moved her hands, the loose cuffs felt cool against her wrists. But the pain in her stomach was growing with a vengeance. And when the waitress served the food, the smell of waffles, eggs, and bacon made her both hungry and nauseous at the same time. She slid down a bit on the padded maroon vinyl. The lack of sleep kicked in, and she let her heavy eyelids close.

"C'MON, KID, GET UP." The guard shook her arm, and she started, cuffed hands crashing painfully into the underside of the table. As she waited for her head to clear, she saw the guard was already standing, a dollar bill lying in between the plates. The bus driver, lipstick reapplied, was returning from the restroom.

For about twenty minutes, Micki had fallen into a dreamless, heavy sleep. Now she was hungry. Very hungry. She looked at the greasy, sticky remains, but it was time to go. She slid across the seat with awkward little lurches, the guard slipping some money to the driver, who went to wait on line for the cashier. Then Micki and the guard were past the front and out the door—the hot, humid air hitting her like an invisible wall.

Back inside the precinct house, they approached the desk sergeant again—a different one since a new tour had begun. And this time, after the two men talked, the guard led her across the large room to the stairway, where they trudged up in silence, passing others on their way down. Worn into a smooth depression in the middle by countless pairs of feet, the marble steps, though permanently covered in grime, seemed out of place.

They entered the detectives' room, where fewer people were milling around and there was considerably less noise. Though a few of the battered-looking desks were empty, two detectives who were typing had people sitting next to theirs while another, talking on the phone and taking notes, was repeatedly nodding and saying "uh-huh" a lot. An empty detention cage, visible through an archway in the far corner, caused Micki's gaze to linger before moving to a fourth cop, who was pouring coffee at a little table in the corner to their right. The guard pulled her along until they stood in front of a door with frosted glass. When he knocked, the murmuring on the other side stopped, and a gruff voice said, "Yeah?"

The guard turned the knob and pushed her into the office ahead of him. "Captain Malone?"

"Yeah. Is this the kid?"

"Yes, sir. And if you'll just sign these papers, I'll be on my way."

With a receding hairline and a touch of grey at the temples, Captain Daniel Malone had deep crows' feet around his eyes and bags underneath, suggesting long hours, little sleep, and lots of stress. His tie—a faded silk, wayward threads poking out here and there—was slung low beneath his unbuttoned collar, while his suit jacket—navy blue, shiny elbows—hung carelessly from the coat tree standing tilted in the corner. Totally surrounded by files and papers, he looked buried behind his desk. He accepted the papers and, after a perfunctory glance, signed and handed them back.

The guard removed the handcuffs. "Anything else you need from me, Captain?"

"No, I think everything's in order. You can go."

The guard nodded, dropped Micki's bag on the floor, and, without even looking at her, left.

Alone in the middle of the office—now the sole object of attention for two strange men—Micki tried to steady her breathing; tried to ignore the second man, the one leaning against the wall near the window. At about six and a half feet tall, wearing jeans and a black T-shirt, he looked like someone who belonged in a movie instead of a police station. He was lean and muscular with a strong face; broad shoulders; and thick, dark hair that was a little on the long side. When she'd first caught sight of him, her heart had skipped a beat. But his brown eyes had narrowed when they'd settled on her, displaying confusion, then anger, as he looked her up and down. Shrinking under the iciness of his gaze, her heart seemed to stop.

Malone got up, walked around his desk, and extended his arm. "I'm Captain Malone. You must be Micki."

Unable to speak, she simply nodded while they shook hands.

He sat on the edge of his desk and tipped his head toward the tall man. "This is Detective Sergeant Baker, your legal guardian."

A sharp pang shot through her as the tall man stared her down. Malone, looking at Baker, raised an eyebrow. Baker turned to gaze out the window, letting his hands slip into his back pockets.

Malone stood up. "I tell you what," he said to Micki as he led her to a wooden bench just outside his office, "why don't you wait here while I talk to the detective sergeant alone. We'll only be a few minutes." He paused in the doorway. "Don't go anywhere; I'm trusting you to stay put." And though he smiled, she thought it didn't look all that sincere.

"Yeah, sure," she said. But as soon as the door had closed, she could hear the other man's voice—so loud the door might as well have been open.

"It's a fucking girl! Nobody said anything about that! All this time you let me believe I'd be dealing with a boy."

His voice barely audible, Malone responded, "I never said it was a boy."

"But you never said it was a girl, either. You knew I'd assume it was a boy. And you never corrected me. Christ, *no one* ever corrected me. I mean, how the hell could I tell from a name like Mickey? It's unbelievable! Now I see how careful you were in the way you said everything: always 'the kid' or her name. Jeez, it's a fucking miracle you never slipped up. In fact, that's the real reason you wouldn't let me see her file before, isn't it; that would've given the whole damn thing away."

"What's the difference?"

"WHAT'S THE DIFFERENCE? Don't give me that bullshit…"

Sitting sideways on the end of the bench, Micki's left ear was close to the door. She jumped at the light tap on her shoulder. It was one of the other detectives, the one she'd seen pouring coffee.

"C'mon. I'm going to put you in one of the interrogation rooms. You can wait in there."

"But he told me to wait here."

"I knows all about it. Don't worry; I'll tell him where you are."

A little overweight, the cop, wearing an old brown leather shoulder holster, had curly, reddish hair and a mustache. Thick, hairy forearms sprouted from rolled-up shirtsleeves, and wet spots had already formed at his armpits. The sports slacks he wore were a bit too tight, and the top two buttons of his shirt were undone. And though it was already hanging loosely around his neck, he tugged at the brown tie that had powdered sugar sprinkled on it.

"But they're talking about me."

"I know. Let's go." With a hint of amusement playing about his features, he held out a hand as if to help her up. Then he took her to a room down the hall on the other side. As he was about to leave, he asked if she wanted some coffee.

What she wanted was one of the doughnuts that had created his tie decoration. "No, I'm okay."

He smiled, then left.

Almost a minute passed before she tried the door, expecting it to be open. But it was locked. She was alone in a locked room. Again. At least this one had windows, though the heavy wire mesh was a grim reminder she was still a prisoner. And the walls—painted the same dull, two-tone institutional green as the rest of the place—were all blank except one, which had a series of gruesome-looking marks and discolorations. She tried not to think about what had made them. Instead she walked around the heavy wooden table that occupied the middle of the otherwise barren space and looked out the window. A homeless man was sleeping amidst the litter in the alley below, ulcerated toes sticking out of filthy socks, an empty pint bottle in his outstretched palm. He wore layers of scarves and coats as if it were the dead of winter, but the heat was oppressive and had sucked out any shred of optimism left her. Why couldn't her legal guardian have been the coffee cop? He seemed nice. Or better yet, Sergeant Kelly. After all, if it weren't for him she'd still be in juvi. Then again, he'd put her there in the first place.

It had been a hot July night and her first time robbing an apartment. Shoplifting, purse snatching, and picking pockets on crowded subway trains had been more her kind of thing, though there were times she'd gone as far as holding people up with a knife. But after an entire day of getting really sick, she hadn't been feeling all that picky.

She'd climbed a fire escape to reach a dark window left open wide, the unseen contents behind it an unknown treasure for the taking. Spicy and rich, the aroma of Spanish cooking had wafted out, but not a sound had issued from within. She sat on the sill, swung her legs over, and eased herself through, hopping down onto some sort of carpet, the stale undertone of cheap perfume almost making her gag. All was quiet until she bumped into a bed and then a chair, heart hammering in her chest while she stood completely still to listen. But after a while, when there was nothing to hear, she started groping along the wall.

If she'd been like the other messed-up girls—or even some of the guys—she would've been out walking the streets for money. But just the thought sparked incredible rage. Well aware of this, Tim had still made her promise not to do it, though by then he was gone, the other promise already broken—the very reason why she needed the cash. But each day was getting harder and harder. So much robbing and stealing just to maintain her miserable little life. And for what?

Hand finally on a light switch, she paused, thinking she heard someone talking very softly. But she brushed it off as paranoia, and wiped away the sweat beading on her face—which had nothing to do with her nerves or the heat. Then she flipped on the light, and the room jumped to life, shockingly bright and stinging her eyes. Shielding them with her hand, she cursed her carelessness: she'd lost her sunglasses somewhere the day before.

Jesus, what a mess. Women's clothes were strewn all over the floor, along with a dirty bath towel and several pairs of high heels. Empty packs of Salems lay crumpled on top of the blanket. Zeroing in on an old dresser with a cracked mirror above it, she quickly ransacked the drawers, finding mostly lingerie, sweaters, and some worthless costume jewelry. She looked around a little longer, then sat down hard on the bed and shivered.

Somewhere in the apartment, a door opened, and the sound of hushed voices returned. She ran to the window and scrambled over the sill. But before she'd even wound her way down to the next fire escape landing, she heard, "FREEZE. POLICE." When she looked up, she saw an overweight cop and his gun framed in a rectangle of light. Below her were two more flights of stairs and then the pavement. She stumbled down the rest of the fire escape as fast as she could, then hit the ground and ran, the cop yelling after her. But, unfamiliar with the area, she got stuck in a dead end. Up ahead was a chain-link fence; behind her, the cop, closing in fast. She wheeled around to face him.

"FREEZE. POLICE," he yelled—as if she hadn't heard him the first time. "HANDS IN THE AIR *NOW*." He'd stopped halfway down the alley and was partially obscured by shadow. And breathing heavily.

She glanced back over her shoulder. But the fence—bits of debris clinging to some of the links, wire strung in large *X*s over several sections—appeared much higher than it had just seconds before. Too high to climb for a beginner like her.

A huge bang made her jump. Her head whipped back to the cop. But he looked like he hadn't moved.

"C'mon, son," he said, "no big deal. Just put your hands on your head and this is all over. Don't make me shoot."

She hesitated: he clearly hadn't gotten a good look at her. And he didn't seem like the Dirty Harry type, either—the kind to want to put a bullet through your brain. Yet she didn't doubt his determination to bring her in, to bring her to justice and all that crap. What she wouldn't know until much later was that, under the circumstances, shooting her—even if she ran—could've ended his career; he would never have done it. But staring down the alley, down the barrel of his gun, the threat had seemed very real. And for a fraction of a second she considered raising her hands. But then she thought about the scars on her face: they might link her to all sorts of crimes. And she'd probably left fingerprints behind on the knife she'd used on Speed…

Motionless, eyes fixed on the cop, she could hear him panting, could practically feel his heart straining to calm down after his brief exertion…

She ran to the fence and started to climb, hand by hand, fingers grasping the links. But she was going kind of slow, having trouble getting any sort of help from her feet—the links in the fence seemed too small for the toes of her sneakers. She felt betrayed: it had always looked so easy when guys did it. She glanced down over her shoulder and saw the cop was right below her, then felt his grip on her foot. And though she tried to pull herself up further, he was tugging hard, inching her lower, causing something sharp to dig into her stomach. Both hands on her ankle, he pulled her down even more, and the little stick turned to severe pain. Kicking blindly, legs flailing, she ultimately kicked him square in the face. He released her foot and grabbed his nose, cursing and bleeding while she continued to pull herself up. She struggled to the top, rolled over, and mostly fell to the other side. Shirt tacky and wet, she crawled only a few feet before curling up in the shadows.

But just a few minutes later, the cop—gasping for breath after running around the block, blood and sweat dripping down his face—was right there. He aimed his gun and used his foot to push at her. "C'mon, get up, you little punk."

The sound of her own breathing was very loud in her ears; his voice, nothing but a faceless, shapeless blur.

"C'mon!" His foot pushed at her again, doing little more than rocking her. With an aggravated grunt, he used his free hand to yank her underweight body up and throw her into the chain links. She slammed against the metal and slid down, the rattle echoing in her brain.

"Stand up, you little piece of scum, and keep your hands on the fence!"

But she remained on her knees, her mind a foggy jumble of pain and sounds.

"PUT YOUR HANDS ON YOUR HEAD," he barked.

She actually managed to do that and immediately felt the pressure of the gun's muzzle at her temple.

"I'd love to pull this trigger right now," he said.

And even with the noise that was rushing through her head, she could hear the sneer on his face—could feel the weight of the bullet in his gun. And all she wanted was for him to hurry up and pull the damn trigger. So the pain would stop. So the nightmare of living to shoot up would stop. Instead, handcuffs clicked around her wrists as he pulled them down behind her, one by one.

"Get up," he ordered.

But when he grabbed her under the arm, she only moaned. Virtually doubled over, her forehead was resting against the fence. In a voice not much more than a breath, she said, "Can't."

Cursing, the cop finally pulled out his flashlight and eased his bulk down till he was kneeling beside her. It was then that he saw the blood running from under her vest and dripping all over her jeans to form a small, dark pool on the ground. It was also then that he realized he'd been chasing a girl and not a young boy, the scars on her face matching a description given by numerous street-crime victims. He set her down on her side.

She closed her eyes.

Using his walkie-talkie, he called for a "bus," talking to the dispatcher while scanning the fence with his flashlight. About two-thirds of the way up, in the dimming rings of the yellowing beam, he could see a section that someone had clipped open. Like a misplaced hook, one piece of link was jutting out, its sharp edge reaching toward the sky. It wouldn't really matter if you were climbing up. But if someone were pulling you down... Her drying blood had stained it. He felt sick.

He removed the cuffs and noted the needle tracks on the inside of her arm: the street's ugly tattoo. What a waste. Then he turned her onto her back and applied pressure as best he could. "Everything's gonna be all right," he said. But he was already covered in blood.

When he heard the ambulance approaching, he put his hand over hers before standing up to meet the paramedics at the street. To this day, he'd swear she whispered, "I'm sorry."

PERCHED ON THE FRONT of his desk, color rising in his face, Captain Malone said, "Now you listen to me, Jim, and you listen good: I went to a lot of trouble to set this up. This kid is high risk, and absolutely nobody wanted her living on her own. But you refused to take a kid in with you. Do you have any idea the hell I went through for that alone? And then there was all the bureaucratic bullshit and the strings I pulled to get the department to agree to this as an alternative to therapy for you in the first place—they weren't exactly taken with the shrink's idea, even less with the special considerations I pressed so hard for. If you back out now, Internal Affairs will reopen their investigation, and you'll be officially back on modified duty—you might even face suspension. Everything you've ever done since you've been on the job will be scrutinized, and I kid you not that your record will be permanently marred and your career essentially over.

"You're a good cop—an excellent cop—and I consider you a friend; I wouldn't have stuck my neck out like this for anyone else. But you need to get your head straightened out. I've seen cops on the edge like you. Push it a little further and you'll end up on the wrong side of that badge."

Jaw clenching and unclenching, Baker stared out the window. "What if this doesn't work out? What then?"

"You *make* it work out."

Baker looked at Malone. "This sucks, y'know that?"

"You want to give me back your shield and your guns right now?"

There was a long pause. "No, sir."

"Good." Malone pushed himself up and handed Baker a manila folder. "Here's a copy of her jacket. It includes some of her file from juvi."

The tall cop—after noting the spelling of Micki's name—opened it and glanced through her record: multiple counts of robbery and aggravated robbery, aggravated assault, burglary, resisting arrest, assaulting a police officer...and a charge that had been given a final disposition of justifiable homicide.

"She killed someone?"

"In self-defense."

"I'll bet. No prostitution charges?"

"No."

"Yeah, right."

With a weary sigh, Malone ran his fingers through his thinning hair. When he spoke again, his voice was much quieter. "Sit down a minute, Jim. I think we better go over some basic ground rules here."

File tucked against his body, Baker folded his arms across his chest and parked himself on the edge of the windowsill.

"You've got a lot of latitude in dealing with her," Malone said. "No one's going to interfere unless things get way out of hand. She's a tough street kid; nobody expects you to handle her with kid gloves. As far as we can tell, she's got no family, no friends. No one's going to be looking out for her except the social worker and Kelly. But once a kid gets placed, Kelly takes himself out of the picture. And with the way things are going at Social Services, the kid'll be lucky if the caseworker sees her even once after today. On the other hand, if word ever gets back to me that she's got serious injuries from you—a broken bone or anything even *close* to that—you've had it." Malone looked meaningfully at Baker, who shook his head slightly and looked out over his shoulder. The sky was becoming overcast. Maybe it would rain. That would be a relief.

"Now, needless to say," Malone continued, "there's to be no sexual contact of any kind, and the burden for ensuring that is totally on *you*. I'm sure, at some point, she'll try to manipulate you. There'll be times when you'll be alone with her in her apartment. Whatever. I don't care if she's standing there naked; you make sure you keep your dick in your pants. Is that clear?"

Baker snorted. "Not to worry, Captain."

Malone appeared less than pleased.

"So what about making sure she's clean?" Baker asked. Unfolding his arms, he stood up and said, "I'll need to frisk her for weapons or drugs, and I'm not about to end up like that uniform, Rodriguez."

Officer Jesús Rodriguez, out of the one-one-two in Queens, had been on the job eight years when he was called to arrest a rather well-endowed woman suspected of shoplifting in Alexander's department store. Uneasy with searching the suspect anywhere near her "private parts," he made the additional mistake of cuffing her hands in front. When he bent down to calm her six-year-old son, who was screaming at the top of his lungs, the suspect managed to produce a small gravity knife hidden in her cleavage. She'd stabbed the officer in the kidney.

"I understand that," Malone said. "You do whatever you have to—whatever's appropriate. 'Appropriate' is the key word here, Jim. Just don't step over the line."

"She's seventeen years old, for chrissakes. It's not like dealing with an eight-year-old little girl. She's, well, y'know…"

"Are you saying you can't control yourself?"

"No! Jesus, I'm not saying that at all, I—"

"Hey!"

Baker stopped.

"You're thirty-six," Malone said, "technically old enough to be her father, certainly old enough to act like one."

"But what if she—without cause, mind you—says I touched her just to—"

"Cover your ass: have other people around as much as you can. They're witnesses. Besides, no one believes you're capable of that kind of thing. If they did, none of this would be possible."

"Lucky me."

"Damn right, 'lucky you.' This is your easy way out, and she was the only kid available."

Baker shook his head. "I can't help it. I'm not comfortable with this; I'm not comfortable at all."

"Well you're just going to have to deal with it."

Pacing in front of the sofa, Baker tapped the file against his thigh. "Great... fine. Fine. You know what?" His voice was rising. "I'll treat her the same as if she were a boy. Right down the line. No better, no worse, no different. That should make everything easy, right? It shouldn't be too tough. She fucking looks like a boy; I'll just pretend she's a boy."

"I'm warning you, Jim; this is not a game."

"Really? Then why am I supposed to be playing 'daddy' to some dumb, punk girl?"

"Make no mistake, she's not dumb. They gave her a battery of tests and she's freakishly bright. It's one of the reasons Kelly was so interested in her."

Baker rubbed his forehead. She was sounding more and more like a little psychopath. "So what's she doing with a name like Micki Reilly? She looks about as Irish as Al Pacino."

"Reilly was the last name of the guy who was looking after her on the street— kind of like a big brother."

"I thought you said she had no friends or family."

"The guy was a small-time drug dealer. Tried to go straight and ended up shot—more like executed, from what I understand."

"And what about this amnesia business? How do you know it isn't bullshit?"

"Several top-notch shrinks all said it's the real thing, though a case like this *is* pretty rare. Personally, I think it's kind of fascinating."

"Yeah, real fascinating. And no one's ever identified her? In all this time, no missing-persons reports ever matched?"

Malone shrugged. "She looks good as a throwaway."

"Still…" Baker's voice trailed off.

"Now, I'm going to get the kid and let the two of you get acquainted. Then I want you to drive her over to her apartment. You can take the social worker with you. By the way, you're all set at the high school?"

"You really want to know? 'Cause I can't even begin to tell you just how thrilled I am to be there."

"You expect me to listen to you bitch about this again? Because this is a *gift*: it puts you—at least on paper—back on full-duty status. With the way it's set up, your jacket'll simply say you volunteered for a special detail—assisted with a test project to help the city look into putting cops in the schools." Malone looked at him fixedly. "Would it kill you to show a little gratitude?"

Baker tapped the file against his hand. "Listen, I really don't want to have to take the kid to the apartment right now. I need some time to myself on this. Can't the social worker take her without me?"

"Jesus! You're a real piece of work, y'know that? But you're going to meet with her now—and without me hearing any more crap about it. Is that understood?"

"Whatever you say."

Malone gave him a sharp look, then stepped outside his office—only to find Micki gone. His face blanched. "Where the hell is the kid? Anybody—"

"I put her in Interview One," said the cop with the mustache.

"Well, go get her!" Malone snapped.

BAKER AND MICKI WERE alone, Malone having gone in search of the social worker, who was now almost twenty minutes late. Standing midway between Malone's desk and the door, Micki wasn't sure exactly what she was supposed to be doing. She felt like she was on display. Baker—arms folded over his chest, manila file still in hand—was casually leaning against the wall and studying her.

She had dark brown hair that fell just below her shoulders, the uneven bangs looking like she'd trimmed them herself. On the right side of her face were two scars, both radiating from her eye: one went from the outer corner diagonally down toward her ear; the other traveled from the midpoint of her lower lid diagonally down across her cheek, practically parallel to the first. Five feet six inches tall, she was very thin, faded jeans hugging narrow hips. And with arms as muscular as a boy's, she wore a cut-off denim jacket as a vest over a sleeveless black T-shirt. Even her sneakers were boys' sneakers: dirty black Pro-Keds. No make-up, no nail polish, and no earrings, rings, or bracelets. But around her neck—not that it really meant anything—was a plain silver cross.

His expression dark, Baker turned his head slightly and spit into a nearby garbage pail.

Her heart seized, though her face showed nothing. Instead, looking bored, she sat down on the mustard-colored sofa, resting her elbows on her knees and her chin in her hands. She stared at the black and green linoleum tiles as if they might yield up some means of escape.

Baker resumed scanning her record. "Nice sheet," he said.

She looked up sharply.

"How much were you shooting?" he asked. Though it was all in the file, he wanted to make her say it, wanted to see if it would make her squirm.

Her eyes narrowed.

He waited.

"Sixty dollars a day," she said flatly.

He nodded. "And in only two months. Very impressive."

Jaw clenched, she looked away.

He closed the folder with a smug little grin.

Nothing more was said, and the silence grew heavy. When Malone returned to the office, there was a tangible, if silent, sigh of relief. Micki stood up.

Glancing from one to the other, Malone asked, "Am I interrupting anything?"

Baker and Micki exchanged dirty looks. Baker, straightening up, said, "No."

A petite woman with sharp black eyes was waiting by Malone's side. Dressed in an inexpensive suit and sturdy leather pumps, she was lowering her overstuffed briefcase from her shoulder to the ground.

"Micki," Malone said, "this is Miss Teresa Gutierrez, the social worker assigned to your case."

The woman held out her hand and smiled. "Hi, Micki. It's so nice to meet you." A slight Hispanic accent colored the melodic voice, and her grip was pleasantly firm. Micki perked up.

"I believe," Malone said to the caseworker, "you've already met Detective Sergeant Baker."

Still smiling, Miss Gutierrez said, "Yes, of course. Hello."

But Baker gave only a minimal nod of recognition to this coconspirator of Malone's. In their brief meeting a couple of weeks ago, she, too, had clearly taken great pains to hide Micki's gender.

"Well, why don't we get going?" she said. "We can talk on the way. I want to apologize for being late, but the case I just came from had an emergency."

Malone said, "No problem," and returned to his desk.

Micki picked her bag up from the floor.

Eyes bright, Miss Gutierrez slung her briefcase over her shoulder and looked toward Baker. "Let's go, then."

But Baker didn't budge. "You two go ahead. I'm sure you won't need me."

Miss Gutierrez's face clouded over. "I think it's important for you to come along. I—"

"I can't right now." Baker stared down at her. "There's something I have to take care of."

Baker's manner was so intimidating that the social worker stepped back. "Well, I—I guess..." But she never finished the sentence. Instead, she tugged at her jacket and smoothed her hair, even though it was already pulled back severely and secured with a large gold barrette. "I'm sure I can get Micki settled in just fine, and perhaps we can all get together tomorrow or Thursday." She turned as if to go, then looked back and added, "I really do think you should come with us now while..." Her voice faded under Baker's gaze. With a considerable yank, she adjusted the shoulder strap of her briefcase. "Yes, well, let's go, Micki. My car is double-parked, and I don't want to get a ticket." She ushered Micki out and smiled at Malone, who smiled back.

MICKI'S NEW HOME WAS in a building on Forty-Fourth Drive in Long Island City, Queens. The two-story brick structure, like its attached twin, had a protruding section with an angular bay of windows. Originally a somewhat dignified pair of single-family rowhouses, the passing years had not been kind to them. After the area had declined, they'd been divided into utilitarian units emphasizing function over form. Their once-proud stature now forgotten, they seemed to be holding on as best they could—waiting for their moment to come around again.

But to Micki, the two together looked like a turreted castle fortress, flanked on one side by the parking lot for an industrial company, and on the other by a vacant store and a corner deli. While there were apartment buildings and other rowhouses to the south and east, the surrounding blocks to the north and west consisted almost exclusively of factories, warehouses, and auto body/repair shops. Off in the distance, Manhattan skyscrapers loomed in a majestic haze. It was like looking at another planet in a science-fiction movie.

They headed up the stoop, where Micki ignored the cracked cement and splintered wood, choosing instead to focus on the stained-glass transoms that accented the first-floor windows of what had once been the parlors. Inside the building, she bounded up the stairs and found the door to her apartment, only to have to wait for Miss Gutierrez to unlock it. Without pausing to first take it all in, she threw her duffle on the little table in the middle of the room and went directly to the kitchen area. It consisted of a mini-refrigerator and an ancient gas stove next to a large, but pitted, sink. The drawers and cabinets—made of cheap, dented metal—contained several lonely pieces of orphaned items prior tenants had apparently forgotten. She rifled through the odd collection as if looking for something in particular, but found nothing much of interest and moved on.

To her right, behind the door of what used to be part of the closet next to it, was a tiny bathroom with only a toilet, a mirror, and a small stall shower. No sink. *No sink!*

She heard some sort of commotion in the street, and crossed to the nearest window, which had been carelessly left open. Whoever had been yelling was already gone, but out on the fire escape was an empty soda can, bent and rusted, that someone had left behind. Sticking her head out further, she looked down through the painted metal slats and saw that the lowest step of the releasable fire escape ladder was hanging just above the building's entrance. When she looked up, she saw the rungs reached as high as the roof. She pulled her head back in, closed the window, and immediately tested the lock, which didn't seem to work very well.

Miss Gutierrez—still standing by the door—had yet to say anything.

Micki's eyes began to dull. Overhead, the light fixture was simply two bare bulbs. And the walls and high ceiling were cracked and irregular from repeated water damage and replastering, a thin coat of fresh white paint concealing little of the underlying layers of dirt. Even the wooden floor was heavily marred and stained, especially in the kitchen area. And when she took a closer look at the small round table beneath her bag, she found the lime-green Formica was full of scratches and burns, the two accompanying metal chairs covered in dirty yellow vinyl that looked like it had never, ever been washed.

A pine dresser had four drawers—all empty—two of which neither opened nor closed all the way no matter how much she pushed, pulled, or wrenched them from side to side. And the bed she'd so looked forward to sleeping in was nothing more than a mattress and box spring sitting directly on the floor, a flat little pillow on the end against the wall. There were no pretty fabrics, no detail or woodwork—nothing at all to try to make the place look nice. The only part of the apartment that held any sort of charm was the turret area. Light streamed in from its three bare windows and fell upon a beat-up wooden desk with a chair, a lamp, and a clock. But no phone. She'd seen a payphone, though, at the top of the stairs in the hall.

Not surprisingly, the rent—which included gas, heat, and electricity—was very low, low enough that her pay would be more than the half she was required to contribute. The remainder of her meager income would have to cover everything else, including food, laundry, and clothes. On the ride over, Miss Gutierrez had emphasized that she was being given a lot of responsibility, and it was up to her to prove she could handle living as an adult. But while the social worker had an optimistic way of talking—as if everything were an opportunity and a challenge—Micki had read the woman's face when they'd first entered the apartment: she didn't approve of its condition. What Micki had no way of knowing were all the other things Miss Gutierrez didn't approve of.

For one thing, the location of the apartment was less than ideal: by subway and bus it was a good forty-five minutes or so from the high school where Micki would be a student. Located in Queens Village—a decent area with a much lower crime rate but higher rents than what the city was willing to pay—the school had been chosen solely for its academic excellence. As for Detective Sergeant Baker, he'd be working at the school so he could keep an eye on Micki. He lived on Manhattan's Upper West Side, nowhere near Micki's apartment—or the school, for that matter. Of course, his commute would most likely be easy since he'd always be driving against traffic. Well, how very, very nice, the social worker thought. For *him*.

The truth was, Detective Sergeant Baker himself was Miss Gutierrez's main concern. During his exceptionally brief interview with her, he'd sat in her office doing little more than glowering and asking repeatedly how much longer their "talk" was going to take. Not once did he ask for any information pertaining to caring for a difficult child or the resources that might be available to assist him. It was obvious he wasn't a willing participant, and, for the life of her, she couldn't fathom why he was being given custody. Twice she tried to elicit the reasons behind his desire to look after a child at this particular time in his life, and each time, while drumming his fingers on the table, he asked, "You *did* speak to Captain Malone, right?" He was referring to her meeting the day before, when the captain had made it very clear that her interview with Baker was merely a formality: Baker would be given custody of Micki regardless of her opinion as to his suitability. And she found him highly unsuitable. A single male with absolutely no parenting skills, he was too young for a girl of Micki's age. He also had a chip on his shoulder. Based on what Malone had said, he was a good cop. But Micki needed a parent more than a parole officer.

This was not the first of Sergeant Kelly's "experiments" Miss Gutierrez had participated in. There had been three children prior to this, and, in each placement, she'd played an integral role. All had been boys a few years younger than Micki, and each had finished all or most of his time before going to live with a solid, double-parent family: a cop and his wife who were eager to have the child. Of course, trying to place Micki in such a home would've been difficult. Compared to those boys, she'd been much more violent and had racked up a hefty rap sheet in an incredibly short period of time. In addition, her behavior in juvi attested to more than the usual difficulty with authority figures.

But Sergeant Kelly was adamant Micki could be straightened out, and, in some ways, Miss Gutierrez could understand why. For she'd read the assessments provided by the psychiatrists—the very assessments used to sway the judge to reconsider the disposition of Micki's case. Yet, compelling as they were, Miss Gutierrez had initially refused to get involved because of the duplicity required;

namely, hiding from Baker that Micki was a girl. It wasn't until Sergeant Kelly had fully revealed the complicating circumstances—the jeopardy Micki was in at Heyden—that Miss Gutierrez had finally acquiesced. Nonetheless, the arguments against doing so had weighed heavily on her for days, leaving her feeling guilty as though she were conspiring to commit a crime. But when all was said and done, it had seemed the lesser of two evils.

In hindsight, she regretted not having talked to Micki while she was still incarcerated in Heyden. But taking the lengthy trip upstate had seemed like a waste of time when she'd have had no input anyway—especially when other, more-pressing cases had been demanding her attention. But now, after meeting the girl, the unorthodoxy of the arrangement was especially troubling. She considered it highly inappropriate for Micki to be living on her own. The teen had hardly begun serving the time to which she'd been sentenced when here she was with too much independence and not nearly enough supervision. And no love.

THEY WALKED AROUND THE neighborhood so Micki could orient herself. Right on the corner was a subway station, and Miss Gutierrez pointed out the supermarket and drugstore across from each other on Twenty-First Street. West on Forty-Fourth Drive, one long block down, was a Laundromat. Through an open doorway, the scent of bleach and detergent flowed out on a steady stream of superheated air.

They returned to Twenty-First Street and went north, into the bank where Micki's accounts would be. Since all of the prerequisite paperwork had been taken care of, the only thing needed was Micki's signature. To get her started, five dollars had been deposited into both checking and savings; the first month's rent had been paid in full. When Miss Gutierrez gave her twenty dollars in cash for groceries and other immediate necessities, Micki folded the two ten-dollar bills, then rubbed them between her fingers. And began to sweat. Until now, the only time she'd ever had any real money on hand was when she'd been about to score a fix. Overcome with nausea, she slipped the bills into her pocket and gripped the new bankbooks tightly. Then shuddered.

"Are you okay?" Miss Gutierrez asked.

"Yeah, fine," Micki said. "Just cold. Y'know, the air conditioning."

The bank manager, rambling on as if neither Micki nor the social worker had said a word, was warning about bounced checks, account fees, and the proper way to use a transaction register. With an anxious little smile, she said, "Well, that's about it. Any questions?"

Back outside, the clouds had totally disappeared, and the sun was beating down as if it were already noon. Micki wanted to return to her apartment and lie down for a while. Instead, they went back to Fourty-Fourth Drive and headed east to Bel Canto, where Micki would be employed as a dishwasher, the same job she'd had at Heyden. Located in the shadow of the elevated IRT tracks, the small Italian eatery was tucked away in what seemed a most unlikely place, its scalloped awning the sole projection over the sidewalk. When Miss Gutierrez had first called upon the owner, Mr. Antonelli, about hiring Micki in some capacity, he'd declined, saying he'd worked hard to create a respectable establishment. Only after it was agreed he could pay her considerably less than minimum wage did he relent. He was the only businessman in the area who'd even considered giving her a job.

The number 7 train thundered overhead as they approached, leaving a trembling silence in its wake. The door was locked, and, when they knocked, Mr. Antonelli himself came to answer. A short, round man with jet-black hair and a neatly trimmed mustache, he was wearing a chef's apron—stained with splotches of red sauce—over a sweaty white undershirt and black suit trousers. Looking frazzled, his voice sounded small and distant as he yelled through the heavy glass door in an extremely thick Italian accent, "We-a closed-a! Eleven-thirty you come-a back-a for lunch-a."

Before he could turn away, Miss Gutierrez—shouting—explained who they were. His entire face lit up. He immediately unlocked the door, and a wave of cool air washed over them, bringing with it an incredible aroma of marinara sauce and baking dough. As he welcomed them inside, Micki's mouth watered and her stomach grumbled.

The little man took Miss Gutierrez's hand in both of his. "Now-a I remember who-a you are-a! Oh, you don't-a know how happy I am-a to see you! Tyrone supposed to work-a today—the double shift, his-a last day-a. But he call and-a say he no come in-a. And-a Juan-a, the other dish-a-washer, he no answer his-a phone-a. So I wash-a the dishes myself-a. Oh, is-a good to see you. Very good-a!"

Micki realized he meant to put her to work right away. It wasn't exactly what she'd had in mind, but the little man could barely contain himself. She looked at the social worker—doing this would probably make a good impression on Miss Gutierrez. And it would definitely help take her own mind off the money in her pocket. Clean for only two months—all of it spent on the inside—she was no longer so sure she could handle her freedom.

THE ICE CUBES CLINKED lightly as Baker swirled the nearly empty, oversized rocks glass, the newly opened bottle of whiskey waiting to be unburdened for the fifth time. After but a moment's hesitation, he freshened his drink, then slumped back into the upright recliner, low on his spine, long legs out before him.

The only light in the room came from the TV; the only sounds, the hum of the fan and the late-night traffic on the streets below. Eyes glazed, he stared at the changing, silent images on the screen: NBC's version of the eleven o'clock news. Even with the sound off, it was depressing. He took a long drink, then glanced down over his shoulder at Micki's folder on the floor, the papers lying inside it in a sloppy pile. What a fucking mess he'd gotten himself into.

When he'd refused to voluntarily see the department shrink, they'd forced him to go, but he'd been so completely uncooperative, the weasel-faced jerk had finally admitted defeat and canceled his sessions—but not without getting the last laugh. For it was the shrink who'd spotted Sergeant Kelly's flyer and suggested to Captain Malone that this might work as a form of "interactive therapy" for Baker. Dr. Tillim insisted this was a valid—though experimental—therapeutic approach, insisted he was sincerely concerned for Baker's well-being. But Baker believed Tillim was simply trying to justify his paycheck. The man probably had nothing better to do than sit around his office all day, reading books and cooking up ridiculous schemes like this one.

Though department policy encouraged cops to seek help if they felt depressed or like their lives were out of control, if you actually did, you were branded with a stigma that forever tainted what was left of your career. So no one went to a shrink of their own free will. Instead, they merely coped however best they could. Every now and then, some poor schmuck ate his gun.

And while Baker was well aware that he'd become more physically aggressive on the job, he found nothing wrong with it. At least not now. When he'd first started on the force, he would've looked at things a lot differently. Back then he'd done everything by the book, had believed in the system. He'd also believed he could really make a difference on the streets. It was hard not to laugh at how idealistic he'd been: James Baker, Lone Ranger of the NYPD. But that had been twelve and a half years ago—1962. Kennedy had been president and man had yet to set foot on the moon. A lifetime ago.

Christ! Some truck driver wouldn't stop leaning on his horn. Baker got up and slammed the window shut. Then he finished his drink and poured another.

Settled in the recliner again, he drew a heavy sigh. Those early years on the job may have been the best years of his life. Sharp and eager to please, his career had gotten off to an impressive start, and it wasn't long till he'd made detective. When he'd chosen to take the test, a cordial rapport with the brass and an excellent record had just as quickly made him a sergeant. And, in due course, he earned a promotion to detective second grade. But with the city falling on harder times, the crime rate was steadily rising, and he'd grown tired of all the corruption around him. His tolerance for departmental politics waned while his sense of being impotent to effect any real change grew. Legal technicalities, plea bargains, and minimal sentencing due to prison overcrowding meant most of the garbage he busted was back on the street in what seemed like no time at all. And they laughed in his face when he brought them in again. The worst were the juveniles, processed through an outdated system that provided no more than a slap on the wrist for even the most violent of crimes.

Eventually he was dishing out some punishment on his own. An unconscious decision at first, he'd started small. But as time went on, things escalated. After a while, he was doing whatever he could get away with, especially when there were no witnesses around. His partner never participated, yet rarely intervened, lips loyally sealed. But accusations were made. And though all of the Civilian Complaint Review Board's rulings were in Baker's favor—either exonerating him or finding the grievances unfounded or unsubstantiated—IAD started noticing a pattern. By the time Baker had broken that punk's jaw, he'd already been the subject of a preliminary investigation. Which turned that one little episode into a big mistake—a really *big* mistake.

Daryl Cole, a twenty-year-old junkie, had aroused Baker's suspicions because he ran when he saw Baker coming down the street. Arrested twice before by Baker—once for narcotics possession and once for armed robbery—Cole had walked on the first arrest because of a technicality and pleaded down to third-degree weapons possession on the second. In the end, he'd spent a grand total of nineteen months behind bars.

When Baker searched him on this occasion, he found jewelry, not drugs, in the boy's pockets—jewelry the boy claimed his mother had given him to sell. But Baker knew Mrs. Cole to be a deeply religious woman. Distraught over her son's drug habit, she would never have given him anything to support it. Baker and his partner took Cole into custody, then went to his mother's apartment to check out his story. There they found the large black woman lying dead in a pool of blood, three stab wounds to the back.

Though they tried to get a confession, Cole, after waiving his rights, would admit to nothing. Instead he laughed and said, "Who the fuck cares? The stupid bitch deserved to die." Baker then lifted him out of his chair and slammed him into the wall with such force that his head snapped back hard against it. After which Cole called Baker a pig and spit in his face. This animal that had killed his own mother for drug money *had spit in his face.* Baker's fist connected solidly with Cole's jaw before his partner pulled him off, the two of them immediately concocting a story. And though Internal Affairs knew they were both full of it, they couldn't prove anything.

The public defender eventually made an appearance to smugly pronounce that "Mr. Cole's" rights had been severely violated; charges of assault and unlawful arrest would be filed against Baker. The pompous little ass virtually waxed poetic as he went into detail regarding the travesties of justice perpetrated against his client at the hands of the police. He planned to file a motion throwing out the murder charge on grounds that the initial search had lacked probable cause, had been purely the result of a personal vendetta. There would then be no remaining evidence to link Cole to his mother's murder: the weapon had never been recovered; the jewelry would be excluded as "fruit of the poisonous tree."

The assistant DA struck a deal: if charges against Baker were dropped, Cole could plead guilty to a lesser charge of manslaughter with a sentence of five to fifteen years. It was unlikely Cole would serve much more than four.

Placed on restricted duty, Baker's drinking increased and his rage grew darker. But Captain Malone—calling in some heavy markers—short-circuited the Internal Affairs investigation and managed to get Baker's full-duty status restored.

The commissioner made it explicitly clear, however, that this was in name only: before returning to his squad, Baker would have to successfully complete Dr. Tillim's "treatment." When Baker had started to object, Malone had shot him a lethal look while the commissioner—his tone noticeably colder—had stated the terms were non-negotiable.

Baker drained his glass and poured another. He should've just stayed in law school. A summa cum laude graduate of an Ivy League university, he'd gone on to study law without giving it much thought. Fighting for justice had always appealed to him. And despite the low pay, he'd wanted to work in the district attorney's office, going after criminals and putting them away. But law school had involved a brutal amount of reading, paper writing, and exams. And having had his fill of academia by then, he'd been restless. When he'd stopped to consider the excruciatingly slow process of the criminal courts—and a system that appeared to bend over backward protecting the rights of criminals—he'd decided to cut his losses, leave school, and pursue something more immediately gratifying: he became a cop.

Being on the front lines with the power to arrest someone—stand up for the victim, right then and there—was an incredible rush. And yet some of the very same issues that had caused him to leave a career in law behind had led to much of his frustration and disillusionment with police work. Maybe what he really should've done was follow his dream and become a writer. But he hadn't written anything in years. Hadn't even tried.

He got up and turned on a light, then shut off the TV and pictured the guys hanging out in the squad room. He missed the job and working the streets, missed working with his partner—or rather, ex-partner by now. Instead, he was stuck heading security inside a large public high school that was overcrowded and difficult to fully monitor. With a student enrollment of nearly thirty-five hundred, the school was on a split but overlapping session. Yet he had a staff of only ten: six men and four women. Three of them—Bill Warner, Denny Marino, and Jack Jamison—served as his assistants.

Warner, who'd be working the early shift with him, seemed like a solid enough, straight-up guy. A former competitive weight lifter, he was taking night classes to finish his Ph.D. in clinical psychology. Marino, however, was another matter. After being rejected for the police academy two years earlier, he'd signed on for this. Always quick with a lewd comment or gesture, he tried to make everything into a joke. If Baker had had his way, one of the women—Angela Love—would've been chosen in his place. And though Marino seemed to annoy Jamison the most, Jamison had yet to object to working second shift with him. Then again, Jamison wasn't much of a talker. In all the time they'd been working together to ready the school for opening, the tall, rangy black man—an honors graduate of Kings College—had said nothing more personal than, "I never read the newspaper in the morning," this big declaration in response to the copy of the *New York Post* Marino had offered him.

Baker went back to the recliner, downed the rest of his drink and set the sweating glass of melting ice cubes on top of Micki's folder, creating a fresh wet ring to join the others already there. Full of material from both the NYPD and the Department of Corrections, the file had taken quite a while to get through, but what had interested him most was the report relating to the homicide. The victim, Andrew "Speed" Davis, had been a six-foot-two, 258-pound Caucasian male, age twenty-six. He'd served time twice for dealing drugs, and the autopsy had shown traces of cocaine and alcohol in his system. According to Micki's statement, she'd used his own switchblade knife against him after he'd attacked her with it. His alleged motive? That he blamed her when Tim—his childhood friend and her "big brother"—had gotten shot. But Baker thought the report was thin and the self-defense scenario suspect despite the evidence to support it—namely, the victim's own fingerprints on the knife. As far as Baker was concerned, Micki was guilty. Because he wanted her to be guilty.

As for the other charges leveled against her, Micki had, in fact, pleaded guilty to all of them. That, and a remorseful attitude, had gone a long way in the state's acceptance of her explanation of Davis' death—the critical factor in the decision to process her as a juvenile. When the doctors who'd treated her in the hospital could only guess at her age—somewhere between sixteen and eighteen—the state had settled on seventeen so she could be placed in Heyden Reformatory for Girls and remain in the custody of the Division for Youth. After a year, she would then be reevaluated to determine if—or for how long—she'd be sentenced to an adult institution.

But Micki had spent the majority of her time at Heyden in solitary confinement—a recurring punishment for a long list of violent outbursts against staff. Only one incident, the very first day of her incarceration, had involved other inmates. And while she hadn't even been at Heyden for two months, the staff, with the exception of the psychiatrist, had formed a united and uniformly negative opinion of her. They stated she was combative, difficult to control, had no respect for authority, and showed no signs of improvement. The fact that she'd tested so exceedingly high, both intellectually and educationally, only bolstered their belief that she was putting one over on the staff shrink. It was their considered opinion she wasn't subject to rehabilitation and would never function well in society. Their recommendation: immediate transfer to an adult women's correctional facility. Baker agreed 100 percent.

On the other side of the fence were Sergeant Kelly and the aforementioned shrink, who'd written: "Micki is an extraordinarily bright child who's become embroiled in antisocial behavior due to unfortunate circumstances and exposure to harmful influences. In a fugue state of extensive duration, she is emotionally and psychologically scarred, exhibiting signs of severe depression with violent and self-destructive tendencies. She's in need of guidance, love, and a stable family environment." Bullshit, Baker thought. What she needs is a good whipping. He chalked the psychiatrist's opinion up to the fact that she was, well, a shrink. What would you expect her to say? But Kelly's stance was baffling. A street cop for something like twenty-five years, he was no pushover. What redeeming quality could he possibly have seen in the kid?

Baker picked up his glass and swirled it around, then drank the water from the melting ice cubes. He didn't give a fuck what Kelly thought or what the shrink believed he should be doing. Micki was nothing more than another delinquent kid playing the system for all it was worth. And while Heyden may have had problems controlling her, he was going to make damn sure she respected *his* authority. He wouldn't take any shit from her and wouldn't fall prey to any snow job, either. Malone said he had a lot of latitude in dealing with her, and he planned to use every inch of it. He'd take the boot-camp approach: there would be severe repercussions for even the slightest infractions. And since he had the right to search both her and her apartment (for which he had a key), he intended to fully exercise that power. He'd spare nothing because she was female; that had been the deal, right? He'd break her down until every shred of self-esteem she had was gone. She was going to wish she were still in juvi. He poured himself a final drink. If she thought she'd found an easier way to finish out her time, she had another thing coming.

Chapter 2

THE ALARM CLOCK'S RING was brash and unrelenting. Micki groaned. Never able to sleep well at night, the hot, humid air hadn't helped. For hours, she'd tossed and turned, finally drifting off just a short time before the buzzer rang. Her limbs felt like lead. Yesterday's double shift at Bel Canto had meant nearly twelve hours of washing dishes and cookware in the sauna-like conditions of its tiny kitchen. Going from the cool dining area into the crowded, airless, overheated back room had been like walking into hell itself. She'd washed dishes at Heyden, but that had been nothing compared to this. The restaurant's automatic dishwasher was too old, too small, and half broken, requiring things to be almost clean before being loaded in. As a result, it was used exclusively for glassware, silverware, and a limited number of small plates, leaving everything else to be done entirely by hand. The innumerable pots, pans, and metal casserole dishes were the worst, usually having some combination of cheese, sauce, and pasta baked on in varying shades of brown and black.

And then there was the heat. Always fired up to the max, there were two huge deck ovens and a large commercial stove—not to mention the steamy water she was using. Constantly in motion, a chef and an assistant chef were adding their body heat along with hers. And with only one marginal freestanding fan and a single small exhaust fan, the air was mostly stagnant—the temperature had to be reaching well over a hundred degrees. Sweat dripped and stung her eyes; her clothes were soaked through in no time at all. And when the night was over—the front door locked, the place empty of diners—she'd gulped down glass after glass of soda before going home to collapse on the bed.

Right before she'd left, Mr. Antonelli had offered her leftover pizza to take with her. But after having had her fill of pasta during her twenty-minute meal breaks, she'd felt too embarrassed. She should've taken it, though. Her stomach was growling, and there was nothing to eat in her apartment. Nothing at all.

With a soft little click, the alarm clock's second hand was ticking off the time, telling her she'd already stayed in bed too long, telling her she'd better get moving. Yesterday, when Miss Gutierrez had given her not only reduced-fare transit passes, but transit *maps*, her jaw must've dropped, because the social worker said, "You just have to take the E or F train to Union Turnpike, then catch the Q44A bus." When Micki didn't respond, the woman—with an unconvincing smile—had added, "It shouldn't be too bad." Micki thought it sounded like a royal pain in the ass, especially since she only had to walk down the street to get to work.

At least the first day of school started late and was merely half an hour—just long enough to pick up program cards and fill out papers. The second day would start late, as well, but last a little longer, with fifteen-minute periods for each class. But Friday, the third day, would be a full schedule, beginning at 7:50 a.m. If she'd had to be there that early this morning, she would never have made it.

She rolled out of bed, drank two glasses of water, and did her usual routine of pushups and sit-ups. But when she went to take a shower, the water was icy cold, even with the hot faucet opened up all the way. Eight minutes later, the water still freezing, she opted for a quick wash at the kitchen sink followed by a dab of deodorant. It wasn't until she was brushing her teeth that she thought about her hair, which was dirty and full of restaurant grease. Well, there wasn't much she could do about it now.

She pulled on her jeans, a fresh black T-shirt, and her vest, the flimsy plastic ID holder Miss Gutierrez had provided going in her back pocket. But as she was picking up her money, she paused to look at the small pocketknife she'd found on her way home from work. Slightly rusted, it was only two inches folded and had a pretty green and black handle. Hidden by a clump of weeds that had pushed their way up through a crack in the sidewalk, her sneaker had sent it skittering across the concrete. Maybe fate had sent it to her—like a lucky charm. She shoved the knife and money in her front pocket, put her sneakers on, and headed out the door.

It felt cooler, at least at first, going down into the subway. Micki held up her transit pass for the token-booth clerk, then jumped the turnstile out of habit. But down on the tracks, it was hotter and more airless than on the street, as if there was less oxygen underground. Alone on the platform—except for a couple by the wall, who were pawing at each other and making out—Micki was watching the commuters on the opposite side. Dressed in stiff-collared shirts and neckties, men were mopping brows with handkerchiefs while high-heeled women transferred weight from one foot to the other, blotting damp make-up with shredding, wadded-up tissues. Faces pinched, people were either checking their watches or craning their necks over the platform's edge to see if anything was on its way to take them into Manhattan.

An F train arrived, heading further into Queens, and Micki stepped into one of the air-conditioned cars, the sweat on her skin immediately evaporating in the dry, chilly air. And though she could've sat almost anywhere, she chose a seat across from two little old ladies with teased-up hair. Side by side, they sat with perfect posture, each holding a black patent-leather purse on her lap. But after they glanced at Micki, they clutched their pocketbooks tightly. When the train stopped at the next station—Queens Plaza—they looked at each other, got up, and sat at the other end of the car, near a man in a suit with a briefcase beside him.

Micki watched as the man pulled out a brown appointment book and jotted something down. She watched the train doors slide together, banging shut. She watched the platform disappear as they began to pick up speed. And when the deafening roar filled her ears again, she realized she'd forgotten to bring a pen and something to write on. Yesterday, instead of buying school supplies and groceries, she'd worked in Bel Canto's steambath. By the time her shift had ended, the stores had all been closed—except for the little deli on the corner. And though she probably could've bought a few things there to tide her over, she'd been too exhausted to think of it then. It hadn't occurred to her this morning, either.

She stared out the window, the murky scenery flashing by: cold, shadowy shapes interspersed with lights shining in a sickly off-white. Here and there, singularly exotic, a bulb was softly glowing blue. And sometimes—beyond the dark, ghostly blur—she could see a vast, empty space with extensive bracings disappearing into total blackness, so that the entire subway system seemed filled with secrets. And maybe nothing was what it appeared to be. Through miles of tunnels and hidden passageways, headlights pierced through an endless night, trains running as if their final destinations were so incredibly important. But, round and round, their wheels stuck to the tracks, they weren't really going anywhere at all.

AT UNION TURNPIKE, MICKI exited the subway and changed to the Q44A, which was sitting at the end of its line. The driver assured her she was on the correct bus, but her stomach squeezed itself into a knot until the clumsy vehicle did a U-turn and headed in the right direction. And though there was quite a ways to go before her stop, her eyes were glued to the street signs passing by—until the strings of stores lining the road turned into homes of all kinds: brick apartment buildings, garden apartments, even private houses—all neat and clean with trimmed hedges, flowers, and well-maintained cars. Sprinklers—gracefully arcing from side to side or rapidly rotating with forceful, even spurts—were watering thirsty, mowed lawns. She turned her eyes away from the window and slumped down in the seat.

The closer the bus got to the school, the more other kids started getting on. Chattering and laughing, they were telling each other about summer vacations. Micki sat in silence. At 232nd Street they all got off, and Micki followed—until it occurred to her that she didn't have to go to school at all. Eyes bright, she stopped in the middle of the sidewalk while kids continued to walk around her. But then her shoulders sagged: with no place to go, twenty dollars wouldn't take her very far. Besides, they'd eventually get her. It didn't take them long after she'd escaped from Heyden.

THE FIRST THING TO come into view was the athletic field. A few kids were already running track and playing ball while behind them rose the back of the school itself. There was no graffiti. No litter on the sidewalks. And as Micki looked around, it finally hit her: the kids who went here all had parents to take care of them, real brothers and sisters, friends to hang out with, rooms with posters on the walls… She stopped again while kids passed by, their voices growing louder till they were ringing in her ears like a warning. Someone bumped into her from behind, a girl who'd been walking backward as she talked to her friends. Micki spun around to find the girl giggling and blushing.

"Oh—like, I'm so sorry," the girl said, though she was looking down at the notebook she'd dropped. Restricted by the miniskirt that showed off her long, tanned legs, the girl was awkwardly stooping to pick up the fallen item, her leather shoulder bag slipping down to her elbow. But when she straightened up and actually looked at Micki, the giggling ceased, and the smile faded. She hurried away with her friends.

Steps slower and heavier, Micki started moving again, feet mechanically following those of the crowd.

A LARGE, THREE-STORY, WHITE-BRICK structure, Newbridge High School was relatively modern and nondescript. Underneath the school's name was a huge clock that read 2:47. Permanently. Micki wondered what time it really was. She proceeded up the steps and through the doors until she saw Baker standing in the lobby. Dressed in jeans and a dark T-shirt, he was observing students as they entered. He motioned with his head for her to wait on the side while other kids paraded past like an offhand sample of teenage fashion: bell bottoms, fatigues, hot pants, skirts, dresses… Several boys with slicked-back hair and motorcycle boots looked like greasers.

From behind a large folding table, two security guards, also in plain clothes, were checking out the students, as well. One of them, a black woman in a polo shirt and khaki pants, got up and stopped a tall boy as he came in with some friends. A few quick questions and then she pointed to the door, shaking her head, her large Afro glistening. Laughing, the boy shrugged, then waved to his buddies and left. When the guard returned to her post, she explained the teen had graduated the year before. A real clown, she still remembered him.

Baker nodded. "Good job, Angela." And once the steady stream of students had died down to a trickle, he told her he was leaving her in charge of the entrance. "Let's go," he said to Micki.

A loud bell rang through the corridors. School had officially begun.

MICKI FOLLOWED BAKER THROUGH the hall, where they made a left around the general office before entering the security office, which was the next room down. Baker, acting as though she already had some clue as to what was going on, introduced the assistant heads of security, who'd returned from their posts so she could meet them. If for any reason he wasn't there, she was to report to Mr. Warner. If neither one of them was available, then Mr. Jamison or Mr. Marino would be in charge.

Warner flashed a warm smile and reminded her a lot of the coffee cop from the day before. Though trimmer and far more muscular, he had the same type of curly hair and mustache, only brown instead of red. Jamison gave her a solemn nod. But Marino's eyes had roved over her body twice already. She gave him a dirty look.

"I'd appreciate it," Baker said to Marino and Jamison, "if you guys would go back and check on things in the hallways."

Promptly heading for the door, Jamison replied, "Sure thing, Chief." Marino, however, tossed his newspaper on the green vinyl sofa, then lingered to leer at her.

Baker stepped between them. "Mr. Marino?"

"Yeah, yeah." But he took his time leaving.

Baker shut the door, then pointed to the farther of two desks along the wall. "Sit down over there."

Micki found a sheet of paper and two index cards—one pink and one white—requesting information for school records.

Tapping his fingers on them, Baker said, "Fill these out."

She looked around the desk, saw a black plastic pencil holder, and reached for one of the ballpoint pens.

He stared down at her. "You came to school without a pen?"

"I worked ye—"

"I don't give a shit. When you come to school, you should be prepared. You didn't bring a notebook, either, did you."

"No," she said quietly.

"No," he repeated.

Hands on hips, he loomed over her while she filled out the forms. And though her ID card had most of the information she needed, a few spaces still had to be left blank. As soon as she was done, he snatched the papers away, saying, "Give me that ID card, too." When he returned it to her, he said, "You know you have to carry this at all times?"

"Yeah."

"Get up and stand over there."

She moved across the room to the spot he'd indicated, an empty space between some file cabinets and another desk. She flicked a glance at Warner, now sitting on the sofa beneath the window and reading Marino's copy of the *Daily News*.

From the top drawer of his desk, Baker pulled out a computer-generated card and a thick booklet that said "Student Guide" on the cover. "This is your program card," he said, holding it up for her to see. "Tomorrow, when you go to your classes, the teachers will sign it. You're to return it to me on Friday. In case you haven't figured it out, this is your homeroom; so if anyone needs to know, I'm your homeroom teacher. Whenever there's an actual homeroom period, you report here. Do you understand?"

"Yeah." He was acting like she was too stupid to understand the simplest things.

"This book," he said, raising it up, next to his head, "will explain everything about the school, including the different schedules. You can—" He stopped and looked her over. "Are those the same clothes you wore yesterday?"

"Different shirt, same jeans."

"Did you even wash today?"

"Yeah."

"Really? Cause you smell, and your hair looks filthy."

"I had to wash in the sink, so I didn't have time to wash my hair."

"You couldn't shower?"

"There was no hot water."

"No hot water," he repeated. "So you think it's okay to come to school like this?" She chewed the inside of her lip.

"Well, let me tell you, then, that it is *not* okay to come to school like this. Even if you have to freeze your butt off, you take a shower and wash your hair every day. You're to come to school *clean*. Is that understood?"

"Yeah."

He put the program card and booklet on the desk, then folded his arms across his chest. His muscles looked even larger than they had before. He said, "I think it's time to go over the rules."

She shoved her hands in her front pockets and shifted her weight to the other leg.

"First of all," he began, "you're to get here by seven thirty-five in the morning so I have time to check you out before you go to class. At the end of the day, you'll report back here before going home."

She wondered exactly what he meant by "check you out."

"There's no smoking anywhere on school grounds."

"I don't smoke."

"You mean there's actually a vice you don't indulge in?"

"I've never smoked."

"You've smoked pot, right?"

"No."

He laughed. "C'mon, you've got needle tracks up and down your arm."

"I've never smoked a fucking thing."

"You're full of shit."

She glared at him.

He unfolded his arms, and his voice became quiet. "Let's get something straight: I don't want to hear you cursing *anywhere*. That means in school or out. Understand?"

"Yeah."

"Furthermore, from now on, when you answer 'yes' or 'no,' you say 'yes, sir' or 'no, sir.' Is *that* clear?"

She seethed silently. It was always the same fucking military crap.

"I *said:* 'is—that—clear?'"

"Yessir."

"You're to call me 'Sergeant Baker' or 'Sir.'"

"Not 'Detective Baker'?" The question had just popped out because she'd never been able to figure out police titles: "detective" always sounded so much more impressive to her than "sergeant."

"What are you, fucking deaf or just stupid? What did I just say?"

She pressed her lips together.

"You're not to carry any weapons," he continued, "and you're not to use any drugs or alcohol. In order to make sure you're complying with these rules, I can search you or your apartment any time I feel like it. And if I have reason to suspect you're using anything, I can have you drug tested, too. It's the same basic drill as parole. Do you have any questions?"

"No, sir." She had stopped looking at him. Instead, her eyes were fixed on the coffee machine atop the little refrigerator by the door. When he said he could search her, he didn't mean—

"Then turn around and put your hands against the wall. I'm sure you know the routine quite well by now."

Her eyes snapped back to see him already coming toward her. Out of the corner of her eye, she saw Warner get up and step closer to the desk on her right.

"Move it!" Baker ordered.

She recalled the security woman she'd seen in the lobby. "Y'can't do this," she said. "Y'supposeda get a female officer if there's one around."

"Well, I've got news for you, Reilly"—his eyes were laughing down at her— "you don't have a female parole officer; you've got me. And it's well within my jurisdiction to do this. So if you don't like it, you can just suck my dick."

"Well whip it out, and let's see whatcha got."

His left hand moved to strike her, and she blocked it—only to feel the palm of his right hand smash across her face. The force of the blow knocked her off balance, making it even easier for him to turn her around and throw her toward the wall. It took all of her strength to keep her face from colliding with it.

Palm pressed between her shoulder blades, he kicked her feet back and further apart. "You don't talk to me like that, you little son of a bitch."

Her left cheek was stinging, and there was a slight aching pain in the bone. She wondered if it was swelling up.

"*Put your head down and keep your eyes on the floor,*" he barked.

Jesus! He was acting like she might actually try to hurt him.

With a rough, grasping motion, large hands patted down her denim vest, then moved underneath and did the same as they slid over the side of her ribs. Reaching around, he placed his hands just below her collarbones. But as soon as they moved, she balked. He slammed his palm into her back again, forcing her to remain in position. Leaning down till his face was only inches from hers, he asked, "Do you have a problem with this, Reilly?"

She continued to stare at the floor.

"Huh? I asked you something! Do you really think I'm trying to cop a cheap feel here? Huh? 'Cause the truth is, you disgust me, and I'd rather not have to touch you at all. But I'm not about to jeopardize my safety—or the safety of anyone in this school—over some bullshit modesty of yours. I can just imagine how many guys have had their hands all over you. Now if you have some problem with this, you go ahead and complain to whoever the fuck you want. But for now, you're just going to have to take it. Is that understood?"

She stared at the floor.

"YOU ANSWER ME WHEN I TALK TO YOU."

Voice flat, she said, "Yessir."

"Now, you don't move. If I have to stop again, I promise you, you'll regret it." He paused as if to let this sink in, as if he wanted to give her some time to consider the consequences. Yet between the two of them, he was the one who was sweating. He placed his palms under her collarbones again, pinkies resting on the rise of her chest. With just the tips of his fingers, he traced the space between her breasts. Then he put his hands below, thumbs touching the underwire rim of her bra, before continuing down. Until he felt the hard object in her right front pocket. He reached in and retrieved it, then swiftly ran his hands over her back pockets, her crotch, and her legs. He straightened up and took a step back. "Turn around."

Her expression cool, she faced him.

He held up the offending item.

"It's just a pocketkni—"

"Shut up! You're not supposed to carry *anything* that could be used as a weapon. Considering how handy you are with knives, I'm sure that, even with this, you could do some nifty work."

Actually, she wouldn't say she was handy with knives. While very effective in threatening people with them, she'd never even cut anyone—except, of course, Speed. It must've been beginner's luck that had made the knife slip so cleanly between his ribs. Nick, "the Knife," on the other hand, was truly handy with knives—and she had the scars to prove it. She could still see him holding the blade only an inch from the tip so he could use it like a razor to slash at her—

"ARE YOU LISTENING TO ME, REILLY?" Baker barked.

Her eyes shot back to his. "Yeah, I'm listenin'!"

"Really? 'Cause you don't look like you're listening. You look like you're thinking about something else. If I were you, I wouldn't be thinking about anything except whether or not I was going to be on the next bus back upstate."

Her lips parted slightly.

"Yeah, Reilly, that's right. This could all be over now. What happens next is up to me. You ought to be thinking about convincing me to let you stay. You ought to be *begging* me to let you stay."

Shifting her weight, she folded her arms over her chest. This was a real power trip for him. He was taking this so fucking seriously. A stupid pocketknife!

"I'm waiting," he said.

She continued to glare at him—but his eyes were laughing.

"In fact," he said, "I think you should get down on your knees and beg."

"Fuck you."

He backfisted her across the face with his left hand, splitting the skin over the same cheekbone he'd hit before. Her head snapped to the side, and the world seemed to spin. Only his steely grip on her shoulder prevented her from stumbling and colliding into a desk. Blindly lashing out to break his hold, she almost hit him in the face. He responded with a punch to the gut. But when his fist met with a solid wall of muscle, their eyes locked. And in that split second before she could retaliate, he yanked her toward him and punched again, only this time high enough to ensure the wind was knocked out of her.

She dropped to the ground, gasping for air that was unwilling to enter her lungs. Crushed by a smooth, round pain and a rush of nausea, she clutched at her stomach.

He snorted. "Now what? You're going to throw up?"

His words, floating around the backs of her eyelids, were mixing with the bitter taste rising in her throat and the ominous little chills that kept running through her mouth.

"So what's it going to be, Reilly, huh? I haven't heard anything yet, but I see you're already on your knees."

Eyes still closed, she could feel him towering over her, a million miles tall. If only she could stand up. If only—

"Well, I guess I have my answer."

"No!"

"What? What was that?"

"I—I don't wanna go back."

"Not good enough."

She could picture the look on his face, the nasty little smile. She wanted to tell him to go fuck himself. But with each jagged, uneven breath, her mind was flooded with images of Heyden, the sudden stillness of the room folding into a dark and empty space. Eyes fixed on the floor, her voice little more than a mumble, she said, "I'm beggin' ya t'let me stay."

Leaning over slightly, he cupped a hand behind his ear. "What? What was that? I couldn't hear what you said."

Fucking son of a *bitch*. Through gritted teeth she said more loudly, "I'm beggin' ya t'let me stay."

"Hmm." He straightened up. "Well, I might as well give you another shot. I'm sure you'll fuck up again soon enough."

Unable to hold off any longer, she threw up the water she'd had for breakfast. She just about never threw up. Even when she really needed to, she had to put her finger down her throat. Of all times for this to happen. Still doubled over, she saw his sneakers walk away, then heard water running. When the sneakers returned, a bunch of brown paper towels—some of them wet—were dropped in front of her.

"Clean up this mess." The sneakers walked away again.

Head heavy, she wiped up the floor with careful, deliberate movements. And though there was pain with each swipe of her hand across the linoleum, she felt oddly numb, as if it were someone else's. When she was done, she slowly stood up and looked around.

Pointing to a door that was ajar next to the desk where Warner was still standing, he said, "In there."

She walked over, but avoided looking at the assistant head of security, convinced that he, too, was reveling in her humiliation.

But Warner was in shock. Stricken silent by uncertainty, he'd merely stood by and watched, hadn't done a single thing to intervene because Baker was a cop. Because Baker's custody of Micki had supposedly been sanctioned by both the juvenile justice system *and* social services. But he felt ill.

Inside the small bathroom, Micki discarded the used paper towels and examined herself in the mirror. Face flushed, eyes a little bloodshot, her left cheekbone—already swelling—was bloody. She washed it, inwardly wincing, then dabbed at it with a paper towel. When she looked in the mirror again, she saw the blood was clotting. She also saw Baker framed in the doorway. She spun around.

"You talk to me with respect," he said.

"Yessir," she said quietly.

The passing bell rang, and he stepped aside. "Take your stuff and go."

But as she was about to leave, Warner grabbed her arm. Body rigid, she fought the impulse to pull away.

"First chance you get," he said, "put some ice on that."

Eyes down, she mumbled, "Yessir." And hurried out the door.

HOW SHE CAME TO be standing at the bus stop, she didn't know. There was no recollection of anything that had happened between the time she'd left the security office and the moment she'd noticed the other kids looking at her and whispering. Several girls huddled together near the curb were being especially blatant about it.

Turning toward them, Micki said, "What're *you* starin' at?"

They immediately backed up. But a boy about her size—jeans ripped at the knees, a pack of cigarettes rolled up in the sleeve of his T-shirt—stepped forward. "Your ugly face," he said.

She dropped what she was holding. "Why don'tcha come over *here* and say that, asshole."

They moved toward each other, but a very large boy, with a blond crew cut and a school football jersey, came between them. "Whoa!" he said. "Everybody just take it easy."

A bus pulled up, and all the kids got on. Except Micki.

The blond boy, standing on the lowest step and leaning out, said, "C'mon."

"Let's go!" the driver ordered. "You're holding everything up."

Micki shook her head no and stepped back. The doors shut, and the vehicle drove away. She felt an odd twinge of regret.

About ten minutes later, another Q44A came along. She flashed her pass, paid a nickel, and found a spot at a window. Then she listened to the motor alternately idle and roar as the bus, stopping frequently, slowly lumbered down Union Turnpike. Seated high above the road, she was looking down at the tops of passing cars. What she was seeing, though, was Baker hitting her, forcing her to beg, making it very clear just what he thought of her.

The bus pulled over to pick up more passengers, coins jingling their way into the fare box, which churned them around in a hidden, rhythmic dance. But crowded as the vehicle now was— little space left, people standing in the aisle—no one was sitting next to Micki. As the bus merged back into traffic, she looked out the window again, aware of the empty seat beside her. Everyone was so quick to judge. Before she'd even said anything, Baker had already made up his mind. But wasn't this supposed to be her chance to prove she could change? Wasn't that what this was all about? Actually, she wasn't sure anymore what this was all about, but, given enough time, she might figure it out.

AFTER SHE'D SWITCHED TO the subway, she took a look at the *Student Guide*. It started off with a short history of the school, which was built in the 1950s. The guide itself looked like it must've been written around then, because the photos, drawings, and text were ridiculously wholesome. Nobody bought this bullshit, did they? A brief flip through the pages showed floor maps, schedules, and course descriptions along with a hefty list of school rules. But when she turned her attention to her program card, the class codes—strings of numbers and letters— were indecipherable. She exhaled heavily; everything was always such a hassle.

The train reached the Twenty-Third Street–Ely Avenue stop, and she exited the station, the sun too bright, forcing her to squint. She needed some sunglasses. Actually, she needed a lot of things, including the money to buy them. She crossed the street, then returned to her program card, trying to match the codes to the course descriptions, barely glancing up as she walked along. When she reached her building, she was so engrossed in what she was doing that she stopped on the sidewalk instead of going inside. And then the card was snatched from her hands.

"Let's see what's so fuckin' interestin'." The thief—a tall, skinny boy with long, stringy brown hair and a bad case of acne—was holding the piece of paper out of reach.

"Hey!" She tried to grab it back.

But his friends, smelling of pot and looking stoned, stepped in to block her— all five of them: three other boys and two girls.

"Oh, look at dis," the tall boy said. "Aren't we fuckin' smart, takin' college level courses at anudda high school. Whatsa matta, our high school ain't good enough for ya?"

"Wasn't upta me," she said.

The boy ripped the card into pieces and threw them into the air.

Micki didn't react.

With a sickening smile, he said, "Sorry, but it wasn't upta me."

The kids all laughed. But as they headed down the street, one of the other boys lagged behind. Overweight, he had unruly reddish-brown hair and glasses, which were crooked after he pushed them up higher with just his index finger. Walking backward, he smiled at Micki and shrugged. "Joey's a real jerk sometimes."

A petite blonde in heavy make-up, tight shorts, and a low-cut tank top grabbed his arm and shot Micki a dark look. "C'mon, Rick."

He smiled at Micki again, then went with the blonde.

Micki looked at the pieces of paper littering the sidewalk.

DESPITE THE FACT THAT she didn't have any ice to apply, the bruise on her cheek didn't swell too badly. It did color nicely, though, all purples and reds. When Mr. Antonelli saw it, he frowned, but said nothing—she was the best dishwasher he'd seen in years.

But the six-hour shift seemed as long as the twelve hours she'd worked the day before. And if there'd been a bed in the basement, she might've considered sleeping there. Instead, she left the restaurant, dragging her feet, the half of a medium pizza with extra cheese still warm inside the flat white box she carried. After what she'd spent at the supermarket that afternoon, restaurant leftovers were looking pretty damn good.

Up ahead, gated shut, was an alley that served as a driveway to a small parking lot for a mirror-manufacturing company. A little group of kids was leaning against the chain-link fencing, and she recognized a few of them. As much as she wanted to cross the street and ignore the hoots and hollers that would surely follow, she continued going straight.

"Hey, I see ya brought me dinna."

It was Joey, the jerk who'd ripped up her program card. He had his arm around a skinny brunette in cutoffs and a halter-top. Rick was there, too, the hot-to-trot little blonde beside him. Micki kept walking.

"Why don'tcha hang out wit' us," Rick offered.

Micki stopped.

The blonde pulled away. "Rick, shut *up*. Whatta ya sayin' that for." Hands planted firmly on hips, she glared at him.

Rick laughed. "Aw, c'mon. Don't be a bitch."

The girl stomped off in her high-heeled sandals, butt swaying side to side. As she passed Micki, she tried to knock the pizza box out of her hands.

"I gotta go," Micki said.

"C'mon," Rick said. "Hang out awhile."

"No, really. I gotta go."

"Curfew?"

"Yeah," she replied, sounding surprised. It wasn't until she got home that she realized he'd probably been talking about a parental one.

She put the pizza slices—unwrapped but still inside the box—in the refrigerator, hoping they'd be safe enough from the roaches. Then she peeled off her clothes, put on the oversized T-shirt she used as a nightshirt, and flopped down on the mattress.

But sleep wouldn't come. Pictures kept running through her head: disjointed scenes from her days in the Bronx mixed with those of Heyden and her life now. Giving up, she turned over and stared at the ceiling.

She remembered when she was in the hospital after they'd stitched her insides back together. They'd put her in a private room with a cop stationed there twenty-four hours a day. The cops never talked to her—kept the door closed while they sat outside, alone. Professional and disdainful at the same time, the doctors and nurses weren't much better. But then one day Sergeant Kelly showed up, out of uniform and with his nose all bandaged. It took a moment till she recognized him. But when she did, she turned bright red, which made him laugh. Then he sat down next to her bed and talked to her. Just talked to her. It didn't seem to matter that she wasn't talking back. Weak from trauma and surgery, she had tubes running in and out all over the place with an IV morphine drip to combat the pain. She liked lying there, looking into his eyes. He had kind green eyes.

After that, he came back to the hospital just once—and found her sick as a dog. One of the doctors, to give her a good taste of withdrawal, had stopped the morphine cold. Sergeant Kelly took one look at her and went storming over to the nurse's station, yelling like hell, calling the doctor a sadistic bastard. Within minutes, they started her on methadone, tapering her down over time till she was completely off.

But as soon as she was discharged, she was taken to Heyden, and things went downhill fast. When they pulled her out of solitary, saying she had a visitor, she thought they were kidding. She didn't even ask who it was. Dirty and disheveled, she wanted to hide when she saw it was Sergeant Kelly. The expression on his face didn't help.

He said, "Hi, Micki"—and seemed to be waiting for her to say something back. She stared out the window instead.

He walked up behind her and quietly asked if they were mistreating her. In reply, she closed her eyes—as if that could make all the bad things go away. And when he gathered the hem at the back of her T-shirt, asking, "Is this okay?" she didn't respond at all. So he gently lifted the material a few inches—just enough to see what he had to—then stroked her grimy hair and said something reassuring, though his exact words were lost to her now. Not long after that, everything changed. They said she'd been chosen for this experimental program, and she'd started counting down the days to her release.

But this wasn't anything like what she'd imagined. In her daydreams, her legal guardian had been understanding and caring, someone protective—like Sergeant Kelly. And she'd always pictured herself being different—not acting like she had in juvi. The only thing she could be grateful for was that Baker hadn't totally lost it on her; the man could easily break her apart. Jesus, what was she thinking back there at the bus stop? What if that had turned into a fight? She could see the bus pulling away again, all of the other kids inside while she stood alone on the curb. Was it her imagination or had that blond boy—the football player—still been looking at her from the window? He'd seemed kind of nice…

She started feeling stressed: boys, sex… So far it had only been ugly. Ugly and cruel. In fact, the thought of someone kissing her in the middle of doing it seemed repulsive. Love—or the thought of love—had to be kept separate. Pure. Untouched. Not that anyone would ever be interested in her that way anyway.

She put her hands behind her head and sighed: as if things couldn't get any worse, she was physically attracted to the fucking cop. But who wouldn't be? That morning she'd seen the reaction of the girls who'd noticed him when they were entering the school: blushes, nervous giggles, whispers behind hands…

She wondered what it would be like to have sex with someone that looked like him.

He was glad, now, that Cynthia was in Los Angeles. These past two nights, sitting alone and drinking whiskey in the darkened living room was about all he was good for. And yet, mind going round and round, the liquor was doing little to sedate him. He could've gone to the gym, could've taken it out on the heavy bag. But that would've risked running into someone he knew. He didn't want to talk to anyone, didn't want to listen to anyone, either. He'd already heard plenty from Warner. As soon as Micki had left the office, Warner had asked, "Are you sure this is the way you want to handle this?"

"I know what I'm doing," Baker had snapped. "Everybody's always coddling these kids, saying they need this, they need that. It's all bullshit. They need the shit kicked out of them. How do you think they handled her in juvi, and look what good it did."

Warner had raised his hands. "Hey, I'm not trying to tell you what to do. I just thought if you wanted to bounce around some ideas, I'd give a listen."

But the truth was, Baker had no idea what he was doing. Everything that had seemed so clear the night before seemed out of focus now. The only thing he knew for sure was that he hated being at that school. It made him think about calling it quits and quietly turning in his shield. But then what? He had no desire to go back to law school, and, at thirty-six, he no longer felt there was a world of opportunity waiting for him. He didn't talk about it with Cynthia anymore because she always said the same thing: "You're too negative. You have to open yourself up and try things. See what happens." Easy for her to say; she was only twenty-seven. Plus her parents had plenty of money. She'd never really known what it was like to scramble around without a safety net. In many ways, he and Cynthia were an odd couple.

They'd met two years ago when he'd been investigating some seemingly credible threats against the director of a controversial film being shot in the city. While checking out some leads on a set in Central Park, he was scanning the perimeter when he caught sight of her entering the holding area. Cast as an extra, she was waiting with some others till she was needed again. He couldn't take his eyes off her. Six feet tall, with honey-blond hair and big blue eyes, she looked like a model. And, later on, he learned that's how she'd gotten started. But despite her perfect proportions, classic features, and natural talent in front of the camera, the fashion world had snubbed her because she refused to play the game—no casting couch for her. Ever. And while she'd been making a good living doing catalog and commercial-print work, she'd become increasingly dissatisfied and unfulfilled. And worried about growing older. So she'd switched her focus. Yet acting was proving equally elusive, fraught with just as many charlatans and predators—maybe more. With the hope of better luck on the West Coast, she'd taken this trip to LA to look for an agent.

But why she insisted on pursuing a career where the chances of making it were so slim—even if you were very talented—he could never understand. She was extremely bright; there had to be a multitude of other options open to her. At least, for now. If she waited too long, she could find herself in his situation. It was also ironic that while she staunchly supported Gloria Steinem, had read *The Feminine Mystique*, and quoted *Ms. Magazine* like it was the goddamn bible, she continued to earn a living as a model. When he'd had the balls to call her on it once, she'd shot back, "It's about having choices. There's nothing wrong with being a model if that's what I want."

"But don't you think being paid to look pretty and sexy just to sell things encourages women to be looked at like sex objects? Aren't you against that?"

The ensuing silence was deadly.

"I *think*," she finally replied, "that if I were a man with a bachelor's in philosophy, I would've been offered at least *one* of the decent-paying jobs I applied for when I got out of college. Then I wouldn't have had to keep modeling to pay my rent. I didn't earn a degree so I could take dictation and fetch coffee."

She hadn't really answered his question. But apparently another one of her "choices" had been to let him open the door for her as they'd left the coffee shop.

He polished off his drink and poured himself another.

Jesus! It had been so easy to hit the kid. Never in his life had he hit a female, but, then again, Micki was different. Still, he hadn't expected things to go that far. And as he stared off into the shadows, he could see her on the office floor again, gasping for breath, throwing up…

He swirled the whiskey around in the glass, then tossed it back.

Tillim's stupid-ass experiment. The way the department was treating him, you'd think he'd beaten the shit out of some innocent old man. All he did was give a murdering scumbag a little of what he deserved. They should be giving him a fucking medal for what he did. Everybody acting like there was something wrong with him. There was something wrong with *them*. Did anyone even take a moment to think of the victim—a good woman, a really decent human being—lying there dead? What about her, huh? What about *her*? So fuck 'em all. Fuck IAD, fuck Malone, and fuck the kid. He was sick of all this shit. In one smooth motion he stood up and hurled the tumbler at the wall. The thick glass left a dent at the point of impact, then hit the hardwood floor, where it broke into several large pieces.

He flopped back into the chair and hung his head. Just another mess to clean up.

RIGHT BEFORE DAWN, THE skies opened up and washed away the brutal heat. Micki crawled out of bed and turned on the light. Twelve calm minutes of coffee and cold pizza were followed by a frantic push to exercise, shower, and get dressed while still making it out the door on time. Before she left, she touched the swelling on her face, but avoided the mirror—not that she ever liked to see herself anyway.

When she got to school, Baker wasn't at the front entrance, so she went to the security office and found him alone. Leaning against the file cabinets, he was drinking coffee from a Styrofoam cup. They eyed each other warily.

"Is that all you wear?" he asked. "Black T-shirts and blue jeans?"

"Why? Are you gonna tell me what I have to wear now, too?"

"No, I don't care what you wear as long as everything's clean. Are those clean?"

"Yeah."

"Yes, *sir*," he corrected.

She looked away. "Yes, *sir*."

He tossed the cup into the wastepaper basket and straightened up. "Let's go. Put your hands against the wall."

Her eyes flew back to his. "Again? C'mon…"

His expression more than jaded, he waited. And waited. Until she complied. And though his touch felt completely professional—same as it had the day before—she thought he was getting off on it, on exerting control over her. When he was finished, she turned around and stared past him.

"Did you put any ice on that bruise last night?"

"I didn't have any."

"Let me see it." He reached toward her, but she recoiled.

Their eyes held.

He snorted.

She glared.

"Do you know where you're going?" he asked.

"Sort of."

"What do you mean: 'sort of'?"

"I dunno, I checked the classrooms off on the maps in that book you gave me; but, y'know, it looks different now. I dunno…" Her voice trailed off.

"Let me see your program card."

She handed it over.

"What the hell happened to this?"

"It—had a little accident."

It took a lot for him not to laugh: "a little accident." The piece of paper looked like a Scotch-taped jigsaw puzzle. The passing bell rang. "C'mon," he said, "I'll show you how to get to your first class."

She looked up sharply. "Really?"

"I'm just in a good mood," he said dryly. "Don't get your hopes up."

As she went from room to room, Micki discovered that Joey had been right: she was taking advanced-placement courses in calculus, physics (a double period with lab), and English. She also had honors American history, economics, gym, and art—but no lunch. She'd have to eat during physics. And with the exception of gym and art, she saw the same kids in almost all of her classes because she'd been thrown into the accelerated science program. Made up of twenty-two boys and four girls, it was a fast track for the most gifted students. While they all looked at her with curiosity, no one said much of anything, though one boy, Greg, came up and introduced himself after history, the last class of the day. Not wanting to have to answer a lot of questions, she said she'd just been transferred from another school and had to go fill out more paperwork right away.

Arms full of heavy textbooks, she returned to the security office and asked Baker if she could get a locker like a lot of other kids had.

"Absolutely not," he said. "That's all I need is one more thing to keep an eye on with you. You can leave your books on the corner of my desk. In the winter, you can use the coat rack over there near the door."

A winter coat. Winter clothes. More things she couldn't afford. "I need a note for gym," she said. "Mrs. Tandy said I needed a note if it would be a financial hardship for me to pay for a gym suit and a lock."

"You've got a job."

"He's only paying me a dollar-forty an hour."

"Isn't minimum wage two dollars?"

"He only hired me 'cause they said he could pay me less."

Tapping his pen on the desk, Baker did a quick mental calculation. He couldn't see how she'd manage even the bare necessities.

He wrote the note. With his left hand. She hadn't noticed that before.

ANOTHER BUSY SHIFT AT work, another slow procession of restless hours in bed. Micki had finally entered the deepest layer of sleep when the alarm went off. Yawning, eyes half closed, she boiled some water only to watch the milk curdle in the cup of instant coffee. But when she got to school, things took a turn for the better: Baker told her to simply turn around and hold her arms away from her body while he patted her down. In time, he'd search her only intermittently and at random.

And so, with the ring of the first-period bell, she became a full-fledged student at Newbridge High. Sitting tall in her first class, loose-leaf open to a clean white sheet, she listened closely to everything her economics teacher was saying. But by the end of the day, after hours of being still and copying notes from the blackboard, she was slouched at her desk, barely listening to her history teacher or fellow classmates. Elbow on her notebook, hand propping up her head, she was doodling around the words she'd scribbled on the page. Thick and fine lines—embellished with tiny, little dots—were crossing and curling around intricate, flowery designs—

The passing bell rang. She raced down the stairs, checked in with Baker, then headed out to face the long trip home. The Q44A came relatively quickly, and an E train was pulling in just as she reached the subway platform. But then, doors open, it just sat in the station for fifteen minutes before running local instead of express. Her books in a pile next to her, she tapped her foot on the floor. What a fucking waste of time. She got back to her apartment and could only wolf down a couple of Twinkies before dashing out again for Bel Canto.

But no sooner had she tied her apron on than diners started coming in to get an early jump on the weekend. Mr. Antonelli—moving between tables, checking in frequently with the kitchen—worked hard to keep the turnover rate high. And as the eatery headed into the heart of the Friday-night rush, groups of tired coworkers gave way to dating couples and families, waiters posting orders in rapid succession. The pass bar filled up, and the atmosphere in the kitchen grew tense. And though Micki's twenty-minute meal break turned into a few forkfuls of rigatoni, she took it as a challenge to have no more than one layer of dirty dishes and pots on the bottom of the sink at any given time.

Shortly after eleven, her T-shirt soaking wet beneath her vest, she finally left the restaurant, the street strangely empty of kids. With only cars passing her by, she saw Saturday stretched out before her like miles and miles of nothing except wide-open space—she didn't have to be back at work until five.

But after spending most of her free weekend hours sleeping, Sunday night came upon her fast. Homework assignments that had seemed like nothing on Friday now looked like massive projects. She sat down and started with physics and calculus, both of which went quickly and were actually kind of fun. English wasn't bad; economics was pretty dry. But history—it was hard to keep her eyes open. Friday's class hadn't been quite so boring because the teacher had used the time to talk about current events—mostly Watergate and Nixon's resignation. The discussion had grown heated, and everyone had had something to say. Except Micki. With only the vaguest idea of what they were talking about, she'd sat at the back of the room, drawing in her notebook and only half listening—same as she had before the class had started. Only then kids had been talking about sports, music, TV, movies, parties, driving… They all knew each other, some of them friends. They went to each other's homes, bought books and albums to share…

In her loosened grip, the pen had strayed, leaving an errant mark upon the page. A small but permanent scar. She glanced over at her needle-tracked skin, then slammed the history textbook shut.

Chapter 3

JOEY OFFERED HER THE bottle again, but she handed it over to Rick, who took an extra long swig as if to prove he was cooler than everyone else. Sitting with her back against the wall in the hidden section of the parking lot, Micki was feeling a little spacey just from breathing in the smoke that hung like a cloud over the little enclosure.

The roach had gotten too small. Rick lit up a fresh joint and pressured her to take a hit since it was his last one. But she wouldn't even touch it to pass it along; Joey had to take it from Rick himself, all the while complaining that he wanted to get something to eat already—he was hungry.

The air was still warm, but it was late, past curfew, and Micki should've been back in her apartment, should've been there a long time ago. But she didn't get up and didn't care much about it, either. There was nothing but homework to go home to. She looked at Rick with his reddened eyes half closed behind his glasses, then looked around at the others. What a waste of time; what a drag. When was something fun ever going to happen?

Johnny stood up and smashed the empty whiskey bottle against the wall, a shock of sandy-colored hair falling across his eyes. He looked really hot in his tight, slim-cut Levi's, but he'd spent time in Spoffard and, more recently, Rikers. A little older and a lot rougher, he and his crew sometimes hung out by themselves. But if Rick scored some weed—which he did as often as he could—they were more than happy to share it with him. Rick was more than happy to oblige since it made him feel cool.

From a window overlooking the lot, a woman yelled, "You kids better get outta here, or I'm callin' the cops."

Micki stood up.

Johnny yelled back, "Why don'tcha just fuck the cops already and leave us alone, y'old bitch."

The window slammed shut, and Micki listened to the inane laughter that ensued, Rick laughing loudest.

"Who was that?" Micki asked.

Rick took another hit off the joint. "Just Mrs. McCrory. Don't worry about it."

"I gotta get goin.'"

"Hey, don't leave. The party's just gettin' started."

"I gotta go. It's past—"

"Ooohhhh." His mouth was in a pout. "It's past ya bedtime."

"Knock it off."

"Little Miss Goody Two-Shoes."

She wanted to punch him. Instead, she started down the alley toward the street. But an old, battered squad car pulled in at the curb, and two young cops— one black, one white—were opening their doors. She froze: there was no other way out of the lot. What a dumb place to hang out.

The black cop was coming toward her. "Just take it easy," he said.

She turned and ran back to the others. "Cops!" she hissed. Things were tossed into the dumpster.

"Okay, everybody up," the black cop ordered. "Turn around and put your hands against the wall."

Appearing bored by the whole thing, the white cop started frisking the boys in a cursory manner. He knew them all by name and talked to them as he went along. The black cop, however, went directly to her. And that was when Micki realized she was the only girl there.

He put his hand on her back and took a careful look at her face. "Haven't seen you before."

"I only moved in last week."

After hearing her voice, he said, "I'm just going to check your pockets. Anything I should know about?"

"No."

He kept his word, then told her she could turn around. And when she did, she saw dark eyes examining her. Slim with close-cropped hair, he didn't look old enough to have been a cop very long. His partner, hulking and closer to Baker's height, was blond with a childlike haircut and a round, ruddy face that made him look even younger. Standing alongside the boys, the white cop was making notes in his logbook.

"What's your name?" the black cop asked.

"Micki."

"Hi, Micki. My name's Officer Roberts."

Her eyes narrowed as they flicked over his uniform and badge. She thought it odd the way he introduced himself—like this was some sort of social occasion.

He smiled, but his gaze was cool: she looked very different than the girls who usually hung around with this crowd. "Have you got some ID on you, Micki?"

His voice sounded so friendly. For now. "Yeah, I got ID."

When she didn't move, his smile broadened. "Can I see it?"

She took a deep breath. "Yeah, sure." She pulled it out and handed it to him.

In the beam of his flashlight, he examined it: official NYPD, though not like anything he'd ever seen before. He looked at her over the card. "You've got a ten-o'clock curfew. It's almost eleven thirty now."

"If I'm on my way home from work, I can be out later."

"I don't really think this qualifies, do you?"

"I—I wasn't drinkin' or smokin' or anything. I—"

"I think you know you're going to have to come with me now." And though his tone was relaxed, the handcuffs were waiting. "Would you put your hands out please, Micki?" When her eyes met his, he saw the hardness in them, the slow-burning anger. Still she gave him her wrists. He said, "Now, I'm being nice and leaving your hands out in front. You're going to be nice and behave yourself, right?"

She shifted her gaze. "Yeah, right."

Roberts called to his partner, "What've you got?"

"Everybody's clean," Wollenski replied. "Though I'm sure"—he indicated the dumpster with his thumb—"we'd find some interesting stuff in there."

Roberts turned his attention to Johnny. "Aren't you still on probation, McBain?"

"Finished yesterday."

"You'd better keep your nose clean from now on. Next time you get busted, you'll be looking at some hard time."

"Oh, I'm so scared."

"A pretty, young boy like you? You should be."

"I'll take my chances."

Roberts shook his head, then addressed them all. "Listen up: if you guys want to party, be smart and keep it quiet. We've got better things to do than bust you for smoking a little pot or drinking. But if you start breaking glass, making a racket, and harassing people, then we have to follow up. Understand?"

"What's wit' her?" Joey asked.

Rick piped in, "Yeah, ya can't just—"

"Shut the fuck up, asshole," Roberts said. "You don't want to know what I can and can't do."

Though he'd taken a couple of steps backward, Rick, with an awkward thrust of his chin replied, "Yeah? Well, we'll just see."

Brushing past him, Roberts led Micki back into the alley toward the patrol car, which was parked at an odd angle in the street. Micki thought she heard someone mutter, "The Po-lack and the nigger, jeez." And while her face colored—deeply— neither of the two cops gave any indication they'd heard anything.

They pulled away from the curb, did a U-turn, then drove the block to Micki's apartment. Roberts got out and took her by her right arm; Wollenski tagged along on the left. As they approached the stoop, Roberts, with another glance at the ID card, asked, "You live in apartment 2F?"

"Yeah, second floor, front. Why?"

They climbed the stairs inside and went to her door. Roberts knocked.

Micki looked at him.

When no one answered, he knocked again, more loudly.

She bit her lip to keep from laughing.

"What's so funny?" Roberts asked.

"There's no one in there."

"Why not?"

"'Cause I'm out here."

"Where's your legal guardian?"

"I dunno."

"Doesn't he live here?"

"No."

"Then who do you live with?"

"No one."

In the dim light of the hallway, Roberts examined the ID card more closely. Only now did he realize that the second address—the Manhattan address—was a separate residence for the guardian, not the address of a Manhattan precinct house as he'd assumed earlier. And yet the card was stamped "JUVENILE." Even more confusing was that next to her date of birth—according to which she was seventeen—it said "estimated." *Estimated?* As he handed the card to Wollenski, he asked Micki, "How old are you?"

"Seventeen."

"Can you get your key out so I can open the door?"

"Why? What're you gonna do?"

"I just want to take a quick look around."

"Are y'gonna let me stay here?"

"Not unless your guardian says it's all right. I'll call him once we get inside."

"I don't have a phone. Y'have to use the one over there." And she lifted her hands to point to the payphone on the landing.

"Can you get your key out?" he asked again.

With grim resignation, she fished it out of the change pocket of her jeans, the chain on the handcuffs rattling.

One look at her apartment, and Roberts was convinced she lived alone: a single twin mattress, a single dresser, one setting's worth of mismatched dishes and silverware in the dish drainer... Though dirty and shabby, the place was surprisingly neat. He went to the payphone to call Baker.

Slumped in a chair at the little Formica table, Micki stared miserably at the pile of unopened textbooks on her desk.

AN UNEXPECTED SHIVER. COOL. Exquisite. Cynthia closed her eyes while Baker's hands glided over her skin. Light, sure, they skimmed her shoulders till the unbuttoned blouse fell to the bedroom floor in a shimmering heap of lilac silk. He felt the tremor beneath his fingers, breathed the scented heat off her body. This was the moment he'd been looking forward to since picking her up from the airport several hours ago. Standing toward the back of the terminal gate, he'd spotted her at the very same second she'd caught sight of him, the color creeping into her face causing his grin to widen.

"Hey, beautiful." He'd kissed her on the lips and hugged her tight. "How was your flight?"

Arms around each other's waists, they'd made their way to the baggage-claim carousel. And while they waited for her luggage, she told him about the man she'd sat next to on the plane. A retired postal worker, the elderly passenger had jabbered on endlessly about his daughter and the grandchildren he'd gone to visit, the son-in-law he hated, and the job he used to do. With only half an hour left till landing, he'd finally taken a nap. But by then, Cynthia had been comatose, her face hurting from the smile that had frozen there.

They exited the airport terminal and headed for Baker's car, the evening air still hot and uncomfortably moist. She commented on how he was carrying her suitcases as easily as if they were empty while she could barely lug them around herself for more than a few feet at a time. When they reached the Camaro, he set them down on the pavement, then ran his fingers through her thick, blonde hair. The strands fell silently back into place, glowing gold in the light of the setting sun.

"I really missed you," he said.

"I missed you, too."

"I wish I could've gone with you; you have no idea…" And he remembered how disappointed she'd been when he'd revealed he couldn't accompany her to LA. Besides going there to look for an acting agent, she'd planned the trip as a vacation of sorts. But Captain Malone, in no uncertain terms, had told Baker he couldn't leave Micki unsupervised; nor could he leave her at Heyden a little longer because then she'd miss the start of school. So Cynthia had gone alone. Without him. But, knowing her, she'd been just fine. Knowing her, she'd probably chatted up half of Hollywood while she was out there.

"It's okay," she said.

Her hand brushed the side of his face with such tenderness that his heart swelled with emotion. He felt the stirrings in his groin—then saw a fiery spark in her eyes, as well. With a look full of mischief, he said, "Y'know, we could just skip dinner and get a room right here at the airport. Then we wouldn't have to wait."

Though she was trying hard not to smile, she blushed a deep rose. "You are so terrible, James Baker!" And she playfully slapped him on the arm.

He laughed, opened the trunk, and threw her bags inside. "So did you happen to meet any movie stars?" To avoid racking up hefty long-distance phone bills, they'd spoken for only a few minutes halfway through her trip.

"Not a one. Didn't even see any; can you believe it?"

"I bet *I*," he teased, "a trained professional with *keen* observational skills, would've spotted a few." He finished arranging the luggage, slammed the trunk closed, then faced her again. "Did you at least meet someone interesting to keep you company? Someone to keep you from getting too lonely without me?"

He'd said it somewhat jokingly, but her eyes had flashed wide before she'd replied, "Not really, just a lot of wannabes like me. You know what that scene's like. So tell me about the school..."

And he'd felt a little catch in his throat, had gotten a sickening, sinking feeling in his gut while the noise from an airplane taking flight overhead had drowned out the rest of her words. Side-lit by the low rays of the sun shooting across the horizon, her features had taken on a harsh, almost sinister, look. Now softened in the muted light of her bedroom, her face was so open—as if she had nothing to hide. His palm gently caressed her cheek.

"You look so sad," she remarked.

He gave her a faint smile before sliding his hands down her back and unhooking her bra—always, for him, the defining moment. Then he pulled off the lacy white undergarment and let it fall, lips kissing her tenderly. With a touch that said he knew every curve of her body, his hands traveled around to her collar bones, lightly grazed her neck, then moved down to cover her small, firm breasts.

She was aware of the rapid beat of her heart beneath his palm, the rush of breath, the spreading warmth and quickened pulse. Her hand ran up the inside of his thigh to cup his crotch and rub the hardness. Then she unbuttoned his shirt so she could feel the skin of his chest against her own.

Kissing, tongues searching, they moved as one, Baker guiding her backward till they reached the bed, where he eased her onto her back. And though they were both still wearing jeans, he straddled her, then leaned down, tongue flicking over her nipples while she let her fingers wander through his hair. Eyes locked, they paused. Then he straightened up and took his shirt off completely. She began unbuckling his belt.

The phone rang.

With sly smiles, they ignored it. But the ringing was persistent, and Cynthia picked up the receiver—only to hand it to Baker. An edge to her voice, she said, "It's your answering service."

At the social worker's insistence that he be reachable at any time, day or night, Baker had gotten an answering service. The instructions he left with the operators were always the same: only forward messages about Micki. This was the first time they'd ever called. While he jotted down a name and number, Cynthia put on a maroon silk dressing gown. She watched his face harden and his eyes darken as he spoke to whomever it was he'd called back, some cop whose name she didn't recognize. She retreated to the brightly lit kitchen to fix herself some tea.

As she moved about, filling the flower-patterned kettle with water and putting it on the burner to heat, she recalled the second—and what was to be the last— time she'd ever gone to meet Baker at his precinct house. A dreary day, she'd been waiting for him to return from his shift. She was seated in Captain Malone's office, the two of them chatting, when she heard a loud commotion. Looking over her shoulder through the doorway, she caught sight of Baker hauling in a struggling, handcuffed suspect he and his partner had arrested. Between the grungy "perp" (as Baker would later call him) and Baker himself, the cursing was so profane she wanted to cover her ears, but refrained for fear of appearing girly. Captain Malone left to find out what was happening while she hung back, just inside the office door.

Though part of her didn't want to look, she watched Baker manhandle the criminal in his custody, the man grimacing in pain yet refusing to comply. But it wasn't until Baker had finished talking to the captain that he actually spied her there. For just a second, he froze, eyes filled with uncertainty. Then he resumed what he was doing, heading for the holding pen, the cursing growing louder but more muffled over scuffling, grunts, and clanging metal. She slipped out of the squad room as fast as she could and took a taxi home—only to hear the telephone before she even got inside.

For the entire evening she avoided him by letting her answering service pick up her calls, eventually disconnecting the phone so she wouldn't be subjected to the relentless ringing. At nine o'clock she plugged it back in and finally answered, full of a fear she'd never felt before. Yet instead of admitting what was wrong, she said she'd left so abruptly because of a shockingly bad headache that had come out of nowhere. But otherwise, everything was fine, perfectly fine. When he reminded her she'd offered to make him dinner the next day, she suggested they meet at the Red Roses Café instead. "Seven o'clock," she suggested—the height of the dinner hour there.

So the following night, they stood on line in the crowded little area near the cashier's, making mindless small talk for twenty-five minutes till they were seated at their suddenly too-tiny table. She felt his piercing gaze boring right into her head.

"Are you breaking up with me?" he finally asked.

She looked at him, his face so handsome. So full of pain.

The waiter came by, and Baker rolled his eyes at the bad timing. But Cynthia, smiling brightly as though the young man hadn't interrupted a thing, proceeded to order. As soon as the waiter was gone, she began buttering a roll she had no intention of eating, but it failed to block out the feel of Baker's gaze upon her. Unable to go on with the charade, she put the bread down somewhat heavily, unconsciously pointing the butter knife at him. Voice shaking, she said, "If you ever lay a hand on me, I will end this relationship immediately."

His brow knitted.

"And forever," she added.

He continued to look at her steadily until his eyes filled with compassion. "As well you should," was all he'd said.

And she'd promptly burst into tears.

WHEN CYNTHIA HEARD HIM slam the phone down in the bedroom muttering, "I'm gonna kill that kid," she began rooting around in the kitchen cabinet to find the honey bear that was playing games, hiding somewhere behind the myriad boxes of teas that occupied the bottom shelf.

Seconds later, Baker appeared in the doorway, tucking his shirttails into his jeans. "I've got to go to Queens. The kid got picked up hanging out with some guys who were drinking and smoking weed."

"The kid" was how Baker kept referring to Micki. In fact, Cynthia had yet to learn the girl's name. She sat down, waiting for the water to boil.

"I'm sorry, Cyn, I—"

"Forget it. Just go. I don't know why I believed you when you said things would be different while you were working at the school. All that's changed is that, instead of someone from the station house calling at all hours, it'll be your answering service."

"What do you want me to do? This is my job."

The kettle started to whistle. She got up and poured the boiling water into her cup. Back at the table, she dunked the tea bag twice, then placed it on the saucer. "It's not like I don't understand. I know that you have to take care of this, but"— she took hold of the plastic bear without picking it up—"well, it's been nearly two weeks since we've seen each other."

"I wish I could tell you I'll be back, but I don't know how long this is going to take."

She squeezed some honey into her tea and swirled it around with a spoon, which she tapped three times on the rim of the cup before setting it down on the bone-white china. But then her shoulders relaxed. Voice softer, she said, "It's okay. Just do whatever you need to. I should try to get to sleep soon anyway. I'm exhausted." But she succeeded with only half a smile.

He bent down and gave her a guilty kiss. "I'll call you tomorrow."

MICKI'S BODY FELT HEAVY and dull, the handcuffs a constant annoyance. She sat on the bench against the wall while Roberts kept an eye on her, his partner having gone upstairs to have some paperwork processed.

But with the tour already over, Roberts was anxious to get home to his wife. They desperately wanted a baby, and tonight was a good night to try—she was waiting up. He glanced over at Micki, now sitting with her elbows on her knees and her forehead in her hands. When she'd heard Baker wanted her brought to the station house, she'd said, "He's gonna kill me." And given how furious Baker had sounded over the phone, Roberts thought she wasn't too far off. He pulled his last piece of gum out of his pocket. He could probably stick around a little while longer—maybe get some answers. Besides, he needed his cuffs back.

AT 12:17 A.M., BAKER showed up in different clothes than what Micki had seen him in at school. Still dressed in jeans, he'd exchanged the T-shirt for a dress shirt, sneakers for brown leather shoes. She sat up straight, and Roberts followed her gaze through the large rectangular archway to the extremely tall man checking in with the desk sergeant up front. When Roberts saw the man turn and stride purposefully toward Micki, he stood up.

But before Roberts could say a word, Baker asked, "Do you have a room that's free?"

"Looks like Interview A is open," and he pointed down the hall, where a door was slightly ajar. He held out his hand. "I'm Officer Roberts. I spoke to you on the—"

But Baker had already yanked Micki to her feet and was leading her away.

Nearly running to keep pace so he wouldn't be dragging her along, she asked, "Y'gonna take these cuffs off me at least?"

"Shut up."

She tried to pull out of his grip. "No! I'm not goin' in there." But he simply tossed her into the room like an old jacket. She smashed into a metal table, her thigh catching the brunt of the collision.

Baker slammed the door shut.

She was barely aware of the throbbing in her leg. It seemed like the only thing she was really conscious of was him. Edging her way to the end of the table, she backed up toward the far wall of the tiny room.

"Just what the fuck were you doing?" he demanded.

He was right in front of her now—she could smell the aftershave he'd put on, could feel the heat radiating from his body. And still her voice came out challenging. Belligerent. "I was just hangin' out. That's *all*. I wasn't drinkin' or smokin' or anything." She shifted her eyes and saw her reflection staring back. A one-way mirror. She looked so small.

"You weren't smoking dope?" He grabbed her vest, pulled her away from the wall a little, then slammed her back. "You reek of that shit."

"That's 'cause everyone else was smokin' it."

"And you think that's okay? You think it's okay to hang out with people doing drugs and drinking?" His face was right in hers, their noses practically touching.

She swallowed hard. "I—I just wanted to hang out awhile. I—"

"This isn't a fucking vacation for you! This isn't about what *you* want. But I'll tell you what *I* wanted. I wanted to spend the night with my girlfriend, who I haven't seen in almost two weeks. I didn't want to be interrupted by a phone call about *you*. Do you have any idea what that felt like?" He slammed her against the wall again. "Huh? Do you know what that felt like?"

Her chest heaved. She hated being tossed around. "I dunno, okay?" she yelled back. "I dunno how it felt!"

"Well, this is how it felt." He rammed his knee up between her legs.

The intensity of the pain took her by surprise. She swung her cuffed hands up. "You son of a—"

But he caught her fists and punched low with his free hand. When she struggled against him, he punched her twice more, hitting the little wall of muscle a little harder each time. And while her face didn't show it, he knew the initial sting was turning more to pain with each blow. He thought about hitting her without holding back, without worrying about what would happen afterward. Instead he released her.

Voice strangely calm, he said, "Besides the fact that you broke curfew, you're not even supposed to associate with kids who drink or do drugs, let alone be hanging out with them *while* they're doing it. Do you understand that?"

Hunched over slightly, she was leaning against the wall. "Yessir."

"Do you have anything to say?"

About to answer, "No," she said, "It won't happen again."

"You bet your sweet ass it won't happen again—'cause there won't be another chance for it to happen again."

Her eyes met his. "But… I…" She straightened up. "Are you sayin' this is over?"

Voice full of contempt, he said, "You want to give me a reason why it shouldn't be?"

She merely gave him a hateful look and turned away. But then she faced him again. "Y'such a fuckin' bastard, y'know that? Y'fuckin' hated me from the minute y'saw me. Why the fuck did they make *you* my legal guardian? I've been livin' here for a week now, and y'haven't stopped by once—"

"So this is *my* fault? You're blaming me for—"

"Y'fuckin' don't get it. It's unbelievable. Well, just f'get it, okay? Go ahead, y'mothafuckin' prick; go send me back t'Heyden. Then y'can go fuck y'girlfriend all y'want. It's nothin' t'me. It's all the same fuckin' shit anyway." She turned her back again.

He paused a moment, then left the room and closed the door, asking a uniformed officer to stand guard outside.

FROM THE OTHER SIDE of the one-way mirror, Roberts had seen most of the exchange. He was sorry the brief phone call from his wife had kept him from witnessing all of it. He followed Baker down the hall to find him scanning the room.

"You looking for me, Sergeant?"

Baker whirled around, and Roberts pulled back.

"You were the one who picked her up?" Baker asked.

"Yes, sir, me and my partner, Officer Wollenski."

"Did she give you a hard time?"

"No, sir, not at all. She was very cooperative."

Baker looked at him steadily, then snorted. "Are you kidding me?"

"She did what she was told."

"And she didn't have anything on her? Nothing at all?"

"No, sir."

"Did she seem high?"

"No. Said she wasn't using anything, and I believed her."

The thing was, so did Baker. He'd put his face right in hers for more than just intimidation purposes. To his disappointment, her breath had been clean: no traces of pot or alcohol, just garlic from whatever she'd had for dinner. "I could use some coffee," he said.

The two cops talked briefly, Roberts pressing for information but getting little for his efforts, only a sketchy picture of what was going on. When he asked what would happen to Micki, Baker said he needed time to think and promised to leave the officer's cuffs with the desk sergeant on his way out. They shook hands, and Roberts headed home. Chances were, he'd never see the kid again anyway.

BLENDING INTO A CORNER of the first-floor stairwell, Baker considered his options. It was pretty much the same as when he'd thought it through over the pocketknife: technically Micki had done enough to justify sending her back to juvi, but Malone would never buy it. He'd be pissed that Baker was taking such a hard line so early, even angrier that Baker hadn't gotten more involved. By now he *should*'ve stopped by the kid's place—several times—if only out of his own self-interest: returning her to Heyden would ultimately leave *him* in bad straits.

A couple of uniforms walked by, smoking, and he nearly asked to bum a cigarette. With about two years of abstinence behind him, it probably wouldn't hurt to have just one. He could almost taste that first puff—feel the smoke filling his lungs. A heavy user for most of his life, he hadn't even been Micki's age when he'd started—his earliest act of real rebellion. He would light up and picture himself in a leather jacket, tearing up the roads on a Harley, a crack shot with all kinds of guns.

He never did learn how to ride a motorcycle.

He rubbed his eyes. He should've been home by now.

MICKI WENT OVER AND yanked out a chair to wait. When no one came for her, she put her head down on the metal table, cheek pressed against the cold, hard surface. But then she pulled her cuffed hands toward her, and rested her forehead on them instead. Any moment now, someone was going to walk through that door and take her to a cell so she could wait some more before the long drive up to Heyden. After everything Sergeant Kelly had done to get her out of that place, she was going back. Over nothing. Her heart squeezed painfully, her scarred veins aching. She wanted to fade into the darkness behind her closed eyes and—

The door opened, and she bolted upright: it was Baker. And for a moment, they simply studied each other. But when he started toward her, she stood up and moved free of the furniture.

"Just take it easy," he said. "Nothing's going to happen unless you can't control your mouth." Misreading her face, he asked, "Is that still a problem? You have something more you want to say?"

She looked away. "No."

"No, *sir*," he corrected.

She rolled her eyes. "Gimme a break. 'No,' 'no, sir,' what's it matter anymore?"

"It matters to *me*." And he picked up her cuffed hands. "I've decided to let this go as a simple curfew violation."

"What?"

He held the little key above her wrists. "You want me to change my mind?"

Though she merely shook her head no, a totally new thought was taking shape: maybe Baker needed her for something.

They left the police station, Baker dropping Roberts' handcuffs off with the desk sergeant.

As THEY DROVE THROUGH the streets, not a word passed between them, the interior thick with silence and the scent of his aftershave. His thigh, long and lean, was next to the stick his large hand was shifting just inches from her knee. Sitting so close, she thought she could feel the air vibrating around him, pulsating with a raw, dangerous energy. And out of the corner of her eye, she could see his profile, her own chest tight from the hard set of his jaw, which was clenching and unclenching while he was thinking about god-only-knew what. He glanced over, and she shrank and withered under his dark gaze, feeling like she was contaminating his private little space.

"Get out," he said, still looking straight ahead while the car idled in front of her building. Then he pulled away without even watching to make sure she went inside.

MICKI STAYED UP MOST of the night to finish her homework and study for an economics quiz. Baker—after picking up a pack of cigarettes from the corner deli—drove home, drank too much, and fell asleep, fully dressed, in his chair.

Chapter 4

AFTER HER LAST CLASS on Thursday, Micki entered the security office for the usual check-in. Over by the window, Baker and Warner were talking about the two juniors Angela had caught popping Black Beauties in the third-floor bathroom. Apparently, one of the girls, in admitting she'd taken the pills from her mother's purse, had said, "The doctor prescribed them 'cause my mom's such a cow. We just wanted, like, to have some fun. School's so, y'know, boring." A couple of uniforms from the local precinct had been called in to pick them up.

"These kids have it too easy," Baker said to Warner. "It's like they have nothing better to do than fuck up their lives."

Micki went over to Baker's desk and dropped off her lab workbook. But the two men had stopped talking. And when she glanced up, she saw them watching her. Looking from one to the other, she asked, "What?"

Baker lit a cigarette.

Her eyes widened. "You smoke?"

Cigarette held between his thumb and index finger—like a joint—he slowly exhaled.

She shifted her weight. "I just, y'know, never saw you smoke before, that's all."

Baker walked over while Warner, some guards' reports tucked under his arm, went to fix himself a cup of coffee.

"Put the books down," Baker ordered. And with the cigarette dangling from his lips, he picked up her left arm and ran his fingers over the needle-tracked skin. Her wrist was still in his grasp when he took the cigarette out of his mouth. She jerked her arm away and stepped back. His forehead creased. But then he simply picked a piece of paper up from his desk and said, "I got a note from your gym teacher. She says you're late every day."

"I get there on time."

"You get to the *locker room* on time, but you're late getting up to class. What's taking you so long?"

"Nothing."

"Look at me when you talk to me."

"Yessir."

He took a drag on the cigarette.

"You think I'm shooting up?" she asked.

"Are you?"

"No!"

"No, *sir*," he corrected.

Fuck you, she thought. But repeated, "No, *sir*."

Actually, Mrs. Tandy had mentioned that Micki was never more than a couple of minutes or so behind the last girl up—not enough time to do much of anything beyond popping a few pills. Baker had searched her locker anyway and found only a wrinkled gym suit. But he wanted to be sure. Leaving his cigarette balanced on the edge of an ashtray, he took a flashlight from his desk and grabbed her shoulder.

She stiffened. "What're you gonna do?"

"Shut up and stand still." He turned the flashlight on. "And keep your eyes open."

She saw blinding white light followed by purple splotches on a washed-out background. Another white flash and more spots in front of her eyes.

Baker let go and tossed the flashlight back. "Why can't you get up to the gym on time?"

"I dunno, I guess I'm slow changing."

"Don't bullshit me, Reilly."

Her eyes flicked over to Warner—still reading reports on the couch—then back to Baker.

"Let's hear it *now*. I haven't got all day."

"I don't wanna change in front of the other girls."

"*You* don't want to change in front of *them*? I would've thought it was the other way around. But this isn't Heyden. Nothing's going to happen in the locker room."

"It's got nothin' to do with that."

"Enlighten me, then."

She flicked another glance at Warner, who looked up.

"Anything you have to say can be said in front of him," Baker said.

But she was starting to sweat. "I—I have scars. I don't want anyone to see 'em."

"Scars from when they stitched up your gut?" He retrieved his cigarette and took another hit.

He must've read her case file with a fucking magnifying glass. "Yeah, from when they stitched me up."

Baker exhaled forcefully. "Lots of people have scars from stitches; they get their appendix taken out or something. I realize yours may be a little worse, but it's really no big deal. I expect you to get changed with everyone else. You're just—"

"I've got other scars, too."

"Oh, really? A minute ago they were just from the stitches; now, suddenly, there are more?"

"I never said they were *just* from the stitches."

"You told me—" Lips pursed, he gave her a dark look. "Okay, so then where are the others?"

If only she had magical powers to make him disappear. "They're on my stomach, too." When his expression didn't change, she added, "And my back."

He dropped his cigarette into the Styrofoam cup on his desk. It sizzled as it hit the thin layer of cold coffee on the bottom. "Show me."

Staring past him she, ever so slightly, shook her head no.

"That wasn't a request, Reilly."

Her gaze slowly shifted up to his, then she took a few steps back. When he started toward her, she retreated further. "Please. Don't."

And he stopped, eyes fixed on hers until his attention was drawn to the scars on her face. He'd gotten so used to seeing them, he didn't notice them anymore. "Would you show Mrs. Tandy?"

She shook her head again.

"Then I can't help you with this; do you understand that? If I don't know what we're talking about, I can't intervene."

She lowered her eyes and shrugged.

"That means you have to get out of that locker room on time. That means I don't want to get any more notes about you being late for gym. Your teacher's going to notify me every time now."

But her thoughts appeared to be elsewhere. She looked small and, for the first time, vulnerable.

"Did you hear what I said?"

"Yessir," she responded quietly.

With a weary sigh, he shook his head.

FRIDAY. ALL WEEK LONG she'd looked forward to this. Her shift at the restaurant was over, and the paper bag she carried was filled with a container of leftover baked ziti. Tomorrow's lunch. Or breakfast. After she slept as late as she wanted to.

It was cool out. With the promise of fall weather just around the corner, she'd have to buy a jacket soon. At least she'd had the sense to start bringing a change of shirts to work. If she'd stepped out of Bel in a sweat-soaked T-shirt tonight, she would've been freezing.

Police sirens wailed in the direction of the bridge. Between the hookers and the drug dealers, something was always happening over there.

"Hey, Micki, how's it goin'?"

Rick, pulling out a pack of Marlboros and lighting one, was leaning against the parking-lot gate. Since Tuesday night's episode, it had been locked religiously after business hours because someone—and everyone said it was Mrs. McCrory—had probably complained to the manager of the mirror company. In another day or so, things would relax again, and the gate would be left open as often as not.

"Where's everybody else?" she asked.

"Down at the wall."

Under the elevated tracks of the 7 train, where Forty-Fourth Avenue intersected Twenty-Third Street, a brick wall was entirely covered in graffiti by the kids who'd claimed it as their own. Micki had walked by once during the day. When no one was there.

"I thought maybe I'd walk ya home since ya can't hang out," Rick said.

"What about Blondie?"

"Sherry? She's stuck at home all weekend 'cause her granny's visitin' from Jersey."

Micki started moving again.

"So d'ya mind if I walk wit' ya?"

"Suit yourself."

They walked a short way in silence, Rick shooting glances at her. "So ya gotta work at that restaurant every day?" he asked.

"Not Sunday or Monday."

"How come?"

"Nobody works seven days a week."

"No, I mean, how come ya gotta work so much? Ya dad lose his job or somethin'?"

"I live alone."

Trying to sound surprised, Rick said, "Really!" But after the cops had taken Micki away the other night, he'd found out what he could from Joey's mother, who was friends with the wife of the super for Micki's building. According to the super, Micki lived by herself and was on parole or probation or something like that. They had reached her stoop, and Rick said, "So, like, maybe I could hang out here wit' ya." While she was looking him over, he flicked his cigarette down and left it smoldering on the cement.

She gave him a careless shrug. "Sure, why not."

Grinning broadly, he followed her into the building and up the steps, where the payphone wore a sign saying, "oUT of OrdEr." They went down the hall, and she unlocked the door.

She was putting her package in the refrigerator when Rick asked, "Ya got any beer?"

"No, just Coke if y'want."

"Yeah, okay. So, like, ya don't drink at all?"

"No." She couldn't think of anything to say. She handed him a glass of soda and poured one for herself.

"So, ya don't drink, ya don't party—what the hell d'ya do?"

She shrugged.

"D'ya mess around?"

"Yeah, I mess around." Which was both true and not true at the same time.

Rick grinned. "Well, maybe we can mess around together."

"What about Blondie? Isn't she your girlfriend?"

Rick laughed. "She's okay, but she's a good Catholic girl. Got real strict parents. She don't do *nothin'*." His eyes narrowed while he took a long drink of soda. "I betcha do everything."

Her voice turned cold. "Not everything."

"Hey, babe, lighten up. Let's just have some fun." He put his glass on the floor and came toward her.

She couldn't move. It was all happening so fast. And even though he was tugging her T-shirt out of her jeans, she was thinking about the blond boy—the football player—still looking at her as the bus was pulling away. But then she was hearing what Baker had said: he thought it was disgusting just to touch her.

Rick reached around to unhook her bra, and she maneuvered herself so that her back was to the window. But his fingers—greedy and cold—were making her skin crawl. She wanted to get away from him, wanted him to stop. And still her hands, soft and warm, were now underneath his shirt, moving slowly over his body.

"Oh, yeah," Rick mumbled. He yanked her vest off her shoulders, pulled her T-shirt over her head, and tugged at the unfastened bra, which fell to the floor. He grunted. No longer camouflaged by the clothes she wore, her chest was large for such a skinny girl. But when he saw the scarred skin below, he stepped back. Face pale, he wasn't smiling anymore.

Her eyes seemed to be looking straight through him. "Whatsa matter?" she asked. "Can't handle it?"

There was a lengthy silence until he said, "Hey, I don't care; I ain't gonna fuck ya goddamn belly." But he went and turned out the light so only the streetlight remained to illuminate the room. He put his glasses on the table.

And all the while, his words were echoing in her head, reminding her of what she once heard when she woke up in the shooting gallery after nodding off. The guy on top of her was saying to his friend, "What the fuck do I care, man? It's just a free piece of ass."

AFTER HE LEFT, MICKI put on her nightshirt and underpants and lay down beneath the blanket. The sex had been fast and disappointing—at least for her. Rick, on the other hand, had appeared more than satisfied. He'd dressed, lit a cigarette, and left as soon as he was done.

Rolled up in a ball, she closed her eyes. But it was hours before she fell asleep.

LIPS WARM AND TENDER, Baker kissed the top of her hair while she lay dreaming, gently breathing in the tranquil rhythms of the night. A strangely peaceful ending to a difficult evening. All through dinner, despite each of his strategically played deflections, Cynthia had pointedly returned to the one topic he'd refused to discuss; namely, Micki. She said she wanted him to share what was currently the all-consuming focus of his life. He said he didn't want to ruin their time together by talking about the kid. Precious little had been left untainted by his current situation; this was where he was drawing the line.

"Are you ashamed of what you're doing?" Cynthia had finally asked when they were back at her apartment. "Because I don't see that there's anything to be ashamed of. Heading security at a large public high school has to be pretty demanding. And being the legal guardian of a troubled teenager is a big responsibility."

"Don't patronize me, Cyn."

"I'm not patronizing you. I know it may sound corny, but it's true. You—"

"I'm a cop, for chrissakes. What the hell am I doing this bullshit for?"

"It's not bullshit. And besides, you're not 'James Baker, the Cop'; you're James Baker, *who just happens to be* a cop. There's a difference. I didn't fall in love with you because you're a cop; I fell in love with you because of *you*—because of *who* you are, not *what* you are." When he was unable to respond, she'd taken his face in her hands and kissed him until his body had responded instead. Afterward, she'd fallen asleep in his arms.

In bed with her now, stroking her hair, he knew she believed every word she'd said. And yet, it wasn't entirely true. What it was, was rather complicated. Oddly enough, the first time he'd asked her out, she'd actually turned him down because of his profession. "Don't get me wrong," she'd said, cheeks mottled, pupils slightly dilated. "It's not that I don't like cops or anything—I just—I don't want any part of what you see."

She could easily have sent him on his way by lying that she already had a boyfriend; she could've just turned him down flat. Instead, she ended up giving him her number anyway. And though, with every phone call, he'd repeatedly reassured her that most cops kept even their wives out of the loop as far as the gritty details of the job went, it took nearly a month—plus a sworn promise never to tell her more than she wanted to know—till she'd finally agreed to go out with him. Only now did he realize just how completely he'd kept his word. For she did, eventually, become curious. But he found himself only telling her the funny stuff, or finding something funny in something that wasn't. He left out the blood and the gore, the filth, the general inhumanity of man toward man—and woman. He left out the danger and the gallows humor. He left out a lot.

Not surprisingly, before it was over, her first visit to his station house had proven to be something of a shock. She'd arrived late in the afternoon, and after he'd given her a quick tour around, she went to get a can of Coke from the vending machine. She was heading back to the bench to pass the time until he was done when two hookers were brought in for questioning about a murder they might've witnessed. All three sat down together, and the next time he looked over, Cynthia was thoroughly absorbed in conversation with the streetwalkers. To this day, her capacity to connect with just about anyone never ceased to amaze him. But when she said something funny and the hookers laughed, the numerous missing teeth of one became exposed by her smile. Baker caught the almost imperceptible flash of horror on Cynthia's face. Unfortunately, so did the hookers. They looked at each other and snickered, one of them saying, "I think she's scared." Baker went over to rescue her.

"Would you mind looking at some photos for me while you're waiting?" he asked, as if she, too, were there on official business. He led her away to sit at his desk and page aimlessly through mug shots till, a short while later, the hookers were taken to separate interview rooms. "They're gone," he said as he closed the book of photos in front of her.

Eyes moist and red, she looked up at him. He wondered if she was going to cry.

"Are you okay?" he asked.

"I'm fine," she said, lifting her chin slightly.

So they went out as planned for a casual evening away from the city: a few games of bowling at an alley in Lake Success, followed by sandwiches at the Silver Moon Diner. By all appearances, an unremarkable date. And yet one he'd never forget.

Having said little during their drive out, Cynthia was being equally silent on the way back, eventually turning on the old AM radio to take the place of conversation. She'd caught Badfinger's "Day after Day" somewhere in the middle, and Baker turned it up, kind of glad now that they didn't happen to be talking. Letting himself drift into the harmonies and mournful guitar, he was soon immersed in the heartache and loss, leading him to reflect that he'd never loved anyone enough to experience that kind of pain. When the track was over, he turned the volume back down and cast a glance at Cynthia, who was staring out the window. And though another song, breezy and light, was already playing, the silence between them was uncomfortable.

"She has a really pretty voice," he said.

"Huh? Oh, Carly Simon—yeah, it's a great voice. Do you have any of her albums?"

"Me? No." He almost snorted.

"I have her first one. I'll lend it to you if you want."

"Oh—uh, sure; that would be nice."

But Cynthia would end up doing better than that, eventually buying him a copy as a gift. And Baker, almost embarrassed to admit it, would grow to like most of it. He eventually became brave enough to buy himself Joni Mitchell's *Blue*. But that night, they simply sat in his car, listening to "Anticipation" as they drove down the highway.

"You've been awfully quiet," he finally said.

"I can't stop thinking about those women I met down at the station house. What kind of life is that? It's horrible; they can't even take care of themselves. God only knows the last time either one of them saw a dentist. I mean, did you see that woman's teeth?"

Baker had already known that this was what Cynthia had been brooding about all evening. He also knew the hooker's pimp had knocked her teeth out on two different occasions: once on a slow night for refusing to take a rough john she didn't like, and once for trying to keep a little money for herself. Baker glanced over again. Eyes full of fear, Cynthia was looking at him expectantly. Stuck in his head was the image of her at his desk, chin lifted like a challenge, telling him she was okay when it was obvious she wasn't. "It's a hard life," was all he said.

Nodding, she leaned back in the bucket seat while the Grass Roots' "Midnight Confessions" started up. "Ooh!" she said. "I haven't heard this in ages." And when she reached over to turn up the volume, some of her hair fell in front of her face. With a subtle toss of her head, she flipped it away. Her eyes met his, and she flashed a smile.

What it was about that particular moment, he'd never know, but his heart leaped then thudded in his chest, a warm glow radiating outward. It traveled up his neck and down his arms, his hands growing hot. Wheel in his grip, he felt the road open up before him, felt the power of the black Pontiac Firebird as the miles flew beneath the tires.

"Are you seeing anyone else right now?" he asked.

"No. Are you?"

"No."

He looked over again, and their eyes held. She'd smiled shyly. He'd smiled back. And when his gaze had returned to the highway, he was still grinning, the city's skyline beckoning, the driving beat of the music making the night feel freshly alive...

As the memory faded, his eyes fell on the night table and the latest book to catch her attention: *The Kybalion: Hermetic Philosophy.* Jeez, what the hell could that be about? Her optimistic, mystically influenced outlook—something he'd initially found charming—usually irritated him now. These days it seemed merely simple-minded: the adult version of believing in the tooth fairy.

He caressed her cheek, and she murmured something unintelligible, a slight smile on her lips. Like an innocent child, she seemed completely untouched by evil. His gaze wandered toward the window and the small, angled squares of light in the distance: transparent panes of glass revealing little dramas to the darkness. Other people. Other lives.

Not once since that night two years ago had his feelings for her ever faltered. But could she say the same about him? He closed his eyes and kissed the top of her head.

A moment later, he shut the light.

By END OF DAY Tuesday, Baker had received three more notes from Mrs. Tandy. He thereupon informed Micki that for every minute she was late to gym, she'd have to spend five minutes in the security office doing nothing but sitting quietly. That meant no reading, no homework, and no sleeping.

"Whatever," she said. But her stomach was already churning. He was throwing away her time. Her *time.* She was lucky if she got even five hours of sleep on a school night. And now, after being just three minutes late to gym, she'd have to sit around the office doing nothing. For fifteen minutes. Fifteen fucking minutes. Wasted.

Baker asked her again if she wanted to show him or Mrs. Tandy the scars, but she said "no" and sat down at the desk across from his, the one assigned to general security staff. And though she started out facing the file cabinets, sitting sideways in the plain wooden chair, it wasn't long till she was watching Baker read reports and write notes. When he chanced to glance over his shoulder, he caught her observing him and swiveled his seat around to face her. Practically eye to eye, they were barely three feet apart, the atmosphere peculiarly calm, as though they'd temporarily called a truce.

"What's the big deal that you won't let me see those scars?" he asked. "Do you really want to sit here every day after school?"

"I just don't want anybody to see them."

"I understand that, but why?"

"Cause they're ugly, okay?" She felt a catch in her throat: she shouldn't have said that.

But he merely looked at her.

She looked back.

Something connected.

Micki's heart started to pound.

But Baker's expression turned cold. He shifted in his seat, lit a cigarette, and leaned back. "Did you turn a lot of tricks when you were using?"

She blinked. "What?"

"What part of the question didn't you understand?"

"I didn't do *any. None.*"

"You're telling me you never even had sex in exchange for drugs?"

"*No!* Y'know why d'ya ask me this sh"—she caught herself—"stuff, if y'don't believe nothin' anyway?"

She was getting so defensive. A street kid. Like it really mattered. But it was a sore spot—a button he could push. He liked having buttons to push. Stretching his long legs out before him, he crossed them at the ankles. "It's always a trip to listen to you, y'know that, Reilly? You're pretty good at sounding like your smart classmates until you get rattled; then the street comes out. And while you may have fooled a lot of people"—he took a drag on his cigarette, then tilted his head back and blew smoke toward the ceiling—"you never fooled me." He swiveled back around and resumed his paperwork. "You can go."

When she retrieved her books from his desk, he didn't even glance up. She wanted to take the heavy texts and slam them across the back of his skull.

MICKI WOKE WITH A start. Sunlight filled the room, assaulting her eyes and forcing her to squint. She had no idea what time it was, or even what day. But a key was turning in the lock. She jumped out of bed and ran to the kitchen. Knife in hand, she wheeled around to face the intruder.

"Put that down right now!" Baker ordered.

All she was wearing was the long, oversized T-shirt she slept in, bikini underpants underneath. She'd seen his eyes flick up and down her body. "No way."

Focused on the ten-inch carving blade she was holding, Baker thought about the small off-duty revolver he carried in an ankle holster. At this distance, if she lunged at him, he'd never get it out in time. "Being an hour late for school is one thing," he said. "But if you don't put that knife down, you're going to be in serious trouble."

"Forget it! Like I didn't see you checkin' me out."

"That was *my* mistake, Reilly, okay?"

Her lips parted: it wasn't exactly an apology, but it was close.

"It didn't mean anything," he said. When she still didn't respond, he added, "It wasn't intentional."

"But you shouldn't be in here when I'm—when I'm not, y'know, dressed."

"You're dressed enough; everything's covered. Now put that knife down. I'm not going to tell you again."

Eyeing him uneasily, she tossed it into the sink.

"Why aren't you at school?"

"I overslept. I must've turned the alarm off in my sleep."

"Like I really give a shit. You get yourself in the shower and get your butt to school pronto, understand?"

"Yessir."

He looked around the apartment. Although it was neat, there was a coating of grime and dust visible on the windowsills and dresser top. A few dust bunnies snuggled in the corner near the door. "This place is filthy. Next time I see it, it better be spotless."

"Yessir," she said.

He turned and left, slamming the door behind him.

Just what I need, she thought. More work.

LEFT ELBOW ON THE armrest of the door, fingers pinching the bridge of his nose, Baker sat in his car with his eyes closed. Whose bright idea was it for him to have to look after a girl? He was totally unprepared for this. By the time he'd caught himself giving her the once over, it was too late. He opened his eyes and started the engine. He refused to think about it anymore.

THE SKY HAD CLOUDED over. Micki hurried up the stairs and into the building. Baker wasn't in the office, but Warner was and gave her a late pass to English class. At the end of the day, Baker told her she'd have to stay an entire hour in the office for being late.

"But it's the first time," she said.

"And I want to make sure it's the last."

She went to the general staff's desk and dumped her books on top. But with nothing to do but go from sitting up straight to slouching in the chair, she started to fall asleep. He woke her with a rough shake of the shoulder, then put her to work, first cleaning the coffee machine, then the little refrigerator. When a glance at the clock showed the hour was finally over, she picked up her books.

"Where do you think you're going?" he asked.

"Time's up."

"Not quite: you were two minutes late to gym, so you've got ten minutes left to go."

"You've gotta be kidding."

"Sit. Down."

"But I'm already gonna be late for work. Mr. Antonelli's gonna have a fit."

"If you can be late for school, then you can be late for work. Now sit down and shut up."

As she was heading back to the desk, she muttered, "Go fuck yourself."

"What did you say?"

"Nothing."

He yanked her around. "*What did you say.*"

She merely glared at him. But then her eyes narrowed further. "I said you could go fuck yourself."

He backfisted her across the face, then spun her around and pushed her toward the bathroom. "I'm going to wash that mouth of yours out with soap."

But when he shoved her forward, she caught the doorframe. "Y'can't do this. I'm not a little kid."

Prying her fingers from the molding, he simultaneously pressed his body against hers. She resisted with all her strength, but he succeeded rather easily in forcing her through. And though she put her hands on the sink and pushed against it, her arms gave way, her hipbones crunching against the porcelain. He turned on the faucet.

"No!" she kept repeating. And when he reached for the soap dispenser on the wall, she elbowed him in the ribs.

Though he hadn't intended to actually go through with anything, now he wanted to grab a handful of her hair and smash her face into the mirror. Until he saw her reflection. Wild-eyed, she had the look of a trapped animal.

He shut the water and threw one arm across her neck, forcing her head back and choking her slightly. With both hands, she grabbed his forearm, trying to free the compromised air supply. But he'd already wrapped his other arm around her waist, and was quickly backing out of the bathroom. He could feel the small ribs underneath his fingers, the tensed muscles of her body as she struggled against him.

"Put your hands down at your sides," he said, "and I'll lighten up."

She gripped his arm even tighter.

Lips right next to her ear, he repeated, "Put your hands down and relax, and I'll let go." And when he was satisfied she'd calmed down, he took his arms away. She went to rub her throat, but he turned her around to face him. Holding her by the shoulders, he asked, "What the hell is the matter with you?"

She looked down at his shoes.

He shook her. "I asked you something."

"Leave me alone!" She could still picture the plainclothes cops who'd laughed as they'd drowned Tyrell in the sink, not knowing she was hiding behind the filthy mattress that was leaning against the wall. But, apparently, Baker hadn't intended to do anything like that to her. At least not here. Not now.

Grabbing her chin, he pulled her face up. "You don't talk to me like that. You're in enough trouble already."

"For what? Cursing a little?"

With a look of utter disbelief, he said, "Yes, Reilly, that's what we're talking about: the cursing, the disrespect… I don't appreciate getting elbowed in the ribs, either."

The taste of blood, from where her tooth had cut the inside of her cheek, was making her nauseous. Voice heavy with sarcasm, she said, "I'm *sorry*, okay?"

"Well, let me tell you, then, that you just bought two more days of this."

Lips pressed together, she looked away. Fucking bastard. Two more days of this. No time to rest, staying up even later to do homework…

The early-session security shift was over. Several guards had entered the office to punch their timecards before going home.

"Get out of here," Baker said.

WHILE MICKI WAS WAITING by the curb on Union Turnpike, it started to drizzle. The cool breeze, chilling her damp skin, raised goose bumps on her arms. And though traffic was moving quickly, no bus was coming for as far as she could see. But she recognized Baker's dark-blue Camaro when it made a left turn onto the street and sped by—leaving her behind in the cold, grey rain.

ALREADY LATE FOR WORK, Micki made a quick detour into Sunny's Superstore, which had really cheap brands of just about everything. She bought an outrageously loud alarm clock as a backup, an inexpensive watch, and an umbrella. On her way out, she noticed a navy hooded sweatshirt hanging on a rack by the door. Lined with some sort of fleece, it felt soft and thick. Yet it wasn't really what she wanted. She left and ran the short distance to the restaurant.

But when she got there, Mr. Antonelli happened to be in the kitchen. Tapping his watch, he said, "You supposed to be here at-a four o'clock-a."

She changed her shirt in the basement, then dashed back upstairs. And within half an hour, she'd caught up with everything piled in the sink from dinner prep and early-evening diners. Mr. Antonelli passed through again and took a look inside the enormous stainless-steel basin. One eyebrow raised, he gave her a respectful nod. She told him she'd probably be late for the next couple of days.

"Is okay-a," he said. "As-a long as everything gets-a done-a." He even smiled. She wanted to smile back. But nothing happened.

Micki finished her homework, then studied for an economics test. It was nearly 2:00 a.m. when she got into bed. After sleeping worse than usual, she was off to school—workshirt on top of her books.

During early session, a couple was found having sex behind the stage in the auditorium; a junior was caught drinking gin in the boys' locker room; and three separate fights broke out, one boy being sent to the hospital with a broken nose. All this in addition to the usual class-cutting and bathroom smoking. When Micki checked in at the end of the day, Baker was in a foul mood.

Without a word, she started cleaning. But as soon as she'd finished with the coffee machine, he sent her next door to the general office to do clerical tasks, not letting her leave until she'd filed the last file the secretary had given her—even though it was way past the hour and ten minutes she was supposed to stay.

She ran to the bus, from the bus to the subway, and from the subway straight to Bel. But the sink was already beyond full, some dirty pots and casserole dishes left to harden on the sideboard. She worked as fast as she could while the restaurant remained busy—not unusal for a Thursday night. But late in the shift, a large group of workers from the Osprey Company's manufacturing plant on Forty-Fourth Road came in and commandeered every open table. The men were so loud they could sometimes be heard over all the noise in the kitchen. But they were spending a lot of money—especially on liquor—so Mr. Antonelli let them order food and carry on for as long as they wanted. Micki didn't get home till nearly midnight.

She plowed through her homework and did a quick review for a physics test. But by the time she settled down to study for an American history exam, she'd run out of steam. She opened the window for some fresh air, only to have the aroma of warm, freshly baked bread come wafting in at full blast from the Silvercup Baking Company. It made her hungry and caused the glossy pages of the thick textbook to seem even more amazingly dull—not quite the effect she'd been looking for. Her heavy eyelids closed, chin falling to her chest and jerking her awake. After several rounds of this, she flopped down on top of the blanket and went to sleep in her clothes.

MORNING CAME TOO SOON, requiring No-Doz on top of two cups of instant coffee. She would've liked another cup, all hot and fresh from the security office's carafe, but was afraid to ask. Instead, eyes on the clock, she absently tapped her foot on the floor. But Baker—wearing a brown corduroy jacket with black patches at the elbows and a wide black tie with brown diagonal stripes—didn't notice. He was busy telling Warner he'd be leaving around one forty-five, shortly before the end of eighth period. "I don't want to be late," Micki heard him say. "I swore I'd be there on time to pick her up. The area's a little sketchy, and they're closing the studio as soon as the shoot's done."

"No problem," Warner said, chewing on a toothpick.

"Make sure the kid stays till at least three."

The passing bell rang, and Micki left.

THE PEN FELT THICK and clumsy in her clammy hand; her mouth felt very dry. She glanced over the test again while everyone around her was busy writing. Though she'd managed to fully answer the first question—"What were the main reasons for the creation of British colonies in North America?"—she'd written next to nothing for the rest. She couldn't even guess stuff since the entire exam was fill-ins and essays. Unlike the physics test she'd taken earlier and had probably aced, she was going to fail this one. Badly.

Physics was so beautiful, so effortless—variables and formulas, the answers just popped out. History, on the other hand, required tons of memorization: names, dates, places… But everything was just swimming around in her head: the Townsend Acts, the Bacon Rebellion… She hadn't had enough time to study. The only thing she'd really memorized lately was the inner workings of the security office's coffee machine.

The words on the test paper looked jumbled, and her eyes kept jumping all over the page. Minutes were ticking by. Baker was such a prick. She glanced at her watch: 1:34.

She stood up and overturned her desk. "I hate this fuckin' school. This is such bullshit. Like I'm ever gonna use this shit in my life." She went over to the bulletin boards and ripped down papers and posters. She tore down the gigantic world map that was hanging in front of the blackboard. Then she headed in the direction of Mr. Ingram, who was backing his way into the corner. But when she swept her arm across his desk, sending everything crashing or floating to the floor, he changed his mind and started toward her.

She picked up the long wooden pointer on the blackboard ledge. Gripping it with both hands, she held it up. "Y'gonna try 'n stop me?"

Frozen, he watched her swing it—as if it were a baseball bat—into the chalkboard, breaking it. But after she overturned his chair and started pulling several drawers completely out of his desk, he motioned to Jeff, the student closest to the back door, to go get help. Slowly, a few at a time, all of the kids got up and moved to the rear of the room.

But to Micki, the room, the kids, the teacher, the blackboard...they all seemed very far away, their voices muffled and garbled as if she were hearing them through water. She felt like she was outside of her body, watching herself; she felt like she was watching someone else. She turned her head and saw Marino—and only Marino—come through the front door. Her heart sank. Nonetheless, she grabbed the yardstick that was still sitting on the blackboard ledge.

"Put that down!" Marino ordered.

"Fuck off."

He picked up the larger of the two pieces of broken pointer.

She laughed at him. "Why don'tcha shove that up yer ass."

Using his walkie-talkie, he called for Baker.

And with a fresh surge of energy, Micki started walking backward between the desks, the ruler at the ready while Marino followed, just out of reach. But at the sound of Baker coming through the rear door, she spun around, and Marino lunged, hitting her hard on the shoulder with the broken wooden rod. She swung back around, but Baker grabbed her and disarmed her before she knew what was happening: one hand gripping her left shoulder, the other twisting her right arm up behind her back. A thread of fire shot from her neck to her wrist, her elbow feeling stressed to the point of breaking. Baker maneuvered her toward the hallway, past her classmates, who were looking on with awe: this was the most exciting thing they'd ever seen at school.

As soon as they were outside, Baker released her and proceeded to shove her along in front of him. They went to the right and he ordered her into the stairwell. Marino, who was behind them, was busy describing the scene he'd walked in on. When he mentioned what Micki had said he could do with the pointer, Baker had to bite his lip, glad neither Micki nor Marino could see his face. The stairwell door clanged shut behind them, the sound echoing down the shaft.

"Okay, Denny," Baker said, "you can go now. I'll take it from here."

"Maybe I—"

"I said I'll handle this myself."

And with what sounded like an even louder bang, the door shut behind Marino.

Across the way was a huge window covered with heavy-gauge steel mesh, sunlight spilling onto the landing halfway down to the next floor. Lying there, on top of the scuffed black linoleum, was a twisted purple wrapper from a Tootsie Roll Pop.

"What was that all about?" Baker asked.

Her eyes darted around the otherwise dark and shadowy enclosure, coming to rest on the candy wrapper in the bright pool of light. She shrugged.

"That's not an answer."

She looked at him dressed in his nice clothes, all ready for his date with Cynthia. "What d'ya want me t'say?"

"Attacking a teacher—"

"I didn't attack him. I didn't touch him. I was just—just—" But she couldn't finish the sentence because she really had no idea what she'd been doing. "I wasn't hurtin' anybody. I just scared him is all."

"I guess you thought that was fun."

His voice sounded so…relaxed. Cordial, even. Micki's heart pounded harder. "Yeah, I thought it was fun, okay?"

"Turn around."

She noticed the heavy gold bar clipped to his tie. Done in a soft, matte finish, there were shiny stripes cut out in—

"I *said*," he repeated, "'TURN—AROUND.'"

When she looked up, she saw only cold, empty eyes staring back. She slowly lowered her gaze and turned to face the railing.

Handcuffs closed, cool and rigid, around her skin, the ratcheting sound magnified a thousand times as it reverberated off the tiles. But then her heart was in her throat, for she was dangling over the banister, his hand gripping the waistband of her jeans, his wrist wedged between her cuffed ones. With the handrail pressing just below her hip bones, her whole body was tilting down, and only his strength was keeping her from diving through the center—an unobstructed, rectangular drop ending four stories below in the basement. The tension in his hold—purposely, it seemed—was wavering, and she imagined him letting go to watch her plummet through the alternating patches of darkness and light.

"Are you having fun?" Baker asked. "'Cause I'm having fun." And for just an instant, he partially released his grasp. In that nanosecond of time, she slid forward a little more and felt the heart-dropping sensation of freefall. A small cry escaped her, then a grunt as he jerked her to a stop. Leaning forward and using his free hand, he grabbed her hair near the scalp and gave it a sharp tug.

She winced.

"Yup," he said, "I'm having a real good time."

When he finally yanked her back to safety, her legs felt like they had no bones. And the cold. She felt so cold. He took the handcuffs off, and she grabbed for the banister. But the metal felt frozen in her palms.

Casually leaning against the railing, he said, "You're going to go back and apologize to your teacher and classmates."

"I hate you," she hissed.

"Aw, you're breaking my heart, Reilly."

She was about to say something back when the passing bell rang.

Baker straightened up. "Let's go before they've all left."

But Mr. Ingram didn't teach ninth period, so he was extending the exam by an extra fifteen minutes to make up for the time lost during the disruption. When Baker and Micki returned to the classroom, he asked them to step back into the hallway so as not to disturb the others. The corridor, full of students hurrying to their next class—talking and shouting, bodies pushing and jostling—was a turbulent rush of energy. Baker appeared irritated. Mr. Ingram, however—one of the young, hip teachers, his long black hair always tied in a ponytail—was simply studying Micki, his face filled more with compassion than anything else.

She looked down at the floor.

The late bell rang, and the passageway was once again empty and quiet—as if there hadn't been utter chaos just moments before.

"She has something to say to you," Baker said.

Micki looked at her history teacher. "I want to apologize for what I did."

"Why did you do it?"

"I dunno. I just—I dunno, but I'm really sorry."

Baker turned to Ingram. "I'm sure she'll get at least two days of suspension for this."

"Actually—if it's okay—I'd like to talk to her alone for a minute."

Baker gave her a sharp look of warning before heading toward the other end of the corridor.

When Mr. Ingram was confident Baker was out of earshot, he asked for an explanation again, adding, "You must've had a reason."

"I wasn't trying to—it had nothing to do with you. I'm—I'm just sorry."

"Is it because you're going through a tough time now?" Eyebrows arched like question marks, he cast a quick glance in Baker's direction.

"I dunno. I guess so."

Ingram tilted his head. "Look, I know you're in a difficult situation. I think maybe you just made a mistake here. If you can give me your word this'll never happen again, we'll leave it at that."

"Y'mean it? Really?"

"Yes, really."

"I swear," Micki said. "I swear I won't ever do anything like that again."

Placing his hands on her shoulders, Ingram smiled. But then he shot an anxious look at Baker. He and a couple of other teachers had talked about the bruises they'd seen on Micki's face. Given all the publicity about the new mandatory-reporting acts, they were feeling very pressured to contact child-protective services. And they had finally agreed to make the call. Until they considered that Baker was a cop. "What's the point?" one of them had argued. "Once the police get involved, nothing will ever come of it. Everyone knows cops protect their own. If anything, it might make things worse." But Ingram felt guilty. He said to Micki, "And I want you to know you can always talk to me, okay?"

"Yeah, thanks." Except she couldn't stand the weight of his palms on her shoulders, wanted to squirm out from under them—but was afraid he'd change his mind.

He gave her a friendly wink, then caught Baker's eye. And with a raise of his hand, he let him know they were done.

BAKER WASN'T PLEASED WITH Mr. Ingram's decision. Mr. Hillerman, the assistant principal, would still get a report about the incident, but with Ingram's request for leniency, it wouldn't have the same impact. As he pushed Micki through the door to the security office, he said, "Don't think you got away with this, Reilly."

She put her books down on his desk.

Warner, who was hanging up the phone, looked at Baker with surprise. "Aren't you supposed to be—"

"Shit!" Baker glanced at his watch. "Cynthia's going to—" He wheeled around to Micki. "You little bastard!"

Warner got between them, hands up in a placating gesture. "Just take it easy, Jim, or you're going to be even later."

Trying to fake his way around Warner, Baker pointed at her. "You're going to pay for this, you little son of a bitch."

Micki noticed that Baker always cursed at her with words usually reserved for guys—not that she minded, though. She hated being called a bitch—or worse. She stared past him.

"Just wait," he said. "You're going to be sorry—*real* sorry." Then he addressed Warner: "Make sure she stays till at least a quarter after three. Have her clean the coffee machine and—and whatever else you can think of." Cursing under his breath, he ran out.

Marino, who'd been hanging around the office, snickered. "Man, you're gonna get yours but good. You're fucking history."

"That's enough, Denny," Warner said. "Shouldn't you be on two-north right now?"

"Tom's up there for me 'cause I needed to check on something."

"Yeah? Like what?"

Marino grinned. "Like how bad she got her ass kicked."

"Get back there *now*."

"C'mon…" But as Warner started toward him, Marino gave a nervous little laugh and backed out the door. "Okay, man, okay. Y'gotta loosen up a little, y'know?"

Warner slammed the door in his face, then turned to Micki. "Come Monday, I sure hope you still think this was worth it."

She shrugged. It was her best universal response.

He grabbed her arm. "What is wrong with you? Are you *trying* to get yourself thrown back in that reform school?"

"'Reform school'? What a joke! It's more like—"

He shook her. "*Listen to me*. You can't afford to play these kinds of games."

"He's not gonna send me back," she said flatly.

Warner pulled himself up. "And why is that?"

"I dunno, but it's true."

He searched her face, then sighed. "You never know when that might change. Right now you might be in some kind of grace period. If I were you, I wouldn't push my luck."

She hadn't considered that. But then she eyed him with suspicion. "What's it to you?"

"I think you've got a shot at making it here. I'd hate to see you blow it."

"Why? What do you care?"

"Micki, some people—"

But just then his walkie-talkie crackled with static, and Micki recognized Angela's voice: "Warner? You there? Over."

"Yeah, Angie, what's up? Over."

Micki went to the coffee machine, dumped the coffee grinds, and pulled out the glass carafe. She jumped as Warner's hand closed over hers, guiding the pot back to the warming pad. "Just leave it, Micki, and go home."

"But Sergeant Baker'll—"

"Don't worry about it. If he finds out, I'll take the heat. Just go home." And he ran out, leaving her alone in the office.

IT FELT ODD BEING there by herself—as if she were trespassing. But it felt peaceful, too. Quiet and peaceful. Micki went to pick up her books, but found herself looking at the things on Baker's desk. There were the usual, standard-issue items: stapler; Scotch-tape dispenser; pencil holder stuffed full of pens, pencils, and Magic Markers... But then there were the more personal objects, the things distinctly his. She ran her finger around the thick glass ashtray he'd brought in just yesterday. Already crusted on the bottom with patches of ashes, the afternoon's butts were twisted and crumpled on top.

She took a quick glance around, then slipped her hand beneath the desk. Under the center section of wood, her fingers found an indentation. She started to pull the drawer open—then paused. And pushed it back. Instead, she picked up the picture of his girlfriend. If anyone was drop-dead gorgeous, Cynthia certainly was. In the photo she was wearing a cherry-red ski outfit with big white ski boots and fluffy white earmuffs. Thick blonde hair cascaded around her shoulders. Smiling brightly for the camera, her cheeks were a rosy pink, a pair of skis and ski poles cradled upright in the crook of her arm.

Micki felt a painful stitch in her heart: she could never be even one-tenth as pretty. She wanted to hate this perfect woman with a perfect body, who probably lived a perfect life and never did anything wrong. But she couldn't. Cynthia's smile was too warm, too genuine. Very gently, she placed the picture back where it belonged, an uncomfortable sensation growing inside her: this woman, who'd never done anything to her, was now standing on some street corner. Waiting for Baker. And scared.

AFTER HE DEFUSED THE situation in the third-floor hallway, where a minor collision outside the boys' bathroom had threatened to turn into a major incident, Warner returned to the security office to finish up. Almost out the door, he spied the nearly empty glass coffee pot and sighed. He didn't need anyone from the late shift making some offhand comment on Monday about burnt coffee. Baker would have Micki's head on a platter. And then his. He threw out the bitter dregs, cleaned the carafe, and set up the machine for a fresh pot.

Within a minute the liquid started dripping down—the rich, dark aroma making him want to hang around and have a cup. But he had a session scheduled at the university's clinic, an elderly woman coming in for an assessment. As a fourth-year student, he'd been seeing patients—under supervision—for quite a while now, but no one nearly as complex as Micki. He often wondered, though, what it would be like to treat someone like her. As it was, he knew precious little. He was cognizant of her amnesia, her stay in Heyden, and her legal status as Baker's ward, but that was all. Baker had said he was "not at liberty to discuss the kid's record" since she was being processed as a juvenile, which meant Warner had to glean what he could from overhearing their conversations. If you could call them that.

Of course, Baker was a puzzle of his own. Warner didn't buy the cop-needs-a-break-after-traumatic-shooting story that was supposed to explain the man's presence at the school. When he as much as told him so, he'd gotten nothing in response but a cold, derisive stare. Always on edge, Baker seemed like a constantly brewing storm of unprocessed rage. And he was taking it out on Micki. But other than stating his opinions privately to Baker, Warner was still hesitant to interfere. It always came back to the same two things: 1) too many people had officially signed off on this, and 2) he had no idea what was really going on. Plus Baker had a completely different way of handling the rest of the student population. On several occasions, Warner had witnessed him in action, breaking up fights or removing disorderly kids from classes. With a minimum of physical force and without ever using handcuffs—a preferable approach for school security—Baker had brought each of the situations under control quickly and effectively. He'd also managed to uncover why the cafeteria register kept coming up short after seventh-period lunch.

Warner had reached his car. He got inside and switched on the ignition. And though he struggled getting out of the tight parking spot, swore at the engine light that was flickering again, and finally drove away—running late if he planned to hit the supermarket before his evening session—he couldn't shake that last look on Baker's face.

He feared for Micki.

And for Baker.

Chapter 5

BAKER PULLED OUT A lighter and—still filtered, at least—a pack of Camels. With a flick of his thumb, he fired one up. Then he took off his old baseball-style jacket—the black leather showing the years of wear—and slung it over the back of an ugly dinette chair. While it was obvious Micki had cleaned her apartment since he'd been there Wednesday, the permanent look of decay was overpowering. Overhead, only one of the two bare bulbs glowed, its yellowed light reflecting harshly in the windows that were devoid of any blinds, shades, or curtains. And the room itself—painted in a dulled, cracking white—was small and sparsely furnished with cheap, hard-used furniture and antiquated appliances. Barring some disaster in the closet, tossing the place wouldn't take long. But what a waste of a Saturday night. If Cynthia weren't still angry because he'd kept her waiting yesterday, he'd be out on a date instead of spending his evening in this dump.

Between leaving the school when he had and then hitting more traffic than he'd counted on, he'd arrived at the photography studio over half an hour late. He'd pulled up in front of the building—an old, converted warehouse in Brooklyn—and had known by the expression on Cynthia's face to just forget about a kiss hello. The large black man standing beside her, however, got a huge hug goodbye before she got into the car. Baker closed her door, then went back around and got in himself. Across the street, a group of boys was sitting on a stoop. Watching them.

Cynthia, who hadn't eaten all day, still wanted to go to the new restaurant that was nearby—some trendy place that had recently opened in the rapidly changing neighborhood of Park Slope. And though she was quick to tell Baker how nice that other man had been—a perfect stranger, simply walking down the street, stopping and offering to wait with her—she was not willing to hear anything Baker had to say in his defense. It had been, to put it nicely, a less than stellar dining experience that had ended with a cold and passionless peck on the cheek.

And then tonight, after he'd finally had a chance to explain what had happened, she'd asked, "Did Micki get suspended?"

"No, but—"

"So what was the big deal? She was looking for some attention, that's all."

"She was looking to make me late."

"And you gave her *exactly* what she wanted. The truth is, you didn't have to be the one to respond."

"But I did; she's my responsibility, Cyn."

"But apparently only when she's doing something wrong. I have to say, it's like you want her to get into trouble. Why can't you at least be a little understanding?"

"The kid's got a rap sheet a mile long—"

"And? She was released early; they're letting her live by herself. So what could she possibly have done that's so terrible?"

"You know I can't tell you that."

"Oh, right. Of course not. God forbid you should confide in me."

Baker had stopped arguing. And when Cynthia had said she didn't feel like going out anymore, he'd left.

He glanced around for something to use as an ashtray, then went and flicked his ashes into the sink before getting started—the sooner he was out of there, the better. Most of the kitchen cabinets were bare. But there were assorted plates, coffee mugs, and glasses in one; some food in another, including two jars of marshmallow Fluff and a jar of chunky peanut butter to keep it company—the ingredients of those gooey sandwiches she brought to school every day. He found boxes of Twinkies and Yodels, bags of snack-sized Milky Way and Kit Kat bars, instant oatmeal and farina, a jar of instant coffee, a box of Rice-A-Roni, a tin of sardines, and two cans of tuna. Half a loaf of Wonder Bread sat on the counter next to a box of aluminum foil and another of plastic wrap.

Beside the sink, in a dusty glass, was a purple-handled toothbrush. Beneath it were cleaning supplies and a box of garbage bags. And the drawers—lined with ancient, peeling contact paper—contained an odd assortment of items: deodorant, toothpaste, a few utensils, a small hammer, and a screwdriver.

Inside the little refrigerator, he found several packages of leftovers from Bel Canto, a carton of milk, a large bottle of Coke, a package of American cheese, a bag of oranges, and a bag of apples. To make sure nothing was hidden, he moved everything around, then opened all of the containers. But not a single thing was the least bit remarkable. And the miniscule freezer compartment, except for an inch-thick coating of frost, was empty. One thing was certain: the kid didn't cook.

Moving on to the bathroom, the absence of a sink was somewhat startling, but explained the contents of the kitchen drawers. And what was present in the tiny room proved disappointing: the toilet, an old flushometer type, had no tank in which to conceal anything; the mirror above, equally useless with no medicine cabinet behind it. When he pushed aside the shower curtain—bright white, the smell of fresh vinyl still strong—there was only a bottle of bargain-brand shampoo and a bar of soap. One above the other, they were sitting in a plastic caddy hanging from the neck of a blackened showerhead dripping at a slow rate, a large rust stain directly below. And the tiles needed grouting. About to walk out, he gingerly picked up the Black Flag Roach Motel sitting on the floor in the corner nearest the door. It was one of several he'd seen scattered around the apartment. Adhered to the sticky interior, an entire family was frozen in tableau. Lovely.

Over at her desk, he rifled through the papers on top: school stuff and a bill for her rent. The drawers were full of more paper plus stationery supplies—and an article she'd clipped from a newspaper: "Warden Resigns in Face of Investigation." It was about Shirley Loren, the now former warden of Heyden—the warden when Micki had been there. According to reliable sources, there had been rumors that charges of abuse were about to be leveled against the woman, and, rather than get dragged through the mud, she'd chosen to step down. The reporter hinted that Loren had political connections who had used their influence to squelch the investigation in return for her immediate resignation and continued silence regarding others' indiscretions. But some of the article was missing while there were pieces of neighboring ones on the top and sides. He flipped it over to see a story—in its entirety—about the impact of New York City's economy on the financial well-being of New York State. Micki had likely cut *this* out for an economics assignment. What were the odds?

Continuing on to the closet, he found a broom and dustpan, an umbrella, laundry in a black plastic garbage bag, and several packages of cheap curtains and curtain rods, one of which had been opened. Why she'd gone to the trouble of buying curtains when she couldn't be bothered to put them up was beyond him.

Only two drawers of the dresser actually contained anything, her entire wardrobe consisting of black T-shirts and an extra pair of blue jeans. There wasn't much in the way of underwear, either, just a bra with several pairs of underpants and socks. All black. What little there was he moved around, unfolding items and checking pockets. Her clothes were small, making him feel big and clumsy.

He lifted the mattress and then the box spring, finding bankbooks and a tiny sum of cash. Nothing unusual in the checkbook, but the passbook documented two deposits. For a total of six dollars.

He lit a fresh cigarette and stood in the center of the room. With no TV and only a small, simple radio, she led a rather spartan existence for a teenager. And though he'd done a pretty thorough job of searching through everything—even going so far as to completely remove all of the drawers—he'd come up empty. Yet something nagged at him, a sense that some basic item was missing. He tapped some ashes into the saucer he'd taken down from the cabinet. Well, his real concern was anything that shouldn't be there but was, not the other way around.

He went over and picked up one of the dumbbells lying on the floor. The number "10" was embossed in the metal. Not bad for a little girl.

WHEN MICKI OPENED THE door, the scent of cigarettes greeted her. Her whole body tensed: someone had broken in. But as she scanned the room and saw her few possessions still there—plus a saucer with cigarette butts lying smack in the middle of the table—she understood Baker had paid her a visit. When she looked around more carefully, she could tell he'd gone through everything. She found herself glancing over her shoulder, half expecting to see him.

It took even longer than usual to fall asleep that night. And what little sleep she had was more fitful than ever.

MONDAY MORNING COULDN'T COME fast enough. Except for when she'd been working, cleaning, or doing homework, she'd spent most of the weekend's daylight hours sleeping—just like she had the weekend before. With time to spare and far less structure, weekends left her mind turning in on itself, endlessly falling through a black and cavernous void. Further and further down she'd spiral, the white-powder craving coursing through her veins till she wanted to rip them all out. It was a relief to finally get up in the dark on Monday and start her routine. The one drawback, of course, was Baker. He was waiting for her in the security office, leaning back against his desk.

She stopped in the middle of the room.

With a glance over his shoulder, he picked up a new pack of cigarettes, then tapped it leisurely against his palm before unwrapping it. He lit one, tossed the pack back, and smiled. "Have a nice weekend, Reilly?" When she didn't respond, he chuckled darkly. "It took a while to figure out how you'd pay for what you did Friday, but eventually it came to me." Inhaling deeply, he let the smoke completely fill his lungs before slowly—very slowly—exhaling. "I've decided you'll clean my apartment for two Sundays in a row. You have to clean it to *my* satisfaction or the day won't count, and you'll have to do it again."

"Whatever."

"In addition, you'll do my laundry, go to the supermarket, take out the garbage, wash the dishes, and"—he took another drag—"you'll start the whole day by making me breakfast."

"I don't cook."

"You will Sunday."

"I'm telling you: I don't know how to cook."

"Be at my apartment by eight."

"Eight o'clock in the morning?"

"Yeah, eight o'clock. And I suggest you be on time." He straightened up, turned around, and began leafing through the files on his desk. His back to her, he said, "You can go."

You can go to hell, she thought.

AT FIRST THE PUNISHMENT didn't look so bad. Although she hated cleaning, it would at least keep her occupied on a Sunday. But between homework, her own housework, and working at Bel, she'd have no downtime on Saturday—no catching up on sleep. It wasn't until third-period gym that the other aspect of the punishment sunk in, the part that had so amused Baker—she was to be his personal servant: doing his laundry, cooking his breakfast… Her face grew hot.

At the other end of the court, the opposing team had just stolen the ball in a game of speedball: a combination of football, basketball, and soccer. So far, it was the best activity they'd had in gym, though it depended a lot on who was in the game. Micki, who was playing goalie, shifted her weight toward her toes and put her hands in a ready position: a charge of girls was coming toward her. Out in front was Rhonda—five foot ten, large hands and lots of freckles—who seemed to have some sort of problem with Micki. Just as Rhonda received the ball not six feet from the goal, the whistle blew—a long, piercing blast—announcing the ball was no longer in play: the girl who'd thrown the pass had committed a foul. Yet Rhonda still hurled it, as hard as she could, straight at Micki's head. Micki blocked it, captured it, and was about to pound it into Rhonda when Mrs. Tandy stepped between them.

"I'm gonna kick your fuckin' ass," Micki said to Rhonda.

"Enough!" Mrs. Tandy said. "Micki, I want you in my office *now*."

Rhonda smirked.

Micki spiked the ball into the ground before following the gym teacher off the playing field.

"Close the door," Mrs. Tandy said and stepped behind her desk.

Micki did as she was told, then stood before the teacher, feeling exposed and ridiculous in the ugly little gym suit.

"I do not want street fights breaking out in my gym class."

"But—"

Mrs. Tandy raised her hand. "I saw what Rhonda did, but that didn't mean you had to respond."

"But I didn't even—"

"Only because I stepped in."

"So what am I supposed to do, just—"

"You're supposed to let me deal with her."

"If you saw that she started the whole thing, how come I'm the one getting the lecture?"

"Because, from what I understand, you're the one who's been in trouble before. My guess is you did something to provoke her. You're to sit on the side for the rest of the class."

As SOON AS MICKI entered the security office, she could tell from Baker's expression that he'd been informed about the incident.

"I didn't—"

"Just shut your mouth."

"But I—"

"Did you hear what I said?"

After a pause, she replied evenly, "Yessir."

"Do you think you could manage to go more than five minutes without being a fucking pain in someone's ass?"

"Do you think you could manage to hear my side of the story before blaming me for everything—or is that too much trouble?"

There was a second of silence.

"That's one hell of an attitude you've got there, y'know that, Reilly? Why don't we just tack on another fifteen minutes to the ten you've already got coming for being late to gym. How does that sound?"

She tilted her head up slightly and glared at him.

"No objections?" he asked.

Mouth clamped shut, she shifted her gaze.

"Good," he said. "Now that that's settled, let's hear it; let's hear what you have to say."

She adjusted the books in her arms.

"C'mon, let's hear it; what do you have to say for yourself?"

"Nothing, okay? Whatever Mrs. Tandy said is how it went down."

He shrugged. "Fine with me." And he seated himself at his desk.

Her eyes threw daggers at the back of his head. When they failed to have any effect, she pulled a sheet of paper from her history text and put it in front of him. "I need you to sign this."

He glanced up. "I need you to" was a strange phrase for a kid to use; adults said things like that. Kids said things like "you have to." He looked at the paper. It was her history exam with a big red F on top and a note saying, "Please see me after class."

"Very nice," Baker said. "What did he want to see you about?"

"He said he'd ignore the F if I did well on the rest of the exams."

"Well now"—Baker skimmed through the mostly empty pages—"wasn't that nice of him." He signed above the F and handed it back, asking, "You've had other tests already besides this one?"

"Yeah, why?"

"Don't ask 'yeah, why.' Just answer 'yes, sir' or 'no, sir.'"

"Yessir."

"You have any with you? I want to see them."

She dropped her books on his desk and started going through her loose-leaf, pulling out sheets of paper. They all had 100s, 99s, or 98s on them.

"Well, I guess you must think you're pretty fucking smart, don't you," he said.

"No, sir."

"Go sit over there until it's time to go." As she turned away, he added, "When I tell you to do something, I expect you to acknowledge me."

"I figure if I do what you say, it's pretty clear I heard you."

He put his pen down and took a very long, drawn-out breath. "I've got to hand it to you, it's like you just don't give a fuck."

"So I've heard."

"Just sit down and shut up."

She went to the general staff's desk—now her official detention desk—and sat down.

A moment later, he shook his head. "You can sit there till two thirty now."

Not wanting to spend the rest of her life there, she said, "Yes, SIR!"

"Keep it up, Reilly, and see where it gets you."

Straight to hell, she thought. The same place I'm going anyway.

Despite what Baker had said, Micki managed not to be a pain in someone's ass for the rest of the week. Baker, though, was doing what he could to get under her skin, mainly by giving her apartment a toss almost every day while she was at work. If he left the school at three forty-five instead of three, he arrived about fifteen minutes after she'd gone to the restaurant. With calculated care, he altered things just enough so she'd know he'd been by. It was subtle. It made her feel as if someone else were secretly living in her apartment.

The only place left where she felt somewhat safe was at Bel.

FROM HIS BEDROOM WINDOW, Baker looked down over Broadway, on all the people carrying on with their lives—having someplace to go. He, however, didn't know where he was going, or if he was going anywhere at all.

He took a drink straight from the bottle and used the back of his hand to wipe his mouth. Malone's call that morning had hit him hard. "Better you should hear it from me, Jim," he'd said. "I know how you feel about Coburn."

It was outrageous: Coburn promoted to lieutenant. He and Baker had gone through the academy together, and Baker had never seen anyone so inept. Yet Coburn had moved up the ranks with ease because he knew how to play the game. And he played it well. Baker, on the other hand, had made enemies as well as friends among the top brass. And all because he did what he thought was right. So now, instead of signing police reports, he was signing fucking history exams. Earlier, when he'd spoken to Cynthia, she'd tried to console him. "After all," she'd said, "I should know how you feel. I'm no player, either, and it's cost me plenty." But it was different for her; she was still in charge of her life, making her own choices. Where were *his* choices? Gone. All gone.

He polished off the bottle, lay down on the bed, and closed his eyes. If they never opened again, it was all the same to him.

Chapter 6

BRIGHT AND EARLY SUNDAY morning, Micki stood in front of Baker's apartment. She needed more coffee. And as soon as possible. After staying up very late to do homework—the homework she should've started before going to work—she'd been so overtired and overanxious that she hadn't actually fallen asleep till nearly 4:00 a.m. When the alarm rang only two and a half hours later, she'd cursed Baker with just about every profanity she knew.

Out the door by seven o'clock, she'd followed Twenty-Third Street down toward Jackson Avenue to catch the 7 train. It came after only a one-minute wait, and she connected with the 2 at Times Square in less than five. The rather seamless commute had left her half an hour early. And since someone had been leaving Baker's building just as she'd arrived, she'd gotten in without buzzing from downstairs. He had no idea she was there. Ear pressed to his door, she heard nothing. He might still be sleeping.

She looked down the hallway, where the walls were a dark shade of beige, the floor an intricate mosaic of old hexagonal tiles. Tacky by comparison, circular fluorescent lights cast an unpleasant glow over it all. And though the four-story walkup was clean, it had that old-building smell, kind of funky but in a nondescript sort of way. Trudging up to the third floor, she'd pondered what it was going to be like hauling groceries and laundry up and down.

She pushed the yellowed ivory-colored button and heard the shrill *brrring* inside. She waited awhile, then rang again. The light behind the peephole disappeared, and then the door opened. Hair tousled, face unshaven, he didn't have a shirt on and his feet were bare. Half-closed eyes confirmed that she had, in fact, woken him up. She took in the well-muscled chest tapering down to slim hips, where blue jeans hung low. Then she noticed the top button of his fly was undone. But when her gaze reached the bulge of his crotch, she became conscious of what she was doing, and her eyes shot up to his.

"Like what you see?" he asked.

Every cell of her body on alert, she held his gaze while several smart answers came to mind. But the words stuck in her throat. Baker seized her arm and jerked her inside the apartment, shoving her back against the door as he slammed it shut. His keys, which were in the interior cylinder of the lock, jangled. Palms flat against the framing on either side, he leaned over and stared down at her. She could feel the warmth of his body, smell the faint scent of old sweat and sleep. And alcohol.

"I wanna go home!" she said.

"Well that's just too fucking bad 'cause you're not going anywhere. You're going to stay right here and do everything I said you'd have to and not a bit less."

The steely, hardened look she gave him was her only defense. How could she have been so stupid? It was so obvious now what this was all about.

He waited a little longer, then added quietly, "And not a bit more." He straightened up and took a step back while her face filled with confusion. "Now, I want you to go into the kitchen over there and wait for me," he said. "I'll be in, in a minute." But as she started to move, he grabbed her by the arm. "And don't you *ever* look at me that way again."

"What about when you—"

"I didn't do anything that even comes *close* to what you just did." Her face reddened, and he let go, waiting till she was inside the kitchen before double locking the door and pocketing the keys.

MOMENTS LATER, WEARING A grey sweatshirt with cut-off sleeves, he entered the kitchen to find her standing in the middle of the room. His tone mocking, he said, "Why don't you take your jacket off and stay awhile." Adding, "Where did you get that?"

"One of the motorcycle stores on Northern Boulevard."

He put his hand out. "Let me see it." Despite the black leather and the brass zippers, it wasn't like the standard biker style that was so popular. And though heavy and well made, there was a ragged, three-inch cut under the collar. He noted the half zipper going around the perimeter of the interior. "This has a removable lining?"

"It's at home."

"This must've been expensive."

"Jeez! I didn't steal it; I bought it yesterday. The guy gave it to me at cost 'cause it's damaged. They were gonna send it back to the manufacturer." What she didn't tell him was that the salesman, a lean biker with tattoos and very long hair, had taken a liking to her, had said he wanted to show her how to ride—leaving to her imagination all the other things he wanted to show her. But she was never going to get on a motorcycle—not after seeing Tim's friend lose his leg in an accident. She could wear the jacket, though.

Baker handed it back. "I'm going to take a shower. I want you to have my breakfast ready by the time I'm done." Seeing her expression, he added, "Nothing fancy, just coffee, juice, toast, bacon, and a couple of eggs—over easy. You can manage that, can't you?"

Eyes on the floor, she said, "I dunno about the bacon. And I can only scramble eggs."

"You're supposed to be so fucking smart, but you don't even know how to fry bacon?"

She looked up. "I told ya I didn't know how t'cook! I said it t'ya twice! So if y'want me t'make all that stuff, why don'tcha jus' show me!"

He struggled to push down his anger. Last night, after Cynthia had canceled at the last minute, he'd really tied one on. Now his brain felt like a rock rattling around inside his skull; his fingers, puffy and uncooperative, had had trouble just trying to close all the buttons on his jeans. "You'd better straighten out that attitude of yours before I get back."

"Yessir," she mumbled, and watched him go off to the bathroom.

WHEN HE RETURNED, CLEAN-SHAVEN, dressed in jeans and a long-sleeved shirt, he was still towel-drying his hair. Halfway into the room, he froze. "Just what do you think you're doing?"

Though it was hardly chewed, she swallowed the bread in her mouth, nearly choking in the process. "Making your breakfast," she said.

"I'm talking about what's in your hand and on the counter."

She looked at the two plain slices of Wonder Bread she held—the outline of her teeth neatly carved in them. Then she looked back at Baker. The aroma of toasting wheat was floating through the air, mingling with that of the perked coffee.

He said, "You don't eat anything here unless you bring it from home or buy it outside, understand? In fact, you're not to *use* anything here without permission unless it directly relates to cleaning."

Holding up the bread, she asked, "So you want me to throw this away?"

"Yeah, I want you to throw it away."

She tossed it into the garbage and dumped the half-filled cup of coffee into the sink. "Y'want me t'puke up what I already had? Would that make y'happy?"

The toast popped up, all golden brown.

Baker sighed and threw his towel over the back of a chair. Seeing his cigarettes on the table, he took one and lit up. "Y'know, Reilly, you got off to a really bad start, and you just keep making it worse. What gets me is that you're only hurting yourself. We could make this three days instead of two—or four or five; I really don't care. You're the one that's going to get stuck with the work; not me. You didn't even set the table or pour the juice yet, did you."

"No, sir."

"And now the toast will get cold while I show you how to cook the eggs and bacon."

Eyes focused on the old grey-speckled linoleum, she said, "I guess so."

"I guess so," he repeated. With a shake of his head, he went to get the frying pans.

AFTER BREAKFAST, HE WENT into the living room to watch TV. She washed the dishes, then started cleaning the kitchen: scrubbing and scouring, sink to table, cabinets to drawers, up and down, inside and out. From time to time, he appeared in the doorway, hands on hips, to watch.

She moved on to his bedroom, wading into a sea of discarded items carelessly strewn about the floor, shirt sleeves and pant legs intertwined in an awkwardly sad embrace. She began tossing everything into an already overflowing laundry basket while Baker, now reading a magazine, could hear her moving around, sometimes mumbling under her breath.

And then there was an extended period of silence.

He went to the bedroom and found her standing on the far side of the bed. Face flushed, she was staring at the floor.

"What's the problem here?" he asked.

Her eyes flashed. "I am *not* picking that up."

"You're not picking *what* up?"

"That!" And she pointed to something blocked from his view.

He strode around to where she was standing.

"I bet you're gettin' a big kick outta this," she said.

On the floor, near the small grey garbage pail, was a used condom. He fought to keep the color from rising in his face. "I'll take care of that," he said. "Strip the bed and change the sheets."

Shifting her weight, she folded her arms over her chest.

"Go on!" he said.

She began taking the pillowcases off the pillows while he bent down to retrieve the offending item. When Cynthia had been on the West Coast, she'd forgotten to take the pill for a couple of days, so they'd fallen back on condoms to play it safe. After it missed the garbage pail, the used one must've gotten buried under all the clothes. Of course, it would have to be that way: one of the few times in over a year that they'd had to bother with one of those, the only time he'd ever thrown so many clothes all over the floor.

Because he'd purposely been a slob.

WITH THINGS NOW WELL under way, Baker unlocked the front door so Micki could come and go as she needed. Down in the basement, she found herself alone in the laundry room, though two washers were spinning down. She couldn't resist checking out Baker's underwear. The white briefs were a given; she would never have pictured him as the boxer-shorts type. But three pair were bikini-cut: two black, one royal blue.

A middle-aged woman in a housedress, wearing a kerchief and pink fuzzy slippers, marched through the door. Micki quickly threw the underwear in the nearest washer and emptied half of the laundry basket on top.

"Oh no, love," the woman said in a thick cockney accent, "y'don't want 'a be puttin' all that together in there like that."

Micki watched as the short, fleshy woman, with the bleached shadow of a mustache, bustled over and started sorting Baker's things into two machines, saying colored items were one wash and whites another. "Else ya colors be bleedin' all over the rest of it, an' 'e ain't gonna take kindly ta that, I promise ya!"

"Thanks," Micki said. She could just imagine what Baker would've done if she'd ruined all of his stuff. She used his change to start the washers, then closed the lid of an empty one and hopped on top.

But the woman, after putting her wet laundry in one of the huge dryers, said, "Is all right ta leave it 'ere, dearie. Nobody's ever pinched me clothes. And there ain't no sense in wastin' good time jus' watchin' the bloody things." She toddled out, and Micki soon followed.

BAKER'S SHOPPING LIST WAS full of items Micki wasn't used to buying: chopped meat, chicken, fresh and frozen vegetables... And because he hadn't specified much in the way of brands or even types, she had to guess exactly what it was he wanted, making the task take much longer than she'd anticipated. Back at his building, she struggled up the stairs with the heavy bags.

Baker immediately scrutinized the receipt and counted the leftover money. "Did you check your change?" he asked.

"It's all there."

"There's a quarter extra."

"I put that in to pay for the bread and coffee I had this morning."

"Is this supposed to make me feel guilty?"

She wanted to say she didn't think he was capable of feeling guilty about *anything* where she was concerned, but all she said was, "No, sir," and started putting the groceries away.

With a sigh, he went back to the living room to watch football, drink beer, and eat his chicken-salad sandwich. When she saw the used bowls, utensils, and chopping board in the sink, her shoulders sagged. But she left them to soak, and went to make up the bed, trying to ignore her stomach, which was growling. On her way to the supermarket, she'd stopped at the corner store—after almost getting mugged—to get something to eat. But she'd only had enough money for a Milky Way bar and a can of Coke.

THE CRISP WHITE SHEETS fit snuggly over the firm, king-sized mattress. She placed the charcoal-grey comforter on top and stuffed the fluffy, oversized pillows into the pillowcases. At Heyden the beds had been nothing more than army cots with mean little mattresses, scratchy cotton, and rough, thin blankets—the one in her apartment just a lumpy mess on the floor. So when she'd been dusting Baker's study, she'd been tempted to lie down on top of the twin bed there, if only to close her eyes for a few minutes. But to slip between these cool, clean layers of linen and fall asleep…

She went to get the vacuum.

WHEN BAKER DEMONSTRATED HOW to iron his shirts, Micki kept her distance. Earlier, when he'd shown her how to cook, she'd appeared equally wary, as if he were going to take the frying pan and hit her over the head with it. But now that his laundry was done, he put his clean clothes away himself—so she wouldn't be snooping around in his drawers.

Finally finished, she put her jacket on, then followed him around as he conducted his review. He inspected every nook and cranny, every knickknack, and every pane of glass. He even ran his fingers over the top of the shower-curtain rod to check for dust. Back in the kitchen, he said, "I have to admit, you did a great job. If it weren't for breakfast, it would've been perfect."

There was a beat before she asked, "Are you saying today doesn't count?"

Feeling like a real dick, he said, "Yeah, I guess so."

"Because of the stupid breakfast."

"Yeah, because of breakfast."

"But I told you I didn't know how to cook."

"It was more your attitude than anything else."

"So you let me work this whole fu—"

He grabbed her roughly by the shoulders. "Just for once, Reilly, do yourself a favor and keep your mouth shut." He let go. "Empty your pockets on the table."

"You think I'd rip you off?"

"I think you'd rip off your own mother if you had one." But he felt a twinge in his chest.

All expression drained from her face, and she emptied the contents of her pockets onto the white Formica.

"Turn around," he ordered.

And while he was patting her down, she looked out the kitchen doorway into the living room—the now very *clean* living room—everything dusted and in its place, floor and rug vacuumed… She wanted to tear the fucking place apart. And then she had an idea. As soon as he was finished, she refilled her pockets and said, "I need to use the john."

He shrugged. "Go ahead."

She headed to the bathroom, locked the door, and put the toilet seat down, letting it drop with a definitive bang. Then she used her apartment key to pierce the upper corner of the lining in the left-hand pocket of her jacket, pushing her pinky through to make the hole a little larger. After waiting a bit, she flushed the toilet to mask any sound caused by opening the medicine cabinet. And there, in between his deodorant and an extra tube of toothpaste, were three prescription bottles, two of which were at least half full. She turned on the water.

She took two pills from the bottle marked "Valium" and three from the one labeled "Librium." The third had only two left, but since it said "Ampicillin," she wasn't interested anyway. She stuffed the pills through the hole in her pocket, replaced the bottles, closed the cabinet, and shut the faucet. When she came out, Baker was standing in the hallway.

"You wait here," he ordered, and went into the bathroom himself. It hadn't occurred to him to remove his medications before she came. And though he examined all the bottles, he couldn't remember how many pills had been left in each to begin with. Except for the Ampicillen. But when he came back out and saw the look on her face, he knew he'd been had: she was daring him to search her again. Wanting him to look foolish. "That's real good, Reilly."

Trying hard to appear confused, she asked, "What is?"

He brushed past her and opened the front door. "Just get the fuck out."

The door slammed shut behind her, and she broke into a wide grin. The day hadn't been a total waste.

She stepped into her apartment and turned on the light.

What a drag.

Baker's place had been full of nice things: comfortable chairs, a sofa, rugs, curtains and blinds... It was a home. A *real* home. By contrast, this single, shabby space—full of old, decrepit furniture—felt more like a cell.

Too tired to even be hungry anymore, she flopped down on the lumpy mattress and sat there with her legs straight out in front of her. She didn't even have the energy to take off her jacket—the jacket with Baker's pills floating around in the lining. She wondered what would happen if she took them all at once.

It was too early to go to bed, but she fell asleep anyway. At 2:00 a.m. she woke up, had breakfast, and tried to do some studying until it was time to get ready for school.

Chapter 7

ON HER WAY HOME from Bel Tuesday night, Micki walked past the empty alley while the wind, kicking up in little bursts, left the leaves shuddering on their branches. Someone was running up behind her, and she turned sharply, only to see Rick.

"Hey," he said. He seemed a little out of breath. He'd barely run half a block.

"I gotta get home," Micki said.

"Why don'tcha come over to my place 'n hang out for the night? Y'can getcha stuff f'school in the mornin'."

"What about your parents?"

"They're in Staten Island, protectin' my aunt."

"Protectin' her? From what?"

"It ain't nothin', really. Just my uncle. The guy's a real ass, always gettin' drunk and sayin' stupid shit, like my aunt's cheatin' on him. He's fuckin' crazy. They got three little kids, the littlest wit' the chicken pox—she don't even have the time. But tonight he smashed some crystal thing her granny gave her, then walked outta the house, sayin' he was gonna come back and kill her."

"Jesus!"

Rick snorted. "Aw, he ain't really gonna do that. But my aunt's scared shitless."

Micki kept walking.

"My bed's a lot better than that piece a crap mattress *you* have," Rick said.

Her homework was already finished—she'd hardly gotten any today. And Baker was always gone before she got back from Bel anyway. She thought about sleeping in a real bed. And maybe the sex would be better this time…

ALMOST ONE THIRTY IN the morning, and Micki wasn't home. Baker sat at the little table, smoking a cigarette and tapping his fingers on the Formica. Just how often did she stay out like this? She probably figured he'd never be the wiser. This was, in fact, the first time he'd ever stopped by so late—a last-minute decision. He'd hung around at the school, had dinner at a McDonald's, then run security for a girls' volleyball game. Afterward, he'd dropped in at a local bar for a couple of beers. It wasn't until he was heading home that he'd considered making this little detour.

He'd gotten to her place at ten thirty-five. By eleven fifteen, he'd used the payphone in the hall to call the restaurant: no answer. All of her clothes were still in her dresser, her stash of cash still under the mattress. She hadn't skipped town. But having run out of patience and cigarettes, he was going home.

The entire drive back, he imagined himself confronting her—planning what he'd say and how he'd say it. But the more he thought about it, the better it seemed to wait until the end of the day, which meant keeping things under wraps in the morning…

Driving around his neighborhood for fourteen frustrating minutes in ever-widening circles, he finally found a parking space at Ninety-Eighth and Riverside Drive.

Just wait till he got his hands on her.

MICKI SAT IN THE dark of Rick's tiny room. She should've known something would go wrong. From what she could hear coming from the living room, Rick's uncle had returned, just as he'd promised—only apologizing profusely. When Rick's dad had given him a hard time anyway, a big argument had ensued with everyone yelling at everyone else until Rick's aunt had demanded his parents leave. Now back in their own apartment, they were still fighting with each other. Very loudly. One of the neighbors had even banged on the wall.

But Rick was fast asleep. As soon as he'd heard his parents coming in, he'd shut the door to his room and gotten under the covers, leaving Micki on the floor beside the bed, hidden from view in case anyone peeked in. She looked at him still lying there, blissfully unconscious, totally oblivious to the racket going on.

Once the shouting match was finally over, Mrs. Galligan went to bed. But Mr. Galligan stayed in the living room, watching some old war movie till three thirty in the morning. And all this time, Micki sat in the dark while Rick slept—a snoring, inanimate lump. It wasn't until she was sure Mr. Galligan had gone to sleep, too, that she found her way out, walking on tiptoe in stocking feet till she reached the front door.

A CRESCENT MOON HUNG lazily over the Manhattan skyline. After Rick's stifling little room, the cool autumn air felt more like winter. Micki zipped her jacket closed, then kept to the shadows while she made her way home through the deserted streets. She slept poorly for a couple of hours, was startled awake by the alarm clock's harsh cry, then forced herself to throw back the blanket and get out of bed. Eyes half closed, she ate her oatmeal and listened to the radio, staring dully at the saucer Baker used as an ashtray. The tiny plate was littered with cigarette butts. *Too many* cigarette butts.

She lost her appetite. Even the coffee was hard to get down.

BUT WHEN SHE GOT to school, Baker didn't say a word, and she left the security office with all of the tension flowing out of her in one huge wave. After that, she started to crash, dozing off in almost every class. By the time she checked in at the end of the day, she was wondering if she'd make it home without falling asleep.

Baker and Warner were by the file cabinets, talking, so she went and dropped her books on Baker's desk. Not sure if she needed to take them all with her, she was flipping through her assignment pad when Baker walked over and made a point of standing next to her. Much too close. She had to tilt her head back all the way to meet the empty eyes staring down at her.

"Where were you last night?" he asked.

Her ears filled with a rush of blood. Then she heard the refrigerator door open and close as Warner, fixing himself a cup of coffee, added some milk. She swallowed hard. "At a friend's. But I was off the street by curfew."

"C'mon, Reilly, you know damn well you're supposed to be at your apartment."

"So now what?"

"So now I want to know where you were."

"I told you, I was at a friend's."

"Male or female?"

"Male, okay?"

"So you have a boyfriend."

His eyes were laughing at her! "He's not my boyfriend," she said heatedly.

His mouth twisted into a smirk.

Her hand clenched around the assignment pad.

"But he's fucking you, isn't he?" Baker asked.

For a split second, her mind went blank. And then she shot back, "So what!"

"So he fucks you, but you're not his girlfriend?"

"He's got a girlfriend, okay?" But her chest tightened: she shouldn't have said that.

"So he takes *her* out, but fucks *you*. Have I got that right, now?"

She relaxed her hand and let go of the book.

Baker's voice became quiet. "I hope he pays you good for it."

Her fist cut upward, catching him squarely in the solar plexus. Face filled with pain and surprise, he doubled over. She stepped back, fist cocked to punch again, but Warner's beefy arms wrapped around her.

Baker grabbed her by the shirt, left hand pulled back to strike. But Warner, lifting her off her feet, quickly pivoted to break Baker's hold and get her out of the way. Glaring over his shoulder, Warner shook his head violently. Only when Baker appeared to have regained some degree of self-control did Warner swing her back around to face him.

"One way or another," Baker said, "I'm going to make you pay for that."

"Like I fuckin' care."

Almost in a whisper, he said, "You will."

The hairs on the back of her neck stood up. Still she forced her eyes to stay locked with his—until his gaze dropped to her torso and remained there. She saw a malicious smile spread across his face. That was when she became aware of the coolness around her midsection. Despite the way Warner held her—arms pinned to her sides—she could, just barely, touch her stomach. She felt skin where her shirt should've been. The material, pulled free of her jeans, was now wadded up between Warner's arms and her chest. Baker was looking at the very scars she'd refused to let him see. Though she knew she couldn't reach, she tried to cover the skin with her hands.

Baker laughed. "Very attractive, Reilly. That must be a real turn on for boys…" But his voice trailed off, the smile fading.

A cold, hard knot in her gut, she watched as he moved toward her. "Stay away from me," she said.

He moved closer.

"Stay away from me, y'fuckin' prick!" And she kicked at him until Warner's large hand clamped tightly over her mouth and nose. When she tried to free herself from his bear hug, he lifted her slightly off the ground, so that her kicking feet dangled.

"You're just making it worse for yourself," Warner said, and she became very still. "Do you want to breathe again?" he asked.

Eyes wide, she nodded while Baker, standing on the side and watching, felt a strange mixture of emotions.

"Then you're going to keep your feet on the floor, where they belong, understand?" Warner asked.

Once more she nodded, and he set her down. He removed his hand, and she gasped for air, ribs straining to expand more fully against the arms that still confined her. Baker, meanwhile, was already leaning down—palms on his thighs to support himself—to examine the scars up close. Micki turned her head away.

Besides the zipper-like signature of the surgical stitching, there were numerous lines in all different directions, the skin altered to various shades of pigment and levels of thickness. When her file had alluded to "some miscellaneous scars" on her abdomen, he hadn't imagined anything like this. He lightly ran his fingers over the damaged skin. Her body recoiled.

Looking up, he asked, "What's all this from?"

She glared at him.

"I asked you something."

"It's none a y'fuckin' business."

The hand that had touched her gently just a moment before, now slammed across her face as if moving of its own volition. The room was spinning inside her head. But Warner, still holding her, jerked her back several steps, beyond Baker's reach.

"*Are you crazy?*" Warner shouted while he struggled to contain Micki. "*Do you really think I'm going to participate in this?*"

Baker raised his hands halfway, showing his palms. "I'm not going to hit her again, okay?"

"*No! No!* It's *not* okay! This is *over.*"

The cop's voice boomed inside the small office: "YOU CAN'T SEE WHAT I'M LOOKING AT. I NEED TO KNOW WHAT HAPPENED TO HER, AND SHE'S THE ONLY ONE WHO CAN TELL ME."

There was a lengthy silence, and no one moved; even Micki had stopped struggling. And the psych grad student recognized something the cop, who was highly defended, was completely unable to see—about himself. Arms still wrapped around Micki, voice low, Warner said, "You don't touch her again while I'm holding her; is that understood?"

Baker nodded.

"I mean it, Jim."

"I swear to you I won't hit her again, all right?" And then he lowered his gaze to meet hers. "I want to know what those are from," he repeated.

"Well I don't wanna tell ya."

"Then we'll all just wait here till you change your mind."

The knot on her cheekbone was swelling; she thought she could feel it changing color, becoming an angry purple-red. For the whole world to see. She wanted everything to just be over already. She wanted to go home. "Stitches," she said. "Stitches from when they sewed my gut back together."

"I want to know what the rest are from."

She looked past him to the window, to the grey sky above the houses across the street. She loved grey skies. Still staring out the window, she said, "Knife cuts."

"You'll have to do better than that."

Micki watched as a well-dressed woman walked down the steps in front of her house. She was holding the hand of a little girl, who was fussing and tugging at the chin strap of her little straw hat. Stopping, the woman leaned over and slapped the child, who proceeded to wail while her mother dragged her the rest of the way to the car.

Micki said, "This guy, Nick, 'the Knife'—that was his street name—he cut me up."

"And why was that?"

When she looked back, Baker's eyes didn't seem quite so cold anymore. "I wouldn't tell him where Tim was. Tim was this guy who—who—"

"I know who he was. What did the other guy want with him?"

"He wanted t' waste him, said Tim had given him up t'the cops. The Knife had just finished doin' time for sellin' smack."

"But eventually you told him what he wanted, didn't you."

"*No!* No, I never told him nothin'. *Nothin'.*"

"Didn't he kill Tim?"

"Yeah, but not 'cause I told him anything."

"Didn't you tell the ADA that that guy Speed attacked you because Tim's death was your fault?"

"It's not the way y'think."

"So tell me, then." And Baker folded his arms over his chest.

Warner, still restraining her, shifted his weight slightly.

Staring at the clock, she wondered if the three of them would really stay there all night. It felt like the room itself was holding its breath. She said, "The day before it all went down, Tim found out that the Knife had been released and was lookin' for him. That's why Tim went hidin' at his girlfriend's cousin's place in Brooklyn."

"So you knew where he was," Baker interrupted.

Her eyes flashed. "Yeah, I knew where he was!"

"Go on."

"If Tim had just left with Mary and gone t'Philly the way they'd planned, he woulda been safe. But he hung around t'come back and get me first. And then… well, that's when…" She looked away.

"Why didn't the Knife just finish you off?"

Her eyes whipped back to Baker's. "That certainly woulda made *you* happy."

"Just give me an answer and keep the smartass comments to yourself."

She shrugged—an almost imperceptible gesture given Warner's hold on her. "He probably figured I was gonna die anyway. I—um—I passed out when he started cuttin' near my eye." Her face reddened, but she continued, "I probably *woulda* died, too, only Willy, this other frienda Tim's, found me and took care a me—cleaned the cuts and bandaged me up. A frienda his stole some meds and stuff from the hospital where he worked. But everything got infected anyway, and I got real sick."

Baker unfolded his arms. "Why didn't you just tell the Knife where Tim was?"

She gaped at him. "I *owed* Tim—*big* time."

"Were you sleeping with him?"

"No! I *told* ya: he had a girlfriend."

"That doesn't seem to be stopping you now."

Her eyes narrowed. "Yeah, well…that was different."

"I'll bet."

"Hey! Tim was like a big brother t'me. He said I reminded him of his little sister, said I even looked like she useta."

Baker chuckled softly.

"What's so funny?"

"You believed that?"

"Yeah, why not?"

"Tim Reilly—that was his name, right?"

"So?"

"So he most likely had fair skin, red or blonde hair, blue or green eyes—am I right?"

"Yeaaaaaaah…" She drew the single word out to the length of a sentence. "So what?"

"*So*, in case you haven't noticed, you don't look anything like that."

"His mom was Italian," Micki replied hotly, "and Tina looked like *her*."

The smug smile disappeared. "So what happened to her?"

"Who?"

"The sister."

"She died."

"I gathered that, but from what?"

Micki was aware of the breath going in and out of her lungs. "A john killed her."

So Tim's little sister had been a prostitute. And though Micki hadn't said it, Baker was pretty sure Tina had been a drug user, too; the two almost always went together. His eyes lost focus as something clicked into place. Almost as an afterthought, he said to Warner, "Let me see her back."

Micki tried to glue her feet to the ground, but Warner, rather easily, turned her around, her unbruised cheek now pressed against the warm, solid wall of his chest. This was the closest she'd ever gotten to being hugged.

Baker squatted down to get a better view.

Micki felt her vest being moved, and then her T-shirt being lifted. Closing her eyes, she concentrated on the thumping of Warner's heart.

But one look at her back, and Baker turned his head away.

Warner's mouth fell open.

When Baker finally spoke, his voice was thick and low. "Did all this happen at Heyden?"

"Yessir."

"You got yourself into a lot of trouble there, didn't you."

"Yessir."

"What did they use on you?"

"A leather strap."

Baker took a deep breath. "What were the cigarette burns for?"

She listened to Warner's heart.

"You must've done something special for those," he pressed.

The only sound in the room was the tiny refrigerator's compressor kicking on.

Baker straightened up, aware of the ache in his knees and lower back. "Turn her around," he said to Warner, then addressed her again. "I asked you something, Reilly, and I expect an answer."

"Well, I don't care, okay? I don't care if we stay here the whole fuckin' night. I'm not tellin'."

"Oh, really!" And with Micki's eyes tracking his every move, he went over to his desk and picked up his cigarettes. Looking at her steadily, he lit one and waved out the match. She started struggling against Warner, a panicked, desperate look on her face. Baker followed her gaze to the cigarette in his hand. Christ! He quickly stubbed it out, and she immediately stopped writhing. But her body remained taut, eyes flicking back and forth between his.

"Do you really think I'd do that to you?" he asked heatedly.

"I dunno, y'hate me enough!"

With a shake of his head, he looked away. "Jesus, Micki." His eyes snapped back to see her stunned expression. "Shit!" And he walked over to the window, telling Warner to let her go.

She hastily tucked her shirt back into her jeans, then retrieved her jacket from the coat tree, putting it on like another layer of armor.

Silence settled over the room.

Baker turned around. "I've come to a decision."

Shoving her hands in her pockets, she shifted her weight, meeting his eyes only briefly before staring past him, waiting for those dreaded words.

"I've decided," he said, "that your social life is your business. If you want to fuck around, go ahead. Just make sure that when that curfew hour hits, you're in *your* apartment. I don't care if someone else is there. Understand?"

Her eyes grew wide. "Yessir."

"And you should thank Mr. Warner, here, for saving your ass. If you ever hit me again, you won't be so lucky."

"Yessir."

"So what's this guy's name?"

"Rick."

"Rick what?"

Distrust welled up in her eyes. "Galligan."

"Are there any others?"

"Others?"

"I don't care if there are others; I just need to know who they are."

"There's nobody else. Nobody else—" But she stopped and, after a pause, said simply, "Nobody else, just him."

"Does this Galligan guy have a record?"

She shrugged and glanced away.

No one said anything.

Baker thought she suddenly looked very small. His voice almost gentle, he said, "You'd better get going, or you'll be late for work." And he actually picked up her schoolbooks and handed them to her. But he didn't let go. For some strange reason, he wanted to tell her that he understood, wanted to tell her—while her eyes were locked with his—that she didn't have to settle for having sex with some lowlife scumbag, which he had no doubt Rick was. Instead, the words that came out of his mouth were, "Just do me a favor, and don't get yourself knocked up."

Roughly tugging the books out of his hands, she said, "Don't worry," and stalked out.

BAKER SAT DOWN, LIT another cigarette, and closed his eyes.

"I'm guessing those scars looked pretty bad," Warner said.

Eyes still closed, Baker responded, "Yeah. They're pretty bad."

Warner moved till he was standing in front of Baker. "It's tough being a hard-ass all the time, isn't it."

Baker looked up.

"Truth is," Warner continued, "I think it's good you finally called Micki by her first name."

"Really? Because I don't; that's going to cost me."

"How? If things were a little more relaxed between the two of you, all of this would probably go a hell of a lot easier."

"I'd rather keep the distance."

"For what? Right now she believes you're capable of burning her with a cigarette. Is that the kind of relationship you want with her?"

"I don't want *any* kind of relationship with her."

"Bullshit."

Jaw muscles flexing, Baker glared at Warner. With tiny, vicious jabs, he stubbed out his cigarette, then stood up and strode across the office. "I'll be back in a little while. I have to go talk to her gym teacher."

THE LIVING ROOM WAS dark except for the elongated rectangle of light that fell through the kitchen doorway. Baker stood at the window, thinking about having a good, stiff drink. But he didn't get one. Too much drinking lately. He looked at the cigarette pinched between his forefinger and thumb. Too much smoking lately, too. Just yesterday he'd switched back to the unfiltered Camels, the slightly smaller pack so much more familiar. He was probably smoking more now than before he'd quit.

Out in the street, four teenaged boys had begun playing saluggi with a little kid's bag of groceries. Pretty mean. Some apples had already fallen out and were rolling away. The boy was starting to cry. But what kind of mother would send her young child out alone to buy fruit in this neighborhood at this hour of the night? About to open the window, Baker saw the older boys were already jogging down the road, laughing and hooting while the little kid tried desperately to find all of the produce that had scattered across the asphalt. Damaged apples and oranges clasped tightly to his chest, he finally ran off.

But it was images of Micki's scars that were flashing through Baker's mind: the discolored, irregular lines; the small, round circles of disfigured flesh… Exhaling smoke through his nose, he tried to imagine taking the burning tip of his cigarette and repeatedly pressing it into someone's skin. Or taking his belt and whipping it, over and over again, across someone's back. He shuddered: the kid had been through some hell. But hey, why should that now be his problem? After all, what could he possibly do about it? And what was the point anyway? How could any vestige of childhood innocence have survived all that?

At least some of her odd behavior now made sense—though Warner had cautioned him, saying that dealing with Micki was like walking through a mental minefield: memories, both conscious and repressed, could trigger unforeseen, over-reactive responses. Warner had also had a few choice words about Baker's ongoing attacks on her self-esteem. "What you see as 'attitude,'" he'd said, "is just a defense. Keep breaking her down and, one of these days, it'll backfire. You might as well put your gun to her head and pull the goddamn trigger."

Putting the cigarette to his lips, Baker breathed the smoke deep into his lungs. At the very least, he had to admit he couldn't figure her out. He would never have believed she'd let herself get cut up just to protect someone. Even when it came to something as mundane as cleaning his apartment, she'd done exactly the opposite of what he'd predicted: the place had never been so clean—even after Cynthia had had her maid clean the place as a gift.

But having Micki underfoot all day Sunday had been a royal pain in the ass. And yet once she was gone, the place had felt empty—just like it now did when Cynthia left after spending the night. He flicked off some ashes and sighed: he was probably getting tired of living alone. Maybe it was time to move in with Cynthia. Get married, even—that is, if they were still together by the time he got up the courage to propose. She seemed distant lately, as if she were trying to pull away. They weren't seeing each other as much, and she was less interested in sex. More often than not, they ended up arguing over little things that had never mattered before. And if he had to pinpoint the moment when all the problems had started, it would be when Micki had entered the picture.

After one last hit, he carefully ground his cigarette into an ashtray. Warner was wrong, dead wrong. He had absolutely no desire to connect with the kid. The sooner he was rid of her, the sooner his life would get back to normal. He ran his fingers through his hair, letting them come to rest at the nape of his neck.

Maybe he'd have a drink after all.

IT WAS A QUIET night at Bel, and she left relatively early, just a little after ten. The street felt dead; the parking lot, abandoned—Rick and the crowd hanging out more often at the wall now. Midway down the block, she crossed Forty-Fourth Drive, then heard the crunch of tires as a car slowly pulled alongside her—a police cruiser. Officers Roberts and Wollenski. She had a powerful urge to run. Passenger window rolled down, Roberts offered a friendly "hello" and asked how things were going. She wanted to tell him that everything sucked, and it was really none of his fucking business. Instead, she said, "Okay," and watched him smile. Then he told her to take care, and the car pulled away.

She crossed Twenty-First Street and stopped at the deli, the little bell jingling above the door as she went in. Frankie looked up from his magazine.

"Hey there, Micki!"

Frankie owned the small store and almost always worked the night hours so he could close up himself. By now she'd been in the place enough times that he knew her by name—and she knew his. She managed an unenthusiastic reply, made her purchase—a box of instant cocoa since she'd used her last packet the night before—and dragged herself the rest of the way home. Then she settled down to homework, plodding through it so listlessly it took her twice as long as it should have.

Yet when she was finally in bed, all wrapped up inside the sheets, sleep was far away. What she saw behind closed eyes was that nasty smile on Baker's face when he'd seen her scarred body. Her teeth gnashed together as she pictured him examining her stomach, then exposing her back. Who the fuck did he think he was? Telling Warner he had to know what happened to her—what bullshit. He didn't need to know a goddamn thing. Her eyes flew open. She should never have given in so easily, should never have told him so much. How long would they really have stayed there like that? And what could he have done if she'd refused to talk? After all, Warner was there to protect her. But then, Warner was the one who'd been holding her—even turned her around for him…

She got out of bed, switched on the light, and filled the pot with water. It probably didn't matter one way or the other. If she hadn't told Baker anything then, he would've just come after her some other time. The man never gave up, always found some way to get what he wanted—she could tell.

The water came to a boil, and she made the hot chocolate—now a kind of ritual for when she couldn't fall asleep. But after two half-hearted sips, she dumped it into the sink, shuffled back across the floor, switched off the light, and crawled her way into bed. Curled up again, eyes shut tight, she felt sheltered in the darkness.

Until a couple started to argue loudly, curses flying back and forth. She got up and looked outside, but the street was empty. When she opened the window wider and stuck her head out, she realized the noise was coming from the basement apartment of her own building. And though she closed the window completely, she could still hear the argument. So she got back under the covers and turned on the radio, catching the deejay carrying on about his girlfriend and some concert they were going to see. "But now," he said, "here's the latest from Steely Dan." And the cool hipster music, unabashedly laid back and self-assured, immediately sashayed out of the little plastic box. She liked to think it was "Micki Don't Lose that Number" instead of "Rikki Don't Lose that Number," though she couldn't, for the life of her, figure out whose number that might be. She didn't even have a phone…

HER BREATHING, LOUD AND *labored, filled her ears, the footfalls of her running feet like a counterpoint rhythm as she raced down the wet blacktop that glistened in the rays of a single floodlight in the alley. To her left was a chain link fence reaching up to the midnight sky in an infinite pattern of metal diamonds; to her right, a brick wall, cold and smooth.*

It was a warm summer night, and darkness surrounded her. But the darkest thing of all was chasing her, chasing her relentlessly. Though she couldn't see or hear it, she could feel it all around, could feel it closing in, greedy for its prey.

Further and further she ran down the alley, a never-ending stretch of unfamiliar road. Until, out of the murky shadows, another wall appeared, spanning the width of her path. Gone was the whispered promise of refuge at the end. She could hear the wind's cruel laughter whipping past her...

She awoke with a start, sweating as if she really had been running for her life, the dream so vivid it was etched in her mind. It was the first one she could ever remember having, though she knew her sleep was fraught with nightmares. Two cups of cocoa and an hour later, she was still awake. She switched to coffee and got ready for school.

Chapter 8

ECOND-PERIOD PASSING, AND BAKER was at his scheduled post in the north wing of the third floor. He watched the pretty brunette—hair falling all the way down to her waist—leave room 372 and walk toward the staircase next to him. Maybe five feet two inches tall, she wore Thom McCann work boots and heavily patched bell-bottom jeans—all very much the trend. But while the two girls accompanying her were chattering and giggling, she seemed unusually preoccupied, clutching her books a little too tightly to her pink embroidered sweater.

Every day Baker watched the three girls change classes together. But for the last several days his attention had been drawn to the absence of the petite one's cheerleader smile. In its place were traces of shame, anguish, and fear—the books once casually cradled now used like a shield. When the three classmates were nearly at the stairway doors, Baker approached her.

"Could you come with me for a minute, please?"

Her two companions, looking envious, exchanged mischievous grins. But her own face scrunched up, lips starting to tremble.

"Everything's fine," he said. "You're not in any kind of trouble. I'd just like to talk to you for a couple of minutes."

Hanging her head, she started to cry. Baker put his arm around her shoulders and gently guided her away, her friends looking on with anxious curiosity.

Micki, on her way to room 323 for calculus with Miss Giannetti, had seen the way Baker had talked to the girl: the concern in his eyes; the protective way he'd put his arm around her. When the late bell rang, she retreated into her math class—feeling a little more dead inside.

BAKER STEERED THE GIRL into an empty room and had her sit in one of the chair-desks while he pulled out the teacher's chair for himself. Forearms resting on his knees, hands hanging down between, he leaned forward. But the girl, arms still tightly wrapped around her books, sat at an angle as if about to get up again. Lips quivering, she was staring at the floor.

"What's your name?" he asked gently.

"Cathy. Cathy Stevens." The constriction of her throat made her high, childlike voice even higher.

"Hi, Cathy."

More like a squeak between sniffles, she said, "Hi."

"What grade are you in?"

"Eleventh."

And that was as far as he got. Though his tone was kind and sympathetic—gently coaxing at most—she burst into tears again and wouldn't reveal what was upsetting her. Eyes squeezed shut, she sobbed uncontrollably. After several minutes, he sighed and asked, "Would you prefer to talk to a woman?"

She nodded.

He stood up and stepped into the hallway to summon Angela over the walkie-talkie.

NOT TEN MINUTES AFTER she'd gone in to talk to the girl, Angie came out to report that Mr. Englars, Cathy's chemistry teacher, had shown her a little more than just how to use the lab equipment when he'd asked her to stay after class on Friday. He'd also threatened to fail her if she told anyone.

Baker stared down the hall. "Did the bastard touch her?"

"No."

"Do her parents know?"

"She was afraid to tell them."

"I want them notified right away. And while I'm calling this in"—Baker looked back at Angela—"I want you to write down whatever she said to you."

"But she doesn't want to press charges; she says she'll deny everything."

"Why?"

"She says she doesn't want word of this to get around. You know how cruel kids can be."

"But—"

Tilting her head, Angie raised an eyebrow.

"We'll see what her parents have to say. At the very least, I want that sick son of a bitch out of this school."

But without requiring any persuasion, Mr. and Mrs. Stevens filed a complaint on their daughter's behalf. And when the story came out, two other girls stepped forward with similar tales. For the rest of the week, this was the talk of the security office till Micki was fed up with hearing about "that poor little girl." After all, she'd been through a lot worse herself—a hell of a lot worse. Yet nobody could care less.

But, then again, that was her, wasn't it.

SWEAT-SOAKED T-SHIRT IN ONE hand, a bag of unclaimed garlic bread in the other, Micki headed home. Saturday nights at Bel were almost always the hardest. But tonight there'd been so much shouting. Tony—the head cook and Micki's favorite person at Bel—had gotten into a fight with Sal, a waiter who Micki and just about everyone else despised. It had started when Sal accused Tony of purposely being slow to fill his tables' orders. Tony then threatened not to fill them at all, asking Sal if he wanted to take the issue outside. Mr. Antonelli, rushing in, yelled at both of them because diners could hear the vulgar exchange taking place in the kitchen. Disappointed that Tony wasn't going to deck Sal after all, Micki "accidentally" spilled a little hot, sudsy water near the out door as Sal was turning to leave. He'd promptly slipped and fallen on his ass. Tony had given Micki a wink.

Eyes now burning with fatigue, she crossed Twenty-First Street and trudged past the deli, accompanied by the pitiful cries of a homeless cat. It sounded like a baby's wails. She hoped the goddamned thing would either shut up or be shot. This was the third night in a row she'd had to listen to this shit. She looked up and saw the light on in her apartment. Jesus Christ, it was nearly midnight. What the fuck did he want with her now?

SEATED AT HER KITCHEN table and smoking, Baker was playing with the empty cup of take-out coffee in front of him. Dressed in a black suit with slightly flared pants, he'd loosened his black silk tie and unbuttoned his collar. When he didn't say anything, Micki proceeded to place her bread in the refrigerator. But warm butter had worked its way through the foil wrap, then leaked through the bag, leaving a large, dark stain on the paper. She wiped her greasy hands on her jeans before hanging her damp T-shirt on the shower-curtain rod. Just as she was about to take off her jacket, he spoke.

"I have a favor to ask."

She tensed. "What kind of favor?"

"First of all, I want to make it very clear that you don't have to do this. But I think it would be a nice gesture since my girlfriend was the one who got stuck waiting on the street when you had your little fun."

Her eyes turned dark. It was bad enough that he was laying this little guilt trip on her, but he didn't even have the decency to be looking at her while he was doing it. "So what's the favor already? I'm not agreeing to anything till I know what it is."

He flicked cigarette ashes into the empty Styrofoam cup, then exhaled a thick cloud of smoke. "Cynthia's having a fancy party tonight, and she hired some people to help. But the woman who was supposed to wash dishes and clean up never came. She called to say she'd been delayed, then never showed up at all. By the time Cynthia realized she wasn't coming, it was too late for the agency to replace her. Now the kitchen's a mess, and Cynthia's running out of dishes and glasses."

"You"—she pressed her fingertips to her forehead—"you want me to wash more dishes?"

"Uh-huh."

"*Tonight?*"

"Yeah, tonight."

"Jesus, I don't believe this!" She ripped her jacket off, then threw it on the floor. "I'm fu—I'm exhausted! I just worked almost seven hours with no break! It's midnight already!"

Baker didn't even glance at her. He took another drag on his cigarette, then watched as he rolled it back and forth between his fingers.

In her head, Micki was saying, "Get some paper plates at the fucking deli and clean the fucking place up yourself tomorrow." But out loud she heard herself say, "Just let me put on a different shirt."

"Sure," he replied.

She gritted her teeth—don't say thank you or anything, you fucking prick—and went inside the bathroom to change. As soon as she came out, Baker stood up and ground out his cigarette.

"Tell me," he said as he watched her put her jacket back on, "do you always change in there, or"—he tilted his head toward the bare windows—"do you sometimes give the neighbors a free show?"

Voice tight, she replied, "I either change in there or I turn out the lights."

"Why don't you hang up the curtains you bought?"

"The screws won't go into the molding. I think there's metal in there or something." She watched as he walked over to the fire escape window and tapped on the framing. Unbelievable, she thought. What the fuck is his problem?

He turned abruptly and headed for the door. "Let's go."

As THEY DROVE TOWARD the Fifty-Ninth Street Bridge, Micki asked, "Am I still gonna have to be at your apartment by eight tomorrow?"

Baker was searching through radio stations and found Stealers Wheel's "Stuck in the Middle with You." After a quick check of the mirrors, he switched into the left lane. "You can pick that up next week."

"So y'mean I can stay home tomorrow?"

He glanced over at her. "Yeah, that's what I mean." Actually, he'd totally forgotten about it. And with the way these kinds of parties usually ran, he might not even get to bed until four o'clock in the morning—and that would be in Cynthia's bed, not his.

The radio crackled and sputtered with static, the song bursting through intermittently as they started across the bridge. When it succumbed completely to the interference, Baker shut it off. Disappointed, Micki leaned back and focused on the view flashing through the bridge girders: Manhattan skyscrapers proudly showing off their lights against a smoky black backdrop. Glittering and glowing, reflected in the water below, they presented themselves with even more spectacle than from the streets of her neighborhood. But she was fighting to keep her eyes open.

"We'll be there pretty soon," he said, "but you can take a catnap if you want."

Yeah, sure, she thought. Mr. Nice Guy. "I'm all right," she said.

DELICATELY PATTERNED CARPET SWALLOWED the sound of their feet as they walked down the hall of the East Side high-rise.

"Don't do anything to embarrass Cynthia," Baker said.

"Uh-huh," Micki responded dully.

He glanced over. Even in the soft light cast by the glass-shaded sconces, her eyes appeared sunken and half closed. He made no remark.

Cynthia herself opened the door when Baker knocked, and before she could stop herself, Micki said, "God!" The aspiring actress looked more stunning in person than in the photo on Baker's desk. Wearing a white satin jumpsuit that accentuated the sleek curves of her body, she'd swept her blond hair up into a fancy French knot. It highlighted her graceful neck and showed off the diamond studs sparkling in her ears. Her height had also taken Micki by surprise: three-inch platform shoes made her a mere three inches shorter than Baker.

Cynthia smiled. "You must be Micki. It's very nice to finally meet you."

Voice so low it seemed she didn't want anyone to actually hear her, Micki said, "Hi."

Cynthia and Baker shared amused looks before Cynthia led the way to the kitchen, saying, "I'm afraid it's really a disaster in there."

As they walked through the apartment, Micki took in not only the beautiful surroundings, but also the "beautiful people" who'd graced the party with their presence—colorful clothes, wild hair, and strange jewelry loudly proclaiming they were "artists." A few glanced back, looking equally curious, but Baker hurried her through the swinging door.

"Jesus!" Micki said.

Dirty dishes and serving trays were piled every which way on every bit of available counter space. In the middle of it all was a waitress in a modified French-maid's uniform, an oven mitt on one hand, hot hors d'oeuvres—just out of the oven—steaming on a cookie sheet on top of the stove. Taking off the mitt and wringing it, the young woman said, "There are no more dessert plates. There are no more plates at all."

Micki slipped out of her jacket and put it over the back of a chair, eyes lighting up when they landed on the appliance next to the sink. "You have an automatic dishwasher!"

"I'm afraid you won't be able to use that for much," Cynthia said. "The glasses are too fragile, and this is my best china—the sterling-silver trim would get ruined."

Micki examined the fancy stemware and fine china: a fucking nightmare. She looked around the sink, then glanced in the cabinets below: no dishwashing gloves. Instead, she discovered the garbage pail, crammed full. After several hefty tugs, she managed to pull the plastic bag out of the container, tie it up, and replace it with a fresh one. Seeing that everyone was watching her, she said, "Go on, I'll take care of everything."

But as soon as they left, she found herself leaning over the edge of the counter, taking slow, deliberate breaths and staring at the chaotic towers of carelessly piled plates and utensils. This was her life; this was what she was good for: cleaning up after people. In fact, this was *all* she was good for. Thursday she'd taken the New York State Regents Scholarship Exam, an all-day affair with six full hours of testing, not including instructions and lunch. And for what? The guidance counselor had already told her that, without a high school transcript, she'd have to wait to apply to colleges. But where would she be a year from now?

Eyes heavy, she stared at the dishes, all jumbled on top of each other, the uneaten food stuck in between. Like little children, they'd left the mess for someone else. The garbage was full, so they didn't bother scraping the plates anymore; too much trouble for them to take the fucking garbage out. It was easy to imagine that waitress saying it wasn't her job. But no one felt it was too much trouble for Micki. Never too much for her. She thought about smashing some of the damned precious china on the floor, but the feeling she was being watched crept over her. Glancing over her shoulder, she saw Baker standing in the doorway. She straightened up and turned on the water.

"Cynthia wanted me to tell you," he said, "that you can help yourself to whatever you want." But he'd caught the despair in her eyes. And if it weren't for the fact that he'd be driving again in a couple of hours, he would've washed away that image with as many drinks as it took.

THE KITCHEN WAS IMMACULATE. Baker was duly impressed, though not surprised. One thing was certain, you couldn't call the kid lazy. Unable to locate her, he felt a tiny rush of adrenaline until he spied her sneakers sticking out from behind the open door. Legs splayed out before her, head resting in the corner, she was sitting on the floor, sleeping. He stepped further into the room and let go of the door so it could swing shut.

"Micki," he said quietly. "*Micki!*" And he gently shook her shoulder.

"Huh?" Her eyes flew open while her head banged against the wall. "Fuck!" She rubbed the back of her scalp.

"Just watch the language," Baker said quietly.

Holding onto the counter, she stood up and scanned the room.

"You're in Cynthia's kitchen," he said.

She looked at him.

"You're in my girlfriend's kitchen. She was in a jam and you agreed to help her out."

"Oh. Oh, yeah. Sure."

He studied her. "Have you ever woken up and not known who you were again?"

"No. No, sir."

"Well, have you ever remembered anything?—y'know, about your past?"

She tucked her shirt more neatly into her jeans. "No. And I don't want to anymore, either."

"Why not?"

"Because: if I had some good kind of life before, I'd just feel bad that I lost it. And if it was bad, well, I'd just as soon not know." She walked over to the sink, where several dirty dishes had been newly deposited. But when she turned on the water, Baker came up behind her and shut it off.

"It's enough," he said.

"But these dishes—"

"It's enough," he repeated.

"I don't believe it!" Cynthia looked around the kitchen. "What an incredible job. I don't know how to thank you." She pressed something into Micki's hand.

Micki shrugged, then eyed the money unfolding in her palm. Forehead deeply creased, she looked at Baker.

"Keep it," he said. "Didn't I tell you you'd get paid?"

"No, sir."

"Oh..."

"Thanks," Micki said to Cynthia.

"Thank *you.*" And Cynthia leaned over to give her a hug. But Micki stiffened at the embrace, and Cynthia shot Baker a look full of concern.

He glanced away.

MICKI WAS SURE SHE smelled the acrid odor of weed as she trailed behind Baker through the smoke-filled apartment. Even out in the hall, it was noticeable. But they took a silent ride down in the elevator, the doorman politely wishing them a good night while holding the door for them as they left.

"How much did she give you?" Baker asked when they'd reached his car.

"Fifteen bucks—almost as much as two whole nights at Bel."

"Cynthia's very generous."

Micki mumbled some vague response, already thinking about the black leather vest she'd seen at the motorcycle store. The denim one she wore was too bulky under her jacket. Not to mention that it was blue. And though she didn't exactly need the vest, she still wanted it, wanted to buy it while she could.

They rode in silence through the streets of Manhattan and onto the Queensboro Bridge. Halfway across, they came to a grinding halt. Up ahead, emergency vehicles' lights were flashing.

Baker slammed his palm against the steering wheel. "Damn it! It's two fifteen in the morning and look at this!" He glanced over at Micki, who was trying to blink back the drowsiness, a guilty expression on her face, as if this were somehow her fault. He said, "It looks like we're going to be here for a while, so you might as well close your eyes and sleep a little. You can put the seat back if you want."

Eyes focused out the windshield, she said, "I'm fine like this."

"But you'll be more comfortable with the seat back."

"I'm *fine.*"

"You're fine?" He snorted. "What's the matter, you don't trust me?"

"I just don't wanna sleep right now."

He stared back at the stalled traffic. Granted, he was a real bastard to her, but as far as he was concerned, this was a totally different issue. It bothered him that she didn't trust him. And it bothered him that it bothered him.

THE NEXT EVENING, WHEN Baker walked through Micki's door, she was at her desk, about to begin her homework. Gripping the back of her chair, she twisted around to see him. Dressed in work boots, his grey sleeveless sweatshirt, and a very faded pair of jeans that were frayed at the knees, he was sporting stubble from a skipped shave. Her blood started pumping faster.

But with nothing more than a careless glance in her direction, he dropped a green metal toolbox on the kitchen table and went to the closet, where he took out the packages of curtains and rods she'd bought. Lit cigarette dangling from his mouth, he opened the toolbox, grabbed a level and a ruler, and began measuring and marking various points on the molding above the fire escape window. He double-checked his work, then plugged in his drill.

Harsh and high-pitched, the noise seemed especially loud in the little room, but Micki moved closer. She liked the definition of his muscles as he pressed the power tool into the thin sheet of metal under the wood. Just as he was about to start at another point, she asked, "Would you teach me how to use that?"

Without looking at her, he responded, "No," the drill's piercing sound punctuating the reply.

Her gaze fell. Then she went over to the table and looked in the open toolbox. There were all kinds of neat-looking things in it: regular and ratchet wrenches, different-sized screwdrivers, a couple of hammers, boxes of nails, toggle bolts… She picked up a pair of needle-nosed pliers.

"Did I tell you you could touch that?" he asked.

She replaced the item she was holding.

"I asked you something."

"I was just lookin' at it."

"Keep your hands off my things unless I tell you otherwise."

She grabbed her jacket from the closet and left the apartment, slamming the door behind her. Running down the steps and out of the building, she decided she didn't care if he finished what he was doing or not. After all, she'd managed just fine till now without the fucking curtains. She hated him. *Hated him.*

BAKER HUNG HIS HEAD and closed his eyes. When he heard the downstairs door bang shut, too, he took a deep breath, then went over to the table and crushed what was left of his cigarette into the saucer. From the upper tray of the open toolbox, the needle-nosed pliers silently rebuked him. He combed his fingers through his hair: there were still three more windows to go.

BURIED UNDER CIGARETTE BUTTS, the misused saucer could barely be seen. Next to it were three beer bottles, two of which were empty and one nearly so. Baker was sitting at the table, a copy of *Newsweek* open in front of him. When Micki came through the door, he glanced at his watch. "One more minute and you would've broken curfew."

"But I didn't, did I." She walked over to the closet and hung up her jacket. "I was hoping you'd be gone by now."

"But I'm not, am I."

She spun around to face him, the look in her eyes causing his chest to constrict. "Where were you?" he asked.

"At Rick's."

"Were his parents home?"

Her voice stiffened. "We were alone."

Baker was aware of how adept she'd become at avoiding straight yes-or-no answers. "Let me guess what the two of you were doing for the past two hours."

"You said that was *my* business."

He sat back and took a drink of beer.

"What's it to you anyway?" she asked.

"You don't question me. Understand?"

She looked away. All she wanted was for him to leave. The last two hours with Rick hadn't been fun at all. Just thinking about it made her want to jump in the shower and scrub her skin raw. She didn't even like Rick anymore. And yet she wanted to have sex. What she couldn't understand was why she still wanted to have it with someone like him. At least it bothered the shit out of Baker.

"Did you finish your homework?" he asked.

"I'll finish it now."

"You'll finish it now? It's ten o'clock. You should be going to bed. Instead, you're going to stay up late and then fall asleep in all your classes tomorrow. Like you usually do." He caught the surprise that flickered across her face. "Yeah, Micki,

I know all about it. A couple of your teachers mentioned it quite a while ago, but they said you were doing so well they weren't too concerned. Then last Friday, I got notes from three of them saying it's become excessive. I should've brought it up then, but I'd had just about enough of you for one week. But we're going to straighten this out now."

"What do you think's gonna happen when you take away the only time I have to catch up on sleep? Last week you had me cleaning your apartment; this week it was your girlfriend's mess."

"You should be getting enough sleep during the week. You shouldn't be so wiped out that you need the weekend to recover."

"Oh, please. Get real. There's no way I can get enough sleep during the week. I'm usually working till at *least* ten thirty, and then I first have to start my homework."

"You should be doing some of that homework before you go to work."

"Maybe, *maybe*—and that's only if the subway isn't having a friggin' meltdown—I have an hour between getting home from school and going to work; that's if someone we both know isn't making me sit around the security office for something."

"That's your own fault."

"Everything's my own fault."

"You said it; not me."

He was always so fucking smug. "Yeah, well, even so; it's hard to get much done between school and work. I get tired, y'know."

He didn't respond right away, and she wondered if he was actually considering what she'd said.

"So when do you go to bed?" he asked.

"About twelve thirty or one, I guess."

"And when do you get up?"

"My alarm's set for six."

"So that's about five, or five and a half, hours. And you're young. You may not feel great, but you should still be able to get by without falling asleep in class every day."

"But I'm not actually sleeping the whole time."

"Well, that's what we're talking about, isn't it? You're staying up and fucking your brains out instead."

"I'm not fuckin' my brains out. Y'know, I've only been with Rick a big three times so far."

"You watch your mouth, if you know what's good for you."

"You said it first."

"It doesn't matter what I say."

She looked away.

Meanwhile, the revelation about Rick had startled him. "So why aren't you sleeping?" he asked.

"I dunno, I just can't sleep."

"What do you mean: 'you just can't sleep'?"

"'I can't sleep' means I can't sleep. Whatta y'mean: 'what do I mean?'"

He pressed his lips together to stop the smile that was threatening the corners of his mouth. "You can't fall asleep, you can't stay asleep, you wake up early…what?"

"All of those."

"All of those," he repeated. "Well, we'll see about that, won't we."

"What's that supposed to mean?"

"So why is it you have trouble sleeping?"

"How the hell should I know?"

"I'm sure we can rule out a guilty conscience."

"This is all so funny to you, isn't it."

With one long swig, he polished off the third beer, closed the magazine, and stood up. "I suggest you start that homework *now*." He cleared the table, took the remainder of his six-pack from the refrigerator, and retrieved the toolbox from where he'd left it on the floor. Pausing in the doorway, he said, "And don't be late tomorrow."

EVEN THOUGH HE WAS gone, his presence still filled the room, as if he were just outside the door, waiting in the hallway. And what the hell did that mean: "We'll see."? She took one of the dinette chairs and tried to wedge it underneath the doorknob. But the back wasn't really high enough, and the rounded metal feet slid out too easily anyway. The desk chair, however, made of wood and with a taller back, worked pretty well. It probably wouldn't hold up to too much force, but it would buy a little time. It would certainly make enough noise to wake her.

But only a few minutes later, she put the chair back where it belonged. After all, what was the point? And for the first time since she'd returned, she took a look at the curtains.

They looked nice.

Chapter 9

SHE BARELY MADE IT to school on time the next morning; each successive Monday seemed harder than the one before. And though it took a lot out of her, she managed to thank Baker for putting up the curtains.

He looked like he was trying not to smirk when he said, "No problem," and walked away.

She stared after him.

IT WAS TUESDAY NIGHT, and she was sitting at her desk, writing in a little memo pad, a legion of tiny pages now filled with small, precise print. After the history-exam disaster, she'd developed her own study method, taking notes every night in preparation for the inevitable tests and quizzes. Each subject's theories, facts, and concepts were neatly organized and catalogued, flawlessly laid out in multicolored splendor. And since the pads were small enough to carry in her jacket pocket, she could study a little here and there whenever she had a spare moment—mostly going back and forth to school. That's how she'd done all of her studying for her economics test tomorrow.

She made a few final notes, then closed her history textbook with a satisfying thud. Ten minutes later, she was in bed.

FROM HIS CAR ACROSS the street, Baker saw her light go out: 12:47. In another half hour, he'd go up and have a look. Holding his cigarette up to the edge of the window, he flicked ashes into the street, some fresh air rushing in with a cool snap against his face. He let his head fall back against the headrest. Surveillance could be very boring. Yet he felt like he was exactly where he was supposed to be, doing exactly what he was supposed to be doing; though it would've been better with a beer to pass the time. With no one to talk to and nothing of interest to watch, he

was chain-smoking worse than usual, literally using one cigarette to light the next. He took a long, languid pull that tasted surprisingly good for so late in the day. But he really had to cut down; Cynthia hated it.

Cynthia. Her party Saturday night had been a double celebration. Not only had she been chosen by some liquor company for a major advertising campaign to be launched in time for Christmas, but one of the agents she'd seen in California had taken her on as a client. Circulating through the partygoers, Baker had done his best to be the proud, supportive boyfriend, talking about what an exciting time this was for her, and how happy he was that she'd finally found an agent who believed in her potential. But behind the words and the smile, he was jealous: her life was moving ahead while his was foundering. And the next time she flew out to LA, well, what if she decided to stay out there? It made sense, didn't it? The heart of the movie industry—and her only acting agent—were there. Nothing was holding her here except him, and he had yet to formalize any kind of commitment between them—much to the dismay of her father, who'd let him know this in no uncertain terms.

But Cynthia would never sacrifice career for marriage anyway. Though not a believer in the "better-dead-than-wed" attitude touted by many in the women's movement, her career definitely took priority. It wouldn't surprise him if she turned the tables and asked him to move to LA. Why shouldn't *he* be the one to accommodate *her*? But he hated the place, could never live there, everyone so laid back and superficial. Just like at the party. Cynthia had chided him, saying he appeared to be working rather than enjoying himself. But he felt so out of place— even with the few people he knew. Everyone seemed to be gossiping about agents, auditions, coaches… And when someone he just met found out he was a cop, they either stopped talking and got away from him as fast as they could or started pumping him for insights they could use for an audition or script—making *him* want to leave.

How different Cynthia was. She was just as comfortable with his cop friends as she was with her actor/model friends. She truly enjoyed people—all kinds of people. Without denying the shallow perspectives held by many of her guests that night, she accepted them for what they were. He simply couldn't wait till they were gone. He hated parties. They were usually nothing more than marathons of

meaningless mingling and insipid small talk. So much mental energy expended for nothing.

And then there was the young actor Cynthia had been flirting with most of the night. The man lived in New York, but had met Cynthia in LA. while both were waiting to see prospective agents in the same office. Not especially good looking, it was his sense of humor that so obviously attracted her. Baker felt like his own sense of humor had gotten buried somewhere. And only last week he'd heard on the radio that, according to some survey, women rated a man's sense of humor higher in importance than looks, education, or income. Great. Just great.

He checked his watch: 1:12. Time to get the show on the road. He got out of the car and, using his foot, mashed the cigarette into the asphalt, a brash gust of wind blowing the chilly night inside his open jacket. Unfortunately, the interior of Micki's building didn't feel much warmer.

Outside her door, he positioned himself to block as much of the hallway light as possible. Then he gently turned his key and eased himself through. But at the first sound of his entry, she jumped out of bed, tripped over the jeans that were lying on the floor, and crashed into the desk. Cursing, she turned on the lamp.

"Take it easy, Micki; it's just me."

"It's just you? What the fuck do y'want?"

"I'm just checking to make sure you're where you're supposed to be."

"Okay, so now y'know." The look she gave him said she was waiting for him to leave.

Instead, he closed the door, walked over to the table, and pulled out a chair. Sitting down low on his spine, he stretched his long legs straight out in front of him, casually crossing them at the ankles. He watched her scrambling to put on her jeans, buckling her belt underneath her nightshirt. "What the hell are you doing?" he asked.

"I'm gettin' dressed. What're *you* doin'?"

"First of all, I don't have to answer to you. Second of all, it's after one o'clock in the morning, so get back into bed and go to sleep."

"While y' here? What're y' kiddin'? No way."

"And why is that?"

"Whatta y'think?"

"You'd better drop that attitude and stop answering my questions with questions."

She threw a glance toward the fire escape window, then watched as he pulled out his cigarettes and lit one.

"I'm going to hang out here for a while," he said. "But you should be sleeping now. So take those jeans off and get back into bed."

"Yer outta y'mind."

He uncrossed his legs and sat up straight, feet flat on the floor and wide apart. "Nothing's going to happen," he said. "So get back into bed."

"F'get it."

Forearms on his thighs, he leaned forward. "I *said* nothing—is going—to happen."

"Well, I don't know that."

Leaning back again, he took another hit off the cigarette and studied her. The oversized T-shirt, which hung down to her knees, emphasized how underweight she still was, its "short" sleeves reaching her elbows and covering up the muscular arms. She looked waif-like. If threatened, she wasn't going down easy, but he knew as well as she did just how vulnerable she really was.

He stood up. "I'm leaving for tonight, but I want you to think about this, because I'll be back."

This last bit of news made her less than happy.

"Gee," he said, "a month ago you were pissed off because I wasn't stopping by. Well, here I am, and now you're pissed off about that." He picked up the Camels and his lighter from the table, then gave her another long look, his eyes laughing.

When the door finally closed behind him, she gave him the finger before sitting down hard on the bed.

HER NEW STUDY METHOD had paid off: Wednesday's economics test had been a snap to prepare for; Thursday's physics exam, as well, though she never really studied for those anyway. And while it was only Friday, she'd gotten both of them back already: 99 on the first and 100 on the second. Sitting in the security office for a special, ten-minute homeroom period, she was drumming her fingers on the desk, waiting for her report card—the first official document that might actually say something good about her. When Baker finally handed hers over, she felt a rush: all Os, for *outstanding,* in her academic courses. Numeric grades wouldn't be coming into play until the next marking period.

But Baker was tapping his finger next to the UN—*unsatisfactory*—she'd received in general conduct. "You'd better pick that up," he said. Then he took the report card back, signed it, and placed it in an envelope to return to the general office.

Elbow on the desk, head in hand, she lethargically flipped through one of her little notepads, using the remaining few minutes as a review for the next period's English exam. Mr. Newsome hadn't even graded the test papers from last week. He gave more tests than any of her other teachers. For *English.* What a jerk.

She sulked through the rest of the day, had a tough night at Bel, then lay down to sleep. Twice she nearly drifted off, only to return sharply to wakefulness, ears straining for any sounds outside her door. At half past midnight, she got up to drink her last packet of cocoa, then went back to bed, putting the radio on low. At least she could sleep late tomorrow.

BAKER SAT IN HIS car, watching Micki's apartment. After Tuesday's failed attempt, he'd decided to give it a few days before trying again. If his date tonight hadn't gone so badly, he would've given it a few more.

Cynthia had been worn out after working all day on a TV soap opera—*Days of Our Lives* or something like that. Though cast in some bit part, she'd explained, over a late dinner, that it was a much more important role than being an extra: she'd been given two lines to say to one of the show's stars. Big fucking deal: two lines. But according to her, this was a significant first step up the ladder. When he hadn't shared her enthusiasm, she'd gone home. Alone. He'd taken a nap.

He got out of his car and stretched his legs. Micki's apartment was dark—same as it had been when he'd arrived almost an hour ago. There was little point in waiting any longer.

TIRED OF TOSSING AROUND on the sagging collection of lumps and bumps that called itself a mattress, Micki switched on the light and checked the clock—it was twenty to two. She turned off the radio, put on her jeans, and had just stripped off her nightshirt when Baker came through the door. Her arms flew to her chest.

Eyes fixed on hers, he took a step further into the room and, without looking, pushed the door shut behind him. She was standing motionless next to the bed—muscular arms crossed over bare breasts, jeans clothing the remainder of a boyish figure. But it was an image he saw only peripherally, for his eyes never wavered—not even an instant—from hers. She, on the other hand, shot a glance down to his crotch. But this time there was no apologetic blush, just a cold, defensive glare.

As to why she'd be going out at this hour, Baker had two theories: either she was meeting Rick someplace or she was going to buy drugs. One way or another—intentionally or not—she was going to tell him. And she would suffer the consequences. He'd make sure of it. He tossed his keys onto the table, the harsh noise slicing through the stillness. She flinched.

"I see you're getting dressed," he said.

"So what."

"So it's nearly two in the morning. Where were you planning on going?"

His eyes had that cold, inhuman look; there was no telling what was going through his head. Trying to temper her voice, she said, "Down to the corner. I just wanted to get something. Woulda taken me five minutes, tops."

"You mean down to the deli?"

"They're open till two."

"What's so important that you have to get it now?"

"I—" But the truth was going to sound too dumb. She needed to come up with something serious. Like medicine. But she already had some aspirin in the kitchen drawer. And Baker knew that.

His expression turned smug.

"I wanted to get a box of instant cocoa."

"Instant cocoa," he repeated.

"It's not the first time. Y'can ask Frankie; he'll tell ya."

"The guy at the deli?"

"Yessir."

"And this couldn't wait till tomorrow? You expect me to believe you're violating curfew for some fucking cocoa?"

She should've lied, should've taken another minute to figure something out. In fact, the perfect thing now came to mind, but it was too late. "I—I still couldn't sleep, and I didn't have any more. I used the last packet a couple-a hours ago."

And though it didn't seem possible, his eyes grew colder. "What the fuck do you take me for?"

In almost a whisper, she said, "It's the truth."

When he moved, she pressed her arms tighter against her chest and backed up against the desk, but he was headed for the garbage pail in front of the sink. He wrenched off the lid and saw, to his astonishment, the torn remains of a Nestlé's instant cocoa pouch with the empty, crushed box underneath. Either she was an incredibly inventive liar—it took balls to come up with something as stupid-sounding as this, which made it all the more believable?—or she was telling the truth. He replaced the cover, then faced the sink. "Finish getting dressed."

Eyes glued to the back of his head, she put on the rest of her clothes. When she told him she was done, he took her jacket from the closet and threw it at her. With mock pleasantness he said, "Let's go shopping."

THE DELI WAS LESS than half a block away, but it was a long, long walk that night, Micki always keeping a good five feet between herself and Baker. As they approached the store, the strange payphone out front caught her eye, and she paused to take a look at it. Encased in an old metal box painted red, it hung midway down the corner where the two graffiti-filled walls of the building met.

Baker gave her a small shove. "Move it!"

When she opened the door, the little bell above it jingled. Frankie, looking up from the large serving tub of tuna salad he was covering, smiled. "Hey, Micki."

"Hey, Frankie." And she went down the narrow aisle toward the back.

Turning to Baker, Frankie asked, "Camels?"—Baker almost always bought a pack when he was there.

"Yeah," Baker responded. But he was staring at Micki while she reached above the refrigerated case and picked out a box from the shelf.

Frankie, putting the cigarettes on the counter with a book of matches, was watching the way Baker was looking at her. When Baker made no move to pay, Frankie asked, "Is there anything else I can get you?"

Picking up the pack but leaving the matches, Baker replied, "No, that's it."

Baker opened his wallet, and Frankie saw the metallic flash of the badge. He'd never noticed that before. He rang up the sale and gave Baker his change, only to see Baker watching Micki again. Apparently, she hadn't liked the first box she'd chosen and was taking down another. His tone somewhat abrasive, Frankie asked, "You need something else?"

Eyes fastened on the returning figure, Baker replied, "I'm waiting for her."

Frankie rang up her purchase. "Everything okay, Micki?"

"Yeah, sure. Say, that payphone out there works?"

"Yeah, it works. Why? Something wrong? You need to make a call?"

"No, I just never seen anybody use it."

Frankie lowered his voice, and with a half-joking, conspiratorial smile asked, "This your boyfriend?"

Micki paled. "He's—he's—um—he's my—um—parole officer."

"Oh!" Frankie flushed slightly while he handed her the change. "Well, that's okay, Micki; everybody makes mistakes." He turned to Baker. "She's a good kid."

"She ever come in here this late before?"

The deli man looked at Micki.

"It's okay, Frankie; just tell him the truth."

"Yeah. Maybe two times." He smiled. "Always for the hot chocolate. She don't sleep too good." He extended his hand. "Frankie Coluccio."

Baker hesitated, then shook it. "Detective Sergeant James Baker."

"Detective?"

Eyes full of disdain, Baker shot a glance at Micki. "I don't usually work in this capacity."

Micki stared down at her hands, which were clutching the paper bag.

"Let's go," Baker said.

She walked outside ahead of him. Maybe Frankie wouldn't like her as much now—now that he saw how much Baker didn't like her. She turned to go home, but Baker yanked her back around.

"You don't leave that apartment after curfew unless the whole fucking building is on fire; do you understand me?"

"Yessir," she answered quietly.

He stared down at her. "You being straight with me about all this?"

"Yessir."

But he couldn't get a read on her. Gazing out over her head, he looked down the street, then over to the left, toward Bel Canto, now dark and shuttered. He exhaled heavily, then started back to her apartment. His brisk pace, coupled with his long stride, was difficult for her to maintain.

Frankie had been watching them through the plate-glass window. Once they were out of sight, he began closing up.

IT WAS MICKI WHO unlocked the door when they returned; Baker's keys were still on the table—which explained why he hadn't just gotten in his car and gone home. Or so she thought. Much to her dismay, he took off his jacket and sat down. And though she had no desire for the hot chocolate anymore, she felt obligated to make it. She turned on the faucet and put some water in the pot. Looking over her shoulder, she asked "Y'want some?"

"Yeah, why not."

Cursing silently, she added more water and turned on the stove, then took down an extra mug from the cabinet. White with pink and green polka dots, it was ugly. *Really* ugly. She'd seen some just like it in Sunny's Superstore. It would be funny watching Baker drink out of that. Her own mug, a glazed cobalt blue, was very pretty—although, right near the handle, it had a small chip where the white stuff underneath showed through. Still, it looked a million times better than the thing she was giving him. She tore open two packets and poured them into the mugs. A fine, sugary dust settled over the mounds of powder.

She leaned against the sink, listening to what little traffic there was outside and watching the pot, which was taking its own sweet time to boil. Baker, smoking a Camel, sat at the table, his chair facing the fire escape window. When the water was ready, she filled the mugs and brought them over. Baker extinguished his cigarette. And though she sat down across from him, she moved her chair slightly so she wouldn't have to look at him directly—not unless she wanted to. But it was a small table, so they were sitting very close—close enough that the air between them felt charged.

The rich aroma steamed up from the mugs. Baker took a sip, then jerked his head back. "Hot!" he said.

But she was staring at her cocoa.

He took to gazing out the window, absently rubbing his thumb along the handle of the cup. Until he took another sip and looked at her. "So—what should I do about tonight?"

She tensed. "What *about* tonight?"

"You broke curfew."

"Well—not really." She said it hesitantly, carefully watching his reaction before adding, "I never actually left the apartment till you were with me." The smile that slowly spread across his face caught her completely off guard, the crows' feet emerging around his eyes making him look rugged and weathered, kind of like the Marlboro man.

He chuckled softly. "I guess I'll have to think about that. But then maybe you want to tell me"—the smile disappeared—"what you were doing looking at me the way you did before. I thought we went over that already."

The dark liquid in her mug—a tiny, circular pool—was still untouched. She watched the reflection of the lightbulb dancing on the surface. Talking to the cocoa, she said, "Yeah, but it wasn't like that. I wanted to... I thought..." She pulled her feet back and wrapped them around the legs of her chair. "I was afraid you..."

But when she couldn't bring herself to say it, he said, "You were afraid I was going to nail you."

She looked up.

"Well, now you have your answer, so keep your eyes where they belong."

She turned her gaze back to the hot chocolate. "Yessir."

"But I'll tell you something," he said, and she met his eyes once more, "another guy in my position probably *would've* nailed you, probably would've done it a long time ago."

"Oh, really? So what makes *you* such a saint?"

He merely chuckled again, though this time it had a dark quality to it. "I'm no saint, Micki, but I try to do what's right."

She glanced over at her bed, all in disarray from the few restless hours she'd spent in it that night.

"I just don't understand," he continued, "why you don't trust me when it—"

"I don't trust anybody," she said.

"Nobody?"

"Nobody. People jus' wanna use you—take whatever they can get, however they can get it."

"Didn't you trust Tim?"

"I…" But she never finished the sentence.

"Let's face it, Micki, I've had plenty of opportunities to take advantage of you, but I haven't done it once."

She shifted her eyes to stare at the cracked wall.

"Have I?" he prodded.

She shrugged.

"C'mon, I want an answer. Have I ever touched you in a—in an inappropriate way?"

"I don't like you touchin' me!" Her eyes were now boring into his.

He lowered his gaze and nodded. When he looked back, his voice was unexpectedly gentle. "You know I have to search you, right? I'm just doing my job—that's all it is. But I—I can understand how uncomfortable it must be for you—having me put my hands on you like that. I certainly wouldn't want anybody doing that to me."

She gaped at him.

"But that's not what I asked," he added quietly. "I want to know if you think I've ever touched you in a"—he leaned back—"in a sexual way. I mean, that's what we're talking about here, isn't it?"

She took one hand off her mug, placed her palm on the Formica, and drew it toward her till it was hanging off the edge of the table by her fingers.

A second later, he did the same. "Well did I?" he pressed. "And I want you to tell me the truth."

She slowly shook her head no.

"So what's the story then?"

"I've still got no reason to trust you."

The ugly spotted mug in front of him was empty. He lit another cigarette and smoked awhile, looking toward the window until he eventually shifted his gaze back to hers. "Did you get raped at Heyden? Did a guard rape you?"

"None a y'damned business what anybody did t'me!"

"It *is* my business. I'm trying to understand why you don't trust me at least a little."

Bullshit, she thought, why don't you go home already and just leave me the fuck alone. But then, hoping it might be enough to satisfy him, she said, "Almost."

"Almost?"

"Yeah, almost."

"What do you mean, 'almost'?"

"'Almost' means almost! It almost happened but it didn't; that's what 'almost' means."

Baker had to force back a smile. He said, "So why don't you tell me what *did* happen."

His face looked different now, the lines softened, his eyes warm. This was someone she'd never talked to before. This was the person who'd gently put his arm around a little girl like Cathy Stevens and gotten rid of the bad guy who'd hurt her.

And Baker knew he'd won. Micki had the look of someone about to confess, the desire to unburden themselves finally overriding everything else. Not another word would he have to say. All he had to do was wait.

"How old are you?" she asked.

The amused smile reappeared. "Where's this coming from?"

"I don't know anything about you."

He knocked some ashes into the saucer. "Thirty-six," he replied. "Actually, thirty-seven soon." Seeing the look on her face, he chuckled. "I'm ancient, Micki."

"I didn't say anything."

"Just wait. Someday you'll be this old."

"I doubt it."

There was a tiny twinge in his heart. But before he could respond, she asked, "So how come you're not workin' the streets? How come you're workin' at the school?"

"Didn't they—"

"Yeah, I know what they said, but I don't buy it."

Baker wanted to laugh. Great cover story the department had given him; nobody believed it. He took a drag on his cigarette, then exhaled slowly. "Let's just say I was having some personal problems, and it seemed like a good idea for me to take a break."

"So didja ever actually shoot someone?"

"Yes."

"Dead?"

His eyes drifted down to the pack of cigarettes he was turning over in his hand. Behind the camel on the front there were palm trees and pyramids; on the back, mostly Turkish domes and minarets. Done in a palette of golds and browns, the scenes looked calm and quiet. Arid. Deserted. He took another long drag.

She began to wonder if he'd even heard the question.

"Yes," he suddenly answered, exhaling the rest of the smoke through his nose and looking very tired. He tapped the pack on the table three times before putting it down and meeting her eyes. "So now tell me what happened at Heyden."

She cleared her throat, then ran her finger around the rim of the pretty blue mug still full of lukewarm cocoa. The apartment seemed unnaturally quiet. "I—I'd gotten in trouble with Warden Loren that day for cursin' her out and takin' a swing at her with a mop. She took me down to the basement and beat me pretty bad with the strap, left me tied and hangin' from this pipe—still wearin' only my jeans—so I could 'think it over.' But not two minutes after she left, Edmunds—a real scumbag, one of the male guards who'd helped her get me down there—came back and started puttin' his hands on my"—Micki swallowed—"on my chest. I mean, my back was all bleedin' and everything, but he didn't care; he was gettin' off on it; gettin' a hard-on. He went, 'Aw, look at what ya did here; ya got me all excited. Now y'gonna havta take care a this.' So—" She shot a glance at Baker.

Resting his cigarette on the saucer, Baker leaned back in his chair, the arm across his body propping up the elbow of the other. With the side of his index finger, he was absently tracing the line between his lips. He angled his head slightly. "So…?"

She looked back at the cocoa and pushed it away. "So I—I didn't say nothin'. I hurt real bad from gettin' whipped. It was the second day in a row this time. I was hopin' he was jus' tryin' t'scare me, that he'd be too afraid a gettin' caught. But then he went around in backa me, held my hips, and rubbed himself against me, sayin' all kindsa shit. So I tried kickin' him back there, but my toes barely touched the ground—I couldn't really do anything. All it did was make my wrists hurt worse and piss him off. He started hittin' my legs with his baton. One leg hurt so bad I thought he'd cracked the bone, so I stopped." She leaned her elbows on the table and combed her fingers through her hair till her forehead came to rest in her palms. "I was in a lotta pain. He went around in fronta me again and undid his belt. He pulled down his fly, takin' his—his dick out. He started playin' with himself, sayin' how he was gonna teach me a lesson better than any whippin' could. But just as he was unzippin' my jeans, the warden came back. She'd usually leave me hangin' there alone for at least half an hour, and I guess that's what he'd been countin' on. He started tellin' her that I'd asked for it, that I'd begged him t'fuck me like that." She looked up.

Baker picked up his cigarette again. "Go on."

In the middle of the table was a ballpoint pen. Micki pulled it over and stopped looking at Baker. "So the warden acted like she believed him. When I tried t'say somethin', she told me t'shut up. And then she jus' let him go, tellin' him it better not happen again." Micki tapped the pen on the table several times. "The warden told me I was in big trouble 'cause I'd solicited a guard f'sex, told me things could get a lot worse f'me than they already were. Said maybe she'd f'orget about it. Started touchin' me, sayin' if I wanted to, I could *make* her forget about it. And then she put her fingers on my lips." Micki drew her head back. "There was no way I was doin' that. I told her she could go fuck herself. That's when she lit the cigarette. At first she jus' held it real close so I could feel the heat. But then she went, 'Maybe y'should reconsider.' I told her I wouldn't, so she burned me."

With the pen gripped in her right hand, Micki pushed the cap up a little with her thumb and index finger, only to force it back down again from the top with just her thumb. She said, "When I wouldn't cry, she went, 'I betcha think y'tough; well we'll see who's really tough,' and she burned me a coupla more times—right on the open cuts. But I didn't cry. I *didn't*." Though she still wasn't looking at Baker, she stopped playing with the pen. "After that they put me in the hole, and I thought they were jus' gonna leave me down there, 'cause nobody'd tell me anything; nobody'd talk to me until three days later when they came and took me out." She placed the pen on the table without letting go. "Still, I knew it was jus' gonna get worse. So when I saw my chance, I—I escaped. Got pretty far, too. Except, after they caught me, they made my life an endless living hell. Till Sergeant Kelly came."

She fell silent. When she looked at Baker, she was hoping to see some trace of the older cop's kindness in him. But his face was blank. Empty. Sitting back, he appeared completely relaxed—as if he'd been listening to someone recount the boring highlights of their summer vacation. Her heart contracted into a tight, painful lump, and she tossed the pen into the center of the table. There was a poor attempt at a smile. "I just made all that up."

Eyes lowered to focus on the cigarette between his fingers, he exhaled smoke. "And why would you do that?"

She shoved her chair back and stood up, causing him to look at her again. "Because—because I wanted ya t'feel sorry f'me."

"Bullshit. If you ever wanted me to feel sorry for you, you would've shown me those scars the first time I asked to see them. Besides, why admit now that you were lying?"

He sounded so fucking cool and…professional. Her voice started to rise. "'Cause y'don't feel nothin' f'me, and y'never will. I bet y'think I deserved everything that happened t'me."

"Nobody deserves to be treated like that." But he was looking at the cigarette again. Voice quiet, he added, "Every word of your story was true and you know it."

"Well—well, I shouldn'ta told ya."

"Why not?"

"'Cause—'cause I bet you'll go and have a good laugh with y'friends over this."

His eyes met hers. "Nothing you just said was even remotely funny."

"Yeah, that's what y'say t'*me*." She looked him over. "You're real good. *Real* good."

"What's that supposed to mean?"

"Y'can play good cop, bad cop all by y'self; y'don't even need a fuckin' partner. F' one minute there, I thought y'were actually human."

He stood up, grinding out the cigarette. "You'd better watch how you talk to me."

"Why don'tcha go fuck y'self."

The back of his fist smashed across her face, which showed no reaction. She even managed not to lose her balance, having purposely braced herself against the table.

Guts twisting inside, he put his jacket on and picked up his things. He said, "You be at my place by eight o'clock Sunday." He waited for a response, got none, and left anyway.

Halfway down the staircase he heard "son of a *bitch!*" followed by the crash of something hurled against the door. He paused for an instant, then continued down.

THE SOUND OF HIS feet on the stairs had stopped briefly, so she knew she'd had an audience. But her book had paid the price. Lying on the floor, pages down, it was opened somewhere in the middle, as if it had tripped and fallen while trying to run away. She went over to pick it up, but found herself crumpled on the floor beside it; first righting it, then skimming her fingers over the hard, glossy cover. The brand new history textbook wasn't new anymore, the spine broken, numerous sheets folded in on themselves. What would Mr. Ingram say when she returned it at the end of the term? Would she have to pay for it? She usually took such good care of things.

She stared at the door and felt her throat constricting. That episode at Heyden was one of her worst memories, something she'd tried very hard to forget. By telling it to Baker she'd given it new life, was once again conjuring up images of Edmunds and Loren snickering over what they'd done—and how they'd gotten away with it. They'd both rubbed it in her face every chance they'd gotten. And now Baker was probably laughing at her, too.

He'd played her. The man didn't give a rat's ass about her feelings, yet she'd completely fallen for his little act—and so easily, too. He must be pretty fucking proud of himself. She closed her eyes. To think he, of all people, now knew what had happened. The shame, tingling and hot, was coursing through her—coursing through her veins.

When she opened her eyes, she was still looking at the door, the dark streets beyond calling out to her. By now she knew her way around well enough to reach the underpass of the bridge without getting caught. That is, unless Baker happened to still be out there—watching. Had he driven away? She hadn't been paying attention to the sounds outside.

Sitting very still beside the book, she hugged her knees to her chest, resting her forehead on them. Waiting.

Waiting it out.

BAKER LET THE CIGARETTE hang from his mouth as he pulled his collar up and hugged himself to keep warm. He should've put the jacket's lining in tonight; the temperature had dipped into the forties after reaching sixty-six in the afternoon. While he was closing the overstuffed little ashtray, some stray ashes took flight. He cursed, swiping them off his thigh, then stared at Micki's apartment. Her lights were still on.

He felt the heat prickling up in his cheeks: he'd been unconscionably cruel. And yet, when the conversation had started, his concern had been somewhat genuine. Hadn't it? But then why did he manipulate her into telling him something she didn't want to? Why did it end up so badly?

He rolled the window down an inch and flicked some ashes into the street.

Christ, the look on her face when she'd checked out his crotch. Never before had he seen such fear of rape being directed at him. He'd felt disgusting. Guilty. Just for being a man. So was that it? Had he been retaliating? Exacting some sort of revenge for her rampant distrust? Or maybe it had just been a ruthless power play, a demonstration of his interviewing prowess: getting her to talk simply because he could. He grunted: the kid had managed to briefly turn the tables. The little he'd disclosed had been far more than he'd ever intended her to know. Recalling her final line of questioning, his jaw clenched.

He was starting to shiver. He turned over the engine to let it warm up, then snorted with self-contempt. After all, he'd forced *her* to dredge up terrible memories just to appease his curiosity. In return, he'd given her nothing. He'd shown more empathy when Cynthia had stubbed her toe on the bathroom door the other night.

What the hell was wrong with him? He knew how devastating sexual assaults were. Because of it, the women's libbers were actually lobbying to change police procedures. They wanted only female officers to take rape victims' statements, and they wanted to ensure no officers at all would be observing the exams. Legally, the examining doctor sufficed to preserve the chain of custody for any evidence collected; yet some officers were still following victims into the examination room, needlessly retraumatizing them. And Baker had been one of them.

He recalled a case from a few years back when a serial rapist had been on the loose in Hell's Kitchen. The fifth in a string of incidents, a forty-three-year-old woman had been assaulted beneath the staircase leading to the basement of her building. The attack had occurred just after midnight when she'd been on her way to retrieve her last load of laundry. Frightened for her life, she'd offered no resistance, though the perp had done nothing more than threaten her. And while many cops labeled rape cases suspect when there were no weapons or bruises involved, Baker had believed her story. Completely. Her emotional reaction, however, had been an entirely different matter.

In the emergency room, he had stood behind her when she was about to be examined. She was wearing a hospital gown with a sheet draped over the lower half of her body to provide "privacy." But for ten minutes, she'd been refusing to lie down, crying and screaming that she wouldn't let them continue while a man—namely Baker—was in the room. She said she didn't care if he was a cop or the goddamned pope. Even now, thinking back, it made him cringe to remember how callous he'd been, saying, "Listen, honey, I can't see a goddamn thing, so why don't you just lie back and relax so we can get this over with already." The doctor—a woman—had given him a deadly look. After that, he'd kept his mouth shut, although he hadn't taken it all that seriously. Because he hadn't taken the doctor seriously. Because she was a woman. He'd mistaken her for a nurse when she'd first entered the room.

As soon as the doctor was finished, he walked out behind her with his bag of evidence, leaving the victim to get dressed in fresh clothes her daughter had brought. The doctor turned to him, saying, "I'd like you to come with me for a minute if you don't mind, Detective," her tone implying he shouldn't even *think* of saying no. He didn't bother to correct her regarding his rank.

He followed her to an empty examination bay, wondering what she wanted and wishing she weren't so short. Though quite attractive—light brown hair and deep-set hazel eyes—she was over a foot shorter than he was. He liked his women tall.

"Do me a favor," she said, "and remove your shoes so you can hop up on the table for me."

He'd flashed an anxious smile. "What?"

"Are you afraid?"

He tried to stare her down.

She was not impressed.

He did as she asked.

Once he was on the table, she had him lie down. Then she made him put his feet in the stirrups and slide his butt all the way to the edge, the clean white paper crackling loudly beneath him until he was positioned exactly the same as the victim had been in order to be examined. Baker knew from the heat in his face that it had turned beet red. And he was still fully clothed.

The doctor said nothing while he quietly got up and put his shoes back on. When he could finally look her in the eye, he apologized.

"I think you should be apologizing to *Ms.* Navarro," she replied.

Baker nodded, then extended his hand, which the doctor had graciously shaken. It was a lesson he'd never forgotten. Until now.

How could he have been so cold? The more Micki had disclosed about her abuse, the angrier he had become, and yet he never let it show, never showed any compassion, either. And even ignoring his response—or lack thereof—what had it cost her to tell her story to him, not only a man but someone who, for the most part, had never been anything but an enemy to her?

Her light went off, and he looked at his watch: 3:07. At 3:30 he'd go. Until then, he'd keep an eye on her building, praying she wouldn't walk out that door. For he knew what he'd done: he'd exposed more scars, cut open some deep wounds on a junkie and left them to bleed. And to think he'd even hit her afterward.

Not too bright.

AFTER MUCH TOSSING AND turning, Micki finally dozed off at seven thirty in the morning, only to get up at noon, tired of jolting awake every hour and trying to force herself back to sleep. She had cupcakes for breakfast and a quick jump in the shower.

Underneath the mattress was the money she'd set aside for the vest she wanted—the entire amount. Except she really hadn't planned on buying it just yet, hadn't quite made the final decision. Still, she took the bills from their hiding place and fanned them out on top of the bed. It made her heart ache. She stuffed the money in her pocket and left.

MUCH TO HER RELIEF, there was a different biker salesman at the store. He didn't comment on her bruised face, simply helped her find the right size vest, then moved on. Saturdays were busy.

She went home, went grocery shopping, then tried to settle down to homework. But it was impossible to sit still or concentrate. Clawing at her every waking minute, the craving was an empty, yawning pit demanding to be filled. She pulled the new vest out of the closet and laid it out on the bed. Rich with the smell of leather, it was soft and smooth under her fingers. She lifted it up. And put it on. But felt exactly the same as she had before. It was just a piece of clothing.

She tried listening to the radio. Eating chocolate till she was nauseous. Sleeping. But the edgy, restless feeling wasn't willing to release her this time. She left the apartment.

Outside, the overcast sky, which was usually soothing, was having little effect. She went to work early, hanging out in the tiny area behind the restaurant—three dented, old garbage pails and a dumpster for company. While she leaned against the brick wall, a slight breeze passed through, eddying the dry, dead leaves at her feet. And then the urge for a cigarette welled up. Though she'd never smoked, she could picture herself doing it. If Baker were standing there instead of her, that's exactly what *he* would be doing.

The metal door opened and Juan, apron wet and full of stains, stepped out. "Hey, Little Micki."

This made her smile. It was a long-standing joke that he called her "Little Micki" when he was but a whole inch taller than she was. "Hey, Juan."

He lit a cigarette and looked up at the thick layer of clouds. "Gonna rain; what a drag. Me and my girl was gonna take a ride on my new bike later on. But at night in the rain... I ain't good enough yet. My bike's a beauty, though. You see her out front?"

Micki shook her head no.

"No? The red Kawasaki?"

"I really wasn't lookin', Juan."

"Shit!" He dashed down the alley. When he returned, he said, "Man, you scare me, y'know? Get me thinkin' maybe somebody rip her off. She cost me alotta bread. I'd freak if someone did that. I oughtta park her back here, but Mr. A won't let me, said there's not enough room." He raised the cigarette to his lips. "How come you hangin' out here now?"

She shrugged.

"You look beat, y'know? Maybe you partyin' too much."

"I'm not partyin' at all, but I'm not sleepin', either."

He gave a quick glance around, then moved closer. His voice much lower, he said, "I got somethin' that'd help you sleep, y'know? I mean, you can party with 'em, but they'll put you out if y'wannem to. You ever do ludes?"

She shook her head no.

"I give you three for five bucks. That's real cheap 'cause I like you."

She had no idea if that was cheap or not, and she couldn't afford the five bucks. But she couldn't afford more nights like the last one, either. "Y'got 'em with you?"

"You got the bread?"

She reached into her pocket, then paused. But the chances of Baker returning so soon were very slim. She took out her money and counted five singles. But when Juan reached for the bills, she pulled her hand away. "Where's the stuff?"

He gave her a sly smile. "You don' trust me, Little Micki?"

"Just get the stuff an' I'll trust ya t'take my money."

He laughed. "I be right back. Don't go in yet." He threw the cigarette to the ground and crushed it with the toe of his work boot. A few minutes later, he came back out with three white tablets inside a tiny plastic bag.

She stuffed the packet inside her jacket pocket. "How many d'ya take?"

"You? You small. Just take one unless you wanna be really wasted." Seeing the strange look in her eyes, he added, "Just be careful; don't take too much."

"Sure, Juan." And she watched him walk away, the kitchen clamor a messy burst of noise when he opened the door to go inside.

She looked up and noticed the darkening clouds. Large and low, they were barely moving, even as another breeze happened by. The air, like her heart, felt heavier now, the leaves chasing each other blindly on the cold, hard ground.

When she left Bel, it was drizzling. Jacket drawn up over her head, she jogged home, changed into her nightshirt, and took one of the pills. But half an hour later, she was still awake. Maybe Juan had gypped her. She threw back the covers and got up. Then couldn't remember why. The walls—washed out, all of the color gone—looked far away and unwelcoming, everything bleached behind a milky-white screen. Centered in its own special space, her mind was floating—and she couldn't feel the floor, her rubbery legs collapsing beneath her. She fell back onto the bed.

This probably hadn't been such a hot idea.

Chapter 10

ICKI WOKE UP THE next morning feeling tired. What a waste of five dollars. She pushed the remaining two Quaaludes through the hole in her jacket pocket. Some people collected stamps.

She arrived at Baker's building and buzzed his apartment, though she could've walked through the main entrance with another tenant again. By the time she reached his floor, he was already standing in the doorway, showered and shaved. He stepped back to let her in and noted the brown paper bag that probably contained her lunch. She took off her jacket and hung it in the closet, then threw the bag in there, as well.

"New vest," he observed.

As if she hadn't heard him, she turned to go to the kitchen, Friday night's bruise—a brushstroke of maroon and red across her cheek—becoming clearly visible. It caused his chest to tighten, but he said only, "Forget about breakfast. Cynthia and I are going out, then I'm taking her home."

Micki glanced at his bedroom door.

"She's still getting dressed," he said. Staring down at her, he added, "I don't want you going through my things while I'm gone, is that clear?"

Before Micki could answer, Cynthia came out, wearing hip-hugger bell bottoms. Hair in loose curls, eyes still puffy with sleep, she looked different without make-up. She smiled—"Hi, Micki"—then put her shoulder bag on the floor and slipped into the brown suede jacket Baker held out for her.

Baker gave Micki a long, hard look.

"Don't worry," she said, "I'm not gonna trash the place while you're gone."

Seeing Baker's expression, Cynthia flashed Micki an apologetic smile. But he continued to look at her darkly. Then he pointed his finger and said, "You watch yourself." And held her gaze a little too long.

Her breath caught in her throat: he knew.

The couple left, Baker locking up behind them, their footsteps and chatter growing more distant as they wended their way down the stairs. Micki stared at the door. She hated being treated like some feral creature raised by wolves. And how could he tell she'd taken something last night? The fuzziness seemed barely noticeable to her. About to start for the kitchen, her eyes were drawn to the upper lock, a double-cylinder deadbolt. She opened the lower latch, turned the knob, and pulled. But nothing happened. The son of a bitch had locked her in. She slammed her palm against the door—"Fucking bastard!"—and marched directly into his bedroom.

She opened the top drawer of his dresser to find socks and underwear plus a small red box that read: "Latex condoms non-lubricated." Tucked in the back, underneath his briefs, was some girlie magazine. She was pulling it out when she heard the jingle of keys. She stuffed the magazine back in the drawer, then hurried out to the hallway—only to realize it had been one of his neighbors. She returned to his room.

This time she went for the wooden box on top of the bureau. Made of walnut, corners worn smooth, it was adorned with the carving of an old galleon. Inside she found his tie clip and a thick silver ID bracelet engraved with his initials—maybe Cynthia had given this to him. The only other item resting on the brown velveteen lining was a gold class ring with a garnet in the middle. Heavy in the palm of her hand, it was too big for even her thumb. She read the letters encircling the dark-red stone: "CORNELL UNIVERSITY." Ivy League. Pretty impressive for a cop. She put it back, closed the lid, and looked around for something else—maybe his uniforms. The closet door had been left open, and she could see them hanging in a neat, orderly row, the sergeant's stripes on the jackets' sleeves creating a pretty design against the sea of dark navy blue. The one at the front—dressier than the others, with all kinds of pins on it—still smelled of his aftershave. She ran her fingers over the bars of patterned colors, wondering what he'd done to earn so many. Acts of heroism and bravery, no doubt.

Acts of heroism and bravery.

She went to the kitchen and started cleaning.

THEY WERE SITTING IN one of Cynthia's favorite midtown restaurants, a Parisian-style café called the Manhattan Crêperie that served the ultra-thin French pancakes in every conceivable form. It wasn't Baker's kind of thing, but the eggs Benedict—made with a crêpe, of course—weren't all that bad. Cynthia had chosen some sort of fruit concoction, a rather meager dish, the raspberry and blueberry sauces now swirling around aimlessly in the melted whipped cream surrounding the uneaten portion.

"Is that going to be enough?" Baker asked.

"It's fine," she said. "You want some? It's delicious, but I think I'm finished."

While he continued working on his eggs, a canny look came over him. "Are you on a diet?"

"I just want to lose a few pounds. The agent in LA said it would be a good idea."

"Oh, jeez, Cyn."

"The camera adds ten pounds," she said. "It's not such a big deal for commercial print, but for film—well, it's like when I was doing fashion work."

He shook his head and went back to his meal. After another couple of bites, he asked, "So did you ever find that book you were looking for?"

"Mmm." Having just taken a sip of coffee, she was nodding. "I went down to Weiser's in the Village on Friday and found a ton of different books on meditation. I bought a couple, but haven't had a chance to start reading them yet."

Their waiter—an elderly gentleman with the prerequisite French accent, well-groomed mustache, and imperious air—came by with the coffee pot. "More café, mademoiselle?"

"Yes, thank you."

He looked at Baker. "Monsieur?"

"Yeah, thanks." And once the waiter was gone, Baker, with a bit of a smile, asked, "So did you buy anything for *me* at that store?"

"Actually," she replied, "I did." When his lips parted, she grinned and reached into her shoulder bag. "Hold out your hand."

He put out his palm, and she placed a round object in the middle. About an inch in diameter, the stone had bands, stripes, and oddly shaped bull's-eye patterns in varying shades of green. As he looked at the polished, irregular sphere, the creases in his forehead deepened. "You bought me a weird, giant marble?"

"It's malachite."

"Malachite?"

"It's a semiprecious gemstone. Spiritually, it can heal, help open up the heart chakra, and bring protection and safety."

"Can it also wash my car?"

"Very funny."

He smiled. "So this thing's supposed to protect me?"

"Uh-huh."

His grin broadened.

Her mouth twisted. Then, with a very straight face, she said, "I *tried* to get one shaped like a gun, but they were all out."

He chuckled. "As long as you tried, Cyn." And he rolled the sphere around in his hand. Closed in his fist, it felt cool and solid. "Thanks," he said, "I like it. I'll find a spot for it at home—it's a little too big to keep with me all the time." While he was putting it in his jacket pocket, a couple walked by, following the maitre d' to their seats. His expression changed. "Oh, hell."

"What is it?"

"I just realized I locked the kid inside the apartment. It didn't even dawn on me when we left. God forbid there's an emergency."

"There's always the fire escape."

"The gate on that window is padlocked. The key's nearby, but she has no idea where it is. For that matter, neither do you."

"You don't really think—"

"No, no, but still…" He tossed his knife and fork into the middle of his plate. What a pain in the ass. Now he felt pressured to go home. And for a moment, he pictured Micki in his apartment. "Christ," he said, "what the hell was I even thinking leaving her alone in there? God only knows what she's doing."

"I'm sure she's just cleaning, exactly like she's supposed to be."

"Yeah, right."

"What?" Cynthia asked. "What's so hard to believe?"

"How is it that you always think the best of people?"

"Maybe because that's the kind of world I want to live in. Why do you always think the worst?"

"It's one of the things that keep me safe."

"Well maybe you need to know when to turn it off!"

Baker drew back.

Cynthia's hand reached out and covered his. "I'm just—I'm just saying…"

"Sure," he said, his voice flat.

"Why don't we get the check," she suggested gently. "Then you can go back and put your mind at ease." She raised her hand to the waiter and pantomimed writing. He promptly arrived with a little silver tray and placed it in front of Baker. But while Baker was busy pulling out his wallet, Cynthia reached over and grabbed the metal dish. The waiter, looking at Baker, raised an eyebrow and practically sneered before moving a few steps away.

"Cyn—"

"No!" After a quick glance over the bill, she placed her Master Charge on top. "It's about my turn again." And when the waiter had taken the tray and was out of earshot, she leaned in, saying, "Besides, you hate this place. You think I don't know you like to call it 'The Manhattan Crapperie'?"

He chuckled, but started to object again.

She cut him off. "You paid the last five times."

"So now you're keeping score?"

"I'm not keeping score; I—" She leaned back. "You still can't deal with this, can you."

"So shoot me. Did you see the look that waiter gave me?"

"So what? What do you care what he thinks?"

Their relationship had nearly ended on the first date because of this. Cynthia, as a feminist, thought they should split all expenses down the middle. Baker, brought up with traditional values, felt it was his job to pay for everything. Never having dated a woman so much younger, he'd never faced this before. After lengthy negotiations, they'd reached an uneasy compromise where Cynthia paid every once in a while.

"Do you think this somehow makes you less of a man?" Cynthia asked.

But before Baker could answer, the waiter returned, presenting Cynthia with the elegant little tray—an imprinted form and her charge card on top. His entire demeanor dripping with disdain, he said, "Mademoi*selle*"—with tremendous emphasis on the last syllable.

Unruffled, her tone completely businesslike, Cynthia replied, "*Merci,*" in a perfect French accent. But Baker noticed that her lips, pressed together tightly, were twitching a little here and there as she signed her name and ripped out the carbon copy. And Baker's eyes began to smile, lips soon pressed together, same as hers. The moment the waiter had disappeared into the kitchen, they both burst out laughing.

OUTSIDE THE RESTAURANT, CYNTHIA raised her hand and hailed a cab.

"Let me take you home," Baker said. "The car's just around the corner."

"You'll only waste a lot of time in cross-town traffic. Besides, the only reason I let you chauffer me around so often is because I know how much you love to drive. But right now"—her palm caressed his face—"you should go check on Micki."

He opened the door for her.

"I love you," she said.

He gave her a kiss, then helped her in. And as the taxi pulled away into the stream of tailgating vehicles, he stood alone on the sidewalk. Feeling adrift.

WHEN HE RETURNED TO the apartment, he found Micki in the kitchen with a sponge mop. He hung up his jacket and put the malachite sphere on a bookshelf in the living room, a matchbook in front to keep it from rolling away. Then he watched as she finished the last few feet. The floor looked sopping wet.

"How long till that dries?" he asked.

She shrugged and, avoiding his gaze, started toward the bathroom to dump the pail of dirty water into the tub. He followed and watched the grey-colored liquid splash against the old white porcelain, leaving a trail of black, sooty particles as it swirled into the drain.

"So were you snooping around?" he asked.

She straightened up and stared him squarely in the eye. "I looked in *one* drawer, your jewelry box, and your closet. Which was open anyway."

His mouth fell open. "You've got balls, kid. Not only do you do exactly what I tell you not to, but you don't even try to deny it."

"Well, I did it, and y'asked me. I don't generally lie, y'know."

He laughed. "You don't generally lie?"

"That's right," she replied hotly. "When have I ever lied to you?"

And as inconceivable as it seemed, he couldn't produce a single genuine instance. The closest he could get was Friday night when she'd attempted to deny the veracity of her story—which didn't really count. "So did you find anything interesting?" he asked dryly.

"Your ring from Cornell."

"And you thought I was just some dumb cop."

"I never thought you were just some dumb cop."

Their eyes held until Baker breathed out in a loud sigh.

"So did I already screw up for today?" she asked.

She looked very tired. "No. Just get back to work." And while she turned on the water to rinse out the bucket, he went to his bedroom, closed the door, and immediately checked the small walnut box. Nestled against the plush lining, his ring, tie clip, and ID bracelet were still there. He pulled open his dresser drawers, yanking on them as though they'd done something wrong. But the contents looked like they always did—not that he was all that particular with his things anyway. He had no idea which drawer she'd gotten into. Slamming the last one shut, he stormed out of the bedroom.

INSIDE THE STUDY, SATURDAY'S mail was waiting for him on the desk—he hadn't picked it up till after he'd returned from the movie with Cynthia last night. There was a bill from Con Ed, his bank statement, some junk mail, and what looked to be a magazine wrapped in brown paper. The name on the return address was Ed Falrone. A sleazy plainclothes cop in anticrime, Falrone was bucking for a detective's shield. His group of friends and Baker's never mixed, though Falrone was forever trying to recruit them. The last time Baker had spoken to him was nearly half a year ago when the man's longtime, live-in girlfriend had called it quits over his habitual philandering. To "celebrate" her departure, Falrone had planned a stag party at his Long Island apartment, inviting Baker to join in. And though Baker never did attend the sordid affair, Falrone wouldn't let up about it. Afterward, he kept boasting about how great it was, detailing the events of the evening, beginning with his trip to a 7-Eleven to get more beer.

According to Falrone, he was on his way home when he picked up a young coed who was hitchhiking—and stoned. He invited her back to the party, where he and his friends proceeded to get her very drunk. "We had the music goin'," and convinced her to take off all her clothes." He snickered. "Man, she was so out of it, she didn't know what the fuck was goin' on. So then we all did her. I even took pictures." In the morning, he drove her to the train station, which was where she'd been headed to begin with. "She didn't remember a thing," he said, laughing. "Even thanked me for a great party."

Baker told him they were all shit—a bunch of lowlifes, guilty of rape. In response, Falrone called Baker a "fuckin' pussy" to his face, knowing Baker, already under scrutiny from IAD, couldn't afford to lose it right there in the station house. They hadn't spoken since, which suited Baker just fine.

Underneath the roughly textured wrapping—a supermarket grocery bag— Baker found a note attached to a layer of smooth brown paper. "Here's something to keep you up when your girlfriend can't—happy birthday." With a muttered "it's not till next month, asshole," Baker tore off the rest of the packaging. When he saw the hardcore-porn magazine Falrone had sent, his jaw clenched and his nostrils flared. He let it fall open to the center, ripped it in half, then ripped each part in half again. He threw the pieces in the wastepaper basket, then shoved the wrapping down on top. Just as he was charging out of the room toward the kitchen, Micki came through the front door with an empty laundry basket. She stopped short. But he went right on past, leaving her to wonder what could have riled him so.

ONLY A SINGLE SHIRT required ironing that week. So, after cleaning the bathroom, Micki hung it from the shower-curtain rod for later. Then she got her lunch from the closet and headed for the kitchen, passing through the living room, where Baker, lounging in the recliner, was too absorbed in whatever he was reading to glance up.

Seated at the dinette table, her back against the wall, she opened up the paper bag and pulled out her sandwich. Heavy with filling, it was a wonderful mess inside the plastic wrap—white marshmallow Fluff and golden-brown peanut butter oozing from between the slices of bread. Her mouth began to water. She pulled off the plastic and took a bite. Eyes closed, she melted into the airy bread; soft sugar; and thick, chunky nuttiness. Salty-sweet. Very dry. She got up to get some water. But as she reached for a glass, her hand froze. She went back into the living room.

"Sergeant Baker?" Her heart was pounding—this was the first time she'd ever called him by name.

He looked up.

"Can I have some water?" Her heart thumped harder.

He stared blankly.

"Forget it," she said, and quickly turned away.

"Micki!"

She looked back.

"You don't have to ask for water."

"Is it okay if I use one of your glasses?"

He felt an uncomfortable sensation around his heart, but his tone came out brusque. "What do you think? That I'd make you drink it straight from the tap?"

She shrugged.

"Yeah, of course you can use a glass."

She hurried back to the kitchen. But only a few minutes later, Baker came in to get a beer. About to take another bite of her lunch, Micki put it down.

He popped the cap off the bottle, leaned back against the counter, and started to drink.

She hastily stood up, wrapping the clingy plastic around the half-eaten sandwich.

"Sit down and finish," he said. "You're allowed to take a break."

"I'm not hungry anymore." She moved toward the garbage pail.

"Leave it. Don't throw it away."

"But I'm not gonna finish it."

"I *said* leave it."

"Fine." She slapped it back down on the table, then stalked off to resume her chores.

He put his beer on the counter and picked it up. Though it only smelled like peanut butter, the sticky filling seemed to be everywhere as he tried to safely remove the sandwich from the plastic wrap. He took a small bite from an untouched corner. Then another. When she came back to get the Lemon Pledge from under the sink, she found him holding it, his fingers full of Fluff.

With a sheepish grin, he said, "I just wondered what these things tasted like. It's good—a little too sweet for me, though."

Her expression was cold. "You've got marshmallow Fluff all over your lips." Then she took the spray can from the cabinet and left.

He went to the sink, threw the sandwich away, and washed the gooey stuff off his mouth. He must've looked ridiculous. But for the first time, he understood he'd lost something.

And it wasn't his dignity he was thinking of.

BAKER HAD MOVED TO the couch to resume his reading, the now-empty beer bottle on the coffee table in front of him. Out of the corner of his eye, he could see Micki spraying the old piece of furniture with Pledge, then wiping it down with rough, angry motions. Exactly what had ticked her off, he didn't know, but it had started while she was eating her lunch. It was getting on his nerves. She finished dusting and started toward the kitchen.

He said, "Get me another beer while you're in there." And though he couldn't see her face, he could see the increased tension in her shoulders, could picture the glare and the clenched jaw.

She stomped off, put the Pledge back, and grabbed a bottle from the refrigerator. When she returned, she set it down heavily next to the empty one.

Baker looked up from his book to see the cap was still on. "Do you expect me to open this with my teeth?"

Her eyes grew darker.

"Go back and open it," he said.

She didn't move.

He held out the bottle. "Go back and open this for me."

"I'm not your fu—"

"Shut up."

"You—"

"SHUT—THE FUCK—UP." And he slammed the bottle down as he stood up. "Y'know, the skin on your face is already pretty colorful, but if you really want me to add to it, I'm happy to oblige."

She stared into his shirt.

"You've got a real problem, kid, and you'd better figure out a way to deal with it. You hate somebody ordering you around? Well, if you don't change your ways, you'll be in the system a long, long time—maybe the rest of your life—and that's exactly what you'll get. You may be tough, and you may be strong for your size, but you're just too fucking small—and not in any kind of position—to play it out like this. Especially with someone like me. I'm sure most of what you got at Heyden would never have happened if you didn't act this way."

Her eyes flashed up at his.

"Now if you don't like this little scenario, here, you should've thought about that before you pulled your little stunt; 'cause you earned this punishment, and you're going to pay it. Maybe you'll think twice before doing something like that again. Now do what I told you, and keep your mouth *shut*."

Chest heaving, her gaze dropped back to his shirt.

Seconds passed.

She shot a sidelong glance at the beer.

He waited.

She looked up, expecting to see a gloating smirk on his face. Instead he looked…concerned. She glanced back at the bottle. With a somewhat tentative start, her hand reached out, then closed firmly around the neck. Backing up a couple of steps, she kept her eyes on his before finally turning and heading for the kitchen.

THERE WAS STILL A good head of foam from when he'd slammed the beer down on the table; so she popped the cap off of a fresh one and returned to the living room. She went to place it on the table, but he intercepted it, fingers lightly brushing hers. She flinched and looked up. Somber eyes were staring back.

"I—I have to go vacuum," she said, backing up again till she was practically out of the room. Then she turned and hurried away.

He gently put the bottle down on the table.

HER ENERGY FLAGGED AS the day wore on, especially since she knew it wasn't going to count. Almost done, she started collecting the trash—the last task of the day. The plastic bag from the kitchen garbage pail was only half full, so she took it with her to empty all of the other wastebaskets into. When she went into the bathroom, the tailored shirt she'd washed was still hanging on the rod—un-ironed. She drew a heavy sigh and emptied the small garbage pail next to the sink.

IMPATIENT TO BE ALONE, Baker shut off the TV and stood looking out the window over the sofa. He heard Micki move from the bathroom to the bedroom, then on to the study. But after several minutes had gone by, he noticed she still hadn't left to throw the garbage away. Oh, shit! He quickly strode toward the little room.

Hands full of the torn pages from the magazine he'd discarded, she was standing over the wastepaper basket. The corners of her mouth were turned down, and her eyes appeared vacant.

He grabbed the papers from her hands and threw them into the bag. "What're you looking at this shit for? You shouldn't see stuff like this."

Staring past him, she said, "I've seen worse."

"Worse than *this*?"

Very slowly, her eyes shifted to meet his. And then the fire ignited: "Speed useta get all kindsa dirty magazines showin' every kinda sex thing anybody could ever think of, always makin' fun a women and puttin 'em down. One even had pictures of 'em bein' tortured. They were disgusting, and I hated 'em, but he'd purposely leave 'em around so I'd see 'em. Tim said it pissed him off, but he never made Speed stop."

Baker felt a sickening pull in his stomach. "Is this what you think sex is about?"

"I think it's what *men* are about."

"Hey! Only warped, insecure guys are into this kind of smut."

"Oh, yeah? Then how come you bought this?"

"I didn't. Some schmuck sent it to me. I would never buy anything like this." And he remembered the first DOA he'd been called to, a drug overdose, back when he was in uniform. It turned out not to be an accident but a suicide: a hooker had OD'd herself on a mixture of heroin and speed, her farewell note the hardcore-porn magazine her pimp had forced her to pose for. Using blood-red lipstick, she'd crayoned over the pictures she was in. When the detectives had finally identified her, she'd turned out to be all of fifteen years old. A runaway from Nebraska, she'd been wearing so much make-up that, after it was removed, her real face had been almost unrecognizable. For days afterward, Baker hadn't slept.

And cops knew rapists lived and breathed this kind of crap, so it came as no surprise when some particularly perverted assault was copied from some photo or "story." Baker thought about the look he'd just seen on Micki's face. He didn't care what anyone said; this shit did damage. He couldn't believe there were liberal assholes who actually supported the smut peddlers hiding behind the first amendment.

"So what about the magazine in your bedroom?" she asked.

"Huh?" His mind snapped back. "That's just a copy of *Playboy*."

"Yeah, whatever."

"I'm telling you, it's just a copy of *Playboy*. Didn't you look at it?"

"No."

"Then why are you—" He paused, a knowing look coming over him. "You've never actually seen *Playboy*, have you."

"So what."

After a brief hesitation, he left the room and returned with the magazine, tossing it onto the desk in front of her. "This is what I read. Take a look at it if you want. What can I say? Men like looking at pictures of naked women." He snorted. "Well, I guess some women like looking at pictures of naked men, too; the women's libbers finally got *Playgirl* for themselves."

"I take it you don't go for women's lib."

"Hey, that's not true."

"Yeah, right."

"Look, I believe women should get equal pay for equal work. And women should be able to have any job they want so long as they're capable of doing it. But, see, that's the thing: they have to be capable of doing it. Like, I really don't give a shit if a fireman's a man or a woman so long as they're strong enough to get me the hell out of a burning building. What pisses me off is when they start talking about lowering strength requirements just so women can qualify. We're talking about saving people's lives, here. If a woman isn't strong enough, she's got no business doing a job like that."

"Yeah? So what about women cops?"

"First of all, being a cop doesn't require a lot of physical strength—though it certainly doesn't hurt. And I have to say, I've known women who were good at working undercover. But until now, most lady cops haven't been much more than glorified jail matrons; most of them haven't been doing the same things as men. The department only got serious about putting women on regular street patrol last year. I'm not really sure if the ladies've got what it takes, but it wouldn't surprise me if they did." Seeing the shocked expression on Micki's face, he gave her a wry smile. "I admit I was pretty skeptical at first: female rookies'll have a tough enough time dealing with a lot of the male cops, never mind the demands of the job. But so far, from what I've heard, most of them have been making the grade. We'll just have to see how it goes.

"See, the thing is, Micki, even if men and women are equals, it doesn't mean we're the same. Some of these feminists say we are, and that's just bullshit." His eyes fell on the magazine. "Take sex, for example. You think I ever worry about getting raped? Or wake up in the morning, wondering if I'm pregnant? Right there it's pretty obvious we're on two different playing fields. Just the fact that our bodies are different means the experience can't be exactly the same. It's not better for one than the other; it's just different. Do you understand what I'm saying?"

"Yeah, I'm not stupid, y'know."

His voice quiet, he said, "No, you're not stupid." He finished emptying the wastepaper basket, then picked up the bulging plastic bag. "I'm going to throw this out. I'll be back in a couple of minutes."

After she heard the front door close behind him, she looked at the copy of *Playboy*. On the cover, the same nude woman was reclining in four different poses, though nothing was actually revealed because of the way she was positioned and how the sheet was placed around her. Micki began turning pages. High-class liquor, cigarette, and clothing ads were interspersed with several pages of letters to the editor, most of them addressing previous articles on political issues, public policy… An ad for Sheaffer pens said: "Tell her you love her. Everyday." She came across "Playboy after Hours," which, after remarking on several bizarre items in the news, went on to review restaurants, records, movies… There was an ad for Bulova watches showing male *and female* executives sitting around a conference table.

When she reached "The Playboy Advisor," the first feature focusing mostly on sex, she scanned the magazine's responses to the readers' questions, the editors actually providing one man with tips on how to give good oral sex to a woman. Overall, there was little of that leering obnoxiousness she'd gotten used to seeing. In fact, in some ways the magazine seemed sort of pro-women. Even the readers' queries and letters in "The Playboy Forum" were different in tone than those of the other magazines. That the letters appeared to be genuine was something in and of itself. She was also amazed that, in fifty pages-worth of material, she'd hardly seen more than two or three bared chests. She looked at the cover again. It said "Entertainment for Men." She returned to where she'd left off.

PURPOSELY TAKING HIS TIME, Baker stuffed the bag into the garbage chute. Why did things always have a knack for working out like this? Falrone sends him a smut rag just once, and the kid's there to find it. He closed the door to the closet-sized room, started back, and almost laughed: what would some parenting expert have to say about his decision to let her see *Playboy*? At her age, if she were male, he wouldn't be thinking twice, but he had no idea what was appropriate for a girl. Of course, after everything she'd already seen, the issue was moot. At least this way she'd know that there were all kinds of magazines just like there were all kinds of men.

Besides, *Playboy* was a quality publication. The articles were good, the interviews excellent—even renowned. He stopped in the middle of the hallway. The interview in this month's issue was with the editor of *Screw*. Not only was the man despicable, but somewhere during the piece, he mentioned an encounter with Linda Lovelace, describing how she'd gone down on him in a "69." He'd said that when her chemise, as he'd called it, had blown away from her body, he'd looked up to see scar tissue running down her chest. Baker remembered the guy stating what a turn-off that had been. Given all the scars Micki had...

Baker ran the rest of the way back, tore into the apartment, and came to an abrupt halt in the doorway of the study—not exactly subtle. And he couldn't stop himself from flicking a glance at the magazine to see what she was looking at.

Her eyes narrowed. "Something in here you don't want me to see?"

A thin, almost sick-looking smile forced its way to the surface of his face. "No, no—not at all." And he leaned on the doorframe, casually folding his arms over his chest.

"You're a lousy liar."

He straightened up. "Look, Micki, this month's interview is with the editor of *Screw*, which, by the guy's own admission, is a really filthy magazine."

"I know what it is."

There was a long pause. "Yeah…well…then you know the guy's scum. Anyway, I think it's obvious from the way the piece is written that *Playboy* thinks so, too. But I'd just rather you didn't read it, okay?"

"If *Playboy* thinks the guy's so gross, then why did they interview him in the first place?"

Baker paused again. "I don't know."

She went back to the magazine, turned the page, and there it was: "Playboy Interview: Al Goldstein, a candid (ugh!) conversation with the outrageous editor of 'screw.'" There were three photos of Goldstein with the caption under the middle one quoting him: "*Screw* leads the league in tastelessness. Our photos are filthier, our articles more disgusting. Our stock in trade is raw, flailing sex. The word love is alien to us. Who needs love? Yuch!" This last declaration touched a nerve, for Micki already had her doubts about men and love. She skimmed through the introductory text preceding the interview itself, and, at one point, it stated how, at seventeen, Goldstein hadn't known if he should kiss his dates goodnight or take them behind the bushes and rape them. Micki's jaw tightened. She turned the page and scanned some more.

Absently tapping his foot on the floor, Baker was unable to recall exactly where the encounter with Linda Lovelace was mentioned. The bit about the scars couldn't be more than a few lines buried in the numerous pages of the interview. Unfortunately, right now, all he could do was stand by and watch. So when Micki rapidly turned past the end of the first segment—apparently she'd had enough—he exhaled. With any luck, she wouldn't bother reading the rest if she came across it later.

Micki picked the magazine up from the desk and started flipping through till she came across the first pictorial. Airbrushed into an ethereal glow, the naked woman in the photos looked beautiful, though the romantic mood in many of them seemed ridiculous given that she was basically saying, "Fuck me."

Suddenly very aware that Baker was watching her examine pictures of naked women, she glanced up. He broke eye contact.

A few pages more and she found a report on men's fashions, accompanied by several photos where the man was fully clothed; the woman, not at all or with her breasts exposed. Micki's body tensed, fresh anger welling up. Though the storyline seemed innocent enough—the woman getting dressed while the man waited so they could go out on a date—it was really nothing more than a nicer version of similar photos in raunchier magazines. Usually shot in some group setting, like a party, all of the women would be topless or naked while the men had all their clothes on. It was a power thing. It was disgusting. And yet the women in the photos (and the cartoons, of course), with their breasts and/or crotches hanging out for all to see, were always smiling like they enjoyed being treated like things, like toys for men to play with: just "tits and ass"—or like they were too dumb to even care.

Micki hated it: the porn; the strip clubs; the way men had to put women down just to get a quick, easy fix for their egos. She remembered how Speed had once come back to the hangout, cursing his head off about the "motherfuckin' meter maid" who'd ticketed him for leaving his motorcycle at a bus stop while he ran into a store to get some gin. "I come out," he said, "and the fuckin' bitch is writin' a fuckin' ticket. So I try to reason with the stupid cunt, but she keeps writin'. She goes"—he made his voice high and snippy—"'Sir, if you disagree with this ticket, you can always contest it.' So I goes, 'Listen, bitch, just show me your tits, and I'll pay the fuckin' thing right now.'" Looking extremely proud of his quick comeback, Speed started laughing.

"Hey, man," Tim said, "not in front of the kid, okay?"

Speed looked straight at Micki and said, "You shoulda seen that bitch's face. Thinkin' she's so fuckin' high and mighty in her fuckin' little uniform. That bitch needed to be taught a lesson, and I shoulda been the one to teach it to her." Tim had said something else, but Speed had already started toward the door. But then he'd looked back over his shoulder at Micki and said, "I think I'll go to the titty bar now for a few laughs."

You didn't have to be a fucking genius to connect the dots.

Returning to the magazine, Micki paged through some more. Why were women always supposed to laugh everything off: the photos, the jokes...? Black people certainly weren't expected to accept being the butt of racist jokes anymore, and guys sure as hell didn't like it when the situation was reversed: Speed had a shit fit when Tim's girlfriend had brought in her copy of *Playgirl*'s very first issue. She'd bought it the year before just to find out what it was like. And from what Micki had seen, the men posing in it weren't even fully naked, their penises always covered by something or other, men—unlike women—apparently deserving to keep some shred of dignity.

Then there were the stupid girls at school who went along with the sexist jokes, trying to be cool or "one of the guys," as if the jokes and stuff weren't about them, that they were somehow excluded—special. But all it did was make it look like girls agreed they deserved to be treated like that. When the guys eventually turned on them—they almost always did—the girls' outrage was kind of satisfying.

But as for the girls who sold their bodies in one way or another—smiling and acting like it was all a huge laugh for them, too—well, that was an entirely different matter. After all, who would want to admit that what they were doing—or being forced to do—was degrading? It made it all that much more humiliating. "I don't care; it's no big deal; it doesn't bother me…" What bullshit. That's why they had to keep frying their brains on drugs and alcohol.

Once, when Micki had been bold enough to confront a few of them, one of the streetwalkers had called her a "silly little girl" that needed to "grow up." But by some bizarre coincidence, only a few days later, that very same hooker had ended up huddled with Micki in a doorway, both of them taking refuge from a sudden summer shower. During those few minutes when they were alone—the hot, sticky air momentarily cooling in the dark shade of the storming thunderclouds—the girl's tough, hard-as-nails pretense fell away, her raw pain pouring out with the rain. Through tears, she started laughing, remembering how—at eight years old, pretending to be a beautiful ballerina with a sparkly tiara and pink satin toe shoes—she'd broken her ankle by jumping barefoot onto the very tips of her toes in the middle of the room. Her mother had been furious. Yet, after her ankle had healed, she was allowed to go for lessons at the local dance school.

But not long after that, her stepfather, who'd always given her the creeps, started visiting her bed in the middle of the night, saying if she ever told anyone, he wouldn't pay for the classes anymore. He said it was her own fault anyway—for being such a tease. So after her fifteenth birthday, when she couldn't take it anymore, she ran away. Dance bag stuffed with leotards, tights, some underwear, and little else, she took a bus to New York City. The entire ride in, she pictured herself dancing on stage at the famed Lincoln Center. Her plan was to get a job giving manicures—she was good at that—and take real ballet lessons. But when she got off at the Port Authority Bus Terminal, she had no idea where she was.

She must've looked as lost as she felt because a well-dressed man approached and offered to buy her a cup of coffee. He told her he could help her. He told her he could make her a star.

"God," she said to Micki, "I was so *stupid*."

The downpour stopped as suddenly as it had started, the sun bursting through the clouds. A small, faded rainbow struggled to climb above the steeple of the church across the street. Without so much as a goodbye, the hooker hurried away. And only one week later, Micki found out she'd jumped off the roof of a fleabag hotel. And broken her neck.

Micki closed her eyes. That could've been her. There were times after Tim had died when she'd felt so unwanted, hated herself so much, that she'd considered turning herself out—as though selling her body was some kind of punishment she deserved. Those were moments of near madness when she would hear a little voice saying, "You know that's what you really are; give it up already. Who do you think you're kidding? You're garbage, just like the rest of them." And part of her, in imagining herself giving in, would feel this strange—and disturbing—sense of relief. Ironically, by cutting her up the way he had, the Knife had spared her: with all of her scars, even the pimps hadn't bothered with her.

Opening her eyes, Micki turned back to the *Playboy* and quickly glanced through two other photo spreads. In general, the pictures were tastefully done and, for the most part, respectful. They were certainly very tame—not even a single beaver shot. She closed the magazine and dropped it back on the desk. But she wouldn't look at Baker.

He, however, was looking at her. The changing pattern of emotions that had washed over her face had left him with a queasy feeling. What the hell had she been thinking about? For several minutes she hadn't even been looking at the magazine.

The silence grew, making it all the more awkward.

"So what's the verdict?" he finally asked.

Mouth set in a hard, bitter line, she shrugged.

"I'll be honest with you, Micki, there's still a lot of male-chauvinist pig in me. I grew up in a different time with different rules. But I try to change when I can."

She faced him.

"I suppose if I were perfect," he went on, "I wouldn't even buy *this* magazine because I'm supporting an organization that has clubs with grown women running around in little bunny costumes to wait on men. But I—I have my weaknesses."

She had the impression he was waiting for her to respond. What was he expecting her to say? In a small, cautious voice she finally offered, "You smoke a lot."

It took him a second to process this seeming non sequitur. But then he threw his head back and laughed while she looked on in confusion. Still smiling, he said, "I smoke *too much*." And he felt the impulse to tousle her hair. Instead he asked, "So, you're finished for today?"

"Yessir."

"Well then, let's take a look."

"What's the point?"

"I haven't made up my mind yet."

"Really?"

"Yes. Really."

And his eyes were almost kind.

AFTER A QUICK CHECK around the study, he moved on to the living room, followed by the kitchen, and then the bathroom—where his shirt was still hanging from the shower-curtain rod.

She blanched. "I forgot about ironing it 'cause it was the only one. But I'll do it right now." And she reached for it.

He stopped her hand. "Forget it."

"But it won't take more than a few minutes. I—"

"No!" His face was set.

Swearing at him in her head, she left to wait in the kitchen while he finished. When he joined her, he was already searching through her jacket, which he'd taken from the closet. Without being asked, she emptied her pockets on the table, and he went through the routine of patting her down.

"You did an excellent job again," he said.

"Big deal."

Grabbing her shoulder, he turned her around. "If you do this well again next week, we'll call it even."

Her jaw dropped. "But—"

Eyebrows raised like two question marks, he said, "You're going to argue with me?"

BY THE TIME MICKI left, the daylight was all but gone. It was getting dark early now. Through stifled yawns, she thought about the history homework that was waiting for her.

She hurried down into the subway and dropped a token into the turnstile—school passes weren't valid on weekends. These little outings—seventy cents round trip—were yet another waste of money. When she checked her pocket, all she had left was a dollar, a quarter, two dimes, and four pennies—and she wasn't getting paid again until Wednesday. But she didn't want to touch her savings anymore. The whole thirty-three dollars of it. Like it really mattered.

The rumble of an approaching train grew louder, and she stared at the subway tracks below. Then she turned her head to look down into the tunnel. Mesmerized by the oncoming headlights.

BAKER WENT TO THE study, pulled his cigarettes out of the desk drawer, and lit up. God, what a relief. During breakfast he'd made a silent pact with himself not to smoke until Micki had left. By early afternoon, he'd known it would be a small miracle if he actually managed to hold out until now. He closed his eyes. Considering he'd spent most of the day sitting on his butt, he was surprisingly exhausted.

When he opened his eyes, he saw the *Playboy* still lying on his desk. Micki would be back next week, and, just like this week, he might end up leaving her here by herself for a while. As it was, he had to remember to hide away the lockbox with his guns, secure the liquor cabinet, take his pills out of the medicine chest... This would be yet another thing to add to the list. While the chances of her finding that one little mention in the magazine were practically nil, he'd feel pretty shitty if she did. Besides, he'd already read everything.

He went to pay another visit to the garbage chute.

ALREADY ON HIS THIRD double whiskey, Baker put Neil Young's *Harvest* album on the turntable and lit a fresh cigarette—his seventh since Micki had left—then settled into the recliner and picked up her file.

Given what had become of Tim Reilly's little sister, it wasn't much of a leap to think that Tim had kept Micki on the straight and narrow, at least as far as sex and drugs were concerned. And from the looks of it, even the heavy criminal activity hadn't started until after Tim's death. That meant Micki had developed a sixty-dollar-a-day habit in only one month, not the two he'd initially thought. It was amazing she hadn't OD'd. But she also hadn't been exposed to the toxic mix of full-blown street life all that long, either.

As for her record, first impressions might've been deceiving there, too: not once had a mugging victim actually been stabbed or slashed, though she'd hit a few when things had gone sour. And yet she could still be extremely violent; Heyden records alone attested to that. But the shrink's assessment seemed more meaningful now: the emotional and psychological scars were increasingly evident, as was the depression, which was reflected in the sleep disturbances and weight loss. Despite a steady diet of candy, pizza, pasta, and peanut butter, Micki now appeared thinner than when she'd first arrived from juvi—even though she'd initially gained a few pounds. She simply wasn't eating enough again. And the self-destructiveness? How many times had she baited him, knowing full well what the consequences would be?

But if the shrink's prescription was as on target as her perceptions, then what the hell was he doing as Micki's guardian? At best he could give some guidance—though not exactly what the good doctor had in mind. And the "love-and-stable-family-environment" shit was definitely out of the question. Of course, the people best able to provide that might never be able to control her; it was naïve to think good intentions and love would solve all of her behavioral problems. He sighed. Sometimes it seemed she just didn't know any better, didn't understand any other way of dealing with things than by using fists and foul language.

About to pour himself another drink, he paused: maybe Warner would be the perfect guardian for her. He was into the psych stuff and strong enough, physically, to keep her in line if he had to. He'd also taken a genuine liking to the kid, though god only knew why. But one thing was certain: no one else gave a shit about Micki. No one from social services had come around to check on her, and neither Malone nor Tillim had talked to her in all this time. Tillim, however, had called Baker twice, each occasion ending up a one-way conversation.

Baker filled the tumbler halfway. Recalling Tillim's awkward attempts to draw him out, he drained the glass with a crooked smile.

The turntable's tone arm, having reached the end of the record, began its convoluted routine of lifting and retracting. Baker closed the folder and stubbed out his cigarette. Shit, how did he let himself get sucked into this? He'd sworn he wouldn't get involved, yet he couldn't help but feel sorry for the kid. He poured another drink and tossed it back. Everything had been a hell of a lot easier when he simply hated her guts. What if she was just conning him?

It was late. He got up and turned off the stereo. He needed to go to bed before the walls closed in, before he thought too much about his life and drank too much of the whiskey. But when he put his head down and shut his eyes, he couldn't fall asleep. The bed was too big and too cold without the warmth of Cynthia's body pressed up against his own. And his mind was still filled with images of Micki. He wondered if she realized he knew—maybe more than she did—just what it was she wanted from him. He felt a tug at his heart. He breathed in and rolled over.

Outside, the street noise continued to change as the shadow side of the city slipped into its midnight skin. Inside, the seconds and minutes crawled by, dark and heavy, skirting the edge of his pillow and the ideas spinning round in his head. Like the brooding, hypnotic beats of a worn-out metronome, his thoughts were keeping time with the song that refused to stop playing—refused to stop repeating—though he tried with all his might to let it go: Neil Young's "Old Man."

Chapter 11

TUESDAY NIGHT'S SENIOR VARSITY basketball game, and Baker was heading security. It was a typical high school event—the squeak of sneakers on highly polished wood; thumps of a dribbled ball; cheers, jeers, and angry shouts; and pulsing pom-poms like giant sea anemones—until an especially tall, well-muscled black forward from Queens Central High engaged in heavy contact with one of the home team's white guards. Surrounded by a haphazard circle of other players and the umpire, the white boy was rolling around on the floor, clutching his ribs, face contorted in a melodramatic display. Queens Central High was predominantly black; Newbridge High, predominantly white. The conflict escalated from a personal, sports-related one to a race-related one in a matter of seconds. The game was called and, with the help of Marino and Jamison, the spectators cleared from the bleachers—though not without the threat of a full-fledged riot. Afterward, rather than sit at a bar alone, Baker called Warner to take him up on a standing invitation to stop by.

Warner lived in a basement apartment near the university where he was attending classes. Baker walked through the door and into an invasion of textbooks, library books, and papers to which the entire studio space had apparently surrendered.

"Sorry for the mess," Warner said as he cleared a spot at the kitchen table. Then he grabbed two beers from the refrigerator.

Looking at the piles all around him, Baker said, "It's fine. What're you working on?"

"A small case presentation, a term paper, and my dissertation.

"You're sure I'm not interrupting you?"

Warner laughed. "*Life* is interrupting me. I feel like all I do in my free time is work on this stuff. So tell me, what happened at the game tonight?"

Baker told him about the incident, they talked a little about work, and then the conversation turned to Micki. After listening to Baker seesaw back and forth, Warner finally asked, "Have you ever considered what it's like to actually *be* her?"

"Huh?"

"How would you feel if you were seventeen years old and entirely on your own without a shred of personal history and no family or friends to turn to? It's a pretty rough deal."

Baker took a drink of his beer and sat back. "Well, it's really not my problem."

"But it is."

"Do you want kids?"

"What?"

"Do you want kids," Baker repeated.

"What does that have to do with anything?"

"Nothing, I'm just curious."

"Well, yeah, I do want kids, but I think it would help if I found myself a girlfriend first to kind of get the ball rolling, don't y'think?"

They both laughed, then drifted onto other topics. And after another couple of beers, Baker left, feeling extremely tired. Still, he found himself detouring to Micki's, driving through Queens neighborhoods where clusters of stores, all closed for the night, looked abandoned and uninviting, most shuttered with graffitied security gates under unlit signs. Here and there—like a misplaced, gaudy island—a fast-food restaurant glared through the boredom, so bright it almost hurt his eyes.

Momentarily stopped at a red light, he looked over at the car to his right. The driver, about twenty years old, was talking to his female passenger. Baker, an invisible stranger in his own glass-and-metal bubble, felt utterly alone. Except for the moon. Glancing upward from time to time as he continued on his way, he watched the earth's satellite—his traveling companion—sliding in and out of clouds as it arced its way across the late-October sky.

BAKER PARKED HIS CAR down the street from Micki's apartment. Though it was only half past eleven, her windows were already dark. He entered her building and trudged up the stairs, noting the telephone's new "OUt oF oRder" sign, which looked, as usual, like a first-grader had written it. The hallway—windowless and narrow, with peeling yellowed wallpaper and uneven linoleum tiles—smelled strongly of bleach, though nothing looked the cleaner for it.

Before he'd even reached her door, he could hear noises—moans—from inside. His fatigue disappeared. Like hell she didn't stay up fucking that bastard! Eleven thirty on a school night! He quietly inserted his key in the lock, then stopped. He'd wait. How long could Galligan last anyway? But as he was pulling his cigarettes from his pocket, he became cognizant of how odd the sounds were. The moans were more distressed than sensual; there were whimpers, thuds, and little cries of "no." He strained to hear what was happening. What if the son of a bitch was hurting her? Forcing her? He turned the key and slipped inside.

Light spilled in through the doorway to dimly illuminate the room. But he saw only one figure: Micki was alone in bed. And though she was unconscious, she was far from inactive, first thrashing around and then curling up tight—yelling, moaning, or whimpering in some nightmarish dream state. He gently eased the door shut, waited for his eyes to adjust, then sat down quietly at the table.

Her bed was an impressive mess, the top sheet and blanket pulled half off the mattress in different directions. He was thinking about waking her, if only to relieve his own discomfort, when she abruptly stopped and opened her eyes. She picked up the alarm clock and tilted it toward the faint light coming in through the curtains. With a groan, she lay back down on her stomach, tucking her arms beneath her and closing her eyes.

Baker slowly exhaled. Motionless at the table, he watched as she shifted, turned, and moved the pillow around on the mattress until she eventually fell back to sleep. But the same violently restless activity soon ensued, sending chills up his spine. This episode, however, was very brief. And when she looked at the clock again, she muttered, "Fuck it," before getting out of bed and switching on the desk lamp. She turned toward the kitchen. And gasped.

"What're you doin' here?" she demanded.

"Just take it easy. I'm not doing anything. Except watching you sleep—if you could call it that."

"Meanin' what?"

"You must've been having a really bad nightmare."

She glanced away, the shadows in her eyes getting deeper. For at Heyden, during the brief time she'd spent in the lower-security cottages, her roommates had made her painfully aware of her nocturnal activities. She could only imagine it had gotten worse. She waited for Baker to ask the inevitable next question, but he never did. Instead, he lit a cigarette and leaned back in his chair. She walked past him, heading for the kitchen. But rather than make cocoa, she got a glass of water. She took a few sips and stared at the back of his head.

"Are you gonna go now?" she asked.

Turned sideways in the chair so he could see her, he replied, "Not just yet."

"Why not? What're you hangin' around for?"

"I'll leave when I'm ready."

"Well, I won't be able to go to bed if you're here."

"If I were going to do something, Micki, I would've made my move while you were still asleep."

She held his gaze, then averted her eyes.

From across the street, there came a loud, metallic rattle as the auto-body shop's garage door opened. A car that had been idling could be heard moving, and then its engine was cut. The garage door clattered closed.

Micki sipped her water while Baker smoked his cigarette. She realized he wasn't going to leave this time. She put the glass in the sink and got back into bed.

Baker went to the desk and shut the light.

LYING ON HER LEFT side, blanket clutched tightly around her, Micki could see the tip of his cigarette brighten each time he inhaled. She tried to focus on the little orange glow and the assortment of sounds coming in from the street. She tried very hard to stay awake. But her eyelids were growing heavy. A short while later, there was a calm steadiness to her breathing.

Voice hushed, Baker asked, "Are you still awake?" When there was no response, he got up and went over to the bed. All of the tension was gone from her face, the scarred skin smoothed out in the soft, diffuse light. She looked younger, peaceful, and—like anyone asleep—innocent. Almost in a whisper, he added, "'Cause if you're still awake, I'll leave. I really don't want to keep you up." But all he heard was the auto-body shop's garage door again, and another car being driven in. Maybe the joint was a chop shop.

He hung around a while longer, even though he'd already seen enough to know that what she'd told him was true: she didn't sleep well. Except for now. For the past twenty minutes she'd barely moved.

THURSDAY MORNING, TWO DETECTIVES and three uniformed cops showed up at the school to arrest three white seniors on murder charges. The boys had allegedly stalked a young black man as he'd left a house only a block away from the campus. Using an old, beat-up Rambler that belonged to one of the boys' mothers, they'd followed him in his Volkswagen to Queens College, where he was a student. He'd parked and gotten out of his car, only to be met with the blows of a baseball bat that fatally crushed his skull. Witnesses claimed the man had been beaten for no other reason than being black.

When word of the killing got around the security staff, there was fear that the incident, if publicized, would fan the fires of racial tension already smoldering in the school. So much for all the peace and love of the sixties, Baker thought. What bullshit that turned out to be.

As he signed the last report for the school's records, he recalled how condescending the local detectives had been until, incensed at the role he was being forced to play, he'd reintroduced himself—rank and all—and flashed his shield. Immediately, their attitudes had changed. And though they'd eyed him with curiosity, they'd kept their questions to themselves.

Baker filed the papers and slammed the cabinet drawer shut. Fucking assholes.

MICKI WAS JUST ABOUT to go home when Marino came rushing into the office.

"Hey," he said as he shrugged off his jacket, "I tried to get back here as quick as I could, but the friggin' doctor made me wait nearly three-quarters of an hour. Man, I could use some coffee." He picked up a Styrofoam cup and pulled out the carafe. Turning toward Baker, he said, "Doc tells me, after taking a ton of blood for tests, that it's probably just some allergic thing—"

The office door flew open as Jamison hurried in to retrieve the walkie-talkie he'd left on the desk a few minutes earlier. The door hit Marino's elbow, causing the coffee he was pouring to spill onto his hand. "Shit!" He let go of the cup, its contents splashing across his jeans and sneakers. As the hot liquid seeped into the denim and burned his skin, he instinctively grabbed at the wet material—letting go of the carafe in the process. The glass pot shattered when it hit the floor. "Shit!" he said again, still pulling at the cloth.

"I'm so sorry. Are you okay?" Jamison asked. "I didn't know you were standing there."

"Shit!" Marino repeated.

Micki was biting the inside of her lip to keep from laughing.

"You think this is funny?" Baker asked.

Marino looked like he'd pissed his pants. Yeah, she thought it was funny, but all she did was shrug and try desperately to keep a straight face.

"Well, since you're finding this so entertaining, you can have the pleasure of cleaning it up."

"I'll help," Jamison offered. "It's my fault—"

"She'll do it herself," Baker said. "You should get back to your post."

"But… Sure, Chief." Jamison glanced at Micki, then apologized again to Marino on his way out.

"Why do I have to clean it up?" Micki asked.

"Because I told you to."

Marino, still standing in the middle of it all, was smirking.

"NOW," Baker barked.

She put her books on the desk and pulled over the white plastic trashcan from beside the little refrigerator. Down on one knee, she threw away the Styrofoam cup, then started picking up the larger pieces of glass while Baker went to get the whiskbroom and dustpan from under the bathroom sink. Literally at Marino's feet, she felt the heat rising in her face. She was gingerly placing her fingers on either side of an especially jagged shard when Baker reentered the room. Marino, taking advantage of the cop's presence, said to Micki, "Why don't you shove that up your ass."

Dropping the glass, Micki sprang to her feet, pushing Marino hard and sending him sailing backward into the door. But Baker grabbed some hair on the top of her head—right at the base of the scalp—and pulled back cruelly. She nearly lost her footing. Face distorted in a grimace, her hands shot up to grasp his wrist. He pulled her backward.

"Fuck it!" she cursed.

Maintaining the tension on her hair, he slammed his free palm into her back. She gritted her teeth.

Marino's grin faded. "Hey, let her go," he said. "It was nothing. Really."

"Go home and change your clothes," Baker ordered.

"C'mon, Jim, I—"

"Get the fuck out of here," Baker said.

As she stood in front of Bel, the breeze blew back her hair so gently it felt like a caress. She brushed the bangs out of her eyes and gazed past the elevated tracks to a row of trees, their dying leaves a warm sunburst of color against the slate-grey sky. The street itself, however—garbage scattered across stained sidewalks, graffiti sprayed on almost every available space—looked ugly and mean.

The number 7 train rumbled past toward the Fifty-Ninth Street Bridge, where it would soon turn off to travel further into Queens. She could picture herself traveling down the road alongside it. But only as far as the underpass. With the possibility of going back to Heyden looming larger than ever, what did it matter if she scored a fix? Eyes closed, she could feel the sweet release, could feel her wretched, lonely existence being carried away into a warm, cocoon-like place of nothing.

She opened her eyes and rubbed her wrist. It hadn't been in such great shape to begin with; now it hurt from Baker having ruthlessly twisted it. But it was what he'd told her afterward that had caused her world to come crashing down: tomorrow he was meeting with Captain Malone to deliver a progress report. "Truth is, Micki," he'd said, "I haven't seen any progress. None at all."

Her mouth had gone dry, the blood turning cold in her veins. She argued she was doing well in school; she argued she was doing so well at work that Mr. Antonelli had given her a raise.

Baker's eyes had narrowed. "When was that?"

Confused by the tone of his voice, her own came out small. "Last night."

"Why didn't you tell me?"

"I—I thought I just had to tell you the bad stuff."

"You tell me everything. *Everything.* Understand?" He hadn't even been pleased that she'd finally be earning minimum wage. And maybe with good reason.

"Micki, you okay?" Mr. Antonelli asked, leaning out the front door of the restaurant.

"Not really," she murmured.

"Eh? I cannot-a hear you."

"I'll be right in, Mr. Antonelli," she said more loudly, and the little man disappeared back inside. Hanging her head, she kicked away a bottle cap with the toe of her worn-out sneaker.

She was such a loser.

BY THE TIME THE entrance buzzer rang, announcing the first arrival, Baker was almost set for the poker game. Though it had been a weekly tradition for years, he'd skipped all but one since starting his job at the high school. When he'd gone the second week after the semester had begun, he'd felt demoted sitting among the men he used to work with—especially his partner, Barry Gould, who'd been teamed with Dave Blanchard in his absence. Baker had lost more money that night than he ever had before, and, since then, he'd avoided not only the poker games, but Gould and all his other cop friends, as well. The one exception—out of necessity—had been Malone. But the isolation had only made him feel worse.

He recognized the knock on the door and opened it to see Gould with a bottle of J&B and a big grin. "Hey, partner!"

Baker smiled, a rush of warmth flooding through him as he accepted the whiskey. Then they briefly embraced with the obligatory pats on the back. A real Mutt-'n'-Jeff pair, Baker was lean, clean-shaven, nine inches taller, and five years older than Gould, who had curly red hair, an ample mustache, and a bit too much weight. Their natures were also opposites: Baker, hot and quick-tempered; Gould, mild and good-humored. But both men were sharp, possessing solid investigative skills and a willingness to do whatever it took to get the job done. They'd made a formidable team. And had bonded like brothers.

"Thanks, man," Baker said. "Make yourself at home. I've just got a few things left to put out."

Gould threw his jacket on the couch and looked at the bridge table holding court in the middle of the living room. With cards, poker chips, and liquor already in place, Baker was putting out nuts, pretzels, and potato chips.

"Y'know, I've missed you," Gould said. "I wish you'd call once in a while just to shoot the shit. I stopped calling myself 'cause I didn't want to push you, but, hey…"

"Sorry," Baker said. "It's just that—well—this whole thing has been really hard on me. Besides, you're working with someone else now."

"So what? That doesn't change a fuckin' thing between you and me. And anyways, Blanchard's a lazy son of a bitch, a real empty suit. He's useless as a partner; I'd be happier alone."

Baker continued setting up.

"I'm tellin' you," Gould said, "this'll be over before y'know it, and we'll be a team again like always."

Not looking all that convinced, Baker nodded. Then he took out his cigarettes and lit one, noting the surprise that registered on his friend's face. A sheepish look spread across his own. "Yeah. This 'therapy' is just doing wonders for me."

"How's it goin'?"

Baker shrugged. "It's going."

When Baker didn't say more, Gould tried asking about Cynthia. But from Baker's brief replies, he gathered that wasn't going too well, either. Apparently, a lot had happened since the last time the two men had spoken. None of it too good.

The buzzer rang again, and Baker hastily stubbed out the Camel before the other players arrived. But since all except Gould and Malone smoked, once the game got going, it wasn't long till he fired up another.

With a broad grin, Batillo pointed his cigar and, in his raspy voice, said, "Hey, look who rejoined the club."

All of the men stared at Baker.

"Yeah, yeah. Screw you," Baker shot back, and busied himself with straightening the stacks of poker chips in front of him.

"Aw, don't get all pissy," Tierney said. "It's just that we were afraid you were gonna stop drinking soon, too."

"Yeah, and then we wouldn't be able to trust you," Martini said.

"We might even have to kill you," Batillo added.

They all chuckled. Except Baker, who said sharply, "Well I can tell you right now that you don't have to worry about that, okay?"

Malone started to deal in the uneasy silence.

"So, Jimmy," Martini asked as he grabbed a fistful of peanuts to toss into his mouth, "you hire a maid or what? You've always been neat, but this place looks fuckin' spotless."

"No maid. The kid's been cleaning as punishment for some shit she pulled."

"Yeah? Well, next time she fucks up, send her over to my place."

"No way!" Tierney said. "That would be cruel and unusual."

They all laughed while Martini shot back, "Yeah? Look who's talkin'."

Within half an hour, all of the tension in Baker's body had disappeared, the cop talk and precinct gossip a little like coming home. And with everything that went on at the school, he had his own share of tales to tell, some quite serious, the rest often funny. By the end of the evening, he understood that his friends were his friends. They'd lost no respect for him, just felt badly that he'd gotten such a raw deal. And though he didn't feel quite the same as when he'd been working with them, he realized most of the judgmental stuff was only in his own head. It made him think about what Cynthia had said.

Then again, it wasn't as if he'd retired. Or been fired.

THE FIRST TO ARRIVE, Gould was also the last to leave. Putting on his jacket, he asked, "So you're meeting with Malone tomorrow?"

"Yeah, why?"

"Nothing, really, just overheard the captain reminding you."

Baker shrugged. "I think he needs some kind of formal status report."

Gould walked toward the door, then paused and turned. "Are you doin' okay, Jim? I want you to tell me the truth."

"I don't know, I guess so. I just can't see where any of this is going."

"You get along okay with this kid?"

Baker snorted. "Not exactly."

"Well, this won't go on forever, y'know. Alls you gotta do is hold the line. Just don't flip out over anything."

"It's a little late for that."

"But—"

"Don't worry," Baker said. "I haven't broken anything yet."

Gould patted him on the back. "I knows you; you're gonna be okay."

They said goodnight, and Baker locked the door behind his friend. But after all the boisterous banter, his apartment felt too quiet. Too empty. Again. Surveying the mess in his living room, he considered being a lazy bastard and leaving it till Micki came on Sunday.

Then he started cleaning up.

THE SKY WAS A brilliant azure blue interrupted by just a few white clouds that looked like mounds of shaving cream. With the sun's rays generating an unseasonably warm seventy-two degrees, Baker considered taking a late afternoon jog through Central Park to catch the autumn foliage. He parked his car, then hurried down the busy midtown street, wondering how long his meeting with Malone was going to take.

But walking into the station house was something of a shock—so familiar and yet not, like returning to his apartment after he'd been away for a couple of weeks. As he lifted his chin in greeting to the desk sergeant, he clipped his badge to his belt, feeling conspicuous and out of place. Yet no one who caught his eye did more than nod or say a quick hello.

He ran up the stairs, two at a time, and knocked on the captain's door, entering at the brusque "yeah?"

Looking up from the statistics he was examining, Malone said, "Jim! Sit down. I'll be with you in a minute."

Baker sat on the old vinyl couch, its ugly yellow color somewhat disarming in the otherwise drab surroundings. The office felt much smaller than he remembered. Not even two months had gone by, but it seemed like a lifetime. He stared out the window. Undaunted by the dirty pane of glass, the bright blue of the sky was fighting its way through the grime. Apparently, no one had told it a nor'easter was predicted to hit by midnight.

"So!" Malone said.

And Baker looked back at the captain, who stood up and walked around to the front of his desk. Arms folded over his chest, Malone leaned back against the battered piece of furniture while Baker, sitting tensed on the edge of the couch, pulled a pack of cigarettes from the pocket of his T-shirt and lit one.

"How's everything been going lately?" the older man inquired.

Exhaling smoke, Baker said, "About the same, I guess."

"Anything new happen since the last time we spoke?"

Baker summarized as concisely as possible—with convenient edits—then stood up and glanced around for an ashtray. Malone pointed to a paper plate with a stale crust of rye bread sitting in the middle of a mustard stain.

"Doesn't sound like there's been much improvement," Malone said.

Baker tapped a small column of ashes onto the plate and raised his eyebrows in a gesture of uncertainty. "Hard to say."

"I'll tell you the reason I asked you to come here today."

Though his cigarette was hardly beat, Baker stubbed it out, then continued standing, hands in the front pockets of his jeans.

"There's another kid Kelly wants to place and—"

Slapping his thigh, Baker said, "You've got to be kidding! What am I, suddenly, a fucking one-man juvenile hall?"

"Take it easy, Jim, and let me finish."

Baker turned and stared out the window.

"This other kid'll be a breeze. He's fifteen years old and was practically an honor student until his parents got divorced. After that he got mixed up with the wrong crowd—started doing drugs and stealing cars. His mother, who he'd been living with, became an alcoholic; his father disappeared. In two weeks he'll be released from Spoffard, but he's got no place to go. The mother's currently doing time for check forgery, and there aren't any relatives to take him till she's out and reestablished as a sober, responsible parent. Seems the family moved here from Ohio three years ago because the mother had a big falling-out with her parents. Even so, you'd probably only have the kid till the beginning of the spring. I think he'd work out a hell of a lot better than Micki has. Not to mention he's a boy. The only drawback to choosing him over her is that he'd have to live with you."

"What? Wait a minute." Baker turned to face Malone. "What do you mean 'choosing him over her'?"

"Well, it's your choice: which kid do you want?"

"I thought you meant—"

"No."

Baker looked stunned. "But then what would happen to Micki?"

"She'd go back to Heyden."

It felt like minutes went by before Baker asked, "What if someone else were interested in taking her? There's someone—"

"A cop?"

"Well, no, he's working security at the high school with me. But—"

"I don't think you understand the whole picture." Malone folded his arms across his chest again. "The only reason Kelly got his way in having Micki released from juvi so early was because, unlike the other kids he'd gotten involved with, it was agreed that whether her first placement worked out or not, she could only have a cop as her legal guardian. Truth be known, no one wanted her. But then you needed a kid, and she was the only one available. Everything about her processing has been completely unorthodox—most of it slipping well under the radar. But no judge is going to allow her to be handled by anyone less than a police officer. She's too much of a risk otherwise. Quite frankly, I think she's too much of a risk, period."

Baker swallowed hard and looked around. "I just—the thought of sending her back there—the things they did to her... I've been having a tough enough time dealing with the idea of leaving her there over Thanksgiving. But to leave her there permanently..."

Malone uncrossed his arms and stood up straight. "Y'know, I figured this was a real no-brainer, that you'd dump that kid in a heartbeat. A month ago you hated her like nobody's business."

"Yeah? Well, I'm not so sure anymore that she's a total waste. Maybe there's someone in there after all. I know she could be jerking me around, but if she's not—"

"Why the sudden change?"

Baker shifted his gaze. "Things've happened."

"*Things?* What kind of 'things'?"

He looked back. "What're you asking?"

"Are you banging her? Is that the difference?"

"Jesus Christ! Give me a little credit! I haven't laid a finger on her. Well, not like that, at least."

"'Not like that'? Then like what?"

"The worst she's ever gotten from me is some bruises, nothing more."

"Oh, jeez." Malone looked away, then looked back. "You care about this kid?"

"I feel sorry for her."

"You feel *sorry* for her?" Blood rushed to Malone's face. "You think she'll feel sorry for you when your career goes down the toilet? If she fucks up bad, it won't look good for you. But you're a winner if your kid's a winner, and this boy I told you about is a surefire success. His behavior in Spoffard's been model, and his delinquency was but a little blip to be erased from an otherwise normal, healthy childhood. Now, I'm going to be frank with you, Sergeant: I don't give a flying fuck about Micki. My only concern is you; it always has been. You're a damned good detective, and I need you back. Since you got your wings clipped, morale in this squad has taken a nosedive, and our clearance rate has gone right down with it. So straighten out your priorities. That goddamn kid's a lost cause, and you're not!"

"I need some time to think about this."

"Well, you've only got till Monday. After that, the boy'll get hooked up with one of the eligible families. There's a lot of paperwork involved. I can't hold them off any longer than that."

"Then why did you wait till now to tell me?"

"Because this time around *you're* the problem. That boy could easily get placed with one of several families eager to take him. As far as social services is concerned you're, by far, the least appealing candidate. But I've been busy pulling strings again."

"Look, I'm not ungrateful, but I—this just isn't so easy. I need some time."

Malone picked up a crumpled paper napkin from his desk and threw it in the garbage. "It's your life."

AUTUMN WAS STAKING ITS claim with wind-driven showers of golden and fiery leaves. They were floating and spinning as the gusts picked up in expectation of the impending storm. But while Baker's feet crunched along the path, pounding out his usual course, the scenery around him was fading. Next week he could still be exercising through this seasonal beauty while Micki might be locked up behind brick walls and barbed-wire fences—back in solitary, no doubt. If she went back there for good, it would probably take her all of one day to manage that.

As he passed another jogger, a man he frequently saw running in the mornings, Baker raised his hand in greeting. Back around June, the same man, going by at a remarkable clip, had shouted to him in a very thick accent, "My son, he just graduated medical school!" The word *just* had sounded like *hhhyust*; the word *medical*, like *medeecal*. And the man's face, glistening from a layer of sweat over a shadow of stubble, had been beaming. Because of his son. Watching the man disappear around the bend in the green glow of late spring, Baker had suddenly wondered whether his own decision to never have kids was a mistake. And now there was this boy Malone was offering...

Stung by a nasty stitch in his left side—his punishment for lifting weights more often than jogging, the cigarettes not helping much, either—Baker slowed his pace. Veering off, he headed back to his apartment, dragging himself up the stairs and cursing the pain in his knees. His sweatshirt was soaked through, and he needed a shower. But more than anything, he needed someone to tell him what to do. The smart thing, thinking strictly of himself, was to get rid of Micki and take the other kid. Micki had been nothing but a combative, streetwise pain in the ass from day one. But every time he thought about trading her in, his mind would throw back proof that he was totally off, completely missing the mark—as if he'd never seen a hint of what was on the other side.

So which Micki was the real one? If she was scamming him, she was doing a hell of a job, was a far better actress than Cynthia would ever be. Plus, that boy had a mother to go home to in the future and lots of people vying to take him in the interim. Micki had no one and never would. No one, that was, except him.

MICKI SPENT THE HOUR before work in a flat and heavy sleep. As soon as her shift was over, she went back to her apartment, changed into her nightshirt, and lay down again, not even bothering to brush her teeth. When the storm started after midnight, it woke her up. She listened to the hard rain strike the glass, the wind blasting by, rattling the old windows and shrieking.

SHE WAS RUNNING DOWN *the alley again, chain-link fence glittering on one side, smooth brick wall on the other. Ragged and harsh in the warm summer night, her breathing had the same steady rhythm as her feet.*

Further and further she flew down the tapering trail, her pursuer anywhere and everywhere in the shadows behind her. And then the air rippled with a long, sorrowful sigh, producing the other brick wall to block her path. Eyes stinging from the gritty dust kicking up from the ground, she could feel herself slowing while the pavement, rumbling and shaking, cracked itself open into a vast, craggy fissure just before the barrier.

She reached the crust at the edge of the pit and stared down at her feet and the chasm below. Chunks of the surface were falling away, the gaping black hole growing wider and wider. But she needed to wait; she needed to stay where she was. Until the last possible moment. Until that razor-sharp point when she alone could make it across. But perhaps she'd already waited too long. Endlessly deep, the gap appeared too large; the crumbling ledge on the opposite side, too narrow. If she jumped now, she could lose her footing.

Alive with flashes and crackles, the atmosphere bristled with a massive static charge. Then the floodlight dimmed, throwing the area beyond into deeper shadow. Hot, foul breath touched the nape of her neck...

Micki woke to the howling of the wind outside, the rain beating harshly against the glass. Wide eyed, she stared into the darkness of her room.

AFTER TWELVE HOURS, THE storm abated, but major roads and highways had been flooded. Strewn with debris and downed trees, they were still closed, precluding the scenic drive to Bear Mountain that Baker and Cynthia had planned. Instead, they went out for a late Chinese dinner and returned to Baker's apartment, debating whether or not to catch the ten-o'clock showing of a movie.

Cynthia thought it would be fun to see *Earthquake*, simply to experience Sensurround, which was supposed to simulate the feel of the real thing. Baker said it sounded dumb and that the movie was probably dumber. So they ended up having sex, then lying around in bed afterward. Eyes closed, stretched out on his back, Baker had his arm around Cynthia. She ran her hand over his chest.

"Mmm," he murmured.

She suddenly pulled the sheet around her and sat up.

Baker opened his eyes. "What is it?"

"Let's bake cookies," she said. "Big, giant chocolate-chip cookies."

"What?" He was grinning.

"I'm starving again."

"You're serious!"

"C'mon, I bet Red Apple is still open; I want to bake them from scratch."

He sat up and kissed her nose.

BAKER DID A MINIMAL amount of cooking, but never baked; so they had to buy almost everything they needed. Following the recipe on the back of the Nestlé's bag, Cynthia sifted, measured, and mixed the ingredients while Baker greased two cookie sheets. Each received one huge glob of cookie dough that was flattened out before heading into the oven.

When Cynthia checked her watch to keep track of the time, it was already 11:13. "Let's see if there's an old movie on TV." They moved into the living room, and Baker turned on the set while Cynthia took off her shoes and got comfortable on the couch. As he started changing channels, she asked, "So do you want to tell me what's been bothering you all night?"

He shrugged and flipped through the stations again. So far, all he'd seen was commercials.

"Talk to me, Jim. Please."

Sighing, he shut the TV and straightened up to face her. "I have to decide if I want to keep Micki or take a different kid instead. Malone told me about a boy he wants me to consider."

"But, I don't understand…"

So Baker sketched it out while Cynthia's expression clouded over. "Well, you're not going to do that, are you? Abandon her like that?"

"At this point, I don't know what I should do. It's not like I don't feel bad about the idea of sending her back to juvi, but I have my career to think about. It'd be a hell of a lot easier on me to take the boy."

Unfolding her long legs from where they'd been tucked beneath her, Cynthia sat up very straight while the aroma of warm, baking cookies filled the apartment. "So you've made up your mind already?"

"No, that's just it: I haven't yet."

"Well—do the right thing."

"It's not that simple."

"It *is* that simple. There's no other choice. It's not fair to her."

"And what about me?" Baker's voice was rising. "Is it fair to me to jeopardize my career when I don't have to? Jesus, I should never have told you about this."

"You're supposed to do what's right, not what's easiest."

"You're so naïve, Cynthia. When are you going to start living in the real world?"

Her eyes flashed. There was a small, defiant toss of her hair. But she got up from the couch with great composure. And when she spoke again, her voice was low. "You go to hell."

Baker's mouth fell open. Not once, in all the time he'd known her, had he ever heard her talk like that.

"I am *not* naïve," she said, "I simply live by my principles." With a cool eye, she looked him over. "I really don't know you anymore; maybe I never knew you to begin with. I always thought you believed in justice and fairness—always ready to help people, protecting those who can't protect themselves."

"What makes you think Micki needs protecting? You have absolutely no idea the things that kid has done."

"Because you won't tell me. But I don't need to know. Whatever she did in the past has nothing to do with where she is now. From the first time I saw her, I knew in my heart that she was basically good, that she had a good soul."

"Oh, Jesus. Now you're going to start in with that mysticism crap?"

Her blue eyes turned darker, and her words began from between clenched teeth: "She just needs someone to help her. She's crying out for some attention, and you're going to turn your back on her."

"You don't know what you're talking about."

"I know *exactly* what I'm talking about." The patronizing look he gave her made her want to smack it right off his face. Instead, she said, "I want to see other people, Jim." When his jaw dropped again, she added, "This has been coming on for quite some time now."

"Yeah, ever since you met that asshole actor out in LA."

There was a spark of pity in her eyes. "It's much more than that. We have a lot of issues that need to be addressed."

Voice full of sarcasm, he said, "Oh, really."

"That's right. You want to hear some?"

"Not particularly."

"Well, that's the biggest one of all." When Baker looked away, Cynthia slipped into her shoes and went to the closet to get her coat. "I think I'd better go."

"I think so."

She was turning his keys in the lock when he asked the back of her head, "Do you want me to call you a cab or wait with you downstairs until you get one?"

Not glancing back, she could picture the annoyed look on his face. "No," she said acidly, and opened the door. "I'll be just fine by myself."

After the door had slammed shut behind her, Baker said softly, "I bet you will."

LEANING OUT THE WINDOW, he could see her exiting the building. As pissed off as he was, he should never have let her go downstairs alone. He had an "understanding" with the local crew that hung out on his street, but she wasn't, by any means, safe; the area was rife with crime. Yet he was worrying over nothing; the woman clearly led a charmed life: a taxi—an extremely rare sight in his neighborhood at this hour—pulled up out of nowhere. He ducked his head back in and slammed the window down.

The cookies were burning. He went into the kitchen and turned off the oven before looking inside and then slamming that shut, too. After a brief pause, he swept his arm across the counter and the table, sending the still-open bags of sugars and flour, the little can of baking soda, the tiny bottle of vanilla extract, the measuring cups and spoons, mixing bowl, and utensils all flying to the floor. In the late-night silence, the noise from the falling metal and heavy glass was deafening. Baker half expected an irate, disapproving bang on the ceiling from his downstairs neighbor—but none was forthcoming.

He stomped back into the living room, pulled out his whiskey, and quickly polished off what little was left. He reached for the J&B Gould had brought, but then closed the cabinet instead. He should go to sleep. After all, the kid would be coming in the morning, the goddamn pain in the ass. Because of her, he couldn't even tie one on when he needed to.

But his sleep was fitful. And at 4:00 a.m., he got up and went back to the living room. After some hesitation, he opened the new bottle. No doubt, this was not how Gould had envisioned his gift being used, but then, Gould didn't know Baker had a drinking problem. Baker never drank on the job and had never gotten truly drunk socially. It was only when he was alone—alone and depressed. Bottle to his lips, he told himself it wasn't such a big deal—nothing he couldn't handle on his own. Yet this was the very first time he'd ever admitted—even to himself—that his drinking was, in fact, a problem.

The whiskey burned going down, the spreading warmth inducing an unusual and uncomfortable tremor. Hand wrapped around the neck, he let the bottle hang by his side.

The hour felt much darker.

IT TOOK FIVE RINGS of the buzzer to cut through Baker's leaden sleep—he'd dozed off only half an hour before. Groaning as he rolled over, he got up and put on his jeans, fumbling with the button before zipping up the fly. He threw on his shirt, not bothering to button it at all.

When he opened the door, Micki drew back. But more than the bloodshot gaze, the uncombed hair, and the state of his clothes, it was his breath that really made her want to bolt.

At first he said nothing, simply stood in the entryway, glaring at her through hooded eyes that were masking the slightly disjointed thoughts and almost imperceptible hint of the headache to come. Strangely sickening, a shimmering aura was flickering back and forth at the edge of his brain.

"Go make me some coffee," he ordered.

Warm and brown, the scent of burnt sugar colored the air as she walked past him into the living room. He followed a few steps behind, then sat down in the club chair by the bookcase.

But at the foot of the kitchen, she froze, gaping at the disaster before her. She pivoted around and started back. "I don't know what the hell is goin' on, but I'm outta here."

He stood up. "Is that right," he said.

She halted a few feet away, still holding her lunch.

"Well, go on, then," he said. "Who's stopping you?"

She remained where she was.

Voice low, speech a little slurred, he asked, "Whatsa matter, Reilly, you scared of me?"

And she wished that—even if it were only for a moment— she could be bigger than he was. "Yeah, I'm scared of you."

A grin spread across his face. "Gee, I didn't think you'd admit that. But, then again, you don't generally lie, do you."

She tried to think of some way to get out.

He snorted. "You're just a fuckin' little pussy."

"Fuck you."

He lunged forward and grabbed two fistfuls of her open jacket, running her backward till he'd slammed her up against the wall. It knocked the breath out of her in a grunt, and there was pain where his fists dug in to keep her pinned.

"Fuck me?" he hissed. "You're gonna fuck me? I could fuck you real easy whether you wanted me to or not. But you'd have a hard time tryin' to do that to me, now, wouldn't you. WOULDN'T YOU."

Her jaded eyes seemed to be daring him.

"ANSWER ME, YOU LITTLE MOTHERFUCKER." But when she merely lowered her gaze, he said, "You better watch what you say, 'cause I'm tired of hearin' the shit that comes outta your mouth. Do you understand me?"

Looking straight up at him, she said, "You're drunk."

He pulled her away from the wall, and she grabbed his upper arms, though her fingers encircled very little of the large, solid muscle underneath. But when she felt her feet leave the ground, she gasped, eyes wide, fingers digging in to hold on. And Baker froze, body vibrating with rage.

A truck rumbled down Ninety-Third Street below.

He released her. "I'm going to the gym." And he turned and went into his bedroom.

She listened to him gathering some things together. She watched him go to the hall closet and stuff the items in a gym bag. She watched him put his jacket on and unlock the door. And then, voice small, she said, "I'll—I'll need to leave the apartment to—to do the laundry and stuff."

He paused, then went back into his bedroom. She could hear him rummaging through several drawers followed by the sound of keys. When he came out again, he tossed them at her, nearly hitting her in the face. "Just make sure you lock up tight when you go out. Both locks. Understand?"

"Yessir."

"I'll be at West Side Workouts if you need me." And with that, he picked up his bag and let himself out, locking the door behind him.

As if nothing had happened, the apartment was quiet. Calm. She looked at the extra set of keys in her hand, then went to retrieve her lunch from where it had landed on the floor. But instead of picking it up, she sat down beside it, slumped in a shapeless heap and hanging her head. When Baker had slammed her against the wall, she'd seen the hate in his eyes—so pure, so intense. And to think she'd recently told herself that he didn't hate her as much anymore, maybe even liked her a little.

She poked at a piece of lint from the rug, then rolled it up between her fingers. There was no way she was going to clean this entire fucking apartment again. Especially with that mess in the kitchen. She looked around. Maybe she should just go home. After all, she could lock the place up. What was he going to do? Tell her she had to clean more days? Send her back to juvi if she didn't? Did it really matter?

She closed her eyes. She knew what would happen if she left. And it had nothing to do with Baker.

When Baker returned, he looked a little green around the gills. Micki took a break from her mopping to watch him from the kitchen doorway. He dropped his gym bag on the floor, took off his jacket, and threw it on the club chair in the living room. Inside the bathroom, he gulped down three aspirin.

Back in the hallway, he paused, his voice low. "I have a splitting headache; I'm going to lie down for a while. I do not want to be disturbed by anything. Do you understand me?"

"I need the shopping list and some money."

He massaged his temples, then pulled out his wallet and dropped two twenty-dollar bills on top of his jacket. "Just get whatever you remember from last time." And he disappeared into his bedroom, closing the door behind him.

Leaving the mop to rest against the wall, she hurried over to pocket the money. She'd finish the floor, then go to the supermarket. She'd already changed the linens on his bed and gotten the laundry started using his stash of coins. But the extra work in the kitchen had thrown her entire cleaning routine off.

Like anyone fucking cared.

She went back to mopping.

ONCE INSIDE THE BEDROOM, Baker stripped down to his underpants and crawled between the cool, fresh sheets. And though he tried several different positions and played desperately with the pillows, nothing eased the pounding in his head. At the gym, he'd punched the heavy bag until his arms had felt like lead, every strike accelerating the onset and severity of his headache. At one point, he was so overcome with nausea that he'd wished he could simply heave his insides out.

He turned over and heard the whoosh and gurgle of a bucketful of water being emptied into the bathtub. It sounded muffled and far away…

AT ONE O'CLOCK, MICKI had her lunch in peace, then continued cleaning. It was nearly four thirty when she finished ironing the last of Baker's button-down shirts. But she hadn't gotten any of her vacuuming done, and she hadn't dusted his bedroom yet, either. Tired of staring out the window, she picked up the book he'd left on the coffee table—a thick, oversized paperback: *The Foundation Trilogy* by Isaac Asimov. Science fiction. Who would've thought? Actually, she was surprised he liked to read anything at all. She sat on the couch and opened it.

But the apartment was growing dark as the afternoon sun, already low in the sky, became hidden behind some clouds. She switched on the nearest lamp, but her eyelids were soon drooping. And after only a few more pages, she set the paperback aside and lay down. The sofa cushions felt comfortable and firm beneath her; the velvety throw pillow, puffy and soft. She closed her eyes and drifted—until she imagined Baker finding her asleep on his couch. She sat up. Elbows on knees, she rested her head in her hands. The extra keys were on the kitchen table; she could still lock the place up and go home.

With a final glance toward his room, she pushed herself up and went to get her jacket.

BAKER AWOKE WITH AN urgent need to relieve himself. He rolled out of bed and stuck his head out the door. Except for a table lamp in the living room, the apartment was dark. And utterly silent. He left the bedroom in just his Jockey shorts, turning on lights as he fumbled his way to the bathroom. After he emptied his bladder, he washed his hands and face, the cold water bracing. But then his vision went white. Leaning against the sink, he could feel his sunken eyes and unshaved skin. He took a deep breath, then glanced at his watch: a quarter past seven; he'd essentially slept through the entire day.

He shuffled back down the hall and into the living room—where he pulled up short. Lying on her side, using her folded-up jacket as a pillow, Micki was asleep on the area rug between the coffee table and the TV. A sharp pang shot through him. He went back to the bedroom to throw on some jeans and a sweatshirt.

THE AROMA OF FRESHLY perked coffee wound its way into her consciousness. Painfully stiff, she got up slowly in the dark; Baker must've shut off the lamp. She dropped her jacket on a chair and walked into the kitchen. Blinking and squinting from the bright fluorescent lights, she saw him sitting at the table, a heavy earthenware mug between his large hands, a cigarette balanced on the edge of an ashtray.

"Is your headache gone?" she asked.

"Pretty much."

"So you don't mind if I vacuum?"

He hung his head. "Forget the vacuuming, Micki. The punishment's over. Why don't you have a cup of coffee, and then I'll take you home."

"So you're saying I don't have to clean anymore? That I'm done? For good?"

He looked up at her. "Yeah, that's what I'm saying."

"'Cause I'm not comin' back here next week; there's no way I'm comin' back."

"You won't have to come back."

"Well, then I'll just take the subway—"

"I *said* I'll drive you home."

She chewed her lower lip. The coffee smelled good. She took a mug from the cabinet and poured herself a cup. "Can I have some milk?"

Another sharp twinge: the kid felt like she had to ask for every fucking little thing now. "Help yourself. There's sugar in the pantry by the door."

"Seriously? You really think you need to tell me where anything is? Besides, I don't even take sugar." She added some milk and started drinking—standing up.

"Sit down," he said.

She took the chair furthest from his.

Baker looked at his watch. "Did you eat anything today?"

"Just what I brought, okay? Nothing else."

"You must be starving. There's some bologna in the refrigerator. Why don't you make yourself a sandwich?"

"I'm not hungry."

"How can you not be hungry when you hardly ate anything all day?"

She shrugged and stared at the coffee.

"If you don't start eating more, Micki, you're going to disappear."

"Well, wouldn't that save a lot of people a lot of grief." She got up, tossed the rest of her coffee down the sink, then stalked out of the kitchen.

After a quick final puff, Baker crushed his cigarette and followed her into the living room.

Her back to him, she was looking out the window.

"What the hell is that supposed to mean?" he asked.

Turning to face him, she said, "Like you wouldn't be happy if I was gone."

Hands on hips, he opened his mouth, then shut it again—he still hadn't given Malone his decision.

Her smile was bitter. "That's what I figured."

"It worries me that you're getting so thin."

"Spare me the bullshit concern. You don't really care; I'm just a job to you. By the way"—her voice was full of sarcasm—"can I say 'bullshit,' or are y'gonna hit me for that?"

He rubbed his temples. His headache was coming back. "I'm going to have another cup of coffee," he said quietly, "and then we're going to leave. Just relax for a little while." But halfway to the kitchen, he paused and said over his shoulder, "And don't ever sleep on the floor again. The couch is a hell of a lot better."

She went back to looking out the window. He hadn't even tried to deny anything.

Across the street, she could see into another living room, brightly lit with all the blinds pulled up. A pudgy man, wearing a colorful Hawaiian shirt, sat reading the newspaper in a large, overstuffed chair. When an equally rotund woman entered the room, holding the hand of a little boy, the man looked up. Smiling with delight, he dropped his newspaper and spread his arms wide. The little boy, giggling and squealing, ran to be swallowed up in a warm embrace.

If only she were someone else.

TRAFFIC WAS HEAVY AS they traveled cross-town on Ninety-Sixth Street toward the FDR Drive. Baker had the radio on low, but was changing stations constantly to avoid hearing the songs he hated most. Switching to AM, he tuned in 1010 WINS to catch an updated traffic report. Micki gave up trying to keep her eyes open and let her head fall back against the headrest.

"Push the seat down," Baker said.

"Huh?"

"On the floor, near the door, there's a lever. Pull it up and lean back."

Not sure what she was looking for, she groped around.

The light turned red, and he reached across, putting her hand on the lever. "Here," he said.

The warmth of his face so close, the feel of his hand over hers—her heart was racing. When he turned his head to look at her, she shyly averted her eyes. He bit the inside of his lip and straightened up. The light turned green. She successfully reclined the seat and fell asleep.

It wasn't until they were crossing the bridge that ugly snippets of their morning encounter began to present themselves to him. He shot a glance at her sleeping figure. Clearly she knew he hadn't been threatening to actually rape her. But when his eyes returned to the road, his jaw was working. And for the remainder of the trip, he didn't look at her again.

DOUBLE-PARKED IN FRONT OF her building, he left the engine running. Micki stirred and opened her eyes. "You're home," he said.

She got the seat upright, unlocked the door, but then paused. For the longest time, she'd planned to say she was sorry once the punishment was over. But after what had happened this morning, what was the point?

"Something wrong?" he asked.

"Nothing's wrong; everything's just great." She started getting out.

He grabbed her arm. "I don't need your snide remarks."

"You don't need *anything* from me. But you are *using* me for something."

Baker paled slightly under the dome light, and Micki's expression turned smug. He released her arm, and she left, slamming the car door behind her.

Chapter 12

B Y THE TIME MICKI got to English class, Mr. Newsome had already written homework questions on the blackboard. But when she went to copy them, she couldn't find her assignment pad; she must've left it behind in Miss Giannetti's room. She raised her hand and asked if she could go back to look for it.

A shrewd smile spread across Mr. Newsome's face. "I'm afraid you'll have to wait until next period passing. I cannot have students wandering around, missing class, because they *say* they've misplaced something."

Fuck you, you asshole, Micki thought, and slouched down to glower at him for the rest of the period. Then the moment the bell rang, she tore back upstairs to the third floor, but room 323 was empty when she got there; even Miss Giannetti was gone. Spying the little book on the teacher's desk, she hurried over to get it.

A teacher she didn't know came dashing into the room. "Just what do you think you're doing?" Using both hands, the woman adjusted her black cat's-eyes glasses, her piercing, pale-grey eyes looking small behind them. She looked down at Micki. "How dare you take something from my desk." Then she pulled at her peach cardigan sweater, causing a smidgeon of lace from her shirt's collar to peek out from underneath.

"But it's mine; it's my assignment pad. I left it here after my calculus class."

"Hand it over, please." Yet when the teacher couldn't find Micki's name in the book, she demanded to see Micki's loose-leaf, as well—to compare the handwriting.

Who the fuck would steal a goddamn assignment pad? Micki thought. The end-of-passing bell rang. "Can I go already?"

The teacher peered down over her glasses. "You need to learn some manners, young lady."

Micki lowered her eyes. "Sorry."

The teacher wrote a late pass, and Micki hurried down to the basement, handing the piece of paper to Mrs. Tandy on her way into the locker room. The crowded rows were already thinning out, metal doors slamming and locks clicking closed. Micki entered her combination, took out her gym clothes, and put her books away until the room sounded empty. But just as she stood up, about to unbuckle her belt, she saw Suzy Parish standing at the end of the aisle in nothing but pink cotton underpants and a matching undershirt. Barely over five feet tall, Suzy was skinny and noticeably flat-chested, her dark brown hair heavily streaked with blonde. A quiet, shy girl, she was something of a loner.

Micki pretended to be rearranging her books while Suzy moved closer. And though it was Suzy who was half undressed, Micki felt the urge to back away and cover up. "What is it?" she asked.

Voice shaking, frosted-pink lip gloss shining, Suzy said, "I like you, Micki."

"Well—uh—I guess I like you, too, but I need to change."

The late bell rang. From out in the hallway, Mrs. Tandy called, "Let's go, girls. Whoever's still in there with Micki, you're late."

"C'mon, Suzy. I really need to change. Just get out of here, okay?"

Suzy twirled some hair around her finger.

"Don't do this, Suzy. *Please.*"

And then, in a voice that was mostly breath, Suzy said, "I want you to kiss me." She pulled off her undershirt. "I want you to—to touch me."

Shaking her head, Micki took a step back. "Y'got it all wrong; I'm only interested in boys."

The smaller girl's jaw dropped, and she clutched the undershirt to her chest.

"I'm sorry," Micki said.

Suzy's pretty face turned ugly. "You better not tell anyone."

"I won't tell anyone."

"Oh, god! I'm dead if anyone finds out."

"No one'll find out; I promise. It's nobody's business."

Eyes pleading, Suzy gave Micki a final look, then ran back to her locker and up to the gym.

When she was finally alone, Micki changed and followed.

THEY HAD A SUBSTITUTE teacher for physics; Mr. Taubenfeld was sick. The period was being spent as a review session. And as if that weren't bad enough, the substitute's voice was a monotonous drone, eventually lulling Micki unconscious. But she was jolted awake by the grip on her upper arm, a grip she knew all too well. Head groggy, eyes half closed, she scanned the faces around her, trying to piece together where she was and what was happening. Absolute silence filled the classroom.

"Get up and take your books," Baker ordered.

Gathering her things together, she wondered if this was all because she fell asleep in class again, though she couldn't imagine the gawky, insecure substitute as being capable of such treachery. Once they were out in the hall, she asked Baker what was going on.

"Shut up." And he roughly steered her all the way to the security office, where he ordered her to put her books down. Feet planted wide, arms folded across his chest, he asked, "You were late getting to the locker room for gym?"

"But I had a pass. I left something in Miss Giannetti's room." All this for being late?

"And what happened after you got there?"

"Nothing. I changed and—" Micki stopped.

"You changed and what?"

"I went up to the gym." But her voice had come out sounding uncertain, and she knew she had that guilty look on her face, the one she always got—as if everything that went wrong in the world was her fault.

"Was Suzy Parish in the locker room with you?"

"Yessir."

"Alone?"

"Yessir."

"And what happened?"

"Nothing."

Baker took a step closer. "I'm going to ask you nicely only one more time, so I suggest you get your answer straight. What exactly happened down there?"

"Nothing," Micki repeated.

Baker struck her across the face, cutting the skin below her eye. Then he grabbed her away from the desk and slammed her against the wall. "That's not what I heard."

"I dunno what you heard, but I didn't touch her!"

"Really? Because I never mentioned anything about you touching her."

"I—I just—"

"Cut the shit. You look so fucking guilty it isn't even funny."

"But I didn't—" She grunted as pain ripped through her, directly under her ribs. Baker had barely moved.

"Y'know, up to now," he said, "all of your fuck-ups have been borderline issues, things that could be written off. But not this. This is something else." And he thought about how close he'd come to putting himself on the line for her. Thank god he hadn't called Malone yet. "I've got news for you, Reilly, this is your ticket back to Heyden. The only thing you have to decide right now is how bad off you want to be when you get there. So tell me what you did, or I'll beat it out of you. I really don't have any problem with that."

"Did *Suzy* say I did somethin' t'her?" Micki was almost positive they'd been alone. And Mrs. Tandy, all the way out in the hall, couldn't possibly have heard them—at least, not clearly.

Baker was silent.

"I wanna know what she said," Micki demanded.

"You want to know what she said? She told Mrs. Tandy that you came on to her while she was changing—backed her into a corner and felt her up."

"And y'believe that? Y'know I'm straight!"

"How the hell should I know what you really are? Maybe you swing a little both ways. Maybe you got so hard up at Heyden that you checked out what it was like with girls. Or maybe"—he lowered his voice—"you just wanted to be the one pushing someone else around for a while."

"Or maybe y'just so fuckin' stupid, y'can't see the truth."

When he crashed his palm against her cheekbone, she jabbed her knuckles into his ribs. And after that, it all became a blur, ending with her hands cuffed behind her, the side of her face and the front of her body smashed into the wall. She hurt all over.

Baker said, "I'm not finished with you yet, Reilly. I warned you about ever hitting me again. You'll be lucky if you can walk out of this room. So now you tell me how it is that *I'm* stupid."

But as he viciously jerked her back by the neck of her shirt and vest, it suddenly occurred to her that her promise to Suzy didn't matter anymore. After all, the girl was a fucking little liar, and, because of it, *she* was the one who was taking the fall. Her words came out in small bursts as she struggled against the pain, trying to say what she wanted to before he started in on her again. "It was *her*—she came on t'*me*—flipped out when I said no—was afraid I'd tell everyone."

And Baker stopped, his stomach dropping as all of the pieces rearranged themselves into a completely different picture. The teacher had been so outraged—and so *sure*—about what Suzy had told her that he'd ignored his own gut feeling that something was off. He hadn't even questioned the accusing girl himself. Seeing how small she was, he'd assumed she'd been easy prey. And yet she hadn't appeared traumatized, just extremely nervous—a huge red flag. Which he'd dismissed.

"Why didn't you say this before?" he asked.

"Promised her I wouldn't. Besides, y'already made up y'mind I was guilty—didn't believe nothin' I was sayin'."

"But I meant it when I said you'd be going back upstate."

With a bitter shrug, she turned away.

Baker called Warner to the office to stay with Micki while he went to question the other girl himself. Before he left, he said to Micki, "You'd better be telling me the truth, or you'll wish you were never born."

"You're too fuckin' late."

DECIDING IT WAS BEST not to talk to Suzy alone, Baker enlisted the gym teacher's help. Outside her office, he gave her the basic game plan, stressing the importance of maintaining a nonjudgmental facade no matter what the girl might say. They went in together, but Suzy looked so frightened that Baker stood in the corner, behind Mrs. Tandy, who took a seat at her desk.

Before either adult had said a word, Suzy, one hand tightly clasped within the other, asked, "So—um—is Micki gonna get kicked outta school over this? I don't wanna have to see her again. I'm scared of what she'll do to me for telling."

"Actually," Mrs. Tandy said, "we'd like you to think very carefully about what happened and tell it again to Sergeant Baker so he can hear it from you himself. These are very serious charges. Depending on what you say, he'll determine whether or not to place Micki under arrest."

"*Arrest*? He can *arrest* her?" Then, turning to Baker, "I mean, you're really a cop?" Despite the buzz around the high school, none of the kids seemed to know for sure.

"I'm really a cop," he stated flatly.

Suzy squirmed. "Cause—um—I mean, I didn't think she'd, like, get arrested or anything…" Her voice trailed off. Fist pressed against her mouth, she said, "I—um—like, I just figured she'd be sent to another school or something."

"If what you told Mrs. Tandy was true," Baker said, "she's going back to Heyden Reformatory for Girls. On the other hand, if I later find out that what you said *wasn't* true, maybe *you'll* end up there instead."

Suzy's eyes flitted from Baker to Mrs. Tandy then back to Baker. She swallowed. Hard. "Well—um—like—um"—her voice became very small—"I dunno." She started to cry.

"All I want you to do," Baker said, "is answer one question for me. And I want the truth, whatever that is. Understand? I want the truth to just that one question. You don't have to tell me anything else. Understand?" he repeated.

Eyes closed, tears streaming down her face, she nodded.

"Did Micki touch you or threaten you in any way?"

Suzy shook her head no.

"You're absolutely sure now?" he pressed. "You're not just saying that because you feel bad about what might happen to her?"

Between sobs, Suzy said, "She…didn't…do anything…to me."

"So everything you told Mrs. Tandy before was a lie."

Suzy nodded.

"Did you tell anyone else about any of this?"

The girl shook her head no.

"Well, thank god for small miracles."

The teacher glanced over her shoulder at Baker, but he walked right past her to the quaking girl, grabbing her arm and forcing her to stand. "I want you to see what I did to Micki because of you."

Eyes wide, mouth hanging open, she let him lead her down the hall to the security office, where he turned the knob, pushed the door in, and pulled her inside. The gym teacher followed.

Micki quickly turned away. But not before Suzy and Mrs. Tandy had gotten a glimpse of her face: split, fat lip; bloodied, swelling cheek... Suzy looked to Mrs. Tandy, but the gym teacher appeared to be feeling faint.

With timid steps, the girl approached Micki. "I—I'm sorry."

Hands still cuffed, Micki whirled around. "Why'dja lie? I would never've said nothin'. *Never.*"

Suzy hung her head and started to shake.

Baker looked at Micki. "Would you like to initiate some kind of disciplinary action against Suzy?"

Micki's eyes shot over to his. "What? What're you talkin' about?"

"She made false accusations, and you've suffered for it."

Tears pouring down, lips in the shape of an "o," Suzy was unable to even utter a plea.

Micki looked away. "Forget it. I don't care."

"Are you sure?" Baker asked.

Micki turned to him with a look of unbridled hate. "*Yeah*, I'm *sure.*"

Baker nodded slowly. "Okay then, Suzy, you can go. But you're not to say anything to anyone. If I hear rumors, I'll make sure the truth is spread around just as quickly."

"Please..."

"It's up to you. Keep your mouth shut."

Mrs. Tandy looked from Baker to Suzy to Micki. "Can someone please tell me what's going on?"

Eyes still locked with Suzy's, Baker said, "I think it's better you don't know."

Suzy looked down at her new pair of brown suede shoes. "May I go now?"

"The period's almost over. When the passing bell rings, you can go to your next class." He addressed the gym teacher: "Thanks for your help—and your silence."

Raising an eyebrow, Mrs. Tandy replied, "I wouldn't know what to say anyway." But before she was completely out the door, she turned back to Micki. "I'm very sorry for what happened. It never crossed my mind that Suzy would lie."

As soon as Suzy was gone, Baker said to Warner, "Thanks for watching Micki."

"No problem. You want me to stick around?"

Micki had already turned to stare out the window again.

"That's okay," Baker said. "Go back to your post."

After the door had clicked shut, Baker walked up behind Micki and lifted her wrists. "If I take these cuffs off, are you going to behave yourself or do something foolish?"

"You can take 'em off." And when her hands were freed, she put them in her front pockets, gritting her teeth so the pain wouldn't show.

"Turn around," he ordered.

Though she did as she was told, it was only to fix her eyes on the little refrigerator and then the coffee machine—the stupid coffee machine with the carafe nearly empty, the liquid inside a brownish-black sludge starting to burn on the bottom—

"I guess I should've given you a chance to explain everything," Baker said, "not jumped to conclusions the way I did."

She looked up. But when it was evident he'd finished, her expression changed. "That's it? That's all y'have t'say? After what y'just did t'me, that's y'whole fuckin' apology?"

Inside his head, a voice was telling him to say he was sorry. What came out was: "It's not like I wasn't justified in believing her, Micki. Look at what you've come from."

Her eyes went black.

Baker walked over to the little refrigerator and removed some ice cubes from the freezer. He put them in a paper towel and held them out. "Put this on your face."

"I don't wannit."

"C'mon, Micki, it'll help with the swelling."

When he moved toward her as if to apply it himself, she slapped his hand away, propelling the ice toward the wall.

"I wanna go back t'Heyden."

"What?"

"*I said I wanna go back ta Heyden.*"

His face went blank. And then: "ARE YOU OUT OF YOUR FUCKING MIND? WHY THE HELL WOULD YOU WANT TO GO BACK THERE?"

"Because I'm tired of all this shit. I'm tired a bein' under suspicion f'every little fuckin' thing. I'm tired a how much y'hate me."

"I don't hate you, Micki."

"No, not much. It was so fuckin' obvious yesterday."

"Yesterday… Look… I didn't…" He ran his fingers through his hair. "At least you've got your freedom out here."

"Y'call this freedom? I might as well be locked up. From the minute I get up, I'm runnin' from one fuckin' thing t'the next. I don't even have enough time t'sleep. I'm so fuckin' exhausted, bein' locked up would be a relief. I mean, it's not like I get t'have any fun or anything—I got no friends. I got—I got nothin' out here."

"You've got nothing there, too."

"But at least I know where I stand."

Stiffening, he pulled himself up a little taller, then lowered his voice. "In case you've forgotten, you didn't exactly do too well at Heyden."

"But there's a new warden there now."

The newspaper article in her desk. "And you think that means it'll be different?"

"Well…yeah."

"Then let me explain something: positions like that often attract people who are warped, or maybe it's the position itself that warps them. I don't know which it is. All I can say is that the new warden might be worse than the old one. Even if she isn't, I'm guessing the rest of the staff hasn't changed. I'm sure your favorite guard is still there."

Micki turned away. But when she looked back, her eyes had narrowed. "I don't get it. How come y'tryin' t'get me t'stay? Isn't this what y'wanted? Y'should be jumpin' up and down, plannin' a goddamn party."

"Because I think you're making a mistake. If I didn't try to talk you out of this, it would weigh on my conscience. Once you go back there, that's it. If you realize later on that you made the wrong choice, you won't be able to get out again."

"Y'think I don't know that?"

But he saw a terrible sadness in her eyes. "Listen to me, Micki, and take some time. If you still feel this way next week, I'll make the arrangements. Otherwise, we'll forget we ever had this conversation."

"I don't wanna wait a week!"

"What's the rush? Afraid you'll change your mind?"

"I'm not gonna change my mind!" Her eyes gleamed darkly. "What is it y'need me for, huh? I wanna know what it is."

He looked at the bruises he'd given her, already ugly—yet just a hint of what they'd become over the next few days. "All right," he said, "I'll level with you: it's true I needed you for something, but I don't need you anymore. So you'd better take what I say very seriously because, right now, I've got no ulterior motive." Of course, he'd put himself in an interesting quandary: as soon as he'd told her she could take a week to reconsider, he'd falsified what he'd just said: Malone needed *his* decision by the end of the day.

The passing bell rang, and Baker hailed Warner on the walkie-talkie. "Cover for me while I take the kid home."

"But I've got a history test eighth period," Micki said.

"You'll take a make-up."

"What am I supposeta tell Mr. Ingram?"

"You? You're not going to tell him anything—I will." Seeing the look on her face, he added, "Don't worry, he likes you. He'll let you take the exam another day."

"But—"

"Micki, you're going home now. You're going to put some ice on your face and anything else that hurts and just take it easy."

"My homework assignments—"

"I'll get your assignments and drop them off on my way home." It was almost comical: one minute, she didn't give a shit about anything; the next minute, she was worried about fucking homework assignments. He threw his jacket on and was pocketing his cigarettes when the memo underneath caught his eye. "There's a school dance for seniors next Saturday night."

"So?" She was struggling to get into her jacket before he looked up again.

"So I want you to go."

"You're kidding, right?"

"You said you have no friends; this'll give you a chance to make some. Maybe you'll have some fun."

"I'm not gonna make any friends, and I'm not gonna have any fun; I'm just gonna stand around all night feelin' like a jerk. I don't belong here; I don't fit in."

"I don't think you've tried."

"Oh, for chrissakes, gimme a break."

"You're going to that dance."

"But I work Saturday nights."

"I'm sure Mr. Antonelli can find someone to fill in. He's got almost two weeks."

"I can't afford to lose a whole day's pay."

"I'll make it up to you."

"I can't believe you're gonna make me do this."

"And I'm working security that night, so you'd better show up."

Jesus fucking Christ, she thought, how lucky can I get?

STILL DRESSED, MICKI WAS trying to fall asleep on top of the blanket. The only position that minimized the pain was lying on her back—which also happened to be the one position she found it almost impossible to sleep in. At least it was her day off from work.

Baker let himself into the apartment.

She sat up and grimaced.

"Did I wake you?" he asked.

Words clipped, she said, "Never fell asleep."

A strange, late-afternoon light filled the room. It accentuated the swelling and discoloration of her face, which had more fully taken form. His chest collapsed, and he could feel the weight of her eyes upon him.

"Y'got my homework?" she asked. It hurt to talk, the bruised ribs resenting the extra breath required.

"How bad does it hurt?" he asked.

Ignoring the pain, she stood up. "Bad enough."

"Do you want to go to the hospital?"

"For what? You're pissed at how I asked you for my homework, so now you're gonna knock me around some more?"

"Jesus! That's not what I meant! I just want to know if you're all right. If you think you need to see a doctor, I'll take you."

She looked away. "I'm fine. Don't need anything. Just wanna be left alone."

He handed her a folded piece of paper. "I'll stop by in the morning to give you a ride."

She opened up the single loose-leaf sheet and looked it over, then tossed it on the desk.

The ache in his chest grew. "If it makes you feel any better," he said, "you got a couple of nice shots in on me." When her eyes met his, he saw a glint of satisfaction in them.

On his way out the door, he paused to glance back. Despite the considerable damage he'd done, he'd still acted with some measure of restraint. He was confident no bones were broken, just badly bruised like the rest of her. But standing all alone in the middle of the room, she looked fragile.

"Jesus!" she said. "What're you waiting for?"

Lowering his eyes, he left.

THE PAIN SETTLED IN for the night and, unable to sleep, Micki thought about the pills in her jacket. Constantly. In fact, one of the reasons she wanted to go back to juvi—the one reason she wouldn't tell Baker—was fear of picking up her old habit again.

It was windy outside, and the tree in front of the streetlight was casting moving shadows on the wall and ceiling. Lying on her back, she was watching the shifting shapes, thinking about the time she'd been so badly cut and slashed that Willy had finally shot her up to give her some relief. And though she threw up the first time, thinking, the hell with this shit, he'd still waited a couple of days before shooting her up again—trying not to get her hooked. But it was too late. That second time— the last time he'd done it for her—the rush was incredible; the high, so sweet.

It wasn't until about a week after he'd skipped town—when the reality of being all alone had sunk in—that she'd scored her first fix for herself, secretly hoping to suffer the fate of many a junkie. Twice, in fact, she'd thought she'd taken enough smack to OD—only to survive with a bigger habit.

She smiled sadly into the darkness—she couldn't do anything right.

JUST PRIOR TO LEAVING the school, Baker called the station house and caught Gould in the middle of some paperwork. When Gould heard about Micki's request to return to Heyden, he said, "So you're off the hook; take the other kid and run."

But Baker said he suspected this was simply more of Micki's self-destructiveness. And while he argued his point, Gould refrained from asking why he cared. Instead, he steered the conversation around to Cynthia. "Call her, Jim," he said. "It doesn't sound like she wanted to stop seeing you altogether. If you still want her, fight for her. And tell her you're keepin' the kid; that should score you some points."

But later, alone in his living room, Baker wondered why he'd argued with Cynthia in the first place, why he'd been unable to admit—even to himself—that from the moment Malone had mentioned the boy as an alternative, he'd known he'd stick it out with Micki. If Cynthia had said "black," he would've said "white." If she'd said it was night, he would've argued it was day—even if the moon was shining right outside the window.

He threw back his drink, the captain's parting comment ringing in his ears: "Mark my words, Jim, you're going to regret this."

THE NEXT MORNING, BAKER found Micki in so much pain that he told her to stay home. But when he returned to her apartment that afternoon, he paused outside in the hallway: she was talking to someone:

"Forget it, okay? I hurt too much, and I gotta get ready for work."

"So? I don't havta pork ya; y'could still get me off—"

Baker opened the door and got his first look at Rick: baggy jeans that were way too long, an old green T-shirt that was much too short, and a denim jacket that looked like it would never close over the bulge of his belly. Nothing like what he would've pictured as Micki's type.

Glasses slightly askew, Rick announced, "It's the fuzz."

"Get your ass out of here," Baker said.

Rick's smirk broadened. "Or what?"

"Or I'll kick it out of here."

"Yeah, right. Like—"

But as soon as Baker advanced, the boy edged his way along the wall, eyes darting between Baker and Micki.

Baker slammed the door after him. "What the fuck do you want with a putz like that? He's a selfish prick, a real asshole."

"It's better than nothing."

"That's bullshit."

"Oh yeah?" Eyes glittering with a bitter heat, she said, "How would *you* know. Look at you—like you've ever gone without a girlfriend if you wanted one."

And in an instant, Baker saw it all very clearly: Rick was playing off of this deep insecurity of hers. She was nothing more than a trophy to him—a conquest. The more he could take advantage of her, the bigger his ego would become.

"You're going to tell me you like this guy?" he asked.

Half rolling her eyes, she looked away.

"Are you at least attracted to him?" When all he got in return was a smoldering glare, he shook his head and pulled out some papers. "Here are your new homework assignments. Did you finish yesterday's?"

"No."

"No?"

"No, *sir*," she said.

"Did you at least start them?"

"No, sir."

"But you're going to work."

"I need the money."

"If you can go to work, you should've been able to get some homework done instead of talking to that shithead."

"He just got here a few minutes ago."

"That's not the point."

"It doesn't matter anymore."

"What doesn't matter anymore?"

"Anything."

When Baker spoke again, his voice was much more relaxed. "Listen to me, Micki, you can't afford to give up, do you understand that? If you give up, no one's going to save you again; there won't be another Sergeant Kelly to come along and rescue you again."

She looked away. "I gotta go. I'm late."

He felt a dull pain around his heart.

She put on her sneakers and continued getting ready. But judging from the difficulty she was having, she was hurting worse than the day before.

"You sure you'll be able to work?" he asked.

"It's too late now to tell Mr. Antonelli I can't."

"Well, you're not to go to school tomorrow." And he stepped behind her to help her on with her jacket.

She avoided looking at him as she left.

THERE WAS A SMALL brown paper bag on the table. Inside, Baker discovered a tube of cover-up make-up that promised to hide unsightly blemishes and provide a healthy, overall glow. Either Micki had forgotten to apply it before leaving or had felt too uncomfortable to put it on in front of him. He placed the tube back in the bag, then started a half-hearted search of her apartment.

TONY HAD BEEN SO wrapped up in his argument with Sal that he'd let an order of manicotti burn. Plumes of steam rising all around her, Micki was now vigorously scrubbing off the charred remains that were welded to the metal casserole dish. As she swiped the side of her upper arm across her sweaty face, she thought about the make-up she'd left sitting on the table. Like wet paint, it would've been dripping down with the sweat—a nasty beige mess getting all over everything.

Mr. Antonelli came in to find out what was taking so long with the customer's order. He happened to glance over at Micki, and eyed her face with alarm.

"Got in a fight," she said. It was what she always said when he gave her that look.

"Is-a no good-a," he replied hotly. "Too many fights-a."

She shrugged, then looked back at her work. And though she could feel him watching her, she wouldn't look up again.

She heard the kitchen door swinging back and forth after he left.

MICKI WENT BACK TO school on Thursday, which was also Halloween. She wore the make-up she'd bought, though it was only partially successful at camouflaging the bruising.

Baker was working the main entrance and said, "Go into the office, Micki. I'll be in before the bell rings."

He came in much sooner than that, however, towing a boy whose long brown hair reached the breast pockets of his khaki army jacket. Faded fatigues and black military-style boots completed his outfit, but he was not a happy soldier. Baker was gripping his arm with one hand, the gun he'd tried to smuggle into school in the other.

"Go to class *now*," Baker said to Micki. "And stay out of trouble."

But it was just the beginning of what was to be a long and difficult day, kids spraying mace in the halls and vandalizing school property. And to top it off, there was a rumor that a large group of black students from Queens Central High was going to descend upon the late session, targeting the white kids as they left—the latest in a series of retaliatory events that had taken place since the infamous, curtailed basketball game. Just last week, three white members of the Newbridge High team had been suspended for beating up a black Central High player as he waited at a bus stop. The most recent game had been closed to spectators.

Before they left the school, students were warned over the loudspeaker to cover up hair with hats or hoods and vacate the premises as quickly as possible; no lingering outside would be tolerated. Police cars surrounded the building, and Baker stayed through the second security shift. But after all the precautions, nothing actually happened.

And though he really just wanted to kick back with a few beers and watch TV, Baker returned to Queens that night after Mr. Antonelli had called—as requested—to let him know when Micki had about an hour's worth of work left. Unaware of the arrangement, Micki walked out of Bel Canto's alley only to stop dead in her tracks: Baker, smoking a cigarette, was leaning against his car, which he'd parked right out front. He had the window open and the radio on, two sports commentators talking about the Ali-Foreman fight—the "Rumble in the Jungle"—that had taken place earlier. Baker straightened up and opened the door.

"Get in," he said.

"Jesus Christ! What the hell am I supposed t'have done now?"

"Nothing. Just get in."

A car full of teenagers drove by and threw an egg, which broke and splattered on the hood of the Camaro.

"Great," he said and threw his cigarette down, grinding it out on the pavement. "Will you just get in, Micki, so I can drive you home?"

"Drive me home? I only live a block away."

"But there's all kinds of bullshit going on tonight. I just saw some kid being chased and hit with a sock full of chalk. Stupid as it sounds, it hurts to get whacked with one of those."

"So?" But as she looked around, she noticed the shaving cream and eggs all over the sidewalk, the walls, the cars...

"*So*—you're not healed much yet."

She stared at him. Was he serious? Only three days ago, he was ready to beat her within an inch of her life. Now he was worried she'd be hit with a bagful of chalk? She got into the car, a painful maneuver in and of itself, then placed the container of leftover ravioli she'd taken—still hot—on her lap.

"Put your seatbelt on," he said.

"For one block?"

The aroma of marinara sauce filled the air, and Baker's stomach growled. He turned the radio off. "Put the damn seatbelt on," he repeated. Then he made a U-turn, drove down the street, and double-parked in front of her building. He watched her go in, and waited until her light went on before pulling away— thinking about having to wash the damn egg off his car so it wouldn't damage the finish.

By the weekend, Micki's pain had substantially subsided. She took full advantage of the free Sunday: sleeping late, lounging around in her nightshirt, and doing homework in spurts while daydreaming in between—mostly about the football player. She wondered if he was going to the dance. Every once in a while, she'd see him in the hall during passing. And he'd smile.

She looked through her clothes, then took the 7 train to Main Street, Flushing, in search of some cheap long-sleeved black shirts and a new pair of jeans—*black* jeans. Just yesterday she'd seen a boy on a bicycle wearing some, and she wanted a pair. But as she made the rounds of the numerous army-navy stores, she found that virtually all of the jeans they sold were blue. She spent almost two hours searching until she came across what she wanted, trying them on as quickly as possible so she wouldn't have to look at the half-naked woman staring down at her from a poster on the tiny dressing room's wall.

On her way home, she stopped at Sunny's to buy more shampoo—then changed her mind and went to the drugstore to splurge on the good stuff.

THE PHONE RANG. SHIT! He'd just sat down with a beer and some pretzels to watch the basketball game. His voice purposely gruff, he said, "Hello?"

"Did I catch you at a bad time?"

Cynthia! "Hold on a sec." Baker hurried to turn off the TV, then got back on the line. "How are you?"

"I'm okay. How are *you*?"

"Fine. I'm fine." There was a split-second pause, then: "Cyn, I've missed you— really missed you. You have no idea how good it is to hear your voice."

"Actually, once I tell you why I'm calling, I'm not so sure you'll feel that way."

His mind raced: what was she going to say? That she was moving to Los Angeles? Marrying that asshole actor?

"I'm pregnant."

Mouth hanging open, he stood there with the phone pressed against his ear.

"Hello? Jim? Are you there?"

HE RESTED HIS FOREHEAD on his fingertips. "Yeah, yeah, I'm still here. I'm just— shocked." When Cynthia didn't offer anything more, he asked, "Are you saying this is mine?"

"It has to be."

"But that's impossible; you're on the pill."

"But I'd forgotten to take it for a few days when I was away, so we were using the condoms."

"All right, so we were still safe then—"

"Nothing's perfect!" she shot back. "Even the pill isn't a hundred percent! Nothing's a hundred percent except not doing it!"

"But we've hardly been having any sex. We haven't even slept together in over a week."

"Seriously? Figure it out! It happened about a month ago!"

This can't be real, he thought, this just can't be real. With a nasty edge, he asked, "Are you sure it isn't Mr. LA's?"

"I'm not even going to dignify that with an answer."

Baker hung his head and took a deep breath. "I'm sorry. I shouldn't have said that. So—so you're going to get an abortion, right? I mean, you always said if this happened, you'd get one."

"I know what I said, but now I'm not so sure. This isn't easy, y'know. It's strange, but there's a part of me that wants to keep it."

His palms were sweating, and he was getting stabbing pains in his chest. A baby. She wanted to have the fucking baby. Maybe. Jesus Christ! A million times they'd talked about how neither one of them wanted kids. He'd really meant it while she, apparently, had not.

"Jim?"

"Uh-huh. Well"—he stood up very straight—"listen, Cyn, I don't want you to worry about anything. Whatever you decide, I'm here for you. If you want an abortion, I'll help pay for it. I'll even go with you; I don't want you going through that alone. And, um"—he took another long, deep breath—"if you want to keep the baby, I'll—I'll help support it and, y'know, do the best I can."

"Thanks, Jim."

"You call me if you need anything, okay?"

She smiled a sad smile he couldn't see. "Sure."

They said goodbye, and Baker, very gently, returned the receiver to its cradle. Then he went over to the couch, sat down, and stared at the blank screen of the TV.

No sooner had Cynthia hung up than the tears started again. Her eyes were red and swollen. And she had a photo shoot in the morning. The doctor had given her the news back on Friday, but, not wanting to fall apart over the phone, she'd waited before sharing it. And yet, she was no more together now than she had been then.

She pushed away some hair that had become matted to her face, then placed her palm against her belly. Totally flat, it betrayed nothing of the process going on inside, a process that could change the course of her life and was bombarding her with feelings she'd never anticipated. Always careful, she'd never worried that much; the chance of getting pregnant had seemed so infinitesimally small. And once abortion had become legal, there'd been a lot less to fear. But while she still firmly believed a soul didn't permanently attach itself to a body until that body breathed its first breath outside the womb, the magic of a possible life could no longer be so casually brushed aside. Maybe it was hormonally induced, this desire to protect the tiny cells growing inside her. Thoughts of a little baby—especially a little baby girl—seemed so precious and bittersweet.

Her fingers, wet with tears, extinguished the candles she'd lit. Then she curled up in a ball, hands in fists against her collarbones. Overhead, her upstairs neighbor's high heels clicked across the ceiling. And back. Then across once more before leaving her in silence—alone with the sound of her own sobbing. How could Jim not know that what she wanted most from him right now—more than anything—was the warmth and comfort of his arms around her?

Chapter 13

I T WAS PARENT/TEACHER NIGHT at the high school, but Baker was only there to oversee security. He'd told Micki that morning that he would meet with her teachers the following Thursday afternoon—Open School Day. She'd seemed less than enthusiastic.

"Is there a problem?" he'd asked.

"No, so why do you have to talk to them anyway?"

Unfortunately, her objections merely piqued his curiosity. But that had soon been overshadowed by the phone call he'd received from Gould: there was going to be an opening in the homicide unit—Ritter was retiring.

As Baker now watched parents filing in, all he could think about was how long he'd hungered for a spot on that squad. Given his current problems with IAD, even if he were still working with Gould, he would never have been considered for the position. But to be doing this bullshit instead, to be so completely out of the running…

When the evening was over, the school finally emptied and locked, Baker got in his car and took the Grand Central Parkway to the Triborough Bridge, heading for the thruway. Cloaked in the night's deep shadows, there would be long stretches where only his own headlights would illuminate the pavement. He listened to the drone of the engine and the tires against the asphalt. He tried to empty his mind. But he kept coming back to Gould's call and then, ironically, the lack of Cynthia's. He hadn't heard a thing from her since Sunday—had no idea which way she was leaning.

He took a deep breath: he'd gotten her pregnant. He could almost feel his shoulders broaden. But the reality of it, the repercussions…

He switched on the radio, then slowed for a toll plaza, rolling down his window to the opening strains of Steely Dan's "Midnight Cruiser." Stopped beside a booth, waiting for his change, he turned up the volume while the Camaro trembled in his grip, grumbling and murmuring, impatient to be released into the blackness up ahead. Then he accelerated back to highway speed and shifted into overdrive, music blasting, miles slipping away, the path before him open wide. But the once familiar thruway seemed foreign tonight—not that anything felt the same anymore. The world had quietly changed while he—still traveling down the same road, waiting for his moment to arrive—had carelessly missed his exit.

He hurtled into the darkness at eighty-five miles per hour. Going nowhere fast.

Chapter 14

NOW THAT SHE WAS actually standing at the top of the stairs, watching other kids go inside in pairs or groups, Micki's stomach started to twist. The senior dance. Who the fuck was she kidding?

Baker, having caught a glimpse of her through an open door, went outside to meet her. "Why don't you come in," he said. "There's nothing happening out here."

"Can't I just go home? I'm so out of place—just look at 'em all." Underneath her jacket, she was wearing a new long-sleeved button-down shirt, her leather vest, and the new jeans. When she'd left her apartment, she'd felt pretty good. But now she was terribly aware of how the other girls were put together: make-up, earrings, colored bell-bottoms, short dresses or miniskirts that were barely visible beneath wool coats… At best, she was dressed like one of the boys.

"I think you look fine," Baker said. Then, quoting a fashion magazine Cynthia loved to poke fun at, he added, "Basic black is right for any occasion." And he grinned.

But Micki didn't smile. "Look, I showed up and gave it a shot, so why don't you let me go home now?"

"How can you say you gave it a shot when you haven't even gone in yet?"

"What's the point? It's not like anybody's gonna dance with me."

About to answer, Baker looked at her—*really* looked at her. Like she was a girl. Her hair was soft and shiny, and she'd trimmed her bangs into a choppy, raggedy fringe. But there was nothing to accentuate her eyes, and her face was still faintly discolored here and there because she'd stopped wearing the concealer she'd bought—the shade hadn't matched very well. And though she'd been spared the typical teenage scourge of acne, the old scars, raised and pale, were like misplaced threads against the fabric of her skin.

Regrettably, her clothes weren't helping: heavy and functional, her black leather jacket was anything but cute or chic, and her old, worn-out sneakers detracted from the new black jeans—her big attempt to dress up. She was what Cynthia's friends would call a fashion disaster. And nothing could be done about it now. Letting her leave would be a mistake, but he should never have made her come here in the first place.

"Y'know what?" he said, "You're already wrong. Because if no one else dances with you, then I will."

"What?"

He walked to the row of doors and held one open.

IN THE LOBBY, THE music was reduced to a dampened throbbing of bass in between loud, intermittent surges of rock 'n' roll that traveled down the building's western corridors whenever the doors to the gym were opened. For safety purposes, the entire east wing had been cordoned off by a large metal gate. Baker took Micki to the security office and unlocked it so she could leave her jacket there. After he'd secured it again, he escorted her further down the hall.

The divider between the boys' and girls' sections had been retracted to create a huge dance floor. In one corner, a boy was playing deejay, changing the records that were blaring out over a rigged-up PA system. In another area, a table was covered with soda, punch, and cookies, a mountain of coats piled behind it. There was a huge mass of bodies gyrating in the middle of the floor while numerous little groups of boys or girls huddled together, laughing and shooting snotty glances at each other.

Micki scanned the crowd. None of the kids she knew from the science program were there. "How soon can I leave?"

"What?" The music was so loud Baker couldn't hear without bending down so his ear was close to her lips.

"When can I get out of here?"

"Not till it's over. I'm going to drive you home."

She did not look happy.

Before he left, he said, "I'll be out front and in the hallway mostly, but I'll check in from time to time."

She wondered if that was meant as a reassurance or a warning.

BARBARA ANDERSON AND TOM Dawber, both of whom worked the late shift, were assisting Baker, several teachers acting as chaperones. The teachers were in charge of keeping things orderly inside the gym while the security team monitored the entrance, accessible hall areas, and bathrooms. Most notorious was the staircase at the farthest end of the corridor. While the actual steps were gated and locked, the doors to the stairwell itself were not. It was a favorite spot for couples to make out or smoke. The bathrooms also saw their fair share of smoking—and not just tobacco.

During the evening, Baker was kept busy confiscating contraband, including cigarettes (which he immediately flushed down the toilet) and a pint bottle of Southern Comfort (which he promptly poured down the sink). But Micki had drifted back into the crowd of kids lining the dance area till she was leaning against the wall near the pile of coats. A black shadow against beige tiles, she was watching other kids dance.

Yet the deejay was playing a lot of great songs, mixing it up between old and new, mostly loud, driving rhythms that made her body want to move. And for the slow songs, couples held each other close, awkwardly swaying back and forth. She wondered what that felt like. The football player was always dancing with some pretty girl whose long hair looked like a flowing sheet of brown silk. But once, when he was passing by, he caught Micki's eye and flashed a smile over his date's shoulder.

Micki took to watching the clock.

IT WAS ALMOST TEN, and the dance was nearly over. Micki, who'd been sitting on the floor since midway through the evening, stood up and stretched her legs. Baker entered the gym and went over to Miss Rindell, one of the teacher chaperones, who then went over to the deejay. But as Baker headed toward Micki, the teacher—nicknamed the Spiderwoman because of her short torso and long, spindly arms and legs—ran to catch up with him. She clutched at his arm, and he paused, bending over to hear what she was saying. When he shook his head no and pointed to Micki, the woman's smile disappeared.

The music stopped, and it was sharply quieter, the deejay announcing he was about to play the final song. He encouraged all of the couples to get out on the dance floor one more time.

"Man," Baker said to Micki, "the last thing I'd want to do is dance"—he tilted his head in the direction of Miss Rindell—"with that one."

"Can we go now?" Micki asked.

"Not yet. I still have to clear the place out. Plus, I think I owe you a dance." The Association's song "Cherish" began to play.

Her face went blank. "I thought you were kidding."

"No."

Color rose in her cheeks. "Forget it."

The corners of his mouth crept upward. "I can't. I'm a man of my word. Besides, you're supposed to be the reason I'm not dancing with the Spiderwoman."

"No—really—I can't. I—I don't know how to dance slow."

"It's easy; you just follow me." He extended his hand, but she didn't take it. Staring down, he asked, "Are you afraid?"

Her eyes turned dark.

His appeared to be laughing.

She placed her right hand in his left, and, with nearly a foot of space between them, they moved into the crowd of dancing couples. Overly conscious of the subtle weight of his palm on her waist, Micki could feel a tiny trickle of sweat edging its way down her back. Baker—though wearing a full suit, complete with tie—looked dry and comfortable.

When she stepped on one of his feet, she looked up sharply, but he seemed to be amused. After the third time, he leaned over and said, "This works better if you're closer." And before she could object, he'd pulled her to him, placing her right hand on his back to match her left, which was barely touching his jacket.

Though she'd stiffened, she tried to force herself to relax—and was only partially successful. Heart fluttering wildly, she prayed he couldn't feel it through the numerous layers of clothes. She tried to focus on the music that was playing—a song of unrequited love. But then her heart started to hurt: no one would ever feel that way about her; no one would ever hold her in their arms the way Baker was doing now. And he didn't even mean it. This was something of a joke to him. She could tell. Still, the scent of his aftershave and the sensation of his body moving with hers were sparking something. She began to feel distressed.

Baker, meanwhile, was reminded of when he'd danced with some distantly related young cousin at a wedding several years ago. Easily as short, Micki was just as shy and nervous. And between her new clothes and (if his nose didn't deceive him) Clairol's Herbal Essence shampoo, she'd clearly had some expectations for the night. But she'd spent the evening alone, just as she'd predicted.

Without realizing it, he held her a bit more tenderly.

For Micki, the music ended both too soon and not soon enough. Kids started battling for coats, and Baker took her back to the security office to wait till he was done. As he was leaving, he used his chin to indicate the refrigerator, saying, "Help yourself to a soda if you want." The door closed behind him.

She could hear the noise in the hallway from kids exiting the school, but the office itself was still. Windows dark and mirror-like, it felt kind of eerie. Inside the refrigerator, she found a carton of milk, two cans of Coke, a Tab, and a Sugar Free Dr. Pepper. She closed the door without taking anything.

Once the gym had finally been cleared, the teacher and students from the clean-up committee proceeded to take over with the custodian. Baker locked the front doors and began his check of the peripheral areas. As he approached the accessible stairwell, he could already smell the pot, a girl's voice seeping out into the hall with it.

"No! How many times do I have to say it? If the stuff's so great, how come you're not really smoking it yourself?"

"'Cause the first hits are the best, and I want you to have 'em. C'mon, baby"—the boy's voice had gone from wheedling to whining—"it'll make you feel real mellow."

Loosening his tie, Baker sighed. He'd had enough babysitting for one night; he wanted to go home and get out of his suit. "Party's over," he announced as he burst through the door. "Just give me the joint and you can go."

The boy hesitated a little too long, and the girl, who'd shrunk behind him, whispered, "Go on, Ben; give it to him. I wanna get out of here." Slowly, with a look that was meant to let Baker know just how uncool he was, the joint was handed over, and the couple hurried out.

A quick glance showed no one else on the landing, and Baker moved on, returning to the lobby. But he was already regretting not treating the incident with greater gravity: alcohol was one thing, but drugs were something else. He was about to go flush the joint away when Barbara Anderson appeared, telling him the girls' room was clear. Seconds later, Dawber showed up, saying he'd checked the boys' bathroom. With the school now locked and secure, the two guards were heading out—and Baker was free to leave. The custodian would shut the school down completely once the clean-up committee was done.

Alone in the lobby, Baker pulled the confiscated item from his pocket—a nice, fat joint and probably very good stuff; the boy had been so reluctant to part with it. He ran his fingers down the tightly rolled paper, then palmed it. And felt a small surge of adrenaline. Looking around, he started walking, then turned the corner. He passed the security office, then the gyms until, at the end of the hall, the stairwell door clanged shut behind him. Shadowy and silent, smelling strongly from before, the empty enclosure seemed far removed from the rest of the world.

He looked at the joint again. Some strange kid's pot. "Fuck it," he said, and pulled out his lighter.

THE SCENT OF MARIJUANA followed Baker back to the office, and Micki's eyes grew wide. But the look he gave her told her to mind her own business. They went to his car and got on the parkway, where he drove more cautiously, even though he wasn't feeling all that high. Just a little disappointed. But then, he'd only wanted to take the edge off anyway. Yet he did feel strange, like a giant man in a tiny car. And his hand was almost numb on the steering wheel.

What if the pot had been laced with something?

They drove from the Grand Central Parkway onto the Long Island Expressway, at which point he turned on the radio. Ominous and dark, the church organ chords from Elton John's "Funeral for a Friend" went crawling up the windows like demonic vines of ivy. He shut the music off, and the car was at peace again. But after they exited the LIE, the local streets appeared unusually long and wide.

Shooting him a harsh look, Micki said, "Y'know you're driving really slow."

"Yeah?" He glanced down at the speedometer, which read all of six miles per hour. He was high as a kite. Red, yellow, and green, the traffic signals looked like huge, brilliant Christmas-tree ornaments. He skated right through a red light, too entranced by its lustrous ruby glow to stop.

"Maybe we should pull over for a while," Micki said.

"I'll be all right; we're almost there." But his voice sounded much lower in pitch, and very slow—though Micki didn't appear to notice anything odd at all.

A short ways past her building, he pulled to the curb and got out. He looked at the lousy job he'd done parking and found this very funny, but didn't laugh. Instead, he said, "I'm not feeling too good. I need to rest a few minutes at your place." The words sounded so serious—so far away. In fact, he wasn't sure he'd actually said them until he heard her reply, "Okay."

Only, he just stood there, staring at the car, unable to recall what it was he was supposed to be doing. Taking hold of his arm, Micki gently guided him toward the stoop. His long wool coat was open and billowed out as the wind blew down the street.

They started up the flight of stairs inside. Baker, hoping to clear his head, tried to silently count the steps he was taking. But before they were even halfway down the hall, he'd lost track. And when they'd reached her apartment, she unlocked the door while he waited behind and pulled out his wallet—to stare at it. Then he stared at the badge inside. Until, like a revelation, he remembered his promise to compensate her for the night's lost wages.

She flicked on the light switch and jumped as the one functioning overhead bulb blew out. Then she stepped inside and left Baker in the doorway, still fumbling around, staring at his money with all those teeny, tiny intricate lines and scrollwork. He'd never noticed how pretty they were. There were two twenties, a five, and three singles. Just how many hours did she work a day? Times minimum wage, which was what? So was eight enough? Twenty, too much? Overheated and sweaty, the math problem was a royal pain in the ass. He decided to go with twenty. What the fuck.

Micki turned on the desk lamp and went back to shut the door. Baker had already dropped the money on her bed and his coat on top. "I'm going to wash up," he heard himself say as he crossed the floor.

He locked himself in the bathroom.

WEEKS AGO, MICKI HAD bought a lightbulb to replace the first one that had burned out. But she'd never bothered to install it. The ceiling was so high that, even standing on the table, she couldn't quite reach. But now, with just the sixty-watt desk lamp working, she couldn't put it off any longer. She took a dinette chair and turned it around to use as a stepladder. Then she took the two largest textbooks she had—history and calculus—and stacked them on top of the Formica. Bulb in hand, she climbed onto the table, which swayed doubtfully beneath her. Very carefully, she stepped up onto the books.

THE BATHROOM WAS SO fucking tiny! Baker loosened his tie some more and looked at himself in the mirror. The perceptual distortions were fading, but it wouldn't be a good idea to drive home just yet. Call someone? Who? Who could he trust? A taxi? Either way, he'd have to leave the Camaro. But if he waited around just a little while longer, he'd probably be able to drive himself.

He looked for the sink and remembered there was none. Never had been. If he wanted to splash water on his face, he'd have to use the sink in the kitchen. About to step out, he unlocked the door, only to pause: he was getting an erection; was suddenly horny as hell. He had to either stay put in this claustrophobic, little bathroom or get the hell out of her apartment as fast as he could.

After a few slow breaths, he turned the knob.

WITH A FINAL TWIST, the new bulb was in place. Micki, standing perfectly still atop the tiny tower of books, was waiting for the table to stop swaying. The initial two textbooks hadn't been enough, and she'd had to climb down and add the physics one, as well. Even so, she'd barely reached on tiptoe.

Rushing up behind her, Baker grabbed her by the waist. "Christ! You could break your neck like that! Why didn't you wait and ask me to do that for you?"

She shrugged, thinking, 'Cause you're too fucking stoned. And she let him help her down. But when her feet were planted safely on the floor, he didn't let go.

Inside his head, a voice was screaming at him to get out, and he willed his hands to release her. She tensed as she tried to step away, but was restrained.

His world was exploding, the walls of the room bleeding into pools of iridescent shadow. High above, he was hanging from the ceiling, looking down.

He saw his hands still encircling her waist, heard the sharp intake of her breath as his lips gently kissed the side of her neck. He felt something inside him give. He nuzzled her ear. "Do you want me to stop?" His large hands, now resting on her belt, felt the slight expansion and contraction as she breathed, her small body muscular and lean, so unlike that of Cynthia, who was tall and thin but soft; so unlike the kind of body that normally turned him on. And yet he could barely stop himself from ripping off her clothes. It took every ounce of self-control he could muster from his drug-addled brain not to act like the animal he felt himself to be.

But she had yet to answer. So strong yet so tender, his touch had sent her pulse racing—a shimmering, visceral excitement spreading like fire throughout her body. And still she imagined herself telling him to fuck off, imagined wriggling out of his grasp and telling him to leave—to get out.

For he needed to get the fuck out.

"Hmm?" he asked again. "Do you want me to stop?" Shifting a little, he pressed himself against her side so she could feel his hardness.

After that, neither one of them moved. Until she slowly closed her eyes and shook her head no. But she could feel her heart breaking. Like a part of her was dying.

She felt his hands glide down over her jeans, then around to the front of her thighs, searching and rubbing till they traveled up, over her ribs, to briefly cup her breasts before gently unbuttoning her new black shirt.

AT FIRST, BAKER WAS so aroused he thought he was going to come before things even got underway. But then his body sank into a strangely disconnected state, making him believe he could last all night. The world seemed warm and fuzzy while his mind was full of fog. But the drugs were wearing off, and he eventually arrived at a singular and unfamiliar place, feeling like he'd woken up from a dream—only to discover it was real. And at the edge of his consciousness, intruding like the unwelcome guest that it was, was the awareness that he was doing something very wrong.

Arms straightened to raise his torso, he stared down at her. Her eyes were closed, and her hands, after slipping down from his back, were resting on his forearms. Greenish-yellow remnants of the two-week-old bruises were visible on her body as well as her face. They blended into the shadows cast by the weak glow of the desk lamp. Now and then, like some austere amulet keeping watch, her plain silver cross shined when it caught a bit of light as she moved.

His eyes followed the curves of her breasts—which looked like those of a fully grown woman. But she was really just a kid—his legal ward, no less. And while his gaze traveled back to her face, he was aware of the fine coat of sweat on his skin and the sound of cars passing on the street below. His rhythm faltered.

Micki opened her eyes, and found herself looking into his. A chill ran through her, and she wanted to cover her nakedness. But he'd already brought her to climax—enjoying it, apparently, unlike Rick, who usually acted like it was a chore if he could even bring himself to bother. And though Baker's passion seemed to have cooled along with his high, she wanted to make him come, wanted him to leave so she could be alone again—untouched.

Baker stopped moving. He looked like he was about to say something. But she closed her eyes and slid her hands down his arms. And while her mind went off to hide in some dark, safe place, she felt herself become one of the girls in those pictures she'd seen. Lightly touching the insides of her thighs, her fingers started moving up. Slowly. Sensually. And it was working; he was getting hard again, hips driving. When her hands reached her breasts, he threw his body back down on hers, thrusting harder and faster until he came with an intensity he hadn't felt in a long, long time—moans loud, body shuddering.

AFTERWARD, THE AWKWARDNESS WAS unbearable, every moment prolonging the act an excruciating eternity. It was embarrassing to lie there, legs still spread apart, while he sat up and held the base of the condom so he could withdraw. Arms crossed over her chest, she stared blankly toward the window. And as soon as he went to throw the rubber away, she grabbed her nightshirt from under the pillow and put it on. Knees drawn up, arms wrapped around tight, she sat on the bed while he quickly dressed.

He picked up his coat from where it had landed on the floor and said, "I need to get some cigarettes." But she was staring into the darkness on the other side of the apartment, the desk lamp, backlighting her huddled figure, making her look to be all of about twelve years old.

And not a single moment could ever be undone.

Barely able to breathe and stone-cold sober, Baker turned away. And left.

But Micki didn't budge—except to rock a little back and forth. She knew it was his car door she heard slamming, knew he wasn't coming back. Finally, she got up to turn off the little light.

It was then that she saw the twenty-dollar bill where it had fallen to the floor.

Chapter 15

No sooner had Baker reached the Manhattan side of the Fifty-Ninth Street Bridge than he turned around and headed back to Queens, parking in the exact same spot he'd had before. Yet Micki's apartment was already dark. Paused on the building's front steps, he broke out in a cold sweat. What the hell was he going to say? He stood on the stoop with the wind kicking up around him, the night weighing heavy in the air. And then a souped-up car gunned by, engine roaring, tires squealing as it fishtailed around a corner.

Head hung low, he turned away, got back in the Camaro, and left.

Sunday was drowning in booze, a river of whiskey flowing steady from the night before. But anytime Baker put the bottle down for too long, he'd see Micki in those moments afterward, hugging her knees to her chest and looking too young, too vulnerable. Looking like someone he should never have touched. The sky was already growing dark, and he hadn't checked in on her once. God only knew what she was doing—maybe shooting up. Or getting smashed, like he was. Too drunk to drive over and see, he drank even more.

But as night descended in earnest on the cold Manhattan streets, he got up from the recliner and staggered toward the window, a terrifying cry of despair welling up from the depths of his being. When it threatened to lay bare the ugly mire that was churning underneath, it was swiftly silenced by yet another long drink. But not for long. He wiped his mouth on his shoulder before lowering the bottle, desperate eyes staring back from the dark pane of glass. Transfixed by the ghostly, ill-defined reflection, he watched as he raised the bottle to his lips again.

He looked away and grunted. He really needed to talk to someone; needed to confess; needed to get it off his chest that he was a self-righteous bastard who'd done the very thing he'd sworn up and down he never would. But who could he tell? If Malone or anyone in IAD ever got wind of this, Micki would be sent back to Heyden in a heartbeat; she would end up paying for his mistake. And his career? That would be over, too. Finished. Finito.

He gulped down more liquor, put the bottle on the table, and picked up his pack of Camels. With a cigarette dangling from his mouth, he fumbled with the book of matches and finally lit one. Jeez, Micki would have to be completely mindless not to recognize his situation. If she chose to take advantage of it, his authority over her was shot. He froze, the match burning brightly in his grip, fingers getting hot as the tiny flame danced its way down the cardboard stick. Maybe she'd planned this all along. He lit the cigarette and waved out the match. That was insane. It would mean that everything she'd ever said or done had been a calculated act of deception.

He picked up the bottle and snorted: it never mattered where he started—this was where he always ended up.

THREE HOURS LATER, BAKER stopped drinking and lay down to sleep; he still had to face the kid at school in the morning.

"The kid"—it suddenly sounded strange. Last night, when he'd danced with her so innocently, he'd viewed her as a child. Later, in his horny, drugged-up state, he'd—conveniently—viewed her the way she liked to view herself: as an adult. She did, after all, live alone with nearly all of the responsibilities. But she wasn't an adult. Not really. And certainly not with him. How he was going to make her see that, he wasn't exactly sure.

SUNK INSIDE A HEAVY, lifeless sleep, Micki didn't wake till almost ten on Sunday—a record for her. But she stayed in bed until she dozed off again.

At one thirty in the afternoon she got up, head hurting when she moved it too quickly: too much sleep. And yet all she could think about was crawling underneath the covers again. Or getting high. It was one or the other. Or both. There was money under the mattress, enough for a dime bag, but she could practically hear Baker calling her a junkie and a whore. Jacket on her lap, she sat on the floor and searched for the pills floating around in the lining. She located three and tried to move them back toward the hole in the pocket. But it wasn't as easy as she'd thought it would be. She considered ripping the damn things out, but then simply stared at the jacket as if it were a broken toy.

Tired of doing nothing, she pushed herself up and looked at the clock, the hours stacked ahead in aimless succession. She got dressed and went outside. Cold and grey. The unseasonable temperatures had come to an end. Without the extra lining zipped in, winter streamed through her jacket as if the leather weren't even there.

She reached the sidewalk and saw Rick approaching, a big grin on his face. He opened the foil-wrapped package he was carrying and said, "Look what I got."

Sweet and rich, the aroma of chocolate greeted her nose. "Brownies?"

With a lift of his chin, he said, "*Hash* brownies."

Her eyes lit up.

THEY WERE BACK IN her apartment, and Rick, looking proud, said, "I put in almost two grams a hash. I figger we can split it."

"Yeah, uh-huh." She cut the single slab of chocolate cake in half and put one part on the counter. She wrapped the other back up and handed it to him. "Get out."

"Wha—? But—"

"Just get the fuck out."

"Hey! I di—"

"GET—OUT." And she went to the door and opened it, eyes looking straight through him.

Face pale, Rick fiddled with the package in his hands. "Whatsa matta wit' ya?" He tried to smile. "Y'on the rag or somethin'?"

"Get the fuck out NOW."

In the hall, he turned and said, "Yer a fucked up bitch, y'know that?"

But she'd already slammed the door.

She returned to the giant brownie, breaking off a small piece and popping it in her mouth. It was awful. Even the rich, fudgy chocolate couldn't mask the taste of the hash. There was too much drug. Maybe it hadn't been mixed into the batter evenly. She wolfed it down as quickly as possible, then chased it with a glass of Coke.

Jacket and sneakers tossed off, she stretched out on the mattress with her hands behind her head so she could listen to the radio and wait for something to happen. But scenes from the previous night kept running around, over and over, in a never-ending loop. Only, she didn't want to think about it anymore, didn't want to remember what it felt like with him on top of her. Inside her. The way her heart had rolled up and stopped beating when she saw the money lying on the floor. He must've put it there afterward when she'd turned away as he'd gotten dressed. He'd paid her. Like a whore. Left it silently for services rendered. Recalling what she'd done at the very end, her face grew hot. Curiously, with everything that had happened, that was the one thing she really regretted.

The disc jockey introduced a song she hated. She turned off the radio and got up to get another glass of soda. But she managed only one step toward the kitchen before the room began to spin. Heart racing, body shaking and tingling, she thought she was falling. She felt sick. With what seemed like her last willful act, she stumbled back to bed.

Flat on the mattress, looking up, she watched the ceiling endlessly expanding, the brown spider-web cracks growing longer and wider. And sounds from the street reached her in a strange disorder of time: she could've sworn she heard two guys say goodbye, have a conversation, then say hello. She kept waiting for some wild and beautiful hallucinations: rainbows of colors or a burst of glittery stars. Instead, she was drifting in a pale, lusterless sea of hopeless detachment.

Not a muscle twitched as she lay there, paralyzed. And unbelievably aroused. She felt desperate to have sex with someone—anyone at all. In fact, someone was knocking. Rick. It could only be Rick. She heard him calling to her.

"C'mon, Micki! Let me in. You in dere?"

And as much as she despised him now, she wanted him to come in and fuck her. But she couldn't budge, couldn't utter a sound.

"Stupid bitch!" And he went away.

Hours later, she woke up in the dark, body stiff but able to move. Yet when she turned on the lamp, the apartment was shot through with danger, everything thrown into shadows and sharp, black corners, the furniture cold and disturbing in the faded light.

She switched on the radio, then sat on the bed, the music pouring out in a brilliant, bold escape from the magical little box. Prancing and shimmying, words and notes tumbled over each other as they danced across the floor, evaporating into air and disappearing into walls. And though she tried very hard to concentrate, things slipped away from one second to the next. By the end of a line of lyrics, she'd forgotten what the beginning was. Nothing made any sense.

Maybe the hash had done some kind of permanent brain damage.

She went back to sleep.

THE ALARM CLOCK WOKE her. Dry and crusted over, her eyelids were stuck together; her teeth, coated with fur. She felt as rumpled and grimy as the clothes she'd slept in. She crawled out of bed, unfolded her limbs, and, with the help of a chair, stood up. After a brief respite, she drank water, then coffee, did a half-assed workout, and showered. But the filmy sheath around her brain was receding at an agonizingly slow pace. Finally dressed, her jaw tightened as she stuffed Baker's money into her pocket. Maybe—if there was any justice in the world—he wouldn't be at school today.

BAKER HAD MANAGED ONLY fitful bouts of sleep. By the break of dawn, he'd given up entirely. Since then, he'd been scrutinizing everything from every possible angle until he was anything but the calm, controlled man he'd hoped to be. Looking out the office window, he saw Micki crossing from the top of the front stairs to the main doors. He went to his desk and ground the stub of his cigarette into the thick glass of the ashtray.

She walked in. "I don't want your damn money." She was holding out his twenty-dollar bill.

His brow furrowed.

"Fine," she said, and strode over to slam the cash down next to the cigarettes on his desk.

"Suit yourself." But he'd noticed the subtle differences: the thick speech, the imprecise motions. "Take off your jacket and push your sleeves up."

With rough, angry movements, she did what he asked, then held her arms out in front, palms up. But as soon as he reached for them, she stepped back. "Don't you touch me!" she hissed.

Heart thudding, he barely glanced at her veins. As if there weren't a million other places she could shoot up. "Turn around, Micki."

"Forget it."

"C'mon, it's just routine like always."

Warner and Marino came through the doorway.

"This is the last time I'm going to help you, Denny," Warner said. "You should've stayed late Friday to finish this and not be taking up my time while I'm on duty. It's—" But the two men froze: the tension between the cop and the kid was palpable.

"I don't care!" Micki said to Baker. "I don't want you touchin' me."

"What's the problem?" he asked.

"'What's the problem?'" she repeated. "*What's the problem?* I don't know if it's Mr. Morality who's gonna pat me down or some guy who drives around, stoned off his ass, and—"

"Fuck you."

"Y'already did."

"Way to go, Jim!" Marino hooted.

"Shut up!" Baker snapped, eyes still riveted to Micki's.

"C'mon, man, no one blames you for bopping the little—"

"SHUT YOUR FUCKING MOUTH, DENNY." And Baker's piercing gaze was now fully trained on Marino.

Marino shut up, backing his way out the door. "Hey, man, take it easy. It was just a joke."

"You breathe a word of this to anyone," Baker said, "and you're a dead man."

Hands raised, Marino said, "No problem. Everything's cool. Already forgotten." And he left.

Baker reached over and dug his fingers into the heart of Micki's bicep. "Let's go next door and have a little chat."

Out of consideration for the intense pain in her arm, she let him take her two units down to an empty conference room. He swung her inside and closed the door.

"Did you think that was cute?" he asked.

"I was just stating a fact."

"You know damn well I didn't mean it literally."

"You took it literally when *I* said it."

His nostrils flared. "You'd better get it through your head that nothing's changed. Like it or not, you'll do what you're told. If you think, for one minute, you're going to hold this over me—"

"I'm not gonna do that."

"Damn right you won't, 'cause no one's going to believe you."

"Oh, really? *They* believed me."

Baker started to sweat: he shouldn't have shot his mouth off so quickly. "Well—no one would care."

"Oh, I think they would," she replied. "I think that social worker, Miss Gutierrez—or whatever her name is—I bet she'd be real interested. And Captain Malone, too." She tilted her head. "Then there's always your girlfriend."

"Yeah? You think so? Well here's a newsflash: it wouldn't mean a damn thing to her. Cynthia and I have an understanding right now." He could feel the heat creeping into his cheeks, the telltale warmth of a spreading blush.

But Micki's face hardened: just one more reason you fucked me, you son of a bitch. She turned to look out the window, at the trees shedding their leaves, then shrugged. "Whatever. Like I said, I'm not gonna say anything."

Baker's head pulled back. "And why is that?"

"Because I wanted it, right?" Glancing over her shoulder she said, "You asked me, and—and I wanted you to do it."

In the span of one brief instant, she'd put herself into the equation and then taken herself right back out, as if what she'd agreed to Saturday night was to let him use her. But it wasn't really like that, was it? He'd satisfied her, hadn't he? His mind became flooded with images: strobing, impressionistic flashes of her naked body moving under his. Disjointed and mostly out of focus, the fragments were drenched in an orange-red haze, the heat of the moment burning itself further into his memory when what he really wanted was to smother it out. He remembered how desperately she'd clutched at him when she came. He watched her now as she gazed out at the cold November day, the light—finding its way through the windowpanes—in streaks across her face. She looked tired and drawn.

The first-period bell rang.

She whirled around. "Y'want me to fuckin' write it in blood?"

Very softly, he said, "No, Micki. Your word is good enough for me."

When she realized he wasn't being sarcastic, her face fell. But Baker wasn't sure what that meant.

The silence grew.

"I don't think any less of you," he offered.

She snorted.

"What are you high on?"

"Nothing."

"Well, then you're hung over from something. You think I can't tell?"

She shrugged.

"What did you take yesterday?"

Her gaze shifted to the window again. To think he had the balls to be questioning her about using drugs after—

"*Micki!*"

Her eyes snapped back to his.

"*Answer me!*"

"Hash," she said.

"I thought you said you never smoke anything."

"I ate it, okay?"

"How much?"

"About a gram."

His jaw dropped. "You ate a whole gram of hash? Yourself? *At once?*"

"So what!"

"So maybe you're lucky to be standing here today."

"Yeah—real lucky."

His voice turned harsh. "You want a reason not to take drugs?"

She glared at him.

"Saturday night's a good reason not to take drugs. I was totally out of control and did something I very much regret. What do you think would've happened if *you* were that high and hanging out with a bunch of boys like you did that night you broke curfew?"

Micki looked away. She knew *exactly* what would've happened. All she had to do was think about yesterday when Rick was knocking at the door; all she couldn't forget was what had been done to her when she'd been passed out in the shooting gallery.

Baker said, "I never would've done what I did if I'd been straight."

Yeah, Micki thought, you've got to be totally stoned to screw a lowlife like me.

As if reading her mind, he said, "That's not what I meant!"

But she was staring at a stubby little pencil someone had left behind on the conference table. It had bite marks all over it, the eraser—

He took a step toward her.

Her eyes shot up to his.

"I don't make it a habit," he said quietly, "of going around fucking little girls." And though his face betrayed nothing, he cringed at the pain that flashed across hers—he hadn't meant to say it quite like that.

"I—I'm not a little girl." And yet her voice had come out thin and uncertain.

"I'm nearly twenty years older than you."

The late bell rang.

"What went on between us," he said, "should never have happened, do you understand that? And it certainly doesn't give me license to do any damn thing I please. I'll respect the same boundaries I always have." His tone relaxed. "If we can't get past this, then it's all over."

But her eyes were fixed on the door, and she was picturing the lone flower that had sprung up several weeks ago behind the chain-link fence beside the bank. A lush, vibrant pink, the petals had basked in the bright midday sun—fine lines, like veins through skin, glowing red. But when clouds had rolled by, the light had dimmed, revealing nicks and tears—little chunks bitten off by tiny rodent teeth or bugs. The following week, the flower was gone, its headless stem sticking up among the ratty, browning weeds. She had no idea why she'd felt so sad about it then. Or now. Her eyes slowly drifted back to his.

"I know this isn't easy—"

"What's the difference anyway." And she abruptly turned around, holding her arms away from her body.

Baker hesitated, then patted her down the way he always did. It was over so quickly it hardly seemed worth all the fuss. Totally sexless. For him.

But for Micki, everything had changed. The sensation of his large hands moving over her, his body so close, sparked memories it never could have before. She wanted to run away. Instead, she was facing him again, head tilted back so she could eye him with a hard, unforgiving gaze.

"Are you all right?" he asked.

He sounded so genuine. He was so smooth! "Sure, why not?" But she turned away.

And for just a moment, he shut his eyes. Then he said, "Look at me, Micki." But he had to yank her around. "*Look at me, Micki!*"

And they studied each other. For quite a while. And though nothing further was said, it seemed as though they'd reached some sort of agreement.

Baker spoke first, his voice low. "Right now, while we're here in this room, you can say anything you want to me. You can rank me out, curse at me—whatever. I promise I won't retaliate. Not now, not ever. But once we walk out that door, all the old rules still apply."

She shoved her hands into her pockets.

"There must be something you want to say."

She lowered her gaze to his chest.

Aware he was towering over her, he went and sat on top of the conference table, legs dangling over the edge, jeans faded, black turtleneck soft and loose. "Don't you have anything to say to me?" he asked again.

But on her way to school, Micki had decided she was going to act like she didn't care. It was hard for someone to gloat over something that didn't bother you. And though she'd done a pretty bad job of things so far, she had no alternative strategy to fall back on. But what she wouldn't give to just tell him off.

Baker watched her staring into space. There was probably a whole slew of epithets about to be hurled in his direction. Maybe she simply couldn't decide what to start with. He was dying for a cigarette.

Her expression turned hard and cold. "I need a late pass."

A little thrill of fear shot through him, and he looked on anxiously as she turned toward him, her whole persona sharp and angular. How she'd surprised him in bed with the gentleness of her touch, a feathery lightness that had sent chills rippling through his body. Hard to believe it was the same person standing before him now.

He hopped down from the table. "Okay, Micki, as soon as we get back to the office." He went to the door and held it open for her. But when she was passing through, he grabbed her arm. "Stay—away—from the drugs. Do you hear me? I can't let it go a second time."

She jerked her arm back, then stalked off down the hall.

He watched the thin, black figure. So angry. So alone. So…silent. As he followed her to the office, he wondered where she'd found the black jeans. He wouldn't mind buying a pair of those for himself.

AFTER MICKI HAD GONE to class, Baker pocketed the twenty dollars, lit a cigarette, and sat down. He was pretending to examine some papers on his desk when he asked Warner, "How come you're still here? Anyone covering one-north for you?"

"Dixon's holding down the fort for now."

Baker stapled two pages together. "So then the second floor is open?"

"Yeah, the second floor is open."

"I see."

Walking over till he was standing right next to Baker, Warner asked, "What the hell are you thinking sleeping with her?" Baker looked up. But before he could answer, Warner added, "And just how long has this been going on?"

"It was once. Just *once*. I did something really stupid Saturday night. Jesus, she could have my shield for this."

"Maybe that's what you want."

"What the hell is that supposed to mean?"

"It means I think you're very ambivalent right now about being a cop. It means that whatever the real reason is that you're stuck here, you resent this job and you resent being Micki's guardian. Part of you wants out, but you're too chicken to make the decision yourself; you're going to let the kid make it for you. I can just imagine what would happen if she tells anyone."

"She already said she won't."

"Well then, I guess you've got nothing to worry about. That kid's got more integrity than anyone I know—certainly more than you."

Baker's eyes flashed. But before he could respond, Warner added, "How could you sleep with her? She's only seventeen years old, for chrissakes."

"It's not like she's a virgin—"

"What the hell difference does that make? Seventeen years old is seventeen years old, and thirty-six is thirty-six."

"Yeah? Well I can tell you she's no innocent, young thing in bed."

"I think you assume too much."

And, silently, Baker agreed. In fact, he agreed with everything Warner had said. Still he heard himself saying, "The bottom line is that I didn't force her. She—"

"Is that so," Warner cut in.

Baker took a hit off his cigarette.

"How much choice do you think she really had?" Warner demanded.

"I asked her if she wanted me to stop. I left it up to her."

"You left it up to her? She isn't even half your age. You're in a position of authority over her. One word from you and she's locked up again. She's at a stage when her hormones are running wild, and suddenly she's got a chance to make it with some guy every female in this school would like to make it with. I'd bet anything, she figured this was the only shot she'd ever get at someone even *half* as good looking as you. And for once, you're offering to make her feel good when all she's ever known from you is pain. That kid's dying for love, and the closest she can get is sex. So you tell me: how much choice did she really have?"

Baker's jaw worked.

"*You*," Warner continued, "*you* had the choice. Not her." He lowered his voice. "You're damaging that kid."

"She's already damaged," Baker heard himself say.

"You're a heartless son of a bitch."

But as Warner started for the door, Baker reached out and touched his arm. "I didn't mean that; I—I don't know what it is about that kid that makes me act this way. I don't want to be like this; I really don't."

"Then get some help." And Warner stormed out of the office.

Baker looked down at the cigarette still burning in his hand. There were ashes all over the floor.

THEY WERE READING *Two Gentlemen of Verona* in English. Micki hated Shakespeare. Voice droning on and on, Mr. Newsome's oversized head was tilting side to side while he made annoying little digging gestures with his pinky to emphasize points. Her notebook filled with doodles, she wasn't listening to anything he was saying. She hated Mr. Newsome almost as much as she hated Shakespeare.

She dropped her pen to the page, sat back, and let the classroom dissolve into a blur. And as if he were standing right in front of her, she could hear Baker's voice again: "I don't make it a habit of going around fucking little girls." Yet she could still feel the softness of his lips against her throat, her chest, her breasts…further and further down…kissing her scars until he'd buried his face between her legs—

"Are you with us today, Miss Reilly?"

"Huh?" Her face reddened at the sight of all the eyes fastened upon her, classmates twisting around in their chairs to look at her.

"I asked if you are with us today."

"Yeah, sure."

There was muffled laughter, but only because at least one student did a major tune-out in Newsome's class every day.

"Then perhaps, if I repeat it yet a third time, you could answer my question."

I doubt it, Micki thought. She hadn't done any homework over the weekend.

The door opened. One of the student assistants from the general office came in and handed the teacher a slip of paper. After a quick glance at it, Mr. Newsome looked up and said, "Well, Miss Reilly, it looks like you've been saved by the note."

Several groans attested to the general opinion of Mr. Newsome's sense of humor.

Eyes still focused on Micki, he continued, "You are to go to the security office immediately. There's no indication as to the purpose of the request, so I suggest you take your books with you."

The messenger left while the color completely drained from her face.

Newsome's mouth became a small, obnoxious smile. "Are you in trouble, Miss Reilly?"

I'm always in trouble, you fucking idiot, she thought. And she hated being called Miss Reilly—at least by him. When students irritated or ignored him, he always called them by their surnames. She pulled her books together, snatched the note from his wimpy hand, and hurried out the door.

ALONE IN THE CORRIDOR, she tried not to panic. It couldn't be all that serious if Baker hadn't come for her himself. Halfway down the stairs, she ran into Angie, who looked her over and said, "You better have a pass to show me." Micki handed her the now crumpled piece of paper, which the guard examined and gave back before waving her on.

But when Micki reached the first floor landing, she slowed her pace, returning to the moment when she'd opened her eyes to find Baker staring down at her, no longer high, no longer the romantic stranger he'd been—the tender interlude over. He'd seen things he had no right to see—had invaded her once more in yet another way, leaving her with some strange sense of guilt. Yet he was nothing more than a parole officer; he'd made that more than clear. And she—well, she wasn't a little girl. No matter what he said.

She arrived at the office, but the door was closed. About to turn the knob, she felt a fresh surge of anger: there was still the issue of the money. She rotated the engraved piece of oval brass and stepped inside.

But only Warner was there.

"Where's Sergeant Baker?" she asked.

Dressed in a light-colored sweater and blue jeans, Warner was standing in the middle of the room. "I'm the one who called you down here, Micki."

"What for?" She took a look at the note wadded up in her fist. It had Warner's signature—not Baker's.

"I thought you might want to talk."

"About what?"

"Why don't you put your books down and make yourself comfortable." And with a slight movement of his head, he indicated the couch.

Instead, Micki put her books on the general desk, then hopped up, swinging her legs over so she could put her feet on the seat.

Warner, feeling like he'd forgotten how to walk, crossed the room and closed the door. Things weren't going the way he'd anticipated. He pulled out Baker's chair—the only one with castors to roll around on—and swivelled it to face her. Sitting down, he said, "Well, this is just as good." But his smile looked forced.

She stared down at him.

"So," he said.

"So what?"

"So how do you feel about what happened between you and Jim?"

Even now, she couldn't imagine calling Baker "Jim." "Did he put y'upta this?" she asked. "Is this some kinda test? I *told* him I wasn't gonna tell anybody anything."

266 ◆ Randy Mason

"He doesn't even know I'm talking to you. And anything you tell me is completely confidential—strictly between you and me."

She snorted. "Yeah, right."

"You might feel better if you talk about what happened."

"I feel fine right now 'cause it didn't mean a fuckin' thing. Maybe ya jus' wanna get off hearin' all the little details."

Trying not to fidget, trying to keep his voice neutral, he asked, "Is that what you really think?"

"I'm not gonna tell ya shit." Cool and calm, her eyes began to look like those of an animal sizing up its prey.

Warner swallowed.

"Y'gonna tell Sergeant Baker I cursed?"

"I want you to feel free to express yourself."

Micki smirked.

And Warner knew he'd never broach the other issue, the one that had been so salient in his decision to send for her.

She jumped down from the desk. "I don't wanna talk, y'got that?"

Her stare was so empty that the hair on the back of his neck stood up. He arose, the chair rolling clumsily away behind him. "That's okay." But his voice was choked off. He cleared his throat. "That's—that's fine. But, y'know, if you change your mind, I'm always here to listen."

"I need another pass," she said.

He felt nervous just turning his back to fill out the piece of paper.

ONCE MICKI WAS GONE, Warner exhaled loudly. He threw away the balled-up page she'd tossed on top of the desk, and closed the door she'd left open behind her. He could almost hear his clinical psych professors chuckling, his supervisor jumping on his lack of insight. More than cavalier, his assessment of Micki had been distorted, a product of his own fears and wishes—something he'd have to explore tomorrow night with his own therapist.

He wiped away the small beads of sweat that had formed over his lip, then turned Baker's chair around and put it back where it belonged. Thoughts of replacing the cop as Micki's guardian were gone. Recalling her stare, a shiver ran through him: were those the eyes of a killer?

AT THE END OF the day, Micki checked in as usual, then headed home. Warner entered the office shortly afterward to cover for Baker so he could leave early to follow.

"I'm worried about her," Baker said as he put his jacket on and pocketed his cigarettes.

Warner's reply was a stony look.

"Hey, I know I fucked up, okay? The best I can do now is try to keep her from fucking up, too."

"How could you do that?" Warner asked. "I still can't believe it. I would never have pictured you as the type."

"I'm *not* the type. I was flying—took some hits off a joint I confiscated, then got wrecked by whatever else was in it. By the time I got Micki back to her apartment, I was too messed up to drive home. When I saw I was in trouble, I tried to get out of there, but things just happened; I couldn't stop myself."

"*Things just happened? You think you're not responsible?*"

"Shit. Don't tell *me* what the line is: *my* decision to smoke that joint, *my* responsibility whatever took place afterward. I'm not trying to defend myself; I'm just trying to explain how it went down."

"All day long, I'm asking myself if I should report this to someone. The one thing stopping me is my fear of what'll happen to Micki if you're taken out of the picture."

"You want to know what'll happen? She's only got two options: me or juvenile detention. That's *it*. I think we can at least agree that she shouldn't go back to juvi."

Warner rubbed his brow.

"I'm telling you," Baker said, "it'll never happen again. It was just the drugs. Jesus, what do you want me to say?"

"What worries me is that you smoked that joint in the first place when you knew you still had to drive her home."

Head down, hands raised, Baker said, "Okay, okay, you've made your point. I've been under a lot of pressure lately; I let it cloud my judgment."

"'Cloud your judgement'? *'Cloud your judgement'?* That's an understatement. And what about your drinking?"

"What *about* my drinking?"

"I wouldn't say I've ever seen you tanked, but there've been plenty of mornings when I've smelled liquor on you. In fact, today it's so bad I can still smell it on you now. You've got to be hitting the bottle pretty hard at night."

"Even dead drunk, I wouldn't do what I did Saturday night. The kid would never be in danger; I know my limits."

Warner took a toothpick from a container on his desk. "I need some time on this."

Baker nodded and lowered his eyes.

"But what about Denny?" Warner asked. "Aren't you worried? Do you really think he'll keep his mouth shut?"

"He's the kind of asshole that doesn't see anything wrong with what I did. He'll keep silent for the sake of 'us boys' sticking together—not to mention he's scared shitless of me." Baker shifted his gaze to the window, then looked back. "I wonder if I could ask a favor."

The toothpick moved from one side of Warner's mouth to the other.

"I really am worried about Micki," Baker said. "I think she needs to talk to someone. I was wondering if you'd give it a try."

"I already did."

"What? When was this?"

"Third period, I'm in the office then anyway."

"You pulled her out of class?"

"What about it?"

"Let's get something straight: no matter what you think of me right now, you can't just pull her out of class."

"I think you've got bigger things than that to be worrying about."

"Really? Because I—" But Baker stopped. "So how did it go?"

"It didn't go at all. She wouldn't talk to me."

"You're kidding!"

"Why does that surprise you?"

"I guess I always thought she liked you."

"But she doesn't trust me."

Shutting his eyes, Baker exhaled. Having her talk to anyone else was too risky.

"If you want to help her," Warner said, "you're going to have to straighten this out yourself."

"Oh, right. Like she's ever going to trust *me* now."

"She just might."

Baker looked up. "What makes you say that?"

Warner shrugged. "I don't know; it's just a feeling."

A glance at his watch, and Baker bolted for the door. "I'd better go, or she'll get home before I get there. Call me later."

The door slammed shut, and Warner threw the toothpick away.

AFTER A QUICK SEARCH through Micki's apartment, Baker returned to his car, which was parked around the corner. Though the location provided an ample view of the subway entrance, it was still far enough away that Micki wouldn't spot the Camaro unless she was specifically looking for it. Or turning down Twenty-First Street to go to the bank. He hadn't thought of that.

But Micki appeared with only a glance to check for oncoming traffic before walking across. He started the car, waited briefly, then drove to the light.

Shit! Instead of going into her building, she'd paused on the stoop. She was staring right at him. It looked like she was about to give him the finger, but then thought better of it. Turning away, she shoved the door open with so much force he could picture it banging against the interior wall and rebounding as she went inside.

But maybe it was better this way. He couldn't exactly spend the rest of the day staking out her apartment. If she believed he was lurking somewhere, waiting, it would probably deter her just as much as if he actually were. Confident she was watching, he turned the corner and drove slowly down the block until he found another parking spot. Sure enough, not five minutes later, she stuck her head all the way out the fire escape window. When she caught sight of him, she ducked back in and slammed the window down.

FUCKING BASTARD! AND YET, if he weren't there, she might've ended up doing exactly what he was thinking.

She paced around the room, then pounded the side of her fist against the heavy, clumsy wood of the dresser. But all it did was make her heart hurt. Cradling her hand, now red and swollen, she lay down on the bed to sleep. And while she would never have admitted it, she was grateful Baker was outside.

BACK IN HIS APARTMENT again, Baker was standing over the telephone. Maybe he'd wait till after dinner. No matter how many times he tried to rehearse what to say, it never sounded right. He started to walk away, then went back and dialed, as nervous as he'd been when he'd called her after their first date. It rang seven times. Just when he was about to hang up, he heard, "Hello?"

"Cynthia?"

"Hi, Jim." Her voice sounded far away. "I guess I should've called."

"No, it's okay. I think I'm the one who should've called. But I just—well, I have something to say." When she didn't respond, he said, "I guess I really don't know how to deal with what's happening; I'm still kind of shocked. And—and I'm confused about us. But I meant it when I said I'd help no matter what you decide—"

"Jim—"

"Even if you don't want to see me anymore—"

"Jim—"

"No, let me finish. I don't want you to think—"

"JIM!"

He fell silent.

"I lost the baby."

"You *lost* it?"

"I miscarried; it started this morning. The doctor called it a spontaneous abortion. It's very common for first pregnancies."

"Jesus! Are you all right?"

"I'm fine. It's like having my period. Only…weird."

"Well, you don't sound okay."

"I'm just very tired."

"You sound depressed." His tone softened. "Did you want to keep it?"

"No, I'd pretty much decided not to, but"—her voice cracked—"but still…"

"Do you want me to come over?"

"I really need to be alone right now."

"Well, can I get you anything?"

"I'm fine. Really. I'll call you tomorrow, okay?"

"Promise?"

"I promise."

He hung up the phone. And felt strangely numb.

He poured a drink, lit a cigarette, and sat down in the living room to watch the evening roll in outside the window. What did that mean, exactly: "It's like having my period, only weird." He'd never been able to imagine what it was like to get a period in the first place—to bleed every month. What a hassle that had to be. When his last girlfriend had had an accident overnight, he'd been shocked by the amount of blood all over the sheets.

His eyes widened. Man, he'd been really dense. That was what was missing from Micki's apartment. For over two months he'd been checking every inch of the place, and not once—not *once*—had he ever seen any of those "feminine hygiene" products: no sanitary napkins, no tampons.

He'd bet anything she wasn't pregnant, but, at seventeen, how could she not get her period? There was no mention of it in his copy of her file. Then again, he didn't have her medical records. He sighed. No sooner did one problem go away than another came along to replace it. Just what was he supposed to do now—ignore it? That was, of course, his first choice. But what if something were seriously wrong? What if she needed some sort of medical attention? Unfortunately, with Cynthia going through this pregnancy thing, he couldn't exactly ask her for help. Which left the school nurse and Angie; they were the only other females he could think of at the moment. But he could hear Cynthia saying there was no reason he couldn't talk to Micki himself. He was a grown man, wasn't he? Micki was *his* responsibility.

And, as usual, Cynthia would be right.

Besides, it wasn't like Micki would have to go into graphic detail. He'd simply find out what, if anything, she knew. If he felt it was necessary, he'd take her to a doctor. He poured another drink. Well, it had waited this long till he even realized what was going on; it could wait another week before he questioned her about it. Things needed to settle down a little first.

The phone rang, and he started, the whiskey sloshing around inside the glass. He rushed over to pick up the receiver, body tensing at the sound of Warner's voice. But when he hung up, he felt that maybe—just maybe—everything would straighten itself out.

He smoked another cigarette before stretching out for a nap.

OPEN BOOKS, INDEX CARDS, and papers full of notes covered the little red kitchen table. Warner massaged his forehead in a futile attempt to ward off the headache he'd felt coming on since lunchtime. But trying to work on his dissertation was pointless anyway: all he could think about was Micki.

Although his knee-jerk reaction had been to get her out from under Baker's authority, it wasn't nearly so clear-cut. Baker could've been lying when he said it was either him or Heyden, but Warner was inclined to believe him. And as much as he deplored Baker's brutality, Heyden sounded even more unacceptable. Either way, it was unlikely another guardian could easily be found. Just thinking about his encounter with Micki that morning made him shudder.

The throbbing in his head was getting worse. Sharply focused behind his left eye, it felt like a dulled stake was being driven through the socket. This was the kind of headache he'd have to sleep off. He stood up and looked at the table littered with academic artifacts. To think he actually felt that, right now, it was best to do nothing.

WHEN BAKER RETURNED TO Micki's at ten to ten, the lights were out. Since she didn't work Mondays, she had all of ten minutes till she violated curfew. He sat in his car, smoking, knowing she could be anywhere, doing anything. He should've kept a tighter watch on her.

Another twenty minutes went by before he shut the radio and opened the Camaro's door. Immediately, he heard two angry voices: one male and one female—though the latter wasn't Micki's. As he crossed the street and drew closer, he could tell the altercation was coming from Micki's building, from the basement apartment that had its own entrance below the stoop. Up till now, he'd never heard anyone else inside the place, though several times he'd caught music—Andy Williams or Perry Como—coming from somewhere on the first floor.

Loud and vulgar, the argument seemed to be escalating. However, once he was inside the entryway, it was significantly hushed; by the time he reached Micki's apartment, completely inaudible. But he could hear Micki inside: the unnerving moans and mumbles, the restless thrashing. He hadn't expected her to be home, let alone sleeping. When he unlocked the door and cracked it open, the ugly row from the basement was once again distinct, carried up on the outside air and through the poorly sealed windows. Micki, however, appeared to be fighting her own private battle in some terrifying dream world.

Heart heavy, he eased the door shut and locked it. At least she wasn't doing drugs.

Or so he hoped.

MICKI DRAGGED HERSELF THROUGH school on Tuesday, talking to no one and never raising her hand. In what little time she had before work, she took refuge in sleep. Baker, having followed her home again, hung around till she left for Bel, then went home himself to take a nap. But after a dinner of sardines and frozen peas, he cleaned his guns and then his ashtrays. As soon as Mr. Antonelli gave him the call, he shut the TV and returned to his car.

Back in Queens, he parked on Forty-Fourth Drive, east of Bel but on the opposite side, facing west. Perfectly positioned. All so he could sit in his car and smoke, eyes glazing over as he watched the restaurant from his bucket seat instead of the Nets game from the comfort of his recliner. Not that things weren't happening: further down the street, a series of kids—mostly boys—were going in and out of an alley. It had to be the one that led to the parking lot where Officer Roberts had picked up Micki. At one point, a large group came out together, including Rick, who had his arm around a trashily dressed blonde—the girlfriend, no doubt. Baker puffed away, free fingers tapping against his thigh while he watched the two laugh their way toward Twenty-Third Street.

Micki finally left the restaurant, and Baker waited till she'd crossed the road before he turned the engine over and followed. While she went into her building, he looked for a space, but was forced to double-park. Slumped down, he lit a fresh cigarette, only to see her apartment go dark less than ten minutes later. Eyes trained on her front door, he shook off the fog and straightened up. When she failed to reappear, he was once more standing in the hallway. Listening.

Wednesday was a carbon copy. Until he dropped his keys on the way out. Swearing silently, he bore a hasty retreat. But the noise had cut through the mangled images of her unconscious. She awoke to the sound of heavy footsteps hurrying down the stairs while her heart was racing so fast it was hard to breathe. Tangled blanket and sheet were thrown off, and she rushed to the window to peek through the curtains. Paused on the concrete, Baker was lighting a cigarette. He waved out the match, then looked back over his shoulder. It seemed their eyes met, though she was sure he couldn't see her in the darkened window. Or could he? He turned to fully face the building, staring up at her, the streetlamp casting a long, black shadow before him. And though he turned and walked away, his shadow seemed to stay.

BY THE TIME BAKER stopped by Cynthia's, it was pushing midnight. Seated at her dining room table, drinking coffee, he felt like he was at a casual business meeting instead of the short date they'd agreed to earlier. And, in time, Cynthia revealed her agenda: she'd continue to see him only if he remained civil about her seeing Mark, as well.

Baker caught himself gazing at one of the paintings hanging on the wall. A Picasso-style canvas in bold colors and striking lines, it presented parts of a face like scrambled pieces of a puzzle. He'd always hated the work. Tonight he couldn't stop looking at it. He tried to keep the bitterness out of his voice when he asked if their plans for Thanksgiving were still on. When she said yes, his heart leaped, then stuck in his throat: according to the terms of Micki's release, he was required to leave her at Heyden while he was away.

THE EARLY MORNING SUN was blinding, and Baker pulled down the shades. Alone in the security office, he was pacing back and forth, waiting for Warner to arrive. Just as he was about to pour another cup of coffee, the other man walked through the door.

"I was wondering if you could help me out with something," Baker said.

Taking off his coat, Warner replied, "Depends."

"Would you consider supervising Micki over Thanksgiving?"

Warner grabbed a mug and pulled out the carafe. "No."

"Really? But why not? If you don't, I'll have to leave her at Heyden while I'm gone."

"Can't do it. I'm sorry." He put the coffee pot back and opened the refrigerator.

"But it won't be much of a hassle; you'd only have to check on her once a day and leave your phone number with my answering service. I don't expect her to get into any real trouble; she'll be working most of the time."

Warner added milk and began to stir the steaming liquid in front of him. "Sorry, but I can't, okay? I just can't."

"I thought you cared about her."

"I do."

"So what's the problem?"

Putting the spoon down, Warner looked at him. "Just forget it, okay?"

"You're so fucking quick to criticize, but you won't actually do a goddamn thing yourself."

"The kid scares me."

"She scares you? What the hell happened the other day?"

"Nothing. Nothing happened, but there's no way I'm taking responsibility for her."

AFTER A BRIEF VISIT to the weekly poker game, Baker parked his car across from Micki's building. Window open, arm resting on top of the door, he was waiting for her to leave Bel Canto. A figure finally emerged from the alley beside the restaurant, then marched into the road. And it didn't matter the distance or that the lighting was poor, he would have recognized that little tough-guy walk anywhere as she made her way down the block, looking ahead at the row of cars on either side—looking for him. She went straight up to the Camaro and leaned over to talk through the window.

"Y'gotta watch me the whole friggin' day 'cause y'got nothin' better to do with y'time?"

He opened the door and got out, but Micki was already halfway across the street. He let her go inside alone while he finished what was left of his cigarette, eventually mashing the discarded butt into the asphalt with the toe of his shoe.

When he entered her apartment, she was hanging up her damp T-shirt from work, pointedly ignoring him.

"I saw your teachers today for Open School Day," he said.

Her back to him, she poured herself a glass of Coke. "So?"

"So they had some interesting things to tell me."

Bubbles were fizzing up in a rush through the dark brown liquid. She'd poured the soda too fast. In a minor eruption, the mocha-colored foam was spilling over, running down the sides of the glass and onto the Formica into a little puddle. She turned to face him. "Yeah? Like what?"

"Like your art teacher telling me students take their work home every few weeks. She was surprised I'd never seen any of yours. What happened to it?"

"I threw it away."

"You threw it away?" When Mrs. Holtzberg had pulled out Micki's folder, Baker had been astounded. There'd been pencil sketches of hands, other students' faces, and a glass—all looking incredibly real. "She's very talented," the teacher had said, smiling. "If she wants to, she could become a professional artist. She'd have to take classes at an art school or college, but she's got the raw ability."

"They're *mine*," Micki said. "I can throw 'em out if I want to."

"But why? You should be proud of them; you should hang them up. I'd hang them up if they were mine."

"Oh, yeah?" Her mouth twisted. "Y'wanna hang one up on your refrigerator?"

Nice shot, he said to himself. But then a curious expression came over him. "I don't know, Micki. Would you *like* me to hang one up on my refrigerator?"

"They're…they're mine," she repeated.

"I see. Well then, there's another issue we need to address: every one of your teachers—every single one of them—informed me that you haven't handed in any homework since last Friday."

"I've been…tired."

"You've been tired? Well, guess what? You're not tired anymore. Now you're going to sit your butt down at that desk and start your homework—and not just tonight's homework; you'll do last Friday's, as well. Then tomorrow you can make up Monday's, and, over the weekend, you can catch up on the rest."

"Y'can't force me to do my homework."

Slamming his palms just under her shoulders, he shoved her back against the counter. "Get over there."

Something flashed across her face. It looked like…betrayal. Inwardly, Baker cringed.

She snorted. "Y'gonna beat me up f'not doin' my homework?"

He shoved her again though there was no place left for her to go. "Is it worth it to you to find out?"

She stood her ground.

"*Answer me.*"

Trapped beneath his gaze, the counter pressing into the base of her spine, she felt very small. "No, sir," she said quietly.

He took a step back, and she moved past him, picking her books up from the table and taking them to the desk. She sat down with a thud and opened her loose-leaf.

"Are you still reading *Two Gentlemen of Verona*?" he asked, for he thought he spied its back cover on top of the pile of texts.

Without turning around, she took a long, labored breath—he was such a pain in the ass!—and answered, "Yessir."

"Jeez, I hate Shakespeare."

She rolled her eyes for the benefit of the window.

"I'm going to the corner to get something to read," he said, and started for the door. "I'll be back in five minutes."

Who the fuck cares, she thought.

Coffee in one hand, a copy of *Newsweek* tucked under his arm, Baker returned. He threw his cigarettes, matches, and keys on the table, then took off his jacket and sat down.

Just make yourself right at home, Micki thought, and continued writing at a furious pace.

"That better be legible," he said. He'd seen some of her classroom notes. Apparently, the faster she wrote, the larger and sloppier her penmanship became. One of her classmates had even nicknamed her the Phantom Scrawler.

Mid-scribble, she ripped out the page, crumpled it up, and threw it to the floor.

He removed the lid from his coffee, lit a cigarette, and opened the magazine.

She started writing again.

MICKI STOOD UP. "I'M done."

Nearly two in the morning, Baker had been on the verge of making a final coffee run. He walked over. "Let me see."

Gritting her teeth, she watched him page through her work while he was standing so close she was breathing in his scent. It brought back the warmth of his skin against hers, the sensation of his body moving underneath her hands—

"What happened to tonight's history homework?" he asked.

"We didn't get any."

"Let me see your assignment book."

She yanked it out from under the physics text and slammed it down on the desk.

He calmly picked it up and flipped through. "You've got two tests tomorrow: physics and math. Did you study for those?"

"Y'don't need to study for that stuff: either y'know it or y'don't."

"But you have to memorize formulas for physics, don't you?"

"I've got it all down cold. Besides, he's been letting us use a reference sheet."

Tossing the pad onto the desk, Baker looked at her fixedly.

"Don't worry," she said. "I'll pass both of 'em."

He grabbed the front of her shirt, twisting it into his fist and pulling her toward him. "I don't want you to just pass, Micki. Till now, you've been getting grades of a hundred or in the high nineties; I expect you to keep that up."

Her heart was pounding, the question in her eyes left hanging in the air.

"So I'm going to ask you again," he said. "Are you really ready for those exams tomorrow?"

She was so tired. And he was taking this school stuff so fucking seriously. "Yessir." she said.

He let go. "I hope so, because I want to see them once they're graded." He went to the table, put on his jacket, pocketed his things, and picked up the magazine. Looking around at the clutter that had overtaken the room, he said, "And straighten this place up."

Fuck you, she thought.

AFTER HE'D GONE, SHE poured her glass of Coke—now warm and flat—down the drain. She cleaned the sticky counter, picked the crumpled paper up from the floor, and put away the clothes that were lying around. But she didn't touch the empty Styrofoam cup from his coffee. Or the saucer he always used as an ashtray. They both stayed on the table. Exactly where he'd left them.

A LIGHT SNOW WAS beginning to fall. Outside the windshield, tiny flakes were swirling in the breezy air.

"What do you care?" That was Micki's unvoiced question. "What do you care if I don't do my homework or study for my tests?" But the real question was, why didn't *she* care anymore?—not that he wanted to hear the answer.

The snow hit the ground, then disappeared. It was too warm for anything to stick. Baker sat a moment longer, recalling the look on her face when he'd shoved her. Even now, it made his stomach turn. He started the engine and switched on the headlights.

Thank god she couldn't tell when he was bluffing.

CONFIDENT THE PHASE OF greatest danger had passed, Baker didn't park in front of Micki's until one o'clock in the morning the following night. He'd already told Mr. Antonelli not to call anymore—not that he could've kept up his little surveillance routine much longer anyway. It had taken a much heavier toll than he'd anticipated.

When he saw Micki's lights still on, he made a pit stop at the deli, then took his time walking back along Forty-Fourth Drive. Coat half-unbuttoned despite the near-freezing temperature, he was mulling over the evening's date, which, from the very beginning, couldn't have gone much worse. He'd been so pleased Cynthia wasn't spending a Friday night with Mr. LA that, spotting a program for the actor's weekend showcase—an experimental theater piece—lying on her kitchen counter, he'd asked her why she wasn't at the performance. When she'd explained she was going to the final show and then the cast party afterward, he'd been crushed.

The misery continued with a short stroll to see a movie that was disappointing, then a drive all the way down to the East Village to an Indian restaurant that was uncharacteristically noisy and crowded. Afterward, they returned to her apartment for coffee and dessert, at which point the conversation had turned inexplicably stiff—as though they hardly knew each other. At half-past midnight, they exchanged a modest kiss at the door, and Baker, feeling patronized and tolerated like an unwanted puppy, left. He was heading up First Avenue, looking forward to the solitude of a drive on the New York State Thruway, when he remembered Micki. Cursing loudly, he'd then crossed over to Second and gone downtown toward the bridge. At least traffic had been light.

He went up the stoop and into Micki's building, the coffee—in a thick paper cup instead of the usual Styrofoam—burning hot in his hand. When he let himself into the apartment, she was at the table in her nightshirt, drinking cocoa. Their eyes locked, and her body tensed.

"Can't sleep?" he asked.

"Whatta y'want?"

"Are we going to go through this every time I come here?"

"Why don'tcha just stop comin' here?"

"Y'know, I'm trying to be patient with you, Micki, but you're really pushing it. Did you at least get your homework done?"

"It's Friday. I don't havta do it till Sunday."

"But I told you yesterday that I wanted Monday's homework done *tonight*."

Her gaze shifted past him. "It's all there."

"Then what the fuck are you arguing with me for?"

She shrugged.

Slamming the unopened container of coffee on the table, he said, "You can be such a goddamn pain in the ass." Then he went to the desk and started leafing through her binder.

Forcing back a smile, she threw the remainder of her hot chocolate down the sink and began to wash the mug. He glanced over and noticed the jeans she was wearing.

"Were you just outside?" he asked.

Still with her back to him, she placed the mug in the drainer. "No, sir."

"Then what's with the jeans?"

She turned around and folded her arms over her chest.

"There's no need for that, Micki."

She shrugged.

Baker's expression softened. "You've been very tired lately."

"Yeah, y'think so? Well, last night y'kept me up till two in the morning doin' homework."

"I think you've been sleeping worse than usual anyway the last few days."

As if you really fucking care, she thought. She walked to the side of the bed that was furthest from him and announced, "Well I wanna go to sleep now, okay?"

"Okay." And he turned and closed her loose-leaf. Then he ran his fingers over its blue fabric cover and, much to her annoyance, straightened up some items on her desk. "When I saw your light on"—he faced her again—"I bought myself a cup of coffee. I figured you'd be up for a while."

So what, she thought. Who the fuck cares about your fucking coffee.

He added, "I'd rather drink it here than in my car."

He wasn't really asking about the coffee. She shrugged again. "Whatever." With her back to him, she began to unbuckle her belt.

Baker went over to the kitchen, took out his cigarettes, and lit one. When he looked back, she was already under the covers. Lying on her side, she was facing the door. He shut the light, sat down at the table, and pulled the lid off the paper cup.

AFTER A FEW MINUTES had passed, Micki opened her eyes and glanced at him. A dark figure, large and silent, he was looking toward the windows, the tip of his cigarette a changing orange glow. Only one week had passed since the senior dance, but it seemed more like years, the memory so strange and out of place she could almost believe she'd imagined it. But she shouldn't have let him stay; should've told him to take his goddamn coffee and go. So what if he knew she didn't trust him anymore? She'd never really trusted him to begin with.

NOT ALLOWING HIMSELF TO look, Baker could feel her watching. He nursed the coffee till it was cold, all the while thinking about how nervous he'd been lately: first sitting at the poker game with Captain Malone yesterday, then tonight when he'd been out with Cynthia. But no one, apparently, sensed any difference in him. And if Cynthia *were* to notice some sort of change, their relationship was so strained she'd probably attribute it to that. He wondered if she was sleeping with that asshole actor yet. He refused to even acknowledge the man's name, forgot it time and again as soon as it was mentioned. He'd just seen it on that damn theater program, and still he couldn't bring it to mind.

The last bitter drop of coffee gone, he looked over at Micki. Lying on her stomach, arms tucked in tight, she was asleep. It was an easy, peaceful slumber, same as the other time he'd done this. He got up and let himself out, hoping she'd sleep just as soundly the rest of the night.

That was, after all, the real reason he'd stayed.

Chapter 16

"**I** GOT MY TESTS back already," Micki said. It was Monday afternoon, and she was pulling papers out of her loose-leaf, creating a pile on Baker's desk.

But he was in the middle of reading a memo requesting his presence at Thursday night's PTA meeting. In spite of a handwritten note that had been added as a personal invitation, he had no intention of going: Thursday was his birthday. Putting the memo aside, he took a look at the exams. Marked in red on the physics test was "100 Excellent!!!"—but the math had only a 94. He tapped his finger on the lower number. "What happened here?"

"I didn't realize there were questions on the back of the last page till the period was almost over. I couldn't finish the last one before the bell rang." When the tests had been returned and her classmate Greg had seen her grade, he'd looked triumphant. In the ongoing competition between them, Micki had always won—until today. Explaining what had happened would've made her out to be a sore loser, so she'd said nothing and let him bask in his victory. But it had rankled. And now she'd have to hear Baker stick it to her after he'd explicitly warned her of his expectations.

Baker lit a cigarette and studied the back of the final sheet—a chaotic mass of equations, calculations, and diagrams. He leaned back and handed her the papers. "Well," he said, "these things happen."

Her jaw dropped.

Eyes focused on Cynthia's picture, he said, "Why don't you get going."

"Sure! I mean, yessir." And she ran out, closing the door behind her.

Baker exhaled a long stream of smoke and played with the ashtray on his desk. Then he pulled out his wallet and removed a card with a phone number on it. He'd already implored Warner once more to reconsider, but to no avail. Gould had too many holiday obligations, though he probably would've refused anyway.

And there was no point in asking Malone. He did, however, inquire about getting in touch with Sergeant Kelly, only to be warned not to: Kelly's wife of nine years—his second—had lain down the law when her husband had gotten too involved with the first boy he'd helped. After all, they had four children of their own who deserved more of their father's attention. So once a kid was placed, there was no further contact. No exceptions. None.

Baker ran his fingers through his hair, then dialed the number with rough, forceful strokes. He made the arrangements for Micki to stay at Heyden, his manner growing increasingly curt despite the fact that he was talking to the deputy warden. As they were finishing up, he said, "I want to make something very clear: I'm only leaving her with you because I have to. If that kid gets abused in any way—"

"None of the children in our care are ever abused," the woman interrupted. "I don't know what—"

"Don't bullshit me," he cut in, and stood up. "I know all about what went on there under Warden Loren. That kid better not get touched, understand? I don't want to find any new marks on her; I don't want to hear that she was sexually assaulted."

"Now wait just—"

"You still have a guard there named Edmunds?" Baker was holding the receiver so tightly the tendons in his wrist stood out like thick cords.

After a slight hesitation, the woman said, "Yes."

"You keep that scumbag away from her. Do you hear me?"

"Really! I—"

"*Do you hear me?*" he repeated.

"How dare you take that tone of voice with me! I don't know what kind of lies she's been feeding you, but I can assure you the children here get quality—"

"Cut the bull."

"Are you quite finished?"

Baker paused. This woman would soon have custody of Micki—for nearly four days. He took his voice down. Several notches. "We'll be arriving sometime around seven or seven thirty in the morning. Is that going to be a problem?"

"Well, seeing how you've been so pleasant, I don't know *why* we wouldn't go out of our way to accommodate you."

"Is that a 'yes' or a 'no'?"

"We'll be ready."

"Thanks so much." And he hung up without waiting for a reply. Squeezed between his fingers, his cigarette was down to a tiny stub. He viciously ground it out in the overflowing ashtray.

ON HER WAY TO the main entrance, Micki ran into the blond football player—who was smiling at her.

"Hi!" he said.

Still walking, she said, "Hi."

He stepped in front and started walking backward. "My name's Bobby. Bobby Reiger. You're Micki, right?"

And she stopped.

"So, like, I heard you're really smart," he said.

"Well, um…yeah, I guess so."

"Cool, 'cause I was kinda hoping you could help me. See, my geometry class is kinda messing me up."

He was large, especially compared to most of the boys in her science class. But the expression on his face—she'd never seen anyone look at her that way before.

When she didn't answer, he said, "Maybe we could get together sometime after school."

Her face fell. "I work every day. Except Mondays. Y'know, like today." Her eyes brightened. "Do you wanna—"

"I can't be late for football practice. The coach is counting on me to run some drills with the team. But maybe next Monday." And he smiled again.

She thought about that the whole way home.

THE LAUNDROMAT WAS VERY crowded, a din of high-pitched chatter rising above the roar of the machines. Saturated with the scent of laundry products, bleach, and cigarettes, the air smelled more cloying and suffocating than usual. Two washers and one dryer weren't working, causing a backup among the regular customers, mostly women with shabby clothes under frumpy coats; a couple of college kids; and a solitary man who never washed more than a pair of jeans, a few shirts, and a handful of socks—no sheets, towels, or underwear. Gross. When it was finally her turn, Micki hurried to the first available washer, but it ate her change without starting. After she'd thoroughly cursed it out while repeatedly shoving the coin tray in with no success, she called over the manager, a worn-out-looking woman with pockmarked skin, frizzy mousey-brown hair, and a considerable gap between her two large front teeth. She reminded Micki of a squirrel. Fixing Micki with a shrewd eye, the woman reached into the small black apron she wore, which sagged under the weight of the coins it contained. She slipped some change into the slots, pushed the tray in, and watched the washer jolt to life.

"Thanks," Micki said.

Palm extended, the manager said, "Y'owe me for a wash."

"But I already put my money in. I told ya: it didn't work."

"Then how come it worked for me?" The Squirrel's hoarse smoker's voice sounded like it was hard—even painful—for her to talk. "Y'think I don't know what you're up to? But that's okay. Just remember that that was your first—and last—free wash."

Everyone was staring at them.

"I'm tellin' ya," Micki said, "I already put my money in. I'm not tryin' t'cheat ya."

Lungs full of phlegm, the woman turned her head to cough, then looked Micki over. "Y'think I was born yesterday, y'little JD?" And she sauntered away.

Micki could feel the heat working its way through her veins. She imagined running after the woman, taking a handful of that stupid, mousey-brown hair, and slamming it down to the ground. Instead, she thrust her hands into her jacket pockets. But with her clothes now stuck in the washer, she couldn't even leave. Besides, the next Laundromat was much further away. She stared after the manager, who was already talking to someone else—the two of them looking at Micki with disgust. And yet, in the dozen or so times Micki had done her laundry in this place, not once had she ever given the Squirrel—or anyone else for that matter—a problem. Still she'd been called a juvenile delinquent in front of everyone. Not that the whole fucking neighborhood didn't know by now that she'd been in juvi.

While her clothes washed and dried, she did some homework, then headed back to her apartment. Arms full of books, laundry, and detergent, she fumbled with her key and unlocked the door, only to be greeted by the scent of Baker's cigarettes, soon followed by the sight of the man himself. So much for the nap she'd been looking forward to; so much for spilling the laundry out on the blanket to savor whatever was left of that warm, just-out-of-the-dryer smell. She kicked the door shut, placed the detergent on the table, and dropped everything else on the bed.

Baker extinguished his Camel before taking the box of detergent and moving it to the kitchen counter.

Micki shot him a dark look: she didn't like people touching her things. And why did he have to move the stupid box anyway? Without being asked, she pulled out her loose-leaf and put it on the table, turning several pages and pointing. "Here, I did almost all my homework already, see? See?" But as she turned more sheets of paper, he stopped her by moving the binder toward him and shutting it.

"Actually," he said, "I'm here because we need to talk about something."

"But I haven't—"

"You're not in any trouble. Just sit down." And he did so himself, pushing her notebook off to the side.

Eye to eye they faced each other across the little table. She was waiting for him to begin. Instead, pinching his forehead, he was gazing down at the lime-green Formica. It was the first time she'd ever seen him appear in any way unsure of himself. When he finally looked up, he leaned forward, left elbow on the table, thumb resting under his jaw with his index finger lying along the crease between his lips. But then he straightened up and lit a new cigarette.

"When was the last time you got your period?" he asked.

"*What?*"

"When was the last time you got your period?" he repeated.

"Don't worry. You didn't get me pregnant."

"That's not what I'm concerned about, Micki. I used a condom with you." But even as he said it, the recent turn of events with Cynthia gave him pause.

"Then why're you asking me that?"

"Because I need to know the answer."

She clamped her mouth shut.

"You don't get one, do you."

"It's none of your business."

"I'm afraid it is."

"Why?"

"Because it's not normal for—"

"I'm normal! I'm normal!" She shoved her chair away from the table and stood up. "I'm just as much a woman as—as—as anybody!"

Great going, Jim, he thought. Left elbow on the table again, right forearm there, as well, he leaned in. He took another hit off his cigarette. "I'm not questioning your femininity. You're very much a woman—"

"Oh, yeah? Last week you told me I was a little girl."

Jesus Christ! The kid didn't miss a goddamn thing! "Look, you're a teenager. An adolescent. You're somewhere in between being a kid and being an adult."

"So I'm a kid when it suits you, and I'm an adult when it suits you."

He sat up in his chair and took hold of the nape of his neck. "Let's not get off track, okay?"

"So then what kind of a question is that?"

"It's a perfectly good question, and I want an answer."

"I'm not gonna talk to you about this."

"Why not? Because I'm a man?"

"Yeah, I—I guess that's part of it. But it's more because you hate that I'm a girl."

"Where the hell did you get that idea?"

"I heard what you said to Captain Malone."

Baker experienced a flash of panic—as if she could somehow have overheard his last meeting with the captain. But she was talking about the day when she'd first arrived from Heyden. He already knew she'd caught part of his tirade then. Breaking eye contact, he tapped the ashes from his cigarette.

Her expression bitter, she waited.

Baker chewed his lower lip, then looked up again. "That was just me being a male-chauvinist asshole, okay? I've gotten past that. I don't have any problem with you being female. For that matter, I don't have any problem talking to you about your period." And what surprised him most was that even the last thing he'd said was true. But she turned away. And when she made no move to discuss it further, he said, "I guess I'll just take you to the doctor's."

"NO!" She wheeled around so sharply he looked startled.

"We're talking about your health. It's important to find out why—"

"I know why, okay?"

"No, it's not okay—not unless you tell me."

She looked at him sitting there. He was so big with those broad shoulders, large hands... He was so...male. "Look, they checked me out at Heyden, and they didn't seem concerned."

Ah, yes, Baker thought, Heyden—the epitome of health care. "So what did they say?"

Rolling her eyes, she looked away.

"*What did they say, Micki?*"

"They said it was probably from shooting up and being so underweight."

"So then you *did* used to get it."

"I remember getting it *once*—about a week after I, y'know, woke up."

Baker leaned back. It could be nothing more than what she'd said, but he wanted to be sure.

Micki watched the smoke that was rising in delicate spirals from the end of his cigarette, forever starting toward the ceiling, only to vanish into the air.

He leaned forward on the table again. "I still want you to see a doctor."

"No!"

That was the second time she hadn't said "sir," and it was the second time he was going to let it go. "If I say you're going to the doctor, then you're going to the doctor."

"No! I'm not goin'. I don't wanna be examined like that again."

"Did something happen when they examined you at Heyden?"

"No, but I heard plenty of stories."

"I'll take you to Cynthia's doctor. He's very reputable; she wouldn't go to anyone who wasn't. Nothing bad's going to happen."

"Yeah, but that's *her*. Nobody'd hurt *her*." Micki's whole body was rigid.

Baker felt that little tug at his heart. He dropped his gaze. When he looked up again, he said, "I'll make a deal with you: I'll call the doctor and explain what's going on. If he says it's okay to wait, then we'll wait. But if he says you need to be seen right away, then you're going for an exam. Does that sound fair?"

Her voice small, she said, "I don't wanna go to one of those doctors."

"I understand that, Micki. But you may have to."

The corners of her mouth turned down.

"I tell you what," he said, "if it ends up that you have to go—and if it would make you feel safer—I'll go into the examining room with you."

"What?"

"I've done it as a cop. I'll be standing in back of you; I won't be able to see anything."

"Y'can't be serious!"

"And one more thing"—he stood up and ground his cigarette into the saucer—"don't just buy a box of tampons and get rid of a few each day. I'll know if you really have your period or not."

"Yeah? How y'gonna tell?"

An amused look crossed his face.

She quickly averted her eyes. "Forget it. I don't wanna know." Cops could get into some pretty disgusting things.

"So do we have a deal?" he asked.

"I—I dunno. I guess so."

He extended his hand.

There was a beat before her own palm went out to meet his, very tentatively, as if he might pull his back at the last second—as a joke. But the large hand engulfed hers, the grip warm and firm. She didn't want him to let go. Yet it was she who pulled away first.

Putting on his jacket, he said, "I guess I'll leave you to your laundry."

But as she watched him walk out the door, a part of her wished he would've stayed.

His apartment was too warm, and several windows were cracked open to allow cold air to enter. Baker could never understand why the super forced so much heat through the radiators. Dressed in jeans but no shirt, he was drinking his whiskey and listening to the soft patter of the rain hitting the window. Harsh and dissonant, the blast of a horn or the wail of a siren occasionally shattered the ocean-like sound of cars passing on the street below.

He'd gotten the name and number of Cynthia's gynecologist, Dr. Silverman, who'd been nice enough to return his call after hours. The doctor had been very cordial, but Baker had wondered how much the man knew about his relationship with Cynthia. And though the temptation had been strong, he'd forced himself not to pry regarding the details of her pregnancy—not that the doctor was likely to divulge much of anything anyway. In fact, when Baker explained who he was, the doctor made no comment at all.

An old-fashioned practitioner with an unhurried, easygoing manner, Dr. Silverman listened carefully to everything Baker told him about Micki, then prefaced his own remarks with a disclaimer of sorts since he'd never examined Micki himself. "My analysis," he said, "is more conjecture than fact. But it's very likely the doctor at the juvenile facility was correct in his diagnosis: habitual use of opiates *can* interrupt the menstrual cycle, as can being underweight. Since the drug use has stopped, her menses might resume if she achieves a more acceptable body weight. You say she appears to be healthy otherwise, so I don't believe there's any cause for alarm. And I don't think it would hurt to wait a few months to see if things might not right themselves of their own accord. However, if her periods don't start again within a reasonable amount of time—or you notice a change in her general health—then she should be seen right away. And since she's sexually active, she should get a regular check-up once a year anyway. It would also be prudent for her to be using some form of birth control. Her cycle could start again at any time, and she'd have no way of knowing until it was too late."

After a pause, the doctor said, "I do have one final thought: there's a possibility that psychological factors are at play here, as well. Since I almost became a psychiatrist, I can't help but throw in my two psychoanalytical cents: given what you've told me about her life and lack of memory, it wouldn't surprise me if, unconsciously, she's clinging to the last remnant of childhood that she has."

"But that doesn't make sense. She's already having sex," Baker said.

"Psychologically and emotionally, there's a big difference between having sex and being able to have a baby."

Silverman's words had struck a chord.

Baker stepped away from the window and dropped into the recliner, staring dully at the dark glass of the TV screen. But inside his head, he was seeing Micki's face, her lips slightly parted, her hair splayed out on the pillow. He saw the flash of the cross between her breasts; felt the touch of her fingers. He was thrusting inside her...

He gulped down more whiskey. What a bastard he'd been. And now to be leaving her at Heyden. But only for a few days, right? Only for a few days. Plus he'd issued a warning loud and clear: "Don't touch the kid; don't touch!" But one hour would be too long a time for her in that place, never mind four days. Still, he had no choice—no choice!—no one would take her.

Cancel the trip. Only solution. But he needed this vacation. Jesus, didn't he deserve a little time off? Time to patch things up with Cynthia? Time to catch his breath and straighten out his fucked-up life? Planned the trip almost a year ago—long before Micki. Long before. How was he to know…?

With the bottle nearly empty and his eyelids drooping, his mind and body were drifting away from the grip of the light and the sounds from the street. He could feel Micki's small hand in his. But as he entered the state between waking and dreaming, it was her eyes that he saw—large, dark, and questioning.

But he had no answers.

Chapter 17

ICKI PULLED THE OBLONG box, covered in Macy's complimentary gift wrap, out of the paper bag. Turning it this way and that, she examined it like some strange, foreign object. Wasted money. She tossed it on the table and went to pour herself a glass of Coke.

Yesterday, as she was about to check in before going home, Warner had run up to her in the hallway. "Did you know that Thursday is Sergeant Baker's birthday?" he'd asked.

"No. So what?"

"Well, it might be nice to get him something."

"Y'mean like a present?"

Warner nodded.

"Y'gotta be kidding! What would I wanna give him a present for?"

"It would be a nice gesture; help smooth things out a little."

"He'll think I'm kissin' his ass."

"No, he won't."

"He fuckin' hates me. I'm not givin' him a goddamn birthday present."

"He doesn't hate you—"

"Really? Then he's doin' a helluva job pretending."

"C'mon, Micki. Think about it…"

So later, she'd thought about it, thought about her talk with Baker the night before, thought about what it might be like if things could change. And in the morning, she'd taken extra money with her, then gotten off at the Elmhurst subway station on her way home from school. When she entered the huge, round department store, she was immediately choking on the heavy scent of perfume. And as she wandered around the first floor, she was overwhelmed by everything on display, acutely aware of the security guard who was trailing around behind her. But she had no idea what to buy. After all this time, the only things she knew about Baker were that he had a fairly large collection of rock albums—pretty hip for a guy his age—and that he liked science fiction. But since she didn't know what records he wanted or which books he hadn't read, she was back to square one.

Seeing a bunch of ties at a counter that stood out like a sanctuary for men amidst the mostly women's-wear departments, she hurried over to talk to the sales clerk. The man gave her a nervous smile, but was still polite, telling her she couldn't go wrong buying a tie. But either too dull, too loud, or too cheaply made, the selection in her price range didn't look very appealing. She had just about given up when she found one she liked: black with crisscrossing lines of gold and white. The clerk deemed it "an excellent choice" and offered to gift wrap it for her. After she'd paid, the security guard had lost interest.

Micki looked at her watch, then guzzled down the rest of her soda. She was late for work. She shoved the box back into the Macy's bag, then stuffed it in a dresser drawer, underneath her long-sleeved shirts.

As if it really mattered.

NOT LONG AFTER SHE left, Baker stopped by. He went through everything and came across her purchase from Macy's, the receipt still in the bag. He saw how much she'd paid and that she'd bought it that very day. But even without the receipt, he would've known what it was. "Let me guess," his father would say with disgust as he'd eye the telltale shape of the box, "it's a tie, am I right?" But his father had had no interests to draw upon—no hobbies, no athletic pursuits. So it was a tie or cuff links; what did the man expect? Especially since, the few times Baker had tried to be innovative, his father had exchanged the gift for a more expensive version—or something entirely different.

Baker lowered his eyes, then put the box back in the bag. Without a doubt, Micki had bought this for him. How she'd found out it was his birthday, he didn't know—though he could hazard a pretty good guess.

LATER THAT NIGHT, WHEN he couldn't put it off any longer, Baker called Mr. Antonelli to tell him Micki wouldn't be able to work during the extended holiday weekend. The restaurant owner immediately started fretting; he'd been counting on her to pick up extra shifts. Baker tried to impress upon the man the serious consequences that might ensue if anyone let it slip about the change of plans.

"Yah, yah. Is okay. I understand-a!" came the irritated response, and he hung up the phone.

Baker poured himself a drink, then dialed Warner, who took his time answering and didn't sound pleased to hear Baker's voice. "This better be important," he said. "It's late, and I've got a lot of work to get done tonight."

"Did you tell Micki it was my birthday?"

"Yeah. So what?"

"Did you tell her to buy me a gift?"

"I didn't *tell* her to do anything."

"But you encouraged her, didn't you."

"I—well I might've said something, I guess."

"You *guess*? She's got little enough money as it is. I certainly don't want her feeling obligated to spend any of it on me. Besides, do you have any idea how awkward this is? She must hate my guts more than ever now."

"I don't think she really hates you. Y'know, she said almost the exact—"

"Just do me a favor," Baker cut in, "and don't interfere."

"Fine," Warner replied. "But watching the two of you circle around, pretending you don't give a shit about each other—it's pathetic; you're both full of it. I suggested she get you something because I thought it might break down the walls a little, open your eyes a bit. Can't you see what you are to that kid?"

"I can't afford to let her get attached to me, and I certainly can't afford to get attached to her. I'm nothing more than a glorified parole officer. Once the school year is up, so is my guardianship."

"And what happens to her then?"

"I have no idea, and I don't care."

"Oh, I see. So come June, you're just going to say, 'So long, kid; have a nice life'?"

"There's no room in my life for a kid."

"Why not?"

"There just isn't—and especially a kid like her, getting into trouble every fucking minute."

"So why don't you help her?"

"Why don't *I* help her? Why don't *you* help her? If you're so fucking concerned, why don't you at least take her for the goddamn weekend instead of making me leave her at Heyden?"

"Let's not get into that again—"

"Why not?"

"Because."

"Well, that's my answer, too: 'because.' If it's good enough for you, it's good enough for me."

"Fine. You win. Are you happy now?"

But that's not how Baker felt when he hung up.

WHEN MICKI DIDN'T BRING the gift to school the next day, Baker was somewhat surprised. But maybe she wanted to give it to him at a more private place and time. Or maybe she'd simply forgotten. She didn't even say anything to him before she left to go home.

But Warner caught up with her when she was halfway to the main doors. "Why don't you hang around till three? Angie baked a cake, and we're going to throw a little party."

"I can't; I'll be late for work." She turned to go, but he touched her arm, and she spun back around. "What? Whatta y'want from me now?"

Warner retreated a step. "Nothing. Forget it."

She gazed at him with a cool, appraising eye. "He found the present, didn't he."

Warner looked apologetic.

"It's all right. I could tell he'd been through my stuff last night." Without waiting for a response, she turned and walked away.

NEEDING SOMETHING TO CUT with, Baker opened Micki's kitchen drawer and took out a large carving knife—the very knife she'd threatened him with the day she'd been late for school. Then he tore off a piece of aluminum foil and put it on the counter next to the package he'd brought.

Angie's devil's food cake with vanilla icing had been huge—huge enough to feed an army. Or so he'd thought. By the time they'd finished with it, barely a quarter had remained. They insisted he take home what was left, Angie suggesting he bring some to Micki. Warner, overhearing, had looked away.

If it weren't for the fact that Micki might think he was simply dumping leftovers on her, he would leave her the entire thing. Instead, he'd give her a very generous slice. That is, if he could cut the damn thing without destroying it. Because of a rather tough, sponge-like crust, the moist chocolate cake was squishing under the knife, the icing between the layers oozing out the sides in response to the pressure: the blade was duller than a butter knife's. Recalling how convincingly she'd held it on him, he gave in to a small smile.

He stabbed out a chunk and wrapped it up. Then he washed the knife and the counter, preparing to go. But the foil package looked very strange sitting all alone next to her books. He needed to leave a note. With a sigh, he went back and ripped a page out of her loose-leaf binder. Pen in hand, he leaned over to write. But he wasn't sure how to begin. "Dear Micki" seemed absurd while just "Micki" sounded too curt. Then again, why even bother with that; it was obvious the note was to her, wasn't it? "Angie baked me a cake," he wrote. "Thought you might like some." He paused. "Sincerely"? "Yours truly"? They seemed equally ridiculous. Maybe he should just write his name. He placed the pen on the paper, but, again, it didn't move. "Sergeant Baker" would look very cold and distant. He'd known Micki for almost three months, and their relationship, though riddled with hostility, was close. And intense. Baker closed his eyes. To think he'd even slept with her. Jesus Christ, he could just imagine how she felt still having to address him as "sir" or "Sergeant Baker." The small of his back started to hurt, and he straightened up.

He could simply sign the note "Jim," but that sounded too casual and not a wise choice, either; oddly enough, for the very same reason "Sergeant Baker" seemed too remote. Maybe he shouldn't sign it at all; after all, she'd know the note was from him. But that might look kind of rude.

He wrote, "Sgt. Baker," and left the slip of paper beneath the cake.

WHEN MICKI RETURNED HOME from work, she saw the curious hunk of foil waiting for her. She read the note and wondered if it was Angie or Baker who'd thought she'd like some cake; the wording was ambiguous. Whatever. Holding up the package, she observed it from several angles, then delicately peeled back the aluminum, exposing the dark, chocolate layers and soft white icing, some clinging lusciously to the foil. After a few seconds, she carelessly wrapped it up and hurled it into the garbage. As she stood looking down at it, still holding the lid of the pail in her hand, her heart started to ache. But she clenched her jaw and slammed the plastic top down anyway. The note, ripped into pieces, quickly followed.

She hung her damp T-shirt from work on the shower curtain rod, then yanked off her jacket. There was homework to do—lots of it. But she found herself sitting on the edge of the bed instead, hugging her knees to her chest.

BAKER STOOD IN FRONT of the couch, gazing out the window at the lightly falling snow. Cynthia, wrapped up in his comforter, was sound asleep inside his bedroom. She'd treated him to dinner at an expensive steakhouse, then given him his present: a beautiful matte-black pen with real fourteen-karat-gold accents; her way, no doubt, of gently prodding him to write again. But that dream—barely a memory now—was long gone.

And Cynthia might be gone soon, too. He could feel her slipping through the ever-widening spaces in his life. When he'd been in bed with her tonight—the first time in weeks—it had seemed more like they were simply having sex than making love. It had never felt that way with her before. And he'd actually worried about how he was performing, how he stacked up to Mr. LA, for he was confident she was sleeping with the young actor by now.

He finished off the glass of whiskey. Maybe she'd agreed to keep seeing him out of pity.

This was not a good birthday. He never liked them anymore anyway, just a reminder that everything he'd ever wanted out of life was receding further and further from his grasp. In three more years he'd be forty. *Forty.* And what did he have to show for it? When he was a kid, he couldn't wait to have a birthday; couldn't wait to get older: one year closer to getting out of that house, one year closer to freedom. He inhaled deeply from his cigarette, letting the smoke completely fill his lungs. It might mean just the opposite for Micki.

But then, the kid didn't even have a birthday; the state was using her arrest date. He exhaled the smoke. He could just imagine how much she'd want to celebrate that. And what would happen when the anniversary of that day arrived?

His guardianship was supposed to terminate no later than the end of the school year. If all went according to plan, he'd return to his squad. But what about her? Shooting back responses to Warner's questions, he'd been so flip. But in this quiet hour, alone in the darkness…

If the state's Department of Corrections wasn't satisfied with her progress, they'd remove her from the Division for Youth's jurisdiction so she could finish her sentence at Bedford Hills—an adult facility.

He stubbed the cigarette out in the bottom of the rocks glass.

To him, she was still a kid.

MICKI DIDN'T BRING THE gift to school on Friday, and she didn't say a word about the birthday cake, either. At nine fifteen that night, Baker headed back to Queens.

The couple in the basement was having another loud argument while Andy Williams, singing "Can't Get Used to Losing You," was blaring from someone's stereo on the first floor. And the payphone was actually working. He called his answering service to tell them where he was, then let himself into the apartment.

Bored with the routine of it all, he went about tossing the small space, the Macy's bag and the gift-wrapped box inside it just as he'd left them on Wednesday. And though the Scotch tape along the folded edges of the wrapping paper appeared untouched, there was no way to be certain it hadn't been tampered with. Eric, his best friend in high school, had been rather adept at opening Christmas presents in advance with no one the wiser. Baker returned the tie to its hiding place and resumed his search, which ended with him pulling the lid off the garbage pail to have a look inside. Half in, half out of the foil, the cake was still visible, scraps of his note sprinkled on top. He replaced the lid, surprised by the jabbing pain in his chest.

"WHAT THE *FUCK* DOES he want?" Micki said out loud when she saw the light on in her window. "He might as well just fuckin' move in already." She trudged up the stairs and went inside, following her usual after-work ritual without so much as an acknowledging glance.

Baker, one ankle crossed over the opposite knee, was sitting at the table and smoking. When she walked over to move her books from in front of him, he asked, "Tough night at work?"

Not meeting his eyes, she said, "Same as always." But that wasn't quite true. Though it might've been her imagination, she thought Mr. Antonelli, Tony, and even Juan, who'd been leaving when she arrived, had all been acting kind of strange—sort of sad, like they knew something she didn't.

Things had seemed off at school, as well, kids in her classes sneaking glances at her, then whispering to each other. Even in the locker room, Rhonda and her best friend, Sonya, stopped talking to study her with unusually keen interest. Rhonda then turned to cup her hand over Sonya's ear while Micki, burying her face in her notebook, pretended not to notice.

But as she was running up the stairs to get to physics—her daily race against the late bell—Micki heard the two of them again. This time they were on the second-floor landing, hanging out in the stairwell like they usually did. They liked to linger there till the last possible minute since their fifth-period class was right next door. With only seconds to go, Micki bounded up the last few steps and saw Baker on the opposite side, making his way down from the third floor. Though it was a regular coincidence of their daily schedules, she ignored him. Like she always did. But Rhonda and Sonya momentarily ceased their chattering—only to start whispering and snickering with even greater zeal.

Micki had plunged through the doors, down the corridor, and on to room 244. But the image of those two had nagged at her for the rest of the day—even through a grueling night at Bel. And now she had Baker to contend with.

She dropped her books on the desk and pulled out the chair.

"I spoke to the doctor," he said to her back.

She turned to look at him.

"He said it would be okay to wait awhile and see what happens."

She turned back to the desk.

"He also said you should be using some kind of birth control."

She faced him again. "For what?"

"If your system kicks in, you won't know right away; you could get pregnant." Both feet on the floor, he was now leaning across the table. "Hey!" he said sharply, "don't you turn your back on me, Micki! We're not through discussing this yet."

She faced him once more, arms folded over her chest, weight shifted to one leg.

"Does Rick use a condom?" he asked.

Her eyes grew darker.

"Answer me," he ordered, adding, "Just say 'yes' or 'no.' You can skip the 'sir' for now."

"No."

"Well then you'd better get him to start, do you hear me? It's a good idea, no matter what. A prick like that wouldn't think twice about giving you VD."

Unfolding her arms, her eyes narrowed further. "Is that why *you* used a condom? You thought I'd give you VD?"

"Is that what you think?"

"Yeah! Yeah, I guess so! It's not like you really give a shit about me."

The heat rose in his face. "Really? Then what am I doing worrying about you?"

"You have to 'cause it's your fuckin' job. You're just afraid if you don't, I might somehow end up bein' a bigger pain in your ass."

He sat back. Every little thing was so fucking complicated now. Leaning across the table again, emphasizing his words with little jabs of the Camel pinched between his thumb and index finger, he said, "I used a condom because I didn't want to risk getting you pregnant." He raised the cigarette to his lips.

She looked toward the kitchen. "Are we done talking about this?"

He leaned back. "Yes—unless there's something *you* want to discuss."

But she promptly sat down and opened her loose-leaf to start her homework. He lit a fresh cigarette with the spent one and continued watching her. She could feel his eyes, like two hot beams, boring into the back of her head.

"I found the package from Macy's," he said.

"So?" She continued writing.

"So I'm going to have to open it. You understand that, don't you?"

She shrugged. "Go ahead." Half under her breath, she added, "I bought the damn thing for you anyway."

"What?"

Twisting around, she threw her arm across the back of the chair. "I *said* I bought it for you anyway."

"But you must've changed your mind." When she went back to writing, he added, "Why don't you return it? You still have the receipt; you could get your money back."

The chair scraped loudly against the floor as she pushed herself away from the desk. She went over to the dresser, yanked open the complaining drawer, and pulled out the bag. With a flick of her wrist, she tossed the box onto the table, where it only narrowly missed the saucer full of ashes and cigarette butts. "Just open the damn thing already."

Baker steadied himself. There was a lot of emotion flying around, and, for once, he was wise enough to know that none of it was what it seemed. He stubbed out the barely smoked cigarette. Best poker face in place, he tore the wrapping off the box. Considering how little she'd paid, whatever was inside wasn't going to be too nice. In fact, it might be quite hideous. But when he removed the top and folded back the tissue paper, he caught his breath: the tie looked way more expensive than it was. "It's *very* nice," he said, and stood up. "Thank you." He took a step toward her.

But she backed away and shrugged. "Yeah, well, whatever."

With great force of will, he shut down the smile that was forming: she would think he was laughing at her. He put on his jacket and gathered his things while she watched him very closely, two deep creases between her eyebrows. Paused in the doorway, he thanked her again before he left.

She went back to her desk and closed her books. She just about never did homework on Fridays.

Chapter 18

ALMOST OUT OF BREATH, Micki was racing up the stairs after gym—everything always seemed so much harder on Mondays. The staircase itself was empty, most kids already at their next class. But she could hear voices ahead on the second-floor landing: Rhonda and Sonya along with Sonya's boyfriend, Reese Parker, a loud-mouthed troublemaker who'd been left back to repeat his senior year.

She was about to open the door when the boy called out, "Hey—Micki!"

Eyeing the little group that was casually leaning against the wall, she wondered if their smirks were permanently plastered across their faces.

"Word's out," he said, "you spent time on the street."

She turned and reached for the handle.

"Word is," he continued, "you used to do guys for money."

She dropped her books and faced the boy as he approached. Rhonda and Sonya's grins grew broader: Baker was coming down the stairs from the third floor.

"So, like, here's a buck," the boy said, pulling a dollar from his pocket and letting it fall to the floor. "Why don'tcha go down and do me." And he tugged at his crotch.

He was still pulling at his groin when Micki hooked him with her left fist. A solid connection, it sent the boy spinning and stumbling backward toward the stairs while Rhonda and Sonya's snickers dissolved into gasps and shrieks. Rushing in with outstretched arms, they barely kept him from tumbling down.

Micki felt Baker's grip on the collar of her shirt. He slammed her into the wall next to the staircase and cuffed her hands behind her. The late bell rang a shrill condemnation.

"You stay put if you know what's good for you," he said. And while he hailed Warner on the walkie-talkie, he hurried over to check on the boy's condition.

Reese's right eye was swelling shut, the surrounding flesh proud with the engorging blood. Underneath was a deepening crescent of red. Still dazed, the boy did nothing more than moan and groan loudly while Baker did a superficial examination.

Rhonda pointed at Micki. "She started it!"

"What? I—"

"Shut up, Micki!" Baker barked over his shoulder.

Warner arrived with the nurse.

Alone by the wall, a forgotten bystander outside the whirl of activity, Micki stopped listening to the lies Rhonda and Sonya were telling, their voices becoming little more than the whining, meaningless static of a broken radio. But the heavy aching in her heart made her want to wrap her hand around the goddamn thing and squeeze until it couldn't feel anything anymore. All it ever did was hurt.

She turned her head, eyes falling on the stairwell window. Large and imposing, rising from the landing below, the glass was brimming with light behind the grimy wire mesh. Presiding with a gritty, urban majesty, it was like a permanently gated portal to a bright and shiny world she'd never know. She shifted her gaze to the metal railing. Even without her hands, she could probably manage to get herself over—

Baker grabbed her by the arm and pulled her downstairs after him. Twice she nearly fell, only to be hauled upward by his painful grip. As soon as they were in the office, he said, "Do you have any idea what the fuck you just did?"

She stared into his chest.

"Huh?" he demanded.

"He said—"

"He *said*? He SAID? You fucking *hit* him. He nearly fell down the stairs— could've gotten killed."

Eyes flashing, she said, "I'm sorry he didn't break his fuckin' neck."

The back of Baker's hand found its mark, and she lost her balance, the worse because her hands were still cuffed. "Maybe I ought to give *you* a black eye," he said. "How would you like that, Micki? Huh? How does that sound?"

"Go ahead!"

Handfuls of her shirt in his fists, he pulled her forward, then slammed her back against the file cabinets. "What's it going to take to get it through that thick skull of yours that you can't go around hitting people just because you don't like what they say?"

She couldn't believe those words were coming out of his mouth. She almost laughed. She said, "Oh, so he gets t'say whatever he wants, and I'm supposeda just take it?"

"Do you know how close you are to getting kicked out of this school?"

"Like I'm the only kid ever got in a goddamn fight?"

Baker lowered his voice. "It's gotten around that you've done time upstate. Somehow, some of the parents have found out, and they're not too happy about it. Do you know what they spent most of last week's PTA meeting talking about?" He paused as if she might actually answer. "You," he continued. "One of the teachers filled me in because I wasn't there. Parents are outraged that you're going to school with their kids. One mother wanted to know why the city was dumping its garbage in her backyard—those were her exact words. That's what people think of you, Micki. And by pulling shit like this, you're proving just how right they are. They want your sorry ass out of here, and, quite frankly, I don't blame them."

Vacant and dull, her eyes had drifted down to his chest.

Warner stuck his head in the door. "The boy's going to be all right; he's in the boys' emergency room with the nurse." He paused before adding, "The assistant principal wants to see you both in his office while he's waiting for Mrs. Parker to arrive."

"Be there in a minute," Baker responded.

Warner left.

Baker removed the handcuffs. "You realize you're going to be suspended this time."

The shrug was almost imperceptible.

Through the scratched and weathered glass of the bus's window, blocks full of houses passed by—some pretty, others not so much. But Micki was no longer thinking about what it would be like to live in one of them. As the scenery swept past like a strip of old and faded film, she kept hearing what that woman had said: that she was garbage being dumped in their nice school, in their nice neighborhood. They wanted to get rid of her. And Baker didn't blame them.

She descended into the subway, where it was dark and dirty, the assistant principal's words coming back to her as a train pulled into the station: "We won't tolerate any more behavior like this… Your being here is a privilege that can be taken away…" When he'd finally gotten around to asking what she had to say in her defense, she'd said nothing. Baker, looking puzzled, made her leave and wait outside the office so he could talk to the assistant principal alone. When he called her back in, Mr. Hillerman informed her she was suspended for the rest of the day and for Tuesday, as well, leaving her with only one day of school before the holiday. Of course, Baker had made sure she understood her suspension wouldn't be a vacation; she'd spend it in the security office, doing homework and making up the class work she'd miss.

The long weekend, which had loomed ahead as an oasis of freedom, seemed tainted by the day's events, as if a large, black cloud had cast a shadow over her. Every minute alone now would be a battle—and it had already begun. Her old friend—her only friend—was waiting for her to come back, calling to her from every cell of her body, out of the very darkness surrounding the train as it hurtled through the tunnels of the underbelly of the city.

At ten past noon, Micki emerged from the subway, fully submerged in her own little hell.

HIS DAY OVER, BAKER left the school and drove to Micki's apartment. Why she hadn't offered any kind of explanation to the assistant principal, he didn't know. But after he'd sent her out of the office, he'd taken it upon himself to tell what he'd observed. The result had been one less day of suspension for her, with a day of suspension for the Parker boy, as well. But considering the lynch-mob climate of the recent PTA meeting, the incident couldn't have come at a worse time.

He parked his car and walked down the street, pausing in front of Micki's building to take in the crisp, dry air. Autumn—his favorite season. Yet each year it seemed shorter, as though winter couldn't wait to cloak the earth in shades of white and grey, leaving the colorful sprays of fallen leaves a brown and brittle remnant underneath. Today, however, the sky was a beautiful cerulean blue, wisps of clouds like soft-spun threads of cotton candy. The breeze shifted slightly, and he smelled the garbage in the pails lined up behind the fence at the foot of the stoop. He hurried inside.

At the top of the stairs, a new "ouT Of oRDeR" sign had been posted on the payphone, though he'd never even seen anyone using it—or fixing it, either. But as he made his way down the hall, his focus shifted, his heart pumping faster. When he turned the key in the lock, his hands were already cold and clammy.

He opened the door to find the apartment dark, the partially drawn curtains creating patches of light within the ambient shadow. He switched on the overhead fixture, and Micki blinked. Sitting on the floor, she was slouched against the wall between the dresser and the bed, one hand wrapped around the neck of a nearly empty wine bottle.

"You're drunk," he said.

Bruised left hand in the shape of a pistol, she closed one eye and aimed it at him. She mimed recoil—"Bingo!"—then put the bottle to her lips and took a drink.

"So you're having a little party to celebrate your suspension?"

She scrambled clumsily to her feet, swaying unsteadily, biting the inside of her cheek to quash the fit of laughter welling up inside her. She had no idea what was so funny; just moments before she'd been in the depths of despair. "I dunno," she finally blurted out, her speech so slurred it sounded like *ahhdno*. Lips pressed together tightly, she was struggling to suppress the silly grin that was bubbling to the surface.

Baker shook his head. "It's just one fuck-up after another with you; you've got no respect for anything. You break rules like they don't exist. Am I supposed to ignore this? I warned you about this, Micki; I told you nothing was going to change because of what happened."

She tried to look serious, but it only made her giggle.

He shook his head again. "I don't know why I bother with you. You're a fucking loser, y'know that? A real—fucking—loser."

And all at once, her eyes became sad. She slowly lowered her gaze, then smashed the bottle against the wall.

Baker felt an incredible rush. Every muscle taught, his eyes were riveted to the weapon she held. "Micki!" But she turned away and reached for the dresser to steady herself. Now in profile, the hand with the broken bottle was closest to the wall. He could charge her, but one small twist of her wrist and he'd be impaled. "Micki," he ordered, "you put that down *now*."

He might as well have not been there. Stepping back from the dresser, she switched her grip on the bottle's neck and held it in both hands, one wrapped around the other.

Frozen to the floor, Baker looked on while everything seemed to slide into slow motion, Micki's arms swinging up above her head in a long, graceful arc. But when the jagged glass reached its zenith—light glinting off the thin, sharp points— he sprang forward, throwing his entire body weight against her. She crashed into the wall, grunting as the air was knocked out of her lungs. Propelled from her hands, the broken bottle's splintering landing was heard a moment later like an afterthought. Glass was everywhere, and Baker kept his body pressed into hers, which was now limp and lifeless. When she didn't respond to his demands to stand up on her own, he bent his knees and threw her over his shoulder in a fireman's grip. Careful where he stepped, he carried her to the table, then kicked out a chair and put her down.

Barely conscious, she was unable to sit up without him holding her there. He placed her arms on the table and her head on top. Then he took a look around. Splattered on the wall, the wine had left a large maroon splotch with slender tendrils dripping down. Chunks, slivers, and tiny bits of glass had sprayed in all directions.

It was a lot to clean up.

THERE WAS TOO MUCH glass on the bed to salvage anything more than the pillow from inside the pillowcase. Everything else went directly into the trash. Systematically moving back and forth across the hardwood planks, he thoroughly swept the floor. He wasn't touching the wall.

Micki hadn't moved since he'd set her down at the table. He picked her up in his arms and carried her over to the bare mattress, a stained and ratty-looking affair. Watching her lying there made him think of psych wards and insane asylums. In fact, right across Union Turnpike, only a few blocks from the high school, was Creedmore State Mental Hospital, its tallest building visible from far around. With its barred, silent windows, it was incredibly creepy. What if they wanted to lock Micki up in a place like that? Already labeled a psychiatric case because of her amnesia, they could just as easily say she'd become a danger to herself. Then again, she'd been drunk.

As if none of it would've happened otherwise.

Without thinking, he turned her onto her stomach. Maybe leaving her at Heyden had a good side to it. For one thing, she'd be under close supervision twenty-four hours a day without much opportunity for a repeat of this little drama. And she might finally comprehend what the consequences would be if she continued to disregard the rules surrounding her release. There was no way she could really want to go back to that place.

But he wasn't fooling anyone: the closer the day of leaving her there became, the more he felt it was a mistake. And as for her safety, people in lockup who wanted to kill themselves, often succeeded despite the high level of surveillance and apparent lack of means.

He put on his jacket, took her homework assignments from his pocket, and left them on the table. Then he picked up the plastic bag full of broken glass and ruined bedding, and shut the light.

It wasn't yet dawn. Still asleep, Micki lay on her side, knees tucked to her chest, a spreading wedge of pale light stretching out across her face. Her eyes gradually opened to see a large silhouetted figure in the doorway. She jumped up, unprepared for the pain that shot through her head.

"It's just me, Micki," said the shadow. Baker switched on the light to see her in the same clothes as the day before, though she must've gotten up at some point to put on her jacket. The apartment was cold.

Squinting, she pressed her palms to her forehead. "What time is it?"

"Five past six. I'm driving you to school. How long will it take you to get ready?"

She thought about being alone in the car with him, in that intimate little space. "I can take the subway."

He shut the door. "You wish. You're not allowed to set one toe on school grounds today without someone being right there to watch you. You're not even supposed to be there."

"So let me stay home."

"After what you did? Fat chance."

"Are you really taking me to school?"

"Where else would I be taking you?"

She studied his face. "I'll be ready in ten or fifteen minutes."

"I'll wait outside."

WHEN SHE GOT IN the car, her hair was damp. The sky was just beginning to grow light. Outside the windows, everything looked cold, sharp, and well-defined. Inside the Camaro, it was nice and warm.

Micki turned her head to look at him. "What happened to my blanket and stuff?"

Eyes on the road, he said, "There was glass all over everything; I had to throw it away."

She faced forward again.

He stubbed out his cigarette and flipped on the radio, catching "It Don't Come Easy"—probably the only Ringo Starr song he'd ever liked. When a commercial came on, he switched to the news while Micki put her colored pens in her jacket pocket and thought about the hours ahead—a whole day stuck in the security office.

"Did you eat anything before you ran out of there?" he asked.

"I'm not hungry."

He shot a glance at the books on her lap. "You didn't bring a lunch, either."

"I'm kinda nauseous."

"You're not going to throw up, are you?"

"I'm not gonna puke."

"Are you sure? 'Cause I'll pull over."

"Jesus Christ, I'm fine."

He changed lanes. "Did you drink all that wine by yourself?"

She noticed a dead squirrel in the middle of the street. Another car ran right over it.

"Did you?" he pressed.

"What?"

"Did you drink all that wine yourself?"

"Yessir."

"Where did you get it?"

She straightened out the books on her lap. "Joey."

"He's one of Rick's pals, right?"

She looked over at him. She'd never mentioned Joey before. But then, Baker was a fucking detective; what did she expect? "Yessir."

"Are you messing around with him, too?"

Her voice stiffened. "I gave him *money* to buy it for me."

Baker shut the radio off. "Jesus, Micki, I wasn't implying anything; it was a simple, straightforward question."

"The answer is *no*."

When they arrived at the school, they pulled into a parking spot around the corner from the main entrance. Micki unlocked the door to get out, but Baker grabbed her arm. "Not so fast."

Heart and head both pounding, she sat back in the seat, staring out the windshield. Baker killed the engine and angled himself in her direction as best he could.

"What the hell did you think you were doing yesterday?"

She shrugged.

He lit another cigarette and stuffed the used match in the ashtray. "What do you think I should do about it?"

She shrugged again.

"Well then maybe you want to tell me what was going through your head when you broke that bottle."

Wearing white shoes, white stockings, and a white dress underneath a short navy wool coat, a woman was walking down the street. She had a white nurse's cap sitting on top of her head like a crown. Micki watched her unlock a red Pinto's door and get in. "I—I was..."

"You were what?"

"I...I dunno."

"I think you ought to talk to someone."

She turned her head. "Y'mean like a shrink?"

"Yeah, like a shrink."

"I'm not crazy!"

"You don't have to be crazy to see a shrink."

"Oh, yeah? Have you ever talked to one?"

Since he'd never actually spoken more than two sincere words to Tillim, he said, "No."

"Well, they've poked around in *my* head enough already. I just wanna be left alone."

"What about talking to Mr. Warner?"

"Forget it."

Baker smoked while Micki tapped her foot on the rubber floor mat.

"Do you want to talk to *me* about anything?" he asked.

Looking through the window at the empty spot where the Pinto had been, she snorted. "Yeah, right." After several more seconds had passed, she asked, "If we're just gonna sit here, can we at least listen to the radio?"

Like a sigh, Baker exhaled the smoke from his lungs, then mashed the cigarette into the tiny ashtray. "Let's go, Micki." And he got out of the car.

Only Micki looked relieved.

FOR THE FIRST HALF hour of her suspension, Micki helped the custodian paint over the Vipers' graffiti. The Vipers were a white gang that periodically spray-painted their logo on school walls overnight. There was a black gang, too—the Demons—but they stayed much more underground and were rarely ever talked about. And yet, just a week ago, Micki had overheard a girl in gym class saying one of the Demons had accidentally shot himself while cleaning his gun. At least, that was the rumor.

The rest of the day was homework and class work, including tests: Warner gave her an English exam during third period; Baker administered a make-up history exam during eighth. Afterward, Baker walked her to the bus stop and waited until the Q44A arrived. As the doors were closing, he said, "Make sure you get here on time tomorrow."

She took a seat and stared out the window. But as the bus pulled away, her hands clutched at her books: the restless, edgy craving had returned.

BEFORE SHE WENT TO WORK, Micki spent almost every extra penny she had buying a new blanket and a set of sheets at Sunny's. But tomorrow she'd be getting paid again, and she couldn't exactly spend it all just to get rid of it. She looked around Bel's kitchen, everyone so busy—just like she was. For now. The upcoming holiday, with all of its unstructured time, had become something to fear.

Chapter 19

LOOKING LIKE SHE MIGHT grab it from him if she had to wait a moment longer, Micki took the pink piece of paper Baker handed her. On it she saw:

Physics—99

Calculus—99

English—99

American History—98

Economics—95

When he saw her copying the numbers down and calculating, he asked, "What're you doing?"

"I wanna see what my average is."

He put his finger next to the UN—*unsatisfactory*—she'd gotten for general conduct. "That better improve next time. It was supposed to go up."

Staring at the desk, she said, "Yessir."

"Otherwise, that's—that's an excellent report card."

She looked up. "Thanks!"

"Yeah, well, give it back to me now so I can sign it."

For the rest of homeroom, he avoided any eye contact with her.

GAZE FOCUSED ON THE ceiling, Micki watched the play of shadows and listened to the sounds coming from the street: an occasional passing car, some kids hanging out... At one point she heard a bottle break; a little later, the rev of a motorcycle engine before it screeched away. But mostly she was concentrating on the radio. As part of a Thanksgiving Day special, the station was playing sets of songs by different bands before it commenced its official countdown of the top one hundred rock songs of all time.

She was hungry again. Though hours till dawn, she'd already been up for quite a while. When she'd opened her eyes and couldn't fall back to sleep, she'd decided to have breakfast, take a long hot shower, then go back to bed. With no school for four days and no work till Friday, what difference did it make if she did things at crazy times? And though the water had become icy cold less than five minutes after she'd turned it on, it hadn't dampened her spirits. Not only had Baker said something nice to her for once, but the desire to shoot up had finally burned itself out. Yesterday, midway through her shift at the restaurant, she'd realized it was gone. And *Baker* would be gone. When asked about his holiday plans, she'd heard him mention to several people that he was taking a trip to Vermont with Cynthia.

The radio was in the middle of a set of one-hit wonders. Marmalade's "Reflections of My Life" came on, and Micki turned up the volume. But as the second verse started, she heard a car slow down, then stop in front of her building. She heard its door open and close. It was Baker. She didn't know how she knew, but she did. Footsteps were coming up the stoop, and then the downstairs door opened.

She jumped out of bed, switched on the desk light, and frantically threw on her jeans. It wasn't even four o'clock in the morning. Wasn't he leaving on his trip today? The footsteps reached the landing and drew closer to her door. His key was turning in the lock while her fly had caught on her nightshirt.

He stepped into the apartment.

They stared at each other across the room. She was still buckling her belt. He closed the door. She shut the radio off. Leaving only silence.

Eyes narrowed, Baker looked her over. When he'd gotten out of the car, her apartment had been dark. Now the light was on and she was wearing jeans. "Anybody else here?" he asked as he turned on the overhead fixture. Then he strode over to the fire escape window, stuck his head out, and looked down.

"Not that I know of."

He closed the window and locked it, then walked over to the closet and the bathroom—both empty. "Why were you getting dressed?"

"I heard the car."

"That could've been anybody; how did you know it was me?"

She shrugged.

"You looked out the window?"

She shook her head no.

A chill shot through him.

She said, "Y'know, you left your car running."

"Cynthia's waiting down there. I wanted to keep the heater on." Micki's shoulders relaxed until he added, "I need you to get dressed and throw a few things in your bag. You'll be staying at Heyden till Sunday."

Her entire body tensed. "Why can't I stay here?"

"You're not allowed to be here without my supervision."

"I'll stay out of trouble. I'll—"

"Micki! I'm in no mood for arguments."

"Is this 'cause a what happened Monday? 'Cause a the fight? 'Cause I got drunk?"

"The decision was made long before then."

He's leaving me there for good, she thought. Not just the weekend. She swallowed hard. "I—I'm supposeda work a lot this weekend—extra shifts an' all. Mr. Antonelli—"

"Knew last week," Baker interrupted. "He's already made other arrangements."

So everybody had known. Except her.

"Get dressed," he repeated. "I don't like leaving Cynthia down there alone."

"Well, she coulda come up, y'know."

Baker pulled out his lighter and lit a cigarette.

"Oh, I see," Micki said. "She doesn't belong in a dump like this."

"Just get dressed, Micki."

She took her shirt and bra into the bathroom to change, then came out and put her sneakers on. With a couple of rough tugs, she yanked her little duffle bag out of the closet from under her laundry. But on her way to the dresser, she stopped to glance at Baker. Leaning against the door, he had one leg casually crossed over the other at the ankle. And his right arm, lying across his waist, was propping up his left as he smoked. Underneath his leather jacket, which was still zipped—unusual for him—she could see the collar of a black turtleneck. And he was wearing a new pair of jeans. *Black* jeans. She resented this for some reason. Her eyes met his, traveled all the way down to his leather boots, then back up to his face.

"What the hell are you doing?" he asked. "Committing me to memory?"

316 ◆ Randy Mason

She went to the dresser. That was *exactly* what she'd been doing. No matter what, she would remember that once—just once—she'd made it with a guy that looked like him. And in her mind, it would always be tender and romantic. No one had ever been that way with her. Probably no one ever would again.

"Hey!"—he grabbed a fistful of clothes out of her hand and threw them back in the drawer—"you only need enough for three days. You certainly don't need these T-shirts."

"They're *mine*. I bought 'em with *my* money that I *earned*. I can take 'em if I want!"

"You're only staying there through the weekend. How many times do I have to say that? Don't you think I'd have the balls to tell you if I were leaving you there for good?"

Her icy stare was cynical.

"Give me that!" And he snatched the bag out of her hand. Cigarette dangling from his mouth, he proceeded to pack whatever he thought was appropriate. "Go get your toothbrush and all that stuff." She did as she was told, then lifted her mattress and removed her money and bankbooks. He went over and grabbed them. "You won't be needing these, either." She glared at him while he stubbed out his cigarette. He was about to return her things to their hiding place when he paused: between the fire escape right outside the window and the cheap lock on the door, just about anybody with half a brain could get into her apartment. He stuffed the money, checkbook, and savings-account passbook in his jacket pocket. "I'll hold on to these so they'll be safe."

"I'll bet."

"I don't need any of your smart mouth right now."

"Yer always such a dick."

His nostrils flared. "Put your jacket on, and let's go."

While she was shoving her arms into the sleeves, she spied her radio.

"Leave it," he said.

"What's the fuckin' difference t'you?"

His palm connected with her body just below the shoulder, jolting her. And then his finger was in her face. "It's a long drive to Heyden. And if you don't straighten out your act, I could make it very uncomfortable for you."

"Like I fuckin' care at this point."

He dropped the bag to the floor. "That's it; I've had it." The cuffs were in his hand. "Turn around."

She held her ground.

"Don't test me, Micki. Because, one way or another, I'm going to get these things on you."

Eyes blazing, she turned and put her hands behind her, letting him slap the metal around her wrists. Then he picked up the bag and opened the door.

She walked out without a final glance. I'm coming back, she told herself. But only part of her believed it.

He hadn't taken her schoolbooks.

JUST AS THEY REACHED the first floor landing, Baker yanked her to a stop. In a frenzied whisper he said, "Don't you *dare* say a word to Cynthia about what happened between us."

"I thought y'said she wouldn't care."

He shook her. "Did you hear what I just said?"

Voice weary, she replied, "I told ya I wouldn't say nothin' t'anybody."

"Yeah, but that was then."

"I got no reason t'hurt her."

"But you've got plenty of reasons to hurt *me*."

"Not at her expense."

Baker lowered his eyes. And for the rest of the way out to the car, the grip on her arm was less severe.

WHEN BAKER OPENED HIS door, Cynthia woke up. From the way he was helping Micki get in—one hand on her head so she wouldn't bump it on the roof, one hand on her arm to steady her—Cynthia knew Micki was cuffed.

"You keep your mouth shut," he ordered Micki. "I don't want to hear a word out of you."

Now sitting up very straight, Cynthia looked like she was about to object, but then faced front again. Baker pushed the back of the bucket seat upright, threw Micki's bag in the trunk, and got in himself. Cynthia shot him a nervous glance.

"Everything's fine," he said. But when he looked in the rearview mirror, he saw Micki's eyes glued to the front door of her building. He shifted the car into first and pulled away.

Once her apartment was out of sight, Micki unwound her body and slouched down. But after a few minutes, she started to twist and squirm: her cuffed hands were pressing into her spine while her lower limbs were mangled. The front seats—to accommodate two pairs of very long legs—were pushed back as far as they could go. She caught Baker's eyes in the rearview mirror and immediately looked away. Three hours—that's all she had left.

NOTHING ABOUT THIS VACATION augurs well, Baker thought. They'd initially planned on arriving at the White Horse Inn by late Thanksgiving Eve; that's how he'd made the reservations last year. But two weeks ago, Cynthia had gotten a call for a television commercial to be shot on the Wednesday of their departure: yesterday. To keep the peace, she'd agreed to leave at this insane hour so they'd at least reach Vermont by early Thanksgiving Day. He, in turn, had promised to let her sleep the whole drive up if she needed to—which seemed highly likely. Apparently, the shoot hadn't ended until after midnight. After *midnight.* He couldn't fathom how a sixty-second advertisement had to take a whole fucking day to shoot. But then, what did he know? He was just a cop. He'd learned to keep his mouth shut about things like that. Their one lucky break was that Heyden wasn't too far out of their way. But what a lousy way to start a trip.

A truck and a run-down van were the only vehicles in sight as the Camaro crossed the Triborough Bridge, Baker skimming along in the right-hand lane. But as soon as they'd reached the other side, he pulled over on a level span of shoulder. Engine still running, he left the car in neutral with the emergency brake engaged.

"What's wrong?" Cynthia asked.

"Nothing." And he got out and pushed the back of his seat forward.

Micki stared at him. "I haven't said a goddamn thing since we left."

"Give me your hands."

It was then that she saw the tiny key he was holding. Her eyes flicked up to his before she twisted around so he could remove the handcuffs.

Without another word he got back in the car, and, once again, they were off.

ABOUT TWO HOURS LATER—THE sky still black but dusted with thousands of stars—they stopped at a Howard Johnson's for breakfast. The restaurant was large and empty, the aroma of coffee, grease, maple syrup, and cigarettes mingling in the air, forever circulating through the ventilation system. The only diners, they were seated in a booth up front—Cynthia on one side and Micki on the other with Baker next to her, facing the door.

Their waitress, who wasn't more than a few years older than Micki, looked like she'd been crying and was about to start again any minute. She asked if they wanted coffee, and Baker said yes for all of them. She filled their cups and said she'd return.

Cynthia, studying the menu intently, said she was starving—which meant she might actually eat an entire English muffin. Already knowing what he wanted, Baker simply glanced over the choices. Micki's menu, however, lay unopened in front of her. And with nothing else to look at—the dark windows more like mirrors—her attention settled on Cynthia. The woman wore no make-up, and there were dark bags under her eyes. Her hair, tied in a low ponytail, hung in front of her left shoulder while oversized hoop earrings glowed rich and warm. She looked like a gypsy. Micki shifted her head and took to staring blankly over the tops of the booths.

Wriggling out of her coat, Cynthia said, "Oh, it's so warm in here!"

Baker merely unzipped his jacket.

Micki was silent.

Cynthia asked, "So, tell me, Micki: what's your favorite subject at school?"

Micki's gaze refocused, eyes filled with such darkness that the woman's smile faltered. Baker, barely breathing, waited: god only knew what kind of profanity was going to come out of Micki's mouth.

"Physics," Micki finally replied.

"Physics! Really!" Cynthia said. "Boy, when I was in high school, you never heard a girl say that. People gave me a hard time just for loving math so much." Cynthia grinned. "The guys better watch out; we women are taking over." And she winked.

Micki's expression didn't change.

"So—um—what do you especially like about physics?"

Micki's jaw tightened. But then she said, "Quantum mechanics. And special relativity. Mr. Taubenfeld, my physics teacher—he's my favorite teacher—gave me a book so I could teach it to the rest of the class."

"Wow, you must be extraordinarily bright," Cynthia said.

But Micki, now looking at the far wall, was contemplating how unlikely it was that she'd ever get to make that presentation.

And Baker recalled the book Micki was referring to, a white paperback with a red circle on it: *Space and Time in Special Relativity* by N. David Mermin. He'd first seen it about a week and a half ago. Even for the accelerated program she was in, he'd thought the topic a bit advanced. Yet he'd never asked her about it—never even asked her, in all this time, what her favorite subject was.

Eyes and nose redder than before, their waitress, dabbing at her face with a tissue, came back to take their order.

"I can't decide," Cynthia said, "between the English muffins and the corn toasties. Hmm…" She played with her ponytail. "I guess I'll have the English muffins."

Handing the waitress his menu, Baker said, "Scrambled eggs with French fries. That comes with toast?"

"And juice."

"I don't want the juice."

"I'll take your juice," Cynthia said. Then she looked at the waitress. "Orange juice?"

"Or tomato or grapefruit."

"Ooh, I'll have the grapefruit."

The waitress nodded, then looked at Micki.

"Nothing."

"I'm paying, Micki, so order whatever you want," Baker said.

"I don't *want* anything."

The waitress collected the rest of the menus. But as she turned to leave, Baker stopped her. "Bring her the same thing I'm having."

The waitress nodded and hurried away.

Doing a slow burn, Micki looked down at the paper placemat. It had a bunch of stupid games printed on it. And then she had an idea. How fortunate that, like Baker, she'd kept her jacket on. "I need to use the john," she said.

He got up to let her out, his jacket shifting to reveal the handle of a large gun in a shoulder holster. Micki's throat constricted: the son of a bitch was such a liar. He had no intention of bringing her back from Heyden. She started for the restrooms, only to find that he was following. Almost sick, she still reached for the door, but he yanked her back behind him and knocked.

"What're you doing?" she asked.

When there was no response from inside, he opened the door and went in. Micki followed. To the left was a row of sinks with the stalls just beyond. Straight ahead was a window of frosted glass.

"Well, this works out fine," he said. "Go on."

"But—but y'can't stay in here."

"Why not? There are doors on the toilets."

"But this is the *ladies'* room."

As if on cue, the door swung open. It was their waitress, most definitely on the verge of a fresh crying jag stopped dead by the shock of seeing a man in the women's bathroom.

Baker, blocking her entry, flashed his badge in front of her saucer-shaped eyes. "I'm sorry, miss, but you'll have to wait a few minutes."

And though it hadn't seemed possible, her eyes widened further.

"Nothing to be concerned about," he said. "We'll be out of here shortly."

Since the girl made no effort to move, Baker essentially closed the door in her face and, arms folded over his chest, leaned back against it. "Well, let's hurry it up here, Micki; somebody's waiting now."

Cursing silently, she went to the furthest stall—ignoring the damn window— and pushed in the door. She looked at the toilet, pictured Baker standing by the sinks, then marched back to where he was waiting. "I changed my mind," she said.

"Gee, what a surprise."

They returned to the booth to find the waitress had just served their food, the table now full of plates and condiments. Micki, mouth in a thin line, stared past Cynthia, who was studying her with a concerned expression: Cynthia's seat afforded a partial view of the restroom area.

When Cynthia turned her gaze to Baker, he said, "I had to go in with her, Cyn." He looked at Micki with an odd mixture of emotions, adding, "And she knows why."

Fuck you, Micki thought.

No one said anything.

Cynthia glanced from Baker to Micki.

No one moved.

Then Cynthia picked up half of an English muffin to smudge the tiniest dab of butter across the top. The knife scraped against the browned irregular edges of the craters. It was the only sound.

Micki was staring across the room.

Baker was staring at Micki.

Until Cynthia, still buttering the muffin, said in hushed tones, "So—um—our waitress just got dumped by her boyfriend; that's why she's so upset. High school sweethearts, they were. He went away to college while she stayed home. He's in his senior year now. Last night he returned for the holiday and told her he'd fallen in love with someone else."

Baker picked up the ketchup and used it to douse his eggs and French fries. Leave it to Cynthia, he thought, to get a total stranger to pour her heart out.

And then the couple began to talk about the weekend: scenic drives, long walks, and evenings in front of a fire. Sunday, before heading back to the city, they'd drop in on Cynthia's parents to have lunch.

"My mom," Cynthia said, "told me it already snowed quite a bit by them. I'd like to rent some skis and do some cross-country at the inn. Would you try it, Jim?"

"I'll give it a shot—have to see if my knees can handle it."

Tuning in and out of the conversation, Micki was catching bits and pieces of the idyllic scenes the couple was painting, her own mind conjuring up images of Heyden. She wanted to tell them both to shut the fuck up. Instead, she drank her coffee. But left the food untouched.

Baker quickly cleaned his plate, the bright-red ketchup left behind like a finger-painted design. Cynthia, eating much more slowly, was still working on her first English muffin, to which she'd added preserves.

The waitress, stopping by to pour fresh coffee, asked, "How're we doing here?"

"I'm done," Baker said.

"Me, too," Cynthia said, and pushed back her plate.

"Are you going to eat any of that, Micki?" Baker asked.

Eyes fixed on her cup, she said, "No, sir."

"It's a shame for that to go to waste."

She looked at him. "So put it on my tab."

He snorted and flashed a wan smile. But Cynthia had caught the sadness in his eyes.

"You can take her plate," Baker told the waitress. "And I'll take the check."

Dawn was breaking. But before they got back on the highway, they stopped for gas. While the tank filled up, the attendant cleaned the windshield and then the back window, the squeegee squeaking across the now-crystal-clear glass. Micki thought of Mr. Paladino, her economics teacher. His special quirk was to sponge down the blackboards and squeegee them dry.

Her heart hurt.

They drove on into the morning, the light playing differently across the scenery as the sun rose higher, patches of mountains left in shadow from clouds that had moved in. Cynthia was sleeping, her hair—having come loose from the ponytail—draped over the side of the reclined seat.

But the signs for Albany were growing more prominent. And by the time the car left the highway, Micki's stomach had worked itself up into such a state that she thought she was getting an ulcer. They braked for the stop sign at the end of the ramp, and Cynthia woke up.

"Hey, Sleepyhead," Baker teased, "could you read me the directions?" He pulled a folded piece of paper from his jacket pocket and handed it to her. She yawned.

Micki imagined grabbing the sheet of instructions and ripping it into tiny little pieces.

Not that that would do any good.

A sparse coating of white covered most of the landscape now, and the sky had clouded over. The guard opened the gate, and they drove along the road leading to the main building. From time to time, Baker glanced at Micki in the rearview mirror. When the full expanse of the facility came into view, he saw the stricken look on her face.

"You okay back there?" he asked.

"I'm just fuckin' great."

"You watch your mouth—"

"Jim!" Cynthia said, lightly touching his arm.

Micki stared at the buildings and grounds she thought she'd never see again. Actually, she had to hand it to Baker: not once had he thrown it in her face that, in a moment of despair, she'd said she wanted to come back to this place.

He stopped the car in front of the largest building, a standard, institutional-looking structure that contained the administrative offices, the cafeteria, and the high-security cells. Surrounding it, in a semi-circular pattern, were several pleasant-looking cottages that housed the general population. It wasn't until he stepped out of the Camaro and looked past the extensive network of well-manicured lawns and recreational fields that he saw the high stone wall topped with barbed wire that enclosed the entire compound. He pushed the back of the seat forward. "Let's go," he said to Micki. She got out while he removed her bag from the trunk. But before he closed the door, he bent down into the car. "I'll be back in a few minutes, Cyn. This shouldn't take long."

Eyes pale, she replied, "Sure." Then, leaning across the seat so she'd be seen, she said, "Bye, Micki."

Micki turned away.

Baker shut the door and took another look around. Under the cold, grey sky, the deserted grounds looked faintly blue. Yet very real. Until this moment, Heyden had been an abstraction, a step removed—like watching some disaster playing out on the nightly news. But here he now was, about to deliver Micki back into the hands of people he didn't know and couldn't trust. She'd been tormented here. He stared down at her, but could only see the top of her head—she was looking back down the road.

"I had no choice," he said quietly.

She shrugged.

No tears, he thought. The kid never cries. For all she knows, I *am* leaving her here for good—and still nothing. He breathed in to ease the tightness in his chest. But the harsh morning air only stung his lungs. "Look at me," he said.

"Jesus, leave me alone already."

"*Look at me,*" he demanded, reaching beneath her chin.

She knocked his hand away and stepped back. "Don't you touch me!"

"Then look at me when I'm talking to you!" His words came out in little clouds of vapor that instantly dispersed into the atmosphere. "Don't make this any worse than it has to be. Behave yourself and things'll go a lot easier."

She couldn't tell if he was talking about her living at Heyden again or simply telling her not to cause a scene right then. Her gaze fell to his chest. After a couple of seconds she said, "I'm very cold."

And indeed, Baker noticed, she was shivering. But it reminded him of his talk with her in the empty conference room: "Say whatever you want to me," he'd offered, and her only reply had been, "I need a late pass."

When he heard the door open behind him, a rush of warmth swelled in his heart, followed by a deep, aching pain.

"Sergeant Baker?" a woman asked.

He turned toward the voice. "Yes." And then to Micki, "C'mon." He followed behind her as they went up the steps and inside.

With the exception of a female prison guard waiting toward the back, the front office—full of grey metal desks, grey metal counters, grey metal filing cabinets, and flickering fluorescent lights—was empty.

Her manner officious, the woman who let them in said, "I'm Deputy Warden Leslie Stanton. I'm in charge while Warden Morrow is away for the holiday." Her demeanor turned even colder when she added, "We spoke on the phone." She didn't offer her hand, and Baker didn't offer his. Big-boned and wide-hipped, the woman had to angle herself a little in order to step behind the long counter that separated the nominal reception area from the clerical section of the room. Out of a file with Micki's name on it, she produced a triplicate-typed form. She told Baker he could give Micki's bag to the guard.

As he handed over the duffle—which was immediately and methodically searched—he said, "I appreciate your taking care of this at such an early hour— and on a holiday, no less."

With a cool eye that said she was having none of it, Stanton pushed the papers across the metal counter. "If you'll just sign these, Sergeant."

He glanced them over and placed his pen on the signature line. After a moment's hesitation, he wrote his name and straightened up.

Addressing the guard, Stanton said, "Search her thoroughly before you take her to C Cottage."

"I already searched her," Baker lied. "She's clean."

Micki's jaw dropped while the guard, still holding her by the arm, paused.

Not trying very hard to suppress her smirk, Stanton inquired, "But you didn't *strip*-search her, now, did you, Sergeant?"

"No, but there's really no need for that."

"I see. Well, let me remind you, then, that you just signed her over into *my* custody. I'm the acting warden here now. *I* am responsible for the safety and well-being of both staff and inmates at this facility, and *I* will determine what is and isn't necessary at this time."

There was something ironic about his receiving this little speech, so much like his own words to Micki when she balked the first time he patted her down. But he hated this arrogant bitch of a woman and the indignity she relished subjecting Micki to. So while everyone waited—the guard now looking annoyed—he reconsidered his options: he could take Micki on his trip with Cynthia—but that was out of the question—or he could cancel the trip and forfeit his money and vacation.

Knowing she was twisting his balls, Stanton's eyes gleamed. And as soon as it was clear he would offer no further objections, she, once again, ordered the guard to go.

Micki took a last look at Baker. Maybe he was going to come back for her after all. But as she was led away, her heart plummeted like a rock into a maelstrom of churning, muddy waters when, behind her, she heard him say softly, "Bye, Micki."

By the time Micki was shown to her cot, Stanton was already waiting. Looking smug, she said, "It certainly didn't take you very long to return to us."

"I'm only here till Sunday," Micki retorted, an angry blush creeping into her cheeks.

"Well, we'll see about that, won't we." And Stanton, head thrown back, cackled as she made her way out.

Chapter 20

"JESUS CHRIST!" THE CAR skidded over another patch of black ice. After a four-inch snowfall the day before, a thin layer of liquid had frozen on top of the highway's surface overnight, leaving sections of the blacktop treacherous. Baker downshifted and shut off the radio. There was no real reason to rush; Warner knew he'd be late today if he showed up at all. He'd already missed work yesterday.

Barely five thirty in the morning, there were hardly any vehicles on the road, and a fine mist hung in the air, scattering the beams of his headlights. He put out his cigarette and peered ahead into the darkness, the solid white line flying by on his left; nothing but a long and, most likely, unpleasant trip home to look forward to.

He wished the whole weekend had never happened.

Thursday, between all the driving he'd done and leaving Micki at Heyden, he'd been wiped out by the time he and Cynthia had reached the White Horse Inn. Still recovering from lack of sleep, Cynthia hadn't been much better off. They'd napped until it was time for the large Thanksgiving dinner, after which they took a ride in a horse-drawn sleigh around the snow-covered grounds. But despite the charm of the setting, the natural familiarity they'd once shared was gone. And, in bed, their bodies no longer meshed the way they used to: Cynthia seemed self-conscious; Baker felt out of sync.

At 2:00 a.m., unable to sleep, he got dressed and went out in the frigid night air to smoke, the wooden deck creaking beneath his feet. Primordial and untouched, the land stretched out on all sides, disappearing into an unseen horizon. He was very aware of being alone. Bathed in light from the glowing orb above, he could feel the power emanating from the darkness, the tall trees standing silent as if guarding secrets in the forest beyond. And then a huge bird, majestic and graceful, flew across the sky, its silhouette visible when it crossed the almost perfect circle of the moon. Earthbound below, he felt small and inconsequential.

The next couple of days were spent much as they'd planned: walking, driving, and cross-country skiing. But Saturday night, as he was lighting kindling in the fireplace, Cynthia finally broached the dreaded subject.

"Let's face it, Jim, things have changed between us. And I guess it's my fault: I can't be involved with two men at the same time. I thought I could handle it, but I can't."

Straightening up, he faced her. "And I—obviously—am the loser, right?"

A couple of tears spilled out of her eyes and down her cheeks. "I'm sorry," she whispered.

The phone's brash ring interrupted, and Cynthia, being closest, answered. And though Baker purposely hadn't left the inn's number with Heyden, he thought of Micki.

Wiping away tears, Cynthia said, "Mom?"

Based on Cynthia's side of the conversation, Baker gleaned something bad had happened. And when she hung up the phone, she looked dazed.

"That was my mother," she said. "My father just had a heart attack." But it wasn't until Baker had wrapped her in his arms, kissing the top of her head and rocking her gently from side to side, that she broke down and sobbed.

They immediately drove to the hospital, where an initial flurry of activity devolved into long hours of waiting and dozing off in uncomfortable chairs—countless rounds of tears, stress, and bad coffee. Every hour, Cynthia and her mother took their allotted ten-minute visits to see her father—first in the ICU, then later the CCU—while Baker stood by with nothing to do.

As the next evening approached, Mrs. Winthrop insisted Baker stay at the family home in one of the guest rooms. "We'll both feel better," she said, referring to herself and Cynthia, "knowing there's a big, strong man around to protect us." And she smiled fondly.

Though Baker accepted, he knew Cynthia's father—a cold, unyielding man who was nothing like his wife or daughter—would never have allowed such an arrangement. If he'd had any say in the matter, he would've cited the appearance of impropriety, even though, closer to the truth, it would've been his feelings about Baker. As a cop—blue collar—Baker wasn't deemed an appropriate suitor.

And then there was the age difference. But Baker was certain that what was really getting under the man's skin was knowing Baker was sleeping with his daughter though there were no plans to marry. And while Baker hadn't been happy that Mr. Winthrop was ill, it had been a relief not to have to see him.

Rolling smoothly down the highway again, he switched the radio back on to ease the now oppressive sense of solitude. Badfinger's "Baby Blue" tumbled out, the first two lines cutting through with painful, uncanny insight. And as he squinted ahead, searching for the exit in the dark gloom of the highway, he wondered if he'd uncovered the real issue behind his problems with Cynthia: they'd been seeing each other for over two years, and he hadn't proposed—hadn't even mentioned the possibility. And now there was this actor in her life… And yet, while Cynthia was herself pursuing acting, Mr. LA had to rank even lower than Baker did on the scale of eligible suitors. At least, according to Cynthia's father. In fact, to Mr. Winthrop, Baker might be looking pretty damn good right now.

As if that actually counted for anything.

BAKER KILLED THE ENGINE. Enveloped in darkness, the juvenile detention facility had taken on a completely different personality. The high-powered security lights illuminating the perimeter brought the barbed wire atop the walls into harsh relief, the graceless main building—now fully dominating the grounds, making the cottages appear secondary and insignificant. Colorless and thrown into shadow, the landscaped evergreens looked almost sinister despite the frosting of snow.

He closed the Camaro's door, which, in the early-morning stillness, sounded unusually loud. Then he breathed in the cold, crisp air and looked at the snow-covered roofs, trying to savor the last few moments he had all to himself. It had been almost meditative to get up in the dark without radio or TV, then shower, dress, and eat breakfast—all in blessed peace—before going into Cynthia's room to kiss her goodbye. Suitcase in hand, he'd then wound his way down the spiral staircase a final time, the carved mahogany banister softly gleaming. Wedged between the salt and pepper shakers on the kitchen table, his thank-you note to Mrs. Winthrop was left to convey (convincingly, he hoped) his regret at having to leave. But after two days full of anxious conversations, running errands, and hanging around the hospital, he'd been grateful for a reason to head back to the city. The drive had been invigorating until he'd hit that first patch of ice.

He approached the main building, and the entrance door opened. But something felt off. And by the time he reached the top of the stairs, Deputy Warden Stanton was standing fixedly in the doorway. Behind her—flickering in and out of shadows cast by a single row of overhead fluorescents—he saw only office furniture.

"Is Micki ready?" he asked.

"Under the circumstances, I'm afraid she'll have to remain here. I would've called, but you didn't leave a number where I could reach you."

He pushed past Stanton. "Where is she?"

"In solitary. Maximum security."

"Maximum security?"

"She destroyed my office and attacked me; that more than warrants her being detained here."

"What the hell are you talking about? What happened?"

"What happened? Nothing happened. She simply acted out the way she always does."

"No." Baker shook his head. "No, there's got to be a reason."

"Is that so!"

"Where's Warden Morrow?"

"It's not even six o'clock in the morning, Sergeant. It was decided yesterday that only one of us need be present to take care of this matter."

And that just happened to be you, Baker thought. Though he barely knew Stanton, he despised her with every ounce of his being. She was a holdover from Warden Loren's days, and her whole demeanor smacked of vicious self-satisfaction.

"I want to see her," Baker said evenly.

"I hardly think—"

"I want to see her *now.*"

There was a tiny twitch of Stanton's lip, a thin film of sweat cropping up on her brow. "I think it would be easier on everyone if you accepted the situation and left without further interference. We both know she should never have been released in the first place. This is where she belongs."

Baker looked at her with disgust. "You don't know anything about what I think, and *I'll* decide where she belongs."

"Deciding may very well not be your prerogative anymore."

"I'm not about to just leave her here—not without seeing her."

"I'd think you'd be happy to be free of the responsibility. From what I understand, you didn't exactly embrace it."

"And just how would you know that?"

With a triumphant little smile, she said, "I have my sources."

"Yeah? Well maybe your sources have their heads up their asses. Now I want to see her, and I want to see her *now*. How many *fucking* times do I have to say it?"

"Well!"—little beads of sweat had broken out in earnest on her puffy face—"I see the two of you have much in common." She patted her short, curly hair, then smoothed the skirt over her wide hips. "Very well," she said. "Follow me."

She led him to a room with no windows and only a table and two chairs. He unzipped his jacket a couple of inches more before lighting a cigarette to wait.

No one had asked him to hand over his gun.

Micki had almost fallen asleep when she heard the sound of footsteps approaching. Taken out of her cell in handcuffs, she was told someone wanted to see her. The ominous and cryptic announcement left her imagination open to the worst possibilities. And though her hands were shackled, she considered resisting.

The guard pulled out his baton. "You'll do what you're told if you know what's good for you."

She thought it should be obvious to everyone by now that she didn't know what was good for her, but she decided she didn't want to feel that wood bludgeoning her anymore. They went down to the first floor and into the administrative wing. But as soon as she saw Stanton waiting at the end of the corridor, she balked. The guard's grip became painful as he yanked her the rest of the way.

Opening the door to her right, the deputy warden told the guard to take Micki inside and remove the cuffs. And when Micki saw Baker, her eyes grew large. She appeared ready to pounce the instant her hands were freed. But then Baker stood up. And after five days of not seeing him, he seemed much taller—and much bigger—than she remembered. She must've been out of her mind the times she'd physically confronted him.

Baker hurriedly extinguished his cigarette.

"What the fuck didja come back for?" Micki asked. "Didja finally get the balls t'tell me the truth y'self? Huh? Y'gettin' a good laugh outta this?"

He crossed the room to shut the door for privacy. Micki scurried as far away from him as she could.

"I *must* object," Stanton said. "She's become extremely violent."

"Then why did you remove the cuffs?" Baker asked.

"Because—well—"

"I know what you're up to," Baker said. "Just get the hell out."

"*I'm* liable—"

"Cut the crap. I release you from liability, okay? The guard's your witness. Now get out."

The deputy warden appeared to have shrunk under his gaze. She left with the guard and closed the door.

Pale and gaunt—her hair a dirty, wild mess—Micki stood before the far wall in an orange prison jumpsuit. Just below the short shirtsleeves, some bruises were visible on her left arm.

Back at the table, Baker sat down and lit another cigarette. "You asked me why I'm here: I'm here to pick you up, just like I promised."

"Y'so full a shit! You were supposeda be here Sunday! Y'said *Sunday*. Today's *Tuesday*."

"I know what I said, Micki, but something happened, and I couldn't make it then; I couldn't get here until today."

"Fuckin' liar! You were never gonna come get me!"

"Then why am I here?"

"You fuckin' tell *me*."

Playing with the pack of cigarettes, he exhaled thoughtfully. "Why did they have to lock you down?"

"What the fuck d'you care?"

"Talk to me," he said.

She looked at him sitting there, so calm. So collected. She imagined not saying anything and just watching him smoke. Until he finally got up and walked out. "I wrecked the fuckin' bitch's office," she said. "And if I could've, I would've ripped her fuckin' head off, too. Okay? Didja get what y'want? Y'happy now?"

"But why did you do that?"

"The bitch told me y'weren't comin'. She knew all along y'were gonna leave me here."

With a shake of his head, Baker said, "No. I called Sunday to let her know about the change of plans. I told her then that I'd be here today."

A sickening knot was forming in the pit of her stomach. "She—she just said y'weren't comin'?"

"I want to know everything that happened and *exactly* what it was she said."

Barely able to breathe, Micki studied Baker's face. For quite a while. And then said, "It was just after dinner when a guard told me Stanton wanted t'see me. He took me t'her office, and she, real obnoxious-like, said, 'I guess by now y'realize he's not comin' today. Looks like y'gonna be here a little longer.' And then she started laughin'—laughin' her ass off. But, like, it was the way she said 'little'—y'know, like she meant the opposite—y'know, like I was gonna be here forever—"

"I understand," he interrupted. "But the truth is"—he leaned forward—"I told her at ten o'clock that *morning* that I'd be coming today instead."

Hands in her pockets, Micki hung her head: Baker was telling the truth. "Yeah—well…I got myself inta really big trouble here; she's not gonna let me leave."

"Well, I'm not going to let you stay."

Her eyes shot up to his.

"Come here," he said.

"I don't smell too good."

"Don't worry about it."

She moved a little closer.

"Did they do anything to you?" he asked.

"Not really."

"Not really? What does that mean?"

"After I went after Stanton, I didn't exactly let 'em take me easy."

The black-and-blue marks. "But did they do anything to you after that?"

"Just stuck me in a cell."

He stood up. "Where's your stuff?"

"I dunno; they made me wear this orange thing the whole time."

Baker strode around the table and yanked open the door. "I want the kid's things brought here immediately. And I want the papers to sign her out."

"After what she's done," Stanton said, "there's no way she can be released back into your custody."

"You think I don't know what kind of head games you've been playing with her?"

"I don't think—"

"I don't give a shit what you think. You get those goddamned papers for me; 'cause I swear, if you don't, I'll make sure you regret it."

Micki's mouth fell open.

"Are you threatening me, Sergeant?" Stanton asked.

"I'm making you a promise. See, I have connections, too—reporter friends at the *New York Times*—and they'd love to get their hands on a story about the shit that goes on in this place."

"You're making a serious mistake!" Stanton's cheeks were mottled with angry, red blotches. But when Baker stood firm, she turned on her heel and headed back to the front office.

He stared after her.

Voice very small, Micki said, "Sergeant Baker?"

Still looking at Stanton's back as she waddled down the corridor, he replied, "What is it?"

"Can I take a shower?"

"Go ahead, but make it quick. I want to get the hell out of here."

MICKI SHOWERED AND FOUND her clothes waiting for her. Outside it was still dark, a thick cloud cover foretelling a grey and dreary day. Taking a deep breath of the cold, clean air, she paused to look at the fresh snow.

Baker threw her bag in the trunk next to his suitcase. As he unlocked the car on her side, he said, "C'mon, get in."

Giddy with her newfound freedom, she almost smiled.

THE BLACK TAR OF the highway contrasted sharply with the white snow piled in mounds on the median and shoulder. Headlights of oncoming cars glittered like diamonds through the misty air. Peculiarly hypnotic, the coarse hum of the tires on the road seemed to blend with the heat coming through the vents.

Baker's voice broke through. "Are you hungry?"

Her stomach was squeezing and grumbling. "I guess so," she said.

"When we get to the next exit, we'll get off and stop for something, okay?"

"Uh-huh."

He glanced over and saw her eyes fastened on the dark scenery. He let it go. "So tell me," he asked, "why would Stanton have it in for you?"

Micki looked at him, but his gaze was focused on the road again. She said, "She and Loren, the old warden, were real tight. Some of the girls said there were rumors it was 'cause of me that Loren got canned. Though I don't get it, 'cause I never said anything—not even to Sergeant Kelly."

The car skidded, and Baker fought to keep it under control. He downshifted. "Put your seatbelt on; there's a lot of ice on the road."

They continued to the next exit, where they left the thruway and found a diner.

THEIR BOOTH HAD A view of the parking lot and the highway. Far away, mountains covered in snow were slowly and resplendently taking shape in the somber shades of dawn. The waitress brought them coffee and asked for their order. But before Baker could say a word, Micki said she wanted pancakes. Baker, having had breakfast, wasn't hungry, but ordered anyway. While he sipped his coffee, he surveyed the other patrons.

A pair of truckers sat at the middle of the counter. They were shoveling food into their mouths while grinning, talking quietly, and throwing furtive glances at him and Micki. At the end of the counter, closer to the restrooms, a grizzled old man sat drinking coffee. And in the corner booth furthest from the door was some sort of businessman jotting down notes in a small, leather-bound diary, a messy collection of papers spread out over most of his table.

Micki was flipping through the selections in the little jukebox attached to the window frame. With a decisive snap, the metal pages clicked against each other as they turned. Most of the songs were current ones she hated or—though it was still a month away—Christmas tunes, their cards a special pinkish red with little sprigs of holly and mistletoe decorating the corners. Almost at the end, buried way in the back, she found a few songs she actually liked, like "Rocky Mountain High" and "Maggie May." But since she didn't have any money, she simply stared out the window and drank her coffee. After spending about thirty-six hours locked up in solitary, just to see the sky and be clean again felt exquisitely rich. Hot, airless, and rank, the tiny cell she'd been in, with no windows and almost no light, had been more like a tomb, every hour like a year.

"Do you really know guys on the *New York Times*?" she asked.

Taking another sip of coffee, he gave her a sly smile. "Yeah, I know a few. But they're not my friends. Stanton didn't have to know that, though."

Micki's eyes gleamed.

The waitress brought their breakfast and returned shortly to refill their cups. Baker, after pouring ketchup on just a small portion of his scrambled eggs, began to eat at a leisurely pace. Micki, drowning her pancakes in syrup, proceeded to wolf them down as if they might be taken away at any minute.

"Didn't you eat *anything* while you were there?" he asked.

Words garbled since her mouth was full, she replied, "Not really."

Finished with the small section of ketchup-covered eggs, his French fries and toast entirely untouched, Baker leaned back and lit a cigarette. When Micki had cleaned her plate, he pushed his toward her. "Go ahead," he said.

Color rose in her face.

"Go on," he urged.

So she moved the plate in front of her and doused, not only the French fries, but the remaining eggs in ketchup.

Baker smiled to himself. Teased innumerable times by people who considered the combination disgusting, he'd purposely put the condiment only on the portion he'd expected to eat himself. Meanwhile, it now looked like a plate of ketchup with eggs rather than eggs with ketchup.

Eating more slowly, she could feel him watching her. Her movements became self-conscious.

He tapped his cigarette on the ashtray. "Why did you act out like that at Heyden?"

"I told y'already."

"No, I mean, why did you do something like that when you knew it would only make things worse?"

Looking at her plate, she shrugged. "I didn't care anymore. I thought nobody..." Her voice trailed off. She poked at her food, then glanced up. "So how come y'couldn't come get me Sunday? And where's Cynthia?"

"She stayed on at her parents' place. Her father's in the hospital. He suffered a heart attack."

"Wow!" With a forkful of eggs hanging poised midair, Micki asked, "Is he gonna be okay?"

But Baker was suddenly aware of his own breathing. Eyes cold, he took another drag on his cigarette. "Just finish up; I want to get going."

She dropped her fork onto the plate. "Y'already sorry y'didn't leave me there, aren't ya. Y'golden opportunity t'be rid a me."

"Just finish up," he repeated.

She pushed the plate away and stared out the window. One of the two truckers from the counter had gone outside. He was getting into his vehicle, a white truck with "Weller's Baked Goods" printed in large black letters. A bakery truck. That's how she'd escaped from Heyden over the summer. When the delivery was very late one day, the normal security routine had been thrown off. She'd snuck out of the kitchen and hid in the truck until it made its next stop. As soon as the doors had opened, she'd jumped out past the astonished deliveryman, her fists gripping bags of bread and rolls. She'd run as fast and as far as she could.

"Anything else?" the waitress asked.

"No," Baker replied as he stubbed out his cigarette. "Just the check." While the waitress tallied the figures on her pad, he slid out of the booth and stood up. "I'm going to the men's room," he said to Micki, "and then we'll leave."

Gazing out the window again, Micki let the waitress clear away the dishes. But she wasn't alone for more than a few seconds before she heard a deep, cheerful voice say, "Hey there, little lady."

She turned back to see the other trucker standing beside the table. Tall and wide all the way around, his smile was as broad and warm as his southern accent. And though his grin was managing to overcome the thick black beard and mustache that obscured most of his face, it did nothing to change Micki's expression. He took the pack of cigarettes he'd just bought from the vending machine and put it in the pocket of his brown, shearling-trimmed jacket. Then he absently checked that the tails of his flannel shirt were tucked into his jeans, which were barely hanging on beneath the bulge of his belly.

Micki thought he looked pregnant—and like something out of a bad TV show. Her tone harsh, she asked, "Whatta y'want?"

"Just thought if things weren't workin' out too well with your friend, here, you might care to ride along with me for a while."

"Get the fuck away from me."

He chuckled. "C'mon, now, girl; I'd treat you right. We could have us a sweet time. A real *fine* time." And then he made the mistake of taking the back of his index finger and stroking her cheek.

With shocking reflex, she slammed his hand down, smashing his knuckles into the table. And while it was too awkward to stand up completely in the booth, she had her free hand drawn back in a fist.

"MICKI!" Baker's voice ripped through the diner.

She let go of the trucker, who backed up, his face still contorted in a mixture of pain and surprise. Coddling his bruised hand, he looked from Baker to Micki—who was now standing beside the booth—then back to Baker, the two of them with their eyes locked together. He noticed the butt of Baker's gun peeking out from under his jacket. Hands raised, he said to Baker, "Hey, man"—he backed up even further—"no harm meant, I—"

"Forget it," Baker said. "Just go."

"Sure, man—thanks!" And he hurried out the door.

No one in the restaurant moved.

"Put your jacket on, Micki."

"Y'know it—"

"I don't want to hear it."

"But—"

"I *don't* want to hear it. Do you understand me?"

"But—"

"DO—YOU—UN-DER-STAND—ME!"

She yanked her jacket off the seat and put it on while Baker picked up the check and threw three dollars on the table as an outrageously generous tip. When he paid on the way out, the woman at the register—still trying very hard to smile—gave him his change with a shaking hand.

As soon as Baker had started the car, he said, "Why is it that you're always getting into trouble? I can't leave you alone for two *fucking* minutes without something happening."

"But I—"

"But you what? Huh? *What?*" He accelerated back onto the highway. "You are *always* in the middle. How can you even *think* of saying it's not your fault when you're always involved. Explain this to me 'cause I just can't figure it out." The knuckles of his left hand—the one that was gripping the wheel—had gone white.

Her voice very quiet, she answered, "I dunno." Staring out the windshield, she wished she were anywhere but with him.

For several miles, they drove in deafening silence until Baker turned on the radio, catching the intro to Climax's "Precious and Few." But just as the chorus started, the car began to swerve: first to the right, then to the left, and then back again. He was trying desperately to regain control when it went into a spin.

And time expanded.

Micki watched the world revolving slowly outside the windows as they crossed lanes—still spinning—heading toward the shoulder. This is it, she thought. This is where my life ends. And as the car floated over the road, her whole body relaxed. But they plowed, rather gently, into the snowbank on the right shoulder and came to a stop. And though she was the only one wearing a seatbelt, Baker's right arm was extended protectively in front of her to prevent her from pitching into the windshield. He cut the engine, and it was instantly quiet—just the occasional swish of a passing car.

"Are you okay?" he asked.

"Yeah. Are you?"

"Yeah."

But when she turned her gaze back to the snow, he saw an odd look on her face. "What?" he asked. "What is it?"

Still staring ahead, she said, "I wish I was dead."

And in that split second following their climactic reprieve from death, all the emotional turmoil that had been churning inside him for days erupted into one slick retort: "Well, so do I."

Her head whipped around. Eyes wide, lips slightly parted, a bitter smile emerged. "Well, hey—we finally agree on something." And before he could respond, she'd slipped out of the car, the slam of the door ringing in his ears.

The moment seemed frozen, like a stilled frame in some strange, incomprehensible movie. And yet in the rearview mirror, he saw her retreating figure, a thin black form walking against traffic in the snow. Large as life. He jumped out of the car.

"Micki, get back here!"

She kept on walking.

"*Micki!* MICKI! YOU GET BACK HERE THIS INSTANT!"

Still walking, she called back over her shoulder, "Fuck you, man. Be smart for once and let me go."

He started after her, creating a larger set of footprints through the crusted top layer of snow. A car, speeding as though the blacktop were bone dry, flew past. He imagined another vehicle spinning out like theirs had, and started to jog.

But at the sound of the more-rapid crunch of his feet, she stopped and wheeled around.

He pulled up short.

It was both super-real and dreamlike standing there under the dark, grey sky—cars intermittently whizzing past, headlights ghostly in the cold, misty air. Safe and warm inside their vehicles, the cars' occupants were totally separated from the scene playing out on the shoulder.

He could feel the chill seeping into his open jacket. "Micki, you get back in that car right now."

"No."

"Don't you tell me 'no'! You get back there right now!"

"Or what?"

They were about five yards apart, and he could see it in her eyes: she didn't give a shit about anything. Reaching across his body, he pulled his service revolver out of its holster and aimed it at her with both hands. "Get back in that car," he repeated.

She didn't move.

"NOW."

Chin tilted up slightly, she said, "Or what? Y'gonna shoot me?"

The large gun steady in his grip, he sighted down the barrel.

But her eyes were laughing at him. "So go ahead... Shoot."

After a few seconds, when he did nothing, she snorted, turned, and started walking away. He remained where he was, still pointing the revolver: a healthy, six-foot-six adult male holding a loaded gun on an underweight, five-foot-six teenaged girl. And he was powerless.

Weapon reholstered, he started after her, and she began to run. But he overtook and tackled her, twisting his body as he did so, taking the brunt of the fall on the edge of his back. Covered in snow, he rolled over, pinning her beneath him. She heard the ratcheting of the handcuffs as the cold metal closed around her wrists.

She laughed at him. "D'ya take those goddamn things with y'everywhere?"

He pulled her up by the back of her jacket collar.

"I bet if y'could," she said, "you'd even wear 'em t'bed—have 'em hangin' from y'goddamn Jockey shorts."

He roughly turned her around, holding one arm tight in his grip.

She looked up into his eyes and lowered her voice. "Whatta y'do with 'em when y'fuckin' y'girlfriend?"

He whipped the back of his free hand across her face, drawing blood.

"Whatsa matta?" she asked. "Y'didn't get any this weekend?"

His fist slammed into her, catching the border of her solar plexus, causing her knees to buckle. Hot and bitter, the taste of bile was mixing with the metallic taste of blood. She gasped for air and pictured herself reexperiencing her breakfast in reverse.

He reached down, grabbed her hair, and pulled her head back. "Y'got any more smart-ass comments?"

But they were interrupted by the brief blare of a siren and a blinding set of headlights. A rotating light flashed red on the snow.

"*Put your hands on your head and step back,*" a male voice commanded.

Baker, who couldn't see anything beyond the headlights glaring in his eyes, did as he was told. Micki, who didn't feel capable of getting up if she wanted to, remained where she was. The trooper, who was approaching slowly, had his gun drawn and trained on Baker.

"I'm on the job," Baker said. "NYPD. My ID is in my front pocket." His left hand began to move.

"KEEP YOUR HANDS ON YOUR HEAD," the trooper barked. "AND LACE YOUR FINGERS TOGETHER. We'll get everything straightened out in good time."

Arms raised, Baker's open jacket was lifted and pulled apart, leaving his revolver fully exposed. The trooper immediately confiscated it, putting it in the back of his own waistband. "I want you to walk over to my car," he said. "Put your hands on the hood and assume the position."

Baker shot a glance at Micki. "You wipe that smirk off your face," he said, "or I'll wipe it off *for* you later."

"MOVE," the trooper ordered. And with his gun still trained on Baker, he made sure Micki was securely handcuffed before helping her to her feet. He put her where he could keep an eye on her, then proceeded to frisk Baker very thoroughly, one side at a time, switching his gun to the opposite hand to keep it pressed against Baker's body. Once he was finished, he pulled out Baker's wallet and took a step back to examine the badge and ID. Then he holstered his own revolver and returned Baker's wallet. But not his weapon. "You want to tell me what's going on here, Sergeant?"

"We spun out on some ice back there, and she decided"—Baker paused, choosing his words—"to be a pain in the ass for a change." When the trooper's expression remained impassive, Baker added, "I'm taking her back to the city from Heyden."

Face still blank, the trooper said only, "Okay." A good six foot four, he had a solid, athletic build and a blond crew cut beneath the wide brim of his hat. He looked as if he'd just stepped out of a recruitment poster. He asked, "Some kind of big case she's a witness for?"

"What?"

"Must be something important for a detective sergeant to be sent as a personal escort."

"Oh—no, it's nothing like that. I had to leave her at Heyden because I went on vacation with my girlfriend this weekend." He looked toward Micki. "Lucky me happens to be her legal guardian for the time being."

The trooper caught the briefest flicker of hurt across Micki's features. "What about her parents?" he inquired.

Baker shook his head no.

"So she lives with you."

"No, she's on her own. But—well—it's more like she's on parole."

"How old is she?"

"Seventeen." When this didn't appear to satisfy the trooper, Baker added tersely, "It's an experiment."

The trooper walked up to Micki. "Y'got any ID on you?"

"Right front pocket."

He pulled it out and looked it over. Without comment, he returned it, asking Baker, "So what exactly was going on here when I arrived?"

"I was trying to get her back to the car."

"So she was running away."

"She... Let's just say she was giving me a hard time."

"I see," the trooper responded, though he didn't see at all. Turning to Micki, he studied the scars and bruises on her face. "Are you sure you're okay?"

The blood on her cheek had already gelled; her lip, now swollen, felt numb. Looking past him, she replied, "Yeah."

"*Are* you giving him a hard time?" he asked.

She shrugged.

His tone became friendly. "So your name's Micki."

"So what."

He smiled. "I have a cousin named Mickey,"

She finally looked at him. The tuxedo stripe on his grey pants made her think of a security guard more than a cop. But that hat! She said, "Who the fuck gives a shit."

Baker took a step toward her. "Micki, I swear—"

But the trooper raised a hand, and Baker stopped. "Don't play tough with me, kid," he said, "'cause I'm not buying it."

Jaw clenched, she shifted her gaze.

"It seems to me," the trooper continued, "that you could use a friend right now. So do you want to tell me your side of this? 'Cause I'm willing to listen."

"He hates me!" she blurted out. "He wishes I was dead! He said so!"

The trooper threw a questioning look at Baker, who, looking heavenward, shook his head.

Micki started to shiver. Cold and clammy, her jeans were damp up to the knees from the snow that had melted underneath them.

"Can you spare a smoke?" the trooper asked Baker.

"Sure." And he reached into his jacket pocket.

But the trooper held up his hand again. "Micki's cold. Why don't you take her back to the car and let her warm up in there. In fact, I'd like you to pull your vehicle out of the snowbank so I know it's roadworthy. After that I'll take that cigarette. Okay, Sergeant?"

With a shrewd smile, Baker did as the trooper asked, leaving Micki cuffed in the car with the window cracked open, the engine running, and the heater on. As an added precaution, he deployed her seatbelt and locked her door, wondering if she even knew how to drive.

The trooper watched Baker stomping back through the snow. The cop was trying to give the impression that the incident was solely a police matter. But it had all the earmarks of a domestic disturbance.

Keeping an eye on his car, Baker offered the trooper a cigarette, then lit one himself. "So is this supposed to be my cooling-off period?" he asked.

"I think you need one."

Despite a rush of heat, Baker flashed an amiable grin. "Maybe you're right. But let me tell you, that kid can push my buttons faster than anyone I've ever known." He filled his lungs with smoke, then examined the cigarette pinched between his thumb and index finger. "Y'know, I managed to quit smoking for two years. *Two years.* But that kid got me started again."

"Really!" the trooper said. "What happened? She put a cigarette in your mouth and a gun to your head?"

Baker looked up sharply, then appeared to laugh it off, giving the trooper a weak smile. "Fair enough."

They both smoked.

"She looks familiar," the trooper said. "Was she the girl that escaped from Heyden over the summer?"

"Yeah, that's right. How did you know?"

"Small world. My uncle's a cop in Rensselaer. She'd made her way to one of the college's summer dorms there, and several students spotted her. My uncle was one of the guys sent to pick her up. He said that when he caught her, she was in pretty bad shape. And with her T-shirt all torn up from running through the woods, he could see infected welts and what looked like cigarette burns on her back."

"And?" Baker had never heard any of this.

"My uncle took her into custody. Once he drew his gun, she surrendered. But having to take her back to that place weighed on him something fierce. A few weeks later, he got in touch with the Department of Corrections, and it started quite the investigation."

"But as far as I know," Baker said, "Micki never even gave a statement to anyone."

"Warden resigned to shut the whole thing down."

Baker grunted.

They smoked awhile.

"You're taking an awful lot of time with this," Baker said.

"I don't like what I saw when I pulled in here. I'm trying to decide what to do about it."

"She can be hard to handle."

"She was already cuffed."

"But way out of line."

"That was a cruel punch."

"I know how much she can take."

"That's not the point."

"Yeah? Well you should've heard what came out of her mouth."

"Nothing she said could justify what you did."

"You can say that because you don't have to deal with her."

"I've got three kids of my own, mister. All teenagers. All boys. All a handful. Do you have any kids of your own?"

Baker looked steadily into the trooper's icy blue eyes and said, "No. But we're not talking about just any kid, here. We're talking about an extremely violent juvenile offender."

"You said you're her legal guardian."

"So what? What's the difference?"

"It means something to her."

Using his middle finger, Baker tapped some ashes off his cigarette.

"Did you tell her you wished she was dead?"

With another look heavenward, Baker said, "It's not the way it sounds."

"*Do* you hate her?"

"No, but—"

"Why are you her guardian?"

Baker put the Camel to his lips and inhaled.

"Let me explain my problem," the trooper said. "What I saw here constitutes assault and battery on a minor—child abuse. Of course, if you insist your relationship with her is strictly as a police officer, we could bring your Internal Affairs Division into this…"

When he stared into the trooper's eyes, Baker saw beyond the words this time. He looked down. "Sometimes I just don't know how to control her."

"No matter what she does, you've got to control *yourself*. If you can't manage that, you'll never be able to exert any control over her."

Gaze still fixed on the ground, Baker nodded.

The trooper's voice grew soft. "She's not lost yet. You know that, don't you?"

But Baker merely looked off into the distance.

The dispatcher's voice cut in from the cruiser's radio, and both men threw their cigarettes in the snow. The trooper reached into his vehicle to respond. Turning back to Baker, he said, "Gotta go." And with measured, deliberate movements, he gave the cop back his gun.

The revolver hadn't felt this heavy in Baker's hand in a long, long time.

"You're her guardian; you've been entrusted with *caring* for her," the trooper said. "Don't forget what that means."

Baker nodded as the trooper got back in his cruiser, turned on the siren, and pulled away.

WHEN BAKER RETURNED TO his car, Micki had already dozed off. A solid shake of her shoulder elicited only an unconscious grunt. Still he managed to get at the cuffs to remove them—even reclined her seat as an afterthought. If he hadn't known better, he would've thought she'd been drugged. But five nights without sleep could explain it just as well.

She slept the rest of the ride back, and it was shortly after ten when he finally parked the car on her street. Snowless, the ground appeared oddly barren. He shut off the engine.

"Micki," he said quietly. "*Micki!*" And he shook her again.

"Mmm."

"Wake up. You're home."

Her eyes opened, then closed.

"I am *not* carrying you up those stairs." He got out of the car, took her bag from the trunk, and opened her door. When the cold air hit her, she mumbled something. He undid the seatbelt, raised her to a sitting position, then let the back of the seat spring upright. But she was still too groggy, and he had to pull her out.

Supporting her on one side, he helped her up the steps. But no sooner were they inside her apartment than she flopped down on the bed. He dropped her bag on the floor and was halfway out the door when he remembered her bankbooks and money. He went back to put them on the table.

THE CHAIN-LINK FENCE GLITTERED *like diamonds to her left while the pattern of bricks on her right had been transformed into the stone wall surrounding Heyden. Spirals of barbed wire looped endlessly into the blackness up ahead. Heart pounding louder than her feet, she flew down the alley, knowing there was no escape, knowing she was trapped—even though she was dreaming.*

So tired. So tired of running. If only this would all just end. She wanted, so badly, to stop.

The brick wall blocking her path appeared more suddenly than it had before, the ground in front splitting in two. Straining to breathe, she teetered on the brink as the pavement before her splintered and shattered, irregular pieces of earth and rock falling through the infinite space of the ever-widening pit. And though there was no discernable source of light, the wall beyond was thrown into deeper shadow as if soon there might be no light at all.

But then a hand reached out of the darkness, reached out across the divide. It was a large hand—a strong hand—but its owner remained shrouded in the surrounding shadows. Palm up in readiness, it grew larger and larger—so huge she could actually step on top and be carried to safety.

Maybe.

The darkness closed in further, cold fingers touching the bare skin of her shoulder. She was falling…

Micki awoke with a start, still feeling the sensation of freefall, still sweating and overheated like she'd been in the dream. Unable to recall getting out of Baker's car, she struggled to her feet and looked around the apartment, which felt much too warm. She took off her jacket and looked at the clock: almost two. She'd missed another day of school.

Three Devil Dogs, some American cheese, and a large glass of Coke that was flat from being in a half-empty bottle too long—and she was still hungry. She returned her money and bankbooks to their hiding place, then opened her duffle bag. And though it might have been her imagination, the odor of Heyden drifted up. She stripped the bed and gathered her laundry together. There would be just enough time before going to work.

ON HIS WAY HOME from the high school, Baker stopped off to find Micki's apartment empty. If the bare mattress hadn't looked so repulsive, he would've stretched out for a nap while waiting for her to return. As it was, she walked through the door less than five minutes later, arms full of laundry, detergent, and schoolbooks.

Pointing to a folded piece of loose-leaf paper he'd left on her desk, he said, "I brought your homework assignments. Those are yesterday's and today's."

"Like I'm really gonna get t'any of it."

"Did you at least do some homework over the weekend?"

"Over the weekend? *Over the weekend? None!* I got *none* of it done 'cause I didn't have any *books* with me. It's a little tough without the books, don'tcha think?"

He'd never packed her books. He massaged his brow. "I'll write notes for your teachers. Do the best you can to make it up by the end of the week."

"I can hardly wait."

Holding his tongue, he turned to go, then paused in the doorway. "What are you saving for?"

"What?"

"In your bank account—you're saving money."

She could feel the heat rising in her face. "College."

He merely nodded, then left.

PHONE IN ONE HAND, cigarette in the other, Baker asked, "How's your dad doing?"

"Much, much better. Thanks for asking."

Thanks for asking? Cynthia was being so formal. A misplaced drop of spaghetti sauce had hardened on the Formica tabletop. He picked at it with his fingernail, and a few ashes fell from his cigarette. He brushed them away. "So when do you think you'll be coming back to the city?"

"Friday maybe."

"How about Saturday? I could drive up and bring you back."

"Don't be silly—that's insane. That would be an outrageous amount of driving in one day."

"I was thinking I'd drive up late Friday night."

"No, that's really not necessary."

"I don't mind, I—"

"No!" Her voice softened. "I—um—I want to thank you for how much you did for my mom and me while you were here. Especially under the circumstances. But the truth is"—she took a deep breath—"and this is hard for me to say, Jim, but"—she paused again—"I don't think we should see each other anymore."

Eyes closed, he rested his forehead against the knuckles of his left hand. Cigarette smoke swirled around his face. "You don't have to sleep with me, Cyn."

"For godssakes, I need some space! Can't you understand that?"

"Yeah, I understand that!"

There was silence on the line.

"Can I at least call you?" he asked.

He sounded so plaintive—so hurt. She sighed. "Just give me a little time first, okay?"

He hung up the phone and finished his cigarette in the emptiness of his apartment. Leisurely and relaxed. As if he had all the time in the world.

THE PICTURES ON THE screen flashed and changed in the darkness, the TV's volume so low it was little more than a murmur. Exhaling smoke, Baker poured another drink. The weatherman was predicting a blizzard tomorrow—like they ever got the goddamn weather right. Probably two whole fucking snowflakes would fall.

He thought of all the driving he'd done in the snow and ice in Vermont, numerous trips taking Cynthia and her mom back and forth to the hospital, out to dinner, once even buying groceries while they'd kept watch over her father. Didn't that mean anything—anything at all? Cynthia had chosen Mr. LA over him, though the wimpy-assed actor hadn't done a goddamn thing through all this. *He* was the one; *he* was the one that was always there for her. But now she was acting like she was doing him a favor by letting him call her. Ungrateful bitch.

He caught his breath and looked about as if someone might've heard his thoughts. Then he hung his head. What a self-centered bastard he was. After all, he'd noticed the slight tremor in her voice, knew she'd probably cried her eyes out after hanging up the phone. And still, all he could think about was how she'd wasted his time, how she'd strung him along for more than two years. Two whole years of his life. Wasted.

Glass after glass, the whiskey vanished until all of the words that were shouting in his brain were beaten down and left to bleed behind a thick and heavy wall. And yet his soul was not at peace. For no amount of liquor would ever still what his heart was saying, or silence what he already knew: that he was losing something precious, something he might never have again.

He shut off the TV and stood in the darkness, thinking about the shape of things to come. For now that Cynthia was gone, the moments of his life would be nothing more than pages ripped from a book and cast upon the ocean to be tossed about by the waves, soaking in the very water that would cause them to disintegrate and sink below to the dark, murky bottom, where no light would ever reach, the meaning lost, the words forgotten, never to be seen or heard from again.

Not that anyone would care.

Chapter 21

MICKI DRAGGED HERSELF INTO the office and dropped her books on Baker's desk. Standing by the sofa, he was having some kind of argument with Warner.

"I haven't had *anything* to drink this morning," she heard him say heatedly.

Hot and uncomfortable in her jacket, she felt like she was half asleep. Why was Baker so pissed? Especially since she could clearly see the mug in his hand.

He walked over. "Nice of you to drop by. You're fifteen minutes late."

Words mumbled, she said, "I need those notes you promised."

While putting his coffee down next to her books, he observed her glassy eyes and flushed face. "Are you high?"

"I think I'm sick."

"You *think* you're sick?"

"I hurt all over, and my throat's sore."

When he reached toward her, she jerked her head back. "Jesus Christ, stand still!" And he pressed his hand to her brow.

His palm felt solid and warm against her forehead.

"You've got a fever," he announced. "You're not supposed to come to school when you're this sick. Don't you have any common sense at all?"

It had never occurred to her that she'd be allowed to stay home.

"Go back, take some aspirin, and stay in bed. And you're not to go to work, either."

"But I need the money."

"You've got some saved; use that if you have to." He looked at his watch. "I'll call Mr. Antonelli a little later and let him know you won't be there tonight."

She grabbed her books and stormed out of the office.

DARK AND THREATENING, THE sky was thick with clouds, the temperature hovering around freezing. For close to fifteen minutes, Micki stood on Union Turnpike, waiting for the Q44A, which finally bumbled its way to the bus stop. She grappled with the steep steps, flashed her pass at the driver and deposited a nickel before heading down the aisle. Though still rush hour, there were a couple of empty seats, and she took one near the back, resting her head against the window's cool glass. Her breath created a patch of fog. But when the vehicle started moving again, the ride was too bumpy, and she straightened up—head soon lolling forward.

She nearly missed her stops: first on the bus, then again on the subway. By the time she got back to her apartment, her throat was so sore it hurt just taking the aspirin. And yet despite how awful she felt, it was still unbelievably delicious to change into her nightshirt, crawl back into bed, and snuggle under the blanket.

HUDDLED BENEATH THE COVERS, wearing her jeans and jacket, Micki was shivering to the point that her teeth were chattering. After the first round of chills, she'd broken out into such a heavy sweat that she'd had to change into a regular T-shirt because her nightshirt had completely soaked through. But the reprieve had been brief.

Someone was knocking at the door—very persistent, as if they knew she was there.

Voice so weak and hoarse it didn't sound like hers, she heard herself ask, "Who is it?"

"It's Juan."

"From the restaurant?"

"Yeah. Open up."

Blanket clutched around her, she shuffled over and cracked the door a few inches.

"Mr. A wanted me to bring you this." He held up a large brown grocery bag. She opened the door further, and he said, "It's soup. Tony said he make it special for you. Everybody hope you feel better. Except Sal." And he grinned. When he realized she was using both hands to hold the blanket, he offered to bring the package inside and put it on the table. Eyeing her more closely, he said, "You lookin' real sick, kid. Maybe you should go to a doctor, y'know?"

She was trying hard not to shiver when she said, "I'll be okay."

His eyebrows pulled together even more. "I dunno… Anyway, I gotta get back." He headed for the door. "You see how much it's snowin'?" He was grinning again.

"Uh-uh."

"Well you should take a look. They say maybe eighteen inches gonna fall. Maybe more. Maybe a record!"

"Uh-huh." The only thing she was interested in was getting warmer.

"Well, I see you, Little Micki. Take care of yourself, okay?"

"Uh-huh."

But as soon as she closed the door behind him, she felt the change taking place: she was starting to sweat. She threw off the blanket, then the jacket, the jeans, and the socks. When she got back into bed, she was down to just T-shirt and underpants. She felt exposed and pulled the sheet up to her waist.

LYING ON HER BACK felt cooler, so she stayed that way, eyes closed, the world swimming feverishly around. Noises trickled in from outside, but different than the usual: shovels scraping sidewalks, a snowplow plodding down the street with its tire chains clanking…

Shallow and slow, breathing seemed difficult, and she found herself focusing on the rise and fall of her chest. Life felt tenuous, as if it might quietly slip away without her noticing. Without anyone noticing. For she was alone. She was always alone. Even when Willy had taken care of her after she'd been cut up, she'd been left alone more often than not, going in and out of a feverish fog much like this one.

Tim would've stayed with her, though; he would've stayed right by her side until she was over the worst of it. Then again, maybe not. Why would he have been any different? She wanted to touch the silver cross he'd given her, but her hand wouldn't move.

The ticking of the clock receded into the background until the room itself opened up and disappeared. Finally free, she drifted into a chaotic ocean of consciousness, streams of thought flowing out in all directions, getting tangled in the fragile threads of reality. She was traveling faster than the speed of light, circling the edge of the space-time continuum, every moment infinitely long while life itself grew geometrically shorter.

Outside, the snow continued to fall.

SCHOOL HAD OFFICIALLY CLOSED at one o'clock on account of the blizzard, yet Baker had waited until virtually everyone else had left before heading out himself. Now kicking himself for not leaving earlier, he navigated the snowbound streets, driving toward Micki's apartment and cursing his luck—and her. If it weren't for her, he'd be on his way home. It was probably just a bad cold, but she *would* have to get sick when there was a major snowstorm going on. God forbid anything should ever be easy with that kid.

Yet by some different stroke of fate, both Forty-Fourth Drive and Twenty-First Street—major roads—had seen the benefit of a snowplow. And someone was pulling out of a spot in front of the deli, leaving a nice patch of relatively bare asphalt underneath. Pulling in right behind, Baker swerved a little over an icy ridge.

The sidewalk and steps in front of Micki's building were completely covered in white with dirty footprints packing it down to varying degrees. He picked his way up the stoop, stomped his feet, then took the staircase inside two steps at a time. Unrestrained, his keys clattered against each other on his overloaded keychain while he let himself into the apartment. Yet Micki, asleep, was surprisingly undisturbed. He noticed the grocery bag on the table and pulled out a large plastic container, still faintly warm. When he lifted the lid, he was greeted by a wonderful aroma: minestrone soup. He moved several items around in the little refrigerator and cleared some space for it on the bottom. Then he sat down at the table, lit a cigarette, and thought about all the snow piling up in the streets. Head tilted back, he blew a few smoke rings toward the ceiling, then exhaled the rest with a heavy sigh: he could've been in Manhattan by now. Whether she woke up or not, as soon as the Camel was done, he was leaving.

But he'd never seen her sleeping on her back before. Covered only by the sheet, she had both arms out on top, the upper area of her left one an extremely ugly mixture of colors. "I didn't let them take me easy," she'd said. His eyes drifted to the half-empty glass of water sitting next to the bottle of aspirin on the kitchen counter, then over to the nightshirt that was hanging across the back of the desk chair—which was sitting in front of the radiator. He sat up straight: he could see the bruised part of her arm because she was wearing one of her regular T-shirts in bed. With a single forceful crush, he ground his cigarette out, then hurried over and placed his palm against her forehead. She was burning up.

"Micki," he said softly. "*Micki!*" And he shook her. When there was no response, he strode into the hallway and found that the payphone—without its usual sign—was actually working. He dialed nine-one-one and reached an operator who sounded brusque: the city, caught unprepared by the extent of the storm, was overwhelmed with blizzard-related emergencies. Only moments before Baker's call, there'd been a multi-car disaster on the upper level of the Queensboro Bridge. The operator further informed him there were no available ambulances, especially for something as undramatic as a high fever. "And given the condition of the roads," she added, "all emergency services will be backed up for an indeterminate amount of time."

"But she needs to go to the hospital, and she needs to go *now*."

"Please stay calm, sir. What's her temperature?"

"I don't know. She doesn't have a thermometer."

"Perhaps she's just sleeping very soundly."

"*What the hell is the matter with you? I don't need a goddamn thermometer to know her life is in danger. The kid's unconscious and totally unresponsive for godssakes.*" He slammed the receiver down.

He ran outside to pull his car directly in front of the building: he'd take Micki to the hospital himself. But someone had double-parked and abandoned their vehicle beside his. He charged into the deli. "Is anyone here the owner of the light-blue Cutlass outside?" But the only customer in sight was a fourteen-year-old boy.

Back at the apartment's payphone, he dialed "0" and asked the operator to connect him to the local precinct. When instructed, he deposited a dime in the slot and listened to it clink and chime its way down the chute. Yet before the call had gone through, he hung up. Even if they were willing to transport Micki as a favor, the roads were too unpredictable: what if they got stranded en route? There'd be no qualified medical personnel on hand.

Checking the coin-return box, he retrieved his dime and dialed the operator again, this time asking to be connected to the local emergency room. And after he'd described Micki's condition to a nurse, he finally got a doctor on the line.

"Have you tried putting her in a warm tub so she'll cool down with the water?" the resident asked.

"There's no bathtub here, only a shower," Baker said.

"Then you'll have to cool her down with alcohol." And the resident explained what that entailed, saying afterward, "Let me see if I can locate someone who could reach you by foot or subway. I think one of the interns might live nearby. In the meantime, you'd better get going. You can't afford to wait."

BECAUSE PEOPLE WERE BUYING all sorts of provisions in anticipation of being snowed in, the stores were doing a booming business. Baker went to Sunny's and picked out a large basin, two towels, a bag of cotton puffs, and the last three bottles of rubbing alcohol they had. The checkout line moved quickly, and he hurried to the drugstore. There he gathered seven more bottles of alcohol plus an oral thermometer, then stood in queue to be rung up. He listened to a woman accusing the pharmacist of overcharging her for her prescription. For several minutes, the argument continued with no progress.

"Excuse me," Baker cut in, "but I have an emergency."

Shooting him a nasty look, the woman said, "We *all* have an emergency."

Baker flashed his shield. "Mine's official police business."

Mouth bunched up, the woman made an exaggerated visual inventory of his purchases before eventually stepping aside to let him pay. When he pulled out his credit card instead of cash, he thought he heard her groan.

Paper bags cradled in his arms, he used his back to push open the heavy glass door, nearly losing his footing on the icy sidewalk as he left. He struggled through the snow and slogged through the slush while gusts of wind blew broken umbrellas down the street. Back in the calm of the apartment, he shrugged off his coat and set up a makeshift workstation by pulling the dinette chairs to the side of the bed: one to sit on, the other for supplies. When all was ready, towels soaking in the alcohol, he looked down at her.

"Micki? *Micki!*" And he roughly shook her shoulder. But neither the shiny eyelids nor the slightly parted lips moved. So after taking a handful of material on either side of her shirt, he tugged and pulled until he'd succeeded in removing the garment and casting it aside. But when he turned back, he froze, his cheeks starting to burn. Until he realized he felt…nothing. His shoulders relaxed and he softly exhaled, his gaze shifting from her bared breasts to her closed eyes. And then the damaged skin on her face.

He set to work.

He wrung the towels out a little, then placed them on her body: hand towel across her chest and stomach; washcloth, folded up, on her forehead. He removed the thermometer from its little plastic container and placed it under her armpit. But five minutes later, when he took it back, his face grew ashen: 105.6 degrees. Her true temperature was at least one degree higher. Sitting by the bed, he continued to diligently soak and apply the towels, the constant chatter in his head temporarily silenced while time crept by in hushed and empty tones. He listened to her breathe.

Night began its approach, and he got up to switch on the desk lamp, the faded luminescence leaving most of the room in shadow. Her features looked so relaxed, as if she were merely resting. Yet she might've died had he gone straight home. She might still. He removed the folded washcloth from her forehead again, then paused to gently brush back some stray strands of hair.

HER TEMPERATURE WAS DOWN to 102.2. Baker grasped her upper arm. "Micki?"

She moaned.

With a fresh surge of energy, he resumed his efforts. But nearly half an hour later, her condition appeared unchanged. He considered calling the ER again, though he'd already called twice to find out whether the doctor had found someone willing to see her. The first call had merely served as a reminder—the resident had gotten sidetracked and forgotten. The second call had proven equally disappointing because the only house-staff candidate had apparently taken his phone off the hook.

Baker removed the towels once more and turned to dunk them in the basin.

Micki's eyes fluttered open. It smelled like she was in the hospital, but it looked like her apartment. She recognized Baker's back. Chilled, she reached down to pull up the covers—and discovered her shirt was off. As Baker turned toward her, she quickly crossed her arms over her chest.

"Micki!"

"What the fuck've y'been doin' t'me?"

A hot spark shot through him. His back ached, he needed a cigarette, and he was hungry as hell. He tossed the freshly soaked towel into the basin. "What've I been doing?" he retorted. "I've been staring at your tits all day 'cause I've got nothing better to do with my time."

The corners of her mouth turned down, and she curled up on her side, leaving him to glare at the bumps of her naked spine. Standing out against the scarred skin, they were a perfectly curved row of bony protrusions, making him think about—of all things—seahorses. He stood up, grabbed his coat, and marched out of the apartment, slamming the door behind him.

As soon as the downstairs door had slammed, too, Micki got up and put her dried nightshirt on. Light-headed and weak, she went back to take a look at the basin by the bed. It was full of alcohol and towels. Despite being such a dick about everything, Baker had been nursing her.

She felt tired. And it was dark outside. How long had she been asleep? Still warm with fever, she shuffled over to the sink and drank a sip of water.

Baker was coming back, wasn't he?

Buffeted by biting gusts of wind, Baker tromped down to the deli.

"Some weather we got here, eh?" Frankie said, smiling.

"Yeah, right," Baker replied. "Give me a ham and Swiss on rye with mustard, and two packs of Camels." Leaving the deli man to make up his sandwich, Baker moved around the store, picking up a six-pack of beer, a box of Tetley tea, and a box of saltines. After a lengthy perusal of the magazine rack, he chose a copy of *Sports Illustrated* and, looking less than enthusiastic, tossed it on the counter. While Frankie was bagging everything, Baker lit a cigarette, eyes falling on the red and blue packs of Tally-Ho hanging from a display on the wall behind the register. He pulled out his wallet. "You can throw a deck of cards in while you're at it."

"You look upset," Frankie said. "Did the blizzard mess you up?"

Baker put some money on the counter, but was still looking in his billfold when he answered, "Kid's sick."

"Flu?"

Now absently staring out the glass door, Baker said, "I don't know."

The deli man—Baker's change in his fist—paused until Baker finally gave him his attention. Then he counted out the bills on top of the counter before putting the coins in Baker's hand. "Tell her I hope she feels better," he said. But when Baker reached for his purchases, Frankie held up his finger. He went to the back and took down a box of instant cocoa. Eyes fixed on Baker's, he dropped the hot chocolate into the bag, adding, "Tell her that's from me."

No hat, no gloves, and no scarf, Baker walked back in the direction of the wind, the sidewalk full of miniature hills, lakes, and valleys made of snow, slush, and ice. And though the precipitation appeared to be abating—he could now see more than halfway down the street—the damage had already been done, the snow reaching almost to his knee, even higher in the drifts. The car that had blocked his Camaro was no longer there, but a nice wall of hard-packed snow had replaced it, courtesy of the snowplow's return.

He wouldn't be going anywhere soon.

Cigarette pinched between his thumb and index finger, shielded from the elements by the rest of his hand, he looked up at Micki's windows and smoked it down to nothing. Then he shook the snow from his hair and headed back up the stoop, where he stomped his feet.

Inside the apartment, he switched on the overhead light, then took off his coat and boots. "Are you awake?" he asked.

"Yessir," she mumbled.

He wiped the thermometer down with an alcohol-soaked cotton puff—which didn't work nearly as smoothly as he'd thought it would—then rinsed it with water. When he'd reached the bed, he said, "I want to take your temperature."

She sat up straight. "I feel better."

"Just do me a favor and put this under your tongue."

Her fever was down to 100.6. Using a funnel he'd made out of aluminum foil, he poured the alcohol back into the empty bottles. After that, he opened the fire escape window further to air out the room; took the minestrone soup from the refrigerator and poured some into a pot; returned the chairs to the table and took out the things he'd bought at the deli; then held up the box of Nestlé's and said, "This is from Frankie," before putting it away.

But Micki was giving him a deadly look: he was going to eat her soup. Without even asking.

Continuing his preparations like a man on a mission, he unfolded the waxed paper around his sandwich and popped open a can of beer. He took her glass from the counter, filled it with fresh water, and placed it across the table. But the apartment was starting to feel cold—he'd opened the window too wide. He went over and closed it within half an inch, letting the curtain fall back into place. And then, as though it really mattered, he smoothed the material out across the rod.

Micki watched him puttering around, doing whatever the hell he liked, never asking, as if he owned the place. Now he was pouring the hot soup into a bowl.

"Put your jeans and jacket on so you don't get chilled, and come sit down," he said. He put the bowl on a plate and surrounded it with a bunch of saltines and a spoon. But when he placed it on the same side of the table as her water, she felt the color rise in her face. She lowered her eyes.

"You feel up to getting out of bed?" he asked.

THEY WERE SITTING ACROSS from each other at the little table. He could feel her gaze upon him. He picked up his sandwich only to put it down. "I"—he glanced away, took a deep breath, then looked her straight in the eyes—"I'm ashamed of what I said before."

Her eyebrows arched up. And when he finally explained what it was he'd been doing, she seemed almost proud of having had such a high fever.

"You were very sick," he said. "*Very* sick—you could've died."

"Well, maybe y'shoulda let me."

He leaned in and thrust his finger in her face. "Don't you *ever* say that again, do you hear me?"

She pressed herself against the back of the chair.

"*Do you hear me?*" he repeated. "I did *not* mean what I said in the car." He tore off a chunk of sandwich with his teeth and started eating. But when he noticed that all she was doing was dipping her spoon half-heartedly in the minestrone, he quickly wolfed down the rest of his meal. "I'm going out in the hall for a smoke."

Once he was gone, she took a sip of the soup. Still hot, the liquid traveled down her throat, the spices burning the raw, inflamed tissue before leaving it feeling soothed. Only it hurt too much to swallow. Ten minutes later, when Baker returned with the scent of cigarette smoke wafting in around him, she was still at the table, the bowl of minestrone nearly full, the plate of crackers untouched.

Hands on hips, he pointed with his chin toward the soup. "Is it good?"

She nodded.

"Why don't you have a little more, then?"

She shrugged.

"Just a little more. It's good for you, Micki. You need to get something in you—keep your strength up."

She eyed the minestrone.

"C'mon, just a little more, okay?"

"I'm not hungry." Yet she picked up the spoon and swirled it around in the vegetable- and pasta-laden liquid.

"How about drinking some of that water, then?"

She put the spoon down, but didn't pick up the glass.

"You're very dehydrated; you've got to drink a lot. Now have some of that." And he pointed to the water.

Both hands around the glass, she lifted it to her lips.

He cleared the table, poured the leftover soup back into the plastic tub, and washed the pot and plate. Micki—not doing anything herself, just watching him from the table—felt uncomfortable. But he appeared to think nothing of it, and continued to fill the pot with water before putting it on the stove to boil. Arms folded over his chest, he leaned against the counter beside it.

The apartment was very quiet. Minutes passed.

"Still snowing," he observed.

Glancing over her shoulder, she looked out the window.

He took her blue mug from the drainer and the polka-dot one from the cabinet. He opened the box of tea and placed a bag in each cup. "Do you know how to play cards?" he asked.

"Cards?"

"Yeah, y'know, like gin rummy or poker?"

"Yeah, I know how to play those. Why?"

"How about a few hands of gin, then?" He poured the boiling water into the mugs and brought them to the table. Settled in his chair, he unwrapped the stiff new deck, softened it, and shuffled. "You know how to play for points?"

She nodded.

"With knocking?"

She nodded again.

"When the knocking card's a spade, points are double, okay?"

"Yessir."

His head pulled back. Then he gave her a small, uncertain smile and slapped the deck down in front of her. "Cut."

THEY'D BEEN PLAYING FOR almost an hour with Micki beating Baker soundly until the last few rounds. While she was dealing the next hand, he tallied the score with satisfaction: "It's about time I started evening things up a bit." He fanned out his new cards and immediately rearranged them, adding, "I'd hate to have to admit I got my ass kicked by a kid." But when he looked up to see her reaction, the teasing, light-hearted expression disappeared from his face. How had he not noticed? Her eyes were glazed, and little patches of red had bloomed on her cheeks. He reached across the table, and she recoiled, then forced herself to let him touch her. Both her forehead and neck were extremely hot. Very gently, he eased the cards from her fingers. "I think you'd better get back into bed."

HE TOOK ANOTHER LOOK at the thermometer, 103.8, then put it aside and set up the alcohol and towels again, Micki following his every move. Seated on the chair that he'd placed by the mattress, he was about to pull down the sheet when he was struck by what he was contending with this time.

He stood up. "Your shirt has to come off." And he turned away to give her some privacy. But when there were no sounds coming from behind him, he looked back to find her the same as before. "I need to put the towels directly on your skin; you understand that, don't you?"

She clutched the sheet to her neck.

"C'mon, Micki, we're wasting time."

She glowered at him.

"C'mon, let's *go!*"

"Forget it."

"If you don't take that shirt off yourself, I'm going to take it off *for* you."

She clutched the sheet even tighter.

Baker moved his chair away. With one smooth motion, he ripped the cheap linen from her hands and cast it back over the blanket at the foot of the bed. But before he could get a hold of her shirt, she'd grabbed two fistfuls at the hem to hold it down.

He sat on the edge of the mattress. "Micki, let go. You've *got* to take this shirt off."

"No!"

"Damn it, Micki, I don't need this right now! Take the fucking shirt off, and let's get on with it!"

Her feverish eyes blazed.

"What's the big fucking deal?" he said. "It's not like I'm going to see anything I haven't already."

"Fuck you." And she curled up with her back to him.

But he forced her flat again, his hands pressing her shoulders to the bed. Leaning over so his face was right in hers, he was about to say something when she asked in a hoarse, half-threatening sneer, "Aren't y'afraid you'll get sick from me, bein' this close?"

"No."

She turned her head away.

But he grabbed her jaw and pulled her face back to his. "Now you listen to me, Micki, I know there's a lot of shit between us, but right now you're simply a very sick kid who needs someone to take care of you. And guess who that person just happens to be at the moment?"

She looked terribly unhappy.

"Now, I'm going to do whatever I have to. No matter what it takes. But it'll be a hell of a lot easier if you cooperate. Believe me, this is just as awkward for me as it is for you."

She snorted.

"I *said*," he repeated, "this is awkward for me, too." And he let go of her jaw.

Her eyes, only half open now, remained fastened on his. But everything else seemed to be sliding away.

"Despite what you think," he continued, "and despite the stupid things that find their way out of my mouth, I am *not* insensitive. I *can* appreciate how you must feel."

And for a few moments, they stayed like that, staring at each other, his face so close, eyes so intense, that her heart started to pound. Slowly, she turned her head away. And released the shirt.

"You need to sit up," he said.

But when she tried, she found herself struggling. He swiftly grabbed her under the arms and raised her to a sitting position. Then he started to lift the shirt. "Put your hands up over your head," he ordered. But even that was too much for her, and he had to roughly tug it off.

As soon as it had been removed, she slumped against him, arms falling on his shoulders. Collapsed upon his chest, she felt heavy. And some of her hair was brushing his neck. But the intense heat of her body, bare skin against his clothes, was bringing back memories of holding Gould's first baby in his arms. With a firm grip, he lowered her down, sliding his right hand in place to cradle her head.

"It sounded like I was arresting you," he said. Though he gave her a self-conscious smile, a terrible sorrow shot through him. And when he'd finished easing her down to the mattress, their eyes locked—only, hers were filled with fear. The two of them were from opposite sides. And no matter what he did, she was too weak to even attempt to put up a fight. He could do anything he wanted. And she was almost completely naked. Hands still encircling her ribcage, he could feel the softness of her breasts against the inside of his wrists.

He tightened his grip. "Everything's going to be all right, y'hear me? I'm going to do exactly what I did before and get your fever back down."

Her fingers, which had feebly grasped his forearms when he'd lowered her, now held on as much as they could—even as he was taking his hands away.

She closed her eyes.

AFTER ANOTHER CHANGE OF towels, Baker took a look at the thermometer: 105.2. "I'm going to call the doctor again." Though her eyes opened to small slits, he wasn't sure she'd understood him. "I'll be right back," he added.

"Unnh." She looked distressed.

"It'll just be a few minutes."

"Unnh!" She closed her eyes again.

Leaving the door ajar, Baker went and placed the call. The doctor he'd spoken to earlier at the emergency room was still there.

"Hold on a sec, okay?" the resident said.

Baker lit a cigarette. He heard some muffled discussion, and then the resident came back on. "I finally got through to a doctor who lives in Forest Hills. You said you're near the subway, right?"

"The Twenty-Third-and-Ely stop is right on the corner." Baker heard more muffled talking.

"Someone's on the other line with him. He says he'll take the train over and have a look at her."

"I'd be very grateful."

"Who says doctors don't make house calls anymore, eh?" the resident joked.

"And, um, this guy's good?" Baker asked. "It's just—well—you said he's only an intern."

"Oh, I never got through to that guy. This is Dr. Orenstein; he's an attending physician here, an excellent doctor. Though I have to warn you: his bedside manner isn't the greatest."

"That's the least of my worries. I can't tell you how much I appreciate this." Baker gave the resident Micki's address and the payphone's number. "How long do you think it'll take him to get here?"

"I'd figure about half an hour or so—unless the subway gets really screwed up."

"Thanks again for all your help."

"No problem. And if you need to, just give a ring back; I'm on call tonight. Couldn't get home anyway, I guess."

Baker hung up, took a few more hits off his cigarette, then stubbed it out against the payphone before returning to the apartment. He reapplied the towels with fresh alcohol and took her temperature again: 105.4.

"Doctor's on his way," he said quietly.

But she lay very still.

Between the top of the turned-down sheet and the end of the towel, which had gotten scrunched up, a small section of her stomach was bare, her left hand carelessly draped over the exposed skin. Without thinking, Baker placed his own hand next to it. When her thumb and index finger lurched forward to grab his pinky, his eyes grew wide. Heart aching, he took his hand and placed it over hers. "I'm right here, Micki," he said softly. "I'm right here."

BAKER OPENED THE DOOR to find a tall, thin man who introduced himself without so much as the suggestion of a smile. And if Dr. Orenstein was at all anxious about the surroundings in which he now found himself, he didn't show that, either.

Micki's fever was down to 102.6. Nightshirt back on, she was sitting up and quite coherent. She was also refusing to be examined. Dr. Orenstein said he was leaving. Baker asked the doctor if he would step outside for a moment while he had a word with Micki alone.

The door clicked shut, and Baker, his voice so low it was nearly a whisper, said, "You'd better change that attitude, Micki. This doctor walked blocks through that fucking mess outside just so he could take the subway here—and you're not even a patient of his. Now you're going to stop being a pain in the ass, and you're going to let him examine you. And if he thinks you need a shot, you're going to let him give you one. Do we understand each other?"

Baker looked very angry. "Yeah, I understand, *okay*?" she shot back.

MICKI ZONED OUT WHILE Dr. Orenstein took her pulse and blood pressure. When he slipped the stethoscope underneath her nightshirt, she stared blankly ahead. Over by the kitchen, Baker stood by and observed, though he thought it odd the doctor hadn't asked him to leave. But then, his presence probably made the doctor feel more comfortable. He was certain it made Micki feel more comfortable.

"How old are you?" Orenstein asked as he poked the otoscope in her ear.

When she didn't answer, Baker volunteered, "She's probably about seventeen."

The doctor paused to look at him. "Don't you know? Doesn't *she* know?"

So Baker explained the situation as briefly as possible while the doctor looked inside her throat and her nose, checked her eyes, and felt the swollen glands under her jaw. Because of the needle tracks on her arm, he asked about her drug use, and when he percussed her back and then palpated her stomach, he had questions about all the scars on her body.

But Micki merely glared, letting Baker explain what he would. When the doctor had shone the bright light in her eyes, she'd felt his breath on her face. It was disgusting. She wanted him to go away.

"And where," Orenstein asked, his eyes now sharply focused on Baker's, "did these black-and-blue marks come from?"

"She got them when she stayed at the detention center over the holiday."

The doctor looked like he was waiting for something more.

Folding his arms over his chest, Baker shifted his weight. "And, um, I don't think she ate much or slept much the whole five days she was there. Maybe that's why she got sick."

"Hmm," the doctor responded, and Baker didn't know if Orenstein was agreeing with him or brushing off his statement as a layman's meaningless comment.

After all was said and done, the doctor declared the infection bacterial—most likely strep. He drew some blood for analysis, took a throat culture, and gave Micki a shot of Bicillen. Baker turned away as she lay down on her stomach so the doctor could inject her in the buttock. She considered this the final indignity.

The doctor then packed his bag, prescribing lots of fluids, rest, and aspirin. Baker lit a cigarette.

His tone harsh, Orenstein said, "Why don't we step into the hallway while you smoke that."

Micki wrapped the sheet around her, seething silently as they talked about her in hushed voices on the other side of the door—a fitting end to this latest invasion of her privacy. But then her gaze fell upon the doctor's medical bag, all smug and unapproachable, sitting by itself on the table. Her eyes lit up. She slipped out of bed and padded over.

Full of scratches and scuffs, the weathered leather made the satchel look incredibly old. It also looked very serious, all black and heavy—not something she should be playing with. But as soon as she undid the latch, it fell open, as if offering its contents for inspection. The stethoscope was too obvious and boring, but the ophthalmoscope was much too big: where would she hide something like that? Where would she hide anything, for that matter? Maybe she could find some pretty pills. She moved the expensive equipment and the tongue depressors aside and found the hefty, nasty-looking hypodermic apparatus the doctor had used to give her the shot. But then, underneath, neatly packaged in sterile wrapping, were some sleek, disposable syringes. Her hands turned cold and clammy. Even as she told herself to get back into bed, her eyes were scanning the room to figure out a hiding place. And then it hit her: the dead space above a desk drawer, on the inside, flush to the front. She grabbed a syringe, closed the medical bag, and hurried over. But the Scotch tape didn't stick that well to the rough, unfinished surface of the wood. And though she used a lot of it, she wondered if it would hold.

She scurried back to bed and dove under the covers—already wishing she'd never taken the syringe in the first place.

WHEN THE MEN RETURNED, Baker's eyes seized upon the medical bag. There might as well have been a fucking spotlight on it. His gaze shifted to Micki, who was sitting up in bed, eyes a little too bright, fixed a little too intently on his.

"So where can I send the bill?" Orenstein asked as he handed Baker his card.

"What?" Baker had been so preoccupied with whether or not to ask the doctor to check his bag that he hadn't heard anything the doctor had said since they'd walked through the door. He took his own business card from his wallet and wrote his home address on the other side. As he was handing it to Orenstein, he decided it probably *would* be a good idea to get the doctor to look over his supplies: better safe than sorry.

But Orenstein had finished putting on his coat and was shaking Baker's hand. Baker heard himself thanking the doctor as he showed him to the door, where he continued to stand, filled with indecision, even as he heard the downstairs door being opened and closed. No sooner did he envision Orenstein as being on the subway than he regretted not having asked. And still he couldn't bring himself to confront Micki. Of course, he could thoroughly toss the apartment at the first opportune moment—even look around quickly now if she went to the bathroom. But in his silence, he felt he'd made a terrible mistake.

USING HIS COAT AS a thin cushion, Baker slept on the hardwood floor. By morning, his back and joints felt achy and stiff. He wanted to go home and catch a shower, a shave, and some decent sleep. When he heard a shovel scraping the sidewalk, he rushed downstairs to pay the boy to dig out his car. Then he made his way to the supermarket to buy some chicken soup.

"I'LL INFORM MR. ANTONELLI you won't be working tonight; I'm sure he's expecting that anyway," Baker said as he put on his coat. "And you're not to go to school tomorrow, either." He paused in the doorway. "If you start feeling worse again, you call me—y'hear?"

She nodded, even as the urge to confess welled up. But she didn't utter a word as the door closed behind him, his footsteps moving down the hall and then the stairs. She hurried over to the bay windows to watch him leave, leaning over the desk so she could see him down the street, clearing snow from his car and scraping ice from the windshield. Then he got in. And drove away. She continued to stare at the empty space—until a dirty black Mustang pulled in and parked.

Baker had gone home.

Chapter 22

SCHOOL REOPENED ON FRIDAY, and it was back to routine for most of the city despite piles of dirty snow and inches-deep puddles of slush. On his way home, Baker stopped at Micki's, but found she'd returned to work. He used the chance to thoroughly search her apartment, only to come up empty: no syringe or anything else she could've taken from the doctor's bag. What he did find, though, were all five cans of soup he'd bought still sitting on the counter where he'd left them.

MICKI WORKED THE ENTIRE weekend when Juan let her take his Sunday shift. Mr. Antonelli sent her home with more soup, saying, "You make-a sure you get some-a good sleep-a." But she turned in much too late and was half awake through most of the night. When she entered the security office on Monday morning, she looked pale.

"You want to get sick again?" Baker asked. But after a cursory pat down, he ignored her, talking instead to Warner about the upcoming holidays.

Micki stood beside his desk, watching the clock, then slamming the door behind her when she left. I'm just a fucking job to him, she thought. He doesn't really give a shit about me; I'm just a job. JUST A FUCKING JOB. Picturing the syringe tucked away above the desk drawer, she smiled, reveling in the tiny success of its concealment: the great fucking detective hadn't found it yet.

AFTER MICKI HAD GONE, Warner asked, "What's she so upset about?"

"Who the hell knows," Baker said.

But Warner, looking into Baker's eyes, thought that wasn't quite true.

AT THE END OF the day, Baker was equally remote, and Micki stalked out of the office. But before she'd reached the main entrance, the football player caught up with her. The hall was empty, so they tried the auditorium's side doors, casting frequent glances over their shoulders until they found one that was open. The houselights closest to the stage were on, and they seated themselves on the floor. But less than half an hour later, Bobby announced he'd had enough.

"This was really great," he said, then closed his loose-leaf and gathered his things. "You explain stuff really well. Will you help me out again next week?"

She shrugged. "Okay." But her heart was beating faster. The gossip around the gym was that he'd broken up with his girlfriend.

They exited the auditorium, and he gave her a quick kiss on the cheek before jogging off toward the stairs. Micki hurried down the hall and turned the corner—running smack into Baker.

"What the hell are you still doing here?" he asked.

"I was helping someone study."

"Where?"

"In the auditorium."

"That's off limits and you know it."

"So where were we supposed to go?"

"Who were you helping?"

"Bobby Reiger."

"The senior varsity football player?" Baker looked like he was on the verge of laughing.

"What's so funny? He needs help with his math."

"I'll bet."

"Y'think I'm lyin'?"

"I think you know you don't belong here now. When you leave that security office, you're to go straight home. Is that clear?"

She left the building with Baker's eyes fastened upon her—cold as the melting snow beneath her feet.

MONDAY EVENINGS WERE USUALLY pretty nice: no Bel, just homework. But it wasn't so great when she was feeling like this. She stared at the packaged syringe.

Just filling it with water she'd get a rush from shooting up—a conditioned response, probably bigger than the one she'd gotten watching Dr. Orenstein insert the needle to draw blood. But afterward—and this was the catch, for there was always a catch—the cravings would be worse. She tore the top open very carefully, pulled the syringe out halfway, and took off the cap.

In the street, some guy started yelling at his kid to either get his ass home now or not bother coming home at all. She looked up at the window. Baker was such a fake, and she'd been stupid enough to fall for it. Again. The vague memory of his hand covering hers only mocked her now. What a bastard.

She snapped the cap back on and eased the syringe down into its now crinkled little sleeve so it could be returned to its hiding place in the poorly constructed desk. With unfinished edges and clunky hardware, the clumsy piece of furniture looked like it had been thrown together in someone's garage. There was enough dead space above each drawer to have made another, much larger, one—the one on the right tending to get stuck before it was even halfway open. By slipping her forearm and elbow into its interior, then angling her hand around, she was able to tape the syringe all the way up near the top. Big and thick, Baker's arm would have a hard time getting in there, especially with all the school supplies inside. Of course, he could merely remove the entire drawer—something she'd once done herself just to be sure it wouldn't disturb anything. Nothing had happened, but it had taken forever to get the warped wood back on its track.

She went to the kitchen and pulled out two half-pound bags of M&M's—one plain, one peanut—and ate till she was too nauseous to continue. Eyelids drooping, mind numb, she flopped down on the bed. And slept.

As the days filed past, Baker retreated further into the bottle, sometimes wishing he could crawl right in. The one feeble attempt he made to move on with his life was asking out the popular Miss Manley, a tall, blond chemistry teacher he'd chatted with briefly a couple of times. With a forced smile and no explanation, she declined his invitation—making him feel like some sort of social pariah.

Slouched in his recliner, he stared at the floor. He'd never imagined he'd be so alone at this stage of the game. He downed another drink and shivered, convinced the chill of the season had seeped into his life for good.

WHEN BAKER ARRIVED AT work on Monday, his head was pounding and his eyes were bloodshot. Micki kept her distance while Warner shot him a long, dark look. And though he'd been hoping for a quiet shift, the day presented him with a steady barrage of incidents instead: two fights erupted in the halls and one in the cafeteria; three juniors freaked out after dropping acid in art class; a senior couple was caught screwing backstage in the auditorium for the second time that term; and, in a rather strange twist of events, Jamison's professional conduct had been called into question. The security guard stood accused of cursing at, and then striking, a student he'd removed from an auto-shop class for being excessively disruptive. Baker couldn't even picture Jamison using bad language, let alone unnecessary force. But the student was sticking to his story. Which meant Baker had one more headache on his hands—one more than he could handle.

BOBBY, WHO'D BEEN WAITING for Micki by the stairwell, ran after her while she was on her way out.

"Hey!" he said. "Got time to give my brain another tune-up?"

"Yeah, sure. But we can't hang out here, I—"

"But I can't leave," Bobby said. "I've still gotta get to football practice, and I'm already gonna be late."

Her heart dropped. "I can't; I really can't. If I get caught, I'm gonna be in big trouble. What about hanging out outside?"

"You kidding? It's too friggin' cold to just sit on the steps. C'mon, nothing'll happen. I mean, we're just studying."

A glance over her shoulder said no one else was around. She followed Bobby down the hall, where the same auditorium door had been left unlocked.

MARINO STEPPED OUT FROM the recessed section of the lobby. Should he tell Baker or not? The kid was just messing around; he could dig that. And she wasn't hurting anyone. But if Baker found out anyway, he'd be in deep shit himself.

He'd give them fifteen minutes.

BOBBY WAS FINDING IT hard to stay focused this time. With the football season nearing its end, the last few games were critical: the coach was going to be pissed.

"I think I got this down pretty good now," he said. "I caught on pretty quick once you showed me how to pull the problems apart." Closing his books, he continued to thank her. A lot. Until two bright spots of pink blossomed on her cheeks. And then he asked her to go to the movies with him Friday night.

A…date? Her mind went blank. "I—uh—I work Friday nights."

"Yeah, but maybe we could go afterward."

"It'll be too late. I'm not done till about ten thirty or so."

"Saturday?"

"Same thing, maybe even later."

He smiled. "How about a kiss, then?" And, leaning in, he pulled her face toward his.

But at the moment their lips touched, Baker exploded through the door. They both scrambled to their feet.

"What did I just tell you last week?" he asked Micki.

"It was my idea," Bobby said.

"Shut up," Baker snapped. "In fact, pick up your books and get the hell out of here."

Bobby hesitated.

Baker took a step toward the football player, who looked dwarfed by comparison. "Do you want me to have a little talk with your parents? Do you want to sit out the rest of your games?"

"No, sir," Bobby responded quietly.

"Then pick up your books and get out of here *now*."

As he gathered his things together, Bobby mumbled, "I'm sorry, Micki." And the door eased shut behind him.

On the floor near Micki's books was a single sheet of loose-leaf paper Bobby had stepped on while leaving. Underneath his footprint was a geometry proof. In Micki's handwriting. But Baker never even glanced at it. Too nauseous to eat anything all day, head still viciously pounding, he could feel his stomach squeezing with hunger. He needed a drink. Badly. "You just can't control yourself, can you," he said.

"What's the big deal? We were just makin' out."

"You think I don't know what goes on in here?"

"We were *just* makin' out."

"But if he wanted to, you would've gone all the way, isn't that right?"

And Micki hesitated. A moment ago, it had all seemed so innocent. But she *had* been wondering what it would be like to have sex with Bobby.

Baker snorted.

"So what!" she shot back.

"You fuck like a whore, that's what."

"And you would know."

The back of his fist hit her hard enough to send her tripping over the pile of books on the floor. "Don't you dare talk to me like that," he said. "Who the fuck do you think you are?" He looked her over. "I bet you couldn't even count how many guys have fucked you."

Micki felt like she wasn't completely there anymore. A part of her was somewhere else. Watching.

"Gee," Baker said. "No answer. Isn't that a shock."

"I don't know, okay? I don't know because—" But she stopped.

"Because what?"

"Forget it."

"Because *what*," he repeated.

"It's none of your business!"

"Oh, but it is," he replied, voice full of feigned concern. "I told you before: everything about you is my business."

"Go t' hell!"

Grabbing a fistful of her shirt, the material pulled tight around her throat, he yanked her toward him. He had a cruel—almost wild—look in his eye. She said, "Y'shoot up, y'nod off—things happen."

Releasing her, Baker laughed. "So you think that doesn't count?"

"It's not like I asked for it."

"Isn't it? You put yourself in a situation like that, you expect shit like that to go down. They used you like a whore; you were just too stupid to get paid for it." And though his face didn't show it, he knew he'd gone too far—*way* too far. But then, he'd lost control before he'd even set foot in the auditorium.

Micki put her jacket on and picked up her books. Voice flat, she asked, "Are y'done with me?"

He simply turned and walked away, leaving her alone in the vast emptiness of the theater.

And if she could've, she would've stood there forever, safe among the vacant seats, deserted stage, and abandoned piano. Instead, having nowhere else to go, she went home.

IT HURT A LOT, what Baker had said. It hurt a little when she withdrew the money from the bank. It hurt for just a moment—a tiny pinprick—when she slipped the needle into her vein.

But nothing hurt anymore.

BEFORE DAWN, MICKI SHOT up some of the junk she'd saved to help make it through the day. She nodded off and barely got to school on time, reporting to Warner because Baker had overslept. When it was time to go home, Warner was also the one to let her leave because Baker had his hands full with a trespasser. Yet she hadn't gotten by completely unscathed: Warner had noticed how agitated she was. Though he hadn't given it much thought in the morning, he was now verily suspicious. He debated whether to say something to Baker or wait to see what Micki would be like tomorrow.

But for Micki, tomorrow would be just like today: dark and lifeless, a bleak and barren wasteland. She shot up the last bit of smack she had, then withdrew more money from the bank and went to work, which seemed an interminable misery. She even broke a plate, the first since she'd been at Bel.

"Is okay-a," Mr. Antonelli said when he saw how distressed she was. But toward the end of her shift, when she started to sniffle, he said, "You no take-a care of you-self-a. You get-a sick again-a."

She shrugged him off, scrubbing even harder at the casserole dish in her hand—waiting till after he'd left to swipe her nose across her shoulder.

HOME ONCE MORE, SHE tried to stay in her apartment—even tried doing homework—but the craving was gnawing at her, crawling through her body. No matter how hard she tried, it was the only thing she could think about. The only thing. So under cover of darkness, clinging to the shadows, she weaved her way toward the bridge, through the dimly lit industrial streets. Three times she hunkered down behind garbage dumpsters: once to avoid being seen by a patrol car, once to hide from a group of unfamiliar boys, and once for no other reason than an overwhelming sense of being followed.

But then she was back in her own little space, where she whipped the belt out of her jeans, tore the syringe and bottle-cap from their taped repose, and cooked up some of the smack. Cotton puff for a filter, she drew the junk into the needle and shot it up inside her vein, the hot liquid pulling her, at incredible speed, through a stream of soft white light until she reached an empty space of total bliss.

The drug paraphernalia was strewn across the table. She had no groceries and her homework wasn't done.

And she couldn't care less.

THE FOLLOWING MORNING, BAKER observed Micki closely: the anxious body language, the evasive glances. Yesterday, when he'd checked her bankbook, he'd seen two consecutive withdrawals.

The passing bell rang, but she didn't leave.

"You're going to be late for class," he said.

"I—I need to talk to you."

Warner, on his way out, caught Baker's eye.

Once the door had closed, Baker asked, "What is it?"

"I…" She looked at the floor, then started again. "I—"

Baker's walkie-talkie crackled to life as Angie reported a major melee in progress at the northwest entrance. One teacher was already injured from attempting to intervene.

"We'll have to talk about this later," Baker said, and dashed out of the office.

Micki stared after him. Later would be too late.

When it was time to go home, Micki told Baker she couldn't remember what it was she'd wanted to tell him. She averted her gaze as much as possible and put sunglasses on before picking up her books. As she was leaving, she passed Warner entering the office.

Baker moved to the window and lit a cigarette.

"What's up with her?" Warner asked. "What did she say?"

Baker watched as she hurried down the steps to the sidewalk. Eyes still focused through the glass, he slowly exhaled smoke. "The kid's using again."

"Heroin?"

"Yeah."

"She told you this?"

Baker looked at the trees, their leafless branches stark reminders of the changing cycle of the seasons: the flow of life—and death. "She didn't have to," he said.

Only the little desk lamp was on, but Micki was sitting at the table, staring at the single fresh cigarette butt in the saucer Baker used as an ashtray. He must've stopped by while she was at work.

Belt wrapped around her arm, teeth gripping the free end to keep it taught, she held the syringe above the bulging, throbbing vein. But tears were running down her face. She'd ruined everything. Out of the corner of her eye, she could see her savings passbook sitting beside her on the table, the meager account cleaned out. Useless. And tomorrow, with no money left, she'd have to tell Baker what she'd done. It would've looked a hell of a lot better if she'd told him today. Not that it would've meant much, but still…

The door flew open, and a large black form stood framed in the hallway light. Baker strode over and ripped the syringe out of her hand, throwing it to the floor and crushing it under his shoe. Unable to move, she let him whip the belt off her arm and throw that on the floor, as well. Then he grabbed two fistfuls of her shirt near the shoulders and yanked her to her feet.

"So this is it?" he asked.

She envisioned him breaking her apart with his bare hands.

He shook her. "I saved your fucking life so you could shove a needle in your arm?"

And as she looked into his eyes, all she could see was hate: he'd hated her from the moment he'd first laid eyes on her. With tears still wet on her face, she swung her fist up in a wide, powerful hook.

And that was when it dawned on Baker that Micki had been crying. *Crying.* By the time he saw her fist, the best he could do was pull his head back enough to prevent getting clocked. Still she clipped his jaw with enough force to rattle him, and he let go.

Throwing punches every which way, she was all over him. In a matter of seconds, more than three months' worth of pent-up fury was being released, her fists coming at him hard and fast. And yet something was inducing him to do nothing more than cover up, his forearms taking a heavy beating as they alternately guarded his ribs, gut, and face—some strikes still slipping in. Painfully.

But there was only so long she could keep it up. And as she tired, Baker looked for an opening. With a sharp forward motion, he trapped her in a boxer's clinch, the momentum of his body forcing her backward. Her heels caught the edge of the mattress, and she fell over, taking him with her. He lifted himself up so he was sitting on top of her, her arms pinned above her head.

Chest heaving, she gasped for breath. There was an awkward moment of silence. And then she said, "Why don'tcha just fuck me again, y'son of a bitch! I shoulda kept the goddamn money last time. Y'think I'm a fuckin' whore, I might as well be smart, like y'said, an' get paid for it."

A sickening chill shot through him, and he could see her slamming his twenty-dollar bill down on his desk. "That money," he said evenly, "was to make up for the pay you lost by not working that night. It had nothing to do with us having sex."

"Oh, yeah, right."

"You got paid for going to the dance and missing work. I said I'd make it up to you, and I did."

And though it seemed very dim, the recollection of his uttering those words came back to her. "Well—well y'still think I'm a whore. Y'said it, didn'tcha?"

Not knowing what to say, he said nothing.

Fresh tears welled up, and she turned her head away, closing her eyes as if that could prevent him from seeing her.

"When did you start shooting up again?" he asked.

Tears rolled across her face.

"Answer me!"

She only sobbed.

Putting painful pressure on her wrists, he repeated, "ANSWER ME!"

She looked back at him. "Two days ago, okay? Two—*fuckin'*—days ago."

"And where did you get the works?"

"You and that asshole doctor—y'were nice enough t'go outside and leave me with a whole fuckin' bagful a needles."

"So then where've you been hiding it all this time?" He watched her face, waiting for the answer—for this was the only real mystery; he'd guessed the rest.

"In the desk."

"No way, Micki, I checked that goddamn thing this very afternoon."

"I taped it inside, above a drawer, right up at the front."

"Oh, yeah? I got news for you, I put my hand up there a couple of times, and I didn't find a fucking thing."

"Well y'obviously missed it!"

The satisfaction she was getting out of this made him want to pick her up and throw her across the room. Instead, he glanced to the side and saw that the right-hand desk drawer was, indeed, open. So he pushed himself up and went over, shoving his hand in to maneuver his fingers into the spot she'd disclosed. At first he felt nothing. But then he thrust his arm in further, over the loose-leaf paper and other school supplies, wood scraping the skin of his forearm till he got his elbow through. Contorting his large hand even more, sweat beading on his face, he reached up a little higher. And the tips of his fingers brushed against the remnants of some old pieces of Scotch tape.

"Shit!" He withdrew his arm and slammed the drawer shut with such force that the pens on the desk—in all their multicolored splendor—went rolling, some of them falling to the ground. "Shit!" he repeated. He'd gotten careless. Careless and lazy. Too lazy to remove the fucking drawers completely because they were such a pain in the ass to put back. How could he possibly have been so stupid? This was such an obvious spot—so *incredibly* obvious. He should've caught this. But he should've done a lot of things. It was as if he'd wanted this to happen.

Her solitary moment of victory fading, Micki curled up in a fetal position and closed her eyes. She was beginning to feel really sick. And though she wasn't watching him anymore, she knew exactly what he was doing. She could tell that he'd turned on the overhead light. She heard the closet door being opened and her duffle bag being unzipped. She heard the jangle of the buckle as he picked her belt up from the floor and threw it inside. Dresser drawers opened and closed, followed by sounds near the kitchen as toothbrush, toothpaste, deodorant, and comb were tossed into the bag. Then came that ominous, final zip: the duffle itself being shut.

"Okay, Micki," he said. "Let's go."

But raising herself to a sitting position suddenly seemed like an unbelievably difficult project, taking tremendous effort. At any moment, she expected him to yell at her to hurry up. Instead, he merely waited—oddly patient—till she was finally standing.

"Y'know, I tried t'tell y'about it this morning," she said.

"Well you should've tried harder."

"Would it've mattered?"

"What do *you* think?"

She lowered her eyes.

"Turn around," he ordered, and promptly patted her down. Then he checked the pockets of her jacket before handing it to her.

She put her arms through the sleeves, all the while looking about. Now that she was sure she'd never return, her crummy little apartment took on a whole different meaning. Eyes filled with tears again, her vision became a blurry, distorted collage of colors and shapes. She fumbled, unsuccessfully, with the jacket zipper.

Baker bent over and gently moved her hands away. As he closed the zipper, two large drops of warm, salty water fell on his skin. He raised his eyes to hers, but she quickly turned her head. And when he straightened up, he felt ten feet taller than her instead of one. He recalled that first night when he'd sworn he'd find a way to break her down. Well, she'd come undone, all right. And he'd never felt so low.

With the bag dangling from his arm, he guided her out of the apartment, down the steps, and to his car. He unlocked the passenger door and held it open.

"Get in."

THERE WAS SILENCE AS they rolled over the Queensboro Bridge, Micki staring out the windshield of the Camaro, a vacant expression on her face. Baker—sweating in his jacket, thoughts spinning around in his head—was waiting, just *waiting*, for her to make excuses for what she'd done; to say it wasn't her fault.

She said nothing.

Once they reached Manhattan, they crept along the pot-holed road clogged with cars, trucks, and the occasional jay-walking pedestrian. At Third Avenue they turned right. When they stopped at Sixty-Fifth Street for a red light, Micki snapped to attention.

"Where are y'takin' me?" The Manhattan precinct she remembered was downtown on the West Side. They were traveling uptown on the East Side.

Baker glanced over. Her body was so taut she looked like she was ready to spring out of the car at any second. He said, "You'll stay at my place till all that shit's out of your system."

"And then what?"

"And then you're never going to use that crap again." The light turned green, and he put the car in gear, jockeying for position among the other vehicles.

"Yeah, right. Just like that. So what am I gonna owe ya f'this?"

He felt himself bristle, but simply gripped the wheel tighter. When they hit another light, he turned his head to look at her. "You'll owe me to stay clean. That's all you'll owe me. That's *all*."

"But you live on the *West* Side."

"We'll go over through the park in a little while. There was too much crosstown traffic after we got off the bridge. I should've just taken the FDR."

Hot and stinging, more tears welled up. And as they pulled away from the light, she turned her face to the passenger window. When he finally parked the car on Ninety-Fifth near West End Avenue, she was still crying.

BAKER LOCKED THE APARTMENT door from the inside and pocketed the keys. He pocketed the key to the fire escape window's gate, as well. He pointed out which sheets and towels to take from the linen closet, told Micki to get settled in the study, then finished the rest of the "safety procedures" he'd used when she'd been there to clean. But when he checked his food supply, it was pitifully low. He sighed.

He put a few ice cubes in a plastic bag, popped the cap off a beer, and went into the living room.

A short while later, Micki found him sitting on the sofa with his shirt off and the bag of ice pressed against his ribs. Her eyes flicked over his torso before settling on his bruised face, which was looking back with reproach. She bit her lip, her own face growing hot.

"You need something?" he asked.

"A nightshirt. You forgot my nightshirt." Picking at her collar and fidgeting with her sleeves, she sniffled, though it was no longer from crying.

"You can use something of mine." He switched the ice to the other side of his body, adding, "But let's get something straight: while you're here, you're to respect my privacy. Don't be going through my things—and I really mean it this time, Micki. In fact, stay out of my room altogether." He moved the ice to his jaw. "But you can help yourself to anything you want in the kitchen—except the beer. Is that going to be a problem? 'Cause I'll get rid of it if it is."

"I dunno."

Baker stared at the dark TV screen; Micki stared at the bookcase and scratched at her arm.

"I'm gonna pay you back for the stuff I use, okay?" she said.

"No, just forget it."

Not knowing where to put herself, she perched on the opposite end of the couch and gazed off into space while he continued to stare at the blank TV—jaw clenching and unclenching.

"Look," he finally said, "I should be shot for saying the things I said to you the other day. I only did it because I knew how much it would get to you, not because it's true." He turned to her and added, "And as far as what happened when you were wasted in the Bronx—well—let's just say you did something really stupid. But that doesn't make it your fault or any less of a crime. You were raped. Period. The guys who did it were fucking animals." His face too cold and starting to itch, he removed the ice and noticed the bag was now half filled with water.

So were Micki's eyes.

IN JUST THREE DAYS, she'd shot up a lot of junk. Sweating, then shivering with chills, she was running to the bathroom and throwing up. When Baker entered the study, he found her in a ball, fully dressed, on top of the blanket. She jumped up and faced him.

"Something wrong with the shirt I gave you? It's the longest black shirt I own," he said.

"It's fine."

"Then why haven't you changed? Don't you want to sleep *in* the bed, *under* the covers?"

"I'm fine," she repeated.

He put his hands on his hips. "Look, this is no different than my being at *your* place when you're asleep."

She shrugged.

"Is it?" he pressed.

"I dunno."

"*You don't know?*" He dropped his arms. "What the hell do you think this is? Enemy territory?"

She didn't answer.

"You think the rules are different here?"

She responded with a cynical twist of her mouth.

"Fine!" he snapped. "For all I care, you can stay dressed like that till you leave. But y'know what?" He paused as if she might actually reply. "Whether you like it or not, you're just going to have to trust me 'cause the truth is"—he paused again, lowering his voice several notches—"you don't have any other choice." He marched out, slamming the door behind him.

She stood where she was till she began to shiver. Then she changed into his shirt and crawled under the covers.

WIRED AND RESTLESS, BODY aching, Micki was unable to do much of anything except lie in bed until she had to go throw up again. All she wanted was a fix. Just one last shot. And then she'd get clean.

What bull.

She started back to bed, passing Baker's bedroom, then paused. Somewhere, in one of his dresser drawers, was an extra set of keys. And if he'd taken his wallet out of his pocket, there would be money, too.

Her eyes grew bright.

EXHAUSTED, BAKER HAD FALLEN asleep on the sofa at two thirty in the morning, the TV a barely discernable buzz in the darkness. In his dream, he was calling Warner to tell him he'd be out for the rest of the week. Then Warner became Captain Malone, and he was trying to make excuses for missing the poker game.

But just as it had numerous times before, the sound of Micki retching roused him. The toilet flushed, and he heard her heading back to her room. But he didn't hear her door click shut when it should have. Eyes still closed, he was now fully alert, ears straining to catch the slightest sound above the low hum of the television set. Something was up; he could feel it. But he'd wait and let her tip her hand.

He could be a patient man.

MICKI CREPT INTO HIS room, the light from the hallway more than enough to see by. Opening drawers and rummaging through clothes, she prayed the small amount of noise she was making wouldn't wake him. She came upon the extra set of keys, and her hand closed triumphantly around them. But when his wallet wasn't on the dresser, she felt a spark of panic before she spied it on the night table closest to the door. Yet as she made her way over, a heavy, oppressive feeling engulfed her, as if a pair of huge, unseen gates were slamming shut. Still, she picked up the wallet—unexpectedly dense, the leather scarred from years of use—and opened it to see his gold shield glinting in the darkness. Her fingers ran across the textured metal, letters and numbers melting into a shiny swirl behind tears.

Three twenties, a five, and four singles. She took them all, then put the five and the singles back. After that, she tiptoed to her room and hastily got dressed, every ambient sound, like the pipes knocking, making her jump. But then her belt was buckled and her laces were tied, and all that was left was to get her jacket.

Out in the hall, she glanced over at Baker, who was flat on his back with his eyes closed, the TV playing for no one. So she continued on to the closet and gently opened the door until, at the halfway point, it creaked. She froze. But all she heard—very, very low—was the background music from whatever show he had on. She poked her head around the wall and could see him still sleeping, breathing evenly in the television's flickering light. And then her jacket was on, and she was slowly turning the lower lock's latch, the small sound ripping through the stillness. Her heart raced even faster. She had a splitting headache. But it was only after she'd slipped the key into the upper deadbolt cylinder that she paused.

"Going somewhere?" Baker asked.

Gasping, she whirled around and, much to her dismay, started crying again. "You don't know what this feels like!"

"So you're going to do—what—go shoot up again? Be a junkie for the rest of your life?"

Tears were streaming down her face.

"It's your choice, Micki. If you want to leave, go ahead. But as soon as you walk out that door, I'll have an APB put out for your arrest. And when you're picked up—which you will be—you'll go through withdrawal in a jail cell instead of here. And no one's going to have any sympathy for you, y'hear me? No one's going to give a shit about you."

Her eyes, the pupils widely dilated, searched Baker's, then closed, tears spilling out. She faced the door and rotated the key, mumbling a choked, "I'm sorry."

But before she'd even turned the knob, Baker had thrown his arms around her, pulling her away and holding her tight. And though she could barely move, she wouldn't stop struggling. He put his mouth close to her ear. "You're not walking out that door until you're straight, do you understand me? And if I have to, I'll break every fucking bone in that little body of yours to keep you here." He paused. "Please don't make me do that, Micki."

Racked with sobs, she hung her head while his arms—two massive bands of muscle—stayed strapped across her torso, keeping her captive against the solid weight of his body. Keeping her safe. From everything. Including herself. So when he started to release her, she blurted out, "Don't"—before catching herself and pulling away.

"Don't what?" he asked.

A hot blush rose in her face.

"Don't let go?"

She backed up, out of reach.

"There's nothing wrong with that, Micki—with wanting to be held; it's not always a sexual thing."

But the rise and fall of her chest became even more pronounced.

"Friends hug, relatives hug; it's perfectly normal," he said.

Turning green, she said, "I havta puke"—and dashed toward the bathroom.

He almost laughed, until he heard her throwing up. He relocked the door and pocketed the extra keys.

ALREADY ON HIS SECOND cup of morning coffee, Baker pulled out the high school staff calendar. Christmas vacation would start after a three-period session on Friday, which meant Micki would miss only a day and a half of school. He'd miss only a little more of work. He looked at his watch and called Warner to say he wouldn't be in. When he confided why, he was greeted with a long, judgmental silence. After a curt: "The kid's safe with me," he hung up and went back to sleep.

A few hours later, a fresh pot of coffee brewing, he called Mr. Antonelli. "Micki's sick again," he said.

The restaurant owner *tsk-tsk*ed. "I tell her she come-a back-a to work too soon-a."

"Yeah—well—I'm keeping her here at my place this time. Maybe next Tuesday she'll be able to pick up her shifts."

"I gonna be open-a Christmas Eve-a, but-a closed-a Christmas Day-a. This-a no good for me, you understand-a? I need-a her to work-a when she's supposed to work-a." He uttered a heavy, guttural sound, then added, "I make-a the other arrangements."

BAKER HAD SEEN ENOUGH junkies in various stages to know what to expect, but living around the clock with someone going through withdrawal was another story. Even worse was the realization that he had little to do but sit by and watch the disgusting process unfold. Once—and only once—he went to the study and opened the door. Teeth gnashed together, she was shivering violently beneath two blankets. He forced himself to stay there for several minutes. Until he wanted a drink. Then he closed the door and settled for a beer.

Smoking incessantly, he was having cigarettes delivered with whatever take-out he ordered, currently puffing away on Lucky Strikes because the vending machine at the Chinese restaurant had apparently run out of Camels. Micki, however, had no interest in food, so he was ordering and eating meals by himself. And on those rare occasions when she said she was hungry, it was solely for chocolate—of which he had none. He eventually gave the pizza-delivery boy a couple of extra bucks to run down to the corner store and get a bunch of Hershey bars for her.

But like a phantom houseguest, she mostly stayed in the study and kept to herself—until Friday morning, when she flew into the living room, startling him out of his reading. He choked on the cigarette smoke he'd just inhaled.

"Y'gotta give me something," she demanded. "Every fuckin' part of me hurts. I can't sleep and—and—it's just too much already. I can't take this anymore, y'understand?"

He looked at her with a shrewd eye.

She wiped at the sweat beading on her face. "C'mon, I'm really hurtin' here."

His reply was a long, affected blink.

"*Didja hear what I said? I can't take this anymore.*"

"Save your breath. You're not getting a goddamned thing."

"CAN'T Y'SEE I NEED SOMETHIN'? I FEEL LIKE I'M FUCKIN' DYIN', YA SADISTIC SON OF A BITCH!"

He returned to his book and cigarette as if she weren't even there. She stomped back to her room, muttering and cursing under her breath, slamming the door behind her. But a short while later—in what seemed like a miracle—she started to feel better.

FOR THE REST OF the day, Micki slept and watched TV. In the evening, after some hesitation, Baker showed her how to use his stereo, surprisingly tolerant of her tendency to play a single song over and over—Derek and the Dominos' "Anyday" being a particular favorite. And yet in the two days they'd been together, barely a word had passed between them that wasn't of the most basic nature or strictly out of necessity.

They were the most intimate of strangers.

NIGHT WAS TURNING INTO morning, and the muted sound of water running in the shower was mixing with the squeaky brakes and rumbling motor of a box truck heading toward its first delivery. A snowplow shovel scraped by. But Baker, lying in the dark, was thinking about Cynthia. And engagement rings. Gould had told him about a family friend who was a diamond dealer: "This guy's gonna give you a great price. I promise. He'll take good care of you."

Sighing, Baker turned over on his side. He was in desperate need of female companionship—more precisely, sex; this was far too long to go without. And yet the thought of picking up some action at a bar was depressing. The last few times he'd done that, he'd ended up feeling lonelier afterward. Besides, until Micki went home, the issue was moot.

He turned over onto his back again and heard her shut the water off. A few minutes later, she left the bathroom. But when he should've heard the door to her room close, there was only silence. The clock read 3:32. He got out of bed and pulled on his Levi's.

MICKI HAD BEEN IN the shower almost half an hour, the steady stream of water hitting her skin with considerable force—strangely pleasant—little liquid beads rolling down in rivulets, over and over. Completely steamed, the medicine-cabinet mirror reflected a fuzzy, fogged-out image. And her fingertips were shriveled like prunes. She dried herself off and made her way through the dark living room to watch the snow falling outside. Under the streetlamps' glow, everything was coated in a pristine layer of white. And like the freshly covered world, she felt incredibly clean and pure. But her heart ached and her body was tired, eyes heavy with the weight of all they'd seen. She felt old.

"Everything okay?" Baker asked.

She spun around.

He turned on a light, his face relaxing into a smile: Her gaunt figure was swimming in black terry cloth. "My robe's a little big on you," he said. When she looked hurt, he added, "It's kind of cute, though. Why don't you roll up the sleeves a little so they won't be covering your hands?"

Instead, she brushed her bangs to the side. And though sunken and sad, her eyes looked clear. She looked clean.

"Hungry?" he asked.

She nodded.

"C'mon, I'll make us some breakfast."

He lit a cigarette and left it hanging from his mouth while he put up a large pot of coffee and toasted a whole package of Downyflakes. Drinking most of the coffee himself, he watched her practically inhale all of the waffles.

THE DAY PASSED SLOWLY. In between long naps, Micki watched TV with Baker: football, drag racing, an interview with a cop who'd testified with Serpico (she fell asleep halfway through that), a *Star Trek* rerun… They played cards and Scrabble. They played backgammon. They barely talked.

Later that night, during a commercial break in a TV show, Micki asked when she could go home.

"Maybe toward the end of the week. We'll see how it goes."

"But I have to work."

"You can go to work. I'll take you there and pick you up afterward. I'm going to tell Mr. Antonelli to call me if anyone sees you step out."

"He knows?"

"He thinks you're sick again. I'll just say it's important I keep a close eye on you. I doubt he'll press me for details. By the way, do you want your watch back?"

"No." While going through the worst part of withdrawal, she'd become extremely sensitive to the ticking of her watch. If it was anywhere near her, that was all she could hear, louder and louder until she had to ask Baker to keep it in his room for her. Just thinking about it now was making her feel queasy again.

Baker went back to his program. But only a few seconds later, he turned his head to find her staring at him. "What? What is it?" he asked.

"Did you always want to be a cop?"

He opened his mouth, then shut it again. Indicating the TV, he asked, "Are you watching this?"

"Not really."

He got up and turned it off. When he was back on the couch, he took a swig of beer, stroked his jaw, rubbed the back of his neck, and finally said, "I was going to say 'no,' but I'm not so sure that's true. Even when I was in law school, I was more interested in finding out stuff about how cops were involved in cases than in being lectured about torts or contracts."

She gaped at him. "You were in law school?"

Baker grinned. "I could've been a lawyer."

"So what happened?"

"One day, I finally admitted that I hated law school and—with rare exception—lawyers. So I quit and went to the police academy instead."

"Have you ever regretted it?"

The smile faded, and his eyes lost focus. "Let's just say it hasn't exactly been what I expected. But, no, I've never regretted it." He put the bottle to his lips and took another drink, then looked at her. "So what're *you* going to be?"

"Me?"

He pointedly scanned the room until his gaze returned to her. "I don't know, Micki, I guess I must be talking to you—I don't see anyone else here." He saw the faintest hint of a smile, and then she seemed almost shy.

"I dunno," she said. "I really haven't thought about it."

"Well you'd better start; you'll be off to college soon enough. You ought to think about applying for the spring semester after you graduate."

She looked at the patterns on the fake Oriental rug. "I used up all the money I'd saved. It wasn't much, but it was something, y'know?"

"With grades like yours, I'm sure you could get a scholarship to any school you want."

"Yeah, right—especially once they find out I have a record."

"If you stay out of trouble, your records will be sealed."

"But—"

"Look, Micki, believe it or not, something like this could even work in your favor. The idea of giving a street kid a chance might be very appealing to some schools—y'know, good publicity, good PR."

She looked up. "Y'think so?"

"Yeah, I do. But you have to straighten out that act of yours."

Her gaze fell again.

"Y'know, you could be anything you want; you know that, right? Except—well—probably not a cop."

She looked into his eyes. "Why didn't you turn me in?"

He felt a catch in his chest. He polished off the beer and stared at the dark glass of the TV. When he turned back to her, his voice was quiet. "I may not have stuck that needle in your arm, but I sure as hell put the syringe in your hand."

Stunned, her expression went blank: it wasn't any of the answers she'd imagined; it wasn't the one she'd hoped for, either. She said, "I—I think I'm gonna go to bed now."

And as she made her way to the study, he wondered what she dreamed about.

ACCORDING TO THE RADIO's forecast, the projected temperature for the day was at least sixty-four unseasonable degrees with the possibility of a record-breaking high. Baker decided it was time to get the hell out of the apartment. He telephoned Cynthia at ten thirty, a time when she was usually well up and about. But her guarded manner signaled she wasn't alone. Claiming he was calling to let her know about Micki, he engaged her in some meaningless small talk before asking her to recommend a movie.

"I just saw a really cool one Thursday night," she said. "It's playing downtown at the Waverly. Kind of offbeat and hip. Funny and sad. Very deep, too. You might even get it."

He decided that that was definitely a shot at him, yet responded with only a good-natured laugh. But as soon as he'd hung up the phone, he lit a cigarette and tossed the pack of matches back onto the nightstand.

He'd sounded pathetic.

FOR OVER AN HOUR, Baker and Micki walked around Central Park in spring-like weather, the light snow that had fallen only two nights before having completely vanished. Folk-rock guitarists and Latin conga players provided background music while people roller-skated, bicycled, and played Frisbee with each other or their dogs.

Finally freed from Baker's smoke-filled apartment, Micki breathed in not only the fresh air—tinged with the scent of moist, dark earth and, occasionally, horses—but all the sights and sounds, as well. It was a heady mixture of colors, rhythms, textures, voices, silvered strings, hoof beats, harmonies, and sirens. They flowed together and drifted apart, dripping down like rain from a summer sun shower. Electric and alive, the park had become a celebration under the bright winter sky.

But everpresent and persistent, as if it were a spoiled brat determined to get its way, the drug demon was tagging along after her. The tension kept building until all she could think about was getting high. From time to time, Baker observed her spaced-out expression and restless, jittery motions. Twice he gently touched her shoulder to bring her attention around, even catching a wayward Frisbee about to hit her in the head. And that was when he realized he should've brought his own Frisbee, which was somewhere on the shelf in the hall closet. Throwing it around would've been a hell of a lot better than all of this aimless walking in silence.

As they headed back toward the street, he said, "I know the park seems okay right now, but don't ever come here by yourself—especially after dark. It's too dangerous."

She looked up. "Really? For who?"

"Yeah, very funny."

On Central Park West they caught the subway and started downtown. Noisy, old, and uncomfortably close, the packed train—a local—made its way haltingly down the tracks, periodically stopping in the tunnels, the lightbulbs overhead flickering or going out completely. Micki, standing and holding a metal strap, started twisting and squirming, unable to get away from the press of bodies that were shifting and bumping hers as the train rocked and lurched. Baker squeezed in front of a disgruntled-looking, middle-aged man in order to position himself directly behind her.

At West Fourth Street they got out and were surrounded by what appeared to be a bunch of struggling musicians, artists, and leftover hippies. Some NYU students who'd chosen to remain in the city over Christmas looked like they were trying very hard to be cool enough to blend in. The theater's ticket line was short and moved quickly. And not five minutes after Baker and Micki had settled themselves inside the auditorium, the lights dimmed. The couple sitting right in front of them lit a joint, and Baker considered leaving. But then he told Micki to get up so they could change their seats to several rows down and to the left.

Stepping sideways, maneuvering past pairs of knees, she shot him a sharp glance. "Aren't you going to make them stop or something?"

"Just hurry up before the film starts."

The movie, *Harold and Maude*, opened with a well-dressed young man attempting suicide while a Cat Stevens song played on a turntable. Baker, shifting his weight in the uncomfortable seat, wondered what on earth Cynthia could've been thinking. But as the story unfolded, he saw a tale of rebirth—of seeing everything in life through a completely different lens. And when it was over, the closing image frozen into a backdrop, he sat through the credits, waiting until the very last note of the soundtrack had faded before getting up. Cynthia's little jab that morning suddenly stung a whole lot more. Just what the hell did she think of him?

"Did you like it?" he asked Micki as they were leaving the theater. During the movie, out of the corner of his eye, he'd seen her looking sad. A few times, he'd even caught her crying. But he'd heard a few giggles in there, too. He'd never heard her laugh before. And when he'd cracked up at the scenes involving cops, she'd looked at him with amazement. "I *do* have a sense of humor," he'd whispered forcefully in return.

After some pizza, they took the subway back, and Micki went right to sleep. But Baker stayed up a while longer, listening to the entire album of *Tea for the Tillerman*.

IT WAS SHORTLY AFTER midnight when Micki awoke, feeling edgy and raw. She got out of bed and pulled on her jeans. Using the hallway light, she padded through the dark living room and into the kitchen, where she flipped on the fluorescents. Full of static and buzz, they stuttered and sputtered to life as if they weren't quite sure they wanted to bother. She scavenged around among the supplies Baker had gotten from the corner store the night before, looking through them twice, as if she might've missed something—finding only one remaining Milky Way bar for her trouble. But there was beer in the refrigerator. And pills in her jacket. She leaned against the sink and played with the now-empty candy wrapper. Tomorrow, with that uncanny ability of his, Baker would know she'd taken something whether he had proof of it or not. She pulled out the bottle opener and the four beers left from the new six-pack.

Seated at the table, she popped off the first cap and began drinking, wondering if anyone really liked the taste of beer. She polished off the second bottle, thinking how creepy the kitchen was at night: the windows all dark, the mechanical hum of the refrigerator almost evil—even more so when the low-pitched whirring ended with a shudder. But halfway through the third bottle, she knocked the metal opener off the table, and it clattered brashly to the floor. Her heart thumped and her mouth went dry. Not a minute later, the living room was flooded with light. Baker stepped through the doorway.

Looking down at the bottle she was holding, she said, "I'm sorry."

He lifted the beer from her hand. "This was *my* fault," he said, and poured the remainder down the sink. Then he opened the last bottle and emptied that, as well. "Next time you're feeling bad, I want you to wake me up, okay? This is not the way to deal with it. And once you go back to your apartment"—he threw the empty bottles into the garbage—"you're to call me if you're getting into a bad head. You can always stay here if you need to, understand?"

She nodded.

"Just call me first, okay? Don't just show up at my door."

"Yessir," she said quietly.

"How long have you been up?"

"I dunno, maybe twenty minutes."

"And you already drank two and a half beers? You must be a little buzzed."

"Not really. Well—maybe a little."

The lines between his eyebrows deepened. "Do you drink, Micki?"

She shook her head no.

"Hmm. Well—do yourself a favor and don't start. You've got all the makings of an alcoholic." And I would know, he thought. "Are you going to go back to bed now, or do you want to stay up?"

"Go t'bed." But when she got to her feet, she felt a little unsteady.

"By the way," he said, "Tuesday night is Christmas Eve. I thought maybe Wednesday we'd go to church." And though he'd made it sound as if he were looking forward to going, he couldn't even remember the last time he'd attended mass.

"I'm Jewish."

He chuckled. But when her expression didn't change, he stopped. "You're serious!" He folded his arms over his chest. "And just how would you know this?"

"The bus on Union Turnpike. When I go t'school, it passes a couple a synagogues." Her speech, though not slurred, had become a bit slow and lazy. "I can read 'em. Y'know—the signs that're in Hebrew."

"But you've been wearing a cross since the first day I met you."

"Tim gave it t'me." And her hand went to touch it, the memory still sharp in her mind: he'd taken it from around his neck and put it around hers, saying, "You remember what you promised me."

Baker studied her: there was an olive tinge to her skin. He'd come to assume she was Italian. Or even Greek.

"Y'know, *I* have a rabbi," he said.

Her jaw dropped. "You're—you're Jewish?"

"Captain Malone."

"Captain Malone's *Jewish?*"

Baker laughed. "It's a cop thing, Micki: a higher-ranking officer who helps you with your career is called your rabbi, and Captain Malone is mine." His voice softened. "I can understand why you want to wear that cross, but I just don't know if it's appropriate for a little Jewish girl."

Micki didn't say anything—because she wasn't sure she liked being a little Jewish girl. Every time she passed one of those temples she'd mentioned, she'd feel a rush of rage—though she had no idea why. Still, as early as the next morning, she was wearing the cross permanently tucked inside her shirt.

MONDAY, BAKER DROVE TO Queens, thinking he'd be in and out of Micki's apartment in a matter of minutes. But once inside he came face to face with a snapshot of what had happened the week before. In the cool light of day, everything looking strangely peaceful and benign. He searched the place thoroughly, then put the needle inside a wad of aluminum foil so he could deposit it—along with the smashed syringe, bottle-cap cooker, and bag of cotton puffs—into one of the trashcans in front of the stoop. Her loose-leaf, textbooks, and nightshirt were thrown into the trunk of his car.

Back in Manhattan, he stopped at the bank before heading to West Forty-Seventh Street—the diamond district. The street was packed with buyers and sellers, shady hawkers standing outside shop fronts, trying to lure people in. Walking slowly down the block, he looked at all the glitter in the windows. And started to sweat.

He went into Building Fifty-Five and was swallowed up by little swarms of people transacting business with the vendors on the main floor. Aware of the plainclothes security guards posted at several points, Baker snaked his way through the multitude of bodies to the booth of Lenny Grossfeld, who greeted him with a wide smile that parted his mustache from the beard he was stroking.

"Ah! So you're Barry's partner," he said. "Another of New York's finest! Come, let's look and see what we can find for you." Underneath bushy eyebrows, his eyes reassured Baker through glasses pushed up high on a nose that wasn't large so much as bulbous. And as he looked down at the rings in the glass case before him, the entire top of his head came into view, allowing Baker to see that the man's curly salt-and-pepper hair surrounded a bald spot that was partly covered by a skullcap.

With both patience and enthusiasm, the diamond seller showed Baker everything in his price range, which, anywhere else, would've been more than he could afford. And once Baker had narrowed his selections down to two, he started going back and forth as though the rest of his life hinged on the decision. After much deliberation, he chose a blend of the traditional and the modern: a brilliant, emerald-shaped diamond in an antique-style white-gold setting. He counted out the money and watched it disappear.

"If she doesn't like it," Lenny said, "you can always bring her here to pick out another."

"And—and what if she says no?"

The jeweler patted his hand. "Then you return it. But take your time. Even a month from now, I'll take it back."

While his purchase was being placed in a black velvet box, Baker asked another question.

"Not me, no," came the answer. "But I could give you the name of someone just down the street. You tell him I sent you, and he'll take good care of you." The diamond seller winked and smiled.

Baker smiled back. Everyone was taking care of him today.

"Are you going to be okay here alone?" Baker had asked. Then he'd given her a phone number and explained he was leaving a set of keys next door with Mrs.

Hernandez. If there was an emergency, Micki was to call her for help. "But don't do anything stupid," he'd said, looking at her meaningfully.

After he'd left, she'd picked up *The Foundation Trilogy*, but couldn't sit still long enough to read. The skittish, junkie energy was making even watching TV impossible. She'd spent most of the day thinking up schemes to get Mrs. Hernandez to let her out of the apartment. Baker's ID bracelet had to be worth something. Or his college ring…

She was considering breaking into the liquor cabinet when it finally hit her: until now—except for Baker's quick, late-night trip to the corner store—she hadn't been by herself since she'd arrived. And as soon as the door had closed behind him this morning, the fragile confidence she'd built up over the last few days had evaporated in a matter of minutes.

She actually needed him.

What a cosmic, fucking joke.

She searched the kitchen for the millionth time, but the only sweet thing left was the Log Cabin syrup. Disgusting as it was to eat plain, she finished it off, but felt no better than before. About to start in on the Wonder Bread, she flashed on her stash of pills. If she could get at just one of the Valiums or Libriums, she'd probably be all right till he got back. But she didn't get her jacket. She didn't move at all. She simply stood beside the counter. Alone in his apartment. Waves of fear washing over her. Maybe this was it. Maybe this fucking torture would never end, and she was going to feel like this for the rest of her fucking life. She picked up a glass and hurled it to the floor. The shattered fragments scattered across the tiles. Then she closed her eyes and felt the tears squeezing out from under the lids. Shameful drops of salty water sliding slowly down her face.

By the time she'd finished cleaning everything up, she could barely keep her eyes open. She wandered into Baker's room and stood in the middle, looking around. And though it was ridiculously big, his uniform jacket—the one still full of colored pins, still bearing the scent of his aftershave—was the item she chose. She liked the heft of it on her shoulders. Back in the living room, with an album on the turntable, she lay down on the sofa, fully shrouded in the heavy navy cloth.

WHEN BAKER RETURNED, HIS apartment was dark and silent. His heart skipped several beats until, deep in the living room's shadows, he caught sight of Micki asleep. By the light from the hallway, he carried the groceries into the kitchen before going back to turn off the stereo's power amp, the glow of its little yellow pilot light reluctantly dying. He glanced over at the cover of the album she'd put on, and was just barely able to make out the Moody Blues' *Days of Future Passed*.

Inside the kitchen, he began putting everything away. Refrigerator and cabinet doors opened and closed; brown paper bags rustled…

Micki woke up. Rubbing sleep from her eyes and blinking, she went to join him. Baker had just picked up a jar of peanut butter when he paused and stared.

The color drained from her face. "Are you mad at me?"

He put the Chunky Jif next to some grape jelly, then pulled a jar of spaghetti sauce out of the bag. "Were you going through my things again?"

"No, sir. I just—needed this."

With his back to her, he put the thick glass jar behind another one in the cabinet and said, "It's okay." But before he went to put a box of rigatoni on the shelf, he looked at her and asked, "But of all things, why that jacket?"

"What do you mean?"

"I always figured you hated that I'm a cop."

She shook her head no.

"Huh! Well, how about helping me put the rest of this stuff away and then setting the table while I cook dinner."

She pulled out a box of Uncle Ben's rice and a jar of marshmallow Fluff. She asked, "Do you like any of that?"—he was holding packages of Three Musketeers and Nestlé Crunch bars.

"In moderation," he replied. "When the checkout girl saw all this junk, she looked at me like I'd gone insane." He put the candy in the cabinet, then turned back. "Especially that." He was pointing to the Fluff.

Micki almost smiled.

HAMBURGERS, TINY TATERS, AND green beans. They sat down together for dinner, both slathering their burgers with so much ketchup that the buns were soaked and falling apart long before the last bite had been consumed.

WHILE MICKI FINISHED WASHING the dishes, Baker retrieved her books from the trunk of his car and dropped them on top of the desk in the study. En route to the kitchen, he found her in the living room, fiddling with the pack of Camels he'd left on the coffee table. She'd already pulled one out and was examining it. He strode over and swiped everything from her hands.

"I wasn't gonna light it or anything; I was just looking!" she said.

"If I ever catch you smoking—and I don't care whose cigarettes they are—I will beat the living daylights out of you."

"What's the big deal? They're legal."

"I don't give a shit if they're legal or not; they're bad for you."

Speechless, she watched him proceed into the kitchen. A minute later, she followed. "So how come *you* smoke?"

Already seated, pen in hand, Baker had his checkbook and a stack of papers in front of him. "When I started, I was younger than you are," he said. "Back then, nobody knew the damage it did."

Opening her mouth to ask why he didn't stop now, she changed her mind and said, "Can I sit here with you?"

"I'm just paying bills."

She didn't budge.

"But I don't mind," he hastened to add.

TUESDAY MORNING, MR. ANTONELLI called to see if Micki could work that night. Since Bel would be closing early for the holiday, it would be a short shift anyway. Without even asking her, Baker told him yes.

"You'll be fine," he said to her as he hung up the phone.

Micki didn't look so sure.

ALTHOUGH BAKER HAD WASHED Micki's clothes, her work shirts were still in her own apartment. On the way to the restaurant, he made a quick stop, checking the payphone to see if it was working while she went inside to grab some things from the dresser drawer. But overhead, the bare bulb glared harshly as if there was something very important she needed to see. And as much as she wanted to leave, she couldn't stop herself from looking. One wall—still stained with wine, lines streaming down like trails of bloody tears—was crying. And over in the corner, snickering, was a piece of smashed syringe Baker had missed while cleaning up. She threw it away, then hurried out to meet him.

She hated this place.

FOR THE FIRST TIME in four months, Micki walked through the front door of Bel Canto instead of the back—Baker, not Miss Gutierrez, by her side. The cop and the restaurant owner finally met, each looking a little surprised by the other's size. Mr. Antonelli insisted Baker have dinner, and Baker insisted Mr. Antonelli let him pay. After a good-natured argument, they reached a compromise.

Micki, meanwhile, had changed her shirt in the basement, then gone into the kitchen, hoping no one would notice her.

"Hey!" Tony said. He had a huge smile on his face. "Welcome back! You look great!"

"Thanks." Except she knew he was full of it. Even after gaining back the weight she'd lost, she looked like hell. Meanwhile, her sweet tooth had become so insatiable that, much as she detested it, she'd actually tried to induce vomiting. She'd overheard some girls in gym class talking about dieting that way. Only marginally successful, she'd given it up after the second try. It was repulsive anyway.

"I'm gonna get fat," she'd once blurted out, and Baker had chuckled.

"Even if you gained twenty pounds," he said, "you'd probably still be too thin. But I'd rather have you fat and straight than skinny and strung out on drugs. Trust me, it'll all balance out. Take one thing at a time." He'd pushed her to start exercising again, saying it would help take her mind off getting high. And sometimes, it did.

Over by the pass bar, Tony was yelling at Sal about an order he hadn't picked up.

Micki put on the thick yellow gloves and opened the faucets, all of the kitchen clamor and familiar smells mixing together with the hot, sudsy water.

She took a deep breath.

BAKER HAD A SMALL antipasto, minestrone soup, veal piccata, and Italian cheesecake, all easily as good as the Manhattan restaurants he frequented. He complimented Mr. Antonelli, and the little man beamed. Before he left, Baker made sure Mr. Antonelli had the payphone's number so he could contact him if

Micki stepped out for any reason—no matter how brief. "She's been so sick, you understand," Baker said.

One hand raised like Peter Falk as Lieutenant Columbo on TV, Mr. Antonelli replied, "Don't-a you worry. I make-a sure Tony keep an eye on-a her." But he gave the cop a savvy look.

Armed with some magazines and more cigarettes from the deli, Baker returned to Micki's apartment. But he was sleepy from the heavy meal. He set the alarm for eight and lay down, trying to keep an ear out for the phone. But it was the clock's bell that woke him with a start, leaving him a bit dazed. Lower back knotted and aching, he stood and stretched, wondering how anyone could sleep on such a horrible mattress every night. He threw the magazines in the trunk of his car, took the short walk down Forty-Fourth Drive, and was soon back at the restaurant, sipping cappuccino while Micki finished up.

"Merry Christmas!" Mr. Antonelli said when they were ready to leave. And after he shook Baker's hand, he went to give Micki a traditional European kiss on each cheek. But as soon as he grasped her arms, she stiffened and pulled back. With a flustered sputter, he let go, but then held out his hand to her, as well, his smile a bit softer. "Merry Christmas-a, Micki! I see you Thurs-a-day." And he locked the door behind them.

"Feel like taking a ride?" Baker asked while the car warmed up.

"Where're we gonna go?"

"To see the Christmas decorations."

"Yeah, sure," she replied absently.

Pulling away from the curb, Baker smiled to himself. "Yeah, sure" was currently one of Micki's favorite expressions. He turned on the heater and said, "Yesterday I noticed some broken glass in the garbage. What happened?"

"I was gonna tell you about it. I just…forgot. I'll pay for it, okay? It was just a glass."

He glanced over, but she was staring ahead. Under the light of a passing streetlamp, her face looked pinched and pale. "Was it an accident?" he asked.

"I broke it on purpose."

They drove a couple of blocks further.

"I guess it was pretty hard being alone," he said. Their eyes met, and he added, "You don't have to pay for it."

With a mumbled "thank you," she turned her head away to look out the passenger window. But when they rounded the next corner, she gasped: house after house was lit with an outrageous display of lights. She couldn't decide which she liked better: the ones done only in white—so pure and magical—or the ones dripping with colors.

Baker grinned. He'd loved it when his father had driven around at Christmas so he could gawk at all the decorations. But that had been when he was little. Before his father had left.

Sun rising, coffee perking, Baker searched through the cabinets for the open bottle of pancake syrup. He could've sworn there'd been a little left before he'd gone to the supermarket Monday. Four waffles sprang up in the toaster, and he put them on a plate in front of Micki—along with a new bottle of Log Cabin.

"Y'gonna see your family today for Christmas?" she asked.

"No." And he went back to put some Downyflakes in the toaster for himself.

"I'm sorry I ruined your holiday," she said quietly.

He placed two steaming mugs of coffee on the table, added some milk to his, and sighed. "I'll admit this isn't exactly how I pictured spending the time, but the truth is—and I honestly can't say why—I really don't mind."

Her face colored, and she became very focused on pouring the syrup into all the little waffle windows.

Later that afternoon, after having spent almost an hour and a half working on her paper for economics—"The Changing Role of Women in the Work Force"—Micki was napping. Alone in the living room, Baker took out the engagement ring for the first time since buying it, its regal elegance engendering neither hope nor excitement. He felt nothing. He closed the box and left it on top of the stereo's power amp.

Stretched out in the recliner, he shut his eyes and listened to Carly Simon's voice floating out of the speakers. But then his heart dropped: he'd chosen an album that opened with a song that was completely unflattering in its assessment of marriage—the album Cynthia had given him.

ARM DRAPED OVER THE side of the chair, lips slightly parted, Baker was asleep when Micki entered the living room. When she noticed the black velvet box on the stereo, she went over and opened it, catching her breath at the sight of the ring. But the record had just ended, and the turntable was shutting down, the mechanical noises nudging Baker awake. He opened his eyes and had to stop himself from jumping up to grab the box. Yet all Micki was doing was moving it around under the lamp so she could watch the diamond's fiery sparks shoot out.

"It's beautiful, isn't it," he said.

She wheeled around.

Baker returned the recliner to the upright position. "I don't mind you looking at it. But just *looking* at it, understand?"

She closed the box and handed it to him. "Are you gonna ask Cynthia to marry you?"

"Yes."

"Wow!"

Her face was so full of awe that he couldn't keep from smiling. "Someday," he said, "someone'll probably ask *you*." But his words felt hollow.

"Yeah, right."

"Why not?"

"Just look at me."

"So?"

"The scars on my face—"

"Are fading," he said.

"So what! I'll still never be pretty. And what about all the scars on my body?"

He stood up and put the box back on top of the stereo. "First of all," he said, "you *are* kind of pretty."

Her mouth fell open, but then her eyes narrowed.

"Second of all," he said, "physical beauty isn't the most important thing anyway. It's what's in your heart and your head that really count."

"Yeah? So then how come you have a girlfriend like Cynthia?"

"You don't think Cynthia has a good heart?"

"Well, yeah, but…"

"But what?"

"Well…"

"You think just because Cynthia's beautiful, she can't be smart, too—is that it?" Baker chuckled. "I don't know which one of us is the bigger male-chauvinist pig: you or me."

Micki lowered her eyes.

"Cynthia may be a model," he said, "but she's also extremely intelligent. She was accepted to every Ivy League university she applied to. She ended up at NYU because she was determined to pay her own way, and they were the only school to give her a scholarship. But when the scholarship wasn't enough, she started to model. And after she graduated, she kept doing it because she wasn't getting offered the kinds of jobs she thought she deserved. Now she's giving acting a shot. I don't really get it, but those artsy, creative things always appeal to her. Personally, I think she'd be happier if she was helping people in some way." His face colored. "Jeez, listen to me going on like this."

Micki shrugged. "I don't mind; I like Cynthia."

"So do I," he said quietly.

"Do you love her?"

"What?"

"Do you *love* her."

Baker felt a tremor in his chest. But before he'd even opened his mouth, Micki added, "If I ask you something, will you tell me the truth?"

"*If* I answer, I'll answer honestly. What is it you want to know?"

"Do men love?"

"Do men *love*?" he repeated.

"Yeah. I mean, do they really feel love, or do they just say that to get into women's pants?"

His face went blank. But then his eyes flashed. "What the hell are you saying? You think men don't have feelings?"

"No!"

He gaped at her. "Oh, so—so we're not human, then?"

She shrugged and looked away.

He shook her shoulder. "Hey—now you listen to me, Micki; I'm not going to lie and say there aren't guys who would do or say just about anything to get laid. At some time or another, most guys'll pull some kind of bullshit. It's not the same for guys; they don't have to attach feelings to sex the way women usually do. But that doesn't mean men don't love. We have hearts just like women."

"Were you satisfied when you had sex with me?"

An icy chill shot through him. "Y'know, *you* had sex with *me,* too. It was a two-way street, wasn't it?"

"*Were you satisfied?*"

He felt lightheaded, the room suddenly unfamiliar. Not wanting to answer, he remained in the safety of silence. Then reconsidered. Not answering would be taken as a "no." Given what she'd just disclosed about how unattractive she felt... He finally said, "Yes, Micki, very much." But there was a strange look in her eyes. Afraid she'd misinterpreted the context of his remark, he added, "You were very sweet."

A childlike sadness came over her, but then she pointed toward the coffee table. "Can I borrow your book when I go home? I don't think I'm gonna be able to finish it here."

Jarred, his heart squeezed painfully. "Sure," he said. "Keep it as long as you want; just give it back when you're done. You like to read?"

"Uh-huh." Her gaze was still fixed on the book.

"Well, when you're finished with that, I have some other books you can borrow." He checked his watch; it was nearly six o'clock. "I guess I ought to start dinner."

"I'll go set the table," she mumbled.

WITH THE PLATES AND silverware all washed and in the drainer, Micki spread her books and notes out in the kitchen so she could work on her paper again. But when Baker walked in about an hour later, she was staring off into space, the page before her a mass of scribbles. He ripped the pop-top off a can of Coke and tossed it into the garbage, a plethora of candy wrappers lying there in a little heap. Sitting down in a chair catty-cornered to hers, he asked, "Did you ever teach your physics class that stuff about special relativity?"

Her eyes slowly focused on his. "What?"

He lit a cigarette. "Did you ever teach your physics class that special relativity stuff?"

"Yessir."

"How did it go?"

"Okay."

"Do you think you could teach it to me?" He chugged down some soda.

"Yeah, sure."

He made a grand, sweeping gesture. "Then take it away."

SHE EXPLAINED HOW MOVING clocks slow down and moving meter sticks shrink. She drew diagrams, wrote formulas, and grew more animated as the lecture wore on. When she was done, he was impressed—and told her so.

A warm feeling welled up inside her.

"So," he said, sitting back, "are you really going to be all right if you go home tomorrow?"

"Yeah, sure."

"Really? Because if you need to, you can stay here longer. I know I said you could go home tomorrow, but that was only if you felt ready."

"I'll be okay. Really."

He angled his head.

"I *will*," she said.

He nodded, stood up, and threw the empty soda can away. "I'll be back in a minute."

While he was gone, she thought about what a liar she was. She was scared to death to be alone in her apartment.

He returned and placed a small white box on top of the papers in front of her.

"What's this?" she asked.

He'd already stepped back and was leaning against the doorjamb, lighting a fresh cigarette. "Open it."

Eyeing it, but not touching it, she asked, "What's it for?"

He laughed "Jesus, I'm getting the third degree, here." But then he took a deep drag, and his expression turned serious. Exhaling smoke, he said, "It's for getting clean—and promising me to stay that way."

A shiver ran up her spine.

"Go on," he prodded. "Open it."

She looked at the box again, looked back at him, then gingerly lifted the lid. Underneath a layer of cotton was a pretty silver pendant on a delicate chain. Her brow knitted. "It's a mezuzah."

When the diamond seller's friend had shown Baker some of these as an alternative to the typical Star of David, Baker hadn't even known what they were. The jeweler had explained they were tiny versions of the things Baker had seen on the doorframes of Jewish homes—objects of protection. The real ones had little prayer scrolls inside while the jewelry had only paper—"in case they're worn in places not fit for Holy Scripture." Though the one that had caught Baker's eye was supposedly for a man, it was really quite pretty, with some filigree work on the upper half.

"It's beautiful," Micki said. And yet she wished he would have given her something neutral—like an angel.

"Well, put it on. Let's see how it looks."

She searched his face.

He took another hit off the cigarette, then raised his chin. Looking out from under half-lowered eyelids, he exhaled smoke. "What," he asked softly, "would be my secret, ulterior motive for doing this? Huh, Micki?"

Voice practically a whisper, she said, "I dunno."

He shook his head. "There is none."

She got up and fastened the chain around her neck.

"It looks nice," he said.

But her expression was sad.

With a little push of his back against the doorjamb, he stood up straight. "You're very tired. Why don't you go to bed now—try to get back to a normal sleeping schedule."

Eyes downcast, she walked past him.

BAKER HAD THE TV turned to the news, but the volume was so low she could hardly hear it in her room. She tossed from side to side until, touching the new silver pendant, she simply stared off into the darkness.

This was her last night here.

She didn't want to go to sleep anymore.

BAKER STOOD UP AND shut the TV. In the silence, he could hear her disquieted motion behind the closed door. Compared to how she usually slept at home, she slept much better at his place, though there were times he'd peek in to find her babbling or moving around, the top sheet and blanket half off the bed. Tonight she sounded more restless than usual.

Maybe he should force her to stay a few more days. Without school, she'd have little structure and no supervision except when she was working—far from ideal at such an early stage. But she was so determined to leave. At some point, he had to let her go; he couldn't keep her here forever. But was this too soon? What was he going to do if she relapsed again? Running his fingers through his hair, he stared out the window. There was something so wrong with that kid. Damaged. That was the word that kept popping into his head.

As quietly as possible, he unlocked the liquor cabinet and poured himself a good, stiff drink. He finished it and poured another. Then he locked the bottle away and went to bed.

WITH MAJESTIC GRACE, THE sun rose into the sky, catching edges of elongated clouds and gilding them. Baker, already showered and dressed, was eating bacon, eggs, and buttered toast. Micki, still in nightshirt and jeans, was having coffee, coffee, and more coffee. She got up to pour another cup.

"Y'wanna save a little of that for me?" he joked.

"There's plenty left," she said and, without taking any, put the pot down with a heavy bang. Then she washed her mug and stalked out of the kitchen.

Baker sighed and shook his head.

EITHER STUDYING OR SLEEPING, Micki kept to herself until Baker said it was time to leave. She was putting on her jacket when he asked, "Do you have everything?"

"Yessir."

"You sure?" He walked back into the living room. Looking around, he spotted *The Foundation Trilogy* on the coffee table and retrieved it. "Didn't you want to take this?"

"Whatever."

His voice turned brusque. "You want it or not?"

"Forget it, okay?"

"Fine!" He took a few steps and tossed the paperback onto the club chair in front of the bookcase. "Let's go," he said, and unlocked the door.

RADIO CHATTER AND CIGARETTE smoke filled the void the entire drive to Queens, where Baker double-parked in front of Micki's building. She got out, pushed the seat forward, and reached in to grab her things from the back seat.

"You've only got ten minutes to get to work," he said.

"I've got my watch on," she retorted. "I know what time it is."

Baker's shoulders relaxed. "Y'know, you can still change your mind and stay at my place tonight."

She straightened up. "I'll be fine."

But before she could close the door, he leaned across the front seat. "You call me if you're having a hard time, y'hear me? If I'm not home, the answering service will pick up and know where to reach me."

"Uh-huh."

"Even tonight," he said. "Don't not call because you feel ashamed or something. I don't mind. I really don't."

"Yessir," she mumbled.

He straightened up behind the wheel.

She leaned in and blurted out, "Thanks for everything," then slammed the door and ran into the building.

"You're welcome," he responded to the dashboard.

Chapter 23

BAKER COULDN'T BELIEVE HE was actually up. Not by much, merely three or four dollars, but it was better than being down a few bucks—or more. Gould's phone rang, and Baker jumped.

"Hey, what's with you tonight?" Martini asked. "Every time that phone rings you nearly pop outta your skin."

Eyes darting between Martini and Malone, Baker said, "I, um—I keep worrying it's my answering service calling about the kid getting sick again. She had such a high fever."

"Oh. Well—sure," Martini said.

"What was wrong with her?" Malone asked.

"Strep throat. Just a real bad case of strep." But when Baker flashed a quick smile, the captain's suspicions were only further aroused.

"Who's in?" Gould called abruptly, anteing up. Then to his wife, who was freshening up the pretzels, "Who was that on the phone?"

"Just Aunt Sylvia asking if we'd be home Sunday. She wants to stop by and see the kids."

"Julie's Aunt Sylvia," Gould said, "is one of the nicest ladies yous guys would ever wanna meet. Just loves to spend time with the kids—babysits whenever we ask."

But Malone's attention wasn't so easily deflected. He would observe Baker keenly for the remainder of the night.

WITH A FLICK OF his thumb, Baker got rid of the ashes hanging off the end of his cigarette; then he rolled the car window down another inch, allowing more of the bitterly cold air to rush in. At two-fifteen in the morning, he was more than ready to go to bed, eyes so dry they felt scratchy and raw. But a light was still shining in Micki's apartment.

He'd worried about her the entire evening, nursing a paranoia that Malone knew what was going on—or had somehow managed to find out what he'd told Gould before anyone else had arrived. For Baker had shown up an hour early, just so he could spill his guts. About everything. "So you made a mistake. Shit happens," Gould had said. But now, looking at the shimmering Manhattan skyline, Baker wondered why it always seemed to happen to Micki.

He got out of the car and locked it, grinding his cigarette into the frozen asphalt, gaze wandering in the direction of Bel, but down Micki's side of the road—the defining border of the adjoining industrial section. Tonight the street appeared darker than usual, though the lighting in the area was poor at best. And while his own neighborhood was far from safe—what with the SROs, the drug pushers, and the clientele they attracted—this one had an air of desolation and danger all its own. Not far away, young male voices were shouting. A police siren blared in the distance, followed by that of an approaching ambulance. A squeal of tires, yelling and cursing, the sound of breaking glass… It was virtually the same scene every night. All night.

He hated this place.

WHEN BAKER LET HIMSELF into Micki's apartment, she barely blinked. Dressed in nightshirt and jeans, she was at the kitchen table, a vacant expression on her face.

"How's it going?" he asked.

Staring at the sink across the room, she shrugged. "Okay, I guess."

"Can't sleep?"

She shrugged again.

"Have you tried?"

She looked at him. "Jesus! Whatta y'want already?"

Nostrils flaring, he reared back, but then said, "I could really use some coffee. You mind if I make some?"

She gave him another shrug—"Whatever"—and returned to staring at the sink.

While he took off his jacket and slung it over the back of a chair, Baker decided that "whatever" had also found its way onto Micki's hit parade of helpful phrases. He filled the pot with water and set it on the stove to boil. Then he put a heaping teaspoon of instant coffee into the polka-dot mug.

"Do you want some hot chocolate?" he asked.

"No, sir."

His voice turned sharp. "You haven't taken anything, have you?"

"No, sir."

Arms folded across his chest, he leaned back against the counter. "You want to drive back with me to my apartment tonight?"

Finally looking at him again, she said, "I'm fine."

"Yeah, I can see that."

The water boiled. He poured it into the mug, added a splash of milk, and sat down. They gazed at each other through the rising steam.

"You're having a rough time, aren't you," he said.

She averted her eyes.

And Baker knew he wasn't going home.

WITH NOTHING BETWEEN HIMSELF and the hard surface of the floor but his folded-up jacket as a pillow, Baker stretched out on his back. Micki offered him her blanket to sleep on, saying the apartment was so warm she wouldn't need it.

"But it'll be on the floor," he pointed out.

"It sometimes ends up there anyway."

And though she was still sitting at the table, he turned out the light and lay down, dozing off, but only briefly. He awoke to find her staring at him. Propping himself up on one elbow, he asked, "What the hell are you doing? Watching me sleep?"

"Were you ever afraid you were going to die?"

"Is that what's keeping you awake?"

There was little light in the room, their forms a deeper shadow in the dark. When she shook her head no, the movement was like a subtle ripple in an ocean of black.

"Well, we're all going to die at some point," he said.

"I don't mean like that. I mean, were you ever afraid you were going to die right then?"

He sat up completely and crossed his legs. "No."

"Even right before you shot that guy?"

"The day I start worrying about my mortality is the day I'd better get a desk job in the department—or find myself another line of work."

"So you're never afraid."

"I didn't say that. I've been scared shitless more times than I care to remember. Truth is, you need a healthy dose of fear or you get careless, and that's when you— or your partner—can get hurt. Or even killed. It's"—he paused—"it's hard to explain, but no matter how dangerous it gets, once I'm in the middle of what's going down, I'm not thinking anymore about what could happen to me. It's like I'm at peace with it. My mind's completely focused on whatever it is I have to do and nothing else."

She pushed the saucer he used as an ashtray a couple of inches across the table, the china gently scraping against the Formica.

"You seem pretty fearless yourself sometimes," he said.

"That's 'cause I got nothing to lose."

"That's not too good, Micki."

She shrugged.

Outside, siren off, a police vehicle drove by, its light flashing red through the curtains.

"What's really bothering you?" he asked.

Covered in the darkness of the night's final hours, the room felt strangely safe. "I need to know what happened to me. I want my memory back. I used to think I didn't care—but I do. You can't imagine what's it's like to know you know something but can't get at it no matter how hard you try."

"You still don't remember anything? Nothing at all?"

"No, and I'm thinking maybe I never will. But then, y'know, sometimes I'm afraid of what it might be."

"Maybe that's why it's better this way."

"I have a right to know!"

They heard another car drive by. And then another. In a small voice, she asked, "How come nobody's come looking for me?"

He felt like his heart was being wrenched right out of his chest. "Why don't you lie down," he said. "You need to sleep."

She finally got into bed and drifted off.

But Baker found himself staring up at the ceiling for a long, long time.

WHEN BAKER DROPPED IN at the precinct house the next day, he searched through the new missing-persons files from the past few months. But no description resembled Micki's—mainly because the dates of disappearance were too recent. And without any new leads to go on, he could spend every waking minute of every day and still not come up with anything. In fact, after her arrest, the only thing ascertained was that it appeared she'd never been in the system before. That alone had been a huge undertaking, detectives sifting through mug shots and old case files from anywhere in the city or its environs. They'd also done the usual screening of local high school yearbooks. There seemed little point in going down those roads again.

Before he headed out, Baker stopped by Malone's office and considered himself lucky that the captain wasn't in. He left a note, then checked around for Gould, but was told he was out on a case. When he returned to his apartment, he thought about calling Cynthia, but decided that if he appeared too pushy, she might break off what little contact they had.

And so, with nothing specific to take up his time, he found himself squandering most of it smoking cigarettes, drinking whiskey, watching vapid TV, and wallowing in a shallow pool of self-pity. And Tuesday was New Year's Eve. As if he weren't depressed enough.

MICKI SETTLED INTO A routine of work, workouts, and long bouts of daytime sleeping. She exercised religiously, sometimes to exhaustion just to get a mild high. Baker checked in on her several times, but didn't stay over again—and her nighttime sleep reverted back to the restless disaster it had always been.

She refused to think about it.

MONDAY, BAKER PULLED HIMSELF together for the few hours of work he had on the school's holiday schedule. On his way back to Manhattan, he stopped by Micki's, then went to a downtown firing range to shoot off a few rounds. He did an intense session at the gym; took a long, hot shower; ate an oversized bowl of spaghetti; and then finally picked up the phone and dialed.

Her voice was bright. "Hello?"

"Hi, Cyn."

"Jim!"

"How's everything?"

"Um—okay—I guess… And you?"

"I take it you have plans for tomorrow night?"

"Mark and I are going to a party in Soho."

Mark. Mr. LA. "Any chance we could get together? Maybe for dinner next week?"

"I—uh—I don't know if that's such a good idea."

"C'mon, Cyn, it's just dinner. What's the harm?"

There was a long pause. "It's over, Jim. Can't you accept that?"

His heart was ripping apart so badly he was sure the jagged-edged pieces would never fit together again. "So—so you don't feel anything for me anymore? Nothing?"

"I don't want to see you because I *do* still have feelings. I'd be reopening wounds that haven't even begun to heal. And it wouldn't be right. I'd feel like I was cheating on Mark."

Cheating on *Mark*! And yet Cynthia's words had exactly the opposite effect of what she'd intended. "I'm only asking," he said, "for a couple of hours of your time. It would mean a lot to me."

There was a fleeting burst of static.

She sighed. "All right. But this is against my better judgment, James Baker. Don't make me regret this."

IT WAS ALMOST NOON when—head throbbing, mouth dry—Baker opened his eyes and failed to recognize his surroundings. In the ribbon of light that emanated from the small space between the closed curtains and the window, tiny dust particles were darting and bobbing. Weightless. Unencumbered. Baker sat up and hung his heavy head in his hands, the previous night's festivities coming back in only little bits and pieces.

Sam Tierney's New Year's Eve party for "swinging singles" had been crowded and loud with the boisterous overcompensation of a lot of people trying to hide their loneliness. Having gotten sufficiently drunk, Baker had succumbed to the advances of a somewhat attractive woman he would otherwise have avoided because, like many of the women invited, she had a thing for cops. It appeared he'd followed her back to her apartment—there was a radio on somewhere and the aroma of perking coffee—but he wasn't sure. After he'd left Tierney's, he must've blacked out.

The woman entered the bedroom, smiling. "Hi there!" She opened the curtains halfway and saw he was already getting dressed. "Don't you want to take a shower first?" she asked.

In the light of day, the woman didn't look quite the same, though she'd clearly taken great pains to reapply her make-up. Tall and nicely shaped, her body was in a youthfully short skirt and a cable-knit sweater sporting a large cowl neck. Her lopsided smile, in a bright coral shade of lipstick, was either endearing or annoying; he couldn't decide which. But worst of all, he had no idea what her name was.

"I really need to get home," he said.

Her smile faded. "I thought we could—y'know—maybe spend some time together today."

God, he hated this. What was he thinking last night? Jesus, he couldn't even remember having sex with her. After a glance around the room—which was wallpapered in large, psychedelic-looking flowers to compliment the thick shag carpet in three different shades of pink—he spotted his boots beneath a vanity table littered with cosmetics and perfume bottles. He retrieved them and sat on the bed to put them on. "I'm sorry," he said, "but I've got some things I have to take care of." Making a point of looking at his watch, he added, "And I'm very late."

She played with the lucite ring on her finger. "Yeah—well—that's okay."

He stood up and threw on his jacket. "I'm sorry," he repeated.

She tugged at the short blonde hair by her ear, then threw up her hands with a forced laugh. "Hey, it was just one of those things." And though she was blinking back tears, she was still trying to smile when she said, "So—so happy New Year."

He gently touched her hair, caressed her cheek, and kissed her. "You take care of yourself." Then he walked through the apartment and let himself out. Once he was in the hallway, he was certain he heard muffled sobs. Or maybe it was just his imagination. Either way, he felt like shit.

ALONE IN THE ELEVATOR, an old model with a pullout door and metal gate, Baker pressed the button and waited. With a nauseating lurch, it began its downward journey, motor whining and whirring as though transporting him took an enormous amount of effort. Just as it was about to reach the lobby, he frantically pulled out his wallet, then heaved a huge sigh of relief.

The condom was gone.

UNDER THE PALEST OF blue skies, Baker hailed a checkered cab to drive him home from Chelsea. Though its suspension was totally shot, the taxi sped over the road, every bump and pothole a source of torture for both his head and his bladder. God help me, he thought, if Micki called after I left the party. He'd given the answering service Tierney's number but not the woman's. At least, he didn't remember giving them the woman's. But when he got home, he called his service to find no messages waiting. He used the bathroom, took three aspirin, drank half a quart of orange juice straight from the carton, and crawled back into bed.

Chapter 24

ONCE THE CONTAINER OF leftover ravioli was safely sealed and inside the fridge, Micki hung up her damp work shirt. Then she poured herself a glass of Coke and sat down at the table, sorry to see the saucer Baker used as an ashtray still empty after she'd dumped it out that morning. Even a single, solitary cigarette butt would've been reassuring. Yesterday, when he'd checked in, she'd been subjected to the nasty fallout from his hangover—probably from too much partying the night before. But then, the whole New Year's Eve thing seemed pretty stupid to her. After all, it was just another night. But she'd worked till nearly two in the morning while people celebrated by getting very drunk and rowdy. And when the clock struck midnight, they'd cheered as if the UN had just announced world peace, yet the only thing that had actually changed was the date on the calendar. Maybe she would've felt differently if she'd had a boyfriend to share it with, but when she'd passed the football player in the hall today—her first day back at school—he'd pretended not to see her.

The knock on the door made her jump. In a harsh voice, she called out, "Who is it?"

"Rick."

It was late; she was tired and had homework to finish.

"C'mon, Micki. Open up. My aunt's in the hospital 'cause a my uncle, and my mom won't stop cryin.'"

Like she really gave a shit about his fucked-up family. Or him. The only person he really cared about was himself.

"C'mon, Micki. Please. Let me in already. I'm real sorry for whatever I did that got ya so pissed off." She was about to tell him to leave her the fuck alone when he added, "I promise I'll make it upta ya."

She opened the door.

THE BUZZER RANG.

"Hey, that must be Santiago," Martini said. "It's about time that son of a bitch showed up. He owes me eight bucks from last week."

Baker got up and pressed the button to release the downstairs door.

"Oh, *yes!*" Martini exclaimed, and used his elbow to push the card just dealt him down in place among the others.

"You are so full of shit," Gould said. "You got nothin' in that hand."

Martini grinned. "Gotta pay to see."

Back at the table, Baker picked up his new cards: a deuce, a five, and a queen. Alongside the pair of tens he already had, they were useless. His front door buzzed.

Throwing two poker chips into the middle, Malone called, "Who's still in?"

With a heavy sigh, Baker tossed in two of his own. "I'll see you." Then he went to greet the newest arrival. But when he opened the door, he said, "What the fuck are you doing here?"

Thick with cigar and cigarette smoke, the air seemed to billow out from his apartment. Micki could hear male voices inside. "I—"

"Eh, Jimmy," Martini called over, "is that Santiago? And are you still in? I raised the pot another buck."

"It's not Santiago," Baker called back. "And I'm out."

"So am I," Micki quipped, and turned to go.

But Baker snagged her by the arm and swung her inside, then slammed the door shut. By sheer momentum, she was carried partway down the hall. There was absolute silence as all five men stopped their game to stare at the severely thin girl wearing a black leather jacket and black jeans. The scars on her face stood out sharply from being exposed to the cold night air.

Heart pounding, Micki recognized Malone, the coffee cop, and one other detective she'd seen that first day in the station house. No doubt, the other two were cops, as well.

"You were supposed to call before coming here, Micki."

Her eyes snapped back to Baker's. "I tried to, but the line was busy."

"So you wait a few minutes and try again."

"I did."

"Bullshit. You—"

"I made a bunch of calls before, remember?" Tierney offered.

While Micki gaped at the cop coming to her defense, Baker's jaw set in a hard line. He exhaled loudly. "Okay, Micki, fine."

"Yeah, well thanks for nothin'. This was a mistake." Books clutched in her arms, small duffle hanging from her elbow, she moved toward the door.

Baker stepped in her way. "And just where do you think you're going?"

"Home."

He snorted. "Fat chance."

"Why? Y'don't want me here."

"For one thing, it's way past your curfew."

"So write me a note."

He tried to stop himself from smiling, but a couple of chuckles could be heard coming from the living room.

Color rose in her face. "Yeah, everything's so fuckin' funny—one big fuckin' joke."

"You watch your language."

"Or what?"

"Don't push me, Micki."

"Fuck—you."

The back of his hand caught her cheek squarely and sent her stumbling, bringing all five guests to sharp attention. Now strewn across the hallway, her books looked like poorly set paving stones creating an uneven path to reach Baker's bedroom. Eyes blazing, she charged for the door, but he grabbed her nearest arm and spun her back around. She responded by jabbing her free fist into his exposed side. Sucking in air, his grip loosened, and she broke free.

Malone, who had already gotten up, was halfway toward the hall.

Micki turned the knob and opened the door about two inches before Baker got her in a bear hug and swung her away, kicking the door shut behind him.

"Let go a me, y'son of a bitch!" And though her arms were pinned in a steely hold, she continued to struggle, legs flailing after he lifted her slightly.

With short, clumsy steps, Baker edged his way toward the study. Throwing her inside, he said, "Get in there." Then he followed, slamming that door shut, as well.

"Let me outta this fuckin' apartment!" Micki shouted. "Y'don't want me here an' I don't wanna be here."

"We both know *why* you're here," Baker yelled back, "and there's no way in hell I'm letting you leave."

"*Y'can't keep me here like a fuckin' prisoner!*"

"*I can do whatever I have to.*"

"*I—*"

"SHUT UP."

"*Y'—*"

"SHUT—UP. WE'RE *BOTH* GONNA SHUT UP FOR FIVE MINUTES UNTIL WE *BOTH* CALM DOWN."

Their voices had carried easily into the living room, where the men looked at each other with raised eyebrows and amused expressions. Malone, who had advanced into the hallway, now retreated to the poker table.

"Maybe we should go," Gould said.

"I don't think that's necessary," Malone responded. "Jim'll tell us if he wants us to leave. Till then, we might as well play."

So the cops, no longer able to hear the voices in the other room, resumed their game, one man short. But Malone wasn't paying much attention. "We both know why you're here," Baker had said. What exactly did that mean?

GLARING AT EACH OTHER as if it were a contest, it was Baker's expression that softened first. He said, "I don't know what it is about you that ticks me off so. I mean, you did the right thing by coming here. Even if you didn't try to call—"

"But I *did.*"

"Okay, okay. I get it. Whatever. Either way, I shouldn't have ragged on you like that. But it's for your own safety that you should call first; it wouldn't be good if I wasn't here to let you in."

Though she merely shrugged, some of the antagonism had left her face.

"Did something happen?" he asked. "Is that what this is about? Because it seemed like things were settling down."

Her eyes fell. Twice she met his gaze only to look away. Then she sat on the bed so she was facing the wall.

Perched on the edge of the desk, Baker waited. When she remained silent, he asked, "Something happen with Rick?"

Her eyes flashed. "How...?"

"Just a lucky guess," he said.

"I'm ruining your poker game."

"Trust me; you're doing me a favor."

She turned her gaze away and stared at the wall again. And then the story spilled out: "Rick stopped by after I got home from work, and we—y'know." She cast a glance at Baker, and he nodded slightly. Eyes back on the wall, she said, "We—were—in the middle when he noticed the necklace you gave me. So he asked me what it was, and I told him. So he goes, 'Baker's Jewish?' And I go, 'No, I'm Jewish.' And—like—he gets this real ugly look on his face and starts callin' me names, like—like 'dirty Jew-cunt.'"

Baker felt a chill and then a searing spark of rage.

"He was—he was still—goin' at it," Micki continued. "And I wanted him t'stop and get off a me, but he wouldn't. And I—I couldn't—he had my arms pinned—his whole fuckin' weight crushin' me—I—"

"Micki!"

Her eyes shot over to his.

"Nobody's blaming you for anything."

"Yeah—well—still... If he hadn't come so fast—in, like, two seconds—I probably could've done somethin'. But at least when he started gettin' up, I managed to kick him in the balls. And while he was dealin' with that, I pushed him into the hall and threw his clothes out after him."

Baker chuckled darkly. "I'd like to rip that son of a bitch's balls off permanently."

Micki's jaw dropped. But then she whispered, "He screamed he was gonna make me pay for it, though."

"You could kick his ass. Besides, he's too much of a coward."

"Himself—yeah. But he'd get his friends to help."

"Like Johnny McBain?"

She nodded.

Stroking his chin, Baker took a long, slow breath.

"Do you hate me 'cause I'm Jewish?" she asked.

"What? How can you even... First of all, I don't hate you. How many times do I have to tell you that? And, no, I don't hate people who are Jewish. I don't hate anyone based on shit like that. I judge people for who they are—as human beings. Do you think I'd have given you that necklace if I had a problem with you being Jewish?"

She shrugged and looked away.

When neither of them had spoken for a while, he asked, "Are you okay?"

"Yessir."

"Are you sure?"

"Uh-huh."

"Do you want to talk some more?"

She shook her head no.

"Then why don't you wash up and get ready for bed. You can grab some clean sheets out of the closet." He straightened up and crossed the room. Hand on the doorknob, he asked, "Do you want me to send the guys home?"

She wanted, very much, to say yes. Instead she answered, "No, sir."

He opened the door and said, "I'm glad you could talk to me about this."

Watching him leave, she thought, Who the hell else would I talk to?

BAKER COULD FEEL HIS friends' eyes upon him as he picked up Micki's things and put them in the study. Then he went straight to the front door, double locked it, and pocketed the keys. He removed his pills from the bathroom medicine cabinet—wondering why he even bothered putting them back anymore—then proceeded into his bedroom, where he pocketed the window-gate key. He was heading for the kitchen when Gould asked him, "Is she okay?"

"Yeah, just a problem with—a boy."

"Eh, Jimmy," Martini said, grinning as he came out of the kitchen with a bag of Milky Way bars, "you've been holding out on us."

"Those are for Micki!" Baker said sharply, hand extended to take them back. But then his face grew hot, and he dropped his arm, a feeble smile appearing. "Kid has a terrible sweet tooth."

From the table, Tierney snorted. "Like that's some big surprise. The kid's a fuckin' junkie."

All the color drained from Baker's face while Tierney blubbered apologies. Snatching the package from Martini's hand, Baker said, "Forget it," and continued into the kitchen.

But for Malone, things were starting to add up.

ANOTHER HAND OF POKER was dealt, excluding Baker, who stood by, smoking. Micki, deliberately ignoring the men in the living room, made her way to the bathroom to quickly wash up and brush her teeth. As soon as she was back in the study, she made the bed and changed into her nightshirt. She had just taken off her jeans when there was a knock on the door.

She froze. Voice harsh, she said, "Yeah?"

Baker came in and shut the door behind him. "Are you about ready to go to sleep?"

"Yessir."

He was taking a drag on his cigarette when his eyes fell on her assignment book. "Did you get all your homework done?"

"I didn't get to my English or history stuff."

With the slightest trace of a grin, he exhaled the rest of the smoke.

She shot him a testy look. "Don't say it, okay? I would've finished if—if things hadn't ended up the way they did."

Grin broadening, he nodded. But his eyes were understanding. "I'll write you a note to get you out of gym tomorrow. You can at least finish your history homework in the security office then. But just this once," he emphasized.

The door swung open, and Micki gasped. But Baker had already backed up as he'd turned toward the entryway—effectively blocking the intruder's view. Micki peaked out from behind him to see Captain Malone.

Baker's voice was cold. "You could've knocked."

"I figured if you were in here, it was okay for me to come in, too," Malone said.

"Can we talk about this outside?"

With mock cordiality, Malone replied, "Certainly." But before he retreated to the hall, he met Micki's eyes with a shrewd look.

Baker stubbed his cigarette out in the ashtray on the desk. "Go to bed, Micki."

"JUST WHAT THE HELL was that?" Baker demanded in a harsh whisper. The two men were standing in the hall, but closer to Baker's room than Micki's.

"I don't see what you're so upset about," Malone said.

426 ◆ Randy Mason

"You have no right to come barging in like that; the kid was only half dressed."

"She didn't seem to mind *you* being there."

"Meaning what?"

Cynical eyes stared back.

"You know damn well," Baker said, "that I go into her apartment unannounced. In all this time, don't you think I've—at least once—walked in on her while she was getting dressed or undressed?"

Malone's forehead creased.

"And when she was burning up with fever and probably dying, who do you think had to take care of her?" Baker asked. "Who do you think had to sponge her down with alcohol till the fever finally broke?"

One of Malone's eyebrows shot up.

"See, the thing is," Baker said, "it's okay for me to see her like that because she knows I'm not going to do anything to her. But you—you she's not so sure about."

"Hey! You watch what you say, Sergeant. No matter where we happen to be, this is official police business; you *will* respect my rank."

"Like you re—"

"Watch it!" Malone repeated. "Your mouth has gotten you into enough trouble, and I've stuck my neck out far too many times to smooth things over. I'm not about to tolerate any kind of insubordination from you. You owe me better than that."

Eyes dark, Baker gazed past the captain—until he heard Micki's door open. A glance over his shoulder found her standing in the hallway. Wearing jeans, she had her jacket thrown over her nightshirt. He whirled around to face her. "Have you been listening?"

Her voice came out small. "No, sir." Which was true, but only because the men had been arguing in whispers. She said, "I can't find the alarm clock."

"I broke it. I knocked it off the desk when I was straightening up a few days ago. Just go to bed, okay? I'll wake you up in plenty of time for school."

She cast a suspicious look at Captain Malone, then went back inside.

"So she's stayed here before," Malone said.

"And obviously in *that* room," Baker countered.

"And for how long was she shooting up again?"

Baker caught his breath. Then sighed—Malone had always been sharp. "Only three days," he answered. "And she came and told me herself." Which was sort of true.

"She's clean now?"

"Yes, sir."

"I'd hate to hear how she was supporting her habit."

"Her savings; she had some money in the bank."

"You should've told me anyway."

Martini yelled over, "Are you guys gonna play anymore or just yap all night like a couple of old ladies?"

Baker watched Malone walk back to the game.

WRAPPED INSIDE THE BLANKET, Micki wondered what Captain Malone and Baker had been talking about. Judging from Baker's reaction, probably her. She closed her eyes. But cigar and cigarette smoke filled the little study like the rest of the apartment, and she could hear the men laughing in the living room, their words unintelligible, their voices intermingling with the sounds of ice cubes against glass, and poker chips in play. And though the door was closed and the lights were out, she felt like they could see her.

She wished Baker hadn't broken the clock radio.

"DAMN KID MUST BE good luck for you," Batillo griped, then relit his cigar.

Grinning, Baker used both hands to scoop yet another pile of poker chips toward him. "She's got to be good for something."

Tierney dealt next, and Baker slowly fanned out his cards to reveal two aces and two queens. Unbelievable for him to be on such a hot streak. But just as the men began to ante up, they heard strange noises. Silence fell, and all heads turned toward the study.

Baker jumped out of his chair, carelessly throwing down his cards. "Kid's got sleeping problems," he said, and ran to Micki's room, leaving the door ajar to let in light. Moaning and pleading incoherently, she was curled up tight in a corner of the bed.

"Micki," he said softly. "*Micki!*" And he gently touched her shoulder. Though her arm lashed out, she remained asleep—still mumbling and whimpering. But when he turned her onto her back, her eyes flew open, and she struck out violently. He pinned her to the mattress, but she continued to fight, her thrashing legs getting tangled in the sheet and blanket.

"It's me, Micki; stop it. Stop it, Micki; it's me. *It's just me.*"

And as her surroundings pulled into focus, she finally went still.

"Let go a me!" she demanded. "Let *go* a me!"

He released her, and she sat up, clutching the blanket around her.

"You were making a lot of noise," he said. "Normally I wouldn't care, except the guys are still playing, and it's—disturbing them." In the dim light, her face looked smaller and more childlike. "What were you dreaming about?" he asked.

She shrugged. "I dunno. I never remember anything. Well—almost never."

"Then what's going on? You usually sleep like a baby when I'm around—at least, compared to this."

"I dunno," she repeated, but her eyes darted in the direction of the living room before she turned her head away.

"The guys?" Baker asked. "Seriously? The *guys*? You couldn't be safer, Micki; they're all cops."

"Big deal."

"They're all *good* cops."

She shrugged one shoulder.

"They're all my *friends*. Do you think my friends would hurt you?" When she said nothing, he shook her till she looked at him. "Do you think I'd let anybody hurt you?"

Lips in a stubborn line, her look was doubtful.

"Answer me!" he demanded. "Tell me the truth: do you think I'd let somebody do something to you?"

Her eyes fell. Quietly, she said, "No, sir."

"You're damn right I wouldn't. Now I'm right outside that door. You've got nothing to worry about, y'hear me?"

"Yessir."

"Do you want some water from the kitchen?"

"No, but do you have another radio I could listen to?"

He took his old transistor out of the desk and handed it to her. Paused in the doorway, he said, "Good night, Micki."

Her heart took a painful leap. "Good night?" she echoed.

"How's it feel being a daddy?" Batillo said, grinning broadly around the cigar clamped between his teeth. With the door left open, everything Baker and Micki had said had been heard in the living room—especially since the men had remained utterly silent so as not to miss a single word.

"Shut up," Baker snapped, and sat down.

"Ooh!" Tierney laughed. "Must've touched a nerve."

Baker lit a fresh cigarette, flung his lighter onto the table, and looked around—but saw only friendly faces grinning back. And as his features relaxed, a sheepish smile emerged. Batillo, Gould, and Malone all had kids; exactly what was he so ashamed of? "Sorry for all the interruptions," he said.

"Don't worry about it," Gould and Martini replied together.

"Jeez," Batillo said, "do you remember that night a couple of years ago when both my kids were upchucking all over the house?"

They all laughed.

"That was the shortest poker night we ever had," Martini said. "I think we played for all of forty-five minutes before running for cover to our cars."

As he shuffled the deck, Gould asked, "Is it all right if we keep playing?"

"Yeah, sure," Baker replied.

"Too bad you had to toss your cards in before," Tierney remarked.

In his haste, Baker had thrown his hand down face up on the table—something he'd never done in his entire life. And it had been such a nice hand to start with. It burned him that Tierney had to needle him about it. He flicked some ashes into the ashtray. "Whatever."

She rotated the radio's dial with her thumb. When she passed a snippet of a classic Young Rascals song—"How Can I Be Sure"—she carefully turned the knob backward, tuning in the station between patches of static. But the old batteries were dying, and the volume began to fade...

HALF AN HOUR LATER, there was a break in the card playing so Gould could avail himself of the facilities. Baker looked in on Micki, then returned to the table. "The kid's out like a light," he reported.

GOULD THUMPED BAKER ON the back. "Take care and"—he held up the leftover six-pack Baker had given him—"thanks for the beer. Oh, and good luck when you pop the question. Give me a call so's I know what happened."

Baker closed the door behind his friend, then hesitated before turning back to the hallway. And Malone. Everyone else had now left.

Slowly wrapping his scarf around his neck, Malone said, "I was impressed with the way you handled the kid tonight."

Baker's eyebrows went up. "Even after I hit her?"

"If one of my boys ever opened up a mouth like that to me, I'd smack him, too—though not quite so hard." He put on his coat. "Tone it down a bit, okay? She's tiny compared to you."

A touch of heat in his cheeks, Baker nodded.

"And I suggest you talk to Dr. Tillim already; it's up to him when you can return to the squad." Malone started to button up. "I'll put in a good word for you, but you're going to have to deal with the man. And despite what you think of all this shit, you *have* changed."

Really? Baker nearly blurted out, for he wasn't aware of any change at all. "You think I could come back next month?"

Malone shrugged. "I really can't say."

But just the possibility caused Baker to feel a little rush—which quickly fell flat. "What'll happen to Micki?"

"Forget the fucking kid already! I warned you about her before, and I was right. My guess is, she won't stay clean for long. Be smart and think about yourself this time." He looked at his watch. "Christ! I'd better get going."

After Malone had left, Baker locked the door and removed the key. Then he went into the living room, which was full of the mess his friends had left behind. Liquor bottles clinked against each other as he put them back in the cabinet and locked it. Then he flopped down on the couch to finish his beer—the last remaining one. With the lightest of touches, he probed his left ribs. And winced.

He went to get some ice.

STANDING IN THE DARKNESS, Micki felt like she'd been hit. Ear pressed to the door, she'd heard everything Captain Malone and Baker had said.

Very clearly.

THE WAIL OF AN ambulance siren woke him. The clock said 3:17, barely an hour since he'd gone to bed. Though the apartment was totally quiet, there was a strip of light under the door: Micki was up. For a while he lay in bed, trying to fall back to sleep. But the longer the apartment was silent, the more restless he became. He slipped into his Levi's and padded over to the kitchen. Eyes half closed, bare-chested and barefoot, he stood in the doorway, trying to comprehend what he was seeing.

Seated at the table, Micki was looking at the back of her hand. Near the base of her thumb were three small cuts, the blood that had bubbled up making them look like parallel strings of garnet beads. Interesting, she thought, how the cutting itself never really hurt all that much, but just a split second later, it always stung and burned like hell.

Eyes now open wide, Baker asked, "What the fuck are you doing?"

She looked up. "I wanted to cut myself."

Pointing to the sharp steak knife she was holding, he said, "Put that down *now*."

"Don't worry," she said. "I'm not gonna cut *you*."

Baker lunged for her wrist, but she jumped up and out of reach, the chair falling over.

"Stay the fuck away from me," she said, "or I'll slash my goddamn wrists—the long way—'n bleed all over y'nice, clean kitchen."

Her eyes were so cold. So empty. The image of them arguing on the side of the snowy highway flashed through his mind. "Don't do anything stupid," he said.

Blood was dripping onto the floor. She snickered. "But that's what I'm best at. That's how I got where I am today."

"There are better ways to deal with your drug habit than this."

"That's not what this is about."

"Then what is it?"

"I'm just one big fuckin' mistake that nobody wants. My life's a fuckin' waste."

"You're still very young," he heard himself say. "Things'll get better."

With a cunning look, she said, "Oh, yeah?"

His heart thudded.

"What's gonna happen t'me," she asked, "when y'go back t'work as a cop?"

He felt like the air had been sucked right out of his lungs.

"I didn't hear nothin'," she said, "when you and Captain Malone were talkin' the first time. But when y'buddies were leavin', they made a lotta noise and woke me up. Then the two of ya were just standin' right outside my door, talkin' plain as day."

Baker tried to recall exactly what he and Malone had said.

"None a this was t'help *me*, was it," she continued. "This was all about *you*. That doctor Captain Malone was talkin' about is a shrink, and I'm just part a some fucked up therapy f'you."

Baker's mind went blank.

Face full of contempt, she looked him up and down. "Y'lied that time y'said y'didn't need me anymore. I still don't get this whole thing, but at least I know where I stand. After y'go back t'work, I'll be locked up in Heyden again—or worse."

"I wasn't really lying; it's kind of hard to explain." He was amazed at how calm his voice sounded. "But I don't see any reason why you wouldn't be allowed to stay on the outside—"

"Oh, please. Captain Malone knows I was usin' again."

"He wouldn't tell anyone."

"Oh, yeah? Why not?"

"Because it would make *me* look bad. I should've notified someone, and I didn't. I should've brought you in."

"But y'felt too guilty, didn't ya."

"I don't want to see you locked up again."

She turned her head away.

"Things aren't going to happen all that fast. Let me see what I can find out."

"Yeah, right." And she tossed the knife onto the table, where it clattered and skidded across the surface.

"Let me look at your hand."

"Just leave me alone."

"You're bleeding."

"It's nothin'. The cuts aren't deep."

"You ought to at least clean and bandage them."

"I really don't give a fuck."

He breathed in. "I'll be back in a minute." When he returned, he had several items that he placed on the counter by the sink. "Come here and let me wash those out."

There was a long pause before she went over and offered her hand. He braced her arm in between his own and his body, anticipating the involuntary jerk as the rubbing alcohol infiltrated the wounds with sharp, stinging pain.

Micki was silent.

"Before you go to work tonight," he said, "you'd better tape something waterproof over these."

"I wear gloves."

"Oh." He felt stupid. He folded a piece of paper towel up and pressed it against the cuts. "Hold this down tight." And once the bleeding had almost stopped, he applied some First Aid Cream—the cool, white paste quickly turning pink where it touched her skin. He put some Band-Aids on, then looked at the clock. "No point going back to sleep now. Why don't you take a shower. I'll put fresh Band-Aids on when you finish."

"I don't wanna go t'school."

"Yeah? Well, that's too bad, 'cause you're going anyway. And in case you were wondering, you'll be staying *here* tonight."

"But—"

"*Don't argue with me, Micki.*"

She turned and marched off.

Baker lit a cigarette and ran his fingers through his hair. Then he washed the blood off the linoleum, though some had permanently seeped into the seams. As soon as he heard the shower running, he unlocked the liquor cabinet and took a large swig of whiskey. This was going to be a very long day.

MICKI COULD BARELY SIT still in class. At times she felt like she'd simply explode if she didn't find a way to get the hell out of the building and get high. But when the passing bell rang, Baker was always waiting in the hall. And after school, he drove her home and hung around till it was time to take her to Bel Canto, giving Mr. Antonelli the now familiar instructions. When she finished work, he drove her back to his apartment.

Sullen, irritable, and belligerent, she was a charming houseguest for the entire weekend, Baker's only reprieve being the time she worked on Saturday. By late Sunday night, when he called Cynthia, his patience with her had worn thin. And yet, when Cynthia said the only night she had free that week was Monday, Baker hesitated: Micki wouldn't have work; it would be risky leaving her alone after school. But Micki said she'd be okay.

So the rendezvous was set for eight o'clock at Sevilla's, a small continental restaurant on East Fifty-Fourth Street. Though Baker would have preferred something with a more elegant decor, most of the finer restaurants were closed on Mondays. Plus Cynthia insisted the setting be casual. "This is not a date, remember?" she said.

He hung up the phone, more convinced than ever that his plan was a mistake. But if he did nothing, Cynthia would be lost to him forever. He took out the ring and watched it sparkle. Yet it was a cold, cold fire that danced and dazzled within the precious stone.

Chapter 25

S CHOOL ON MONDAY WENT well. Micki went home, did laundry, some homework, and a little cleaning before she lay down to take a nap. But when she awoke, the darkness around her seemed to be breathing. Watching. She switched on the light, but could still feel it. Underneath. Waiting. Waiting for her to give in.

She should never have told Baker she'd be all right.

For the second time that day, she forced herself to exercise—even jumped around to some music. But all she could think about was getting high. Lying on the bed, she listened to the radio, hugging her knees to her chest and rocking. Until she finally got up. And left the apartment. With nothing but her jacket, she hurried down the hall, past the payphone with its new "out of order" sign in the usual, childish scrawl. Outside, the temperature had dipped precipitously, and she zipped her jacket up as high as it would go.

When she reached the corner, she dropped a dime in the telephone in front of the deli, and, after about the tenth ring, Baker's answering service picked up. She explained she needed to get in touch with him, but the operator told her he'd left no forwarding information.

"If you like," the woman said, "you may leave your name, number, and a brief message."

"I'm at a payphone, and it's urgent."

"If you'd like to leave your name—"

Micki hung up, then leaned her forehead against the cold metal box. A gust of wind blew down the street, and she shivered. She thought about the short walk down to the bridge.

"Hey, Micki." Holding open the heavy glass door, Frankie was talking to her from the deli's entrance. "Why're you standin' outside like this when it's freezin'? Somethin' wrong? The phone don't work?"

"No, it works fine."

"'Cause you can come inside and use the phone in here."

"It's okay, Frankie. I'm—I'm gonna head over to the Seven train."

"You're sure now…?"

"Yeah. Thanks anyway." She gave him a weak smile and started for the subway. Angels came in strange forms these days.

IT WASN'T MUCH FURTHER to the IRT station. Hands in her pockets, Micki walked quickly, trying to ward off the cold and make it to Baker's before curfew. A couple of cars passed by, but she was the only person on the street—except for a man who was half a block ahead. Short and wiry, he was wearing a beat-up, heavily studded leather jacket with a wallet chain hanging between his back pocket and his belt. His motorcycle boots looked too big for his feet, and he was moving very slowly. *Too* slowly. As the gap between them continued to close, she got the feeling she should backtrack to the corner, take a turn, and disappear. But going all the way around the block would waste too much time.

Though breathing faster, she walked more leisurely, studying the pavement and tracking her shadow, which was rotating around her as she went from one streetlamp to the next. When it was clearly visible in front of her once more, she strode purposefully forward, keeping to the furthest part of the broad, cracked cement—giving the man as wide a berth as possible. But after she passed him, she noticed his shadow wasn't falling behind. And when she crossed the street, she watched his distorted, two-dimensional projection follow hers.

She spun around, and he immediately stopped, his upper lip curling into a confident sneer. But something was already happening inside her: she could see every detail on his face and hear the tiniest of sounds. Muscles relaxed, breathing even and slow, her entire being was suspended in a deep, impenetrable calm. Muted and far away, a white-hot anger burned softly, but otherwise her mind was amazingly clear—razor sharp in a realm of profound stillness. Time had stretched, and she felt at one with every atom in the universe, even as her senses remained fully trained on the man in front of her. She was acutely aware of the most subtle shifts in his energy, completely immersed in the moment—no fears and no thoughts. Except one: if he came at her—if he attacked her—she was going to take him out. She was going to kill him. Just like she'd killed Speed.

The man's smug bravado faltered, the sneer fading on his pockmarked face. And though his eyes betrayed him, he pulled out his cigarettes and, very casually, lit one. Then he took a few steps backward—eyes still locked with hers—before turning to walk away. As fast as he could. He even looked behind him a couple of times to make sure she wasn't following. When he went around the corner and was out of sight, time contracted back to normal and her heart started to pound. She turned and jogged the rest of the way to the station. Shivering.

JUST AS SHE REACHED the elevated platform, the 7 train was pulling in. She jumped into the nearest subway car, joining only a handful of other riders. At Times Square she got off to transfer and, while waiting for the uptown IRT, gave Baker's number another try. But as she stood there with the receiver pressed against her ear, she became aware of a transit cop studying her. Distracted by the voice on the other end of the line, she inadvertently made eye contact. They stared at each other while she left a message with Baker's answering service. But by the time she hung up, the officer was already heading toward her.

She bolted and could hear him chasing after her in his heavy black shoes— keys, cuffs, and miscellaneous hardware clinking and clanging, voice bouncing with his stride as he kept yelling at her to stop. And though she raced up the steps, she had to pause on the next level, not sure which way was best, heart sinking as a precious moment ticked by. Running again, she dodged several startled civilians, then saw another cop coming at her from the direction of the token booth. She turned hard and immediately swerved to avoid careening into a couple with a baby stroller. The cop behind her grabbed her jacket and slammed her against the wall.

HAIR DONE UP IN an old western–type style with several loose tresses softly touching her face, Cynthia looked stunning though wearing only a simple pair of slacks and a pastel turtleneck. Overdressed by comparison, Baker wore a black suit, white dress shirt, and the tie Micki had given him.

The meal had been fine, the conversation awkward, the sweat beneath his collar getting worse with every pause. And when the waiter brought their coffee, his heart thumped as he felt the little velvet box, so soft and innocent, in his pocket. He took it out, even as the voice inside his head tried to reason with him, telling him to put it back, telling him to leave it be. But there it now was on the table.

"What's this?" Cynthia asked.

"Open it."

But when she lifted the lid, her eyes turned stormy. "How could you do this?"

"I thought it would make you happy. I thought that's what you wanted: to get married. I thought we broke up because you thought I'd never ask."

"You're unbelievable! How is it that everything I tell you goes in one ear and out the other? Didn't you hear me say we had problems to work out? Don't you remember saying you didn't want to discuss it?"

"I thought *this* was the problem—that I hadn't proposed." They were arguing in angry whispers that threatened to become overheard by other diners. "I love you, Cynthia, don't you understand that?"

"Do you know how long it's been since you actually said that to me? You can go for weeks—months—without saying it once."

"I assumed you knew how I felt. I thought it was obvious from the way I acted."

"Oh, really? Like leaving me standing on some horrible street corner, waiting for you after you promised—*promised*—you'd be there to pick me up?"

"Jesus! Are we back to that again?"

"I said I'd take a cab or catch a ride with someone else, but you insisted—*insisted*—you'd pick me up instead."

"I told you: I lost track of time because I had to—"

"That's just it: you didn't *have* to do anything. You were simply obsessed with taking your anger out on a seventeen-year-old child. Someone else could've handled the situation; it didn't have to be you."

"It did have to be me—"

"Oh, god, it's not just that! There are lots of things. You think I don't know you have a drinking problem?"

"You talk like I walk around drunk all day."

"You may not walk around drunk all day, but you drink too much. *Way* too much. It's a crutch."

"It's not a crutch."

"It *is* a crutch."

"I just need it to relax sometimes."

"Sometimes? Try *all* the time. Every day now. It's so much worse than when we first met. I used to assume you drank because you couldn't handle the pain you felt from your job. Until recently, I took it for granted that you had deep feelings you couldn't express. Now I realize you're just afraid to be vulnerable by showing any kind of emotion at all—even to me. And there's something very cold and cruel in you, something I never let myself notice before."

"And what brought you to these startling revelations?"

"When I saw the way you treated Micki. You've been so callous when it's obvious how much she needs—and wants—some love from you."

Baker snorted. "When we took her upstate, you were scared to death of her."

"So what? So maybe I'm not as worldly-wise as I like to think I am. Big deal. The things I said are still true; you have no compassion for her."

"You have no idea how I've taken care of that kid. When she was sick, I even saved her goddamn life. I—"

"But you're unwilling to face anything on an *emotional* level. There's nothing there. *Nothing*." She paused. "Y'know, I have never seen you cry."

"That's what this is about? That I won't cry like some—some…"

And while he searched for a word that wouldn't be too vulgar, Cynthia stood up and threw her napkin on the table. "It's no use talking to you; no use at all. You'd better take a good, hard look at yourself, Jim, or you'll be alone the rest of your life." She grabbed her coat and purse from the adjacent chair and stormed out of the restaurant.

And out of his life.

Face hot, feeling like everyone was staring at him, Baker paid the check and drove home. The only thing that kept repeating in his head was Cynthia's references to Micki; everything always came back to the kid. In fact, his first real fight with Cynthia had been about her.

He thought of all the trips to Micki's apartment, worrying if she was using again, worrying if she was all right. The kid was a fucking pain in the ass. And for what? For *what*? In trying to save her, he'd lost the only woman he'd ever really loved. If it hadn't been for Micki, none of this would be happening—*none of it*! He could've gone to LA, and Cynthia would never have taken up with that asshole actor. Nothing would've changed. *Nothing*.

He circled around his block several times. Twice, while waiting at a red light, someone stole a space he'd spotted. When he was finally unlocking his apartment door, the telephone rang and he rushed to answer it. But as he listened to the caller, his face grew darker.

"I'm not picking that fucking kid up now," he said.

The cop on the other end of the line tried appealing to Baker's sense of justice: the kid hadn't really done anything wrong; it was just a slight curfew violation. And they weren't supposed to keep someone—let alone a juvenile—in a holding pen for more than a few hours.

"I really don't give a shit. Let her stay in lockup overnight. Maybe it'll knock some sense into that thick skull of hers." The more the officer tried to reason with him, the more stubborn Baker became. And he'd just emphasized to Micki the importance of calling first. She was a goddamn pain in the ass. A FUCKING—PAIN—IN—THE—ASS! She couldn't get one fucking thing right. "I'll get her in the morning," Baker said, and slammed the phone down. Then he ripped off his tie, kicked off his shoes, and pulled out his whiskey. Settled in the recliner, he muttered, "Let the fucking kid rot there."

THE LARGER HOLDING PENS were in the basement of the station house. Adding to the dungeon-like atmosphere were small, secured windows set up high on the far stone wall outside the cells. Headlights from passing cars flashed by, causing the shadows cast by the bars to stretch to twice their length and move across the dimly lit space over and over again. Traffic noise and indistinct voices came from the street, mixing with the sounds made by prisoners and cops.

Being both a juvenile and female, Micki was in a cell that was separated from the others. It had a hard, narrow ledge—and nothing else. She was cold, uncomfortable, and alone. "I don't want to see you locked up again"—isn't that what Baker had said? She stared at the dirty bars. He was such a fucking liar. Always had been. And every time she'd let herself believe him—even a little—she'd been a fucking idiot.

When a mouse scampered across the floor, she pulled her feet up. After that, she simply stared into space.

"YOU ALL RIGHT IN there?" the cop asked. This was the third time he'd checked on her, and she'd barely moved. She never looked at him, either, just kept staring at the wall. "Hey"—he moved closer to the cell—"why don't you sleep a little. It'll make the time go faster. Hey—kid—look at me."

"Fuck off."

The cop bristled. "Have it your way. You're—" But he stopped and softened his tone. "Look, it's really not so bad; you're getting picked up in the morning."

She turned away.

BAKER DRANK THE REST of one bottle and nearly half of another before deciding it was time to go to sleep. Leaving the whiskey on the floor beside the recliner, he stumbled into the bedroom and, still in his clothes, flopped down on the bed. When the alarm rang at five forty-five, he groaned and reset it for over an hour later, but was no better off when it rang again. After a great deal of effort, he sat up on the edge of the mattress and fumbled around, searching for his cigarettes. He went and found them in the living room, where he lit one and ran his fingers through his hair. It was already a quarter after seven.

He called Warner at the school to say he wasn't sure when he'd be in. "And the kid'll be late, too," he said. "I've gotta go pick her up."

Sounding more annoyed than concerned, Warner asked, "You okay?"

"Yeah, I'm fine. I'll call you later." And he hung up before Warner had a chance to ask anything else. Then he called the precinct where Micki was being held, and asked if someone could drop her off at his apartment when their shift was over; there was no way he could come get her in his present condition. The desk sergeant told him not to sweat it; he'd arrange something.

Nauseous, head throbbing, Baker dropped into the recliner and picked up the bottle. The liquid inside was a rich, warm gold. He'd always liked the color. After a moment's hesitation, he drank a little more. Just to take the edge off.

BY MORNING, WHEN THEY took her out of her cell, Micki had convinced herself that everything that had happened was her own fault. While she was putting on her belt and relacing her sneakers, she kept looking around for Baker.

"I'm going to take you home," said the young detective who handed her the rest of her things.

Her whole body relaxed, and she put on her watch and cross. But when she picked up Baker's necklace, the pendant twisting back and forth as it dangled from its thin silver chain, she felt a flash of anger. She fastened it around her neck anyway.

They rode in silence in the detective's car until Micki realized they were going to the Upper West Side. Bolting upright in the seat, she said, "This isn't the way to my apartment. I live in Queens."

"I have to hand you over to your father."

"He's *not* my father."

The detective shot her a curious glance. "I still have to turn you over to him. Sorry."

You're sorry, she thought.

AFTER THREE CUPS OF coffee, Baker showered, shaved, and dressed, but still felt like shit. When the downstairs buzzer rang, he struggled to his feet to respond. A few minutes later there was a knock on his door, and he opened it, extending his hand. "James Baker."

"Roger Daton," the younger man replied. And they shook.

"I really appreciate this."

"No problem."

"Want some coffee?"

"No thanks, I'm beat. Just want to get some shuteye."

"Was any paperwork started on her?" It was Baker's only acknowledgement of Micki's presence.

Shaking his head no, Daton motioned with his hand in a friendly, dismissive gesture. "Don't worry about it."

"Thanks."

But Micki had caught the spark of irritation in Baker's face. "Can I go?" she asked. "I'm already real late for school."

"You're not going anywhere just yet."

"Well, *I'd* better get going," Daton said.

Baker shook Daton's hand again. "I owe you."

"It was nothing—not even out of my way." Then to Micki, "Bye, kid."

The door closed behind the other detective, but neither Baker nor Micki spoke. Baker was waiting till Daton was well out of earshot; Micki simply knew better than to provoke Baker when he was in this kind of state—Cynthia's answer must've been no.

"Your mouth stop working, Reilly?" Baker finally asked. "No smartass comments for once?"

She retreated into that small, distant place within herself.

"You have totally fucked up my life," he said. "Do you understand that? You've *ruined* my life. There isn't one goddamn moment when you're not fucking something up."

"I'm sorry," she mumbled.

"You're sorry?" he said. "You think that makes up for everything? You're useless; you're a worthless piece of shit. Why do you think no one's ever come looking for you, huh? It's because no one wants you." Seeing the look on her face, he snickered. "Awwww, what's the matter, little junkie? Did I hurt your feelings? You want to go shove a needle in your arm?" She swallowed hard, and he snickered again. "Or maybe you want to go cry? Huh? Do you want to cry? You're real good at crying, sitting there about to shoot up, crying your eyes out. Oh, yeah, poor little junkie, my heart bleeds for you. Well I'm finished with you, y'hear me? I don't give a fuck about you anymore. You get your ass out of here and go to school. But just you watch your step because, first chance I get, I'll send you right back where you belong. You're street scum and always will be." He marched into his bedroom and slammed the door behind him.

Micki stood very still, feeling like a thin sliver of broken glass was slowly edging its way through her heart. It would've hurt less if he'd simply hit her. But maybe it was better this way. At least everything was very clear.

Taking soft, careful steps, she went into the living room, gaze lighting upon the bottle beside the recliner. She snatched it and hurried back to the hall closet, where she opened the door as far as she could without causing the hinges to creak. Body half inside, arm extended all the way, she successfully extracted Baker's gym bag, then stuffed the bottle underneath his boxing gloves and zipped the duffle closed.

Eyes empty, face blank, she left.

Chapter 26

RUSH HOUR. MICKI FELL in among the throng of subway commuters, the platform full of passengers heading downtown just like she was. As the train left Ninety-Sixth Street behind, it stayed at a crawl, passing through an abandoned station, work lights casting a sinister glow on the multicolored art unknown kids had left behind. Unlike the graffiti in the subway car itself, which was mostly a chaotic mass of tangled-looking lines in black spray paint or Magic Marker, these designs were pretty, nearly all of them huge. She used to wonder why kids did it—why they had to write all over any empty space they could find. But now she wished she'd left her own name scrawled somewhere. Anywhere.

The train lurched and picked up speed, but she felt no sense of urgency. And when she changed at Times Square, she walked right past several cops—completely relaxed. She was just a kid with a gym bag among a motley crowd of people.

And no one bothered her.

IT FELT ODD TO be in her apartment when she'd normally be in school. Not that it mattered. She wouldn't go anyplace looking like this. A quick shower, a pass of the comb through her hair, and then she put on her black jeans and her favorite black T-shirt.

On the floor beside the bed, already waiting, was the tall bottle of whiskey next to a short glass of water, both looking like they thought they should be somewhere else. But when she sat on the mattress with her jacket in her lap, she knew everything was exactly where she wanted it to be.

The jacket's winter lining zipped out easily and was carelessly tossed aside. Then she grabbed a handful of the silky material underneath and ripped it apart, all the while apologizing in her head. Two Librium and one Quaalude immediately dropped onto the blanket. But she had to search around—even into the arms of the jacket—for the rest. Except for one Valium, she recovered them all.

She flipped on the radio and began turning the dial, but settled on WNEW when the initial scan proved fruitless. She could wait till something good came on; Baker would be sleeping off his hangover. But then she got up and wedged the desk chair underneath the doorknob. Just in case.

With the radio stuck in a commercial break, she took a look about the room: the crappy kitchen that needed cleaning, the wine-splattered wall, the textbooks on her desk with her unfinished homework… She was nothing but a failure. Though she'd tried so hard to be something else, it had all come back to this. Sergeant Kelly would be so disappointed. But then, he probably didn't even think about her anymore. And no one was going to miss her much, either. Mr. Antonelli and Frankie liked her, and most of her teachers liked her, but their lives wouldn't change without her. Not the way hers had changed when Tim had died. The corners of her mouth turned down, and her hand reached up to the little silver cross around her neck. She felt Baker's pendant, too. With one vicious tug, she broke its delicate chain, then got up and hurled it into the street. After slamming the window back down, she returned to sitting on the bed.

And then she finally heard what she was waiting for, a song—a message—sent out over the airwaves: the Youngbloods' "Get Together." As if it were radiating light, it was filling the room with a mystical essence, with a magic so real she could almost touch it, could almost feel it glowing as it flowed all around her, taking her someplace far away. Someplace where the world wasn't ugly.

She could see herself at the top of a hill, looking out across a lush, green meadow that was shimmering in the heat, her skin warm and browning. Skirting the trees, a soft, gentle breeze swept across the land, over the grass and the colorful flowers, which swayed gracefully, their open blossoms alive with the buzz of bees and the sweet scent of summer. And for a moment, she was a part of it all, as eternal as the sun shining down from above, as pure as the drops of liquid that glistened like jewels as they clung to the grass at her feet.

But when she looked off toward the mountains in the distance—their snowy caps a bright, cool blanket—she saw herself for what she really was: just a whisper of breath in the vastness of space; a dull, flickering light against the brilliant blue of the sky…

She looked at the drab, stained walls of her apartment. It was time for her to go.

Using as little water as possible, she swallowed the pills before uncapping the whiskey, first taking little sips, but soon gulping it down.

Her heart hurt and the tears fell silently.

The song had ended.

She shut the radio and continued drinking until she needed to lie down, curling up and clutching the pillow in her arms. The usual noise drifted up from the street, and, somewhere, a bird was chirping. But mostly what she heard was her own breathing.

It wouldn't be long now. She could finally rest.

TRY AS HE MIGHT, Baker couldn't get back to sleep. He tossed and turned until he eventually got up and reheated the remaining coffee. Strong and bitter, the mud-colored sludge refused to improve despite any addition of milk. It should've been dumped in the sink. But he sat in the kitchen, chain-smoking, till all of it was gone. He called Warner again.

"I really feel like shit. Do you think you're going to need me at all today?"

"No," Warner replied, his voice tight. "Just stay home."

"What time did the kid get in?"

"Micki?"

"Yeah, Micki!" Baker snapped. "Who the hell else would I be talking about?"

"She didn't get here yet."

"*What*?" Baker pushed his chair back and stood up. "Why didn't you call to let me know?"

"I figured she was coming in with you. You said you had to go pick her up."

"Christ! I'm going to kill that fucking kid."

But instead, Baker froze. For in that moment, he knew what she had done.

SIMON & GARFUNKLEL's "HAZY Shade of Winter" kept playing over and over in his head like a movie soundtrack as he raced through the streets, portable red light flashing on the roof of his car while he leaned on the horn since he had no siren. He'd purchased the used Camaro just before the incident with Daryl Cole.

Afterward, bitter and disheartened, he'd never bothered to have a siren or two-way radio installed. But now he regretted it. Very much. And he should've at least dialed nine-one-one before leaving his apartment; should've had the police and paramedics go to Micki's immediately. Now, without the radio, it was impossible to notify anyone unless he pulled over and stopped—which he couldn't bring himself to do.

Vision blurry, head still throbbing, he was making his eyes scan back and forth twice as much as they normally would. He practically held his breath while negotiating the intersections. But most cars were clearing a path for him as he tore ahead, horn blaring, light flashing...

Screeching to a halt in front of her building, he left his car double-parked, then flew up the stoop and the stairs, two steps at a time. He jammed his key into the lock, turned it, and was startled when he slammed into the door. Perhaps the key hadn't turned all the way. He tried again—with the same result. But he'd felt the panel give.

"Micki!" He pounded with the side of his fist. "*Micki! You open this door!*" When he got no response, he stepped back and kicked it in, crashing into her apartment. Surrounded by broken pieces of the old wooden chair, he was momentarily confused by the sight of his own gym bag on the floor—boxing gloves half out, her jacket all ripped up beside it. Lying on the bed, she looked lifeless. He hurried over and pushed away the pillow, which had fallen partway out of her arms. Freed from underneath, the overturned whiskey bottle went rolling noisily across the hardwood planks.

Her pulse was weak and irregular, her breathing very shallow. He slapped her face several times and called her name, then got up and ran down the hall. There was no sign on the payphone, so he lifted the receiver and dialed nine-one-one. With the handset to his ear, he shut his eyes, and bowed his head. And heard... nothing. He smashed his palm against the heavy metal box. "*Fuck!*"

WHEN THE PAIN IN his knees got too much, he stood up and began pacing back and forth between the bed and the window. Where the hell was the damn ambulance? He'd called from the corner phone over ten minutes ago. He stopped and picked up Micki's jacket to examine the ripped material more closely, then heard a little ping as something fell to the floor. Catching sight of the tiny blue object rolling away, he captured it under his boot. But before he'd even picked it up, he knew it was a Valium—*his* Valium. Just as it had been his whiskey.

He understood the torn lining.

He closed his eyes and recalled the horrible things he'd said that morning, then knelt down and leaned over the bed again. Soft and faint, her breath was a vanishing trace of warm air against his cheek, her pulse weaker and more uneven, a ghostly beat beneath the pallor of her skin.

And then she stopped breathing.

His eyed widened, the thready pulse still palpable under his fingers. And as if he'd done it a thousand times, he checked that her airway was clear before lifting her neck so her head tilted back. Pinching her nose shut and placing his mouth over hers, he breathed into her lungs, regretting that his own breath reeked of alcohol. And though an ambulance siren was growing louder from far off in the distance, it seemed like hours till the paramedics' feet were trampling up the stairs.

"She stopped breathing, but she's still got a pulse," he said to the two men that ran in, pushing him aside. "And I'm almost positive now," he added, "that she took some pills with the whiskey."

The younger man with long, dark hair was applying the mask of a breathing bag while the short man, checking her pulse, asked, "Like?" Then he raised her eyelids and shined a small flashlight into each pupil.

Baker said, "Uh—Valium probably and—uh—I—I don't know." Now that someone else was there to take control, a huge, smothering wave was washing over him.

The short paramedic wrapped a blood-pressure cuff around her needle-tracked arm. "What about heroin?"

"I don't think so, but I can't say for sure."

Using a walkie-talkie, the short man radioed information back to a doctor at the hospital. Snatches of it registered in Baker's ears: "respiratory arrest…blood pressure sixty over palp…pupils dilated…requesting permission to administer a course of Narcan followed by saline IV…" While the men continued with their work and transferred her to a gurney, Baker heard himself asking, "Is she gonna be all right?"

"Hard to say," the short one said. They began to move her out of the apartment. "Is that your car out there with the cherry on it?"

"Yeah," Baker said.

"Then you can follow us to the hospital. We're taking her to Old Queens County General."

"Is she gonna be all right?" he heard himself ask again.

THE RIDE TO THE hospital was a blur. A zombie on automatic pilot, Baker followed the wailing, flashing ambulance in front of him like a baby duck following its mother, realizing too late he should've exercised his option to remain by Micki's side. What if she died on the way?

But once they reached the emergency room, he felt completely useless. Medical personnel were swarming around, cutting away clothes and yelling instructions to each other while they rolled her into one of the treatment cubicles. A nurse handed him a little paper cup. Inside, he found Micki's cross. He opened his mouth to ask where the other necklace was, but then shut it without saying anything. And out of nowhere, some woman in a nurse's uniform was asking him for Micki's name and address, her most salient concern being the insurance information. He felt a sharp pang: Micki was probably covered under his own insurance as a dependent. His *dependent*. How could he have been so blind?

In between answers, Baker kept demanding to know about the doctors taking care of her. Were they qualified enough? They weren't just house staff, were they? Where was an experienced doctor? What were they doing to her?

Overhearing the belligerent onslaught of questions, an attending physician came over and sent the woman away. "Hi, I'm Dr. Mikulewicz," he said, extending his hand.

"Jim Baker." And they shook. "I only want to be sure she's getting the very best care."

Just shy of six feet tall, Dr. Mikulewicz looked to be in his early forties. He had piercing blue eyes and a full head of thick, black hair. "I understand," he said, "and I can assure you she's in good hands."

"But I don't want someone learning on her; I want someone who knows what they're doing." As Baker continued to watch over the doctor's shoulder, he saw fresh concern among the medical staff, heard anxious, clipped orders coming from a nurse. He asked, "What are they doing to her now?" He tried to step past the doctor, who deftly blocked his way. "I want to know what's going on!" Baker demanded. "I have a right to know what's happening to her!"

With a gentle touch, Mikulewicz put his hand on Baker's arm. "I'm going to have to ask you to wait outside in the waiting room."

Baker's eyes flashed wide.

"Please," the doctor said.

Baker attempted to glare the man down—until his entire demeanor changed and he stood very tall. "But I'm a cop."

Mikulewicz looked surprised, then confused. "I was told you're her guardian."

"I am."

"But—" And then a savvy, yet compassionate, expression came over the doctor's face. He asked, "Are you here as a cop or as a family member?"

Baker closed his eyes and felt the ER chaos spinning around him. Smaller and smaller, he was getting further and further away… He opened his eyes and struggled with the words: "Family member."

"Then you'll have to wait outside."

Baker swallowed hard.

"I'll let you know how things are going," Mikulewicz said. "I promise." When Baker didn't move, the doctor added, "Please don't make me ask those uniformed officers to escort you out."

Baker's eyes darted over to the two young patrolmen standing three cubicles down. To pass the time, they were cracking crude jokes while the person in their custody was being treated. Baker took a deep, ragged breath. "That won't be necessary." Then he walked in the direction the doctor had pointed, his legs feeling like they belonged to someone else.

FOR AN ER WAITING room, it was only moderately crowded. Baker sat down in an aqua-colored chair made of molded plastic. To his left was a young couple, the woman crying into the man's shoulder while he did his best to comfort her. To his right was a tired-looking woman in a dark wool coat covering what appeared to be pajamas—her three preschoolers running, screeching, and giggling while she tried, unsuccessfully, to get them under control. A sullen-looking teenager in a hooded sweatshirt under a faded denim jacket was directly across from him, smoking, mindlessly tapping a pack of cigarettes on his thigh while eyeing him with suspicion.

Baker lit a cigarette himself. In between tense drags, his jaw worked, clenching and unclenching while his harsh, unwavering stare—though directed at no one—caused the youth to get up and move to a seat across the room. But Baker barely blinked. He shifted his gaze to focus on the little children, now sitting on the floor and coloring, fighting bitterly with each other over the crayons as though the world was going to end if they didn't get the colors they wanted. Feeling a fresh surge of pain, he turned his eyes toward the windows and the bright light streaming in through the oversized panes of glass. But what he was seeing was Micki washing down the pills with his whiskey, hugging the pillow and waiting—all alone in that crummy, little apartment—to die.

Lit cigarette still between his fingers, he hung his head in his hands.

And cried.

EVERY TWO MINUTES, BAKER checked his watch and glanced at the door in anticipation of the doctor's return. He drank coffee and chain-smoked and periodically paced around the room while reflecting, disapprovingly, on the man he had become. He decided he must've been temporarily insane. A profound quiet now possessed him as if Micki's suicide attempt had shaken him free of some evil spell. No wonder Cynthia hadn't wanted to marry him. If he were her, he would've felt the same way.

Dr. Mikulewicz came through the door, and Baker sprang to his feet.

"She's stable now, so she's being transferred to the ICU," the doctor said.

"Is she awake?"

"It may be a while, yet, till she regains consciousness."

"But she's gonna be okay, right?"

"When we pumped her stomach, no pill fragments remained, but we got her blood pressure back up, so things are looking good for now."

"Can I see her?"

"Just for a moment. Once she's settled in upstairs, you can visit her there—briefly. She's still intubated and on a ventilator."

Baker nodded. Yet when he saw her, the tears welled up again. She looked so small and pale, smudges of charcoal on her face, like a little kid who'd gotten dirty going out to play. The orderlies were moving the gurney. He felt he couldn't breathe.

"Is there any way this might've been an accident?" Dr. Mikulewicz asked. "It's obvious she has a history of drug abuse."

Baker shook his head no.

The doctor looked at him steadily. "Okay, then. I'm going to see if I can contact Dr. Lerner in our psych department. Micki will probably have to stay there for at least a couple of weeks. But if you could talk to Dr. Lerner today, it would be a big help. She'll want to have as much background information as possible before she sees Micki for the first time."

So Dr. Lerner was a woman. A female shrink. That was probably better for Micki. They started walking in the same direction the orderlies had gone.

The doctor said, "If you have a minute, I have a few questions I'd like to ask you myself."

If I have a minute? Baker thought. Where the hell would I be going? But knowing the doctor's cordiality was merely a prelude to something unpleasant, he turned to face Mikulewicz and said, "Shoot."

"Micki has a lot of scars on her body. I need to know how she got them."

"All of that happened *before* I became her guardian."

"And how long has that been?"

"Since September."

"And you're related to her how?"

"I'm not."

Mikulewicz nodded. "I see. Is there anyone who could verify the presence of those scars prior to September?"

Baker's expression turned dark. "I don't have to stand here and—" He caught his breath.

The doctor waited.

"I'm—I'm sorry," Baker said. "I know you're just doing your job." And it made him think about not only Dr. Orenstein's cursory inquiry when he'd examined

Micki, but also all the teachers who'd ever seen her bruised face—in those instances, by his own hand—but had never brought it to anyone's attention.

Baker provided the doctor with a brief sketch of what he knew, pointing out that whatever scars Micki had had before Heyden would've been documented in both her post-arrest hospital records and her juvenile police records. The remainder—those inflicted while she'd been incarcerated—would most likely not be documented at all. To protect the guilty. But the only person, besides Micki, who could corroborate his own statement would be Warner, who'd witnessed the incident when Baker had first seen the scars himself. The doctor took Warner's phone numbers, and they moved on.

When they had arrived at the elevator bank, Mikulewicz said, "Let me page Dr. Lerner now and see what we can arrange today. Meanwhile, the ICU is on the third floor; just follow the signs." As he turned to go, he added, "I'll be in touch."

BUT THE PSYCHIATRIST WAS available to talk with Baker immediately. So before he had a chance to see Micki again, he left the ICU and took the elevator up two more floors. One of the nurses unlocked the door to the ward and led him down a short hallway. At first it seemed like any other hospital wing, but as he passed the dayroom, his stomach started to turn. A young woman, sitting stiff as a board, was staring off into space while, in the corner, an old, disheveled man was slapping his face repeatedly. Baker turned his eyes away. He suspected that when he passed by on his way out, they'd both be doing the exact same things. He followed the nurse through another set of doors to a row of offices down a long, empty corridor.

She stopped and pointed. "Second-to-last door on the right." And then she left.

Walking down the passageway alone, Baker felt a lump growing in his throat. The closer he got to Dr. Lerner's office, the worse it became. Her door was slightly ajar, and he knocked.

"Come in," said a woman's voice.

He stepped inside. "I'm Detective Sergeant James Baker—Micki Reilly's legal guardian. Dr. Mikulewicz sent me to see you."

"Yes, of course. I'm Dr. Lerner." Her smile warm, she stood up from behind her desk and extended her hand to shake his. "Won't you sit down?" She motioned to a pair of old, upholstered chairs while she took her seat in a tall-backed, leather-looking one.

He tried to smile, but the pain in his heart grew worse, so he sat down and crossed his left ankle over his right knee. When Dr. Lerner didn't say anything, he cleared his throat and tilted his head toward the couch against the wall. "Am I going to have to lie down on that?"

"Not unless you want to," she said.

She exuded a subdued youthfulness that had caught him off guard. Dressed in a slate-blue tailored suit, the skirt hemmed just above the knee, she was slender, her brown hair framing her face in soft waves. He'd expected a greying, sixty-year-old woman—complete with bun, glasses, and a German accent. Placing his foot back on the floor, he took a pack of Camels from his pocket and removed one. Paused with the cigarette halfway to his lips, he looked at her.

She handed him an ashtray.

He put the thin metal dish—which was more like a shallow, fluted cup of aluminum foil—on the small table between the chairs. He put the cigarette in his mouth. With what appeared to be tremendous concentration, he tore a match from his matchbook and carefully closed the cover. But his chest felt very tight, and he did nothing more than breathe. Until the tears started streaming down his face.

"You're very sad," Dr. Lerner said softly.

Eyes clamped shut, he took the cigarette out of his mouth and simply nodded. In a voice strangled to the point of cracking, he whispered, "This is all my fault."

Since Dr. Lerner had squeezed Baker in—in between appointments—they talked for only ten minutes so as not to make her next patient wait. With all there was to tell, it was barely enough time to give her more than a few sketchy details about Micki's life and the events immediately leading up to the suicide attempt.

Lerner said, "I'd like to have sessions with you and Micki separately as well as together."

Mouth so dry it was difficult to speak, he said, "You want to talk to me about Micki, though—right?"

"I'd also like to talk about you."

He looked down at the floor, then nodded.

Standing up to signal their time was over, she said, "I'll arrange my fees in such a way that this won't be a financial hardship." He was putting his cigarettes back in his pocket when she added, "Micki's an interesting case."

HAVING FOUND HIS WAY back to the ICU, Baker sat by Micki's bed and smoothed her hair while the unceasing noise—whispered chatter, medical monitors, and ventilators—pushed his stress level up another notch. Technically, he was allowed to visit only ten minutes every hour, but his good looks usually bought at least five more, the nurses pretending not to realize how long he'd been there. Overly cautious, as if she might break, he touched her cheek very lightly, the cool skin fine and soft. Until his fingers traveled over the scars. Tears welled up again, and he closed his eyes.

An interesting case.

VISITING HOURS IN THE ICU ended at seven o'clock, but Baker hung around until ten, smoking cigarettes in the now-empty adjacent waiting room. Like mother hens, the young nurses fretted over him, telling him to go home and get some rest. He eventually agreed. But it was Micki's place he went to since it was closer to the hospital. Once there, he realized his mistake: the payphone still wasn't working. So he went to the corner and placed a call to his answering service, hoping the hospital might've already tried to contact him. When the operator told him he had messages, he snapped to attention, only to crash when she added it was from the day before.

"Yesterday?" he repeated. But then it occurred to him that he hadn't checked in since having dinner with Cynthia.

"Yes, sir. Actually there were two calls that came in. According to our records, one was at nine forty in the evening, but the caller left no name or number. Then there was another at ten-o-two from a Mickey—no last name—stating he—oh, I'm so sorry: *she*—was on her way to your apartment. Oh, I guess that message isn't very useful anymore."

Baker's throat constricted, and there was a burning sensation in his chest. When he'd gone to the restaurant, he'd completely forgotten to leave a forwarding number. And Micki had called. Needing him. His voice came out weak. "I'll be home within the hour. Until I check in again, please pick up any calls immediately."

THE WALLS IN MICKI'S apartment closed in around him. It felt like a million eyes were watching. He picked up her jacket, ripped the inner lining out completely, then did the same to her vest, taking them with him for his tailor to fix. Pretty creative, her little hiding place; he'd never suspected a thing. She must've lifted the pills from his medicine cabinet the very first day she came to clean, then carried them around for months, never using them. Even when she was going through withdrawal.

He got in his car, turned over the engine, and pulled away from the curb.

He hadn't given her nearly enough credit.

WHEN HE REACHED HIS apartment, there was still no message from the hospital. Without even taking off his jacket, he headed over to the liquor cabinet. Out of his own brand, he grabbed the bottle of Jack Daniels—Martini's favorite—then paused. He unscrewed the cap, only to close it again. For almost a minute, he simply stood there. Then he put the bottle back and locked it away.

That morning he'd had his very last drink.

BAKER'S SLEEP WAS FITFUL, his dreams surreal versions of the day's events. In the wakeful periods between nightmares, he found himself dredging up everything that had ever happened with Micki, everything he could've seen if he'd only opened his eyes.

He wanted to rip his own heart out.

At 2:00 a.m. he flung back the covers: he needed to return to the hospital. The premonition was so strong that he didn't shower or shave, and with no traffic on the roads, the drive was short. But once he arrived, he was at the mercy of the nurses, who initially rebuffed his request. Looking unabashedly pitiful, he pled his case, then waited while the women talked amongst themselves: it was a breach of ICU rules to let someone visit outside of official, posted times, but at such a quiet, early-morning hour, who was to know? The teen's life was still hanging in the balance, and the rugged, handsome cop was so distraught. The nurses granted him ten minutes and no more.

She had yet to take a breath on her own.

THE CHAIN-LINK FENCE SHIMMERED *in the summer heat while the stone wall's endless loops of barbed wire looked unforgivingly cruel and bleak. Heart straining and weakening with every beat, she ran, gasping for air as if in a scorched and arid desert. Sweat was trickling into her eyes, burning and stinging, further blurring the hazy, heat-ravaged landscape. Yet she felt so terribly cold. And so tired. She longed to lay down and sleep. Forever. And all she had to do was stop. Whatever was chasing her was not far behind, determined to finish what it hadn't before, determined to destroy the very light that was burning inside her. And for the first time, she understood that what she was running from was death.*

The wall appeared in the distance, and the ground ahead of her ripped apart. But this time a mist—thick, black, and foul—rolled in to swirl beneath her feet, long wisps reaching out like greedy fingers to wrap around her legs. Unable to breathe, her limbs too heavy to move, she waited to be engulfed by the twisting, turning vapors— only to be carried upward on a pillow of air and gently delivered to the brink of the precipice. Sleepy, she looked down into the void while shadow fell over the brick wall beyond.

And it was then that the mysterious hand reached out—out of the shadows from across the divide. Palm upward, it began to grow until it was so large it could carry her safely across the chasm. But she was drawn to the infinite darkness that was spreading out below: just one more step and she would disappear. Into nothingness.

Still perched on the edge, her mind soft and lazy, she watched the hand withdraw, returning to normal size while the gap between them widened. But as time ran out, it was the hand's owner who leaned forward, reaching for her, his face finally entering the light.

Baker.

Filled with rage, she jumped into the ravine, even as he seized her arm and plunged into the darkness after her. She experienced a euphoric sense of triumph at the realization that she was taking him with her into death. But as they hurtled through the pitch-black space, it rotated, becoming a tunnel, causing them to float instead of fall. Arms outstretched, she was weightless, gliding like a bird through the boundless tubular corridor.

Up ahead, dazzling and bright, a tiny light appeared, incredibly small but growing larger. It was throwing off sparks and cutting through the darkness, leaving sprays of glowing embers like little trails of glittering gems. Baker's hand, holding on tightly, had slipped down to hers, but she no longer cared that she was dragging him along. Her entire being was fixed on that light. It was beckoning her to enter, summoning her to come home. It was the light of Heaven. She'd heard about it once on the radio.

But the brilliance was already fading. And she began to hear odd sounds and voices—authoritative ones, not the angelic ones she'd been expecting. Contorting her body, she tried to pull back, but Baker floated past and pulled her forcibly behind him. Faster and faster, they accelerated toward the light, the noises growing louder and louder—

Micki's eyes fluttered open, and a strange gurgle escaped her throat. Though disoriented, she knew she was very much alive—and staring at Baker, his hand still tightly gripping hers. She started to thrash around, but Baker pinned her down. She tried to scream, but nothing came out. People in white surrounded her, and Baker disappeared. She closed her eyes.

At least the son of a bitch was gone.

Chapter 27

THROUGHOUT THE MORNING, MICKI faded in and out of consciousness. Baker sat in her room—in the clumsy, motel-style chair—watching her sleep and listening to the heart monitor's beep. His mind was empty; his body, heavy and depleted. Whenever he noticed any sign that she was coming to, he got up and left—something that confused the nurses to no end. But shortly after noon, while he was staring out the window, Micki opened her eyes to see his back.

"Get the fuck outta here," she said. Her voice was a painful-sounding rasp—a consequence of the endotracheal tube they'd removed.

He spun around to see her struggling against the restraints.

"I fuckin' hate you," she said.

"I don't blame you."

"Go fuck y'self."

"I'm glad you're alive, Micki."

"Yeah? Well I'm not, y'son of a bitch. I wanted out. Who the fuck asked y't'interfere, huh?"

Heart aching, he left—and had his first real session with Dr. Lerner. He sat down, lit up, and didn't stop talking until the outpouring of words had highlighted almost every abuse he'd ever heaped upon Micki. Finally pausing, he said, "I can't believe that was me; I can't believe that I could do those things. But from the minute I saw her—no even before that—I hated her. Really hated her. And once I met her, I hated her even more."

"What made you feel that way?"

"I don't know; I guess I resented Dr. Tillim's whole therapy scheme—I thought it was total bull. Plus I was fed up with the leniency of the juvenile justice system. I'd made up my mind from the start to hate the kid, whoever they were."

"But what made you hate her even more once you'd met her?"

He exhaled a large stream of smoke. "Well, for one thing, the fact that she was a girl. Nobody'd let on to me about that; they even went out of their way to actively cover it up. But I have to say, they knew what they were doing: I took it as an insult to have a female charge." He gave the doctor a wan smile. "That is, until I realized what a tough little bastard she was. But I hated her just the same."

"Yes, but why? Do you remember any of the thoughts that came up?"

The smile faded, and he shook his head. "I don't know."

When Baker offered nothing more, the doctor asked, "Have you ever hit one of your girlfriends?"

"Jesus, no! Never. I never—*never*—hit a female before hitting Micki."

"But you hit men."

"No. Well, yeah. I mean, I started hitting perps—y'know the scum I apprehended. That's what got me into this mess." And he went on to briefly relate the episode with Daryl Cole. "But you have to understand: I *want* to be Micki's guardian now. I didn't then, but, y'know, I've changed my mind."

"What's different now?"

Baker shifted his weight in the chair. "I guess, y'know, I feel sorry for her and all. She needs someone."

"I see."

Baker stubbed out yet another spent cigarette and went to light a new one while the doctor observed the tremor in his hands. "Sorry for subjecting you to all this smoke," he said. "But since I stopped drinking yesterday, I've been smoking like a fiend."

"What made you decide to stop drinking?"

"I think…I think this was a wake-up call." Taking a short pull on the freshly lit Camel, he appeared about to say something else, only to stare down at the cigarette, which he was rolling back and forth between his thumb and index finger. Finally, his voice small, he said, "I—I had sex with Micki once." When he shot a glance at Lerner, he was caught off guard by her neutral expression. And as she waited for him to speak again, a singular, undefined space gently opened up between them.

The doctor became the only person besides Gould to ever hear what had happened that night.

"But that was it," Baker said as he finished. "That was the only time. I never had any sexual contact with her after that. Or before, for that matter. None. Zero.

If I hadn't been so wasted, I would never have done what I did then, either. When I started coming down, I was—I was horrified…" His voice trailed off, and his eyes drifted. Seconds passed before he said, "It seems like that was years ago. Things changed so much after that."

"In what way?"

"I started seeing her more as a kid. Pretty ironic, huh?" He drew heavily on the cigarette, then tapped it sharply on the edge of the ashtray. Exhaling, he said, "But I know it hurt her terribly—y'know, my having had sex with her like that. She wouldn't admit it, but I knew. And she's already pretty messed up when it comes to men." He looked straight at the doctor again. "She thinks we don't have any feelings—well, any nice feelings like love and all that stuff. She thinks we only pretend. I guess I didn't help much as far as that goes."

"I'm afraid our time is up for today."

In fact, they'd gone over by nearly another session's worth. Yet Baker stood up reluctantly.

"If it would be at all possible," Dr. Lerner said, "I'd like to meet with you at least three more times this week. This is a very complex situation, and it's important that I get as complete a history as possible. I'd get most of it from Micki herself except she's refusing to talk to me. I'm hoping that will change once she's transferred here later today."

"Sure. Of course," Baker said. "Whatever you need." And he left the ward feeling a little less stressed. Until he got on the elevator and considered what he'd done: agreed to talk to a shrink. Willingly. Three more times. In one week.

When he stopped by Micki's room again, she was still in restraints. She closed her eyes and kept them that way as if he weren't there. And eventually, he wasn't, finally taking his cue and leaving. He felt like all of the hospital staff were watching him—talking about him. And not in a good way.

And of all things, the damn social worker had called the high school that morning. Earlier, when he'd checked in with Warner, he'd gotten the message that Miss Gutierrez wanted to meet with both him and Micki to see how things were going. What the hell was he going to tell the woman? He'd intended to ask Dr.

Lerner for advice, but by the session's end, he'd completely forgotten. Well—fuck it; there was nothing he could do about it now.

He drove home and checked in with his answering service, then threw himself on the bed. And finally slept.

He had just started climbing the stairs when his flashlight died. Swearing silently, he waited for his eyes to adjust, then continued up, gun drawn, feet carefully planted, the air around him fetid and cold. When he reached the second floor, he heard a crash and then his partner cursing from the other side of the building, something heavy clattering down the fire escape there. Moving toward the sound, he entered a large room to see the suspect near a broken-out window, aiming a small pistol at a downward angle.

"Don't do it," he heard his partner say.

But the man merely snickered. "You're a fuckin' pig, man. You're dead—"

The .38-caliber Smith & Wesson exploded twice in Baker's hands, flashing fire, the sound reverberating through the cavernous, empty space. And the moment of silence that followed—absent of breath, borne of darkness—slipped away, unseen, into the farthest corners of his mind.

As if to be forgotten.

Baker's eyes flew open.

BAKER STOOD IN THE dark by the living room window, Elton John's *Tumbleweed Connection* playing on the stereo. After sitting in silence for hours that morning, he needed something to listen to—definitely not the TV. He stroked the scratchy bristles on his chin. He needed a shave, too.

His ears pricked up as the haunting notes of a plucked harp marked the introduction to "Come Down in Time," one of two songs on the album that were like a religious experience to him, sparking the creation of vivid, otherworldly landscapes—hidden places—that belonged to him alone. This one led to images of tall blades of grass rustling softly in waves under a sepia-colored moon, an intense, indefinable energy pervading the dark, ghostly scene. He closed his eyes and listened with reverence, the music and words inducing, like a reliable drug, heightened feelings of sorrow and loss.

He took a deep breath. He needed to call Cynthia. Needed to tell her what had happened.

But just as the song was ending, giving way to the next, he heard two men get out of their cars and begin arguing on the street below. From the increasing volume and frequency of cursing, he could picture the escalating altercation, the macho posturing and threatening gestures. But he wasn't going down there. For all he cared, they could blow each other's brains out. Over a fucking parking space. What assholes.

His cigarette was beat. He stuffed the stub into the empty soda can he was holding and turned on the lamp. Then he picked up the receiver and dialed.

"Hello?"

"Please don't hang up, Cyn."

"Give me one good reason why I shouldn't."

"Micki tried to kill herself."

"Oh, my god..."

With a slight quaver in his voice, he said, "I really fucked up this time; I really did." After a pause, he added, "I'm sorry for—so many things. You were right in just about everything you ever said to me."

"Oh, Jim..." And she could feel his sadness, could picture him standing there, alone, in the dark.

And he could hear that she was crying. He told her which hospital Micki was in and where it was. "But if you're going to visit," he said, "don't go alone. Take"— he tried to remember the actor's real name—"Mark with you. Or you can always deliver a message through me. I'll be going there every day."

"Tell her I send my love."

Baker ended the call, his heart aching so badly he had to sit down. But eventually he got up to flip the album over. Back at the window, he watched the people down on the street going on with their lives as if nothing had changed; as if nothing had happened; as if what had happened was nothing at all. Bowing his head, he closed his eyes, the music pulling him into "Where to Now St. Peter?"...

He was in a small wooden boat on a river, colored leaves cascading down under a grey autumn sky. Warm and relaxed, he drifted downstream, water sparkling now and then as sunlight peaked through the clouds. But the grey turned black as the

moonless night completely swallowed the sun, the river now an ocean, his boat a tiny
spec. Darkness all around, there were no lights to bring him in. The world was silent.
Except for the water that was lapping against the weathered wood of the boat.

BACK AT WORK, BAKER was distracted and feeling guilty for being at the high
school, though there was no point in hanging around the hospital all day. He called
Miss Gutierrez's number and drummed his fingers on the desk while waiting for
the line to connect. When the receptionist told him the caseworker was out in the
field, he felt like a huge weight had been lifted. At least, temporarily.

Hoping to see Micki before his session, he arrived at the hospital early,
stopping at the gift shop first to pick up a pack of cigarettes. Stuck on line for the
cashier, he noticed the array of stuffed animals on display. A cute white bunny
with long, floppy ears caught his eye, and he thought about his conversation with
Mr. Antonelli the previous day. The restaurant owner had been fuming because
Micki hadn't shown up for work the night before—hadn't even called so he could
get a replacement. But after Baker explained why, Mr. Antonelli had made little
clucking noises, saying, "She never-a happy. I never see her-a smile. Always look-a
so serious. Is-a no good-a; she's-a too old for her age-a."

Baker purchased the bunny and headed up to the fifth floor, where the nurse
who unlocked the door to the ward mentioned he ought to bring Micki some of
her own clothes to wear.

"Has she seen Dr. Lerner yet today?" he asked.

"No, sir. I'm sorry."

His face fell. "Then she hasn't talked to her at all?"

With a subtle shake of her head, the nurse said, "No."

"And what about the restraints?"

"They were removed last night, but she became violent and had to be sedated.
So far today, she's been behaving, so she's in the dayroom."

As soon as he entered the community area, Baker spotted Micki at a table
in the far left corner. Slouched in a chair, she was wearing green hospital scrubs.
He walked toward her, trying to ignore the other patients: the unkempt, middle-
aged man who kept touching himself all over as if to make sure all of him was

still there, the grey-haired woman rocking back and forth on the floor near the right-hand wall.

Micki was sitting quietly, staring vacuously. But before Baker was halfway across the room, her head whipped around.

He said, "Hi, Micki." She turned her back to him. He walked around in front of her. "How do you feel?"

"How d'ya think I feel?"

"Do you mind if I sit down?"

"Yeah, I mind! Why don'tcha just go home and leave me alone."

"I want you to get better."

"I'm not sick."

A woman who looked to be in her thirties started shouting, "I'm so good I could've should've stood on the wood hood. Bleed greed the deed. Maybe we three can see the tree and free some tea..."

"Why don't you talk to Dr. Lerner so you can get the hell out of this place?" Baker asked.

"I don't need a shrink. I'm not crazy."

"You need to talk to someone."

"I need to be dead."

"Don't talk like that!"

"Or what?"

There was silence till Baker said, "Mr. Antonelli hopes you feel better soon."

She grunted.

"And Cynthia sends her love."

Micki's eyes blazed. "Does the whole fuckin' universe know I'm here?"

"Just the people who care about you."

She jumped to her feet. "Nobody fuckin' cares about me!"

"That's not true!" And he thrust the bag from the gift shop toward her.

Her eyes narrowed. "What's that?"

"It's—a present." But all at once, his idea seemed incredibly stupid, and he wished he could take it back. He awkwardly lowered his arm. "I just thought it was cute, and you might, y'know, like it." He tried to smile, but succeeded only halfway. Then, eyebrows raised, he pulled the bunny out and held it up.

"That's a fuckin' toy!" she said. "That's for little kids!"

"Not just for little kids—Cynthia has a stuffed animal, a little teddy bear."

"Fine. Give it t'me."

He handed it over. Very slowly.

With a vicious twist, she ripped off one of the big, floppy ears.

Baker cringed.

"Thanks," she said. "I feel so much better now."

But he'd seen the flicker of hurt in her eyes. Heart aching yet again, he could only stand there and blink.

BAKER HAD BARELY SEATED himself in Dr. Lerner's office when he launched into a recap of what had just happened.

Looking somewhat perplexed, she asked, "What made you buy her something like that?"

"I thought maybe she needs to know it's all right to be a kid." And then he told her not only what Mr. Antonelli had said, but what Cynthia's gynecologist had mentioned back in November.

Lerner asked Baker how he knew Micki didn't get her period. When he told her he'd actually discussed the issue with Micki himself, the creases in Lerner's brow deepened. "I'm getting the impression," she said, "that yesterday you presented only one side of the story. I would've thought there was nothing positive at all in your relationship with her."

"I figured you just needed to know the bad stuff."

"Everything is important. I need to understand all the different aspects of how the two of you interact—the good as well as the bad." Eyes softer, she said, "For today, why don't you tell me about some of the good things."

So Baker described moments when he'd bonded with Micki in one way or another, amazed by how many there were. But then he paused. Massaging his forehead, he said, "I'm starting to see a pattern."

Lerner nodded. "What kind of a pattern?"

He wondered if he was going to get a headache. He said, "Every time I get close to Micki, I come back with something abusive."

"What do you make of that?"

The first thing that popped into his head was that he resented Micki getting something he'd never had. He puffed away on his cigarette, trying to think of something else to say, then shrugged. "I don't know."

The doctor was silent.

"I don't. I really don't."

Lerner's expression turned shrewd.

Shifting his weight in the seat, Baker said, "But, y'know, even those times when Micki and I are getting close, we're often very—I don't know how to put it—harsh? Confrontational? It's, y'know, not exactly sweetness and light."

"There are at least two reasons for that, but one of them is quite simple: you're not Robert Young, and she's not Shirley Temple."

There was a beat before Baker threw his head back and laughed.

Dr. Lerner smiled, then announced they were going to have to end for the day.

Baker hurriedly extinguished his cigarette and stood up. Then remembered Miss Gutierrez. After he described his predicament, he said, "What am I going to tell her? She hasn't seen me—or Micki—since Micki's first day. By then I'd already made a terrible impression on her. I'm afraid that, because of what's happened, she'll—well, she'll take Micki away from me."

Standing between her chair and Baker, Lerner felt incredibly small. "Why don't we sit down again for a moment," she suggested. And when both were once more seated, she said, "I'm not going to lie and say that's not a possibility—because it is." Watching his face closely, she added, "In fact, someone looking at the bare facts of this case would probably be inclined to do just that. *However*"—and she put a lot of emphasis on that word—"there's much more going on here than what's apparent from a superficial review. And whenever possible, I work as hard as I can to keep a family together."

When he heard her refer to him and Micki as a family, his heart leaped.

"I'd be happy," she continued, "to talk to the social worker—"

"Miss Gutierrez," he said.

"Miss Gutierrez," Lerner repeated, "and discuss my current assessment and expectations given what I've observed. I know how understaffed and overwhelmed these caseworkers are. I doubt she'll object to letting me formulate a recommendation based on how I see things progressing over the next few weeks."

His shoulders relaxed. "That'd be great."

"Let me ask you something, though," the doctor said. "What would you do if I later told you I'd determined Micki would be better off with someone else?"

It felt like all of the air had disappeared from the room. Voice strangled by the painful lump in his throat, he replied, "I guess I'd have to accept your decision. The last thing I'd want to do is cause the kid more pain. But I'll do anything—*anything*—to become a better"—he paused and glanced down, his neck getting hot—"parent-type person for her. I mean, that's the only reason I'm here. For almost a year, now, the department's been trying to get me to talk to their shrink, but I haven't said more than two words to that asshole." Baker's face reddened. "But I don't think you're—y'know—I mean, he really is." Lerner nodded, and he caught the amusement in her eyes.

She got up from her chair. "Let's see how things progress, okay? Why don't you give me Miss Gutierrez's phone number, and I'll let you know what I arrange with her."

Baker rose and shook her hand. "Thanks, Doc."

WHEN HE FOUND THE door to Micki's apartment unlocked, the hair on the back of his neck stood up. He was sure he'd locked it behind him when he'd left—he always did. He went inside and flipped on the light to find the place in shambles, the smell of stale urine and spoiled food assaulting his nose. But worst of all were the two black swastikas spray-painted on the wall above her bed—or rather, what was left of it. Baker's eyes grew dark. He turned around and marched outside to call it in to the one-o-eight.

As SOON AS THE apartment had been processed and the investigators were gone, Baker contacted an emergency locksmith service and began the cleanup process, which, from the looks of it, was going to take a lot of time. The floor was littered with bits of glass and broken china along with spilled soda and leftovers taken from the refrigerator. The chairs, table, and desk were essentially dismembered; the bureau and desk drawers, smashed into firewood. Reeking of urine, the bedding and mattress sported huge gashes while the pillows had been ripped into shreds. Her money was gone; the bankbooks, destroyed. And, scattered all over the room, as if they'd exploded out of her loose-leaf binder, were pages of notes and homework. Amazingly, the majority weren't too badly damaged, just rumpled or stained. He picked up a pair of her underpants, now torn and covered in ketchup. Her only other bra had been cut in two.

It was nearly an hour before the locksmith arrived. By then, Baker had managed to get the mattress, box spring, and smaller pieces of broken furniture down to the curb. Maybe tomorrow, Gould or Warner would help him remove the bureau and desk.

"Whoa," the man from AAA LICNY Locksmiths said as he walked through the door.

While he continued to pick several loose-leaf sheets out of the mess, Baker said, "Yeah, well, I need this place secured so this doesn't happen again. I want a high-quality deadbolt, and I want to replace the cylinder that's already on the door. I also want the fire escape window to be measured for a gate. How long will that take to get in?"

"Two to three weeks."

"I need it in two."

"I'll see what I can do. You realize I'm gonna need cash for the locks, but I can take a check as a deposit for the gate."

Baker looked inside his wallet. He'd gone to the bank during his lunch break, but this would pretty much wipe him out. "That's fine," he said. "In the meantime, I want that window nailed shut. I'll come back tomorrow with some two-by-fours to board it up until the gate is ready."

"I can't—"

"Just let me borrow your hammer, and I'll do it myself."

The locksmith shrugged. "Sure."

WHEN HE GOT HOME, Baker took the clothes he'd managed to salvage from Micki's place and headed down to the laundry room. Then he dozed off in the recliner, setting his travel clock to wake him when the washer, and then the dryer, were done. Afterward, he stripped down to his Jockey shorts and fell into bed without even brushing his teeth.

IT WAS NEARLY MIDNIGHT, and Micki could hear the staff preparing to change shifts. After refusing to eat anything all day, she was sitting up in bed, listening to her stomach and thinking about what might happen if she fell asleep. She feared the psycho patients as much as she feared the staff. Maybe more. Heyden was hellish, but this place was totally creepy. Not knowing which was worse, she had no reason to cooperate. They were probably going to ship her back to juvi just as soon as they decided she was okay.

She gritted her teeth. Old Man Andrews was starting to shriek again. The bastard probably did this every goddamn night. Well, one thing was for sure: she couldn't stay in this place *too* long, or she really would go crazy.

WHEN MICKI AGREED TO see Dr. Lerner the following morning, the orderly looked mildly surprised. But as soon as he left, she lay down on the doctor's couch and promptly fell asleep for a fifty-minute nap.

"I'M NOT LEAVING UNTIL I see her," Baker said. He was standing on the edge of the common area with one of the nurses, who was reminding him that hospital staff couldn't force a patient to see a visitor—and visitors were only allowed in the dayroom.

"Tell Micki," he said, "that if she wants this stuff, she's going to have to see me to get it." In addition to bringing her some of her own clothes, he'd stopped by Macy's on his way over so he could buy her new underwear. Feeling completely ridiculous, he'd lumbered around among the racks of frilly undergarments until he'd eventually given in and asked a salesgirl for help. At least he'd had the presence of mind to note sizes before throwing away the vandalized items. When he told the clerk to show him something black, she promptly produced some lacy lingerie, and his face grew hot.

"It's for a kid—a teenager," he said. "She's too young to be wearing something like that."

"Oh, this is for your daughter," the salesgirl had said.

To which he'd simply answered, "Yes."

But now that Micki was refusing to see him, he'd use what little leverage he had. "Tell her," he said to the nurse, "that I'm sure she'd like to wear something other than green hospital scrubs."

Micki—looking thinner, dark circles under her eyes—finally emerged.

"Aren't you eating?" he asked.

"They said you brought some stuff for me."

Indicating an empty table in the middle of the room, he said, "Why don't we sit down over there and talk awhile."

"I've got nothin' t'say t'you."

"Please, Micki—"

"*I fuckin' hate you,*" she shouted. "*Why is that so fuckin' hard f'y't'understand?*"

He thrust the bag toward her.

She snatched it from his hand and shuffled away.

He turned and headed toward Dr. Lerner's office, where he could stand alone in the hallway, licking his wounds till it was time for his appointment.

DEBBIE WAS A NINETEEN-YEAR-OLD who'd been admitted because she'd taken a bunch of aspirin in a token suicide attempt. When Micki returned to her room, she found Debbie inside, holding the damaged bunny.

"Gimme that!" Micki said, swiping it away. Then she dropped the bag from Baker and grabbed the girl's arm, swinging her out into the hall.

"Ow! You're hurting me!" Debbie cried.

"Stay the fuck outta my room an' keep y'fuckin' hands offa my stuff." And while Micki put the bunny back in its bag, Debbie went to rat Micki out to the nurses.

SUDDENLY MUCH TOO WARM in his black turtleneck, Baker decided not to mention Micki's outburst to Dr. Lerner. But since that was all he could think about, he had nothing left to say. He pulled out his cigarettes and lit one, asking, "So—so do I have to talk about my childhood and all that kind of stuff?"

"We *should* talk about that at some point, but it doesn't have to be now."

"Yeah. Well, might as well be now, right?" He tugged at the knit collar of his shirt as if to stretch it out. "Um—I don't know where to start."

"Just tell me what it was like for you growing up. What was your family like? Were you happy?"

"Not exactly—no. No, I wasn't happy." He took a drag on the cigarette, then began to paint a picture of a sad little boy who grew up in a cold, unloving home. His father, while dreaming of being an inventor, had traveled constantly, selling some sort of health tonic he claimed had been blessed by the pope—a complete lie. Marginally successful as the latter, an utter failure as the former, he had to listen to his wife—Baker's mother—forever harp on his inadequacies and his inability to maintain her in the kind of lifestyle she felt entitled to.

Neither parent had any genuine capacity for empathy or compassion, leaving Baker bereft of even a shred of emotional comfort or support. His mother, in particular, trivialized everything, from his disappointments to his illnesses and injuries—unless, in one way or another, it brought *her* some attention. If he was depressed or upset, she'd say, "You have to pick yourself up by your bootstraps!" or "That's the way life is; don't make such a big deal out of it!" If he was sick, she'd tell him some other little boy was much sicker than he was. And if he complained, she'd say *her* life had been much worse when *she'd* been a little girl, eyes readily filling with tears for herself. In fact, every little problem in her life was a full-blown crisis, full of melodrama and self-pity. He, on the other hand, was harshly reprimanded or punished for any show of emotion, his mother always succeeding in spoiling what few moments of happiness he could have had.

Though they were, by income, on the upper edge of the lower class, the family somehow managed to live in a modest house in a middleclass neighborhood. As a child, he didn't know enough to question how that was possible. And though his parents drilled it into his head that money was tight, he noticed that his mother got things like a new mink stole or a new diamond ring, got her hair done every week, and had a cleaning lady to take care of the home—and him. Naomi was a large black woman with the patience to deal with Baker's mother and a genuine affection and tenderness to care for the little boy. Dr. Lerner came to see that Naomi was responsible for partially ameliorating the negative psychological impact of Baker's parents. She was, in many ways, Baker's mother. But before he'd reached his teens, Naomi had returned to her family and her deeply religious roots in the South, and had purposely, it seemed, lost contact with Mrs. Baker. When he was older, Baker came to comprehend just how much he owed Naomi, and how much he loved her. He tracked her down, only to find she'd passed away years before from a heart condition.

"Did Mrs. Cole," Dr. Lerner inquired, interrupting him, "remind you of Naomi? Is that why you became so enraged by Daryl's comments?"

A look of astonishment swept over Baker's face. "Probably. I never realized that before."

"And perhaps you felt guilty that you couldn't protect her from her son."

Baker's voice grew tight. "I feel like I can't protect *anyone*. Even when I know someone's no good, I've got to wait until they hurt someone—even kill someone— before I can go after them and get them off the streets. And then, before you know it, they're right back out."

"So you feel like your work is pointless."

"A lot of the time, yeah. And what makes it worse is that people hate cops— they *hate* cops. They hate *you*. All they have to do is see the uniform or the badge. They don't even know you, but they hate your guts. You go to answer a call and people are throwing things at you from windows or roofs: bottles, garbage, even empty refrigerators. Sometimes all it is, is a setup—they ambush you. And still you're trying to protect them. You'd think they'd at least have some respect for the job. You put your life on the line, and for what?" He inhaled from the cigarette, then slowly exhaled and lowered his voice. "It's all a fucking waste; it's all for nothing. The whole justice system is like one goddamn revolving door."

"You do your best," Lerner offered.

"So what the fuck is that worth?"

"What would it be like if there were no cops at all?"

Baker grunted, then stubbed out his cigarette. Seconds later he lit another and went back to his narration:

There had been almost no displays of affection between his parents, and what little he'd seen had appeared artificial and contrived, leaving him—even as a small child—uncomfortable. He himself was rarely the recipient of any tokens of endearment, frequently hit and almost never hugged by his mother. And he didn't know which of those was worse—stiff and smothering, her hugs were more for show than anything else. The inherent insincerity made him want to break free and run away—though he never did. Unfortunately, his father was no better, never taking much interest in his son, always anxious to be back on the road, conning strangers. But to Baker, his father was a stranger. Their interactions were awkward and self-conscious. Baker had carried on more significant conversations with people he'd barely met.

When he was twelve, his father left at his mother's request. But because his father professed to be a practicing Catholic, his parents never divorced. Baker was aware, however, that his father had had affairs while on the road and would, no doubt, have girlfriends once he had his own apartment. This hypocrisy left Baker angry and ashamed. But from that point on, whether he wanted to or not, he saw his father once a week for an obligatory dinner and a night of two-handed blackjack or poker. It was probably more time than he'd ever spent with his father. But just as empty.

He continued to live with his mother, who, several years prior to the separation, had returned to work as a legal secretary. Because of her schedule, he got used to coming home to an empty house and taking care of himself—even when he was sick. He made his own breakfast and lunch, and often cooked dinner—though he almost always ate alone. He cleaned, did laundry, went grocery shopping, and also did things his father had previously taken care of, such as taking out the garbage and draining the boiler. But the task he hated most was going to the bank every week to cash his father's support checks. He was the only child in the neighborhood from a broken home. And while his mother treated him more like a servant than a child—even interrupting his homework to make him come upstairs to change the channel on the TV—she never stopped telling him what a burden he was, even going so far as to scream at the top of her lungs that he'd ruined her life, making him wonder if his birth had been an "accident."

The one bright spot in his young life was school. An overachiever, he received from his teachers the praise and attention he craved, even as his mother continued to find fault with everything he did. Despite—or because of—his academic accomplishments, she repeatedly called him stupid. And when he made the track team, she could only snipe that his brains were in his feet. The better he did, the more contempt she had. He took to forging her name on his report cards just so he wouldn't have to show them to her anymore. She never even noticed.

"She slept a lot, too," Baker said. "Every day she'd come home from work, have her Chivas on the rocks, and lie down. Almost any time I ever talked to her—no matter how important the issue—she was lying down, half asleep. It was like I was annoying her just by existing."

"It sounds like your mother was depressed," Lerner said.

"So what! So was I! She had a kid! A responsibility! She always acts—to this day—like she was the sacrificing mother. But ultimately, when you get right down to it, she was simply doing what was best for *her*, or whatever was needed to keep up appearances. I don't think she ever wanted a kid. She always put herself first. What really gets me is that she honestly believes she was a good mother. Jesus! I was more like *her* mother."

"Do you still keep in touch?"

"Barely. She's still denigrating everything I do, so why would I want to talk to her? When I was going to law school, all I heard from her was how low-class lawyers are and that, these days, anybody can become a lawyer. So now that I'm a cop, she looks down on me because it's blue collar. I think it embarrasses her: it's not 'sophisticated' enough for her. She's always got her nose up in the air. She keeps asking me when I'm going to get a *real* job."

Flicking ashes from his cigarette, he shook his head. "She's cold—cruel. Whenever I've made the mistake of seeking some comfort from her, she's just thrown it back in my face and twisted the knife in deeper."

"Like? Can you give me an example?"

"Like a few years after I joined the force, when we were on the phone and I was extremely stressed out. She asked me what was wrong, and I told her how depressing it is to see people throwing their lives away, doing sick things to each other. I told her how, just that day, I'd found a dead baby in a dumpster. I told her how I couldn't get it out of my head. Such a tiny thing—a newborn—still covered in blood, lying on top of a bunch of chicken bones. I kept seeing its little face practically buried beneath the flies and the bugs…and the stench. My mother's response was, '*You* wanted to be a cop! *You* picked it!' That was it: no empathy, no sympathy, no…no nothing. I fucking hate her most of the time. I don't even talk to her much anymore—stopped trying to have real conversations with her ages ago."

"And what was it that made you stop?"

"I finally realized she was never going to change."

"Yes!" Lerner said. "Yes, that's very good! People don't change unless they want to, and then they have to be willing to work hard in order to make it happen. Even if we know that intellectually, we often don't get it emotionally. We keep repeating the same things over and over with the same people—or people just like them—getting surprisingly angry when we get the same results." She cocked her head. "Maybe in some ways Micki's lucky."

"What? What do you mean?"

"She has you, and you're here."

Baker grunted.

Half a minute went by.

"So what about your father?" Lerner asked.

"He died when I was twenty-five." Baker took a hit from his cigarette, then tossed off a painful smile as he exhaled. "Y'know, I guess it's pretty obvious that I've repeated with Micki a lot of the things that were done to me; although"—he glanced away, his expression somber when he looked back—"I stopped, or started to stop, some of them already. On the other hand, physically I've been way ahead of my mother."

"You mentioned your mother hit you."

"Yeah. A lot. I was small for my age until high school, which was when I started building up my muscles. Came a time she hit me and I just laughed. After that, she was too scared." He shrugged. "Still, the worst she ever did was use a hairbrush on me, though she used to threaten all kinds of shit like: 'I'll bash your head against the wall,' or 'I'll knock your teeth out.' And when I was little I used to believe she'd actually do it. She was so enraged. I'd imagine what it would be like to have my brains splattered across the wall and my skull caved in. I'd think about how much she had to hate me." He shifted in his seat and snorted. "Listen to me going on like this. I mean, what's the big deal since she never really did those things, right?"

"So you think only severe physical abuse is harmful."

"I don't know—well, yeah."

"Then emotional and psychological abuse—or neglect—don't count?"

Baker looked uncertain.

"How much have you physically abused Micki?" she asked.

His eyes flashed. "A lot. You know that already."

"And that time when you, as you put it yourself, 'beat the shit out of her' because you thought she'd molested another student—did she try to kill herself then?"

"No."

"And this time, when she actually did attempt suicide, how much did you hit her?"

Muscles taught, he said, "I didn't! I didn't touch her at all!"

"So which do you think hurt her the most: your fists or your words?"

Baker clenched his jaw, but was soon forcing back tears. He tried to continue smoking, then gave up and blurted out, "Micki hates me."

"She's very angry."

"Yeah, but she hates me, really hates me now. She screamed it at me."

Lerner's face looked back with compassion. "If you didn't mean so much to her," she said, "she wouldn't be so angry."

GOULD STOPPED BY MICKI's apartment to help Baker board up the windows and clear out the larger pieces of broken furniture. They went to the deli to pick up a six-pack, and Frankie asked after Micki since he hadn't seen her for several days. Back at the apartment, once they'd been working again for a while, Gould noticed he was the only one drinking.

"I wonder if those assholes got in here with a key," Baker said.

"Who would Micki give a key to?"

"No one. But when I arrived, the windows were all locked, and the door hadn't been picked or forced in any way. I'm just not buying that they climbed in through the fire escape. I asked the guys working the case to check with the super—find out who has access to his keys."

"What about prints?"

"They only lifted a few usable ones out of the entire mess. Except for one, they were all Micki's—or mine."

"And the one?"

"Rick's, which, since he'd been in her apartment before, leaves us nowhere. When they brought him in for questioning, he denied everything, sat there smirking the whole time."

"Did they lean on him?"

"His father's attorney was there. But, man, how I'd love to get my hands on that little prick."

"Do yourself a favor—"

"I'm not going after him," Baker interrupted. "Not now, anyway."

Gould shot him a look, but said nothing, the black swastikas staring at him from the wall.

BAKER DIDN'T EVEN BOTHER having dinner that night, though he stopped by the liquor cabinet several times just to stare at it. It would've been easier to simply throw all the bottles away, but then the next time he hosted the poker game, he wouldn't have any liquor in his apartment—and his friends would all know…

Fingers tapping on the armrest of the chair, he chain-smoked and stared at the TV. But the cheesy canned laugh tracks were only irritating, the commercials even worse. He shut the set off and picked up his pack of Camels, the last of three he'd bought that day. He had all of two cigarettes left. Two. Christ, this was a bitch. He put on several layers of clothes and went out jogging in the frigid night air.

IT WAS DARK IN the Quiet Room, as they called it. Micki strained her ears to catch the slightest sound lest someone be returning—not that she could do anything if they did. Unlike her previous episode, they hadn't put her back in her room all shot up with tranquilizers. Instead, they'd stuck her here, strapped to the bed in unforgiving all-points restraints—completely defenseless. She could be raped—or maybe just tortured, like what she'd heard about at Heyden over Thanksgiving. Apparently, the latest thing was tying a girl down to an infirmary bed, then injecting the muscles of her arms and legs with some kind of drug that made them cramp up tight, causing unbearable pain that lasted for hours—but left no trace.

Time dragged on, and she stared at the ceiling…the walls…her toes… She forced herself to stay awake, cursing Baker for not letting her die. Life was nothing but hell. Tears welled up, but she forced them back: after all, who was she crying for? She was worthless. Just like Baker had said.

She wondered if you could simply will your heart to stop beating.

Chapter 28

COLD AND GREY WITH a light snowfall, Saturday dawned. Baker rose early, did laundry, then drove to Queens. First stop: the hardware store.

ALMOST LATE FOR HIS appointment, Baker was hurrying through the psych ward. Under his black leather jacket, he wore a blue work shirt and a very old pair of Levi's—both generously speckled with beige paint. He'd also brought a bag with something to give to Micki, but when he passed by the dayroom, he noticed she wasn't there.

He reached Lerner's office, flopped down, and immediately dove into a detailed description of Micki's vandalized apartment. When he was finished, he pulled out a pack of Camels and drew the ashtray toward him, saying, "I don't think it would be such a good idea to tell her what happened just yet."

Lerner nodded.

"Has Micki seen you?" he asked.

"Not really, no."

"What happens if she won't talk to you?"

"It's a little too early to be worrying about that."

Baker lit a cigarette and fell silent. And though merely smoking, he exuded an overtly intimidating aggression the doctor hadn't seen before.

"How's the alcohol withdrawal going?" she asked quietly.

He shrugged. "It's worse at night. And the weekend was tough. But I'm holding up okay."

"What do you do when it gets difficult?"

"I usually work out at the gym or go for a jog."

"What about your friends?"

"What about them?"

"Do you call them?"

"For what?"

"For support."

Exhaling smoke through his nose, he snorted. "There's no reason for me to bother my friends."

"It might make it easier for you when you're feeling shaky."

"I can handle this myself."

"Perhaps. But I think *alcohol* was your friend—the one you could always turn to, the one you could always count on. And now that friend is gone."

Baker closed his eyes.

"What are you feeling now?"

He opened his eyes. "I'm not feeling anything, okay?" And he turned his gaze to the window.

After a lengthy silence, Lerner asked, "Did your father drink?"

"Not really."

"But you mentioned your mother drinks."

"Yeah, but when I was a kid, she drank even more. Didn't get noticeably drunk or anything, but every day she'd have a few drinks—large drinks—and either be meaner or lie down for a while. Like I said, she slept a lot."

"Do *you* think she was depressed?"

"Yeah, I suppose. Her life didn't exactly turn out the way she expected. But she took it out on me like it was my fault." He inhaled from his cigarette. "I feel sorry for her sometimes. In some ways, she's kind of pathetic. But it doesn't make what she did all right."

"No, it doesn't. But by understanding her, she isn't evil, just a severely flawed human being who made mistakes—most likely the product of her *own* childhood."

"She's a selfish, self-centered bitch. She acts like the whole fucking world revolves around her. She thinks she should be waited on hand and foot. She made me feel guilty for every penny she ever spent on me, every minute of her time that I took—like I owed her for it. Everything she did for me made her a martyr in her eyes; that's why I tried to do everything for myself. And still I worked so hard to win her approval—to make her love me. When I was very little, I was disgustingly good, but it was only because I didn't feel loved by either one of my parents. I was afraid that if I didn't do everything perfectly, my mother would just get rid of me."

"Did you really think she'd throw you out in the street?"

"It seems outrageous now, but, back then, I believed it. Jesus, all I wanted was a little love from her—real love—but I didn't get shit."

"You're very angry at her."

"So tell me something I don't know!"

Almost an entire minute passed.

Lerner asked, "How would you describe your current relationships with women?"

"Okay, I suppose. What do you mean?"

"How long do they usually last? Do you fall in love easily?"

"Do we really have to talk about this?"

"Why don't you want to talk about this?"

"What does this have to do with Micki?"

Lerner tilted her head. "Do you understand what your therapy is about?"

He leaned back, crossed his left ankle over his right knee, and took a long drag on his cigarette. "To make me a better guardian for Micki."

"That's true, but I see that as a natural outcome of the process as a whole. The problems you have with Micki aren't the result of poor parenting skills, per se; they're a symptom of larger issues that need to be resolved. By talking about things, you can gain insight into the patterns of your behavior and what's caused them. That, in turn, will eventually lead to change."

Baker tapped his cigarette against the ashtray. "How long is this going to take?"

Lerner tried not to smile. "Why, are you in a rush?"

"I don't want to lose Micki while I'm working on getting my head straightened out."

"The most important thing to me is that there's progress being made. Before all of this happened, you'd actually made some progress on your own; it just wasn't enough."

"I—" Baker sat up a little straighter. "Oh."

"And if it makes you feel more comfortable," the doctor continued, "I can also tell you that I'm very impressed with the work you've done here so far."

"Really?"

"Yes, really."

Baker's smile was almost shy. "I'm going to be at the hospital every day, so I can see you as often as you want."

Lerner pulled out her appointment book. "I think twice a week is enough for now. Let's see what we can arrange."

"WOULD YOU TELL MICKI I'm here?" Baker asked. The diminutive woman he was talking to looked so young he'd first thought she was only a candy-striper. Staring down at her white cap—which looked like a giant, upside-down cupcake liner—he still wasn't convinced she was a real nurse.

"She's not in any condition to receive visitors right now," she said.

His body tensed. "What the hell does that mean?"

"She's resting."

"Resting from what? She doesn't do anything here all day except rest."

"I'm sure tomorrow—"

"I want to see her now."

"Tomorrow—"

"*I want to see her NOW.*"

"Visitors are only allowed in the dayroom and—"

"Call Dr. Lerner and get her permission for me."

"I can't—"

"Fine! Then I'll go back to her office myself and—"

"Okay, okay." The young woman's face started to pucker. "I'll call her, okay? Y'know, this is my first day here."

After a brief exchange between the nurse and the doctor, one of the regular staff members escorted Baker to Micki's room. Lying on her side, she was clutching the paper bag with the bunny in it. And though her eyes were open, they didn't even blink to acknowledge Baker's entrance.

He walked over and, without thinking, gently stroked her hair. "Hey, Micki, how's it going?"

She didn't answer. But she didn't recoil, either.

He looked at the nurse. "Is she sedated?"

"No. Following the last time we did that, Dr. Lerner was very specific that she not be given any meds."

Baker dropped the bag he'd brought, pulled up a chair, and sat next to the bed. "So why is she like this?"

"She hurt another patient—"

"Badly?"

"No, it was more threatening than anything else. But when she was confronted by the staff, she became verbally, and then physically, combative. Since we couldn't medicate her, it took three orderlies to get her under control."

When Baker couldn't completely suppress his grin, the nurse glowered at him. She added, "She was kept in restraints overnight, then released this morning. She's been like this all day."

Lightly touching Micki's face, he asked, "Are you aware I'm here, Micki?"

"Uh-huh."

"And you know it's me? Sergeant Baker?"

"Uh-huh."

He stroked her hair again, and her eyes fluttered. "It's all right," he said, his voice soothing. "Close your eyes and sleep. I'm going to stay here awhile. I promise to wake you up before I go."

Almost immediately, she drifted off. But he continued to smooth back her hair. Next time she said she hated him, it probably wouldn't hurt quite so much.

BAKER HAD JUST ENTERED his apartment and was hanging up his jacket when the phone rang. "Oh, Jesus!" he said out loud. "What is it *now*?" Then he picked up the receiver. "Hello?"

"Jim?"

"Hi, Cyn. Everything all right?"

"Well, yes. Why do you ask?"

"Because everything around me is going to hell."

"Oh…um… How's Micki?"

"She's not adapting too well to the hospital."

"Gee, I'm really sorry to hear that. It must be horrible in there. What does she do all day?"

"As far as I can tell? Not much."

"Well, I'm calling because I bought a book for her and was hoping you wouldn't mind bringing it with you the next time you go. I'll leave it with my doorman—that way you can pick it up whenever you want."

So it was too much trouble for her to see him for the five fucking minutes it would take to give him the goddamn book. "That's fine," he said.

"I thought about going over there to give it to her myself, but"—she took a deep breath—"but I just can't. I don't think I could deal with it."

He lit a cigarette and his voice relaxed. "It's okay, Cyn. Really. I understand. I'm sure it'll mean a lot to her just to know you've been thinking about her." When Cynthia didn't respond right away, he knew she was trying not to cry. He added, "Don't worry about it." He thought he heard the sound of a tissue being pulled from a box. "Are you okay?" he asked.

"Yes," she finally answered. "Yes, I'm fine. How are you?"

"I'm hanging in there. Look, I've got something in the oven, and I think it's burning."

"Oh! Well, I'd better let you go, then. I'll bring the book downstairs now in case you want to pick it up later."

What Baker wanted was a drink. He finished his cigarette, changed his clothes, and went out for another late-night run.

SITTING IN HIS RECLINER with a cup of coffee, Baker flipped back and forth through the pages of *Songs from the Journey*, the book Cynthia had bought for Micki. When she'd mentioned the volume several months ago, it had sounded like just another one of those spiritual mumbo-jumbo things, so he'd acted disinterested. As he examined it now, however, he noticed each "chapter" was actually a poem written like song lyrics. There were verses, choruses, and sometimes a bridge. He picked one at random and began to read. And then a chill raced up his spine:

> At this lonely stretch of sky
> Grey with clouds that hide the sun
> I face the one that I've become
>
> As I drift along the sea

With the birds that fly above
They call your love back home to me

I know now I'll never be
All the things I hoped to be
Wish that I could have more time
But time grows short, you'll never know
Like fired guns, the river runs

Through the forest green with leaves
Barren branches lie in wait
For chilling breeze of winter's sleep

And this path that points the way
Through life and death, I cannot choose
It calls my name, I'm not to blame

I know now I'll never be
All the things you are to me
Wish that I could have more time
But time grows short, you'll never know
Like fired guns, the river runs...

Sunday. Standing up as he approached, Micki eyed Baker's beige-speckled clothes with venomous curiosity.

He gave her a crooked smile. "I'm a mess, huh?"

In return he got a cold, empty glare. Then she held out the bag he'd left the day before.

"They don't fit?" he asked. "I bought the same size as the pair you have on now."

"I don't wannem."

"But they're black. And they cut off your only black jeans in the ER."

"I can't afford to buy anything."

"You don't have to pay me for them—"

"*I don't wannem.*"

He breathed in. "Well I can't return them 'cause I already cut off all the tags. So you might as well keep them."

She tossed the bag onto the table and looked away.

He put *Songs from the Journey* and his copy of *The Foundation Trilogy* down. With a tap of his finger on the paperback, he said, "I figured you might want to finish this. And this other book"—he pointed—"is from Cynthia."

Eyes out of focus, she was staring into space.

"By the way"—he tried to move into her line of sight, but she turned her whole body to avoid him—"did I tell you Frankie says hello?"

She shoved her hands in her pockets and shifted her weight to the other leg.

Baker sighed. "Why won't you talk to Dr. Lerner, Micki? She's very nice."

She looked at him. "Are *you* talkin' to her?"

"Yeah."

"About *me*?"

"Sometimes, but also about me."

Jaw tight, she crossed over to the large windows with their thick wire mesh, then folded her arms over her chest.

"So what've you been doing to keep busy?" Baker asked.

But the only thing he heard in response was the television that was mounted on the wall in the far right corner. It was perpetually on, the volume turned down low.

"See anything good on TV?" he asked.

He could hear the phone ringing at the nurses' station.

"Do you want me to tell Frankie or Cynthia anything?" Baker pressed.

But Micki wouldn't talk to him anymore, not a single word no matter what he said or did.

He walked up behind her and leaned over, his face right next to hers. "What is this, huh? You're never going to speak to me again?"

Lips pressed together tightly, she shrugged. But her eyes looked sad.

He straightened up. "You let me know if you need anything, okay?"

A Dr. Manwani was being paged to the ER.

Voice full of sarcasm, he added, "You can even write it on a piece of paper so you don't have to actually say anything to me."

Her head whipped around, and their eyes locked—but only for a second.

Then she turned to look out the window again.

SINCE THE HOSPITAL WAS overheated, Baker had brought Micki her black sleeveless T-shirts. When she entered the psychiatrist's office Monday morning, she was wearing one of them with her new black jeans. She walked over to the window, and gazed outside. It looked bitterly cold. She glanced back over her shoulder.

Dr. Lerner smiled and went to close the door.

Micki turned toward the doctor. "You're seeing Sergeant Baker, too?" she asked.

"Yes."

"What's he sayin' about me?"

"I can't tell you that without his permission, just as I can't tell him what *you* say unless you agree to let me. Why don't you sit down." About to take her own seat, she hastened to add, "But not on the couch. I won't let you use your therapy sessions for naps."

"Why should I sit down? I don't wanna talk t'you."

"Then you're free to leave."

After a beat, Micki shot back, "I'm tired a shrinks askin' me all kindsa questions like they're tryin' t' help me when they're just curious f'themselves."

"But I really do want to help you."

"No y'don't. This is just y'job. Y'get paid f'this, don'tcha?"

"I have to be able to pay my rent, Micki, but I earn my living as a psychiatrist because I genuinely want to help people."

"Yeah? Y'wanna help me? So prove it."

Lerner raised an eyebrow.

"I need t'sew somethin' but they're afraid t'let me have a fuckin' needle." Through a small tear in the paper bag she was clutching, a bit of white fur showed.

"You'd have to do the sewing in here, then," Lerner said.

Micki lifted the bag.

"Let me look in my purse," Lerner said. "I usually have one of those miniature sewing kits with me." The doctor rummaged through her pocketbook and produced what appeared to be an oversized matchbook. She handed it over.

Micki opened the cover. Inside were different colored threads wound around a piece of cardboard that had two needles stuck through a tiny piece of gold foil. "Thanks," she said. Eyes gleaming, she added, "But I'm gonna need a pair a scissors, too."

If Lerner had had nothing to go on but her own gut instincts, she would've denied Micki the scissors while explaining that she needed more time to get to know her. The teen's muscular arms; scarred face; and tough, angry demeanor left the doctor uneasy, especially knowing how violent she could be. Yet Baker had presented Micki in a very different light. Of course, given his size and strength, he had a great deal less to fear. Lerner stared savvily at her patient, then went behind her desk and retrieved a pair of scissors. She proceeded to hand them over as if she were bestowing the key to the city.

Micki looked impressed. She sat down, threaded the needle, and began sewing, trying to leave the plush animal in the bag as much as possible. With deft, tiny stitches, she worked at a quick and even pace.

"You sew very well," Lerner observed. "Where did you learn that?"

Eyes on her work, Micki shrugged. "Who the hell knows. I have amnesia except for the last eight months or so. But I'm sure you already know that. And no," she added, "I have not remembered anything."

Lerner noted the marked change in Micki's speech, but said only, "That must be very hard for you. How does that make you feel?"

Shrugging again, Micki continued sewing. Completely absorbed in the task, it wasn't long till she was finished.

"That's the bunny Sergeant Baker gave you, isn't it," Lerner said.

Since it didn't matter anymore, Micki removed it from the bag. Full of innocence, its cute features stared back. Her own face turned sad.

"Do you want me to help you?" Lerner asked softly.

Micki started to cry.

IN HER NEXT SESSION, Micki recounted what her life had been like in the South Bronx. When she was done, she said, "Everything I did then was bad. Everything. I did terrible things."

"You were trying to survive with no family and no memory—afraid to trust anyone," Dr. Lerner said. "That doesn't make what you did all right, but at least, from what you've told me, you never seriously hurt anyone."

"I killed Speed, didn't I?"

"It sounds to me like you were more than justified. You were trying to save your own life."

"But what he said was true: Tim died because of me."

"And just how do you figure that?"

"If Tim hadn't gone back to get me, he would still be alive. So it's *my* fault—*my* fault he's dead."

"So you feel guilty. You feel responsible."

"Yes."

"You also seem very determined to convince me of what a bad person you are."

"I'm just telling it like it is."

"But people make their own choices, Micki. It was *Tim's* decision to try to protect you. He must've cared about you very much. Perhaps you should consider what that means."

After a few seconds, voice childlike, Micki asked, "What does it mean?"

"It means he thought you were worth risking his life for; that's very impressive. Perhaps you owe it to him to do something meaningful with yours."

"Well, my real family couldn't have thought very much of me; they abandoned me, didn't they? In all this time, no one's come looking for me. What does *that* mean?"

"There's no way to know since we have no idea what happened to you *or* your family. What's interesting, though, is that you blame yourself for everything—whether you deserve to or not. I feel like you've condemned yourself."

"'Cause I hate myself; I'm just a junkie and a whore." But Micki gasped.

Lerner studied her new patient. Baker had mentioned Micki's sensitivity to the latter issue—and how he'd cruelly exploited it. "What makes you say you're a whore? You told me you never did that; you said you'd always kept that part of your promise to Tim."

"I—I did. I did keep my promise. I—I don't know why I said that—especially that word. I hate that word; I really hate it."

"What does it mean to you?"

Micki tapped her foot on the floor. "It's just—it's just so full of contempt; it's just, y'know, a put-down, like you're dirt if you're a hooker—like you're not a human being anymore. I've seen the way they're treated, like they don't have brains or feelings or anything. Like they're just things to be used. Nobody cares about them. But—but they *are* real people, and they *do* hurt."

Lerner wanted to go deeper, but the session was nearly over. She said, "We're going to have to stop for today, Micki. But I want you to think about something: you're not forever what you were. Look at your life now: you're a top-notch student; a reliable, hard worker; you're responsible, honest—"

"But I started shooting up again."

"Life is not a straight road. The idea is to constantly be working toward transforming yourself into what you want to be. If we were forever chained to our mistakes, if we could never move beyond our past, life would have little purpose. Anyone, at anytime, is free to change. You just have to find the right path."

BACK IN HER ROOM, Micki finally looked at the book Cynthia had bought for her. She opened it up in the middle and read the page she'd picked:

> Looking out my window, I
> See all the people passing by
> And in my hazy, dreamlike mind
> They seem to fly
> But here inside, the darkness grows
> Until the night can take me home
>
> And so the question in my heart
> Of every path I chose to start
> And all the dreams of all the days
> Along the way
> I fear I've very far to go
> Until the night can take me home
>
> Rose and blue surround a golden dawn
> The sun has drawn this enchanted place
> Silver rain falls softly from the sky
> The moment dies, all is gone without a trace
>
> A dark wind blows across the sky

And I'm abandoned to the night
As through a vast and empty space
The journey waits
Endangered soul, I walk alone
Until the light can take me home...

Chapter 29

"WHAT THE HELL HAPPENED to my loose-leaf?" Micki demanded. "And those aren't my textbooks!" She was pointing to the two replacements.

Baker sighed: the lie he'd prepared was never going to fly. "Someone broke into your apartment, and most of your things were ruined. I asked your teachers for the new books."

"What? But my apartment—" Her face went blank. "Whatever."

"And Greg gave me his notes for you to copy. He says he hopes you get better soon because it's no fun taking tests without you."

"So now the whole fuckin' school knows I'm locked up in a psycho ward?"

"They think you have mono."

"Well isn't that just great." She looked at the pile of school materials. "Why did you bring this shit anyway? What the fuck am I supposed to be studying for?"

"You've got finals coming up."

"Oh, yeah, like I'm not goin' back to juvi as soon as they say I'm not crazy anymore."

"You're not going back there, Micki."

"Yeah, right."

But after a while, when Baker's expression didn't change, she asked, "So how am I gonna take my finals if I'm still in this place?"

BAKER CLOSED THE DOOR. "The kid's not eating anything! She's getting much too thin. Doesn't anybody notice? This is a fucking hospital, for chrissakes; can't you do something?"

"She started her therapy," Dr. Lerner said.

Baker's face brightened. "Really?" He walked across the room and sat down.

"And I'd like your permission to tell her things you say when I consider it appropriate."

He paused. "If it's something I say about her, that's okay. But I don't want you telling her anything about my family or girlfriends—y'know, stuff like that."

Lerner nodded. "That's fine. Tomorrow I'll ask the same of her. This will help move things along until you start having sessions together."

"So what about her not eating?"

"It's quite common for people's eating habits to change when they're severely depressed: they either overeat or under-eat. And from what you've described, not eating seems to be a pattern with her."

He lit a cigarette. "Yeah, that's true. I think I told you how, except for a few rare occasions, she wouldn't eat in front of me."

"Did those occasions have anything in common?"

"Not that I can see."

"You can't find any similarity in those examples?"

Baker shook his head.

"That's interesting," the doctor said.

"What's interesting?"

"I'm sure your deductive powers as a detective are quite impressive, yet this is a blind spot."

With one hand hanging carelessly off the end of its armrest, he leaned his head back against the chair and looked out from under half-closed lids. Then he put the cigarette to his lips. And exhaled the smoke through his nose.

"Let's approach this from another perspective," Lerner said. "Perhaps you could tell me how you think the pattern of her *not* eating in front of you started."

"Probably when she first came to clean my apartment. I yelled at her for eating some bread." His face colored. "Jesus, I was such a dick."

"But why would that stop her from eating her *own* food in front of you?"

Baker shrugged.

"If you provide nourishment to someone, it's a caring—nurturing—thing," Lerner said. "But the incident in your kitchen sent a very different message. And because of your attitude and behavior toward her, Micki took it to the extreme."

He inhaled another lungful of smoke.

"What happens," the doctor queried, "if someone stops eating?"

Grinning while he exhaled, he said, "They lose weight—most women's dream come true."

"But not Micki's," Lerner countered. "She's already too thin."

His grin faded, and he straightened up to tap the cigarette against the ashtray.

"What happens," Lerner asked, "if someone continues not to eat?"

"You mean, for a long time?"

"Yes."

"I guess they'd starve."

The doctor raised an encouraging eyebrow.

"To death," he added.

"Because…" Lerner prompted.

"You need food to sustain life." He looked quizzical at being asked to state something so obvious.

And then the truth hit home.

HE FOLDED CYNTHIA'S SILK dressing gown into a neat rectangle, placed it on the living room chair, then ran his hand over the soft material that had so often draped her body. She'd left a message with his answering service, saying she wanted to pick up whatever items she'd left at his apartment. When he'd called her back, she said she'd stop by at eight.

There weren't all that many things to collect: the dressing gown; a pair of slippers; comb and brush; toothbrush; and a change of clothes, including sneakers. But each one was a reminder of what he'd lost. He lifted the silk robe and pressed it to his face so he could breathe in her scent. When he opened his eyes, they fell upon the malachite sphere sitting on the bookshelf. He went over and picked it up. Closed in his fist, it felt cool and smooth, same as it had the day she'd given it to him. "It helps open up the heart," she'd said. Tears welled up, and he put the stone back before wiping his eyes with the back of his hand. He cried so easily now… A strange, garbled laugh caught in his throat.

The downstairs buzzer rang, and he pressed the button to let her in before going to check himself in the bathroom mirror. His eyes were noticeably red. Running around the apartment, he turned out as many lights as he reasonably could, only to then wonder if she'd think he was trying to set a romantic mood. He sighed.

When she appeared at the door—empty-handed—her manner was cool and overly polite. "How's Micki?" she asked.

"She's fine." And he went to get a shopping bag.

"Did she like the book?"

"I don't know," he said. "She's not really talking to me."

While he was placing her belongings into the bag, Cynthia's eyes wandered around the room until, face flushed, she pointed to the coffee table. "The book's right there! It's unbelievable how you can just lie to me like that!"

Baker's voice was calm. "That's mine, Cyn. I gave Micki the copy you bought and got this one today for myself."

Her jaw dropped.

"I'm not as thick-headed as you might think," he said.

"Oh, god, I'm so sorry. I shouldn't have jumped to conclusions like that."

"Don't worry about it." He handed her the shopping bag. "Do you want some coffee or something?" But even as the words came out of his mouth, his eyes became moist again, and he quickly turned away.

Cynthia, meanwhile, was already declining, saying she had to rush off somewhere; she had a taxi waiting. But when he turned back, he found her studying him.

"It's quite dark in here," she said.

"I...I have a headache."

"Oh. I'm sorry. I—"

"It's nothing, really. So how've you been?"

She shrugged. "I've been better."

"Why? What's wrong?"

Chin thrust forward and slightly raised, she glanced to the side as she put the bag down on the floor. Then she straightened up and looked back. "I broke up with Mark."

"You what? What happened?"

"He asked me to marry him, and I said yes. Then everything changed. He expected me to move to LA with him, give up my career, and start a family—even though he knew I'd decided I *didn't* want to move to LA and had no desire to have children. It was as if my life—my dreams—didn't matter anymore, only his. Nothing was even open to discussion. He's incredibly sexist and self-centered. I guess I never noticed because we were always so busy laughing. He seemed so intent on making me happy when we were still 'courting,' as they say. I should've realized he was only playing a role." Voice bitter, she added, "He's a very good actor."

"I'm sorry."

"Are you?" she retorted.

He angled his head.

She lowered her gaze. "I—I don't know what's gotten into me. That was totally uncalled for." She looked up and tried to laugh. "I'm certainly apologizing a lot tonight."

And as she closed her eyes and fought back tears, Baker's hand started to reach out. But then he swiftly drew it back, saying, "That's okay, I think I've got a few shots coming to me."

When she opened her eyes, she saw a sad but affable grin. She smiled amid the sniffles. "I don't know why I'm telling you all this."

"I'm still here for you, Cyn. I know I really blew it the first time around, but I'd like it if we could stay friends. Would you give me another chance?"

Palm down, she held out her hand. He sandwiched it between his.

For the next two sessions, Micki talked to Dr. Lerner about her drug use. She talked about Rick. Her classes at school. It helped to pass the time.

Toward the end of Thursday's hour, the doctor remarked, "Not once have you mentioned Sergeant Baker."

Eyes fastened on the gap between the floor and the bottom of the door—a thin strip of light disappearing and reappearing as several people walked by—Micki said, "Because I hate him."

"Then perhaps we should discuss finding a different guardian for you."

Micki looked up.

"Well," Lerner continued, "until the state deems you to be eighteen years of age, you'll be required to have one. If Sergeant Baker is so unacceptable, we should work toward finding someone better suited for the job."

"But—but they could end up being worse and—and I wouldn't know till it was too late."

"I see," Lerner replied.

Clamping her mouth shut, Micki looked away.

"So you don't usually go too long between girlfriends."

"I guess not. This is probably the longest for me." Baker picked up his book of matches and tapped it on the table before placing it on top of the pack of Camels.

"Have you dated at all since you broke up with Cynthia?" Lerner asked.

He was holding the lit cigarette between his index and middle fingers. With a flick of his thumb, he deposited some ashes into the ashtray and shifted in his seat. "Not really. I had a one-night stand New Year's Eve, but that's about it."

"Someone you already knew?"

He took a drag and shook his head no. "I met her that night. Quite honestly, I don't even remember having sex with her. I drank so much, I must've blacked out."

"Then how do you know you slept with her?"

"The next morning, I woke up in her bed. And the condom was gone from my wallet."

"You always carry a condom with you?"

"Only when I'm unattached, so to speak."

"And then you carry one all the time?"

"Just if I'm going out and there's a chance I'll—chance I might need it." He shifted in his seat again.

"Did you use a condom with Micki?" Lerner asked.

"Yeah, sure."

"Even though you were so high?"

"It's automatic, an ingrained habit with me. I don't even think about it."

"So the night of the dance, you purposely took a condom with you."

Pretty sharp, Baker thought. "I guess I was thinking that, y'know, I might get it on with someone: a single teacher or a mother who came as a chaperone." He shrugged. "I admit the odds were small, but it was just in case. Better safe than sorry."

"Then you never actually thought about sleeping with Micki before it happened?"

"No."

"Never?"

"No!" Once more, he shifted in his seat. "Well, I guess I can't say never, but it was just, y'know, hypothetical, wondering what it would be like." A bit of color bloomed on each cheek. "Guys do that all the time."

Smile demure, eyebrows arched mockingly, Lerner said, "Really!"

Baker laughed, and his shoulders relaxed. He said, "When it came to stuff like that, I always saw her as a kid; I knew exactly where the line was drawn. I made sure I never touched her in any way that could be construed as sexual, especially when I was searching her. Besides"—a hint of resentment crept into his voice, for he wasn't sure if Lerner believed him—"she's just not my type."

"What about when you danced with her that night?"

He stared blankly at the doctor, aware of the heaviness around his eyes. "I feel very tired," he announced.

"You don't want to talk about this," she said.

He continued to smoke, the light from the window deepening the lines etched in his face. "I felt sorry for her. Just like she'd predicted, she spent the night alone, and no one danced with her. I did feel a little tenderness, I guess, and, I dunno, I suppose there was some sort of sexual—what would you call it—tension? How could there not be? But it was all very chaste, really. If I hadn't gotten high, nothing would've happened." He mashed the cigarette butt into the ashtray. "I hate myself for what I did. I mean, she doesn't trust anyone—do you know that?—but she'd finally begun to trust *me*. And then I went and did that to her." He was still crushing the cigarette, grinding it into the metal dish though it had long since gone out. He said, "It's no wonder she hates men." He looked up. "She's never actually said it, but I think it's pretty obvious."

"She's been badly abused by men. There's a lot of rage inside her."

"The warden at Heyden abused her, too. And she's female."

"My guess is that the abuse she's suffered at the hands of men has been far greater than what she's suffered at the hands of women. And for her, there's a whole other element when it crosses gender."

Baker nodded, lowering his eyes, not knowing why he'd even voiced such a weak argument until, looking up, he said, "But *I'm* male."

"So I've noticed," Lerner said, "though I think Micki has put you into a category all your own."

"Is that good or bad?"

Lerner got up and pulled the shades down most of the way to block the setting sun, which had edged its way in line with the office. "What is it that worries you?" she asked.

He lit another cigarette, eyes wandering around the space while the doctor regained her seat. Bathed in the warmth of the light passing through the ochre-colored fabric, the room—which had heard so many voices, felt the beats of so many hearts—seemed filled with the sadness of all the words left unspoken. He said, "I want her to accept me as—as…" He threw a glance at Lerner, then boldly looked her straight in the eyes. "I want to be a father to Micki."

"I think that remains a possibility," the doctor said.

"Even after I slept with her?"

"Yours is not a typical case. You had a very different relationship with her then. And as terribly wrong as it was, there were a lot of mitigating circumstances surrounding what happened."

Though his mind seemed to be racing in all kinds of directions, he tried to take in what the doctor was saying. But now that there was a crack in the dam, another fear spilled out: "So tell me why she would even *want* a father when, for as far back as she can remember, she's been on her own without one."

A compassionate look in her eye, Lerner replied, "Because for as far back as she can remember, she's been on her own without one."

THE NURSE LET HIM into the locked ward and escorted him to the dayroom. When he'd seen Baker at the poker game last night, he'd been shocked: his friend had lost a noticeable amount of weight, and there had been heavy pouches under his eyes. All of the guys had asked politely after Micki, but when Baker's responses had been thin, no one pushed for details. After all, it was only after they'd applied considerable pressure that he'd agreed to show up at all.

But then Tierney noticed Baker was only drinking club soda, and asked, "You on the wagon?"

"You got a problem with that?" Baker shot back, and, shortly afterward, he'd left.

The younger detective now followed the nurse toward the back of the room. Psych wards gave him the willies, and he clutched at the paper bag in his hand. A skinny old man stepped in front of him, thrusting his face in his, and he jumped.

"Betcha can't see me," the man said, "'cause I'm invisible. Yep!" And he broke into a raucous cackle, providing a perfect view of a totally toothless mouth.

"Mr. Kertz, go sit by the TV and leave the visitor alone," the nurse ordered.

He grinned. "You only know it's me 'cause y'can hear my voice, right?"

"Mr. Kertz!"

Head hung low, the old man loped away.

Drawn out of her reading, Micki looked over to see what was happening. Leaving her book on the table, she stood up, eyes turning dark at the sight of the coffee cop.

"Hi, Micki," Gould said.

Her eyes darkened further.

He held out the paper bag. "I brought you some chocolate." When she didn't take it, he added, "I remember Jim sayin' you like chocolate."

Her stare was deadly.

Gould put the bag on the table and suggested they sit down, reminding her of her meeting with Warner. Instead, she slipped her hands into her pockets.

He swallowed hard. "Okay, look, I'll get right to the point. Jim's not only my partner but my best friend. Alls I wanna know is why you won't talk to him. I mean, it's killin' him. He's not eatin'; he's not sleepin'. Give the guy a break, okay? Just talk to him. He"—Gould caught himself before he divulged something Baker wouldn't have wanted him to—"he's doin' the best he can."

She shifted her weight.

"He deserves better than this from you."

Her eyes sparked, and she took her hands out of her pockets. "*He* deserves better than this? That son of a bitch told me I'm a worthless piece of shit. So fuck him and fuck *you*." With amazing speed, she picked up the bag of candy and hurled it at the cop, who put his arms up to protect his face. While the contents scattered all over the floor, the orderlies descended upon her.

"Okay, kid," one of them said, "you just earned a few hours in the rubber room." Which was what they called the padded cells.

Gould's shoulders sagged as he watched them dragging her away. Thinking only of Baker, he'd committed the cardinal sin and jumped in with only half the story.

And now he'd have to tell his partner what he'd done.

WHEN THEY CAME TO take her to her session, Micki was on the floor in a corner, staring vacantly, streaks running across her face where tears had fallen. After punching and flinging her fists into the padded walls, she'd scratched her face and then, more deeply, her arms, digging her short, ragged nails firmly into the skin before ripping them cruelly through her flesh. There were parallel rows of raised welts—dark, clotted blood on top of the ones on her arms. But she wouldn't let the nurse clean the wounds, even as the orderlies tried to hold her still. They called Dr. Lerner to inform her of the delay and were told to bring her to the office as she was.

"It's all right," Lerner told the orderlies standing in the doorway. "You can go."

"Are you sure?" the taller one asked. He cast a sharp glance at Micki, who'd already seated herself.

"We'll be fine," Lerner said.

Once they were gone, the doctor waited for Micki to speak, but she only stared out the window.

"Do you want to tell me what happened?" Lerner asked gently.

Slowly turning her head till her eyes met the doctor's, Micki whispered, "I hate myself. I don't wanna live anymore."

"What're you feeling?" Lerner asked.

"No matter how hard I try, everything I do turns out wrong. Somebody's always blaming me for something. And—and underneath it all, I feel used and—and dirty." Tears streamed down her cheeks. "Nobody loves me, and nobody ever will. I just don't wanna hurt so much anymore."

"Tim cared about you—"

"And now he's *dead*."

"Sergeant Baker cares about you—"

"No! No he doesn't!" Micki's eyes were blazing. "He hates me! He said I ruined his whole fuckin' life. He thinks I'm shit."

"He wouldn't be visiting you here if he didn't—"

"*Don't you get it?*" Micki screamed, "I'm a fuckin' *job* to him. And he *needs* me; he needs me so he can get back to workin' the fuckin' street. They're just usin' me for some kinda fucked-up therapy for him. Everybody just uses me; nobody gives a shit about me. His fuckin' cop friend comes here worryin' about *him*."

"So you're just part of Sergeant Baker's job."

"Yeah."

"And he's a cop."

Micki's eyes narrowed. "Yeah, so?"

"Would you say he's a good cop?"

"Whatta y'mean?"

"Is he good at what he does?"

"Yeah, I guess so."

"How do you know?"

Micki shrugged. "I dunno. He's a detective. And a sergeant. And he's got a lot of those ribbon things."

"Hmm, I see," the doctor responded. "Tell me something, then: when he caught you about to shoot up, did he arrest you?"

"No, but—"

Lerner put her hand up for silence. "Did he send you back to Heyden?"

"No, but like I said—"

Once again, the doctor raised her hand. "Did he at least ask you who your dealer was?"

"Well...no."

"Huh!" Lerner said. "He doesn't sound like a very good cop to me."

As Baker approached, Micki stood up—which was her way of telling him to leave. And yet, this time she studied him through different eyes. Haggard and thinner, the effect the last two weeks had had on him seemed genuine. She'd been shocked to learn he could've been rid of her a long time ago, could've switched her for another kid. And since that opportunity had come and gone before they'd had sex together, his decision couldn't be written off to guilt. She felt all mixed up now. Hating him had been so much easier before she knew all this.

Seeing her expression, Baker would've given anything to know what she was thinking, but it was the scratches on her cheeks and the bandages on her arms that commanded his attention.

"What happened to you?" he demanded.

She pushed *The Foundation Trilogy* across the table. "I finished this," she said.

"*What happened?*" he repeated.

"I need another book."

Sighing, he picked up the paperback. "Did you like this?" he asked. When she didn't respond, he said, "I liked it. Y'know, it's always hard at first to get into science fiction stuff; you've got to learn all the made-up names and words. But you get used to them after a while, don't you?"

Her eyes had drifted toward the TV, where a Spic and Span commercial was playing.

"I just want to know if I should bring another science-fiction book," he said.

Now staring out the window, she mumbled, "I wanna get outta here."

He seemed startled. "Are you really working with Dr. Lerner, Micki?"

She turned to face him, then looked up into his eyes. She wanted to ask if what the doctor had told her about him was true. But then maybe he'd lie—just like he could've lied to the doctor. Her eyes dropped, and her gaze became unfocused.

"I'll bring you another book," he said softly.

BAKER HEADED STRAIGHT FOR the nurses' station, demanding to know what had happened. The plump, middle-aged woman with wire-rimmed glasses and crimson-colored lipstick sounded aggravatingly blasé. "She scratched herself."

"I can see that. I want to know why."

"She had a visitor, then became unruly and was put into one of the padded rooms. Although we were checking on her regularly, she managed to do that in between. We should've put her in a straight jacket."

Baker already knew about the provoking incident; Gould had called him at the school. What angered him was that no one from the hospital ever thought to keep him apprised of episodes like this. "Is Dr. Lerner available?" he asked. "I'd appreciate it if I could have just a few minutes of her time."

"Let me see."

Caught off guard, he said an extra-courteous, "Thank you," and, after waiting patiently, was told the doctor could see him briefly when her current session was finished. But once he was inside her office, Lerner summarily informed him she was not at liberty to discuss anything—Micki hadn't given permission yet.

Baker shook his head. "When can she get the hell out of this place?"

"I'd like to release her as soon as possible, but I can't do that until I feel confident she's not a danger to herself. I also need to know that she'll accept your supervision. Her reticence to allow me to relate even the most basic information to you isn't helping. Although I would've preferred to wait a while longer, perhaps we should try a session with both of you together. Could you be here Monday at one o'clock?"

"I'll get someone to cover for me."

"I'd keep this to yourself, Sergeant—otherwise, Micki might not show."

The investigation into the break-in at Micki's apartment had come to a grinding halt. Considered a low-priority crime for that precinct to begin with, there simply wasn't enough evidence to proceed. And early on, despite Baker's hunch, the detectives assigned to the case had ruled out any connection to the super of Micki's building. They said he lacked motive for vandalizing one of his own apartments and had no kids of his own to be involved. On the other hand, Baker had argued, why was he being so completely uncooperative?

So that Saturday, Baker washed some of his own clothes at Micki's Laundromat. Trading on his good looks, he chatted up several of the women there and got them talking. A lot. And under the guise of hunting for an apartment nearby, he eventually uncovered the connection between the super's wife and Joey's mother. When the dryer was done and his shirts were folded, he threw the clean laundry into the trunk of his car, then sat in the bucket seat, drinking coffee and smoking. Until he had an idea.

"I know why you're really here," said the wizened, scrawny man. "You're that kid's parole officer. You think you're so smart tryin' to act like you're some undercover cop, but I know what's goin' on. All yous guys are the same, wantin' to pin every goddamn thing that goes wrong around here on the neighborhood boys. But the truth is, it's that delinquent kidda yours that's causin' all the problems. She's the one on parole, right? Not Joey. She prob'ly trashed the goddamn place herself. I'm not givin' you one red cent for whatever the hell you're doin' over there. You should be givin' *me* money."

Baker had named no names, yet the super—eyes bloodshot, nose red and pitted like an alcoholic's—had mentioned Joey. His tone mild, Baker asked, "So where's the key to her apartment? I'm sure you wouldn't mind showing it to me."

"Like I told those detectives: I threw it away 'cause some jerk—prob'ly *you*—changed the lock on her door. Jeez, don't yous guys ever talk to each other?"

"That key went missing, didn't it."

"Get the fuck offa my property. I don't havta to talk to you." And he slammed the door in Baker's face.

Baker turned and walked back to his car. Regardless of whether the key had ever played a role or not, the super was protecting those boys—out of loyalty to his wife's friend or out of fear. Either way, the case was essentially dead. When Baker got home, he called Officer Roberts. "Can you make those boys' lives miserable for me?"

ON SUNDAY, BAKER BROUGHT Micki a copy of J.R.R. Tolkien's *The Fellowship of the Ring*—now one of the most popular books at the high school. Feeling like a stubborn puppy dropping toys in front of its disinterested owner, he also gave her the homework he'd forgotten to give her on Friday. Day after day, he'd been faithfully handing over assignments, though he'd stopped borrowing Greg's notes a while ago—she wouldn't even take those. She'd sort through the papers, toss the notes to the floor, then look at him with a defiant glare while crumpling the remaining sheets—her homework assignments—into a tight little ball in her fist. That was, until today. For the first time ever, he saw her actually glance them over.

"I want to take my finals," she said.

His brow creased. "Really? You've been studying?"

"I started yesterday, okay? But I'll be ready by the end of the week."

He looked at her closely. "I'll see what I can arrange."

Chapter 30

IT WAS SNOWING AGAIN, but the dirty, mesh-covered glass robbed the snowflakes of most of their magic. Micki sighed: another Monday in the hospital. With each passing day, the routine of her outside life seemed further and further away. She left the window and walked through the dayroom, then down the corridors to Dr. Lerner's office. She could hear the doctor talking, then recognized Baker's voice.

She stepped inside. "What's *he* doing here?"

Both heads turned.

"I think it's time you had a session together," Dr. Lerner said.

"This is *my* session; I don't want him here."

The doctor walked past Micki and closed the door. "Please sit down."

Eyes smoldering, Micki took her usual chair.

The doctor seated herself.

No one said anything.

Micki looked at Baker. "What's with the stupid hat, huh?"

When he'd grabbed his jacket from the closet on his way out that morning, Baker had spied his Yankee baseball cap on the shelf. Thinking it might lighten the atmosphere, he'd taken it. "I don't know, Micki; I just felt like wearing it. I'm a Yankees fan."

Micki turned to Dr. Lerner. "He just wants to give you the impression he's Mr. Nice Guy."

Though Baker was trying as hard as he could, he couldn't keep himself from smiling.

"See?" Micki said, her voice rising. "He thinks it's funny; he thinks everything's so fuckin' funny."

"It's just"—Baker tried desperately to control the nervousness that was fueling his behavior—"you always have these names for me: Mr. Morality, Mr. Nice Guy..."

Micki jumped up and confronted the doctor. "I'm sure you think he's done everything the way he should've. I bet he made himself out to be some kinda fuckin' saint who's had to put up with god-knows-what kinda shit from me." Neither Lerner nor Baker said anything, though Micki noticed Baker's expression had turned grave. "Did he tell ya how he hits me?" Micki asked.

"Yes," the doctor responded.

Shock flitted across Micki's features. But then, voice rising further, she said, "Yeah? Well did he tell ya how he once beat me so bad I could hardly move, and it was all f'nothin'?"

"Yes, he did."

Micki flashed Baker a dirty look before once again addressing the doctor: "Well, did he tell ya how he fucked me?"

Baker jumped up. "Why do you always have to say it like that? That's not how it was."

"Yes, it is!"

"No, it isn't!"

"You were so fuckin' stoned y'would've fucked a goddamn horse if that was the only thing available."

Chest heaving, Baker paused. "Okay, Micki, I'll admit it: I was completely wasted and horny as hell, but that doesn't mean I wasn't aware that I was with *you*."

"Oh, yeah, right."

Voice low, he said, "Let's tell it exactly how it was, okay? When I started crashing, I wanted to stop because I knew what I was doing was wrong. I wanted to stop *before* I came, but *you* wouldn't let me."

"I just wanted t'keep things even."

"Keep *what* even? You mean because of the money?"

Her eyes narrowed. "No, not because a the money. I didn't even see the goddamn money till after you left."

"Then what're you talking about?" But all at once, a cunning look crossed his face. "You wanted me to come because I made *you* come, isn't that right? If I was being such a selfish prick, how come I made sure to satisfy you first?"

She glared at him.

"Why can't you answer that?" he asked. "Why can't you admit that I made you feel good?"

Micki could see him kissing her scarred body.

"Why can't you admit," he said, "that I was making love to you—"

There was a loud, crisp smack as her palm connected with his face. Of the three of them, Micki looked the most stunned: lips slightly parted, eyes large and round. What astonished her most was that Baker had simply stood there and taken it. He'd made no move to block it, and not a single muscle had twitched to retaliate.

Voice hushed, she said, "I don't wanna talk t'you anymore." And she ran for the door.

He cut her off. "Don't leave, Micki. Please."

"Get outta my way."

"You're not leaving till the session's over."

"Says who? Y'can't make me stay if I don't wanna. Y'got no authority here."

"I've got no authority here? It doesn't matter where the hell we are; you're still my kid."

She drew a sharp breath.

He looked stricken.

"Micki!" he called, reaching out.

But it was too late. She was running down the hall, having slipped out the door while he'd been momentarily paralyzed.

When Baker turned back toward the doctor, his face was filled with pain. "I guess I didn't handle that too well."

The doctor's expression was kind.

Lips trembling, he tried to smile. "I guess I should've worn a different hat."

With the rest of the session now his alone, Baker withdrew into silence. "This is never going to work, is it," he finally said.

"Why do you say that?"

"Look at what just happened. It's never going to go away; that night's going to haunt my every minute with her."

"Only by getting all of this out into the open will you be able to put it to rest. I realize it's painful and unpleasant, but it has to be done."

He lit a cigarette. "And then what?"

"What do you imagine?"

Body tense, he shifted his gaze past the doctor. "Y'know, she's still attracted to me."

"And you see this as a problem."

Looking at Lerner like she was crazy, he exhaled a long trail of smoke. "Yeah, I see this as a problem; I see this as a *big* problem."

"Then why did you wait so long to bring it up?"

Baker shrugged and looked away again.

"How do you know this?" Lerner asked.

"I know, that's all. I can tell."

"You think she wants to sleep with you again?"

"No! No, of course not." And though he didn't need to, he flicked a few ashes into the ashtray. "Y'know, she's never even come on to me—not before that night or after. In fact, she's always been very careful to, y'know, keep herself covered up and stuff. Even when she was sick. It was a real battle to get her to let me put those towels on her. God"—shaking his head, he closed his eyes—"she was so afraid of me." And in the stillness of the office, he felt the stillness of Micki's apartment again: the heaviness in the air, the darkness reaching out of the corners…

"The reason I'm not concerned, Sergeant"—Baker opened his eyes at the sound of Lerner's voice—"is that, based on what I've observed and what you've told me, her attraction to you will never be a problem as long as you don't act on it."

"But I *did* act on it."

"Even ignoring that you were high, your relationship to her then was very different from what it is now: you didn't see yourself as playing the role of a father; you were acting almost exclusively as a parole officer. Yes, it was a despicable abuse of your position of authority, and reprehensible given her youth and the difference in your ages. Let's be clear: as her legal guardian, what you did was incestuous. Make no mistake, if you were to commit such an act now, I would rip her away from you so fast your head would spin."

"I would never…"

"And it goes without saying that I trust you won't ever get high like that anymore, either."

"I wouldn't do anything that stupid again. She's too important to me."

"Do you understand how important you are to her?"

"Now I do."

"You're only *just* realizing it?"

He took a rough drag off the cigarette. "Okay, so maybe it's that I'm finally admitting it—accepting it—now. I want to be there for her."

Lerner looked at him pointedly. "Then you have to stop running away."

MICKI WATCHED BAKER FROM the window—a black figure tramping through dirty winter white. She wondered what he'd said after she'd left.

She retreated to her room to sleep. It was barely two in the afternoon.

THAT NIGHT, BAKER UNLOCKED the desk drawer containing his important papers. He pulled out a manila envelope buried all the way underneath and examined one of the documents inside. The first thing that caught his eye was the name on it: Mickey Reilly. A closer look showed it had been altered; someone had used correction fluid, then typed over it. Holding it up to the light, the "i" underneath the "e" in "Mickey" became visible. He snorted, then skimmed through the text. His guardianship remained in effect until she reached her eighteenth birthday or until such time that formal, legal action was taken to terminate it; whichever came first.

He returned the envelope to its place in the drawer and wondered if all of the other copies he'd signed had been altered, as well. After he'd read the first one, he wouldn't have looked at the rest very carefully. On some technical level, the deception probably compromised the validity of the documents. But it didn't really matter. He was the only person likely to contest them. He was also the last person on earth who actually would.

"WHY DID YOU SLAP Sergeant Baker?" Lerner asked the next day.

Micki gave a lethargic shrug.

"You must've had a reason," the doctor pressed.

"He shouldn't talk to me like that."

"Like what?"

"Like *that.*"

"Why not?"

Micki gave her another shrug.

"If you could, would you sleep with him again?"

"No!"

"Why not? It sounds like he was a good lover—"

"*Shut up.*"

"What's the matter?" Lerner asked.

"I don't wanna talk about this."

"Why not?"

"It's *wrong.*"

"Did it feel wrong when you were doing it that night?"

Micki hesitated. "It felt...I don't know...I... Once the stuff he'd smoked started wearing off, it felt bad."

"I don't understand."

"When he was stoned, it was like he was someone else."

"And when he was no longer high?"

Micki stared at the books on Lerner's shelves. Practically whispering, she said, "I wanted to hide." She looked back. "I—I really don't wanna talk about this anymore."

After several seconds had passed, Lerner said, "I heard you've been studying, that you're planning to take your finals at the end of the week."

"Two on Friday and three on Saturday. The nurses are gonna give 'em to me. I have to take 'em in one of the padded rooms." Seeing Lerner's expression, she added, "Well, if I'm not gonna be dead, I might as well not fuck up the one thing I got goin' for me."

"Hi, Micki."

She'd been staring out the window, watching visitors and hospital personnel navigate the slushy puddles lining the roads below. When she spun around, she saw the owner of the voice she recognized but couldn't place.

"Do you feel up to talking for a few minutes?" Captain Malone asked.

"Are you gonna tell me to talk to Sergeant Baker, too? 'Cause I already told the other cop ta"—she paused—"t'leave me alone."

He tensed. "What other cop?"

"I dunno his name, but he said he's Sergeant Baker's partner."

Malone relaxed. "That's Detective Gould. No, Micki, I'm not going to tell you to do anything, although I *would* like to know why you won't talk to Sergeant Baker."

"'Cause I hate him."

Arms in a classic Jack Benny pose, Malone stroked his chin. "Is that why you—is he the reason you're here?"

She looked so deeply into his eyes that he drew in his breath.

After a long pause, she said merely, "I was very depressed."

Malone exhaled and dropped his arms. "Y'know, nobody wants you to take your own life, kid."

"But no one particularly cares if I live, either."

His heart twinged. And he finally saw Micki as a real person, not just some peripheral entity in Baker's life. Voice quiet, he said, "That's not true."

"Yeah, whatever."

"I hope you feel better soon."

She shrugged and turned away.

Malone lightly touched her arm, and she jumped.

"I meant what I said, okay?" he added.

Eyebrows pulled together, she responded a little too forcefully, "Okay!"

"Okay," he repeated softly, and gave her a sad smile. "Bye, Micki." And he quickly strode across the dayroom.

She waited till his navy wool coat had disappeared, then turned back to the window to watch the world go by some more.

"IT WAS ONE OF those weird winter days when it doesn't feel extremely cold, but you can see your breath, y'know?" Baker lit a cigarette and crossed his right ankle over his left knee. "Gould and I were staking out this suspect's old neighborhood. We were were sitting in a car and drinking coffee. There were two other detectives where the suspect had been hanging out more recently, but I had a hunch he'd go back to his old digs. With the body count rising, we needed to get this guy, and we needed to get him fast." Baker filled his lungs with smoke, held it, then exhaled. "And I wanted to be the one to get him. He'd killed four people in three stores in six days—went in to rob a place and didn't even give the poor slob at the register a chance, just blew his brains out, took the money, and ran. Blew away one customer, too. Didn't give a shit who he killed; didn't give a shit about anything. Not surprisingly, only one witness was willing to take a look at the mug shots. The guy they picked out was a long-time junkie—never violent before, all his priors petty thefts. And while we thought the witness might've made a mistake, they insisted it was him. So we started checking him out. And when we learned his girlfriend had recently OD'd on some bad smack, we figured something in him must've snapped."

Shifting in his seat, Baker recrossed his legs the opposite way. "Anyway, we see the guy turn the corner and start walking toward us. But then he makes us and bolts. We end up chasing him for a few blocks until he runs into this abandoned building. It's totally disgusting inside and, except for this one beam of light coming through some busted boards over a window, it's also really dark. Gould and I are both breathing hard from running, and the mist from our breath is kind of glowing in that light—kind of creepy. Anyway, we can hear the guy racing up the steps. Gould goes back out and heads for the fire escape in the rear to cut him off. I find the stairs and start up when my flashlight dies on me. The stairs are almost pitch black, and I don't hear the guy anymore. But just as I reach the second floor, I hear a crash and Gould cursing. And it sounds like he's dropped his gun; I can hear it clattering, heavy, down the fire escape. When I go toward the sound, I enter this huge room and see the suspect's back. He's standing in front of a window, and I can tell he's pointing a gun at Gould—who's telling him not to shoot. But the guy says, 'You're a fucking pig, man. You're dead.' And then I hear two gunshots. They sound far away, like from some other part of the building. It takes a moment till I realize I'd pulled the trigger. Twice. And I'm watching this guy stagger forward a couple of steps and then crumple to the ground. Slowly. I mean, that's how it looks 'cause everything seems to be happening in slow motion.

"As I go past the guy, I kick his gun away. His eyes are closed, his face all sunken and sallow. I can see he's still breathing, but there's a lot of blood—and I know he's not getting up. Meanwhile, Gould, who's right outside the fire escape window, is in shock. When he heard the gun go off, he thought he'd been shot. He's okay, actually, except for a twisted ankle and some bruises—he'd slipped on some ice. But when I get back to the perp, he's dead. Two rounds and I'd taken him out."

Baker pulled hard on the cigarette, then exhaled the smoke in a long, steady stream. "It was all so unreal. Over and over in the academy, I heard how most cops never fire their weapon in their entire career, let alone hit someone—or kill them. By the time the shooting happened, I'd drawn my gun so many times, I'd grown comfortable with the idea that I'd never actually have to use it. And then, when I understood I'd killed someone—well—I kept second-guessing myself because I never gave any warning. Just shot him. I mean, no one else was questioning it—"

"You said yourself," the doctor interrupted, "that this man had already shown he had no regard for human life; he'd killed without reason or provocation. If you'd taken the time to issue a warning, your partner would probably be dead now. You did what you had to."

"That's easy for you to say; you're not the one who pulled the trigger." Baker ground the cigarette into the ashtray. A second later, he lit another. "I'm going to die of lung cancer."

"You're under tremendous stress right now. Let's first concentrate on alleviating some of that, then we'll deal with the smoking."

Baker grunted and played with his lighter, then tossed it onto the table. "Anyway, that's when I started drinking so much. It helped block out the images and the sound of the gunshots that kept ringing in my ears. I didn't want to see anything anymore. I didn't want to feel anything anymore. But even with the drinking..." His eyes lost focus, and he hung his head. They sat in silence until he said, "I have"—he took a deep, ragged breath—"I have blood on my hands now." He looked up. "That piece of garbage forced me to take a life—to *kill* someone. To kill *him*."

Lerner waited, letting the moment fill the room and settle slowly to the ground. Then she said, "That's a heavy burden to carry."

"Yeah, well... I can tell you that that day became the dividing point in my life. After that, everything seemed different. Especially on the job. I started getting more physical, and it didn't bother me one bit. Quite the opposite: it felt good. Gould never took part, but always looked the other way. He felt he owed me his life. He would do anything for me. Still would."

"Did you talk to anyone about what you were going through?"

"Not really, no. At some point, Captain Malone got concerned and made me talk to the department shrink. But I simply said all the things I had to in order to remain on active duty."

"Why didn't you tell him the truth?"

"I didn't want to end up on the rubber-gun squad."

"The what?"

"The rubber-gun squad. That's what we call it when they take your gun away and assign you to some desk job."

"What about your partner?"

"I didn't want him worrying that he couldn't depend on me."

"Your girlfriend?"

"I didn't want Cynthia to think I was weak."

"Is it so terrible to need someone's help?"

Baker shrugged. "I've always done everything for myself."

"That's because as a child you didn't have a parent you could count on; you were your own parent. In some ways, you were your mother's parent. By doing everything yourself, you didn't have to deal with being let down, and you didn't have to owe anyone anything. It also distanced you from your mother's sense of entitlement. But you can't go through life that way. It's impossible; people need each other. Tell me something: how did you feel when Micki showed up at your poker game that night?"

"Furious. I told you how angry I was."

"Yes, but that was when she first arrived. After that, when you knew why she was there and how hard it must've been for her to be asking you for something..."

"I felt...touched. Protective."

"And why was that?"

"I felt needed."

"You *like* feeling needed," Lerner said. "It's one of the reasons you became a police officer. In general, people like to feel needed because then they know they mean something to someone."

Baker grunted.

Half a minute went by.

"Sometimes I can't get the shooting out of my head," he said. "It's like I'm back in that moment all over again. I—I still have dreams about it."

"Can you tell me one of the—"

"Can we talk about something else?" Flicking ashes from his cigarette, he shifted in his seat.

The doctor's voice was gentle. "When you feel ready, we'll explore this further. But I want to point out that you appear to feel guilty simply for being at the right place at the right time—for doing your job and wanting to do it well."

Baker looked toward the window. A pigeon tried to land on the icy ledge, then flew away. He said, "Just for once, I wish that my hunch had been wrong. Then Gould and I would've been waiting there for nothing."

"You've got women's intuition."

He gave her a lethal look. "Don't let that get around."

Lerner's jaw dropped. "I—I would never…"

He started to grin.

Her face reddened, but then she broke into a wry smile. "My lips are sealed. But that brings us back to something you said during your first session. You'd mentioned that while you'd already made up your mind to dislike Micki before you'd even met her, your feelings intensified significantly as soon as you had."

Baker's grin faded. "I realized I'd been tricked. I hadn't been expecting—and didn't want—a girl."

"I think it was more than that. I think you *intuitively* knew something about her that was triggering those feelings. I think she reminded you of someone."

"You mean like the guy I shot—the one I was just telling you about?"

"Could be. Does that ring true for you?"

"Not really."

"Then what does? *You* have to be the one to decide."

"Maybe the guy whose jaw I broke. That's when the shit hit the fan. He was a junkie, too—and he'd killed someone." Stubbing out his cigarette, he said, "I don't know; I'm not sure."

"Then who else?" Seeing Baker's expression, she added, "It can be more than one person. For that matter, it can be many people. The mind doesn't limit its associations."

"Please don't tell me it's my mother…"

Lerner chuckled. "No, not your mother. We psychiatrists don't connect *everything* back to your mother."

"So who?"

"I'd like you to think about that."

"Is it really that important?"

"Very much so."

CAPPED INSIDE THE BOTTLE, the Jack Daniels—a perfectly smooth, rich amber—seemed to be glowing. For ten minutes, Baker had been staring at it. How many times had he gone through this same little scenario? But tonight the compulsion felt stronger—almost desperate. At first he couldn't understand the backslide; he'd been doing so well. But talking about the shooting must've dredged up the very feelings he couldn't handle sober in the first place. As soon as he'd gotten home, he'd unlocked the cabinet, ruing his initial decision to keep the bottles: fuck it if the guys had to bring their own. But having the liquor around gave him a sense of power—proof that he, not the alcohol, was the one in control. Of course, at times like this, he was no longer so sure. Jesus, he should just lock the fucking bottle away already. But it would be such a relief to take one tiny sip—

Something crashed to the floor in the apartment above, and he started. He shoved the bottle back in the cabinet, locked the door, and put his keys on the dresser in the bedroom. But on his way out, he stopped by the night table to stare at the phone. Then he picked up the receiver. Though he was about to call Dr. Lerner, he dialed another number instead. Warner didn't answer. He dialed again, but reached only Aunt Sylvia, who was babysitting at Gould's. Taking a deep breath, he dialed the number that he should've tried first.

"Hello?"

"Hi, Cyn. Did I catch you at a bad time?"

"HOW CAN YOU SAY he cares about me when he treats me the way he does?"

"He has a lot of problems," Dr. Lerner said, "and, unfortunately, he's taken a great deal of them out on you. But he's very sorry for what he's done."

"That's such bullshit," Micki responded. "Not once has he ever said, 'I'm sorry.' His few apologies have been nothing but half-assed excuses."

"But he *is* sorry—"

"Why are you defending him?"

The doctor's tone was soothing. "I'm not defending him. I'm simply trying to show you there's another side to this; things aren't so black and white."

"Yeah? So his hitting me doesn't mean anything?"

"It's wrong, Micki; it's very wrong. But it doesn't mean he doesn't care."

"He treats me like nothing more than a goddamn prisoner. Y'know how many times he's handcuffed me?"

The doctor paused. "What would've happened if he hadn't?"

"What?"

"Well, let's take, for example, the time you ran away on the side of the highway. If he hadn't handcuffed you, what would've happened?"

"How the hell should *I* know?"

"Humor me," Lerner said dryly. "Just tell me what you *imagine* would've happened."

"Like what?"

"Well, would you have surrendered and returned to the car because he told you to?"

Micki snorted. "No way. I would've done whatever I could've to get away again."

"Such as? Hitting? Punching?"

"Yeah, so?"

"So then what would Sergeant Baker have done?"

Chewing her lower lip, Micki could see where this was going. An edge to her voice, she said, "He would've tried to stop me."

"Which, if he wasn't going to use handcuffs, would mean what?"

"I guess he'd've hit me back."

"And what do you think the final outcome of that would've been?"

"He's twice as big as me!"

"Yes, he is. And he's well aware of just how easily—and how badly—he could hurt you."

Micki broke eye contact.

"And speaking of his size," the doctor continued, "even on the snow, it must've been terribly painful when he tackled you. He has to weigh well over two hundred pounds."

Glaring at Lerner, Micki said, "It didn't hurt at all."

Eyes large with mock surprise, the doctor said, "That's amazing! How could that be?"

"'Cause I fell on top of him," Micki retorted.

"But *he* tackled *you*, isn't that right?"

"Yeah, but somehow I ended up on top."

Lerner's voice was soft. "Do you think that was by chance?"

"So what?" Micki shot back. "So what? I mean, what the fuck does that mean? It's all just for show. It's all just bullshit."

They sat in silence till Lerner asked, "Is it true you think men don't have any real feelings?"

"Did he tell you that?"

"Yes."

"Yeah. Okay. So I said it."

"Do you believe it?"

"Yeah."

"You think this about all men?"

"Yeah."

"Even Tim?"

Micki shrugged one shoulder.

"He died trying to protect you."

Micki's eyes turned sad.

"And what about Sergeant Kelly? Why do you think he helped you?"

"I have no fucking idea, okay?"

"You don't believe it was because he cared?"

"It could just as easily've been that they needed some sorry-assed, scapegoat kid for Sergeant Baker's therapy."

"So all men are heartless bastards, is that it?" When her question was met with silence, Lerner said, "Maybe that's why your boyfriend—"

"He's *not* my boyfriend."

"But Rick *was*—past tense—your boyfriend, wasn't he?"

"No! Never! I would just have sex with him; that's all. It didn't mean anything; I *told* you that."

"Is that all you want?"

Though Micki wanted to answer yes, she found she couldn't say anything.

"If all men are shits," Lerner said, being unexpectedly crude, "then it really doesn't matter who you pick, does it. And choosing someone like Rick is actually a way for you to confirm your theory about men. More importantly, not having any emotional involvement also means you're never close enough to get hurt."

"Oh, please," Micki shot back. "All that love stuff is phony. Who needs it anyway?"

"You do," the doctor said. "In fact, that's why you're here."

Chapter 31

A PADDED CELL SEEMED like a very fitting place to take finals. Unfortunately, the closeted little space—four walls of uninterrupted white bathed in a sickening fluorescent glow—soon turned oppressive. And yet, question after question, Micki filled in blanks, picked the best choices, calculated answers, drew diagrams, and wrote essays in a large, messy handwriting.

When she finally put her pen down, it was late Saturday afternoon.

And she couldn't keep the grin off her face.

Chapter 32

ANOTHER NIGHT OF NOT sleeping, another morning of not eating. For Micki, Monday was like any other day until, halfway through her session, Dr. Lerner broached the issue of discharging her from the hospital. Tuesday, after a daytime excursion to the high school to take the New York State English Regents exam, Micki could spend her final night on the ward. Assuming all went well, her last session as an in-patient would be Wednesday. With school still in recess, she'd have time to gradually readjust to her regular life: first returning to work, then starting the new semester after the weekend. Her therapy would be reduced to one session on Mondays after school.

Before the doctor had even finished explaining the plan, Micki agreed to it. But the next day, when she went to take the test, the world outside seemed different, as if everything had been slightly altered. To avoid having to talk to anyone, she waited in the security office as long as possible before going to her assigned room. But students had been grouped alphabetically, and no one from her science program was even there.

And though she was no longer feeling all that confident, when Wednesday morning rolled around, she small-talked her way through her session, packed her things, and headed out of the hospital.

"Did you say goodbye to everyone you wanted to?" Baker asked as they walked through the parking lot.

Not having said goodbye to anyone, she replied, "Yessir."

He caught his breath.

They drove through the drab, graffitied streets without even the radio to negotiate the space between them. When he started searching for a parking spot, she said, "I can go up myself. I just need my key."

"I'm going up with you."

Eyes throwing daggers through the windshield, she silently cursed him.

They climbed the stoop and then the stairs inside, everything looking smaller and shabbier than she remembered, the smell of the building's interior causing a flood of memories that swiftly drowned her sense of freedom. But then she was standing in front of her door, holding out her palm while he produced a shiny new set of keys that he dangled above it.

"I put in a really good deadbolt and changed the cylinder on the other lock," he said. "But I want you to understand"—he finally relinquished the keys—"that it's going to look a lot different. The place was pretty much trashed."

Her eyes dulled, and her shoulders sagged. But when she went inside and turned on the light, she gasped. In place of her old, ratty mattress was a real bed, complete with Harvard frame and two fluffy pillows. It had a brown blanket, cream-colored sheets, and—folded neatly at the foot—a rust-colored afghan. The walls had been painted a warm beige, and her old curtains had been replaced with new ones in a crisp white linen.

When her gaze came to rest on the fire escape window, he said, "I put that gate on for security."

She shifted her attention to the kitchenette table, its mocha-colored Formica blending nicely with the dark brown seat cushions on the accompanying chairs. Then she took in the dresser and desk made of plain stained wood. There was a matching night table that had—a phone? She pointed to it.

"The bill goes to me," he said. "Just do me a favor and don't start making calls to China." But his grin quickly dissipated in light of her expression. "I'm not going to use it to check up on you," he said. "If you don't want to, you don't ever have to answer it. It's here in case you need to talk to someone—or you need to call for help."

"How am I supposed to pay you back for all this?"

"I don't expect you to pay me back for *any* of this."

"But I'll owe you—"

"Nothing," he interjected. "You don't owe me anything. I did this because I wanted to."

She continued to glare.

"It's okay," he remarked dryly. "You can still hate me."

She turned away.

Talking to the side of her head, he said, "I bought you some groceries. But this"—he took a ten-dollar bill from his wallet—"should tide you over till you get paid again."

She faced him. "I don't need your money. I—" It was gone, of course.

"If you want to, you can pay *this* back when you're able to."

Avoiding his eyes, she took the cash and shoved it in her pocket.

"Are you going to be okay here tonight?" he asked. "Do you want me to stay? Or I could come back later. You can always stay at my place if you want to."

"Y'can't watch me every fuckin' minute. If I really wanna shoot up or kill myself again, there's nothin' y'can really do about it."

He felt like he'd been hit. He went to the door. And left.

From the window, she watched him as he headed down the street.

UNABLE TO SLEEP, MICKI sat at the kitchen table, trying to read *The Fellowship of the Ring*. But she kept looking around the newly decorated apartment, feeling like a stranger in someone else's home. Nice as it was, it was just another example of how everything in her life was always changing—and how nothing was ever really hers. Even worse, now it felt like everything was *his*. She went to make a cup of cocoa, pausing to stare at the small white teakettle sitting on the stove. He'd bought her hot chocolate, too.

Fuck it. It was his fault she'd tried to kill herself, his fault she'd ended up in the hospital. Therefore, somehow or other, it was also his fault that her apartment had gotten trashed. In the end, all these new things merely made up for what *he* owed *her*.

She filled the kettle with water and set it on a burner, then took down an oversized white mug and poured a packet of cocoa into it. Virtually everything had been replaced, right down to the towels and dishes. The cobalt-blue and clowny polka-dot mugs were gone. The cereal bowl with the faded rose on the bottom was gone. But tucked away in the closet, there were also a couple of weird, new things; namely, a sleeping bag and what seemed to be an empty—yet locked—metal box. And for the first time ever, there were barred windows that weren't meant to keep her in, but rather to keep others out. Yet despite the added security, she actually felt less safe now than she did before. A small shiver rippled through her: she was all alone.

As she waited for the water to boil, she leaned against the counter and eyed the telephone on her desk. A plain black rotary model, it sat there, waiting patiently, like a device left behind by aliens. Earlier, while getting ready to go to sleep, she'd gingerly lifted the receiver to listen to the dial tone.

The water hadn't boiled, but she turned off the stove and then the light, took off her jeans, and crawled back into bed. Snuggled under the covers, she almost giggled as she pictured Baker wandering around stores, picking out stuff and color-coordinating things.

Then she started to cry.

HE LIT A CIGARETTE and leaned back in his chair, waiting for his hot chocolate to cool down. Bold and black, Micki's number stared at him from alongside the phone on the kitchen wall. She probably wouldn't pick up anyway. He could drive over to see if she was all right, but he could just imagine the frosty reception that would get.

He wondered if she liked everything.

CLOUDED OVER AND WINDY, Thursday's outlook was bleak. The knock on the door jarred her out of her reading. She closed the paperback and checked her watch. It was almost time to leave for Bel.

Voice gruff, she said, "Who is it?"

"It's me, Micki."

She opened the door with her brow deeply knotted. "Did you forget your key?"

Gazing at her steadily, Baker said, "No."

She stepped aside to let him in.

"How do you feel?" he asked.

"I have to get ready for work." She sat on the bed to put her sneakers on.

"Did you sleep okay? Was the bed comfortable?"

"Yessir." She stood up and busied herself by checking pockets for money and ID. Then she grabbed her jacket from the closet and put it on. "Well, I gotta go now."

Still standing beside the table, he said, "Okay."

"Whatta y'want?" she demanded.

"I just want to know how you're doing."

"Are y'gonna stay here?"

"For a little while, yes."

"Are y'gonna toss the place?"

"Yes."

She grunted in reply as she opened the door. But then, in a monotonic flurry of words, she said, "Everything looks real nice—thanks." And she slammed the door behind her before running away.

When Baker heard the downstairs door slam, too, he pulled out his cigarettes and lit one.

Micki wasn't feeling as good as he'd hoped.

SINCE BAKER REFUSED TO leave his apartment that night, the guys made a last-minute change of venue and held the poker game at his place. Gould, stricken with the flu, stayed home. But no call came from Micki, and Baker broke even.

After the others had left, Malone hung around, helping to clean up. He was pouring uneaten pretzels back into a bag when he said, "I'd like to know what happened with the kid."

Baker put down the glasses he'd been collecting and looked at his superior. "I'm surprised you waited this long to ask."

"I was hoping you'd *want* to talk to me. But now that she's out of the hospital, I have to have some answers."

Lowering his eyes, Baker shook his head. Then they sat down, and Baker told his story—or at least as much as he could safely reveal. When he was finished, he said, "I can't explain it, but sitting in that emergency room was like waking up from a bad dream."

Malone nodded, and they both fell silent.

"Y'know, I asked her if she tried to kill herself because of you," Malone said.

Baker's eyes widened. "When did you see her?"

"When she was still in the hospital."

"Jeez! She never said a word. But I guess that shouldn't surprise me; she's still not talking to me."

"I asked her about that, too."

"And?"

It was hard for Malone to keep a straight face. "She says she hates you."

Baker's face fell.

Chuckling, Malone slapped the younger man's shoulder. "Don't take it so hard. Typical angry teenager."

Baker's mouth fell open.

"She said she was just very depressed," Malone added.

"What?"

"When I asked her if it was your fault," he said. "That should tell you something, *Detective*." They stood up and walked together, Malone retrieving his coat from where he'd thrown it on a chair. About to open the door, he said, "So you really care about this kid."

Baker's voice came out choked. "Yeah."

Smiling, Malone thumped Baker's back twice. "You take care, all right? And I want you to talk to Dr. Tillim. And I mean *talk*—not just sit there like a vegetable for an hour."

"Okay," Baker replied.

"Okay!" Malone echoed, grinning broadly as he left.

THE FOLLOWING AFTERNOON, THE Long Island Expressway became a parking lot when an overturned tractor-trailer spilled its load of dishwashing liquid across most of the westbound lanes. By the time Baker reached Long Island City, Micki was already at Bel, so he drove on into Manhattan and went home.

But with only the muted, tinny sound of a neighbor's radio coming through the wall, his apartment felt too quiet. Again. He dropped his keys and wallet on the night table, lit a cigarette, and stood beside the phone. Overcome with feelings of loss, he listened to the Five Stairsteps' "O-o-h Child"—until the neighbor shut the radio off.

Then he lifted the receiver and dialed.

"Dr. Tillim's office," a woman said.

GETTING BACK INTO THE swing of things at Bel Canto wasn't so easy, the stress and heat much worse than Micki remembered. When her shift was over, the short distance back to her apartment didn't look nearly short enough.

She heard the usual sounds from the group fooling around in the mirror company's parking lot, so she quickly crossed the street. But then she was afraid that Frankie might catch a glimpse of her, so she hurried past the deli, too: she couldn't take any more of the sad smiles and awkward words.

"Hey, bitch!"

Almost home, she recognized Johnny McBain's voice as it ricocheted down the street, directed, she was sure, at her. Not turning around, she continued on at the same pace. But once she was inside her building, she bolted up the steps and into her apartment, locking the door behind her.

WHILE THURSDAY'S SHIFT HAD dragged on and on, Friday's flew by with the restaurant's usual end-of-the-workweek rush. Micki was under the gun from five thirty on. On her way home, she finally stopped in to see Frankie, who gave her a big smile and welcomed her back. She bought a large black-and-white cookie and left the deli feeling better—until she saw the little party gathered to greet her on her stoop. She observed herself walking confidently toward the gang of four, noting that Rick wore his usual asshole smirk, mirrored by that of little Blondie, who sat next to him. Joey looked nervous, while Johnny's eyes were cold.

It was Johnny who spoke. "How was the nuthouse, bitch?"

"Y'gonna get outta my way 'r what?" Micki asked.

As soon as Johnny stood up, so did the rest.

Her heart was pumping faster. If they all came at her at once, she didn't stand a chance. Plus Johnny had been fighting on the streets all his life.

Johnny said, "Ya tell ya P-O—"

"He's not a parole officer," Micki said. "He's a Manhattan cop."

Johnny's reaction wasn't what she'd expected: he snorted. "Well then ya tell that *pig* to get the local fuzz off our backs; 'cause if he don't, we're gonna take it outta ya ass. Ya got that?" He lit a cigarette, and Micki felt cold. All at once, they scampered past her, Johnny hissing, "Do it, bitch!" while deliberately knocking into her. When she turned, she saw the reason for their hasty retreat.

"What was that all about?" Baker asked.

Micki had no idea. But when she looked up, Baker's head and shoulders seemed to be blocking out the night sky. For a moment, she considered repeating Johnny's threat. But then all she said was, "Nothing."

"It didn't look like nothing to me."

She merely shrugged and went into the building.

Inside her apartment, she put away the spaghetti she'd taken from Bel and the cookie she'd bought at the corner. She hung up her jacket and her damp T-shirt from work. "I'm real tired," she said.

"I won't be staying long."

"Y'got my report card?" Baker had spared her the trip to school, saying there was no point in her traveling all the way there just for a fifteen-minute homeroom period.

"I've got your new schedule, too." And he pulled them both out of his pocket.

Taking a deep breath, she unfolded the pink piece of paper and checked out her grades:

> Physics—100
>
> Calculus—99
>
> English—99
>
> Economics—99
>
> American History—98

"That's a great report card," Baker said.

She pointed toward the bottom. "But I only got an 'N' in general conduct." An N meant *needs improvement.*

He smiled. "That's better than what you got last time. I'm very proud of you."

An unsettling warmth swelled inside her.

He opened the door to leave. "You make sure you keep this double locked, y'hear me?" When he was halfway out, he heard her say, "Yessir," and he stiffened. But he closed the door behind him anyway and continued down the hall.

ONCE HE'D REACHED THE street, he stood on the sidewalk, soaking in the atmosphere and getting a bad vibe.

Micki wasn't safe.

SATURDAY, MICKI SLEPT SO much throughout the day that her head hurt. Yet every time she woke up, she felt agitated and exhausted. And though Bel was busy that night, the hours went by slowly. She left to go home and saw Johnny and one of his friends being loaded into the back of a squad car while the rest of the kids stood by to watch. As she crossed the street, Rick spotted her and yelled out, "Ya dead, Micki! Y'got that? Fuckin' dead!"

"Shut your mouth, asshole," Wollenski ordered.

SUNDAY MORNING, BAKER CALLED Cynthia to see if she wanted to get together. She said she was trying to learn two scenes for an off-Broadway audition and planned to spend all day doing it. To her astonishment, he offered to help her run lines.

And so that afternoon, feeling adventurous, Baker tried his hand at acting. His role was that of a rebel college professor in the first scene and an overzealous prosecutor in the second. Cynthia portrayed a coed protest agitator. Though Baker considered the script flawed and the dialogue stilted, he immersed himself in the process as best he could.

As the rebel professor, he had an unrequited crush on Cynthia's character that translated into insulting hostility during the first scene's encounter. "You're not a woman, you're a man in a dress!" he had to say nastily. But after the first read-through, he asked Cynthia, "Don't you think that's a chauvinist thing for this guy to say? Isn't he supposed to be Mr. Equality—this enlightened, pro-women's-lib guy?"

Appearing impressed, she said, "By the end of the play, he's exposed as an opportunistic hypocrite."

Of course, on the next go around, it was that very line that Baker misread: "You're not a man," he said, "you're a woman in a dress!" Aware that it had come out backward, his forehead creased.

She smiled.

Trying to stay in character and set it right, he ad-libbed. Horribly.

She giggled.

He tried again, but it was even worse.

After that, they both broke down and laughed so hard they had tears in their eyes.

"BREAK A LEG TOMORROW," Baker said at the door.

"To tell you the truth," Cynthia said, "I'm not so sure I want the part. I think the play's pretty bad."

He chuckled. "So do I, but I didn't want to say anything."

"It's just that there's supposed to be some big name backing it. If that's true, it could get a lot of attention and lead to better things for someone like me."

He nodded.

She sighed. "Actually, I'm not so sure I even want to pursue acting anymore. I'm tired of always running around, looking for the angle, the gimmick, the big break. I wonder if it's all worth it. Maybe I should be doing something else."

"Like?"

"Teaching."

"Teaching!"

"I know, I know. It's like I choose a new career every week."

Baker shrugged. "So what? At least at the rate you're going, you're practically guaranteed to find the right one."

"Very funny."

He smiled. "So what do you think you'd teach?"

"Maybe math. Y'know: geometry, trigonometry, algebra…"

"High school kids."

"Yeah, high school kids—teenagers."

"There'll be a lot of young boys with broken hearts."

Cynthia laughed.

He stifled the impulse to kiss her goodbye, but she surprised him with a peck on the cheek. And for the whole ride home, he tried to convince himself that it was just a friendly kiss and nothing more.

Nothing more.

MONDAY WAS A SHORT school day with truncated periods, its sole purpose to have students sign into classes and collect textbooks. As Micki was getting ready to leave, Baker said, "I'll stop by later to take you to your appointment."

"I can get there on my own."

"It'll take forever by mass transit."

"I—"

"*Micki, don't argue with me!* I said I'll take you. Starting next week, I'll have to take you anyway. I'm not about to let you leave your last class early just to make your appointment."

"I don't wanna go with you!"

"Well that's just too bad. Whether you like it or not, you're going to have to suffer through my company for a little while each week."

"I hate you."

His voice quiet, he said, "So you keep telling me."

She stalked out of the office, two hot blotches of color on her face.

She was staring at the floor.

"How do you like your apartment?" Dr. Lerner asked.

Micki looked up. "You knew?"

"Yes."

"Well, I don't like having to take stuff from him."

"Then you don't like it."

"Well—I dunno." Micki fidgeted. "I decided he owes it to me."

"I *see*. How interesting." And after listening to Micki explain her reasoning, Lerner said, "So you feel your suicide attempt was Sergeant Baker's fault."

Micki nodded.

"Then his opinion must mean a great deal to you."

Eyes narrowed, Micki looked away. Seconds passed in stormy silence. Until she suddenly asked, "What's the point of living? I mean, what's the point of doing anything? You're just killing time one way or another until you die. When you come right down to it, it's all meaningless."

"There are reasons why you feel this way right now. Further down the road, you may be able to see things differently. Ultimately, we're the ones who give life meaning, and, sometimes, even the smallest pleasures can make it worthwhile. "

"I just want it to be over."

"It's our connections to other people that make us want to live. I think you feel all alone."

"I *am* all alone."

"You have Sergeant Baker."

With a roll of her eyes, Micki slouched down in her seat, then glared at the wall. Finally, she asked, "How the hell do I know what he's really thinking?"

"You still can't tell?"

"I'm afraid to trust him. I don't wanna take a chance again."

The doctor's voice was gentle. "I think the truth is, you're afraid you *do*."

BAKER DRANK A CUP of bitter coffee in the hospital's cafeteria before returning to his car to wait. Sitting alone in the Camaro, he felt utterly rejected. And yet, when he'd searched Micki's apartment Thursday, he'd found the bunny he'd given her stuffed in the back of a dresser drawer—the torn ear repaired with tiny, careful stitches.

As she rounded the corner, he put the car in gear to meet her. But when she opened the door, her mood was as frosty as the blast of air that rushed in.

"Are you hungry?" he asked.

She slammed the door shut. "It's only four o'clock."

"So what?"

"I wanna go home."

He drew a heavy sigh and ordered her to fasten her seatbelt.

AFTER A LATE DINNER of cold pizza in front of the TV, Baker took a walk down Broadway, then headed over to Riverside Drive, beside the park. He was more aware than usual of the shoulder holster strapped against his body. When he looked through the bare branches of the trees, he could see a single star—a planet really—shining brightly against the dusty velvet of the clear night sky.

A cat darted past, disappearing into the shadows of one of the old, prewar buildings lining the road. Proud and stately, the brick structures were full of people winding down the day, the thick, solid walls helping to keep out the cold and the crime while the warm glow of incandescent lights softened the harsh edges of the city that lay crumbling on the other side of the windows.

A couple of cars passed by, the occupants of one throwing some garbage out a window. And then a boy and a girl—teenagers—appeared from around the corner. Walking hand in hand, they looked so young. And so in love. After that, the place was empty. Quiet. And under the distant sounds of traffic and the haphazard gusts of wind blowing in from the Hudson River, he could hear the Critters' "Don't Let the Rain Fall Down on Me" as it poured out of an open third-story window. He lit a cigarette and walked over to stand beneath it.

When he returned home, he made some coffee, planning to watch the news for a while before going to bed. Instead, he found himself sitting at his desk with a pad of paper and the pen Cynthia had given him. For the first time in over a decade, he started to write.

A FEW MILES AWAY and across the river, Micki was standing at the window, watching the empty street and listening to the radio in the dark. The stupid-ass cat was wailing away again, reminding her of Old Man Andrews on the psych ward. She almost had to laugh: no matter where she was, nothing seemed all that much different. And maybe it never would. Lately she felt like she just went round and round in her therapy sessions, never getting anywhere.

A motorcycle gunned its way down the block, and then Rick and Joey came walking along, smoking and drinking beer out of bottles in paper bags. Though she couldn't be seen, she stepped back from the window, still hearing the taunts and obscenities they were yelling up to her apartment. To think she'd once wanted to be friends with them. Her life felt like a tangled mess of mistakes she couldn't get out of.

The Four Tops came on the radio, singing "Reach Out I'll Be There," and she went over to turn up the volume. But when she caught herself staring at the phone, she looked away. Closing her eyes, she tried to picture the Four Tops, tried to picture them watching over her and following her through the darkness till she made it safely home. But she could still see Baker's face, could still hear his voice underneath the harmonies and the driving bass. Eyes edged with tears, she sat on the bed. And hugged herself tightly against the deepening chill that had overtaken the apartment.

Chapter 33

"Is Micki ever going to stop being so angry at me?" Baker asked. "Nothing's changing."

"Why do you expect things to be changing?" Lerner countered.

"'Cause it's different now. *I'm* different now. And look at how I fixed up her apartment. I mean, c'mon, that has to tell her something."

"So you think she should implicitly trust you now? This wouldn't be the first time you've shown her kindness in one way or another and then did a one-eighty."

"But this is different."

"How can she know that? Have you actually told her how you feel?"

"Well—well, no, but I think it should be obvious by now, right?" But even as he said it, he recalled how Cynthia had rebuked him so harshly for never saying what he felt. He slid down a little in his seat. "I think I'm afraid to."

"What's the worst that could happen?"

"She'd laugh at me, and I'd feel like an asshole." He lit a cigarette, then flashed a weak smile. "I guess I'd still live." But then his face grew sad. "I don't know. I have to say, I wouldn't buy it if she did. I know the kid wants me to care about her."

Lerner waited. But after nearly a minute, Baker merely announced he had an appointment scheduled with Dr. Tillim that Friday.

"How do you feel about that?" Lerner asked.

"I think I can talk to him now, especially 'cause the captain thinks I'm ready to return to the squad. And things are going okay with Cynthia, too; we had a nice time together Sunday—just as friends."

"How do you feel about *that*?"

Baker shrugged. "It hurts. A lot. But it's better than losing her altogether." Eyes downcast, he played with his lighter while the heat crept into his face. "I can't help it," he said. "She kissed me goodbye—just on the cheek—but I'm already thinking maybe I still have a chance. It's"—he fought back the emotion welling up—"it's hard to let go."

Lerner's voice was soothing. "Nothing's set in stone. Just let things be. You might be surprised by what happens."

"Yeah." But he sounded doubtful. Then he sat up straighter and tapped the ashes from his cigarette. "Y'know, I've been thinking about what you said—about Micki reminding me of someone."

"And what have you come up with?"

Eyebrows and shoulders raised, he showed the palms of his hands. "Nothing. The only thing I can think of is what I already told you: Daryl Cole. But the more I think about it, the less convinced I am that it's him. Do you really think she reminds me of someone? Like I said, I had plenty of reasons to hate her sight unseen."

"But when you met her, you reacted very strongly, and it was an instantaneous, gut reaction. I'm convinced she triggered a connection on some deep level."

Shaking his head, Baker exhaled a long stream of smoke, then stubbed out his cigarette.

"Perhaps it'll help," Lerner offered, "if I give you a description—a list of traits and attributes. But if you disagree at any point, feel free to stop me." Baker nodded, so Lerner began: "Is extremely intelligent; is extremely independent; has difficulty with authority figures; has difficulty trusting; has a hard time showing any emotion besides anger; expresses anger through violence; is muscular and aggressive; has strong survival instincts, yet can be extremely self-destructive; has a drug-addiction problem; was badly abused; had, for all intents and purposes, no parents; has a number of good friends, though isn't able—"

"Whoa!" Baker interrupted, raising his hand. "Micki does *not* have any friends. There are some people who like her, but I wouldn't exactly say she's friends with anyone."

"I'm so sorry," Lerner replied, "I guess I didn't explain myself very well." Eyes gleaming, she stared straight down into his soul. "I haven't been describing Micki, Sergeant; I've been describing you."

STILL REELING FROM HIS session, barely able to keep his eyes open, Baker struggled up the stairs to his apartment. It was only six thirty. He could easily nap for an hour or so; Micki wouldn't be leaving work till at least ten o'clock. He wanted to get back to Queens in time to make sure she got home okay—a temporary solution to what might be an ongoing problem.

He shrugged off his jacket, pulled off his shoes, then called his answering service. And with the alarm clock set, the radio's volume low, he flopped down on the bed and closed his eyes.

THE KITCHEN DOOR SLAMMED shut behind her, and she stepped out into the cold night air. It helped cut through the fog inside her head. Tuesdays at Bel were often slow, but this had been one of the worst. Every time she'd looked at the clock, scarcely ten minutes had passed. Between the heat and the boredom, she'd spent the night fighting to stay awake.

But when she came out of the alley, she was instantly alert; she couldn't afford to be careless on the street. In fact, anytime she was outside her apartment now, she was twice as vigilant as she'd been before. She might as well be back in the South Bronx.

There were no sounds coming from the mirror company's parking lot, but she started diagonally across the street anyway. Not more than three steps off the curb, she saw Rick, Joey, and two other guys appear out of the shadows on the opposite side. She stepped back on the sidewalk and walked past the driveway, seeing no one and hearing nothing from within. But Rick and the others were keeping pace with her—watching her. The hair on the back of her neck stood up. Just as she was about to check behind her, something hard smashed against her skull.

GROANING, HE REACHED FOR the alarm clock. Damn thing was so annoying, ringing and ringing. He tried to shut it off, but nothing happened. Oh, fuck: it was the phone. He sat up and switched on the light, squinting as it stung his eyes.

"Hello?" His voice sounded thick and raspy.

"Sergeant Baker?"

The male voice was familiar, and Baker snapped to attention. He checked his watch: 10:37. He'd overslept. "Who is this?" He shut off the radio.

"Officer Roberts. I'm calling about Micki."

"Oh, shit! Is she all right?"

"Well, yes and no."

"Shit!" Blood was throbbing in his temples.

"She was jumped on her way home—hit in the head and knocked out. But she's basically okay. I'm at the ER with her now, and she's fine—just a mild concussion."

"That's all?" Now standing, Baker was pacing back and forth in the perimeter allowed by the tethering length of the telephone cord.

"Well—there's a little more to it. It seems they came up behind her—"

"Who?"

"Can't say for certain; Micki didn't see who attacked her. But my guess would be McBain, though I'm sure they were all in on it. She mentioned that Galligan was among some kids who were following her from across the street. Y'see, Saturday night we approached McBain on a disorderly and ended up arresting him after things got out of hand. When Micki passed by on her way home, Galligan yelled out to her that she was dead. Did you know they threatened her when she came home last week?—told her if she didn't get you to get us off their case, they'd make her pay. 'Take it out of your ass' were their exact words."

Struck cold inside, Baker recalled the little scene he'd interrupted on her stoop. "Go on," he said.

"After they knocked her out, they dragged her all the way to the back of that parking lot where they like to hang out. Someone—and it sounded like Mrs. McCrory, though she wouldn't give her name—heard all the commotion and called it in. When the old lady saw what was going on, she must've yelled to them that we were on the way, 'cause none of the boys were there when we arrived. As much as she'd love to see the whole lot of them put away, I don't think she could've stomached standing by while Micki got gang-raped."

Baker felt sick. "But you said she was all right. Now you're saying that they—that they…" He couldn't finish.

"The old lady scared them off in time. The doctor said there was no penetration."

No penetration. So cold and clinical sounding. "You're at Old Queens County General?"

"Yeah, but—" Roberts hesitated.

"But what?"

"Well, she asked me not to call you."

"She *what*?" Pacing again, Baker picked up the base of the phone and almost threw it against the wall.

"She asked me not to call you, said she didn't want you to know."

Baker was breathing so heavily Roberts could hear it on his end of the line.

"I tell you what," Baker said, "you take her home, but don't tell her you spoke to me; let her think I don't know. Tomorrow I'll straighten this out in my own way."

The image of Baker with Micki in the interrogation room months before flashed through Roberts' mind. "Take it easy with her. Don't forget, she's got a mild concussion."

"Did the doc say it was okay for her to go to school?"

"He said she should stay home and rest, but she kept pushing till he said it probably wouldn't hurt. But definitely no gym."

Baker grunted. Micki knew if she skipped school, she'd have to make up a reason why. "Just take her home, but don't say anything. And make sure her apartment's safe before she goes in."

Baker hung up, but continued to pace around. Tomorrow things were going to change.

When Micki came into the office the next morning, Baker said, "You look tired."

"I didn't sleep well."

"And you're late."

"I *said* I didn't sleep well."

"Don't you talk to me like that." He stood up and crossed to the file cabinet to return a folder.

"Or what?" she challenged.

Slamming the file drawer shut, he turned to face her. "Do you think I don't know what happened last night? Did you really think they wouldn't call me?"

With a fresh look of insolence, she shrugged.

"You're still seventeen, and I'm still your legal guardian."

"I wasn't doin' anything wrong, so what's the difference?"

"What's the difference? You got hurt didn't you?"

"It was nothin'."

"It was nothing? By the time they found you, you were half undressed and unconscious—almost gang-raped. And you call that nothing? What the hell is the matter with you?"

"It's none a yer business."

"Christ! How many times do we have to go through this? You're supposed to tell me everything. *Everything*. I shouldn't have to hear about this from someone else."

"Yeah? Well *I* think I shouldn't have t'tell y'about somethin' like this at all. Why should I, huh? Just so y'can get y'rocks off—"

His palm struck her cheek. Hard.

She felt a sickening sensation in her skull, and the beginning of a new headache.

"Fuck it!" he said, slapping his thigh. "I swore I'd never hit you again, but you get me so pissed off."

"Yeah, right," she mumbled.

"Yeah, right!" he retorted. He grabbed her shoulder. "When was the last time I hit you, huh? When? C'mon, tell me."

She glared at him.

His expression turned smug. "You can't even remember exactly. For chrissakes, Micki, things have changed; can't you see that?"

She snorted.

"Jesus, what's the matter with you? Don't you understand that I care about you?"

She rolled her eyes. "Oh, please."

"Hey! I mean it. I know I made a lot of mistakes, and"—his heart was banging against his ribs—"I'm sorry—really sorry—for the things I did." This caused her to look up. "But I can't undo it all, I can only go on from here and try to do better."

He'd actually apologized—actually said the words "I'm sorry."

"Don't you have anything to say?" he asked.

Her mind went completely blank.

The seconds ticked by while his throat constricted and his chest squeezed painfully. He said, "Well then you listen to me, and you listen good: no matter what you believe or don't believe, don't you *ever* talk to me that way again. You'd better show me some respect, because I've had it; do you understand me?"

Her heart fell. It was all just words. In the end, it was the same old shit.

"Do you understand me?" he repeated.

Voice flat, she responded, "Yessir."

His head pulled back while he sucked in air. "Y'know what? I don't want to hear anymore of this yes-sir-no-sir bullshit. Just answer 'yes' or 'no' like a normal person. And don't call me Sergeant Baker anymore, either. My name is Jim, and that'll be just fine." When her jaw dropped, he suddenly felt like he was all alone on a stage, not knowing where to stand or what to do with his hands. He took hold of the back of his neck and said, "Um, why don't you go home and rest. Roberts told me the doctor said—" But his words hung in the air, her reddened, freshly slapped cheek staring back at him. "Jesus Christ! Are you all right?"

Her head hurt. "Yessir."

Squinting, as if he might see the truth more clearly, he scrutinized her face. "Are you sure? 'Cause I still think you should go home. It's only the second day of real classes; it's not like you're going to miss much."

"I'm all *right*."

But by the middle of second period, which was now American History 2, Micki told Mr. Ingram she wasn't feeling well, and returned to the office. Baker—at his desk, his back to the door—was on the phone.

"Yeah, sure," he said to whomever he was talking to. "Listen, I'll call you later, okay? I gotta go." And he resumed his paperwork.

Micki, standing behind him, was waiting for him to turn around: he had to know she was there. But Baker, rifling through papers as if looking for something, was waiting for her to address him—hoping she wouldn't just tap him on the shoulder.

Silently, she said his name: Jim. She imagined saying it out loud. What if he hadn't really meant what he'd said? What if he'd already forgotten he'd said it? Her heart thumped, and her face grew warm. It was making her head hurt again. She blurted out, "Baker?"

He turned to face her. "What is it, Micki?"

"I...I..."

"It's okay," he said. "You can call me Baker if you want."

"Um...I think you were right. I think I should go home."

He nodded. "Give me two minutes while I get Warner to cover for me."

"I can take the subway..." Seeing the look on his face—and the tilt of his head—her voice trailed off. She put her jacket on and waited.

THEY TURNED ONTO FORTY-FOURTH Drive, and Baker searched for a parking space. When they were inside her apartment, he told her to throw some things together so she could stay at his place overnight.

"Why can't I stay here?" she said. "I wanna go to sleep *now.*"

"You'll feel safer at my place."

"What about work? I can't leave Mr. Antonelli without someone for tonight. Juan took off till Friday and—"

"You shouldn't be going to work tonight anyway. If worst comes to worst, *I'll* fill in."

"Yeah, right."

"I'm sure I can handle it." Jeez, he thought, it's just washing dishes. How tough could it be?

CLOUDS ROLLED IN AS they drove through Manhattan, bright sunlight giving way to muted grey. When they pulled up to Baker's building, James Taylor was singing "Blossom" on the radio. Baker double-parked and left the engine running. He reached into his jacket pocket and pulled out a set of keys with a miniature NYPD-detective's shield attached to it. It was not the spare set she'd seen before.

"Here," he said, handing them to her. "I don't have time to go up with you; I've got to get back to work. Just make sure you double lock the door after you go in. Or if you go out, for that matter."

"Oh! I thought you were going to… Yeah. Sure." But though she had her bag and her books in her arms, she still hadn't opened the door.

"You want to hear the rest of the song?" he asked.

"You mind?"

He shook his head and pulled out a cigarette. Side by side they sat and listened, their expressions somber. Then he twisted in his seat to face her. "I want you to promise me you'll never try to kill yourself again."

Chest heaving, she looked down.

"Promise me, Micki."

Tears fell, and she closed her eyes.

He reached over and gently touched her hand. And though she flinched, she didn't pull away. "Call me if you need me, okay?" he said quietly.

WITHOUT MUCH CHOICE, AND with only a prayer that business would be slow, Mr. Antonelli let Baker take over for Micki that night. But when the cop headed into the kitchen, he found it shockingly hot. It was also incredibly small, as were all the people in it—except him. The tight, cramped, steamy quarters were not what he'd expected. He borrowed one of Tony's T-shirts to work in, but it was too small and too-soon soaked with sweat. To add to his misery, he couldn't even smoke when he wanted to. Twice he managed to run out for a few quick puffs, wondering if he'd catch his death of pneumonia from the shirt's moist fabric chilling against his skin in the cold winter air.

Just as things were calming down from the evening rush—the bottom of the sink finally visible through the piles of plates, pots, and pans—a steady stream of odd little groups came in to finish off the night. It wasn't until the clock read 10:22 that he hung up his apron and ripped the thick rubber gloves off his sweaty hands. After he'd changed back into his turtleneck, Mr. Antonelli offered him his pay. He told him to hold it for Micki.

He left Bel and walked the way Micki would to go home, checking out the now gated and empty parking lot where she'd been attacked the night before. Looking up at the adjacent buildings, he wondered which one of them contained Mrs. McCrory. Without her stepping forward as a witness, there was no hard evidence to charge any of the boys with anything. Earlier he'd spoken to Roberts about pressing her to give a statement.

"Forget it," Roberts had said. "Remember, she's got to keep living here. We're grateful she at least tips us off the way she does. For an old gal, she's pretty feisty."

Baker stood quietly before the shadow-filled lot. Not a minute later, he was marching off to his car.

IT WASN'T LONG TILL he found the three boys he'd seen on Micki's stoop. They were partying with some others at a wall under the elevated train tracks, a fire they'd made in a large industrial drum keeping them warm. Of the three, Baker knew only Rick, but it wasn't hard to guess which of the remaining two was probably McBain.

He drove past, all the way to Queens Plaza South, then back up to Forty-Fourth Avenue, killing his headlights and rolling quietly to a stop just shy of the corner. From this vantage point, he could see the boys without being easily observed himself. Laughing, they were passing around a bottle and a joint. The little scum-sucking pricks were acting like they ruled the world. He wished he could make sure none of them ever laughed again. But he could only go so far. And he could only go after one. And while McBain had most likely initiated the actual attack, it was Rick who'd started the whole thing—Rick who'd been such a pig to Micki in every way.

Baker cracked his window open, zipped up his jacket, and pulled out his cigarettes to wait.

SHORTLY BEFORE MIDNIGHT, THE boys' party broke up, and Baker was in luck: while the other boys marched down Twenty-Third Street toward Forty-Fourth Drive, Rick was headed north toward the Queensboro Bridge—alone. Based on things Micki had told him, Rick was probably off to score more weed, going there now to show the others just how cool he was. Fucking asshole.

The cop turned down Forty-Fourth Avenue and drove back to the wall. Then he turned onto Twenty-Third Street with his headlights off and came up behind Rick. Rick, appearing to possess no street sense at all, seemed unconcerned or unaware that a car was following him. It wasn't until Baker stopped and got out that Rick even bothered to glance over his shoulder. He then darted across the street in a stiff, nerdy gait, but Baker quickly overtook him. Grabbing the boy, he spun him around and slammed him up against the chain-link fence. Overgrown with weeds and piled with litter, it clinked and rattled loudly. But there was no one there to hear.

The teen attempted an arrogant, cocky smirk.

Baker said, "You'd better wipe that shitty-assed grin off your face right now, dickhead." Then he yanked Rick forward and turned him, pushing him, face first, against the fence. After he kicked the boy's legs back and apart, he patted him down. Thoroughly. His catch: a small blue pipe with a rolled-up, sandwich-sized plastic bag containing only the remnants of some grass. He turned the boy again and pushed him back into the jangling links. Holding up the items and shaking them, he said, "This is kid stuff." Then he threw everything over the fence.

The smirk returned to Rick's face.

Baker could feel the heat growing inside him. How easy it would be to take the boy down to the ground, grab a handful of hair, and smash that ugly face of his into the concrete till it was shredded and raw. Voice low, he said, "You think I don't know what you did to Micki? You and that punk McBain? You think I don't know it was you who set her up last night? You and your friends who trashed her place?"

Rick's smirk grew broader. "What if it was? Ya can't prove shit." And as Baker's eyes narrowed further, the boy's face filled with glee. "What's ya sudden interest anyhow? I thought ya hated her." He snickered at Baker's silence. "What she do ta get ya all hot 'n bothered, huh? Give ya a blow job?"

With both hands, Baker grabbed the boy's jacket and whirled him around to the street side of the pavement, ramming him up against one of the metal stanchions that supported the elevated subway tracks. Rick's head smacked against the cold steel, and his glasses flew off, landing amidst some litter. Yelping and grunting, he gurgled and sputtered as Baker's large hand encircled his throat to pin him in place. His eyes were bulging.

A glance down, and Baker could see, even in the dim light, a spreading patch of darkness at the boy's crotch. "Looks like you had a little accident there, Rick. But I can tell you right now"—he shoved his face in the teen's—"if anything else happens to Micki, you're going to have an even bigger accident. Do you catch my drift here?"

Face ashen, the boy was mute.

"Answer me, you motherfucking asshole."

In a strangled voice, Rick said, "Uh-huh."

"In fact, from now on," Baker continued, "you'd better look out for Micki. Because if anything happens to her—anything at all, whether it's your fault or not—I'm coming after you and McBain. You tell him that. You tell him that I will personally shove both your dicks down your throats." With a forceful push, Baker released him and casually lit a cigarette. "Now go home, you little piece of shit, and change your diapers."

Rick rummaged through the pile of litter to find his glasses. But once he'd put a little distance between himself and the cop, he stopped and pointed, a tough-guy expression plastered clownishly across his face. "Ya gonna pay fa this! Ya can't—"

"I can't *what*, you fucking idiot? There's no one around. It's like this never happened. Now get your stinking ass out of here and tell McBain what I said."

"I—"

Baker feigned throwing down his cigarette as if to go after the boy.

Rick ran away as fast as he could.

"Fucking putz," Baker muttered, and walked to his car. But even if Rick was too stupid to get it, McBain would back off, which was all that really mattered. Rick was no match for Micki on his own, and he knew it. He was also too much of a coward.

Driving by the underpass, looking for the entrance ramp to the Fifty-Ninth Street Bridge, Baker noted the drug dealers, pimps, and prostitutes that were congregated in the area. The hookers—dressed in little more than cheap lingerie, high heels, and very short fake-fur jackets—had to be freezing.

Many years ago, one frigid January night when he'd been on patrol, he arrested a whole bunch of them near the Lincoln Tunnel for no other reason than to get them out of the cold for a few hours. But he wasn't sure he'd really done them any favors. They'd probably caught hell for getting locked up. Pimps couldn't care less if their girls lived or died so long as they made money up to their last dying breath. And the hookers, like shackled slaves, went along with it—which was hard to comprehend unless you knew the whole story:

Typically beaten and gang-raped for days—often forcibly hooked on drugs for good measure—runaways were broken down by pimps before being turned out onto the street. After that, with dead eyes and jaded smiles, they did what they were told, usually joking and teasing crudely with the johns. And the cops. But buried deep underneath the loud, vulgar talk and the thick, garish make-up, Baker was certain that the pale, frightened shadows of the girls they'd once been were still there. Were still crying. Were still praying to be saved.

Seeing them be ravaged by drugs, rapidly age, and often die within a few years—sometimes by their own hand—was hard for him to take. He hated pimps and had roughed up more than a few—pretty badly, too. But unlike cops who were nothing more than thugs with badges, cops like him had to walk a fine line—had an unspoken code. And had to live with their choices. But the world was changing: more and more people felt there was no place at all for aggressive police behavior. But if you weren't on the job, you really couldn't understand.

He drove over the bridge with no regrets over what he'd just done. If anything, he wished he'd gone further.

A lot further.

THE SOUND OF A key turning in the lock woke her up. Eyes full of sleep, she sat up on the couch and said, "You're back so late."

"I had to take care of something." His voice turned teasing. "Why, you worried about me?"

Looking shy, she shrugged. "Just thought you'd get back earlier."

"How do you feel?"

"I'm okay."

He glanced at her clothes. "You should be in bed by now, Micki."

"Yeah, I guess so." She stood up. "How did it go at Bel?"

He grunted. "I don't know how the hell you work that job *and* go to school. I'm completely wiped out."

She started toward the study. "You get used to it."

When she passed in front of him, he asked, "Do you want to talk about what happened last night?"

She paused. "Not right now."

Eyes kind, he nodded. "By the way," he said, "you don't have to worry about anyone bothering you anymore."

THE NEXT MORNING, WHILE they were putting on their jackets, he asked, "Do you have everything?"

"Uh-huh. Here"—she took something from her pocket and held it out—"here are your keys."

"Those are *your* keys," he said.

The lines between her eyebrows deepened as she reexamined them. "No they're not, they're *your* keys." And she held them up so the little detective's shield dangled down. "See?"

"I haven't used that keychain since I made sergeant." He looked at her meaningfully. "Those are *your* keys to my apartment."

Opening her mouth to object, she paused: her keys to his apartment.

"You can come here whenever you want," he said. "You don't have to ask, and you don't have to have a reason. Although, if it's after curfew, I want you to call so I can come get you."

All she could manage to say was: "Okay."

Chapter 34

DESPITE WHAT BAKER HAD told her, Micki was constantly looking over her shoulder, jumping at the slightest unusual sound. And at work the next day, all she could think about was what the boys had done to her. Her face—already flushed from the hot, steamy water—turned a deeper shade of red.

Before she left the restaurant, she wrapped a sharp steak knife in a cloth napkin and tucked it up inside the sleeve of her jacket.

CYNTHIA PICKED UP THE phone on the second ring and, without hesitation, accepted Baker's invitation to get together that Saturday night. After he hung up he reflected, with mild amazement, that she'd had no plans. He turned on the TV and made himself comfortable in the recliner, glad the weekly poker game had been postponed a day. And though the last half hour of the ten o'clock news was boring—only fluff—he didn't have the energy to get up and change the channel. He was thinking about how nice it would be to have a new TV—one with a remote control—when a field reporter launched into a story about a group of volunteers reaching out to homeless people on the streets. All things considered, it wasn't that dull of a piece, but he was unable to sit still, a ball of anxiety festering in the pit of his stomach. "Oh, shit," he said. Not a minute later, he was heading back to Queens.

AFTER A QUICK CONFIRMATION that Micki wasn't in her apartment, Baker zeroed in on the one location that offered the best chance of catching Rick. It would've been his own choice last night had fate not intervened. Situated in a residential part of Long Island City, it nearly guaranteed success if not a clean getaway. And with any luck, Micki's target, who lived the furthest south, would be by himself for at least one full block, the structure of the elevated train tracks providing her with some minimal cover. But in addition to the risk of witnesses, it called for waiting around without any clue as to when the boys would actually be heading home. It required a lot of patience.

Baker jogged down Forty-Fourth, past Bel, to the corner. He then crossed twice and headed south on Twenty-Third, sneakered feet moving silently down the east side of the street. But with so few cars driving by and no one in sight, the area felt abandoned. Until the back of Micki's shoulder stuck out momentarily from behind a riveted steel support. He stopped and stood very still.

But she'd caught a glimpse of his approach when he'd been two blocks away. After a couple of minutes had passed and he hadn't walked by, she stole another quick peek, only to catch her breath: he was barely fifteen feet from her.

Dressed in black like she was, he said, "Hi, Micki."

She stepped out from behind the stanchion and faced him. Eyes as cold as they were empty, she asked, "How the fuck didja know I was here?"

All of his senses were heightened, every muscle ready to react. Yet instead, with forced casualness, he pulled out his cigarettes and lit one, cupping his hand around the tiny flame. He gave her a wry smile. "You don't expect me to reveal *all* my secrets, now; do you?"

"That mothafuckin' bastard's gotta pay f'what he did t'me!"

"I know how you must feel, but—"

"No! No, y'*don't* know. Y'*can't* know a fuckin' thing about how I feel!"

Cigarette halfway to his mouth, he paused. "Okay, I can't," he said. "But this is not the answer, y'hear me? This is *not* the answer."

"That son of a bitch's gotta pay!"

"Listen to me, Micki: if you go after him, *you're* the one who's going to pay—and for the rest of your life. In the end, he'll still win. Everything you worked so hard for will be gone."

"Yeah, that's how it always is, isn't it. It always comes back to *me*. So what're y'gonna do now? Huh? Y'gonna turn me in?"

"You haven't actually done anything yet. That's the whole point: just walk away."

"Yer always a fuckin' cop."

"No, Micki, not always." There was a beat before he added, "And not now."

She seemed to deflate as she lowered her gaze.

Walking toward her, he said, "Give me the blade."

Her eyes shot up to his.

One eyebrow arched, he said, "Lucky guess?"

She let the knife slide down, then handed it over. While he was examining it, she removed the napkin from inside her sleeve.

"Did you take this from the restaurant?" he asked.

"I planned on returning it," she snapped.

Trying hard not to smile, he said. "I'm sure you did. C'mon"—he patted her on the back—"let's go home."

AS SOON AS THEY were inside her apartment, Baker said, "Why don't you stay at my place."

She took off her jacket. "I'm not gonna try anything else, okay?"

"I know that, Micki." Yet if it weren't to prove his trust, he would've insisted she go back with him.

"I'll be all right," she said.

"You call me if you need me." He pointed to the phone. "That's what it's there for."

But shortly after he left, she knew she was far from all right. She hated leaving it like this: Rick and McBain getting the best of her the way they had—having the last laugh. Everyone was always fucking her over, and she was never able to even it up.

Stretched out on the bed, still in her street clothes, she turned on the radio, searching up and down the dial. But the song—the message—never came.

At half past two, she put on her sneakers and jacket. She couldn't take it anymore. She wanted to get so fucking high she'd never come down. She'd cashed her paycheck and could feel the little wad of money in her pocket. But when she grabbed her keys—all of them now on the key ring Baker had given her—she was confronted by the miniature detective's shield. Gold with blue enamel, it looked just like the real ones, only much smaller. It used to be his, used to hang out in his pocket all day while he did his job.

Her eyes slowly drifted from the keys to the phone. Shiny and black, it sat on the desk, patiently waiting, silent and forgiving like a long-neglected, misunderstood friend. She put the keys down, lifted the receiver, and held it to her ear. The dial tone droned loudly, resonating inside her head. She twined the thick, coiled cord around her finger, then released it, watching it snap back into place while she shifted her weight from side to side. She felt like she was about to burst right out of her skin. How much easier it would be to just hang up and walk out the door. Yet she remained where she was, hypnotized by the grating, buzzing monotone.

She watched her hand reach out, finger slipping into the dial at the number four. She moved it around sharply, then let it go. And though the ratcheting sound it made was very businesslike and serious, the clear plastic disk rotated lazily back. After six more numbers, she heard the mechanical clicks of the line connecting, followed by the ring. But then she whipped the phone away from her head, leaving the receiver hovering above the cradle. Suspended between her thumb and index finger, it was still ringing, faint and thin.

"Hello?" His sleepy voice sounded miles away.

She put the receiver back to her ear.

"Hello?" he asked again—but much more harshly, for all he was hearing at the other end of the line was dead air. "Jesus Christ!" He was about to slam the phone down when, all at once, he could picture her standing there. "Micki?" he asked.

Voice small, she responded, "Yeah?"

Throwing off the blanket, he swung his feet out and sat bolt upright on the bed. "Are you okay?"

She could barely speak for trying to hold back the tears. "Not really," she managed to whisper.

THERE WAS HARDLY ANY traffic, and it wasn't long till he was at her door, overnight bag stuffed with towel, toiletries, and a change of clothes.

Knocking softly, he called, "Micki?"

"Yeah?"

He let himself in and found her sitting on the bed, fully dressed and staring across the room.

"Did you go out?" he asked.

"No, sir."

He tossed his bag on the table, "Then what's with the jacket and the sneakers?"

Eyes still fixed on the sink, she said, "You told me not to move until you got here."

He looked at her more closely. "Did you take something?"

"No, sir."

He squatted down in front of her, forcing her to meet his gaze. "You know you don't have to answer me that way anymore."

She looked very sad.

"Have you slept at all tonight?" he asked.

She shook her head no.

"Do you want to talk?"

She shook her head again.

When he straightened up, a sharp pain shot through his left knee, and he silently cursed it. Then he took off his jacket and opened the closet door. "Why don't you get ready for bed. You can still catch a few z's."

She watched him pull out the sleeping bag and the grey metal box from the shelf. After he removed his ankle holster and emptied the bullets from his gun, he locked them all inside the box and put it back. There was a tug at her heart.

Almost whispering, she said, "I'm sorry."

"For what?" One of the ties on the sleeping bag had knotted up. His attention was focused on undoing it.

"Making you come all the way out here again."

He glanced up. "You've got nothing to feel sorry about. You did exactly what I told you to. You did the right thing." And he continued to patiently work at the knot, feeling it loosen as he picked and pulled.

"I'm scared," she blurted out, and looked surprised at hearing her own voice.

He paused to look at her. "Of what?"

"I dunno," she breathed.

Nodding, he returned to the knot, which came free. He unrolled his bed on the floor and said, "Maybe that's good in a way."

"*What?*"

"Maybe," he said, "you finally feel like you have something to lose."

Chapter 35

D R. TILLIM WELCOMED HIM with a smile. "Take a seat."

Only half awake after being up most of the night, Baker entered the office, shut the door, and fell into one of the old, beat-up chairs. But for the first time ever, he greeted Tillim with something less than a dirty glare, wondering if the man wasn't smarter than he'd given him credit for.

Probably not.

He settled himself and lit a cigarette. The fifty-minute hour had begun.

"HEY!" MALONE SAID, USHERING Baker into his home. "How did your appointment go?"

"Hello to you, too," Baker said, taking off his coat.

"Yeah, all right: Hi—How are you—I'm fine—How did your appointment go?"

This elicited a chuckle, and Baker said, "It's hard to tell, but I think it went okay."

"So you'll see him for a few sessions?"

"Actually...um...well...Tillim didn't seem to mind my continuing to see Micki's shrink. I cleared it for her to talk to him about me."

"*Continuing* to see Micki's shrink?"

"Well—yeah. I've been going for a while now."

"C'mon, you guys," Martini called from the living room. "We don't wanna wait till Christmas comes around again to deal the next hand."

"Keep your pants on," Malone yelled back. Then to Baker, "Did Tillim ask for your guns?"

"No, but from what I've heard, he leaves that to the department: *you're* supposed to take them from me."

Malone grunted and rubbed his forehead. "Well, he obviously didn't tell me you were seeing the kid's shrink. And I'm going to pretend that you didn't tell me, either. That being said, is it helping? You, I mean. Not the kid."

"It's helping both of us."

"Well—that's good. I have to say, you look more relaxed."

"By the way, I hope you don't mind that I gave Micki your number in case she needs me."

"How's she doing?"

"She's coming along."

Malone nodded and started to turn away, but Baker grabbed his arm. "I—I never really thanked you," he said, "for everything you've done for me."

Malone's expression softened, and he patted Baker on the back.

"What's goin' on over there?" Tierney shouted. "Another private party, or are we invited? We're startin' to wonder about you two."

The men headed into the living room.

Taking his seat, Baker asked, "Where's Gould?"

"Home sick—said it's a stomach bug this time. First his kids, then his wife, now him."

"Another reason to stay single," Tierney quipped.

"Bullshit," Martini said. "It's just that no decent woman would ever have you."

"Shut up," Tierney shot back.

The rest of them grinned.

"Deal!" Baker called, rubbing his hands together. "I feel lucky tonight."

SNOWFLAKES TWIRLED IN THE light of the streetlamp, the sidewalk below looking like it had been dusted with powdered sugar. Micki watched in the dark as the tiny crystals danced in the air, then fell to the ground, getting lost amongst the others. Supposedly, no two were ever exactly alike. Just like fingerprints.

She stepped back from the window and flopped down on the bed. She was so tired of her life. It was so empty—so pointless. And, pretty as it was, the newly decorated apartment was still nothing more than a place to live. Temporary. Like everything else. It didn't belong to her, never did and never would. At least if her memory came back, she'd have something to hold onto, something to call her own. She'd even asked Dr. Lerner about hypnosis; it looked so easy when they did it on TV. But the doctor had said, "There are reasons why you can't remember, Micki; your mind is protecting you. Forcing things to unfold too rapidly could prove dangerous."

Micki got up and turned on the light. And though she didn't really want to do homework, she opened her physics textbook anyway, eyes wandering now and then to the piece of paper tucked under the phone. "Captain Malone," it said in Baker's handwriting, with the number printed beneath. He'd offered to stay over again, too.

She closed the book, changed into her nightshirt, brushed her teeth, and got into bed. Outside, the street was quiet, the whoosh of an occasional passing car sounding lonely. She always wondered about the people who were traveling so late: Where were they going? Who were they hoping to see? Twenty minutes later, she was still awake and listening to a truck idling on the street below. After another quarter of an hour had dragged by, she went to the closet and took down Baker's sleeping bag.

"Gotta go," Baker announced, putting out his cigarette and standing up.

Practically whining, Tierney said, "It's still early. Y'gotta give us a chance to win some of that back."

"Sorry, boys"—Baker grinned, waving around the forty-six dollars he'd won—"but I've got to go check on the kid. You'll have to wait till next time."

With little traffic to contend with, he drove from Malone's house, in New Jersey, to Manhattan via the George Washington Bridge. Then he took the Harlem River Drive, the FDR, and, ultimately, the Fifty-Ninth Street Bridge into Queens. When he arrived at Micki's building, her windows were dark, so he let himself in as quietly as possible and stood by the door. Once his eyes had adjusted, he could see her sleeping. *Soundly.* About to leave, he paused to take a closer look: she was nestled inside his sleeping bag.

He left the apartment. Smiling.

SATURDAY, BAKER ROSE EARLY. He went to the grocery store, did some laundry, worked out heavily at the gym, then stopped by Micki's to leave her Cynthia's phone number.

Lying in a heap on the bed, Micki barely managed to say hello. When Baker suggested they go to a movie the following afternoon, she shrugged.

He told her to be ready by two.

"Is MICKI MAKING ANY progress?" Cynthia asked as they settled themselves on the plush white couch.

"She was, but now I'm not so sure." Baker looked down and swirled his glass of Coke. The ice cubes rattled around against each other. He looked up again. "So when do you find out about your audition?"

"Oh, I…" Cynthia's hand went to the string of crystal beads around her neck. "Um, okay. Well—I already know I didn't get it. They said I read well, but look too old."

"Ouch."

She laughed and made a funny face.

He smiled.

"Believe me," she said, "it's a relief. That play was awful. There's a reason they say 'be grateful for the roles you don't get.' Besides, I've made up my mind to start graduate classes next fall."

Soda held high, he said, "Then I propose a toast to one of the best mathematics teachers New York City schools will ever see." With a ceremonious flourish, they clinked their glasses together and drank.

Chin and eyes motioning toward his Coke, Cynthia asked, "How long has it been?"

"About a month."

"A month! Let's celebrate: Anthony's Grill—my treat. And no negotiating."

"How could I reject an offer made by such a beautiful woman?"

"You can't," she said, and went to get her coat.

FLAMES LICKED THE LOGS and crackled in the fireplace. A spray of sparks glittered for an instant and was gone. Stomachs full, they sat on the floor with their backs against the couch and watched.

"So what's really going on, Cyn?" Baker asked, eyes fixed on the flickering light. "I know you much too well. Whenever you're as bright and cheery as you were at dinner, you're covering up for something."

She sighed. "Too much change too fast. And every time I look back on my relationship with Mark, I feel so foolish—"

"Don't," he interrupted. "You got swept away in a fantasy because you were so hurt." He absently stroked his chin, then added, "By me."

"Well, then," she said, "there's my career. I feel my decision to quit acting is right, but it still hurts. I had such high hopes, and I worked so hard." A small, bitter-sounding noise escaped her throat. "I think it's called 'getting nowhere fast.'" He turned to look at her, but she'd already turned away. "I'm certainly feeling sorry for myself, aren't I." And she quickly wiped at some tears.

"You're mourning the loss of a dream," he said gently. "There's a difference."

She looked back. "It was a foolish dream!"

"No," he said. "No, it wasn't. I've come to realize that just pursuing a dream—whether you succeed or not—is pretty courageous. There's no shame in not reaching a goal, only in not trying."

"But I'm giving up."

"I don't think so; I really don't. I think you've come to the end of this part of your journey, and it's brought you to something else. You said it yourself: it's simply time to move on."

Sniffling, her eyes lit up, and she laughed. "Listen to you; you sound like me."

He smiled. "I'll take that as a compliment." But then the smile faded, and he looked back at the fire.

The flames continued to snap and pop.

"What're you thinking about?" she finally asked.

Still gazing at the fire, he took a deep breath, held it a moment, then let it go. "I was thinking," he said, "that I owe Micki my life."

With a slight tilt of her head, Cynthia asked, "What do you mean? You saved *her* life—twice."

He turned to Cynthia with such pain in his eyes that her lips parted as if to say something, but no words came out. He looked down, eventually turning his face away. She reached over and tenderly caressed his cheek, the back of her fingers lingering at the edge of his jaw. When he turned toward her again, their eyes locked. And then the only sound was from the logs shifting in the fireplace, the flames burning brighter after throwing off another shower of glowing embers.

Baker breathed in. "I'm sorry, Cyn, but I've gotta go. I don't have this 'just friends' thing down a hundred percent yet." But as he started to gather his feet beneath him, she lightly touched his arm.

"You don't have to leave," she whispered.

Chapter 36

OVERCAST SKIES THREATENED SNOW, but the weather reports claimed it wouldn't start till after midnight. Baker was late. Standing at the window, Micki was watching the street and thinking about sleeping some more until he got there. Maybe he'd forgotten. A yellow VW Beetle *put-putt*ed by in search of a parking spot, and then she spotted the familiar blue Camaro pulling up behind it. Her heart jumped, and she watched as Baker double-parked in front of her building. Cigarette dangling from his mouth, he was looking at something in the newspaper while he headed for the stoop. She threw her jacket on, checked her pockets, and grabbed her keys. As soon as he knocked, she opened the door.

"Never just open the door," he said. "Always ask who it is first."

"I saw you from the window."

"Are you ready?"

"Uh-huh."

"Why don't you grab your books and throw some stuff in your bag—you can stay over at my place tonight."

"Why?"

"Change of scenery, that's all."

He stepped inside to flick some ashes into the saucer.

She gathered her things together.

BECAUSE MICKI LIKED RIDING in the car and listening to the radio, they drove all the way up to Westchester for a three twenty showing of *The Return of the Pink Panther*. This latest movie with Peter Sellers as Inspector Clouseau was supposed to be the funniest yet, and they weren't disappointed; the hapless French policeman was at the top of his form.

Afterward, they went to a nearby diner made up to look like a medieval castle, a coat of arms flying from a banner on top of the roof. Inside, while waiting for the hostess, they watched oversized cakes go round and round in a glass carousel. They were soon seated in a booth, where they took off their jackets and examined the menus. When the waitress arrived and pulled out her pad, they both ordered burgers, fries, and Cokes.

They were munching on crackers when Micki said, "I don't like the new patrol cars."

"The turquoise ones?"

"Yeah."

"Why not?"

"Because of the color."

"But the old white-tops—with that awful green and black—are so ugly."

"But these are too pretty—too *friendly*. I mean, they're *police* cars."

Baker chuckled, and their platters arrived. They took turns pouring ketchup all over everything.

"So tell me something," he asked after taking a bite, "'cause I've been curious."

Micki's chewing became cautious.

"I know how you got your last name, but I've always wondered how you got your first name." Sipping his soda through a straw, he raised his eyebrows.

Micki put her burger down, then picked up a French fry and swirled it around in the pool of ketchup on her plate. Eyes glued to the French fry, she asked, "Have you stopped drinking?"

"Yes."

She looked up. "Not even beer?"

"Not even beer."

"How come?"

"Because I have a problem with alcohol."

She returned to playing with the French fry, which proceeded to break in half, its hot, white center releasing aromatic steam. She looked up. "You have to swear you'll never tell anyone."

Caught with his mouth full, he swallowed what he was chewing and wiped a bit of ketchup off his lips. "Okay."

"No, you have to actually *say* it."

Though most of his face bore a solemn expression, a gentle smile was creeping its way into his eyes. "I swear I won't tell a soul, Micki—cross my heart and hope to die."

She rolled her eyes, then took a deep breath and put the French fry down. "Okay—so...the place I fell asleep in 'cause I thought it was safe—y'know, that first night that I can remember—that was Tim's hangout. When he found me there, he was *really* pissed. I woke up with a knife to my throat."

"Jesus! Really?"

"Yeah—well—he said, 'Gimme one good reason why I shouldn't slit your fuckin' throat right now.' Of course, I couldn't, and, I dunno, I thought I was good as dead. But then the next thing I know, he asks me my name. And I thought if I told him the truth—that I couldn't remember—he'd never believe me. So—um— on the floor, there was all this garbage, y'know? And I noticed this old magazine that was open to an article about Mickey Mantle. So—so I just said, 'Mickey.'" Looking at Baker expectantly, she twirled the upright ketchup bottle around on top of the table.

His knitted brow relaxed while a grin began to emerge. "But you spell it M-i-c-k-*i*."

"Well, I didn't want anyone to *know*." God, he could be so dense.

Throwing his head back, Baker laughed, and Micki looked at him with an uncertain smile. He said, "Mickey's a normal enough name—more so for guys— but still, I don't think *anyone* would've guessed where you got it from."

She shrugged, mouth twisting with mild irritation.

He added, "Thank god it wasn't an article about Yogi Berra."

And though she hung her head to try to hide it, Baker could see she was laughing.

Breezing to a stop by their booth, the waitress inquired, "How are we doing here?"

Gaze fastened on Micki, Baker replied, "We're doing just fine." The waitress moved on, and Baker leaned back, affecting the mannerisms of Inspector Clouseau "in disguise" as Monsieur Guy Gadbois: his shoulders, eyes, and cheeks twitched, his face sometimes assuming an almost pained expression. Then he raised his glass of soda, and, in his best Clouseau voice, said, "Here's-a loo-king at-a *you*, kid!"

Micki giggled.

Micki turned onto her back. Though she'd fallen asleep several hours earlier, she was now wide awake and staring at the ceiling.

For just a moment, she feels a pulling sensation in her leg, as if it's about to knot up. And then she's completely paralyzed and on her left side, someone pressing heavily on her right shoulder. Left pudgy cheek squished into the mattress, it's hard for her to breathe, and only one eye, wide with terror, is open.

But now she's looking down from the ceiling and feeling nothing—she's numb. The room is squalid; the only furniture, the bed. But she can see herself on it, no more than an infant, her naked little body still clothed in baby fat. Behind her, a man is standing, hips thrusting while, out in the hallway, there are others—including her father. And something is changing hands. But the man in the room is doing something horrible to her. He hates her and wants to punish her for being female—even though she's so tiny.

Once again in her little body on the mattress, her heart is racing so fast and so hard that she thinks it'll burst. Bright flashes of light are coming from the direction of the door.

And then it's over. Micki's back in Baker's apartment, still staring at the ceiling. She's starting to remember.

The next morning, Baker made eggs and toast, but was the only one eating them. Micki's breakfast was a Nestlé Crunch bar that she was poking around on the plate in front of her. Chewing slowly, he eyed her selection, then her. She refused to meet his gaze. Halfway through her "meal," she lost interest and merely sipped her coffee, directing a vacant stare at the middle of the table.

Baker put his toast down with a heavy hand that knocked the butter knife off his plate. He needed this shit like a hole in the head. "What's bothering you?"

Still staring at the Formica, she shrugged.

"Hey!"

She looked at him.

"What's wrong?"

She studied his face: the dark eyes, the deepening lines... But all she said was, "Nothing."

He let it go. Maybe this was some strange rebound effect from the pleasant time they'd had yesterday.

But he didn't think so.

TWO UNIFORMED OFFICERS WERE leading away the senior Jamison had caught attacking a junior girl on a staircase that led to the basement. This was the second attempted rape since Baker had been at the high school. Seated at his desk, he was starting in on some paperwork when the phone rang. He was surprised to hear Malone's voice on the line: "Good news, Sergeant."

"ARE YOU WARM ENOUGH?" Baker asked.

"I'm fine," Micki said, looking out the passenger window. Baker was driving her to the hospital for her weekly session, but all she really wanted was to go home and sleep. All day long, the images from the night before had intruded on her thoughts—even during a surprise physics quiz.

Sleet was falling steadily, and Baker pulled up to the hospital's entrance so he could let her out before he parked. She released her seatbelt and unlocked the door, but then hesitated. "Would you come up with me?"

"WHAT A PLEASANT SURPRISE," Dr. Lerner remarked as Baker followed Micki into the office. "To what do I owe this?"

"Is it okay?" Micki asked.

"Yes. Though in the future, I'd prefer to schedule family sessions separately—in addition to your private ones."

Family sessions! "I—um"—Micki took off her jacket—"I just thought I'd give this another shot."

Already seated, Baker lit a cigarette and flashed an anxious smile, though no one was even looking in his direction.

When Micki had settled herself, the doctor asked, "What is it you'd like to talk about, Micki? My guess is, you had something particular in mind."

With everyone's eyes on her, she fidgeted. "Yeah. Well—I dunno. Things—seem different now. I wanna know if it's real."

"In what way are they different?" the doctor asked.

"Y'know…" But both the doctor and Baker remained silent, so Micki said, "He's more—relaxed about stuff. And he doesn't, y'know, even search me anymore." Then looking at Baker, she added, "He still searches my apartment, though."

"I'm worried about you using drugs. I know it isn't easy staying clean."

"Then how come you stopped the other?"

"Because I feel I can trust you not to bring contraband to school. And because—and because it makes me uncomfortable now."

"Yeah, well, whatever."

The doctor said, "You don't sound convinced."

"Well, why should I be? He can say anything he wants. How do I know if he really means it?"

"You don't think I'm being honest?" Baker asked.

Micki shrugged.

"Why would I lie?"

"Maybe you just want me to think you like me now so I won't try to kill myself again. I'm sure that didn't go over too well with—with—y'know."

"So you think this is all an act? So I'll look good?" Baker's voice was rising.

"Why not?"

"So yesterday I was only *pretending* to have a good time?" Shaking his head, he shifted his gaze and stared at the wall. "Jesus, Micki."

She looked at him sitting there with his right ankle crossed so casually over his left knee. Cigarette smoke was wafting toward his eyes, and he was squinting slightly as he took another hit. "I dunno, okay?" she shot back. "I dunno anything anymore! How do I know if y'really feel anything?"

He nodded while he exhaled a large stream of smoke and stubbed out the Camel. Still looking at the ashtray and grinding out the cigarette, he said, "I breathed life back into you." His voice had come out choked, and he turned his face away.

Her mouth fell open. Voice so low it could barely be heard, she said, "I just— I—I dunno. You're only my guardian 'cause y'have to be."

Both feet now planted firmly on the floor, he leaned forward so his forearms rested on his knees. "Captain Malone called me this morning. He said I can go back to my squad whenever I want."

Lips in a thin line, she averted her gaze, eyes alighting on the doctor's bookcase and Freud's *The Interpretation of Dreams.*

"I told him I'd wait until the school year ended."

She turned back. "What?"

"I think it would be best if I were there until you graduate."

She was almost unaware that the question "why?" had escaped her lips.

He lit another cigarette. "Because you could use some stability in your life."

Still looking stunned, she said blankly, "Oh."

Lerner asked, "How do you feel about that, Micki?"

"I dunno," she replied. "How am I supposed to feel?"

"Well then, how do you feel about Sergeant Baker?" Lerner asked. "Last time you were both here, you were very angry at him."

Micki glanced at Baker, then looked back at Lerner.

"You were especially angry," Lerner continued, "about his having had sex with you."

Micki took to staring at her hands, which were sitting in her lap.

"How do you feel now?" the doctor asked.

There was only the ubiquitous, careless shrug.

Body tense, Baker smoked.

"I'd really like you to answer," the doctor pressed.

"I—I guess I don't feel so angry anymore," Micki said.

"What's different?"

Micki stared out the window. The sky was completely overtaken by clouds. "I dunno. I'm not sure. It all seems so far away now, and—and I don't think he did it to hurt me."

Feeling a familiar stab of pain, Baker closed his eyes.

But before Micki had a chance to say more, flashes of the previous night's images returned, and her eyes grew panicked. When she caught Lerner observing her, she felt as though the doctor could see right into her head.

"Our time is up for today," Lerner said. "But perhaps you'd like to schedule another appointment this week, Micki?"

"I have to work."

"Perhaps Saturday morning."

"It'll almost be Monday again anyway."

"I understand," the doctor said. "I'll see you next week, then."

Baker looked from one to the other.

"And I'll see you tomorrow," Dr. Lerner said to Baker with a smile.

"Yeah, sure," he said, grinding out his cigarette and standing up.

BUT THE NEXT DAY, Lerner was called away on a family emergency, and Baker ended up badgering Warner for insight into Micki's odd behavior.

"For chrissakes, give it up," Warner finally said. "I can't answer these questions. You know Micki far better than I do. I may be getting a Ph.D. in psych, but I'm not a friggin' mind reader."

Baker went home, took off his jacket, and went to pour himself a drink. When the liquor cabinet's door refused to open at his tug, his face filled with astonishment. He straightened up, retrieved his cigarettes, and lit one, smoking fiercely. Then he threw some things in his gym bag and hurried out.

"YOU BETTER THINK THIS through very carefully," Gould cautioned.

"I have," Baker replied. Phone cradled between his head and shoulder, he was about to light a cigarette, then returned it to the pack.

"Well—you better be one hundred percent sure before you say anything. If you change your mind and take it back, it's gonna be a million times worse than if you never said anything in the first place."

"So you think I should leave things the way they are."

Gould sighed. "I can't answer that. Alls I know is it won't hurt nothin' to do nothin.'"

"I'm thinking about what Micki needs."

"You better be thinkin' about what *you* need, too."

I am, Baker thought.

"It's gonna affect you," Gould continued. "We're talkin' major lifestyle change."

"Not really."

"Jeez, I don't know. What's the rush? What's another week? Wait so's you can talk to the shrink about this."

"Yeah, okay," Baker said reluctantly.

Gould's tone brightened. "Do you realize that, two weeks from today, I'm gonna have been married ten years?"

"Ten years? Shit!"

"We'll be throwin' a little party the Friday after next. Bring Cynthia if you want. By the way, did you—um—ever return the ring?"

"I couldn't. I felt like such an ass."

"Lenny'll still take it back—seein' hows you're my partner and all. You know that, right?"

Baker took a deep breath, "I think I'm going to hold on to it for now."

"Yeah? So things are going good, eh?"

Picturing the grin on Gould's face, Baker smiled himself. A kid started crying in the background.

Gould said, "I gotta go but I'll give you a call in a few days." And he hung up.

Baker got a can of Coke, then sat in the dark, drumming his fingers on the armrest of the chair. He wanted to talk. To Micki. He couldn't explain the sense of urgency. But it wouldn't go away.

Chapter 37

MRS. TANDY BURST INTO the security office, a sullen-looking Micki beside her.

"I'll call you back, Cyn," Baker said into the phone. He hung up and extinguished his cigarette.

"I *will* not tolerate any violence in my gym classes," the teacher said. And as Baker stood up, she added, "The slightest provocation and she gets physical."

"What happened?" Baker asked evenly.

"One of the other students—"

"Rhonda," Micki interrupted.

Mrs. Tandy flashed a withering glare at Micki, who then clenched her jaw and stared past Baker. "One of the other students," Mrs. Tandy began again, "apparently said something Micki didn't like. Micki shoved the girl so hard she went flying backward halfway across the floor, where she tripped and fell over an exercise mat."

With the image of Rhonda falling on her ass still fresh in her mind, Micki had to bite the inside of her lip to keep from laughing.

The teacher said, "Maybe she thinks that because of that…unfortunate incident last term, I'll look the other way when she behaves like this. I'm making it clear right now that that is *not* the case."

"I understand," Baker said. "I assure you it won't happen again."

"It better not, or I'll have her dropped from the class. Which means"—she turned to Micki—"you won't graduate in June."

The humor vanished from Micki's face.

"I'll see to it this doesn't happen again," Baker reaffirmed.

With a pronounced lift of her chin, the gym teacher turned abruptly on her red-sneakered heel and left.

The cop and the kid stared each other down, Micki reflecting miserably that certain unpleasant experiences in her life seemed to continually repeat themselves. She noted the rise and fall of Baker's chest. He looked extremely angry. And disappointed. Actually, that was something new.

"What happened?" he demanded.

"What's the difference." She turned away, putting her books on his desk.

He yanked her around. "Answer me. I asked you what happened, and I expect an answer."

"Rhonda didn't think I could hear, but she whispered to Sonya that the only reason a boy would ever go out with me is to fuck me."

"Oh, Jesus, Micki; for chrissakes. But she didn't touch you, did she?"

"All I did was push her!"

"What's it going to take to get it through your head that you can't go around assaulting people just because you don't like what they say? Didn't we go over this already? It wasn't even that long ago."

"I'm not gonna just stand around and listen to that shit."

"Then say something back if you can't walk away. But keep. Your hands. To yourself."

She glared at him, then looked out the window.

"What the hell is the matter with you?" he asked. "Keep this up and you won't graduate; you could even be expelled. And then what, huh?"

Stone-faced, she was staring at a dead-looking tree across the street.

Baker's expression went dark: she was ignoring him! "You'd better—" But he stopped, eyes growing wide. He reached out and tried to draw her toward him, but she stiffened and resisted. Still holding her by the shoulders, he shook her slightly till she met his gaze. "Do you think," he asked, his voice low, "that because I'm angry that means I don't care about you anymore?"

Her eyes narrowed.

"Do you think," he continued, heart pounding, "that means I don't"—he took a deep breath—"love you anymore?"

Face full of panic, she tried to wrest herself from his grip.

But he held on tight while the remainder of the words spilled out: "Because I do love you, Micki—like you were my own kid, my own flesh and blood. And I'm only angry because I don't want to see you make the same mistakes I made."

In a sudden burst of noise, a couple of kids ran down the hallway, giggling. Baker let go of Micki, strode over, and shut the door. As he walked back, he asked, "Do you want to know the real reason I'm here instead of with my squad?"

There was a spark in her eyes.

"It's because I couldn't control my anger. I may've been angry for the right reasons, but the things I did were wrong. I"—aware of how closely she was looking at him, he started to sweat—"I actually broke a guy's jaw once, a perp I had in custody. He was a cold-blooded murderer, a real scumbag. But because of what I did, the entire thing went to shit. In trying to save my ass, the DA's office let him plead to a nothing sentence." His eyes bore down into hers. "And I have to live with that."

Her brow creased. Deeply.

"Please, Micki. I don't want you following in my footsteps. Not like that, anyway. And look at you: you're so young; you've got your whole life ahead of you. Don't fuck it all up."

She turned away.

His shoulders sagged. "I really don't know what else to say; I really don't. Y'know, I'm only your legal guardian till you turn eighteen, but—" Micki looked back, and his heart started hammering in his chest again.

"But what?"

"Well…"

"'Well' what? What're you gonna tell me? That I have to have a full-fledged parole officer for the rest of my life?"

"Well, there'll probably be a lot of legal hurdles, but—but—"

"But *what*?"

He ran his fingers through his hair and heard himself say, "I—I want to adopt you."

There was a beat before she said, "You *what*?"

Though he felt as though the ground beneath him had fallen away, he heard himself still talking. "At the very least, I want you to think about coming to live with me."

"Live with you? How d'ya know y'won't change y'mind tomorrow? People fall in and outta love all the time, right?"

Baker caught his breath. "That's romantic love, Micki. This is different."

"Yeah…well…I dunno. I…I dunno…"

He felt a painful lump in his throat. "Look, I'm not going to pressure you. Take your time and think about it. All I need from you right now is a promise that you're going to try really hard not to get into trouble like this again."

The passing bell rang.

"You have English class now?" he asked.

"Yeah."

"How's Mrs. DeGroot?"

"Better than Newsome."

Baker nodded. "Go on, then. I'll see you later." But as he watched her leave, he wondered how long it would be till he got his answer.

THAT NIGHT MICKI HAD a dream:

She was a little kid. Her father wanted to buy her and the other kids stuff to eat. The other kids were two boys that were her friends, and another girl. But she went to buy herself two cans of Sprite and was upset to see the clerk had opened both without her permission. Not much more than a closet, the store was crammed full of magazines and candy bars, odd novelty items hanging down from the ceiling. She reached into her pocket, proud she had her own money to spend. But while getting out some change, she began to feel strange, as though she was observing herself putting the shiny coins on the counter. The space felt much larger than it had just moments before.

Back outside, the pavement was baking, the sun so hot the sky was white. She saw that her father and the other kids had gone on top of some sort of double-decker bus that was moving slowly down the street. Alone on the sidewalk, she walked alongside them, noise and people streaming all around in the circus-like atmosphere of Times Square. Then the boys started waving, and she felt she had to wave back— had to smile—as if she were having a good time, like they were all playing the same game. But the boys, joking and laughing, were now wearing motorcycle helmets and superhero costumes as if it were Halloween, while she was still wearing her old T-shirt and shorts.

Keeping pace with the bus, she continued walking, knowing she was supposed to meet them all at Entertainment World—an "adult" entertainment place. The boys had no idea where they were going—or what it meant. But she did. She knew exactly. Unlike the other kids, who would remain safely on the bus—remain children—she, streetwise and jaded, was already much older than her years. Walking along, she continued to wave, even as she kept a wary eye on the street. She realized she didn't need to be following the bus to find Entertainment World. She already knew where it was.

ON FRIDAY, BEFORE MICKI left for work, Baker showed up at her apartment to give her Cynthia's number again, but this time on a list with several others, including Malone's and Gould's.

"You hold on to these," he said, raising up the index card and waving it slightly. "I'll be at Cynthia's tonight, but I'm not sure for how long. If you need me, try my number first. If you get the answering service, call hers."

Distant and dull, Micki's response was: "Uh-huh."

"Are you depressed because it's Valentine's Day and you don't have a boyfriend?"

Her eyes flashed. "I'm through with boys!"

"Micki—"

"You think I'm kidding?"

"I think you just need some time to heal; I can't picture you as the type to stay celibate for the rest of your life. Besides"—he tucked the list under a corner of her telephone—"boys around your age tend to be especially big assholes anyway."

"Yeah? Well, I'm thinking that maybe what Rhonda said was true."

His tone was gentle. "Don't say that. Y'know, I'm sorry about what happened over that Reiger boy in the auditorium. He seemed like a nice kid. You ever see him at all?"

"No." And she looked away.

Baker bowed his head.

The silence grew heavy.

He looked up. "I've got to buy an anniversary gift for—a friend. I'll be going out to Fortunoff's in Westbury on Sunday; I thought maybe you'd like to come along. You could help me pick out something."

"Me?"

"We could spend the day out there, and then you could stay over again like last week."

She gave him a canny look.

As he was leaving, he said, "Have a good night at work."

Over at the window, she watched him cross the street, get in his car, and light up. He always looked so confident. So self-assured. What could he possibly want her for? What if he woke up one day and decided she was nothing more than a burden—a mistake?

What if he woke up.

THAT NIGHT, MICKI HAD another dream.

Wearing black patent leather Mary Janes and a short, crinolined dress, she couldn't have been more than five. Her hair was cropped to just below her ears.

Her father, standing over her, said, "The dress'll have to come off. It's dirty."

Feeling very small, she tried to hold back the tears. She didn't want to take off the dress. "No, it's not!" she argued in her high-pitched voice, for she'd been extra careful to keep it clean.

"Yes, it is," her father insisted.

And when she looked down, she saw that it was all stained.

ALL OF SATURDAY AFTERNOON, the snow and sleet kept coming down, making the walk to work a slippery, nasty mess beneath her worn-out sneakers. For the entire shift, Micki kept to herself more than usual, then went home and spent a restless night—fearful of dreaming, fearful of waking.

When she saw Baker's car on Sunday, trolling down the street in search of parking, she suddenly resented the intrusion. Instead of saving him some trouble by going down to meet him, she planted herself on the bed and glared at the wall. What was the point of going to the stupid store with him anyway? But when he knocked, she opened the door and found him smiling down at her.

And the day seemed full of possibility.

THE DRIVE TO LONG Island was a breezy escape under a sky of turquoise blue—engine humming, radio blasting. With few cars on the road, they cruised along at sixty for most of the trip. Once inside the store, Micki was awed by all of the things on display: fancy knickknacks and fine jewelry, shiny silver tea sets and glittering crystal, kitchen gadgets, clocks, watches... But too afraid to actually touch anything, she kept close to Baker while they combed through the floors.

They settled on a large, earthenware bowl heavily decorated with patterns of small vines and leaves in brown, gold, rust, and forest green. And though Micki was the one who'd spotted it, she still had no idea who it was for—and never asked.

By the time they got back to the city, the sun was disappearing below the horizon, igniting an incredible mixture of fiery pinks and blues. Micki did some homework while Baker watched hockey on TV. When she finally joined him in the living room, a commercial was on, and she picked up a novelty catalogue that was lying around on the coffee table. There were pictures of bathmats, mugs, bookends, bookmarks, purses, wallets, hangers, coasters... She jumped up and ripped the catalogue in half. Then she took one part and ripped it in half again.

"What the hell are you doing?" Baker asked.

Shaking with rage, she shouted, "I hate this shit! Why the fuck is it everywhere? It's *everywhere;* every fuckin' place y'look!"

Standing up and holding out his hand, he said, "Give it to me." The page that had sparked her reaction was in two large pieces on top. When he put it together, he saw a picture of ice cubes shaped like naked women's breasts with the caption: "A bevy of beauties to brighten up any beverage." Another picture showed a roll of toilet paper depicting a woman stripping further with each square. Yet another advertised a deck of cards illustrated with women in various positions and in various states of undress.

"What's the big deal?" he said. "It's just a joke."

"Fuck you." She stormed out of the living room and into her bedroom, slamming the door behind her.

Mouth hanging open, Baker stared after her. Then he tossed the torn pages onto the coffee table, went to the study door, and knocked. "Micki?"

"Go away!"

He entered the room and saw her sitting in the dark on the floor. She had her back against the bed, arms wrapped around bent knees. When he switched on the desk lamp, she turned away, pressing her left shoulder against the mattress.

"Leave me alone," she said.

He sat down cross-legged on the floor in front of her. "What's going on here?" he asked.

Tears were rolling down her face. "I wish I was dead."

"Because of *that*?"

Eyes full of fury, she said, "How would you like it if they were selling ice cubes shaped like—like—like your—y'know..."

He let the image fill his mind, then chuckled. "I don't know. I, um, I have to tell you that—well—I think this is one of those things that doesn't quite have the same effect when you reverse gender." When she didn't say anything, he added, "I suppose there are lots of reasons for that."

"But you think that kind of shit's okay?"

He opened his mouth to answer, then placed his elbow on his knee and rubbed his forehead instead. "I don't know. Maybe not." He tried to imagine himself as a woman. "I guess it *is* kind of obnoxious."

"Men *hate* women; that's the truth, isn't it? I mean, look at all those sick magazines."

"Only *some* men hate women. And, yeah, some men like that stuff because it's a put-down. But some men just don't realize that it would upset anybody. They see it as a joke; that's all."

"Like *you*," she retorted. "So that makes it okay?"

He rested his index finger across the crease between his lips, then said quietly, "No. No it doesn't." And he was reminded of an old Greek fable he'd once heard as a kid. When he said he wanted to tell it to her—at least, as best he could remember— her expression became guarded.

"Two boys," he began, "were playing by a pond, throwing rocks to see who could hit the most frogs on the head. After a while, an old man happened by and said, 'What on earth are you doing?' One of the boys answered, 'Don't worry; we're just having some fun. It's just a game.' So the old man said, 'To you, it's just a game, but the frogs hurt for real.'"

It took a second before Micki's face relaxed. "So you understand what I'm saying, then, right?"

"Yeah, I guess so. But your reaction is sort of out there—*way* out there. I mean, I know women who don't like any of that stuff—or the magazines for that matter. But I've never seen anyone react the way you just did." Yet, in his mind's eye, he saw himself ripping up the smut rag Falrone had sent him.

Looking down, she played with the grey shag carpet. She was always surprised at how rough it felt beneath her fingers.

"Have you ever talked to Dr. Lerner about this?" he asked.

She shrugged.

"What does that mean?"

She merely shrugged again.

"Well—do you know why it gets to you this way?"

"It's wrong!" Eyes still on the rug, hands clenched into fists, she felt fresh tears welling up. As she wiped at her face, she said, "You must hate the way I cry so much now."

"It doesn't bother me."

"Yeah, right. You probably think I'm weak—and—and naïve—can't handle the big, bad world."

He snorted. "Not exactly."

She looked up at him, her face full of pain.

His eyes turned sad. "What I think," he said, "is that right now you've got… open wounds. You're sort of falling apart so you can put yourself back together."

When the tears continued to roll down her cheeks, she turned her head.

"Listen to me, okay?" he said. "It's all right for me to see you like this. I'll never tell anyone anything—except maybe Dr. Lerner."

She changed positions so she was sitting cross-legged like he was. A childlike expression was looking back at him.

"Sometimes," he said, "you're like a little girl." When she started to object, he interrupted. "I *like* the little girl, Micki. I like all of you. And that includes whatever you were before and whatever you'll become as a young woman. I take them all, sight unseen—unconditionally." As her eyes became edged with tears again, he reached forward to gently stroke her face. Then he pulled her silver cross out by its chain until it came to rest on top of her shirt instead of under it. When his hands were once again on the carpet between them, she moved her right one forward just enough so their fingers touched. He gave her a reassuring smile, then stood up. "I'm going to start dinner. Why don't you take a few minutes, and then come set the table for me."

Watching him leave, she thought about what he'd said: "You're falling apart so you can put yourself back together." She worried that maybe she was just falling apart.

IN THE DARK OF early morning, Micki woke up, remembering the end of a dream:

A whole squad of uniformed police officers were walking toward her on a Times Square subway platform, two of the men pushing an empty baby stroller. It was her stroller from when she was a baby.

Short as it was, the dream was disturbing, and though she wanted to go back to sleep, it was difficult to block it from her mind. All at once, she sees a young girl, brightly lit, standing in a long, dark corridor. Her hair, wavy and blonde, is being tossed back by a fan-blown breeze while around her, side-lit and misty blue, is a rolling fog—like in a movie. The girl's eyes widen in horror, and Micki's heart starts to pound: she is looking at herself.

The scene shifts, and now she's somewhere else, lying on her stomach in an empty room. She feels a pulling sensation in her leg, and it starts to cramp up, reminding her of the episode as an infant. But then she's hanging above the bed, looking down at herself and seeing that the dress she's wearing is dirty. Even worse is the filthy blonde hair, the grime no longer camouflaged by bright light: it's a wig.

Back in her body, she feels as if she's waiting—waiting for something terrible to happen. And though she tries as hard as she can, she can't lift or turn her head, her entire body dead, like she's been drugged. There's a quick flash of blue neon on the wall, its shape the outline of a girl's head. Oversized musical notes are burning...

And then she's back in Baker's apartment, heart thumping, eyes open wide. And though she has yet to see his face, Micki hates her father.

BREAKFAST MONDAY MORNING WAS strained, almost an exact replica of the week before. Baker tried first coaxing, then pressuring Micki to talk, ultimately demanding to know what was wrong. Retreating into a shell, she felt guilty for her silence—as if she were lying.

"Maybe—maybe you could talk to Dr. Lerner at the end of my session," she offered.

"Sure," he replied. But his tone was decidedly cool.

She withdrew even further.

And so for the entire drive to the high school, he was left to wonder if he were to blame. Apparently, he wasn't going to find out anything until her session that afternoon.

The school day stretched ahead like a prison sentence.

AFRAID HE'D MISUNDERSTOOD, MICKI said, "I need to see Dr. Lerner alone first." They'd left the parking lot and were approaching the main entrance to the hospital.

"I'm well aware of what you meant," Baker snapped. Walking quickly, he ignored that she was running to keep up with him.

Micki stopped in her tracks. "You're angry with me, aren't you."

He halted, his back to her, the leather of his jacket expanding and contracting as he breathed. With a slap of his thigh, he spun around, about to fire back a response—until he saw the pain in her eyes. He closed his mouth, took out his cigarettes, and lit one, cupping his hand around the match. In the soft, mid-afternoon light, his tall, lean figure stood out sharply.

Micki felt very small.

He exhaled a large cloud of smoke that dissipated instantly in the cold, dry air. "I'm not angry at you."

"'Cause I—"

"It's all right," he interrupted. "You go on ahead. I'll get some coffee in the cafeteria, then head on up myself. I'll wait in the hall. You come get me when you're ready."

So they entered the hospital together, but Micki went up in the elevator alone.

DARK AND BROODING, MICKI walked into Dr. Lerner's office and sat in the seat she always chose.

No one said anything.

A door slammed somewhere.

Lerner waited.

Micki said, "Um—yeah—I dunno." She could already feel the tears stinging her eyes. "Things are starting to happen."

Lerner's voice was gentle. "What kind of things?"

Outside the window, the sky was a blank wall of grey: no birds, no sun…Micki tried to shut out all the images that were running through her head. Once she put everything into words—heard it out loud in her own voice—there'd be no going back. But she couldn't keep it locked inside her any longer, either. "I think," she said, "some of my memory's coming back."

THERE WASN'T ENOUGH TIME. Micki wanted to talk to Dr. Lerner more herself, but Baker was surely waiting in the hall by now. Eyes and nose red from crying, she checked her watch for the third time.

"Do you have to leave early?" the doctor finally asked.

"No, but—well, I was hoping you could explain to Baker what's been happening to me. He's angry 'cause of the way I've been acting."

"There's no need to hurry your session, Micki. No one's scheduled next hour. After you're done, I'll have plenty of time to talk with him. But I think you should tell him these things yourself."

"No!"

"Then maybe you should wait until you can."

"No! Please—I—I need him to know *now*."

"Why is it so urgent?"

Micki started crying again.

Normally, Dr. Lerner wouldn't have played intermediary. While she might have given a parent or guardian a generalized update on a juvenile patient, she wouldn't have served as an informational conduit. The very fact that a patient was unable to broach an issue with someone, usually indicated they weren't emotionally ready to accept the consequences. Plus, Micki's conclusions painted a horrific scenario that devastated her self-esteem—even though she'd been utterly blameless. And just a child.

Heart heavy from all she'd heard, the doctor looked at her patient, her gut telling her to do as she'd been asked. "Let's finish the session first, and then we'll discuss this again."

IT WAS TEN TO four. Just when did Micki plan to bring him in? Pacing the hallway, Baker was playing with a pack of cigarettes in his jacket pocket.

The door opened. "You can come in now," Micki announced.

But as he walked through, she edged past him. He grabbed her arm. "Where are you going?"

Face pasty-white but blotchy, eyes wide and dry but red, she said, "I'm gonna wait out here."

He opened his mouth to object, then shut it again, letting her go and slamming the door after her. With a thud, he fell into the chair beside the one she'd vacated just moments before, then whipped out his pack of Camels and lit one, deciding it didn't matter anymore how many fucking cigarettes he smoked. As of Friday, he'd been trying to cut down, but since breakfast, he'd had so many that he was already into Wednesday's rations. Wearing black jeans, a black turtleneck, his black leather jacket, and a black expression, he sulked.

"You're upset," Lerner observed.

"Well, why shouldn't I be? I don't know what the hell is going on with that kid. Did you know that I asked her to live with me?"

"No, I didn't."

"I was going to talk to you about it first, but things just sort of…happened." Eyes piercing into hers, he asked, "Do you object?"

Her expression was kind. "No."

"Yeah—well—I don't get it, okay? Yesterday we had a nice time—a really nice time—and she stayed overnight. But then this morning she was totally different, all upset and depressed, pretty much giving me the silent treatment. Last week it was the same thing. *Exactly* the same. And what really gets me is that she won't talk to me. I can take anything so long as she doesn't shut me out. I thought I had an understanding with her, but I guess I was wrong." He took a furious drag on his cigarette, then exhaled the smoke through his nose. "And look—look at this! She won't even stay in here to talk with me *now*. I mean, what the hell am I supposed to think?"

"Perhaps I should tell you what it is she couldn't say to you herself."

"Sure. Go ahead. Knock yourself out."

The doctor paused, then said, "Micki had some very disturbing dreams recently. But even more importantly, these last two weekends—when she stayed at your apartment—she had flashbacks."

Baker's brow furrowed. "She dropped acid?"

"What?"

"LSD flashbacks?"

"Oh! Oh, no. These are memory fragments of traumatic events. You've probably heard about this sort of thing with Vietnam vets. The experience is very vivid. It feels like it's actually taking place in the present."

Baker sat up straight. "So she's remembering stuff."

"Yes, but these are horrible memories."

He slumped back. "So being with me—staying at my apartment—is triggering horrible memories. Great. Just great."

"I think you're misinterpreting this."

"Oh, really? And just how do you figure that?"

"It's only because she feels safe enough now—safe enough with *you*—that these things are being able to surface."

He let this sink in. "So what is it she remembers? Or are you not allowed to tell me?"

"She wants me to tell you the flashbacks as well as the dreams, but I need to know if you're ready to hear them."

Nodding, Baker adjusted his weight in the chair, then sat back to listen.

WHEN THE DOCTOR WAS finished, Baker was silent, his mind still racing, everything he knew about Micki falling into place. Put into a different context, her odd and over-reactive responses had taken on a completely new meaning. The pain in his heart was unbearable.

"You're certainly very quiet," the doctor stated. "Have you nothing to say?"

"What's there to say? What does *Micki* say? What does *she* make of all this?"

"First I'd like to hear how *you* put all the pieces together. I'm interested in your professional opinion."

"I'm no expert in interpreting this kind of stuff."

"I think you're trying to avoid the issue."

Extinguishing his cigarette, he said, "It's sick. I don't even want to say it."

"Please."

He took a deep breath. "I'm basing this, you understand, on more than what you've just told me; I'm taking everything into account." The doctor nodded, so he continued, "I think her father pimped her out—sold her for sex since she was just a little baby. I think he had photos or movies taken for kiddie porn, too." When the doctor said nothing, Baker began to feel disconnected—as if time had stopped inside the little office. He could feel his face growing hot: perhaps he'd been way off base.

But then Lerner slowly nodded. "Micki sees it that way, too."

His eyes grew moist.

They sat awhile until the doctor stood in closure. "I can't tell you any more than that."

Baker remained seated.

Her voice gentle, Lerner said, "I'll see you tomorrow, Sergeant, and we can continue then."

"I just—I need a minute."

"Why don't you let Micki see how you feel?"

"Because she already saw me about to cry last week. Right now I think she needs me to be strong." And the very act of stating that seemed to pull him back together. He arose, feeling even taller than usual as the doctor passed to open the door. Then he stepped into the hallway, and the door clicked shut behind him.

Micki was standing just in front of the opposite wall, her expression vacillating between a defiant "fuck you" and a desperate plea for comforting.

Arms outstretched, he said, "Hey, kiddo. Come here."

Her lips started to tremble.

He took a step forward, opening his arms wider. She flew into them with such force that it was more like the full-body check of a hockey player than a child accepting a hug. But he held her close, and she buried her face in his chest.

"Everything's going to be all right," he said as he smoothed her hair.

She knew as well as he did that that was a wish more than a prediction. But it was exactly what she needed to hear.

WHEN HE FLIPPED ON the switch, the entryway was flooded with light, the apartment beyond still draped in shadow. Silent. Empty. Baker locked the door behind him.

Gym bag, drugstore purchases, and jacket were tossed onto the club chair while he made his way to the kitchen, going straight for the Coke. Ice cold, full of fizz, two glasses disappeared, one right after the other as he gulped them down, relishing the burn. Then he took out a brown paper bag, the pungent aroma of its contents seeping into the air and causing his stomach to growl. An unexpected guest in his refrigerator, the leftover half of a sandwich inside would never know the pleasure of even a single overnight stay.

He took it out and placed it on the counter, layers of heavy white paper wound around it, tightly folded, neat and precise, as if it were a present. Once unwrapped, it sat proudly and fearlessly in the middle of the plate while he licked his fingers clean of the golden-brown mustard that had oozed out from beneath the top slice of bread. He brought it to the table and picked it up with both hands. But despite his mouth watering and his stomach rumbling, he sank his teeth very carefully into the thick pile of spicy beef on rye. Gould hadn't been lying last month when he'd said the place he was recommending—a small establishment in Rego Park— had some of the best kosher deli in the city. And as Baker took another bite, a grin spread slowly across his face.

After the session with Dr. Lerner, he hadn't wanted to take Micki straight home. He'd suggested getting something to eat and, to his surprise, she'd agreed. And though it was obvious they were driving quite a bit out of their way, Micki didn't say a word. Baker parked half a block down at a meter, and they hurried out of the cold to be greeted at the door by warm, humid air saturated with the scent of hot pastrami and knishes. Alone on a nonexistent line, they stood next to the cash register, where a sign said "please wait to be seated."

A kitchen door opened, and a waiter with little hair but lots of wrinkles, grunted at them and said, "Follow me." Shuffling forward, he led them into the midst of the fully mirrored walls of the tiny restaurant while Micki pointedly stared straight ahead at his skinny, stooped back. But when they'd reached their table and were waiting for him to put their menus down, Baker caught sight of their reflection, a grin spreading across his face much as it had just now. He'd nudged Micki and motioned with his chin for her to look at the silvered glass, as well. Side by side, the two of them looked like different-sized versions of each other.

Their overstuffed sandwiches arrived in short order on thick white plates that were placed on the table with a heavy clunk and a curt, "Enjoy." Neither Baker nor Micki actually ate much of anything, and neither of them said much of anything, either—big gaps of silence in between small talk. And yet, it didn't feel awkward.

Late afternoon turned into early evening, and other patrons, most of them elderly, began arriving for dinner. Baker asked the waiter to wrap up the rest of their meals and they'd left. Then he'd dropped Micki off at her apartment. But only because she'd insisted.

He finished off a third glass of Coke, surveyed his empty plate with disappointment, then called Dino's Pizzeria for a small pie to pick up. After that he hung his sweaty gym clothes in the bathroom and his jacket in the closet before putting away the drugstore items—including a new box of condoms. With all of the conflicting studies and stories about dangers and side effects, Cynthia had become increasingly concerned about staying on the pill. She'd switched to an IUD, but wasn't entirely confident in it yet. And after what she'd just been through, well, would he mind using condoms, too, for just a little while longer?

As he was slipping the box inside the dresser drawer, pushing it underneath some underwear and socks, his eyes fell on the copy of *Playboy* tucked away in the back. Heavy, glossy, and slick with its own sense of style, it was something he'd always taken for granted—simply bought without giving it a second thought. But nothing in the world existed in a vacuum. This magazine was the genteel end of a spectrum of materials for which, and from which, a lot of evil and ugliness had been, and would be, perpetrated on women. And young girls. Even little baby girls. Baker closed his eyes. He wanted to crawl into bed and go to sleep.

When he left to pick up his pizza, he made a quick detour to the garbage chute first.

UNABLE TO SLEEP, MICKI stood in the darkness, letting the moonlight wash over her. Spilling in through the window, the pure white light felt soft upon her skin, and minutes passed illuminated in the cold, spectral glow.

She wondered what Baker was doing.

After her session, when she'd gone with him to the deli, he'd asked about her classes, about her teachers, about Tony and Sal at Bel… But eventually he'd asked if she'd be afraid to stay over at his place again. She told him "no." At this point, it seemed just as likely she'd have a flashback at her own apartment as his. She'd rather be at his place anyway—though she didn't tell him that. Besides, she might not have another flashback for a long time. Dr. Lerner said her mind would only unveil as much as she could handle, and she was finding it difficult to deal with what she already knew.

She got back into bed and bundled herself up in the blanket, feeling very much alone until she recalled Baker's arms wrapped around her. She'd felt safe there. Very safe. But he couldn't hold onto her forever.

Chapter 38

OVER THE NEXT FEW weeks, Micki gained some weight and stabilized there. Although still very thin, she no longer appeared gaunt. She also began asking Baker questions:

"If I live with you, will I have to change schools?"

"No, of course not. You'll go in with me in the morning."

"Okay, I—" Her eyes grew wide. "Oh…" This was the reason why he hadn't returned to his squad right away. But it wasn't until the following day that she asked, "What about my job?"

"If you really want one, you can get one near me. But until you graduate, you don't have to work at all unless you want to; I can more than afford to take care of you." When she looked skeptical, he added, "There are guys with my salary who support a wife and kids. Believe me, it'll be fine. I can always moonlight."

"But why do you want to do all this? I mean, what's in it for you?"

And so he tried to explain that being a parent was supposed to be a giving thing, that the giving itself made you feel good. He said he didn't expect anything in return, but then added, "Well, maybe a little love and appreciation would be nice."

Chewing the inside of her lip, she looked away.

A few days later, she asked, "What if sometime I wanted to, y'know, um, have a friend over?"

Trying to keep a straight face, he asked, "A friend of the *male* persuasion?"

"Um—well—yeah."

"I suppose…I suppose that would be okay; I'd rather know where you are and who you're with than not. What about you?" he asked. "How're you going to feel when I have Cynthia spend the night?"

And Micki tried to imagine what that would be like, for she'd never thought about it before, had never considered that he would ever ask her such a thing, either. "I'd be okay," she finally said.

And so it went until she had nothing more to ask. Still, he didn't get his answer. Yet they'd fallen into a comfortable pattern: she spent Sunday afternoons with him and stayed overnight, sometimes Monday nights, as well. She also made good use of his laundry room, more than happy to stick it to her Laundromat. Baker forced himself to be patient.

Then one day, after school, she said she needed to talk to him. *Alone*—for Marino was in the office on the phone. But once they were in an empty classroom, she couldn't meet his eyes for more than an instant. His heart sank, the atmosphere suddenly as oppressive as the room's drab interior.

"I—" She stole yet another quick glance, only to note the hard set of his jaw. After she awkwardly cleared her throat, she said, "I got my period." And then she turned her head to fully look at him, only to see his face had gone blank. Her own face grew hot: he'd *told* her to tell him this if it happened; it wasn't like she'd ever want to. This was, after all, a very female thing. To have to tell him this while he towered over her...

"I—I wasn't expecting you to say that," he said. "But that's great."

"Yeah, oh joy!" she shot back.

He chuckled. "I admit it doesn't sound like much fun, but"—his expression grew serious—"it's a good sign, Micki. You know that, right?"

She shrugged, then watched his gaze shift to the far end of the floor. She could practically see the wheels turning in his head, spinning around feverishly. When he finally looked back, her face was full of suspicion.

He said, "I know I told you that you wouldn't have to go to the doctor—"

"I'm not going! You said I wouldn't have to go if—"

"I know what I said. But the truth is, you're already sexually active, so you should be getting regular checkups anyway."

"But I'm *not* really active now, right?"

He gave her a shrewd look.

She folded her arms across her chest. "How come you didn't say this before?"

"Because I..." He put his hands on his hips. "Look, I'm not going to make you go this very minute. But in a year, if you haven't gone already, I'm going to insist."

Micki didn't respond. She was too busy trying to grasp that, a whole year from now, Baker fully expected to be a part of her life.

THAT SUNDAY, OVERNIGHT CLOTHES packed and waiting on the bed, Micki was scribbling furiously, finishing as much of her history homework as she could before Baker arrived. In the middle of answering the third of five questions, she heard a car door slam, and she closed the heavy textbook along with her loose-leaf. She heard Baker's voice as he approached the stoop, and then another male voice—which she recognized—answering back. When she peered out the window, she could see the top of Gould's head behind Baker's. Her nostrils flared. This was *their* time together—and Baker hadn't even asked. She listened to them making their way up the stairs, but she didn't open the door until Baker knocked.

Seeing her expression, his smile faded. "I—um—I forgot my smokes. I'm just gonna run down to the corner. I'll be right back."

Micki gaped while he beat a hasty retreat. Then she clamped her mouth shut and gave Gould an acid glare. With crisp, purposeful strides, she went over to the desk and sat down to resume her homework.

Not knowing what to do with himself, Gould remained in the doorway. Eventually he entered the apartment and closed the door. "Okay," he said to her back, "Jim's little routine was pretty lame. But the truth is, I wanted to come here so's I could talk to you."

Without turning around, she replied, "Well, you're here and you're talking to me, so I guess you got your wish. Now you can go home."

Micki couldn't see, but Gould was fighting back a smile. He walked up beside her. "Look, Micki"—he lightly placed his hand on her shoulder—

She leaped up, nearly overturning the chair while he jumped back, heart skipping several beats.

"Don't you touch me!" she hissed.

"I'm sorry," he said. "Alls I want is to apologize for what I did when you were in the hospital."

"Well, y'already apologized; the nurse told me so."

"I don't feel that was good enough."

"I say it is, okay?"

"No, it's not okay, okay? You're the most important thing in Jim's life, so I need to make it right with you. I did what I did because I was only thinkin' of him. Y'have to understand how tight him and me are; we go way back."

Micki's face said she couldn't care less.

"C'mon, I owe him my life."

"What?"

Gould's eyebrows shot up. "Y'mean he never told you?"

She eyed him cautiously.

He pulled a chair out for her, then sat down on the other one himself. After a moment's pause, she joined him.

THERE WAS SILENCE: GOULD had finished. Not once had Micki interrupted or even asked a question, though her features had undergone several subtle transformations during the telling.

"Yeah, okay," she finally said.

He was careful that only his eyes were smiling when he said, "Just so's I'm sure: you and me are okay, then?"

Chair legs scraping against the floor, she stood up. "Uh-huh."

He stood up, as well.

But then her eyes narrowed. "So how much do you know?"

Using his thumb and index finger, he absently smoothed his mustache. "I know some—not everything."

"Yeah? Like what?"

"I know what happened that night between you and Jim."

She looked away.

"No one else knows."

Her eyes flashed. "So whatta y'think, huh?"

"I think Jim made a terrible mistake that he'll never forgive himself for."

There was a flicker of shock before her eyes narrowed again. "But whatta *you* think of *me*?"

All sorts of things started going through his head. In their brief time together, she'd revealed far more than she knew. There was so much he wanted to say. All that came out was: "I think you're gonna be all right."

But he'd stated it with such empathy that Micki's expression changed. And when Gould held out his hand, it reminded her of when Baker had done that. The beefy grip was firm, and she felt an odd little thrill before they released.

He moved toward the window. "I have to give Jim the sign that things went okay."

"Yeah? What's the sign?"

"I stand so's he can see me, then run my fingers through my hair."

Sure enough, Micki could hear the downstairs door. As Gould turned back, she asked, "And what if things hadn't gone okay?"

"Then I would've just stood at the window, lookin' sad and pathetic."

"Sounds real sophisticated."

His manner solemn, Gould said, "Sure. Y'don't think we spent all these years on the job for nothin', do ya?"

And as if they'd known each other for the longest of times, they shared a sly grin that slowly became a full-blown smile. Baker let himself into the apartment, and looked at them both with mild amazement. Then he pulled some tickets from his jacket pocket, fanned them out, and held them up. "What do you say we all go to a Rangers game?"

"You've got four," Micki said. "Is Cynthia coming?"

"Malone's meeting us there."

"I'm not going."

Gould and Baker exchanged meaningful glances.

Gould, heading for the door, said, "I'm gonna wait downstairs." But halfway out, he paused and leaned back in. "I hope you change your mind, Micki." He left without waiting for a response, and she wondered if that implied Baker was going either way: with or without her.

"Why don't you want to go?" Baker asked.

"How do you think I'm gonna feel goin' to a hockey game with three cops?" But the stricken look on his face made her lower her eyes.

"You're not going with three cops," he said heatedly. "You're going with me and two of my friends."

She hung her head. "Captain Malone doesn't like me."

"He doesn't really know you, Micki; that's why he wanted to come. And considering the way he's seen you behave, if he's willing to give this a shot, I think it's only fair you do the same."

She looked up and glowered at him.

"And you can just call him Malone," Baker added.

"Yeah, whatever."

"Jesus! You can't go through life with all these walls up all the time. I mean, you can, but you'll miss out on a hell of a lot."

She rolled her eyes.

The creases in his forehead deepened. "C'mon, Micki. I can't have my life all split up into fractured, little pieces."

"Why not?"

"Seriously? Please. This is important to me."

With a sigh full of misery and defeat, she said, "Fine."

His face lit up.

She was surprised to find herself smiling back.

MICKI HAD A GOOD time.

Chapter 39

GYM BAG IN HAND, Baker was almost out the door when the phone rang. He paused. It had been a long day. Not ten minutes into first period, there had been yet another bomb threat credible enough to have the entire school evacuated and the local precinct called in. And that had only been the beginning.

While the phone continued to ring, he took a deep breath, then went back to answer it.

"Hey, partner," Gould said. "Blanchard just went home with some kinda fuckin' backache for a change. It's like fuckin' clockwork anytime anything's about to go down. Anyways, now we're one guy short, and we're gettin' ready to bring in some armed-robbery suspects supposed to be holed up in a squat on West Thirty-Ninth. One of 'em looks good for that candy-store shootin' I been workin'. Captain's askin': you want in?"

BAKER'S VEINS FELT LIKE electrified wires. Standing in a filthy, crumbling tenement hall—gun drawn, every nerve on fire—he was waiting for the door to be rammed open and the melee to begin. He never felt more alive than when he was facing the possibility of death.

The door gave way, and they rushed in, shouting, "POLICE! GET DOWN ON THE FLOOR *NOW!*"—which startled their three suspects plus two other men they hadn't counted on. With jackets on to ward off the cold, the five had been sitting on the floor, drinking whiskey and divvying up money. Cash scattering all around, four of them clumsily scrambled to their feet while the fifth, reaching for a gun on the upside-down box beside him, got shot in the shoulder by Tierney for his efforts. Three then surrendered to Gould and Martini, but Baker had to run after the last one, who'd overturned a broken-down bookcase and was heading for the dark back room.

"FREEZE," Baker commanded.

One leg out the window and one still inside, the man glanced down over his shoulder and caught sight of the uniformed officers positioned below the fire escape. Lips in a snarl, he then looked back at Baker, the hand hidden by his body inching backward along the windowsill.

"PUT YOUR HANDS UP," Baker barked. "LET ME SEE THOSE HANDS!"

But the perp's palm—still blocked from view—crept back a little further on the bumpy, peeling paint, the edge of his thumb sliding up the side of his rump. There was a tiny shift in the material of his open jacket, and he worried about the almost imperceptible alteration it might have made in the outline of his figure. But eyes steady on Baker—a large, faceless mass in the darkness—he felt his fingers touching solid, cool wood; felt them wrap around the textured grip…

Baker's voice broke through the trancelike power that seemed to have overtaken the room. "Keep going for that gun"—he cocked the hammer of his .38—"and I swear it's the last thing you'll ever do on this earth."

THE ENTIRE OPERATION HAD taken place in a matter of minutes, but it would be at least another couple of hours before the adrenaline wore off. In the past, after taking care of paperwork, Baker would've hung out at the bar with the rest of the guys. Instead, he made his trip to the gym after all, lifting weights and punching the heavy bag till all of his excess energy had been spent.

Still sweating heavily and feeling like he'd overdone his workout, he dropped his jacket and gym bag on the bed, stripped off his clothes, and stepped into the shower. The steaming-hot water felt cleansing—redeeming—and he turned to let it wash down his face. Afterward, in just his jeans, he wolfed down leftover Chinese food and slaked his thirst with three glasses of Coke. Then he put Simon & Garfunkel's *Parsley, Sage, Rosemary and Thyme* on the stereo and shut off all the lights in the living room except one.

KEY IN HAND, MICKI stood poised in the third-floor hallway, the aroma of something spicy hanging in the air. But it couldn't have been anything Baker had cooked; she was quite familiar with his entire, and very limited, repertoire. Arms full between schoolbooks and a couple of bulging, dangling bags, she still managed, with great difficulty, to glance at her watch again, though it did little to help her make up her mind. For nearly ten minutes she'd been standing in front of his apartment doing nothing more than listening to stray noises from the street, arms growing tired and two fingers turning numb. He did want her here, didn't he? "You'll have plenty of time to be on your own soon enough," he'd once told her. "This is your last chance to be a kid, Micki. Take it before you lose it." That last statement had hit her hard.

She slipped the key into the upper lock and turned it.

BAKER AWOKE WITH A start and jumped up, only to grab onto the liquor cabinet. With his vision full of scintillating white particles, he couldn't see a thing. And someone was breaking into his apartment. No—no, couldn't be; he could hear the sound of keys. He stumbled through the soft glow of the living room into the shadowed hall and dark foyer, where, silhouetted in the open doorway, Micki was fumbling for the switch. He reached across and flipped it on, blinking and squinting in the bright glare.

She shifted the books in her arms to keep them from falling, not sure what to make of all the lights that were off. Bare-chested, jaw set squarely, Baker looked as though he'd been sleeping, his half-closed eyes neither happy nor unhappy to see her.

"I quit my job," she blurted out, then quickly added, "I mean, I'm not here *because* I quit my job; I told Mr. Antonelli last week that yesterday would be my last day." And in her mind's eye, she could still see the little man's face clouding over as she'd broken the news. He'd looked really angry, had probably thought her ungrateful after he'd been so good to her. Just thinking about it now, she was getting the same sinking feeling she'd had then. But when she'd told him the reason why, his face had just as quickly beamed. "Is-a good-a! Is-a very good-a! I'm-a so happy for you!" And before she'd had a chance to stop him, he'd grabbed her and kissed her once on each cheek. But now, facing Baker, she wondered if she'd made a terrible mistake.

His voice husky, Baker said, "Either way would be okay with me." He cleared his throat. "All that matters is that you're here." But there was no emotion in his voice.

"Is someone *else* here?"

"Now?"

"Yeah."

"No. Why?" And all at once, his mind was sharp, taking in the moment's significance.

"I dunno. You look like—well…" She shrugged one shoulder. "I just wouldn't want to be—intruding."

"You can't be intruding in your own home."

Her heart fluttered like a tiny butterfly opening its wings. And yet she was still unnerved by something—something about Baker himself.

"I went out on a bust with the guys today," he said quietly.

A police siren wailed through the open window in the stairwell.

Eyes and chin indicating her overburdened arms, he asked, "So what is all this, huh? Y'know, you didn't have to drag everything you own on the subway. In case you've forgotten, I *do* have a car."

Trying to hold back tears, she said, "I—I didn't wanna wait, and—and I didn't wanna have to go back there again." Yet she was still stationed in the doorway—standing on the threshold.

His tone softened. "Well"—he reached down to take her books—"I think you'd better come in, then."

And so she took a step inside, letting some of the darkness fall away, letting the warmth of his presence—like the welcome rays of a strong November sun—seep into her heart, her blood, her bones.

About the Author

A TEENAGER DURING THE turbulent 1970s, Randy Mason grew up in New York City, where she has lived most of her life. *Falling Back to One* is her first book.